WILD RAPTURE

BY
**KAY
McMAHON**

ZEBRA BOOKS
KENSINGTON PUBLISHING CORP.

ZEBRA BOOKS

are published by

Kensington Publishing Corp.
475 Park Avenue South
New York, N.Y. 10016

First printing: February 1985

Printed in the United States of America

For my parents, Lottie and Charles

Prologue

April 10, 1804
near Williamsburg, Virginia

The last rays of fading sunset gone, the countryside grew quiet with the coming of night, save for the creatures who roamed the dark in search of food, scurrying from the path the single carriage took down the road. Though spring had left its mark on budding trees and tiny wild flowers in the meadows, this night bore a chill in the air, a silent omen of doom. Its horses lathered from their quick pace, the dark coach raced onward, jostling its passengers and swaying the lanterns inside. The hour being late, no other carriage passed them, which slightly appeased one of the two men who rode inside the elegant landau.

"I still think I could have handled this without your help," the larger of the two grumbled.

Dark, penetrating eyes glared at him. "I rather doubt it, or we wouldn't find ourselves here now. You've messed up once already on your own, and my plan is too important to allow

7

some merchant to stand in our way." He looked back outside at the black shadows of the trees lining the road traced in silver moonlight.

"Then tell me what you plan to do. He claims to have proof," the older man rallied.

"Exactly my point. *He claims!* That's why you must meet with him. You are to hear him out, get him to show you the proof, if there is any—which I doubt—and take it from him."

"Then what?" the first bellowed. "Wait for the authorities?"

"Of course not, you fool. If there is such evidence, he'll die with his knowledge."

"Just like that?"

A calculating smile creased the other's mouth. "No. I intend to make it look like an accident. But it must be done carefully. He's not a stupid man. He'll expect you to try something, and that's why I'll wait in the carriage until after you've gone inside, to make him think you've come alone. I'll be listening by the window, and when I'm sure of his claim, I'll create a disturbance to draw him outside. That's where I'll kill him."

"But how will that look like an accident?" his cohort argued loudly.

The man leaned back comfortably in the carriage seat, his arms folded over his chest. "Who is to say we must leave him there? We can always move the body."

His companion shifted his weight nervously. "I don't know—what if he isn't alone?"

"He will be. It's part of the agreement and he's an honorable man. We aren't."

A worried frown raced across the older man's face. Something would go wrong. He was sure of it.

Checking his timepiece with the mantel clock, Dru Chandler snapped the lid closed and returned it to his waistcoat pocket. He made one last entry in the diary, blew out the candle, and stood, lifting the book from his writing desk to cross to the armoire. Opening its doors, he pushed aside the clothes and reached inside. The secret panel slid easily to reveal the small cubicle behind it. Putting the book in place, he sealed the compartment again, readjusted the garments before it, and closed the wardrobe doors, hearing the clatter of a carriage outside the house. He turned, looking toward the window of the room. *Right on time.*

Part One

Chapter One

March 7, 1806
Jamestown, Virginia

A chill born of early morning settled over the countryside, first rays of sunlight blotted from the sky by gray, swirling fog, damp and foreboding, hailing the outset of an affair of honor. There were no sparrows chirping and no rabbits in the thicket. A stillness prevailed. In the distance a blackbird cawed. In a clearing near the road, six men gathered to discuss the rules. Ten paces, turn and fire. A fair duel, the only way when one man's honor had been disgraced.

Fletcher Courtney removed his coat and hat and gave them to Arnold Simmons, his longtime friend, a trembling hand accepting the pistol held out in return. Beads of sweat dotted Courtney's brow, in spite of the raw bite in the air. He knew in a moment he must aim the weapon at another, and he prayed his skill would be greater than his foe's. A silly game of cards, an accusation against his honesty, a challenge, all seemed a dream of long past.

Courtney checked the powder and load, stalling for a moment's thought, a searching in his mind to justify this act. Baron Kelzer Von Buren, a Hessian for England during the

Revolutionary War, had claimed Courtney had cheated. But when Courtney denied the charge, in truth, offered to play the round again, the baron had violently refused, swearing Courtney had tried to trick him, thinking the baron ignorant of American games. The lines on Courtney's brow deepened, his pale blue eyes troubled. A foolish statement. Fletcher Courtney thought nothing of the kind. Though of German blood, the baron had married one of the richest women in Virginia ten years earlier. While his titled lands lay near Hamburg, the baron very seldom returned there, and had spent the greater part of the past years on the vast plantation near Jamestown, even after the death of his wife. And playing cards had always been Baron Von Buren's favorite pastime.

Courtney looked up, noticing the muted orange ball through the dense surrounding trees fighting to penetrate the gloom. It seemed a fitting backdrop to this stage of discontent, for before the first ray of warmth touched the earth, a man would die.

Summoned by the judge, Baron Von Buren and Fletcher Courtney approached, leaving their witnesses to stand away. The sixth man, a surgeon, waited near the carriages, his black bag of instruments held in one hand. One final instruction, and the men turned to stand heel to heel, pistols raised at their shoulders, waiting for the count to begin.

"You won't live to see the sunlight," the baron growled over his shoulder as the judge moved away. "You'll die owing me money. Would you like to know how I intend to collect?"

Fletcher Courtney closed his eyes. The baron did not have to say it. He knew. A man with a weakness for gambling, Courtney's earnings had dwindled to nothing. The night past he had hoped to fatten his purse, swearing that if good luck befell him, he would seek other ways to put food on the table. And it *had* graced him, until Baron Kelzer threw his cards in Courtney's face, calling him a blackguard, a liar and a cheat. With no money, a small rundown cottage on a worthless piece of land, Fletcher Courtney thought of the only thing of real value he had ever had in his life—Amber and Andrea, his twin daughters. The baron meant to have one as payment.

"Why Herr Courtney, I do believe you're trembling," Von Buren laughed. "Can't you bear the thought of one of your

14

daughters warming my bed?"

Bile rose in Courtney's throat, gagging him. If Von Buren chose Amber, he would have a fight to the end, for although the maiden had reached womanhood in years and figure, the wild, headstrong girl remained. No, Amber could take care of herself. It was Andrea's state of mind for which he worried. As different from her twin as winter to summer, Andrea had displayed a soft and gentle nature. Similar to fine crystal, Andrea would break if abused.

"Gentlemen, begin. One—" the judge's voice rang out.

Courtney took a step, his eyes still closed, the pistol held firmly in his hand. A tightness gripped his throat and he fought to catch his breath.

"Two—"

Visions of his frail wife came to mind, interwoven with the fair and innocent face of Andrea. So many compared the two.

"Three—"

Dear God, give her strength if she be the one.

"Four—"

A tear trickled down Fletcher Courtney's cheek, moistening the ugly scar that ran the length of his jaw.

"Five—"

And forgive me for what my roguish ways have brought to you. Know I love you both, dear sweet daughters.

"Six—"

Angeline, I have done you wrong. My cursed life killed you, took the very breath from your soul.

"Seven—"

He opened his eyes, his vision blurred with tears, to see the morning sunlight penetrate the gloom.

"Eight—"

If nothing else, I will see this through, I will be the victor and swear myself to a life of being the adoring father. I pledge to make up for all the evil things I've done. He steeled himself, swallowed his tears—

"Nine—"

He smiled bravely at Arnold Simmons, who stood near. Courtney's confidence faded at the shocked expression on the man's face.

"Ten—"

Fletcher Courtney turned, readying his pistol, his face instantly frozen in horror, for Baron Von Buren already faced him, trigger pulled, the muzzle pointing at Fletcher's heart. The powder exploded in the stillness, scattering birds from lofty treetops into the crystal clearness of the sky.

Four black carriages dotted the hillside of the Jamestown cemetery. A splattering of rain descended upon the mourners gathered around Fletcher Courtney's grave, the minister's voice droning out the prayers, committing his soul to God and offering peace to those he left behind. Two identical figures cloaked in long black capes, multiple folds of the hoods hiding their faces, stood near the minister, one unmoving, the second trembling with her sobs for the death of her father. Had anyone ventured to peer beneath the shroud of the first, they would have shuddered with fear. Pale blue eyes, unblinking and without a single tear, stared coldly ahead, unseeing. Amber Courtney would not cry anymore. She would see the baron brought to justice.

Amber had always hated Baron Kelzer Von Buren. He stood for everything she disliked about people of wealth—their greed, their power, their indifference for those below their station. On the rare occasions when her father took the twins to Jamestown as young girls, they had oftentimes had the misfortune of meeting the baron, of enduring his scorn, the contempt he hurled at Fletcher Courtney about his manner of dress and his inability to master the game of cards. Being very young, both girls had huddled in the corner of their buggy listening to his deluge of vicious, sneering insults, until Fletcher Courtney humbly climbed in beside them and set the rig in motion toward home. When the baron's wife died and rumors raced about the countryside concerning the woman's accidental death, Amber often wondered about it, certain no one could live with the man for very long. And like so many others, she considered the possibility that the woman had purposely thrown herself down the flight of stairs to escape him.

As time passed and the twins grew to womanhood, Amber

often journeyed to Jamestown to look for her father after an absence of two days, knowing she would find him contentedly curled up in an alley, sleeping off his overindulgence in ale and a bad night at the gambling tables. The people of Jamestown laughed at Fletcher Courtney. A crowd would gather to watch his daughter labor with the uncooperative man, satisfied to stay where he was, regardless of those who witnessed her efforts, Her heart aching for the broken, defeated man, Amber's pleas would turn to rage at hearing the cruel and scornful laughter of the onlookers. When she could bear it no more, she'd whirl on them, screaming. Most would slowly move on, all except the baron. Dark brown eyes, unblinking, seemed to burn with his lust for the woman, raking over her, baring her to the soul. Though most feared him, Amber despised him. Not once would she back away, certain if he spoke one word she would strike out at him. And now he had murdered her father.

Amber lifted her eyes to stare at the three dark figures standing opposite the gravesite. Mr. and Mistress Bartholomew Webster, neighbors, and Seth Tyler. Poor Seth, Amber thought. She suspected he loved Andrea and that she returned his love, but that his pride kept them apart. The amount he earned working at the general store in Jamestown scarcely supported himself, and, until he could offer a wife more, he would harbor his feelings for Andrea in secret. Foolish, Amber mused, for she knew wealth was of minor concern to her sister, yet he worked day and night to save what little he could. For Andrea's sake, Amber hoped it would not be long. Andrea needed his pampering, his love. And someday, maybe, Amber would find her own.

Feeling someone's gaze upon her, Amber blinked and looked at the woman at Seth's side. Gertrude Webster smiled softly in return, forcing Amber to study her hands folded in front of her. Andrea adored the old woman, but Amber always felt nothing but contempt for her. The Webster plantation ran adjacent to the Courtneys' small property, and hardly a day went by that Amber didn't see the slaves working in the fields. As children growing up, the Courtney twins had made friends with several of the young blacks, a common bond of poverty shared between them. Then, one by one, the young children had disappeared, either sold to another owner or dead of the plague or the beatings they endured. Rich people meant large plantations and large plantations meant slaves. She hated both and what they did to the children, and her only consolation lay in the rumors she had heard about a group of people working to aid the slaves in their effort to flee northward to freedom.

Amber's gaze moved to the grave before her. A simple wooden box with rope handles. No silk pillow cushioned his head. A pauper's grave. Amber closed her eyes. Maybe so, but Fletcher Courtney would be buried with a special richness: the love and admiration of his daughters.

"Rest now, Papa," Amber whispered. "You and Mama are finally together again."

The rain increased its methodical pounding, and, once the minister gave a final prayer, the small circle of mourners moved toward their carriages, Seth hurrying to catch up with the twins.

"Andrea," he called, reaching out for her hand when she turned to face him. "I wish there was something I could do."

"You can," Amber snapped. "You can help me prove Papa was murdered."

"Amber, please," her sister begged, "not here."

Seth's handsome face crimped with their exchange. "I don't know how I could. Nor that anyone would believe us, Amber. The baron is not without influence."

"Yes. Money buys everything. Even silence," she hissed.

An uncomfortable moment passed while Seth quietly shifted his weight from one foot to the other, Andrea chewed on her quivering lower lip, and Amber stared off in angry consideration. Finally Seth cleared his throat and looked at Andrea with a weak smile.

"I must be getting back to work. Mr. Wilson gets angry when I'm gone for very long."

"I understand," she nodded. "Will you come this evening for dinner? It's been such a long time."

"Of course," he said softly. Lifting Andrea's hand to his lips, he placed a gentle kiss upon it, wiped a stray tear from her cheek, and walked away, hurriedly climbing into his rented uggy. Andrea watched until he had driven out of sight.

The shock of her father's sudden death, her sister's bitter refusal to accept fate as it was, and the impossibility of openly expressing her love for Seth caused Andrea's tears to overtake her again. Sobbing, she permitted her sister to help her into the carriage, slipping to the far side of the seat to weep in hushed agony.

Lifting her skirts to place a foot to the carriage step, Amber paused when someone called her name. Her tall frame tightened when she spotted Mrs. Webster hurrying toward her.

"My dear child," the old woman consoled, "if I can help in any way—"

"Thank you, Mrs. Webster, but we'll manage," Amber replied crisply, turning back to climb in next to her sister. Taking the reins, she snapped them once and set the buggy in a brisk pace down the road.

"You shouldn't have been so rude," Andrea scolded, dabbing her eyes with a worn handkerchief. "You misjudge the woman. You misjudge all who have more than we. Mrs. Webster has never been anything but kind to us, and I'm sure she truly wants to help."

"If anyone truly wants to help," Amber mocked, "they'll see justice done. Baron Von Buren must pay for murdering Papa."

Andrea twisted the corner of the white cloth into a knot and asked weakly, "Will that bring Papa back?"

Blue sparks flashed in Amber's eyes, yellow curls bouncing when she snapped her head around to glare at her sister. "Don't you wish to see Papa's murderer punished?"

"Of course," Andrea rallied, her darker blue eyes staring back in astonishment. "But the baron is a wealthy, powerful man with many friends." She looked at her lap. "We have nothing. Only each other. I fear what he may do if you publicly accuse him."

Amber opened her mouth to retaliate but thought better of it. Andrea was suffering enough without hearing Amber's tirade on the baron's ethics and moral upbringing. They rode the rest of the way home in silence, Andrea quietly grieving, Amber plotting revenge.

19

When the road divided, a scarcely used path jutting off to the left, Amber guided the mare onto it, hauling back sharply on the reins when she spied an unfamiliar carriage drawn up before their cottage.

"Who is it?" Andrea asked worriedly.

Amber masked her fears, leaning to pat her sister's hand reassuringly. "Only someone who wishes to express their sympathy at our loss," she guaranteed, the declaration sounding shallow in her ears, for deep inside she suspected different. She snapped the reins and the buggy jerked forward, a fearful doom gnawing in the pit of her stomach.

"Amber, I'm frightened," her sister avowed nervously as they moved closer, her gaze affixed to the stately carriage waiting outside.

Plush velvet seats, leather window coverings, brightly polished brass lanterns on either side of the door, a coat of arms of equal luster signifying ownership loomed out at the twins, radiating the vehicle's wealth. Seemingly unaffected by the drizzle, the coachman sat rigidly in the driver's seat, eyes staring straight ahead as though no other carriage had arrived. Amber's tawny brow lifted, appraising the eloquent cut of cloth to his clothes, for, dressed in her finest, Amber doubted her clothes were worth half of his.

"We know no one who could afford to travel in this manner," Andrea half whispered, clutching her sister's arm. "What do they want?"

"One way to find out," Amber frowned, reining their buggy in to the small stable in back of the house.

After unharnessing the mare and tossing a pitchfork full of hay into the stall, the twins silently started for the house, their skirts lifted to avoid the mud that threatened to stain their hemlines. Acrid smoke from the chimney stung their nostrils as they approached the front door, and, although Amber longed for privacy, she silently thanked their guest for stoking the fire. Its warmth would chase away the chill and soothe her troubled mind.

First to reach the cottage, Andrea lifted the latch and went inside while Amber gazed once more at the elegant coach, its driver still positioned mutely like some giant stone figure adorning the courthouse in Williamsburg. What magic word would bring him to life, she wondered indifferently and turned to go inside.

Andrea had stepped no further than two paces into the room, her bright blue eyes wide, her face drained of all color. Surprised by such display in her usually impeccably mannered sister, Amber followed the direction in which her sister stared. Leaning casually against the mantel of the fireplace, Baron Kelzer Von Buren nodded his greeting.

Dressed in silks and velvets, high black leather boots, and white powdered periwig, his attire belied his military background and complimented his fifty-one years. Well over six feet tall, round, full-chested, he carried himself proudly and with authority, never allowing anyone to get the upper hand and put him at a disadvantage. Large-boned and with the hands of a giant, he was feared by many men, who believed he could crush their skull with a single well-placed blow. His comrades stood in his shadow, never testing him, only doing as he instructed without a moment's thought to consequence, fearing his wrath more than the price they might pay for any injustice caused. Women cowered beneath his regard, spineless pawns in his pursual of wealth and supremacy, frightened into submission by the commanding glare of his dark, almost black eyes, a hint of glowing red seeming to herald the fires of evil in them. All who knew him stepped aside, the annals of his fierce combat of the last thirty years demanding their respect and caution. All, except one. A young woman two less than a score of years, her own determination and fire stiffening her moves, her hatred of him flashing sparks in her pale blue eyes.

"You!" Amber choked, rage strangling the breath from her. "Get out of our house. Out, I say!" Her hand clutching the doorlatch, she swung the door wide. It easily glided on its well-oiled hinges to slam against the wall. Its thunder reverberated tenfold in the closeness of the tiny house.

"Come now, Miss Courtney. You mustn't be rude," he sneered, straightening to collect the box of snuff from his pocket, long, lacy shirt cuffs swaying with the movement. "We have business to discuss."

"We have nothing to discuss," she shouted, flipping back

the hood of her cape.

One pinch to each nostril, he dabbed a handkerchief to his nose and returned the box to its place. "Oh, but we do. I fear this is bad timing, but since your father owned so many, I only wish to make certain I will not be cheated by some overzealous collector."

"Whatever my father may have owed you, sir, he more than paid for with his life."

The baron chuckled. "His death does not bring silver to my purse." He leaned over the only upholstered chair in the room and dusted its seat with a trio of brisk waves from his handkerchief. Lifting the tails of his coat, he sat down and crossed his knees.

Amber bolted across the room to stand before him. "And had you not murdered him, sir, he would have put that silver in your purse."

The baron raised a dark brow. "Murder? Can you prove that?"

"Yes!"

"How?" he asked easily.

"Mr. Simmons. He was Papa's friend. He'll know why there was a need for a duel. Papa would have told him."

"Simmons?" he questioned, toying with the white curl of his periwig dangling near his cheek. "I thought someone told me he decided to visit relatives in England." Von Buren flicked a piece of lint from the knee of his dark velvet breeches and set a cold stare on Amber.

A stirring in his loins, Baron Von Buren recalled his reason for calling on the Courtney twins. Six months of planning and a well-executed plot put them at his mercy. He was to take a wife. He wanted Amber Courtney. The beauty of a grown woman with the fire of a rebellious girl had always inflamed his desire. What fun to tame such a woman. His gaze lustily devoured her comeliness. Long golden hair the color of the sun, high cheekbones touched with a shade of pink, square jaw, full, sensuous lips, took second place to the most captivating pale blue eyes he had ever seen. The only difference between the twins. Dressed in the riches he could afford, she would honor him with her presence by his side. He glanced at Andrea,

ho hadn't moved since entering the cottage. But then, on the
her hand, this tall, lanky wench would cause no trouble. Out
fear, she would do as he instructed. He smiled to himself.
nd he could always have Amber as his mistress. Ah, yes. The
est of both.

The sense of doom that had assailed her earlier returned in
eater force, and Amber stumbled over her words. "When
he returns—"

"Not when, my dear, *if*," he added, fingertips tapping
gether. "And I rather doubt he will." He smoothed a wrinkle
om his already perfect attire and stood, returning to the fire-
lace where he lifted the clock from the mantel to examine it.
Your father wagered heavily on our game, Miss Courtney.
ow do you intend to repay me? This is the only thing of real
orth in the entire house and it's not one-tenth of what's due
e."

"What's due you cannot be measured in silver," Amber
issed, sparking venomous laughter from the baron.

"There are others who agree, I'm afraid." He returned the
ock to the shelf. "However, since money was what he
agered and there were several witnesses, I expect to be paid
e same way. Otherwise—"

Amber glanced back at her sister, then returned her glare to
on Buren. "Otherwise what?" she asked guardedly.

The baron turned to face her, resting an elbow on the
antel, his bejeweled hand dangling earthward. "Otherwise
ne or both of you will find yourselves in debtors' prison."
learing their rapid intake of breath, he studied the neatly
anicured nails of his hand, adding, "Of course, the sale of
his house and small plot of land still would not meet the debt
ou owe, and if you're put in prison I'll never receive payment.
o, I have a better idea."

Amber stiffened, a sense of foreboding tickling the hairs on
he back of her neck. "Which is?" she asked cautiously.

His dark eyes raked over her, the gleam of victory burning in
hem. "That Andrea becomes my wife."

Andrea's face paled at the announcement, her knees weak,
nd she fell back against the table behind her. Amber, how-
ver, boiled in outrage.

"How dare you," she raved, her fists clenched as if to strik him. "You murdered our father and now expect my sister t willingly marry you in return for debts you claim he owes You, sir, are insane!"

A sinister smile twisted the baron's mouth, accentuating hi rugged features, the cleft chin. "I merely seek payment of debt due me. If not, I'll see you thrown in prison. I hav enough witnesses to see my threat carried through." His dar eyes stormy, all mirth vanished from his face. "You have n choice."

"Oh, yes, we do," Amber returned, not the least stunned b his effrontery. "We'll see you're paid, but in no way will yo ever claim my sister. I'll see you dead first!"

The baron threw back his head and roared in laughter "You're quite the tigress, aren't you, my little Amber?" H reached out to stroke the back of his fingers against her cheek only to be presented with a stinging slap to his knuckles. H laughed again. "I've always loved a good contest and I see n reason not to have one now." He moved toward the door. "I' give you one month to find the money you owe me or Andre will become my wife." He paused, turning back, his gaze briefl appraising the humble dwelling. "You must admit, she woul live like a queen compared to what she's had until now. An who knows," he added, his merriment overshadowed by hi obvious lust for Amber in the dark tenseness of his eyes, "w might even allow you to live with us."

"Get out, you lecherous guttersnipe," Amber demanded her body trembling with her fury.

He smiled. "Yes, it should be quite interesting." He set hi gaze on Andrea, devouring her beauty from head to toe. "Tak good care of yourself, my dear. I want you healthy for ou honeymoon." Hearty guffaws echoed in the small room a Baron Kelzer Von Buren lifted the latch and stepped outside marching proudly to his carriage without a backward glance. sharp command to the coachman set the rig in motion, an within moments only the steady dripping of rain from th eaves disturbed the quiet.

*   *   *

Andrea sat before the crackling blaze in the hearth, her red-rimmed eyes swollen, her lip quivering and wringing the handkerchief she held in her hands into a long, wrinkled spiral. Repeatedly she glanced at the doorway leading to the bedroom she shared with her sister.

"Amber, I wish you wouldn't go," she said again, for she had spoken of nothing else the past two days since Amber had announced her plans.

The narrow archway filled with the shapely figuré of her sister clad only in her camisole. "I must," Amber assured her, securing the last curl in place with a hairpin. "I see no other way."

"But maybe Seth—"

"Seth what?" she barked. "What can he possibly do but stand aside? He admitted he hadn't enough money to pay our debts. And if he married you, Baron Von Buren would simply claim me."

Andrea twisted the handkerchief around her finger. "I know," she whispered, a single tear racing for her chin. "But we've never had to do something like this before in our lives. Papa would be so ashamed."

Amber hurried to kneel at her sister's side. "Papa would do the same if it meant saving us from that awful man."

Andrea turned tear-filled eyes on her sister. "Oh, can't we just leave?"

"And where would we go? Where would we stay? The only relative we have is Papa's cousin." Amber smiled teasingly. "Would you like living on a ship with a man who steals for a living?"

"Don't mock me, Amber," Andrea snapped.

Amber reached up to lovingly brush away a strand of hair from her sister's brow. "I wasn't," she whispered. "You're my best friend. I'd never do anything to hurt my little sister."

"Five minutes," Andrea exploded. "I'm only youngest by five minutes."

A bright smile wrinkled the corners of Amber's mouth as she bounced to her feet to stare mischievously at Andrea.

"You never let me forget it, do you?" Andrea sighed, a smile of her own drying her tears.

25

Turning on her heel, Amber sauntered back to the bedroom. "No," she threw back over her shoulder. "Nor that of us both, I'm the most lovely, witty—" She disappeared into the other room and immediately stepped back out to add, "and humble."

They exploded into laughter.

"Now be sweet, little sister, and help me into my gown. I want to reach Williamsburg before noon."

Knowing of no way to persuade her sister differently, Andrea rose to do as bade.

Chapter Two

Nicholas Chandler stood at the docks of Williamsburg, shirt sleeves rolled to his forearms, several papers dangling from his fingertips, and longed to be sailing on the ship weighing anchor. His ship, one of several belonging to the Chandler Shipping Lines. Would the desire ever fade? It hadn't for his father's cousin, Sean Rafferty. Papers raised in the air, Nicholas shaded his eyes from the bright sunlight with the back of his hand, smiling fondly at the man issuing orders. Nearly sixty years old, Sean Rafferty had as much spirit and drive as he had had when he and Nicholas's father, Dru, sailed the seas as pirates. How things had changed. A respected man, Sean walked the streets of Williamsburg equal to any man of class, none daring to speak of his sordid past, since they feared the Chandler name more than any other, save Remington. Alanna Elizabeth Remington, his grandmother, and probably one of the richest widows in the entire commonwealth.

"Ahoy there, Nicholas."

Blinking away his thoughts, Nicholas waved at the man who now stood by the railing of the ship. "Smooth sailing, Mr. Rafferty."

"Thank ya," Sean called. "We'll be comin' back before ya know it. I be figurin' just in time ta see ya wed." Blond curls dusted with silver shimmered when he laughed.

Until the moment it actually happened, Nicholas felt certain Sean would continue to remind Nicholas that the time stipulated in his father's will had nearly run out. Four weeks were all that remained. He must take a wife or risk losing his entire fortune. His eyes clouded in thought, recalling the tense conversation he and his father's cousin had exchanged after Dru's death. At first Nicholas hadn't been able to understand why his own father would cut him out from any inheritance whatsoever. It seemed that he hated his son. But, as always, Sean Rafferty had soothed things over, explained that it wasn't at all as it appeared. Dru Chandler had led a roguish life, sailing from port to port, woman to woman. He had wasted his youth, he had claimed, and nearly allowed himself to lose the one woman he truly loved by refusing to settle down. There was more to life than wild adventures, a satisfaction one could find only if one found roots, made a mark, left heirs to carry on the name. Dru worshipped his children and didn't want them to miss the things he had. One dark brow arched, enhancing the deep brown intensity of Nicholas's eyes. It was a game Dru Chandler played, for, although sincere in his desire to see Nicholas return home where he belonged, he had added a touch of humor, of irony, to his conditions should his son not comply. The shipping lines would go to Nicholas's sister, to be managed by her, by her husband should she marry, and Nicholas would become nothing more than hired help. He shook off the idea and smiled up at Sean.

"Then you'd best set sail, Mr. Rafferty." He waved good-naturedly and watched the giant ship slowly glide to deeper waters.

"He's right, you know."

Nicholas started at the soft tones of a woman's voice behind him. He turned to find its owner. "Grandmother," he smiled, reaching out to wrap her small, frail form in a gentle embrace. "What brings you to Williamsburg? Is Kate with you?" He guided her toward the office at the end of the pier.

"Yes. Your sister's at the inn seeing to our rooms," Alanna said. "And you know me, I wouldn't wait. I had to see you."

Nicholas laughed. "I haven't changed a bit since you saw me

28

three weeks ago."

Alanna stopped, resting a small, wrinkled hand on her grandson's chest. "That's not why I came, Nicholas."

"I know," he answered, his smile fading.

"Well?"

Nicholas sighed, fighting to hide his irritation. "Grandmother, would you truly wish to see me wed to just anyone? I want to own my father's shipping line, to pass it on to my son, but not if it means marrying someone I don't love."

"But what about Heather? You've been seeing a great deal of her."

Nicholas smiled crookedly. "She's been seeing me, Grandmother. I fear there isn't a woman in tens of miles around that doesn't know of my situation and wishes to better her own."

"Oh," Alanna whispered, starting off again. Several moments passed in silence before she drew the courage to add, "If only your father hadn't made so foolish a request."

"I had two years to find a bride, Grandmother. And it wasn't foolish. He only wanted to see me settle down."

Alanna laughed warmly. "How many times I told your father you only followed in his footsteps. He was thirty-four before he married your mother, and you're only twenty-seven." She shook her head. "A wilder sort than he you'll never find. Imagine. A pirate, of all things." Her eyes took on a look of sadness. "I thought he'd near perish when your mother died giving birth to Katherine. He loved her so." She stopped to look at him. "You have her eyes, Nicholas. Everything about you is your mother's. That's why your father loved you deeply. You reminded him in every way of Victoria. I wish she could have seen Katherine." She laughed softly. "I always told Dru that I expected Katherine to be speakin' a wee bit of the brogue when she first talked, so much like her father." Alanna choked back her tears. "And now this. If only he hadn't been killed."

"Don't think about it, Grandmother," Nicholas insisted compassionately. "And now that you've seen me, why not return to your rooms and rest? I'll join you later after I've finished work and we can sup together; you, me, and Kate. All right?"

Round, dark eyes looked up at him, the face lined with age, black hair streaked with silver. "All right. We have a little shopping to do anyway," she smiled, tugging at her cape. "It's certainly chilly today."

Nicholas helped his grandmother into the carriage and waved goodbye, thinking how warm the morning really was. He turned and walked to the office.

Lost in the endless rows of figures listed in the ledger spread out before him, Nicholas failed to notice the presence of someone in the office doorway until knuckles rapping against the framework startled him. He glanced up apologetically.

"I'm sorry, Mathew. What is it?" he asked.

Mathew Calloway had been hired to keep the books for the company, but, because he sought perfection, many times he asked Nicholas to double-check his work. And Nicholas had yet to find a single mistake. That was what truly bothered Nicholas. For the past two months, their shipments had come up short when they docked at their destination. Only small amounts, one or two crates, but all the same their figures differed from one shipping point to the next. It posed no danger yet, but it was something he couldn't overlook. This plus the guilt he felt for all the years he had spent sailing the oceans, living in London, Paris, Spain, even Morocco, where he had purchased land. He had been drawn home only by his father's death. This guilt was the reason Nicholas threw himself into his work. He vowed to honor Dru Chandler's memory and in doing so left himself little time to find a suitable wife. He frowned. Maybe Mathew had finally found something.

"I hate to bother you, sir," Mathew said, reaching up to push his wire-rimmed glasses further onto his nose.

"It's quite all right," Nicholas assured him, laying aside his quill.

"There's someone here to see you." Mathew's gaze darted from the floor to Nicholas to the nail of his thumb.

"Well, show him in," Nicholas said, hiding his smile. Would the little man ever get over his fear of Nicholas Chandler?

Mathew tiptoed further into the room. "Not him, sir. A woman."

"Oh," Nicholas sighed, falling back into his chair. Who was

it this time? Since rumors of Dru Chandler's will had flooded Williamsburg, an endless stream of suitable maidens and their hopeful mothers sought an audience with him. Although his patience ruled, Nicholas was in no mood now to tolerate another. His brows furrowed, marking his disgust. "Not now, Mathew. I have work to finish and I'm meeting my grandmother and Kate for dinner. I barely have time to return home and change." He bent over the papers on his desk and added, "Tell her to make an appointment for next week."

"Yes, sir," Mathew said. "I'll take care of her."

An hour later, Nicholas dropped the quill in the well, the visitor forgotten, and stretched back in his chair, his eyes catching sight of the clock hanging on the wall across from him. If he hurried, he could make it home, change into fresh clothes, and return to the Chesterfield House in time to avoid excuses for his tardiness. Hastily he stood, jerked his coat from the back of the chair, and started across the room, rolling down the cuffs of his sleeves and calling out Mathew's name. They met in the hallway.

"I'll see you tomorrow morning. Lock up for me, will you?"

"Yes, sir," Mathew nodded.

Shrugging into his jacket, Nicholas paused at the front door and turned back, one hand resting on the latch. "Oh, by the way, did you have any trouble with the woman?"

"Well, she wasn't too pleased. Said she couldn't wait a week." Mathew thoughtfully scratched his chin. "You know, Mr. Chandler, I think this one is different."

Not only did Mathew have an acute skill at managing the books, but a talent in judging people, something on which Nicholas had often relied. He relaxed and centered his attention on the man. "How so?"

"Well, her name is Amber Courtney. She's from Jamestown."

Nicholas shrugged. "I'm not familiar with the name."

"I wouldn't have been either, if it hadn't been for the rumor I heard a few days ago."

Nicholas grinned. "Since when does Mathew Calloway listen to rumors?"

"Very seldom," Mathew laughed. "But the lady's presence

31

rather confirmed it."

"All right, I'm listening. You've never been wrong before. Tell me what you think."

"Miss Courtney's father fought a duel with Baron Kelzer Von Buren and was killed. Apparently he owed Von Buren money, and I imagine she came to Williamsburg to seek a loan to pay off her father's debts. What puzzles me is why she came to you. I would think she'd try a bank."

A lazy smile curled Nicholas's lips. "Mathew, you're slipping."

"Sir?"

"I think it's rather obvious. Who more than anyone else in this area has enough money to loan and has a problem of his own? By marrying me, she could offer a solution and a way of paying what she owes." He turned abruptly and opened the door, calling back over his shoulder as he stepped outside. "No, Mathew, my good man, she's no different than the rest. See you tomorrow." He waved farewell and set off toward the livery stable and his horse.

Warm, steady rays of late afternoon sunshine followed Nicholas as he walked the narrow streets of the waterfront, pausing as he always did when he came to the end. Before him stood an iron fence surrounding a marble stone with a brass plate covering its surface. "In the memory of Beauregard Travis Remington, a man who gave his life for the freedom of the United States, 1780," it read. Williamsburg had honored Nicholas's grandfather by erecting the plaque on the very site of Beau Remington's heroic death, while his body lay at rest in the family cemetery on Raven Oaks. Rereading the words, Nicholas experienced his usual regret at never having known his grandfather, even though his memory lived on in the hearts of those who had.

I'll not shame your memory, Nicholas pledged silently. Nor my father's. The Chandler Shipping Lines had been Beau Remington's gift to his daughter and Dru on the day of their marriage. Nicholas's father had built it into a thriving business the first year solely on his own, intending to pass it on to his firstborn, his son. Nicholas knew he must not let that wish go unfulfilled because of his unwillingness to settle down. He turned away, feeling the weight of his burden, and headed for the stable.

The ride to his house, a mile out of town, took only a short time. He stopped outside the front steps, slid from the saddle, and flipped the horse's reins over the hitching rail, vowing to be gone only a few minutes. He took the stairs two at a time and entered through the front door, not bothering to close it behind him, and removed his jacket before he had crossed the foyer.

"Anna," he called, pausing at the foot of the wide spiraling staircase. A frown settled on his brow when no answer came to his summons, and he glanced briefly toward the door leading to the kitchen, spotting a piece of paper folded and sitting on a nearby table. Crossing to it, he picked it up and began reading.

Mister Chandler,
    I hope you'll forgive me for leaving before you had your supper, but I fell terribly ill. I've gone home to bed. I'll send my son by tomorrow morning to tell you how I am.

Anna

"Perfect timing, Anna. Of course, you'll still feel guilty even when I tell you that I had planned to eat at the Chesterfield House tonight," he smiled, knowing his cook cared more about his health than her own. She must have been very sick to leave early. Stuffing the note in his pocket, he turned and hurried up the stairs to his room.

Golden streams of fading afternoon stole in between the draperies, and Nicholas quickly shed his shirt and breeches for clean ones, pausing before the washbowl to rinse away the day's grime from his face and neck. Pulling a fresh jacket from the armoire, he ran a brush through his hair, then left the room in a rush, awkwardly donning his coat when he reached the top of the stairs once more. He stiffened instantly when someone called his name, a woman's voice he didn't recognize. With the absence of candlelight and windows in the foyer, he found himself straining in the shadows to see the face of the woman standing in the entryway.

"Who are you?" he demanded crossly.

"I'm sorry, sir, but I really had to speak with you right away. I couldn't wait until next week."

"Oh, I see," he said irritably, adjusting his shirt collar beneath his coat. "Miss Courtney, isn't it?"

"Yes, sir."

"Well, I'm afraid you'll have to wait." He started down the stairs. "I was just on my way out."

"Sir, I wouldn't bother you if it wasn't a matter of urgency," Amber pressed, still silhouetted in the doorway, her face a shadow. "And I'm certain I can offer a suitable deal for both of us."

I'm sure you can, too, he mused, heaving an angry sigh, then said aloud, "Sorry. But I've heard all the 'deals' I care to hear. I'm certain yours is no better than any other. Now, if you don't mind—" He held out a directive hand toward the front door, only slightly affected by the way she bowed her head and appeared to fidget with her purse strings.

"I'm—I'm prepared to beg, Mr. Chandler." The declaration came weak and strained.

Nicholas's hand slapped against his thigh. "You don't hear very well. I said I'm not interested."

"But how do you know if you won't even give me a chance to explain?" she persisted bravely, her head tilted to one side.

He could almost see the tears in her eyes. This method had been used countless times before and it never failed to irritate him. "And if I agree to listen, will you promise to leave as soon as we're done? I don't want to be late." He would give her the usual five minutes to state her terms, then briskly dismiss her on a hopeful note, as he had all the others before her.

"Yes, sir," Amber quickly answered.

"Then come into the study." He turned sharply and crossed the foyer ahead of her. "And close that door. I don't need anyone else walking in unannounced," he barked, stepping into the next room where he blindly found his way to the desk and a hurricane lamp.

The orange glow of the candle danced about the room, and Nicholas begrudgingly rested a hip on the corner of the desk, crossing his wrists over one thigh patiently to hear her story.

But once Amber Courtney appeared in the study doorway, the soft shades of lamplight falling on her face, Nicholas's anger and vexation vanished. Honey-blond hair falling in thick curls about her face, an ivory complexion, tempting lips, slightly parted, a tall, willowy frame and heavenly blue eyes confronted him. She was without doubt the most beautiful woman he had ever seen. He blinked, recovering, and motioned for her to sit down in the chair near him.

Amber had learned about Nicholas Chandler from one of the merchants in Williamsburg after all her other attempts had failed. He was said to be the richest man for miles around, with a good head for business. If anyone would help her, he would. She had imagined him to be older than her father, possibly bald, and wearing a gray suit with buttons straining against his rounding belly. But the man who faced her now was far from any vision she had conjured up, and she wondered at the sudden pounding of her heart. The flickering light of the lamp alluringly caressed his powerful features, casting a bronze reflection on his suntanned face and neck. Thick dark hair curled defiantly against his brow and accentuated the wide cheekbones and thin, straight nose. But her gaze was drawn almost immediately to the full mouth, now set in a hard line, and she noticed the way the muscle of his square jaw flexed in suppressed irritation. Pulling her attention away from him, she hurried to the chair he had indicated and sat down. But his strong, masculine attraction destroyed her will not to look at him again, and she found herself appraising the fine cut of his clothes that clung so revealingly to his wide shoulders and well-proportioned arms, suddenly curious what it might feel like to have his hand gently trace the outline of her cheek. She blinked, wondering if he had seen the slight blush that burned her face. She doubted it, since he seemed to be studying her clothes.

A special skill in managing a huge business such as his father's necessitated a keen eye for detail, and Nicholas applied that skill now, in an instant noticing the frayed shawl and the outdated, yet neat gown Amber wore. Obviously, the woman had little wealth, and Nicholas braced himself for the newest approach in convincing him she should be the one he married.

"What can I do for you, Miss Courtney?" He recalled her full name and wondered if her mother had chosen it for the color of her hair.

Amber smiled politely. "My younger sister and I live near Jamestown. We don't travel to Williamsburg very often, I'm afraid. That's why you've probably never heard of us."

Nicholas returned her smile. She certainly was pleasant enough. But he wondered how long it would take for her to come to her reason for gracing him with her presence.

"I'll come right to the point, Mr. Chandler," she said, failing to see the twitch at one corner of his mouth. "My sister and I are in dire need of a loan."

"A loan?" he repeated. So Mathew was right. On that point, anyway. And he had to admit it was a novel strategy.

"Yes, sir."

"I'm not a banker, Miss Courtney. I'm not in the habit of lending money." He made to rise, stilled when she raised a hand.

"Sir, hear me out, please." She scooted to the edge of her chair. "My father died just recently and left us with more debts than we have money. One of the men to whom we owe gives us one month to repay him or he'll claim my sister's hand in marriage."

"A true gentleman," Nicholas mocked.

"I only come to you because I will not let this happen. The man is overbearing and cruel, and will surely abuse my sister." Amber looked to her knees. "I've never asked anything of anyone before."

Nicholas studied her a moment, then calmly asked, "How old are you?"

Surprised by his interest, she relaxed slightly. "Eighteen."

Dark brown eyes studied her a moment. "Did your mother send you here?"

"My mother is dead, sir."

"You mean this was your idea?"

"Yes."

"How did you find out where I live?"

Amber toyed with the strings of her purse again. "I—I followed you."

"Then nobody knows you're here?"

She shook her head.

He stood, rounded the desk, and settled in the chair behind it. Well, he might as well get it over with. "How do you intend to repay the loan, Miss Courtney? If you had anything of value to sell you would have done so and had no need of seeing me."

"I'm willing to work it off."

A suspicious smile crimped the corners of his mouth. "I already have a cook and housekeeper."

"But surely you could use another," she said, her eyes wide and hopeful.

"Sorry."

"But there must be something I can do in exchange."

He leaned forward, cupping his chin in his hand as his elbow rested on the desktop. Go ahead, say it, he thought. I can marry you and save your inheritance, Mr. Chandler. Then an idea struck him. He would play the game out to the end. He would force her to say the words, knowing if he suggested such an answer she would only act the innocent. And after all, he was a little tired of Heather anyway. He rose, circled the desk and took her hand, pulling her to her feet.

"I think we can figure something out."

Amber resisted only slightly. "W-where are we going?"

"Well, I don't imagine it would be very comfortable here."

"Comfortable?" she asked, stumbling when he jerked her forward. "For what?"

Nicholas laughed almost sinisterly. "Discussing a way for you to repay the loan. That is why you're here, isn't it?"

Worry knotted the young woman's brow. "Y-yes, but—"

"Then come along. I haven't much time."

They crossed the foyer and started up the stairs. But once they reached the top, Amber yanked her hand away. "Sir, I don't think—"

Nicholas stopped and turned to face her. "That the price you must pay is worth saving your sister from marriage? I'm not an ogre, Miss Courtney. Surely it won't be that unpleasant." He seized her wrist and dragged her through the first open doorway. When he released her to seal in their privacy by securing the lock, Amber hurried to the far corner of the room.

"But, sir, this is rape!"

"Quite the contrary. If finding the money you need requires you to make love in getting it, it will not be rape, for you will not fight me but easily give in." He leaned back against the closed door, arms folded over his chest. "Unless, of course you have another source for borrowing money."

A victorious smile lightened the ebony depths of his eyes certain at any moment she would break for the door and flee his house, never to be seen again. Several minutes ticked away He watched her closely in the dying glow of sunset trailing in through the window, the wide grin suddenly replaced by a sagging chin, for in the muted light of the room he saw her gently lay her purse on the dresser, kick off her slippers, and begin to unfasten the buttons of her gown. His pulse quickened. Somehow he hadn't expected this from her. She seemed different Why, he couldn't answer, but looking at her, he put her above all the rest. He forced himself not to move. Surely she had a plan. But what could it be? Then it hit him. Of course! She would come to him later, claiming she carried his child, and force him to marry her. But didn't the little fool realize it would be too late by then?

The muslin gown slid from her shoulders. His heart beat louder. He didn't move, watching, waiting. The petticoats joined the dress on the floor as she stepped out of the white circle of cloth and kicked it away. Did she tremble or had he imagined it? As if to ease her modesty, something he truly doubted she felt, she loosened the thick mass of curls to cascade them over her shoulders and hide the full curves of her bosom. But when shaky fingertips reached for the strings of her camisole, a wild stirring exploded in Nicholas's loins. As though drawn by some unexplainable force, he slowly crossed the room to stand before her. Placing a knuckle beneath her chin, he forced her eyes to meet his, surprised to see the tears shining in them. A game? A trick, perhaps? Suddenly it didn't matter, as he lowered his head to gently kiss the sensuous lips The fire of passion burned uncontrollably within him, for never before had any woman fanned the lustful spark that raced through him now. He twisted his mouth across hers, his arms encircling the slight form to pull her tightly against him and he could feel the wild beating of her heart. *What madness,* he thought. No woman could so fully entrap him as this young minx had done, chase away all reason, break down his barrier of caution.

His hands raised to cup the delicate lines of her jaw, then traveled slowly down the long column of her neck, his fingers lightly touching the smooth flesh of her bosom pressed against the restricting camisole. He found the strings, unlaced them, and set free the full, ripe breasts. But when he bent to sample their sweetness, she pulled away.

"No! I can't—"

His kiss smothered her objection, his embrace hampering her struggles to escape. He had not heard, he did not sense her change of heart, for his lust consumed him, possessed him, drove him to take what she had offered. In one swift move-ment, he stopped to sweep her in his arms, and with agile grace carried her to the bed and laid her upon it. When he stood back to disrobe, she scrambled to her knees and crawled to the far side of the bed, the wall at her back. She began lacing up the camisole, a startled squeal escaping her when he suddenly appeared before her, knocking her hands away to undo the task she had started.

"Please, Mr. Chandler," she sobbed. "You mustn't." Slender fingers tore at the ones that sought to strip her. "Please, I'll find another way."

Her cries went unheeded, as though spoken in a dream, for Nicholas did not falter in his desire to have her. She lashed out at him, raking her nails across the hard muscles of his chest. It only seemed to excite him, urge him on. In one merciless tear, he ripped the garment from her, entangled both hands within the thick mane of golden curls, and crushed her to him as they fell against the feather mattress.

Amber Courtney had dared to follow the man when he left his office earlier only on the premise of striking a bargain, a satisfactory solution where both sides were concerned. When he rode out of town, she had slowed her buggy, hesitant to continue, but the urgency of her mission spurred her onward. He had left the main road, riding down a long drive and dis-mounting outside a huge manor, dark and foreboding in the last rays of sunlight, as if warning her to take care. She hadn't. In fact, she had walked right in without permission when no one answered her summons. He had been angry with her. She had known he would be, for not doing as he had instructed, but she had assumed he would understand once she explained. She had tried every banker and wealthy merchant in Williamsburg before seeking him out. He was her last hope. She had thought he understood her dilemma, was willing to think of something that might work, until he led her up the stairs, to this room, to suggest she exchange the one thing that was hers alone to give for the sum it would take to free Andrea. She had been appalled at first, wanting to slap his arrogant face. But when he reminded her that she had nowhere else to turn, no other method to acquire a loan or quicker way to pay it back, Amber considered the logic behind his proposal. One night with this man in trade for Andrea's lifetime with Baron Kelzer Von Buren. If that was what it meant, she would do it. Then he kissed her, sending rampant, unfathomable shivers up her spine. He took her breath away, for she had never imagined a man's touch, his caress, could stir such strange desires in her. His hands moved to the strings of her camisole and sanity returned. No, she must find another way. Not this. She couldn't let him have the one most precious gift she possessed. Sobbing disapproval, reclamation, she fought him with all her strength, suddenly finding herself crushed to his chest, their naked flesh searing when they touched.

His lips pressed urgently against hers, suffocating her, stilling her cries, while his hands freely explored the curves of her back, waist, hips, to finally rest on her buttocks. Panic knotted her stomach. She could feel his manhood throbbing hotly against her thigh. A scream lodged in her throat. She must stop him. But how?

Without warning, he rolled, curling her beneath him. He kissed her hungrily, his tongue darting into her mouth. Her eyes flew open, shocked by such an act. She moaned, struggling to push him aside, but his weight held her down. She clawed his back, feeling the warm trickle of blood beneath her nails and hearing his startled cry of pain. Cruelly, he seized her wrists, twisting her arms above her head, his mouth finding the

40

fullness of one breast, his tongue teasing its peak. Such invasion sent a tremor of revulsion racing through her. Tears burned her eyes. She wanted to fight him, show him she was no whore only playing with him, that she would be the one to decide, but her arms grew numb, her strength weak.

She cried out, demanding he stop, but the words never reached her lips, for he had slipped an arm beneath her and she knew he would not listen, that the time for reasoning had ended. His knee parting her thighs, he raised her hips to meet his thrust. She screamed, pain shooting through her, and felt him rise above her, his body still, unmoving. She refused to look at him, certain he enjoyed the torment he forced her to endure, her tears of anger and humiliation stealing between her lashes to trail hot paths down her face. She lay stiff, fearful, confused when he gently touched her cheek with his thumb to wipe away the moist tokens of her shame, the hurt she experienced. She chanced a look at him, the horror beginning again when she saw the desire burning in his eyes, and he lowered his head to kiss her passionately. He moved deeper, faster, his breathing labored, and Amber wondered if he would tear her apart with his lust. She moved her head from side to side, eyes squeezed tightly closed, praying it would end, that it had all been a fierce, monstrous nightmare and she would awake in her own bed, alone.

Of a sudden, he lifted from her and left the bed to dress. She didn't move, afraid he would use her again, hoping that if she remained silent he would forget her presence. She listened to him move about the room, holding back the tears fighting so desperately to break free. Then stillness surrounded her and she bravely opened her eyes, thinking he had gone, her terror beginning anew when she discovered he loomed over her, watching, a dark, angry scowl emphasizing his rugged features.

"If you thought to trick me, madam, you have failed," he whispered caustically. "There have been many before you, and no doubt many shall follow. Dress yourself and be gone, for I do not intend to pay for what others give freely."

Shame, outrage, a multitude of sins exploded in Amber's mind, but none would surface victorious to command her words. Her chin quivering, she turned her face away to hide her tears and quickly found her clothes, covering her nakedness from his damning glare. Clutching her slippers to her bosom, she fled the room, raced down the staircase and out into the enveloping arms of night.

Nicholas stared at the empty doorway for a long while, a painful frown hooding his dark eyes.

The mile ride from his house to Williamsburg always offered Nicholas time to reflect on problems concerning the shipping lines. He seldom considered anything else, since few other topics took priority. However, in the stillness of early evening, trotting down the deserted road, the thoughts of what had just happened filled his head and formed the angry frown on his face. He had shared intimacies with plenty of other women in his life, a few duchesses and wives of nobility, even milkmaids in his younger days, all discreet and totally honest affairs. No commitments, no false promises of love, and never once without the woman's consent. So what made it different this time? Why did he feel the guilt that tore at his insides? Hadn't she offered herself? Yes, he had suggested the kind of payment she should use, but had it not been acceptable she could have refused. Nicholas nudged his horse into a canter. Is that what bothered him? Usually the women with whom he shared a bed had been the ones to entice *him*. It had never been a business transaction. Lord knows he could have had countless others to choose from if that had been his desire. So why Amber Courtney? What made her special? Why would he suddenly be the aggressor? Could it be he sensed she truly didn't wish to give herself to him but felt compelled, that his ego needed proof of his charm, his way with women, and she had posed a threat? The muscle in his cheek flexed with the thought. Is that why he wouldn't stop when she had begged him, certain she simply played a game at his expense? He studied the road ahead of him as the stallion raced along, recalling his pain when he lit the candle in his room and found the bloodstains on his bed. *A virgin! My God, she had been a virgin.*

The lights of Williamsburg dotted the horizon before him

42

and he kicked his horse into a gallop. Would he ever be able to return home again, to his room, and not think of what he had done? Yes, in time he could, for what they had shared, the guilt he experienced, had been equally her fault. She must have known, have willingly accepted her fate, or she would have fled his room when given the chance.

"Damn," he growled. "Stop thinking about it!" Leaning forward in the saddle, he moved gracefully with each pounding step of the stallion, never slowing the steed until he reached his destination. He would dine with his sister and grandmother and thoroughly enjoy the evening. He would not allow Amber Courtney to invade his mind again.

Outside the Chesterfield House, Nicholas hauled back sharply on the reins and came to a sliding halt. Dismounting in a rush, he tied off the horse to the brass ring of the hitching post and took the front steps two at a time. But once he reached the inn's main entrance, he paused, took a deep breath, and straightened his jacket before calmly walking inside.

As usual, the inn's dining hall brimmed with patrons enjoying the delicacies for which the Chesterfield House was noted, and he didn't see his grandmother and sister at first until one of the serving maids pointed them out to him. He followed the winding path between the countless groupings of tables and chairs, his concentration so great that when he passed by the third he inadvertently brushed the shawl draped over the back of one chair to the floor. Scooping it up, he stood to offer his apology, noticing the tattered edges of the garment that marked its age. He frowned briefly at the hint of recognition, then looked at its owner, his pulse quickening when he saw the pale blue eyes staring back at him. Would he ever be free of her?

"What are you doing here?" he demanded tersely.

Amber Courtney had seen Nicholas the minute he stepped into the dining hall. Her heart pounded, certain he had followed her and stood searching the room for her whereabouts. Dear God, he didn't intend to air her disgrace publicly, did he? No, he had made it quite clear he was finished with her. He had gotten all he wanted and sent her on her way. Then what had changed his mind? She watched a serving maid approach him and share a few words before he started off toward her table. She wanted to jump to her feet and run, escape his biting words, hide her shame, but it was too late. He was only a few feet away. Why didn't he look at her? She blinked, realizing he had spoken.

"W-what?"

"I asked what you're doing here?" he repeated impatiently.

Shaken by his obvious surprise at finding her here and knowing that her fear that he had come for her was unfounded, she nervously looked to her hands folded in her lap, mumbling the first words that came to mind. "I didn't know you owned this inn."

"I don't. I had just imagined you would have run for home by now. In fact, I would suggest it."

Piqued by his callousness, Amber's true nature surfaced. No one would order her about. She lifted cool eyes to glare at him. "What I intend to do is none of your business, so don't try to intimidate me," she said bravely, her words belying the smile on her lips. "But if it will guarantee me that I will have privacy again, I'll tell you this much. As soon as I've finished my tea, I will leave here. Where I go afterward is something I don't care to discuss."

"To try your wiles on another unsuspecting victim?" he sneered.

Amber's eyes widened, shocked by his insinuation, but her temper quickly ruled. "If anyone has played a ruthless trick, Mr. Chandler, it was you. I imagine it is the only way you can woo a lady into your bed." She hissed the accusation in a whisper so only he would hear, then leaned forward. "Tell me. Is it true?"

He raised one dark brow questioningly.

"That you must rape to have a woman?"

Having his character and manliness disputed, Nicholas straightened, glaring down at her through half-closed eyes. He tossed the shawl over the chair seat and stalked away.

"Nicholas, we were worried about you. You're so late,"

Alanna Remington said once her grandson sat down at the table next to his sister.

"And I apologize," he smiled softly, though it proved an effort. "I—I had some unexpected business to take care of."

"From your expression when you walked in here, I would say it went badly," she observed.

"Depends on one's point of view," he grunted. "But let's not talk of me. How have you been feeling?"

On the day of Kate's birth, Alanna Remington had vowed to show no favorites. But her love and devotion to Beau overruled her pledge, for in every word, movement, gesture, and striking resemblance, Nicholas mirrored his grandfather. It was as if she had watched Beau grow from childhood to the troubled man she saw before her now. She could sense Nicholas's moods without a word spoken, and she knew when not to press. In her heart she loved him more than Kate, but she justified this by his resemblance to the husband she had lost so many years ago. Nicholas kept her young, her memories alive. And she wanted more than anything else to see him happy.

"I've felt better. This time of year always causes an ache in my bones," she added, pressing a small fist in her side to ease the discomfort. "I imagine Mr. Rafferty has the same problem."

Nicholas chuckled. "Not so he'd admit it. He still thinks he's young enough to sail to England with no ill effects." He leaned back in his chair and stretched. "So what brings you and my sweet little sister to Williamsburg?"

"Katherine thought she needed a new gown."

"Another? She has enough now to last out the year," he teased, glancing over at his sister to find her attention drawn elsewhere. He relaxed, crossing his arms over his chest and grinned mischievously. "Am I that boring that you'd ignore me, Kate?"

Startled by the sound of her name, she jerked her head around to acknowledge the summons, eyes wide and apologetic. "I'm sorry. What did you say?"

"I asked what gentleman has so obviously caught your fancy that you'd totally shun my company?"

A light blush settled over the young girl's face. "No gentleman, Nicholas. I was only studying the woman you stopped to talk with."

Reminded of Amber's presence, Nicholas shifted uncomfortably in his chair, avoiding a look her way.

"I must say, she's the best you've considered so far," Kate continued, studying Amber again.

"Considered?" he barked. "For what?"

"A bride," Alanna remarked, smiling. "And I quite agree." She, too, appraised the stranger's beauty.

"Well, I'm sorry to disappoint you both. I'm not considering her, as you so delicately put it. She's merely a business acquaintance."

"Her?" Kate asked, surprise changing the pitch of her voice. "From the way she's dressed, I'd say she'd be a poor partner. In more ways than one."

"Careful, little sister, your claws are showing," Nicholas rebuffed, amused by her straightforwardness.

Kate's narrow face paled. "Oh, I didn't mean it that way, Nicholas. She's very beautiful. But from the appearance of her clothes, I don't see how she could afford any business dealings. Look at her. All she's having is tea."

Nicholas chanced a look in Amber's direction to affirm his sister's observation, then motioned at one of the serving maids. After whispering his instructions, he turned to face his company.

"What did you do?" Kate asked suspiciously, a playful gleam sparkling in her steel-blue eyes.

"As I was told earlier, it's none of your business," he said firmly, causing a childish pout to form on his sister's face. He smiled secretively. Although Kate tried to act her full sixteen years, he could always manage to provoke her, easily winning any argument when she'd choose to sulk rather than debate the subject. Someday she'd make a beautiful wife, even with one minor flaw.

"I pray I live long enough to see you two friends," Alanna sighed, shaking her head.

"We are, Grandmother. Sometimes it's just hard to tell,"

Nicholas grinned, reaching over to squeeze his sister's hand.

"Only when you don't treat me like a child," Kate scoffed.

"You're not," he assured her, "and I wasn't." He lifted her hand to place a gentle kiss on the fingers curled around his own.

"Yes, well very soon I'll have my revenge, dear brother. When I own the shipping lines, I'll work you morning and night for a tuppence." The gleam in her eye denied her declaration.

"Of that I have no doubt," he laughed.

Their conversation interrupted by the serving maid who brought Nicholas a cup of tea, he waited for their privacy once more, then looked at his grandmother. "Have you ever heard of a man by the name of Baron Kelzer Von Buren?"

"Oh, good heavens, you're not dealing with him, are you?" Alanna asked disapprovingly.

"No. I've never met the man. I was simply wondering if you knew anything about him."

Alanna arched an opposing brow. "Well, rumor has it he married his wife for her father's estate, though Lord knows he was rich enough already."

"But I've heard he seeks a wife," Nicholas said, instantly satisfied Miss Courtney had lied.

"It's quite possible. His first wife died about two years ago. She fell down a flight of stairs in her home and the authorities called it accidental. Some say she took her own life, though no one knows for sure. He's an evil sort, loves to gamble, and has fought countless duels. He seems to thrive on others' misfortune."

Nicholas remained quiet a moment, silently chastised for damning the young woman when he truly knew so little about her. He glanced up at Alanna and smiled. "If you know so much about the man, why don't I?"

"Nicholas, when was the last time you went to a social gathering of any kind?"

Nicholas shrugged resignedly. "Yes. I guess you're right. Spending all my time at work prevents my hearing any gossip." A serving maid passed their table with a cup of bread pudding topped with a mound of whipped cream. He watched her set it down on Miss Courtney's table, exchange a few words, and walk away.

"Nicholas."

He glanced back at Alanna, realizing his attention had been pulled away. "I'm sorry. What did you say?"

"I said I'm having a dinner party in about a week. You will come, won't you? And spend the weekend?" she asked hopefully, her eyes suddenly drawn to someone standing at his elbow.

He looked up, somewhat surprised to see Amber Courtney glaring down at him, the dish of bread pudding in her hand.

"Please excuse my intrusion, but there seems to be a mistake. I didn't order this dessert, nor do I take handouts. *I* always pay for what I want," she growled, the implication unmistakable. Without hesitation, she overturned the bowl to allow the sticky dessert to land with a plop in Nicholas's lap. "Good day, ladies," she said politely, looking from Kate to Alanna, then turned, and, plucking her shawl from the chair, she proudly walked from the room, all eyes following her departure.

Learning of the possibility that Amber Courtney might truly be in need of money during the conversation he held with his grandmother, and then having the reality of that likelihood pointed out by his sister's observation that Miss Courtney had only ordered tea, Nicholas had felt a twinge of compassion. That and the foolish notion that he could buy her off so easily had prompted his purchase of the bread pudding. His mistake, obviously, had been in allowing her to know from whom the gift came, but even more in underestimating her. In that instant when he realized what she intended, anger flooded over him, that she or anyone had the nerve to refuse something he offered. But as the cascade of browns and whites poured earthward, a new, more powerful emotion hit him. With his elbows resting against the table, he stared at the disaster in his lap, its tepid dampness quickly soaking through his velvet breeches. He had been told to cool his loins before, but never in this fashion, and, knowing he deserved it, the whole idea struck him funny. Especially when he glanced up to find the shocked look of dismay on Kate's face and how his grandmother's eyes twinkled as she hid an obvious smile behind her handkerchief.

"If you'll excuse me, ladies, I have an urgent matter to take care of," he said calmly, his lower lip quivering as he fought to conceal his mirth. With a napkin, he removed what he could of the bread pudding from his clothes, stood and nobly walked away, his shoulders bobbing slightly with his laughter.

"Katherine, my dear," Alanna sighed happily, "I think we've found her."

Chapter Three

Andrea Courtney stirred, mumbling incoherently when her sister left the bed they shared, rolling over to drift off into blissful slumber once more. The sun had barely risen, spreading its muted yellow light across the sky to announce the beginning of another day. Ordinarily, its cheerful subtle influence was reflected in this young woman in her smile or the light tune she hummed as she heated water in the kitchen for their morning tea. But not today, for Amber felt anything but happy. She had returned home late last night in a dark mood, and Andrea had quickly retired to bed, knowing when it was best to leave her twin alone. Amber had only offered to tell her that her efforts to find money had failed, and that in the morning she would think of something else to rid them of the baron. Now that daylight chased away the shadows, it also took with it Amber's thoughts of succeeding in her mission. She kindled the fire, poured fresh water in the pot, and hung it over the flames before stepping outside on the back porch to listen to the merry chirping of the sparrows.

How could everything have gone so wrong, she wondered, smelling the sweet aroma of wildflowers and damp grass. And how could she have been so foolish? Moisture glistened in her eyes. "I'm so ashamed, Papa," she whispered. "I only did it for

Andrea. How was I to know he lied?" Biting her lower lip, she briskly wiped away her tears, vowing Nicholas Chandler would never be the cause of her grief again. What had happened was yesterday and she must think of today—tomorrow. In time, the bruises he had inflicted and the soreness of her thighs would vanish. She would put the incident in the back of her mind. She would never dwell on it again. She would never recall the gentleness of his kiss, the stirrings he had aroused, the way her flesh had seemed to burn wherever he touched her, or those dark, lustful eyes, handsome features, hard, powerful muscles—She blinked, a rush of heat scorching her cheeks. Turning abruptly she went back inside to see about her tea.

"Good morning, Amber," her sister said quietly from the kitchen doorway.

Amber glanced up, forcing a smile. Andrea would not learn what had transpired between her and Nicholas Chandler. The soft, gentle soul wouldn't understand and would probably blame herself for it until her dying day. She moved to the table and sat down. "Did you sleep well?"

"Yes. Did you?" Andrea asked, stepping into the room. She went to the cupboard where she took down the tin of tea leaves and two cups.

"Oh, yes, quite well," Amber lied, remembering how she had tossed and turned, driven from their bed when the first sunlight had appeared in the room. "I hope I didn't wake you."

"No, you didn't," Andrea said, placing the cups on the table and returning to the hearth. "May I fix you something to eat?"

"No, thank you. I'm not really hungry. Maybe later." She watched her sister lift the kettle from the hook, move to the table, and pour the steaming water into the cups. Amber thanked her once more and tested the tea, guardedly observing her sister return the kettle to the fire, the young woman's steps short, spine stiff and her mood tense.

"So," Andrea said suddenly, sitting down opposite Amber, "have you decided what we shall do?"

Amber shrugged. "No." She took another sip of tea.

"Well, I have."

Amber glanced up curiously. She didn't like her sister's tone.

"We'll sell everything and go away. Some place where the baron can't find us," Andrea said bravely, her eyes averted.

"And where would that be? A nice idea, but foolish," Amber mumbled into the cup raised to her lips.

"Then what do you suggest?" Andrea snapped. "So far you've managed to wear out your slippers walking around Williamsburg."

"I don't know," Amber exclaimed angrily and stood. Crossing to the window, she pulled aside its clean but tattered curtain. "But I'll think of something. We still have over three weeks. And if I have to, I'll shoot the baron first before I'll allow you to marry him."

"Oh, Amber, don't talk like that," Andrea moaned.

"And why not?" She squinted in the sunlight. "Who says I can't be as heartless and dishonest as Baron Von Buren?"

"I do."

Amber glanced back at her sister.

"It's not in you. Oh, sure, you scream and holler, but you'd never hurt a soul—Amber?" She called the name twice more before the distant look in Amber's eyes disappeared.

"Dishonest," she mumbled.

"What?"

"Maybe I'm not heartless, but when driven to it I can be dishonest."

"What do you mean?"

"If I can't borrow the funds we need, I'll steal them!"

"What?" Andrea gasped, her face paling.

Amber's lips curled upward as she thought about carrying out such a plan. "And I know just the perfect victim. An arrogant, uncaring, self-centered—"

"Who do you mean?" Andrea broke in worriedly, producing a satisfied grin on her sister's face.

"His name is Nicholas Chandler."

"Of Chandler Shipping in Williamsburg?"

"The same."

Exhibiting a rare emotion, Andrea's brows knotted together. "That's the most foolish idea you've ever come up with, Amber Courtney. How do you intend to get away with it? They probably guard the office at night, and he more than likely keeps his

53

money in the bank anyway!"

"Oh, don't pop a seam, Andrea. I'm not going to rob his office. I intend to be more subtle." Lost in thought again, she hurried to the small writing desk in one corner of the room and searched its pigeonholes for what she needed. Extracting a blank piece of paper, she sat down at the workplace and began scribbling a message. "I hope he can read," she muttered, more to herself.

"Who?" Andrea questioned, thinking her sister mad.

"Papa's cousin, Paxton," she answered, without looking up.

"The pirate?"

"Yes."

"Why are you writing to him?"

Amber finished the passage, returned the quill to the well, and lifted the paper before her to reread. "If I can find him in time . . ." she murmured. "The last Papa heard of him, he was sailing near Boston." She glanced up at her sister. "I hope he hasn't been arrested."

"Amber!" Andrea exploded, stomping a slippered foot to the floor. "What do you intend to do?"

"If Paxton agrees, I intend to split the profits fifty-fifty."

"What profits?"

Crossing to the fireplace, where she took down one of the tapers from the mantel, Amber bent to light it, saying, "Don't ask. And don't breathe a word of this to Seth. The less both of you know the better." Returning to the desk, she allowed one drop of wax to fall on the letter and pressed her father's seal to it. She blew out the candle and smiled. "Yes, I think everything is going to be just fine."

Bright sunlight sparkled in the waters, warming the earth and chasing away the crisp bite of the early morning air. The dock at Williamsburg bustled with workmen unloading the newly anchored ship, counting each piece, stacking and sorting. Tea from England and fine cloths from Paris numbered just a few of the treasures, and Nicholas Chandler surveyed their progress as he always did, certain the time had come to warrant the purchase of another ship. The seemingly endless caravan of wagons rumbled their way to the end of the pier, waiting to carry the goods to the merchants eagerly expecting the newest shipment of cargo.

"It's all here, Mr. Chandler," Mathew beamed, holding up a fistful of papers as he walked closer. "They sure made good time. Nearly a week early."

Nicholas's suntanned face took on a healthy glow as he digested the bookkeeper's words. "Yes, I know. I'd say it's time we got ourselves another ship, don't you?"

Mathew's lips pursed in serious thought. "I suppose. But if I were you, sir, I'd find where those shortages are coming from first."

Nicholas sidestepped a sailor carrying a large crate. "They're minor, Mathew. I'm not truly worried about it. We'll find it." He held out a hand, silently indicating the documents Mathew possessed. "I better enter those. You find out from the captain how soon he'll be ready to sail again. I want that load of cotton off the pier before Carter decides to have someone else ship it."

"Yes, sir," Mathew answered, hurriedly setting off to do as instructed.

Nicholas smiled faintly, thinking how angry Mr. Rafferty would be when he returned. For the past two months, Nicholas had cunningly avoided using Sean and his crew for the longer voyages, and Nicholas realized they were close to having heated words to discuss the issue. But Nicholas worried what a lengthy trip would do to Sean Rafferty. Though Sean never complained, Nicholas had furtively observed the man's growing discomfort in his shoulders and knees. Some mornings Mr. Rafferty failed to hide the pain he felt, even though he smiled brightly or challenged Nicholas to an arm-wrestling match. Nicholas loved Sean Rafferty as much as he had loved his own father and would never be the cause of the man's death by sending him on a voyage across the ocean. He smiled covertly, envisioning the quarrel they were sure to have.

Sea gulls overhead pulled Nicholas's gaze to them, and he noticed how the sun raced to reach its peak in the crystal blueness of the sky. His smile faded, his fingertips gently rubbing the tender wounds on his chest. *Her* eyes were nearly that color, and the long flowing mane of her hair matched the golden streams of the sunlight. He hoped this injury she had inflicted would leave scars. He deserved them. And more. How was he to know she was a virgin? He had assumed that she had tried the ploy on others and only wanted to show her that he would not be fooled. He had raped her! Hadn't she cried out for him to stop? Hadn't he sensed the gentle upbringing she must have had? She was no practiced harlot, but innocent of the art of lovemaking, the joys it could bring. If only he hadn't been so insensitive! He sighed heavily, praying his guilt would quickly pass, since he doubted he would ever see her again. Slapping the papers against his thigh, he turned sharply for his office and collided with a young boy standing behind him. Such an unexpected move caught the youth off balance and tumbled him to the wooden planks of the pier.

"You clumsy oaf! Watch where you're goin'," the child snapped, struggling to find his feet again and the floppy hat that had flown from his head.

Nicholas easily reached down, caught the boy's elbow, and yanked him upward to full height, only four or five inches shorter than his own six feet. "I'm sorry, I—"

"Let go. You're hurtin' me." The wiry adolescent jerked free, plopped the hat in place, brushed the dirt from his already rather soiled breeches, and looked up, his pale blue eyes widening in a sea of dirt smudges.

"Is something wrong?" Nicholas asked, taking in the youngster's rowdy appearance. Despite the boy's height, Nicholas judged him to be only thirteen. He had no need to shave and his skin was smooth and fair, with short cropped blond hair curling about his face. His shirt hung loosely from his narrow shoulders, bright patches of another cloth sewed at the elbows. Bare legs beneath the knees of the baggy attire disappeared into shoes much too large for his small feet. Nicholas twisted a dark brow disapprovingly, yet something slightly familiar about the child gnawed at his memory.

"Ah . . . you Nicholas Chandler?"

Nicholas folded his arms over his chest, one knee bent as he replied, "Yes. Do I know you?"

The boy's eyes widened all the more. "No," he barked,

somewhat fearful. "I—I mean there's no reason ya should."
He looked to the scuffed toes of his shoes. "I—I didn't mean to
snap at you, sir. I sometimes forget my manners."

Nicholas studied the boy a moment longer, then dismissed
his musings, blaming the long hours he had spent at work for
causing him to mistake his acquaintance with anyone of this
sort. "No harm done," Nicholas replied quietly, dropping his
arms as he made to move toward his office, only to find his way
blocked by the lad, a bright smile shining in the pale blue eyes.
"Was there something else you wished to say?"

Short blond curls bobbed up and down. "I need a job."

Nicholas's dark eyes glowed. "Doing what? Making a nuisance of yourself?" He noticed a slight curl on the boy's upper
lip.

"I'll work hard," he hissed.

Nicholas shook his head. "Sorry." He took a step to pass,
stopped by the boy's insistence when the child blocked his way.
"Don't you understand English?"

"Of course, I do," the boy rallied, then forced the smile to
return. "Look, ya don't have ta pay me much. I just get hungry
now and then."

Nicholas's gaze swept over the slight form. "Obviously you
don't need it for a better suit of clothes. The ones you're wearing should be good for another year or so."

The smile changed to a sneer. "I ain't like most of you—
you—" he decided on a gentler title, "rich folk. Clothes ain't
important."

A hand shot out to wipe a smudge from the tip of the boy's
nose. "Nor a bath," Nicholas speculated, testing the grime
between his thumb and forefinger.

"Hey, if I do a good job what do you care how I look?"

"I was thinking more on the order of smell."

"So stay upwind," the boy jeered.

Nicholas pressed his lips together, voiding the smile. "I
intend to." He paused a moment, then shot past the youth,
hoping to end their conversation. But before he could find
safety inside his office behind a closed door, the boy ran past
him to stand in the way with outstretched arms.

"I could sweep up."

"Someone already does."

"Run errands."

Nicholas shook his head.

"Work on one of your ships—"

"No!"

The boy thought a minute. "Where do you live?"

Nicholas's shoulders drooped. "I own a house just outside town. Why?"

"Well, I could drive your carriage for ya. You know—to work in the morning, home at night."

"I ride a horse."

"Oh," the boy whispered, his head lowered in defeat.

Nicholas leaned to see the boy's face. "Where are your parents?"

Bobbing shoulders revealed his apparent lack of knowledge. "They dumped me when I was—a—thirteen."

"Thirteen?" Nicholas chimed, recalling his earlier impression. "How old *are* you?"

Without thought, the boy replied, "Eighteen."

"Ha!" Nicholas exploded. "If you are, you're a year older than me!"

The pale blue eyes failed to look at him.

"Where do you live?"

Again the boy shrugged. "Around."

"Sleeping in alleys or haylofts, no doubt. Do you know what could happen to a boy like you, running around without protection? You'll find yourself some pirate's cabin boy."

A grin creased the smudges of dirt on the boy's cheek. "Yeah. That's why I'm lookin' for a job. If I had a little money, I could find a place ta live—"

"Oh, all right," Nicholas moaned, "you've got a job. But one argument, one negative shake of that dirty head of yours and you're out on your ear. Got it?"

"Yes, sir," the boy chirped. "Where do I start?"

"Come back around five o'clock—"

"Tonight?" he wailed, his face reflecting his dislike of night work.

Papers clutched in his hand, Nicholas rested the fist on one hip.

"Yes, sir," the boy amended. "Tonight."

"Meet me here. We'll have something to eat and discuss your duties. What's your name?"

A look of near panic raced across the boy's face and disappeared. "Edgar, sir, Edgar MacDonald."

"Edgar MacDonald?" Nicholas quoted doubtfully.

The lad smiled with a lift of one shoulder. "Didn't like my real name. I changed it."

Nicholas stared at the boy a moment, then waved him aside. "At five o'clock, Edgar. Don't be late," he called back over his shoulder, disappearing into his office.

A wide smile curled the corners of Edgar's mouth upward, a look of satisfaction mixed with a strange air of mischief sparkling in the pale blue eyes. Slapping his hands together, he rubbed them vigorously as if pleased with himself as he turned and walked away.

"Good night, Mr. Chandler."

Nicholas looked up and nodded. "Good night, Mathew," he said. "See you in the morning."

"Yes, sir. May I walk out with you?"

Nicholas laid aside his quill and stretched. "Thanks, Mathew, but I'm waiting for someone."

"All right then, I'll be going." Glasses punched back into place, gray coat lifted to his shoulders, Mathew waved and left the doorway, the clicks of his footsteps fading in the distance.

Nicholas looked at the small clock sitting on the counter opposite him. Five o'clock exactly. He cocked a brow, wondering if punctuality would be one of Edgar's virtues, when the doorway darkened again with another form.

"Five o'clock," Edgar pointed out, stepping into the room. "Just like ya said."

"Yes, so I did," Nicholas replied, noticing Edgar's appearance hadn't improved. If anything, he seemed dirtier. That vague awareness of a previous acquaintance with the youth flashed across his mind and disappeared. He blinked, observing how streaks of dirt ran down the boy's legs and into his shoes. Oh well, the job Nicholas had in mind might possibly cure that. He stood. "Hungry?"

"Guess so," Edgar returned.

Lifting his coat from the chair, Nicholas eased his broad shoulders into it and picked up his hat from the corner of his desk. "It won't be much. Just a little ham and sweet potatoes. You like bread pudding? We can stop by the Chesterfield House and pick some up on the way."

His back to the boy, Nicholas failed to see the smirk on the youth's face before Edgar blinked, realizing what Nicholas had said. "On the way? Where?"

"To my place." He motioned toward the door. "Shall we go?"

Round blue eyes stared back at him.

"Well?" he added, setting the boy off at a reluctant pace.

Once Edgar stepped outside the building, he started down the street toward the center of town. With a clumsy gait, his oversized shoes clunking against the wooden sidewalk, he paid his new employer no heed, as though lost in a world all his own.

"Where are you going?" Nicholas called, watching the child stop abruptly and turn around. "I live outside of town, remember?" he asked. "Too far to waste time walking." He moved to his horse, which was tethered to a rail.

Casting a worried glance in all directions, the boy shoved his hands into the pockets of his breeches, his attention centered on the stallion, then on Nicholas, then back on the horse. "I—don't mind walkin'," he said weakly.

"Nonsense," Nicholas scowled. "The horse can manage the two of us."

Edgar rocked slightly on his heels. "Yeah, well, I ain't really hungry. Why don't ya just tell me what it is ya want me ta do and I'll get to work."

"What's wrong? Don't you know how to ride?" Nicholas asked, one hand resting on the saddle, the other on his hip.

The street urchin kicked at a pebble near his toe.

"Well, it's nothing to be ashamed of," Nicholas encouraged, mistaking Edgar's silence to mean the affirmative. "Come on. You sit in the saddle and I'll ride behind you. Then there won't be any chance of your falling off."

"I—don't—"

"Edgar. Remember our agreement?" Nicholas asked. "Now either get on the horse or find another job."

Edgar's mouth opened to respond, then snapped shut at the challenging tilt of Nicholas's head. Looking back over his shoulder, as if seeking some sort of rescue and finding none, Edgar's thin frame sagged in defeat. Grudgingly he came to stand next to Nicholas.

Bending, Nicholas cupped his hands together for the boy to place his foot and easily lifted him to the saddle. Such a light form, he mused, oddly experiencing a twinge of sympathy for the boy's plight. Apparently finding an adequate amount of food had been his biggest problem, for he doubted the boy's weight surpassed that of a small bale of cotton. How could a mother and father discard their kin without a care? And his clothes! Had the child ever known the luxury of fine cloth? Or a bath, for that matter? He mentally shrugged off his thoughts, knowing it would change if he had anything to do with it. Untying the reins, he handed them to Edgar, grabbed a handful of the horse's mane, and skillfully swung himself up behind the boy.

"Get rid of the hat," Nicholas ordered tersely.

Edgar stiffened. "Why? Ain't doin' you no harm."

Angrily snatched from the boy's head, the offensive item found itself crushed to the boy's chest by Nicholas's firm grip. "I can't see past it. If you wish for us both to stay mounted, you'll do as I say."

Strong, hard muscles curved around Edgar as Nicholas reached for the reins and spun the horse around, setting it off at a brisk trot down the road.

Although the streets teemed with people on their way home either afoot or in their carriages, Edgar failed to notice. With his eyes trained on the road ahead, he sat rigid in the saddle, his mind oblivious to all else. Nor did he feel the attention Nicholas gave him, the way he leaned back just enough to study the dirty, slim shape of his companion. The mud-caked hair mixed with golden strands aroused Nicholas's curiosity, for it hinted at a fine beauty, resembling various shades of sunlight, in a thickness seldom seen. He fought off the temptation to touch it, repulsed by the lack of care the child gave it, and wondered at the butcher who had taken scissors to it. Then another detail sparked his interest. Although the boy was covered with grime from head to toe, Nicholas grew acutely aware of the lack of any odor, which would surely accompany such an uncleansed body. In fact, the child had a pleasant, inoffensive scent that caught him unawares. Soap? Could the fragrance possibly suggest some time spent soaking in a tub? He tilted his head to one side, discreetly appraising the pale whiteness of the youth's neck below the unkempt mop before the tattered shirt hid it from view. Nicholas's dark brow, tipped golden by the sun, raised bewilderingly with his discovery. A spot customarily skipped, deemed unnecessary by children, was here quite clean. What sort of child was this Edgar Mac-Donald?

"Do you have any brothers or sisters, Edgar?" he asked aloud.

"Could have, I guess," the boy replied.

Nicholas chuckled. "Don't you know?"

"I told ya, my parents dumped me off a long time ago. They don't care about me and I don't care about them. How much further is it to your place?"

"Not far," he said absently. "Edgar, surely you know whether or not you had any brothers or sisters. You couldn't have been that young not to remember."

The narrow shoulders drooped. "All right, all right. I have a brother. Now are you satisfied? And if ya don't mind, I'd rather not talk about it."

"Why?"

The boy stiffened. "Look, I don't go poking into your business, so just stay out of mine."

Nicholas smiled, dismissing the boy's secret past as nothing of real concern. "Do you know how to cook?"

Edgar twisted in the saddle to glance back at his employer. "I suppose. Why?"

"I'd like to change my clothes when we get home. I thought maybe you could see to our meal while I do." Once Edgar looked away, Nicholas smiled brightly. "We could delay it a bit if you'd like to wash up." He felt the child stiffen at his suggestion.

"I know how ta eat with a fork. Don't need ta wash my hands."

"I was thinking more of your entire body. How can you go around all day looking like you do?"

"Easy. *I* don't care what I look like."

A low rumble of mocking laughter pierced Edgar's toughened exterior. "That, dear Edgar, is obvious."

The road stretched out before them as they left the outskirts of town, and Nicholas nudged his horse into a canter, bringing a squeal of fear from the lad. "Don't worry. I won't let you fall," Nicholas guaranteed, slipping an arm around the boy's tiny waist.

"Get your hands off me," Edgar shouted, pulling at the strong, unrelenting hold. The grip tightened.

"Stop that," Nicholas stormed. "You will fall if you don't sit still."

"Then let go of me. I'm not a baby. I know how to ride."

Nicholas's face mirrored surprise. "Then why did you say you didn't?"

"I never said it. You did."

"All right. *I* said it. But you never denied it. Why?"

"'Cause I didn't want ta sit this close to ya. Rich people make me nervous."

Nicholas's cheek twitched in suppressed retaliation. "Would you rather run alongside?" he asked quietly.

Edgar remained silent.

"Then shut up and hold on."

As if to test the lad, Nicholas spurred the stallion into a full gallop, racing down the road at a breakneck speed, allowing the horse full rein until they came to a drive that veered off to the left. Grabbing both hands full of the horse's thick mane, his hat forgotten as it flew from him, Edgar leaned in, riding with the grace and skill of a master horseman, his mouth clamped shut, eyes affixed to the course Nicholas chose to take, for instead of the wide, smooth path, he reined the horse onto a narrow trail in the woods surrounding them. Willow branches lurched out at them, stung Edgar's bare legs, and threatened to whip the pair from the saddle. They raced across a clearing, down a ravine, and up the other side, bearing down on the log fence before them. Edgar's eyes widened at the sight, certain the horse could not carry them both over the height of the barrier, feeling the steed's strong muscles beneath him flex as they reached it. In one sleek move, the horse lunged, cleared the fence easily, and landed with a jolt on the other side.

"All right, all right. Ya proved your point," Edgar screamed. "Now slow this animal down!"

Ignoring the boy's request, Nicholas kicked the horse harder, sending them off as if the devil himself chased them. The drive crossed in front of them but Nicholas chose not to take it, dashing through a stand of oak trees instead until the way before them opened up to a wide, empty yard, in the center of which stood a huge, stately manor. Just when Edgar decided the man intended to race them in the front door and out the back, Nicholas jerked hard on the reins. The stallion immediately obeyed, nearly burying his hindquarters in the ground as it came to a sliding halt.

"You're right," Nicholas agreed, slipping down over the horse's rump. "You ride quite well." He flipped the reins over the brass hitching post and started up the steps, calling back over his shoulder, "Aren't you coming?"

Edgar sat a moment longer, catching his breath. A leisurely ride on an old plow horse hardly compared to the experience he had just encountered, and if he never rode in such a manner again it would be too soon. Rubbing a finger beneath his nose, Edgar swung a leg over the saddle and jumped to the ground.

The wide front door of the manor stood open, as Nicholas had left it, and Edgar stopped just outside, uncertain whether or not to enter, his chin sagging as he took in the view. A shiny marble floor spread out before him, masked slightly by the multiple colors of the oriental rug lying upon it. Opposite the door, a long, circular staircase wound around and disappeared into the second story, a stained glass window on the landing flooding every color of the rainbow into the room. Overhead hung a crystal chandelier, its multitude of teardrops reflecting the wealth and craftsmanship of such a treasure. Against one wall stood a long, dark buffet, above which hung a large painting. Enthralled by the beauty of its subject, Edgar absently entered the foyer to get a closer look. White lace sparsely covered the woman's shoulders and the soft swell of her breasts, a startling contrast to the ebony richness of her hair and her dark, smiling eyes. A friendliness and grace surrounded the portrait, reflected in the slight upward curve of the full mouth. Although Edgar had no knowledge of whom the woman might be, he felt oddly cheated of the honor.

"It was painted on the day she married my father."

Edgar glanced up to find Nicholas at the top of the stairs, bare to the waist, a fresh shirt dangling from his fingertips. He looked back at the painting.

"She's beautiful," he whispered.

"Thank you. You're not the only one to have that feeling," Nicholas added, descending the staircase. He came to stand next to the boy. "She had a special beauty much like her mother, my grandmother. It came from within." He smiled softly, in thought. "I want to marry a woman like her, but I doubt I'll ever find one. Not in time, anyway."

Edgar glanced up, surprised. "What do you mean, in time?"

Resting a bare arm around the boy's shoulders, he said, "Never mind. It doesn't concern you."

Edgar quickly wiggled free. "Stop touchin' me. I told ya I don't like rich folk gettin' too close."

Nicholas studied the dirt-streaked face. "What do you like, Edgar?"

"I like to look at the way you rich people waste your money." A thin, dirty hand reached out to capture a delicate vase sitting on the buffet, painted with bright flowers and colorful birds. Edgar rolled the vase in his hands. "How much ya pay for this?"

Nicholas quickly snatched it from the boy and returned it to its place. "Its value outsums any amount you can imagine."

"See what I mean?" Edgar reiterated. "A waste. What good's it do ya, huh? I'll wager ya don't even stick flowers in it." He selected a figurine made of alabaster. "And this. Whatcha do with this? Clunk unruly children on the head with it?"

Nicholas cast him a vexed look. "I'm thinking about it."

Edgar returned the item to the buffet with a thud and said, "Are we gonna stand here all night trying ta outwit each other,

65

or are ya going to show me where I get ta work?"

"The latter, since I see no contest otherwise," Nicholas replied, lifting his shirt to his shoulders.

The boy's pale blue eyes narrowed at the insult. "I don't have ta stand here and take this, ya know."

"Very astute, Edgar. Just close the door behind you when you leave," Nicholas said flatly, starting off across the foyer.

"Hey, wait a minute. I didn't mean that."

Nicholas stopped and turned around. "Didn't you?"

The boy's chin fell several times as he fought to find the words. Unsuccessful, he lowered his head and picked the crusted dirt from his palm.

"Then I suggest your first task shall be to keep your mouth closed, your hands to yourself, and do exactly as I say, or you'll find out just how far it is to walk back to town. Understand?"

Edgar nodded sheepishly.

"How well do you know how to cook?"

"Enough ta get by," he mumbled.

"Good. Then that much of it is settled," Nicholas replied, turning for the hall.

Edgar's narrow face wrinkled. "Of what?" he asked suspiciously.

Pausing in the doorway of the kitchen to look back, Nicholas pressed a hand against its frame, his other stuffed in the pocket of his breeches while he studied the boy. "Anna Wilson does my cooking and light housework. She is ill and probably won't be back for a few days. It really isn't much of a problem, since I can eat in town, but I would appreciate something for breakfast. Then there's—"

"You dragged me all the way out here ta fix your blasted breakfast?" Edgar shouted.

Nicholas sighed, subduing his irritation. "If you'd kindly hold your tongue, I was about to explain your other duties." He glared challengingly at the urchin until Edgar looked to the floor in silence. "Mrs. Halstead comes in every day to do the main housework. She is away now visiting relatives, and with Anna being sick I need someone to help out for a while. Or don't you think you can handle the job?"

"That's sissy's work," Edgar muttered.

"Well, you can hardly expect to do a man's job," Nicholas argued. "You are not strong enough. Now come with me. After we've eaten, I'll show you where you can sleep."

"Sleep?" the boy exploded.

"Yes, sleep. You're staying here with me," Nicholas replied before turning to disappear from the doorway.

The boy's small mouth dropped open, but no words to argue came to his mind.

Chapter Four

Cool morning air drifted into the room through the open window, gently caressing Amber's bare arm sticking out from beneath the coverlet. Moaning at the interruption of her slumber, she flipped the quilt over her head, content to lie in the darkness for a while longer and listen to the chirping melodies of the mockingbirds and thrushes outside her bedroom. She loved playing audience to their recital and often lingered in bed long after Andrea had risen to stoke the fires for breakfast.

Instantly and painfully aware of her surroundings, she sat straight up in bed, coverlet clutched beneath her chin, and stared at the closed and locked door, wondering how she had slept at all. She tilted her head to listen for any sounds coming from another part of the house. Silence prevailing, she breathed a sigh, relieved to learn she had awakened first. She scooted off the bed and, out of habit, went to the small dressing table to brush her hair, her breath leaving her in a rush when she saw her reflection in the mirror. Slowly drifting to the stool before it, she sat down, tears burning her eyes, one hand raised disparagingly to the yellow curls encompassing her face. What sorrow she had known when she had cut each golden lock to reach no longer than her ear, a smile she didn't feel turning the corners of her mouth upward to soothe the dismay of her sister.

"It will grow back, Andrea," she had assured her. "It's only a minor sacrifice for a greater goal."

Looking at the mass of tiny curls, stiff with dirt, she fleetingly wondered at the sanity of her ruse. Nicholas Chandler was not a stupid man. One slip on her part, a failure to use the words of a young boy, and he would know her game in an instant. And she must never let him get too close. Her gaze moved downward to the rags lying on the floor near her feet. Her clothes, Edgar's clothes, the ones she had trapped herself into wearing. How awful she felt in them, how she longed to discard them for the clean muslin of her gown, the full skirts rustling about her ankles. She glanced at her reflection, spying the dirt marks on her nose and chin. How she yearned to bathe, to soak away the grime, feel clean again and smell of lavender-scented soap. How long must she pay the price? Her shoulders squared, she frowned at the image staring back at her. Until it's finished, she scolded silently. Bending down, she grabbed the formless garments from their place to get dressed and fix breakfast before the master of the house came looking for her.

Amber glanced up from the table at the sound of someone's entering the kitchen. Dressed in a dark blue coat and breeches, a softer shade for both his shirt and stockings, Nicholas made a striking appearance. The fine cut of his clothes fit him perfectly, clinging to the hard muscles of his shoulders and thighs, accenting the narrow hips and flat belly. Her breath caught in her throat when she noticed how the dark blue fabric stretched across his manhood, as though making a proud display of what he could offer. She gulped, quickly looking away before he discovered where her gaze had lingered and think it strange.

"Sleep well?" Nicholas asked, sliding into a chair opposite her.

"S'pose," came the disinterested reply.

Noticing a new smudge of dirt on her face, Nicholas frowned. "I'm sure your room was clean. How did you manage to find that?"

Amber glanced up irritably. "What?"

"That," Nicholas said, reaching over to wipe her chin.

Amber jerked back. "What do you care? It's my face."

"Yes. But I have to look at it."

A smirk appeared on Amber's mouth and Nicholas sighed, knowing what the gesture implied. "I can't very well go around talking to the wall. Though Lord knows it would be more enjoyable." He poured hot water over the tea leaves in his cup from the pot sitting before him. "Take a bath today," he announced suddenly, then added, "and do something with that hair. It looks awful." He missed the quivering chin of his companion as he reached for a biscuit and spread fresh butter over it. He took a bite and looked up, noticing how Amber absently twisted a finger in one curl. "Does it feel like straw? It certainly looks like it," he said out of the corner of his mouth.

Angry blue eyes glared up at him. "Didn't your ma teach ya not ta talk with your mouth full?" she snapped.

Nicholas gulped the wad of food. "She taught me a lot of things. One was to care how I looked. Obviously your mother didn't." He concentrated on the biscuit again.

Tears stung Amber's eyes at his mention of her mother. Angeline Courtney might not have been as beautiful as his mother, or as rich, and she hadn't dressed in the finest of gowns or attended grand balls, but she had been a lady nonetheless. She had taught her daughters grace and charm and had groomed them as best she could on what little they had. Only a desperate need drove Amber Courtney to dress as she did. Yes, she could bathe as he ordered, rid herself of the grime, but nothing else about her would change. She despised him, and no amount of soap and water would wash away that feeling.

"Start by making the beds," Nicholas instructed, rising from the table, a second biscuit in his hand. "Then see to the study. It's the only room I really use other than my bedchambers, and I'm rather messy, I'm afraid. But don't touch a thing on the desk." He started for the door, pausing to look back once he reached it. "I'll be home in time for dinner. Try to fix something palatable, if you can manage."

Amber looked balefully at him, a sneer more akin to a growl curling her lip. "Yeah, well, don't be surprised if I ain't here when ya come home," she spat, punching holes with her finger in the one remaining biscuit on the plate.

"Oh, please," Nicholas mocked, "don't give me cause to hope." Turning sharply, he made his exit before an angry retort could come to Amber's mind.

Listlessly, she washed the breakfast dishes and put them away before she begrudgingly headed for the stairs on her way to Nicholas's room and the duty of straightening up, recalling their conversation over dinner the night past. To seal her disguise of boyhood, she had argued with him, saying a young man's work should be at the pier or cleaning stables, not chamberpots. The discussion lasted only that long, for Nicholas promptly informed her that he already had someone to care for the stable and if the child wanted work, he would do as told. Little did Nicholas know that his announcement was well received, for Amber truly disliked the idea of currying horses or cleaning manure from the stalls. She would have preferred being near his office and the chance of overhearing anything concerning his shipments, but she realized that to insist on it might tip her hand. She would have to be patient. And there was always the possibility she could learn something from Nicholas himself. One corner of her mouth crimped in disgust. Of course that meant spending time with him, something she wished she didn't have to do, since her presence seemed to provoke the man, and she wondered if possibly it was his only side, a serious, grouchy nature. It didn't matter. Once she was through with Nicholas Chandler, his manner would change to that of a raging demon from hell.

Passing through the foyer, Amber spotted the vase sitting proudly on the buffet. She paused beside it, gently running a fingertip over the raised surface of painted flowers, a devilish smile creeping over her young face. Latching on to the brightly colored object, Amber tossed it in the air, caught it in one hand, and skipped happily up the stairs, her treasure tucked beneath one arm.

"Will you be coming in tomorrow, Mr. Chandler?" Mathew asked from the doorway of the office, his jacket tossed over one arm, hat in hand. "It's Sunday."

"No," Nicholas replied, closing the ledger. "I'll take this home. I have work there to do anyway, and I can finish this up at the same time. Enjoy your day off, Mathew."

"Thank you, sir. I wish you'd do the same."

Nicholas looked up and smiled. "You have a wife and three lovely girls to keep you busy. If I sat around all day, I'd go mad."

"Then come to the house for dinner," Mathew offered eagerly.

"And interfere with your time alone with your family? No, thank you. You needn't try to entertain me. If I grow bored, I'll find something. Now get going or your wife will be angry . . . at both of us."

"Yes, sir," Mathew nodded. "At least allow me to walk out with you."

Nicholas laughed. "Now that much I'll agree to."

The dark leather book imprisoned in the crook of his arm, Nicholas lifted his coat from the chair and followed his book-keeper from the office, waving farewell when the man turned and started down the walkway. Stuffing the volume in the pouch tied to his horse's saddle, Nicholas stood back and stretched, noticing how the sun seemed to burn the landscape as it slid ever so slowly earthward. Another week had slipped away, and, while he stood there inhaling the fragrance of the salt air, he experienced the recurring twinge of remorse. In three weeks he'd no longer have the right to make decisions concerning Chandler Shipping. He thought of his father, and a dark, suspicious frown shaded his eyes. Only Mr. Rafferty and he questioned the fire that had claimed the life of Andrew Chandler. Black hair turned silver had been the only evidence of his age. A quick wit and a keen business sense had been his traits until the very last, and Nicholas could not, would not believe his father had fallen asleep at his desk and in his dreams knocked over the lamp that in turn ignited the papers surrounding him. Yet no clue had proved otherwise. If only he hadn't worked late that night, alone. If only Mr. Rafferty had chosen not to sail to Boston that morning. If only Nicholas had stayed by his father's side, not played the dandy in the English

73

court. If—Nicholas's face twisted in rage and complicity. Jerking the reins free of the hitching post, he swung himself up into the saddle, kicked the horse's flanks, and raced off toward home.

"Well, well. Who do we have here?" Heather Branford smiled, the feather of her hat bobbing as she appraised the youth standing before her from head to toe.

Amber's lip curled.

"Are you some poor relation come to mooch off Nicholas?"

"I ain't no relative of his," Amber snapped. "Whatcha want?"

"I came to speak with Nicholas. Is he home?" Her hazel eyes, haloed by a mass of mahogany curls, looked past Amber.

"If he was, he'd answer the door."

"Oh," Heather pouted, her eyes suddenly sparkling with a new thought. "Do you expect him soon?"

"He said he'd eat here."

Her thin lips stretched into a smile. "Then I'll wait," she announced, stepping past Amber, who refused to move.

"Could be a while," Amber grunted, swinging the door closed. "An hour. Maybe two."

"I don't mind," Heather said, happily. "I'll wait in the parlor."

Before Amber could refuse, the shapely figure glided across the marble floor and disappeared into the next room, followed by the curious street urchin. Leaning a shoulder against the door frame, hands shoved deep in her pockets, Amber watched the unexpected and unwanted company remove her lace gloves and bright blue bonnet before crossing to the sofa to sit down. She wasn't the same woman Amber had seen Nicholas dining with, the one whose hand he had held and kissed. This one wasn't nearly as beautiful.

"Who are you?" Amber asked.

The woman looked up, smiling politely. "Heather Branford. Who are you?"

Amber shrugged dismissively. "You ain't the same one I've seen him with before." She grinned, deciding such a voiced observation might wilt her ribbons some.

Heather smoothed the folds of her skirt. "It doesn't surprise me. Nicholas is quite sought after. Every unmarried woman in the area seeks his approval."

"For what?" Amber exclaimed, straightening sharply. The idea repulsed her, and she truly saw no need for any woman to chase after such an arrogant—

"Why, haven't you heard? Nicholas must find a wife within three weeks or lose his inheritance," Heather offered, the picture of innocence shining in her round, hazel eyes. She studied the satin bow of her hat. "He hasn't much time for me, I'm afraid."

Amber's mouth fell open. So that's what he had meant when she promised a deal and he stated he'd heard enough of them. He thought the woman seeking a loan was only playing some sort of trick. Three weeks! No wonder Nicholas snapped at Edgar. He had more important things on his mind than some little troublemaker looking for a job. Amber covered the giggle that found its way to her lips. Served him right. She hoped the pompous ass would lose everything. He'd soon learn what it meant to have to beg. Amber looked back to the woman sitting quietly across from her. Better still, she decided, she'd like to see the man shackled to some spiritless wench like this, all honey and sweet and—

"What's the matter," Amber said aloud. "They cuttin' in on your time?"

Heather stiffened, her thin face reflecting dismay. "No. It's nothing like that. I love Nicholas."

"Oh, yeah," Amber chimed, "you and twenty others, I'll wager."

Heather opened her mouth to deny any misdoings on her part as the thundering clamor of racing hoofbeats drew their attention outside the manor.

"Ah," Amber remarked, "your lover returneth." Pleased with her banter, Amber watched the woman shrivel unhappily, then turned back to the foyer in time to see Nicholas come through the front door. With a bounce to her step, Amber started across the room to advise her employer of his guest, pausing at the disapproving look she received.

"I thought I told you to bathe."

Amber's cheek twitched. "I didn't have time. I've been entertaining the future Mistress Chandler," she sneered triumphantly.

Nicholas's eyes clouded, the news adding to his already irritable mood. Without bothering to ask his guest's name, Nicholas went to the buffet and laid his book on it, pausing as he examined the length of its shiny surface.

"Edgar," he called hesitantly, turning around. "Where's the vase?"

Stuffing her hands in her pockets again, Amber slowly ambled closer. "Oh, that. Well, I kinda hoped ya wouldn't miss it."

"Edgar," Nicholas growled. "Where is it?"

She retreated a step. "Don't act like ya snagged your stocking. It was an accident."

The sun-darkened face paled. "An accident?" he repeated slowly.

"Yeah. My hands were wet."

"You broke it," Nicholas moaned.

Amber grinned sheepishly, nodding, and looked to the floor at her feet. "Ya don't have to pay me for today—"

"Pay you?" Nicholas bellowed. "You little fool. All the money in the world couldn't replace it. It belonged to my mother. She made it. Its value was only the cost of the clay, but it was priceless to me."

Amber's breath seemed to leave her. "Oh," she whispered. "Why didn't you say so before?"

"What difference would it have made? It's still broken."

Amber's lower lip trembled. "I'm sorry—Mr. Chandler."

"Sorry," Nicholas snarled. "What good is being sorry? Go see to dinner while I greet my guest. We'll discuss this later."

"Yes, sir," Amber mumbled, turning away.

She crossed the foyer toward the kitchen, then paused to look back. Nicholas stood before the buffet staring at the portrait of Victoria Chandler. Overcome by strange feelings of empathy for this man, she turned, head down, and quickly made her way to her room.

Amber knelt beside the bed and pulled a bundle from

beneath it that was wrapped in a pillowcase. She unfolded the corners, her smooth brow wrinkling as she gazed upon the vase in her hands. If she returned it to its place, Nicholas would know she had stolen it. And it had no value should she try to sell it. She sighed, disheartened. This wasn't going at all well. Not like she had imagined. In the comfort of her own cottage, with her sister by her side, it had seemed so easy. She would don her best gown, travel to Williamsburg and seek the help of a banker or wealthy merchant. Her face burned with the thoughts of her foolishness and of how things had actually turned out. But vowing not to submit, to admit defeat, she had devised a better plan. She would cut her hair, disguise herself as a boy, and claim revenge on the man who had stolen her maidenhood. Her chin trembled. With the help of Barlow Paxton, she would learn which of the ships belonging to Chandler Shipping carried a valuable cargo large enough to be worth stealing, then sell it up north and split the profits with Paxton. After their task was completed, she would return home, pay off Von Buren, and settle down to live happily without anyone's knowing what she had done. A tear fell on the painted surface of the vase she held in her hands. A business transaction. That was all. Stealing from his ships wasn't the same as stealing his mother's vase.

"Edgar."

Amber stiffened. Nicholas was in the kitchen. Hurriedly, she rolled the vase in the cloth again and shoved the parcel under the bed.

"What are you doing?"

Her wide blue eyes stared up at Nicholas standing in the doorway of the room. "I—ah—thought—I kicked something under there. I was just looking."

The muscle in his cheek flexed, his dark eyes still glaring his anger with the boy.

"Have you fixed anything to eat?"

Amber came to her feet and moved away from the bed and her secret. "Yeah, ready any time ya want it."

Nicholas took a long, deep breath and let it out slowly, as if trying to ease the tension that tightened his entire body. "Then serve it in the dining room."

"Why? Kitchen's just as good."

Nicholas gave the youth dangerous look. "Because I always serve my guests in the dining room."

"Guests? You mean she's staying?"

"That's right. Any objections?"

Amber looked down, the corner of her mouth twitching. "No."

"Good. Then see to it right away."

"Yes, sir," came the disapproving grumble.

Nicholas turned to leave, then stopped abruptly with a thought. "You may have tomorrow off. In fact, I think it would be wise if you make yourself scarce for a while. After you wash the dishes, I suggest you leave the house. The only thing saving you from a sound thrashing is the fact that I believe it was an accident. But if you get in my way, I might change my mind."

"Yes, sir," Amber mumbled, unable to look at him.

"Be back here on Monday morning after eight o'clock. I'll be gone by then." He turned quickly and exited the room, leaving Amber to stare after him in quiet penitence.

Nicholas finished his fifth glass of wine, feeling its warming effect spread over him and numb the piercing tone of Heather's constant chatter. He stared over at her sitting opposite him on the sofa, her own glass of wine empty. He stood, took the goblet from her without asking, and went to the buffet to refill them. He liked Heather. No one could deny her beauty or the stirring she always managed to arouse with her innocence. He smiled one-sidedly, listening to the dark liquid trickle into the glass. She was far from innocent in the true sense of the word. He had often sampled her charms and no doubt would do so tonight. It obviously had been her reason for coming. Although she never spoke of it outright, she had often hinted of the consequences they would pay should she find herself with child, his child. But it had never really bothered him. If it happened he would marry her, if no other woman claimed his heart before then. Handing Heather her glass of wine, he returned to his chair to quietly indulge in the only thing that seemed to please him of late, smiling or nodding periodically at his guest to disguise the absence of attention he paid her.

He had truly wished to be alone tonight, to spend a quiet evening in his study to sort out his thoughts. But finding Heather waiting in the parlor changed his mind. Although they shared very little in the way of interests and could hardly share a meaningful conversation, he enjoyed her lightheartedness, the coquettish manner and subtle way she lured him to the bedchambers. He smiled dreamily.

"Nicholas?"

Blinking, he glanced up at her. "What?"

"I asked if your young houseboy lives with you."

"Yes." He stood and went to the buffet to pour another drink. "But I told him to take tomorrow off. In fact, he should be gone by now. I told him he could leave just as soon as he finished in the kitchen." He tried three times to replace the stopper in the wine decanter, finally setting aside his glass to use both hands to accomplish the task.

"Did he cook that delicious meal?"

He picked up his goblet and turned around, frowning when his eyes failed to focus. "Mmm—yes, he did," he answered quietly, then smiled. "It's a surprise, isn't it? Wouldn't think a dirty brat like that could—could handle it."

"Yes, well, I think he handled it better than you're handling your wine," she observed when Nicholas took a step and stumbled sideways.

"Huh? Oh, yes. I'm sorry. I didn't think I had that much to drink."

"Maybe you should go to bed," she suggested demurely.

Glass raised to his lips, he smiled into it, then swallowed the contents. "Yes. Maybe—I should."

"Would you like me to help you up the stairs? You're seeming to have a difficult time on your own."

"Would—you? That would be awfully—kind of you," he said, playing along. Just once he wished she'd fight him. Oh, well, a tumble in bed with a woman would always be the same. A faint smile appeared. Not all, he remembered. There was one. . . . He allowed her to take his glass and set it aside, and then slip her arms beneath his to brace him. They started for the stairs.

"You know, Nicholas, I really shouldn't be doing this," she smiled sweetly. "What will everyone think if they find out?"

Draping his arm across her shoulders, he let his fingertips rest against the pale flesh of her breast exposed above the decolletage of her gown. "That you are a very—giving woman."

"Nicholas!" she half scolded, half laughed, lifting her skirts to ascend the long staircase.

The dancing flames in the sconces beside them cast long shadows that spilled smoothly over the banister and treads to fall against the marble floor of the foyer, interrupted by the slight form that stepped in the way. Amber watched the duet with apparent disgust curling her lip until they disappeared into Nicholas's bedchambers and closed the door behind them.

"Here, let me help you," Heather whispered, pushing his hands aside when Nicholas made to unbutton his shirt.

Her agile fingers quickly undid the garment, the smooth palms of her hands pressed against his chest and up to his shoulders to slip it from him. A heady aroma of perfume and rose-scented soap assailed him, breaking down his intent of gentleness. She ignited a fire in him, one he had never before experienced with her, an unexplainable need to possess her. Clasping her face in his hands, he pulled her to him, his mouth covering hers hungrily. She moaned when his fingers found the buttons of her gown, eagerly helping him unfasten the last when it seemed to resist, and shimmied from it. He kissed the corner of her mouth, her chin, her neck, his passion mounting. Quickly finding the strings of her camisole, his head spinning with desire and his immoderate consumption of wine, he pulled them loose and freed her from the garment.

Silver moonlight through the window brightened the room, flowing in to caress all it touched. Having shed the rest of his clothes, Nicholas held her to him, their naked bodies pressed as one. Through half-glazed eyes he studied her, blinking when a soft shade of blue stared back, golden hair shimmering across her shoulders. His lips formed the name, but no sound escaped them.

Her slender fingers entwined with the hair at the nape of his neck, pulling his lips down to meet hers. The vision faded, his lust consuming him. Lifting her gently in his arms, he carried her to his bed, his step wavering slightly and bringing a trio of giggles from his delicate burden. They fell together on the feather mattress. He trapped her beneath him, and his mouth found the peak of her breast, its nipple taut, her hands urging him to savor the sweetness a moment more. She opened her thighs to meet him, a journey he had traveled, a secret he had found many times before. Impatient not to wait a single heartbeat longer, he thrust his manhood into her, hearing her groan with pleasure. He moved faster, his desires exploding within him. Near his peak, his mind flooded with the illusion that had haunted him earlier, lifting him to heights he had never before reached.

"Amber," he moaned, his voice a husky whisper.

Heather stiffened beneath him. "What? What did you say?"

Knowing the name he had called had not been hers, yet uncertain which one he had chosen, his passion died in the cold reality of the moment. "Heather," he offered weakly. "I said 'Heather.'"

"No, you didn't," she growled, pushing him from her. She left the bed quickly and found her clothes. "I know you see other women, but I thought only I shared this pleasure with you." Fighting with the buttons of her dress, she moved toward the door, then looked back. "How could you?" she cried.

Lost in the shadows of the room, he vaguely saw her lift the latch and pull the door wide until the blinding light from the hallway sconces flooded in. Her figure passed before it and an instant later she was gone.

"He-eath-er-," he moaned, propped up on one elbow in the center of his wide bed. "Damn!" He fell back against his pillow, his head spinning all the more. In the next minute, he breathed the steady rhythm of slumber.

A pair of bright blue eyes secretly watched Heather Branford storm from the house, their owner unaware of the turbulence that had just occurred and why.

Nicholas rolled over onto his back, squinting in the bright sunlight that stole into his room, certain the pounding in his temples would remain until the last rays of sunset faded in the western sky. He obscurely remembered what had happened after dinner the night past, that he'd had too much to drink and that Heather and he had wound up in bed. His arm shot out to test the space next to him. Empty. He relaxed. He enjoyed the moments they shared this way but hated waking up next to her. She always played the virgin robbed of her maidenhood. A minor thing, but one that annoyed him. As he lay there thinking about her, he considered another flaw in her character. She was much too understanding. She never argued, always did whatever he wished, and he got the feeling she did it only to satisfy him. He liked Heather and had more than once considered her above all the others for a wife. However, he surmised a life with her would be uneventful. Especially after the grand balls of Europe and the violent storms on the high seas. Nothing could compare, he feared, leaving the ache for adventure stirring in the pit of his stomach. Would he ever be content to settle down?

Nicholas yawned, wincing with the pain so minor an act provoked, and pulled the coverlet up over his head, the faint ringing of church bells in the distance. Was it noon already? His body ached, his eyelids heavy with unfinished slumber, as though he'd only slept an hour. His lips were dry, and he ran his tongue over them, flipping down the quilt when even this got in his way, wondering if, during his sleep, someone had stolen into his room and forced an entire bale of cotton down his throat. Maybe if he ate something— His eyes opened slowly when the fresh smells of tea and biscuits floated in to greet him as if summoned by his own thoughts. He sat up, cradling his head in his hands. Had God sent an angel of mercy to see him through the day? He didn't care just as long as she spoke in a whisper. Or could it be Heather? Not likely. She had never fixed breakfast for him in his life. Forcing himself to rise, he scanned the room through one half-opened eye to spot a pair of breeches lying on the floor. So what if he wore them yesterday? Bending down ever so slowly, he hooked a finger in the cuff and returned to the bed, easing himself to its feathery softness. Breeches in place, he looked about for a shirt, but decided against it, since his need for something to drink seemed of more importance. Barefoot, he left his room and started down the long staircase, one hand held securely to the railing to steady himself.

"I'll never drink again," he moaned softly for the hundredth time.

When he reached the marble floor at the bottom, he paused, touching cool fingertips to his brow. He needed to lie down. Looking back up at the endless row of treads, he decided the effort it would take to climb them would be more than he could manage. He moved his attention to the hall leading into the kitchen. This route would be much easier. Lifting a foot toward his destination, he walked slowly, keeping his head straight as even the slightest movement seemed to hammer the blood in his temples. But before he reached the doorway, he heard the laughter of women and paused to listen, uncertain from which direction it came. When it died away, he decided that he had imagined it, and shrugged off his curiosity as he started through the archway to the kitchen, pulling up short when he found his grandmother, Kate, and Edgar sitting around the long trestle table, the two women listening intently to something the youth had said.

"Grandmother?" he frowned.

Alanna glanced up from her cup of tea, surprised by his presence, and smiled almost immediately. "Oh, good morning, Nicholas," she said, her cheerful greeting quickly altered to a concerned frown once she saw his ruffled hair and tired, bloodshot eyes. "Are you all right?"

Acutely aware of his manner of dress, or lack of it, he lifted his arms across his chest. "The evils of manhood, I'm afraid. I'll be perfectly fine by this evening. I'll get a shirt—"

"Don't bother," she replied with a shake of her head. "We've seen you this way before. Come, sit down, and have breakfast with us.''

Moving slowly, he crossed the room to accept the cup of tea she offered. ''I wasn't expecting you,'' he apologized as he eased himself into a chair opposite her. ''Is something wrong?'' He tested the coolness of his drink, then tilted the cup higher, swallowing nearly all of the brew before he relaxed with a sigh, his eyes closed.

''Only that we wanted to remind you that you just have three weeks left before I take over the Chandler Shipping Lines,'' Kate broke in, fighting the smile that tugged at her lips.

He opened one eye to look at her. ''The way I feel right now, you'd be more than welcome to it.''

Her steel-blue eyes glowed with amusement. ''I can hardly wait. After all these years, I'll be able to tell you what to do. What fun.''

His lips stretched into a silly grin. ''Oh, yes, what fun,'' he mimicked, looking over at their grandmother. ''I give her two months before the company is broke.''

''Oh, really?'' Kate threw back at him. ''And why do you think that? I intend to hire a very capable manager. Of course, if you can't handle the job—''

''And what makes you think I'd accept?''

''How else will you support yourself? I won't give you any handouts, and I'm sure Grandmother won't, either,'' she predicted confidently with a lift of her nose in the air.

He watched her a moment, then spoke softly. ''Maybe I'll turn pirate like our father.''

''Nicholas, you wouldn't!'' she exploded, all mirth gone.

Always enjoying the easy manner with which he could embarrass his sister, he played on, no trace of mockery shining in his eyes. ''Why not? It was good enough for him. And I'm sure Sean Rafferty would agree to go along.''

''No, he wouldn't,'' she argued. ''He's too old for that sort of thing.''

Nicholas shrugged. ''Then I'll find myself a rich woman who'd take in a boarder.'' He wiggled his brows suggestively.

A red hue quickly settled in Kate's cheeks at his brashness, and she opened her mouth to remind him that men of his class wouldn't behave in such a shameless manner when she saw one corner of his mouth twitch upward. Clamping her own shut without a word, she concentrated on the plateful of biscuits sitting before her, wondering if she would ever be able to best him at anything.

"Well, I don't think we'll have to worry about it, Kate," her grandmother sighed, refolding the napkin in her lap.

Nicholas glanced up with a smile. "Oh?" he asked. "And do you know something I don't?"

Her brown eyes so much like his own stared back devilishly at him. "Only that if you're not careful, you'll find yourself at the altar for another reason."

The laughter faded from his eyes. "What do you mean?" he asked guardedly, a creeping suspicion knotting his stomach.

Grinning, Alanna rested one arm against the edge of the table, hands folded, and allowed only a slight hint of humor to lace her words. "Really, Nicholas. I thought you knew the possible consequences of—shall we say for modesty's sake—being alone with a woman."

His chin down, Nicholas stared over at his grandmother through furrowed brows. "Yes, I'm well aware of what could happen, but I fail to see why you bring it up."

Reaching for her tea, she winked at the youth at the end of the table. "We were told you had a visitor last night," she stated simply, then lifted the cup to her lips.

The sallow color of his face and neck darkened a bit as Nicholas slowly turned a damning glare on the wide-eyed ragamuffin sitting near his sister. His nostrils flared, the muscle in his unshaven cheek twitching, he forced himself to remain calm, if only for his grandmother's sake. But he was sorely tempted to teach the impudent brat a lesson. He wanted to bolt from his chair, attack the child and blister his backside. What he did in his own home was *his* business and something this little urchin would soon learn not to repeat if it meant he couldn't sit down for a week as payment for acquiring the knowledge. He stiffened suddenly. "I thought I told you to take the night off."

The heat of his rage directed at her, Amber felt every inch of her flesh burn with his unspoken warning, thankful that his grandmother and sister were there to protect her should he lose his temper and decide to vent his wrath physically. Unable to endure his piercing glare, she studied the wood graining of the tabletop. "I—I didn't have no place to go," she muttered.

"So you decided to spy on me and tattle to anyone who would listen," he growled.

"Nicholas," his grandmother intervened, "don't be so rude."

Turning back to wrap his hands around his teacup, he grumbled, "Rude isn't all I'd like to be."

"Well, don't be angry with Edgar. He didn't tattle, as you put it. We were only talking and I asked him if you were still working late every night or had decided to enjoy some free time for a change."

Only his eyes moved when he looked at her. "A simple yes or no would have done," he snarled.

"Oh, Grandmother," Kate interrupted, enjoying the fact that someone had for once made her brother's life a little uncomfortable, "don't try to smooth things over. It won't do any good. Nicholas likes being grouchy."

He cast her a sideways glance, then glared at Edgar again. "I'm only grouchy when someone makes me that way."

"Oh, you're only grouchy when you're hungry," Kate pointed out, grabbing a biscuit. "Here,"—she tossed the roll at him—"eat this and spare us all your bad humor."

His reactions dulled by the pain in his head and his dislike of airing his personal life, he failed to catch the biscuit in midair, his temper smoldering when it hit his arm, fell to the table, and rolled onto his lap. He stared irritably at it a moment, his wide shoulders drooping with his annoyance, then silently retrieved the defiant piece of food and pointedly ignored the giggles coming from the young woman at the end of the table.

"See why he isn't married, Edgar?" Kate laughed, leaning toward the youth. "What woman in her right mind would want to wake up to that every morning?"

Amber smiled weakly in return, avoiding a look Nicholas's way. His style of dress had upset her the minute she saw him

86

standing in the kitchen doorway, blatantly reminding her of the night before. She had hidden in the foyer listening to his conversation with Miss Branford until she had heard the woman offer to help Nicholas to bed, then fled for safety in the shadows of the tallboy on the opposite wall. She couldn't explain why, but as the couple had ascended the stairs, a strange feeling had overcome her, and for an instant she had thought it was jealousy. But of what? Surely she could not have been envious of another woman's being with the man who had raped her! In fact, the thought that any woman would willingly fall into bed with him turned her stomach. Didn't Heather Branford know a scoundrel like this only used her, as he had used the innocent woman seeking a loan and nothing more? She peered secretly over at him, noticing how the muscles of his arm and chest flexed when he reached for the jar of honey sitting on the table before him. Her pulse quickened and she frowned, looking away, and wondered at its cause. He wasn't the sort of man she had imagined would excite her. Why, he didn't even have the good manners to dress himself properly in the company of others! Feeling horribly uncomfortable and quite out of place, she cleared her throat and stood.

"If you'll excuse me, I got things ta do," she said quietly, hoping no one saw the blush she could feel burning in her cheeks. She made to step away, halted by Kate's hand clutching hers.

"Wait. I'll go with you," the pretty face beamed up at her.

A dirty brow wrinkled in surprise. "But—but I'm gonna clean."

"Good!" Kate grinned excitedly. "I'll help. I'd much prefer your company to my brother's anyway." She cast Nicholas a haughty lift of her nose and smiled broadly when he returned her banter with an irritated curl of his lip. "And he and Grandmother have things to discuss which always bore me." She turned back to her companion. "You don't mind, do you, Edgar?"

Amber shook her head slowly, confused by the young woman's offer to do menial chores. She had always thought women of wealth pampered themselves in lavish baths or practiced the arts of stitchery and needlepoint, too uppity to do anything below their class. Could it be Katherine Chandler had ulterior motives? But what? Mentally, she shrugged off the question, knowing that if Kate did, Amber would soon find out. She moved toward the door, her eyes trained on her steps and averted from the half-naked man at the table already engaged in conversation with his grandmother.

"Where do we start?" Kate asked enthusiastically a moment later as they walked across the foyer.

"Mr. Chandler's room, I guess," Amber mumbled, wondering what the two of them would find to talk about for very long. But when they reached the bottom of the stairs leading to the second story, Kate paused at the credenza and gazed up at the painting hanging above it.

"She was very beautiful, don't you think?" Kate asked, tilting her head from side to side to appraise the subject smiling back at her.

Surprised that the young woman would choose to discuss her family with a stranger, Amber frowned, forcing her attention from Kate's lovely profile to that of her mother. The woman in the portrait radiated a kind of warmth that sparked a twinge of regret in Amber for never having met her, and, without any hesitation, she agreed with Kate's declaration.

"Yes, she is indeed. You must miss her."

Kate shrugged. "Not really. You can't miss something you never had."

"What do you mean?"

"My mother died giving birth to me. I never knew her."

"That's awful," Amber blurted out.

"So I've been told. But my grandmother was always there, and between her and my father, they raised me." She grinned over at Amber. "And, of course, Nicholas. You know, with the father that I had and my obstinate brother, I'm surprised I didn't turn out worse than I am."

"I don't see anything bad about you," Amber argued, suddenly relaxed in the young girl's company. "Why do you think that?"

"Papa was such a tease. And after Mama died, he devoted all his time to me. Spoiled me, I'm afraid. But it was his way of easing the pain, Grandmother said." She sighed, looking up at the painting. "He loved her very much. We used to all live here in this house. Then after Papa was killed,"—her voice cracked—"I went to live with Grandmother, and Nicholas took over the house."

Her curiosity piqued, Amber dared ask, "Tell me about your brother."

Kate laughed. "Have we got that long?" She started up the stairs. "Well, Nicholas was eleven when I was born. We were good friends, even though he was so much older than I. When he turned seventeen, he left home. Papa said he couldn't blame him. He did the same thing as a young man, wanting to see the world. He'd come home once a year and try to work with Papa, but before long he'd sail off again. Then Papa started worrying about him. Said he wanted Nicholas to settle down, to enjoy the things a wife and family could bring." She smiled, following Amber into Nicholas's bedchambers where they set about cleaning and straightening the room. "That's when he came up with the idea of his will. Grandmother told him it wouldn't work. And so far it hasn't." She paused in her duties to cross to the window and stare outside, deep in thought. When she spoke again, her voice revealed the sorrow she felt. "I think Nicholas blames himself for not being here when Papa died." Turning back to Amber, she said quite matter-of-factly, "I don't like Heather Branford."

Nicholas's discarded shirt held in her hand, Amber glanced up quickly in surprise. "Why?"

"Oh, she's nice enough, but she's only after Nicholas's money. She'd never really love him."

"She said she did."

Kate went to the bed and tugged the covers in place. "I can imagine how many times some woman has said that to him. They've never really meant it."

"No one?"

"Well, if they did, he never believed them. Nicholas wants a woman he can love as much as Papa loved our mother. That's why he'd risk losing the shipping lines. He won't be tied to anyone just for the sake of money." She giggled. "And that's why I tease him so. I know he wants to do what's right. I'm just trying to hurry him along."

"You almost make me feel sorry for him," Amber grunted.

Laughing, Kate turned to her companion, her fists on her hips. "You don't like him very much, do you?"

One shoulder bobbed.

"Well, I can't say I blame you. He is sorta mean at times."

Mean, Amber thought sarcastically. That's not the half of it. He's rude, arrogant, domineering, and heartless. He'd take anything he wanted without a care to others. She wondered what his sister would think if she told Kate that Nicholas had suggested she repay a loan by spending a night in his arms. She shook off the temptation of telling her.

"You said your father was killed," Amber replied, changing the subject. "How did it happen?"

Kate went to the small writing desk in the corner of the room and sat down in the chair behind it. "There was a fire at the warehouse one night almost two years ago. The authorities said Papa must have fallen asleep at his desk and knocked over a lamp." She reached out to run a fingertip along the plume of the quill sitting in the well before her. "Nicholas and Sean Rafferty don't think so," she whispered, her words heavy with grief.

"They don't? What do they think?" Amber asked, coming to stand near her.

"They won't talk about it to me, but I overheard them one time. They think he was murdered but can't prove it."

How Fletcher Courtney died, senselessly, brutally, callously, and the hours she had watched over him, sharing his pain, came rushing back to Amber's mind. *Murdered but couldn't prove it.* Did the Chandlers know who was responsible for their father's death? Amber knew who had killed a gentle, loving man: her father. And she too couldn't prove an injustice done. But at least she knew who had committed the crime, and she swore an oath to see him pay. Holding back her grief, the common bond between her and Kate, Amber reached out to touch Kate's shoulder. "I'm sorry. I shouldn't have pried."

"It's all right, Edgar. You didn't know," Kate said, an understanding smile on her lips as she patted the sympathetic hand. She took a deep breath and stood up quickly. "Don't you think we should get to work?"

Amber nodded, a strange compassion for this young woman she hardly knew pulling at her heart.

When they had finished with Nicholas's room and stepped out into the hall on their way to the parlor, Amber paused to glance back inside, her eyes immediately drawn to the wide four poster bed in the center of the huge space. She hadn't thought about it all the while she dusted and picked up his clothes from the floor, caught up in Kate's words as she was, but her time with Nicholas had been in that very bed. A knot formed in her throat. And Heather Branford had shared the same intimacies. Her gaze drifted to the soiled linen shirt she held in her hand. He had discarded her for another as easily as he did a change of garments. *Were all men the same?*

"How old are you, Edgar?"

The question startled Amber out of her private world of remorse, and she awkwardly grabbed for the doorlatch to swing the door shut and block out the vivid reminder of her earlier transgressions. She cleared her throat, wadded up Nicholas's shirt, and stuck it under her arm, smiling up at Kate and responding without consideration.

"Eighteen."

"Eighteen?" Kate echoed. "You certainly don't look it. Are you sure?"

One side of Amber's mouth turned upward. For some odd reason, she wished she could tell Kate the truth, imagining the surprise on the girl's face when Kate learned this boy wasn't at all as he appeared.

Mistaking the lopsided grin, Kate laughed. "I know how you feel. I wish I was older at times."

"Why?" Amber asked, deciding not to argue the point as she followed Kate down the stairs.

"Sometimes I wish I was married, had someone to love me."

91

"But you do!" Amber exclaimed.

"You mean my grandmother and Nicholas? It's not the same. I want to know the love of a man."

Kate missed the troubled look on her companion's face as she led the way into the parlor. Nor did she see the way Amber's hand absently touched the garment tucked in the crook of her arm. If she had, she might have questioned her, and right now Amber had no answers.

"I don't mean to be rude, Grandmother," Nicholas whispered, flinching when the shrill sounds of Kate's and Edgar's laughter grew louder, "but I'd really like to go back to bed if you don't mind."

"I understand, Nicholas," she sympathized, reaching over to pat his hand. "Your grandfather spent many Sunday afternoons recuperating from his foolishness." She smiled up at Kate when she and Edgar hurried into the room, noticing they still enjoyed a secret they had shared by the gleam in their eyes. "We'll go just as soon as we tell you about our surprise."

"Oh, yes, I nearly forgot," Kate grinned, pulling Amber down into the chair next to her. "Nicholas is going to love this."

Somehow Amber felt she was intruding on matters concerning the family, but she also realized Kate would not permit her to leave. She picked up her cup of cold tea and stared into it, feeling as if the minor act allowed privacy for the others.

"Surprise?" Nicholas repeated.

"Yes, We're having a dinner party this Saturday," Kate volunteered.

"And that's the surprise?" Before either of them could answer, he raised a hand to acknowledge his sudden understanding. Alanna Remington's surprises always meant someone new had been invited, someone she was certain would please him but rarely did. He loved his grandmother very much, but at times she tested his limits. "Somehow I know already, I hope," he said dryly.

Alanna's eyes sparkled. "Yes, as a matter of fact, you do.

"You met her the other day. Amber Courtney."

Half-swallowed tea lodged in Amber's throat, choking the breath from her. She gulped, and it went down the wrong way, bringing tears to her eyes and a surge of strangled coughs. Fighting for air, she grabbed a napkin and covered her mouth, certain her world had come to an end.

Chapter Five

Irritably, Nicholas rose from behind the desk in his study, a fistful of papers clutched in one hand, his teacup in the other, and headed off for the kitchen. No matter how many times he tried he could never make a satisfactory tasting brew, and this morning was no exception. He decided to try again. But the dark scowl that drew his brows together stemmed from a different cause. His grandmother's sudden announcement that she had invited Amber Courtney to spend a few days at Raven Oaks and her insistence that he join them had caused a knot of worry to form in the pit of his stomach. He couldn't very well decline the invitation without an excellent reason, and he dreaded meeting Miss Courtney again in the stark brightness of day. How do you apologize to a woman for raping her?

"Excuse me, Miss Courtney," he mocked, "but about the other night. Please forgive me for forcing myself on you. I couldn't help myself, for you see, I've gone a little mad."

His upper lip curled into a snarl. Dear God, what *would* they talk about? But then again, maybe she wouldn't accept the offer, knowing he might be there. He threw his head back, his gaze looking to the heavens, one hand tossed in the air. Of course, she'll be there. If she wanted money, wanted *him* desperately enough, she wouldn't miss it for the world. He stormed into the kitchen and slammed the cup down on the table.

I'm surprised no one has thought of it before, he mused. Move in on my family, win their respect, and let them do the work. After all, what man wouldn't listen to his dear, sweet grandmother? Well, Miss Courtney, you'll have a hard battle to win, for I intend to spoil it every chance I get.

He filled his cup with fresh tea, picked up his papers, and started for the study again. And now this. Where was Edgar, anyway?

"Thanks, mister," the young street urchin called halfheartedly, watching the hay wagon with its driver lumber down the road. Amber's narrow shoulders hung in marked defeat, arms at her sides, feet shuffling as she made her way down the long drive leading to the Chandler house. She hated wearing the baggy shirt and torn breeches and shoes too large to be comfortable. If only it would end soon. She sighed heavily, knowing Andrea was right. They should leave Jamestown and all their problems. But where would two young women go without money and not have more grief befall them? Thank God one favor graced them. Only their father and mother had ever been able to tell them apart. And, for this reason alone, Amber had accepted Mistress Remington's invitation. Andrea would go in her place. The last thing she wanted was to throw suspicion on them, and refusing Mistress Remington's offer would certainly do just that. The corner of Amber's mouth twisted, recalling the heated exchange she and Andrea had had the night past when Amber had told her sister of the plan and of how Mistress Remington had come to know Amber Courtney.

"I can't do it," Andrea had stormed. "They'll know by the way I behave that something's wrong. I've never been as outspoken as you. They will suspect."

"Then apologize for my behavior and explain how distraught I was, that I usually don't conduct myself in such a manner," Amber had suggested. "They don't really know me and they'll never guess."

The late night hours had faded into early morning before

Amber had convinced her sister everything would go smoothly and they had retired to sleep the few hours before the sun made its showing. But Amber had lain awake, stomach churning, nerves jittery, and tears filling the corners of her eyes. It had taken her a long time to decide, and although she saw no other way she regretted having to make her sister assume her identity. Especially when Andrea, poor, sweet, innocent Andrea, knew nothing of what had happened between Amber and Nicholas Chandler. She feared he would speak of it again and state his change of mind, that if she agreed to accompany him to his room he would arrange some means of payment, as she had already suggested on their first meeting. What would Andrea think? But then, Mistress Remington did not appear to be the kind to allow such behavior under her own roof. Certainly not with Kate there. Yes, that was it. She would tell Andrea to befriend Kate and avoid Nicholas at all costs, explaining that only he might recognize the real Amber Courtney. She had relaxed with the thought and drifted off into fitful slumber.

Amber had donned Edgar's attire that morning, reiterated the importance of Andrea's avoidance of Nicholas Chandler, and started off for Williamsburg, hoping that with luck Paxton would arrive before Friday.

Crossing the wide veranda to the front door of the house, Amber somberly and without hesitation lifted the latch and pushed the door open. Startled when she met Nicholas standing on the other side, several papers held in one hand, a cup of tea in the other, her knees buckled and nearly spilled her to the floor.

"Where have you been?" he asked tersely. "It's almost noon."

Recovering from the unexpected presence of her employer, Amber's lip curled disdainfully. "At the theater, watching a play. What did ya think?" She swung the door easily on its hinges, letting it close with a thud.

"Very amusing," Nicholas returned, one corner of his mouth crimped in a lopsided, disapproving sneer. "I told you to be here after eight, not eleven."

"And ya told me you'd be gone," Amber observed.

"Oh, I see. So you decided to get a full day's pay for half the work."

"Pay me what ya want," she grumbled, head down as she started past, her curiosity aroused when she heard Nicholas sigh.

"Look, I was worried. You said—"

Amber's head shot up, surprised laughter escaping her. "Worried? About me?"

Nicholas stiffened. "Yes. You said you had nowhere to go, then you disappeared without a word and didn't show up for work this morning when I told you. What was I to think?"

Amber's brow wrinkled. "You should think good riddance."

The angry lines on Nicholas's face softened. "Come into the study," he instructed, turning away before Amber could object.

He rounded the huge desk in the center of the room and put his teacup and papers on it before sitting down in the leather wing chair. He motioned for Amber to sit opposite him and waited until she had done so before leaning in to fold his arms along the edge of the desk.

"For some reason I feel the need to apologize," he began.

"For what?" Amber exploded, laughter tingeing her words.

Nicholas glanced up, his dark eyes warmed by his smile. "Because I'm taking out my problems on you. In less than three weeks, I must find a bride or lose my father's shipping lines."

"I know that," Amber shrugged. "Your lady friend told me. Must be kinda hard ta tell which one really loves ya or wants your money. It's dumb."

"Why do you say that?"

"'Cause love ain't got nothin' ta do with money."

Nicholas fell back in his chair. "I knew there was a reason I liked you. We think the same."

Amber's slim frame stiffened, her eyes narrowed. "Oh, no we don't. If we did, ya wouldn't be living like ya do."

"Oh? And how would I live?"

"Ya wouldn't be wasting money on trinkets."

Nicholas' amusement sparkled in his eyes. "What would I do with my money? Give it to people like you who won't work

98

to better themselves?"

Amber's lip curled. "I work enough ta feed myself. I don't have ta dress all fancy to be happy. Tell me, Mr. Chandler, are you happy? Does all your wealth lighten your heart? If you died this minute, could you honestly say you lived your life to the fullest? No regrets?"

Resting an elbow on the arm of his chair, Nicholas pressed a fist to his chin, deep in thought. Regrets? He had plenty of them. Money had never meant anything to him, contrary to what this little ragamuffin thought. He had spent it carelessly and continually all the while he had sailed the seas and lived in Europe. The only time he had put any amount to good use was in the purchase of land in the foothills of the Atlas Mountains in Morocco. But even that had been a whim to outsmart Yaakob, a mountain warrior who preyed on the local farmers and sheepherders. Nicholas had hired a large number of the nomads to protect his property and the villagers, but only to anger the huge warrior. No, it wasn't the money he sought to inherit, but the honor of his heritage. And now that he thought about it, he had never been happy. Oh, he'd had a pleasant enough childhood; he had loved his father and mother, but when Victoria died giving birth to his sister, his ties with home had been broken. He had felt a need to explore, to search for something, a desire he couldn't suppress nor understand. He had lived recklessly, wildly, leaving his imprint anywhere he went, and a trail of broken hearts to mark his path. Not once had he found a love that touched him deeply, passionately, with finality. He blinked, looking at the dirty face staring back at him. Maybe this little beggar recited the words to describe what he himself truly felt inside. Money had nothing to do with love. And all the ladies he had courted never saw past his wealth to the inner man, and instinct had always warned him in time. He sighed. Why should he be punished for wanting to share a love with a woman, as his father had with his mother?

"It's a shame I can't find a girl who thinks like you," he said suddenly.

"What?" Amber shrieked. Had he recognized her ploy?

"If I could, I'd marry her. At least I'd be sure she wasn't after my money. Just as I'm sure of you."

The youth appeared to have trouble drawing a breath. "Well, you're wrong there, Mr. Chandler. Your money would be the only thing that would interest me about you. You'll have a long wait before you find a woman who feels different."

Laughter rumbled deeply in Nicholas's chest. "You really do carry a grudge, don't you?"

"A grudge? Against what?"

"Against people of wealth. Tell me, do you group us all together?"

Amber shrugged, her cheek twitching with a sneer. "Guess so. Never had no cause not to."

"Then I think it's time you saw the other side."

"Of what?" Amber asked hesitantly.

"Of 'rich folk,' as you call us. My grandmother is having a dinner party, and you're going along. Maybe I can teach you a few manners and point out the benefits of having money."

Amber's breath left her in a rush. Gulping for air, she bolted from her chair. "Oh no, I ain't." She moved toward the door.

"And why not? Afraid?"

"I ain't afraid of nothing. I just ain't going, that's all."

Nicholas smiled, reaching up to stroke his chin. "If it's because you have nothing suitable to wear, I'd be more than eager to purchase a new suit of clothes for you. It would be money well spent just to see a clean face."

Amber stopped inside the doorway and glared back at him. "Yeah, that's the only reason ya asked me ta go along. Ya want me ta take a bath. Well, forget it." She turned away.

"Edgar," Nicholas called, a stern warning tone in his voice that stopped Amber before she'd taken a step further. "Part of our agreement was that you not argue with anything I tell you."

Amber spun around. "What's eating fancy got to do with cleaning your house?"

"It's what I order. And if you wish to continue working for me, you'll not say another word."

Amber's chest heaved with suppressed retaliation. She glared at Nicholas, the words she wished to speak shining clearly in her eyes.

"That's better," Nicholas nodded. "And since we must leave

100

in three days, you and I will go into town this afternoon to buy your clothes." He leaned forward, spread out the papers on his desk, and picked up the quill from its well. "You may go."

"Yes, sir," Amber hissed, turning on her heel to exit the room.

The last column of figures added and entered in the ledger, Nicholas returned the quill to the well, leaned back and stretched, catching sight of the clock on the fireplace mantel. Two-fifteen. No wonder he was hungry. He'd worked right through without a thought to time. Rising, he crossed the study and headed for the kitchen, determined to eat something, then find Edgar and ride into Williamsburg. A smile lit up his face. It would be interesting to see the boy in something other than his dirty rags and scuffed shoes.

Finding the kitchen empty, he set about fixing something to eat and several minutes later sat down at the table to enjoy the plateful of scrambled eggs, biscuits with honey, and a cup of tea. He ate hungrily, unaware of anything around him until the silence that seemed to fill every corner of the house hammered in his ears. A dark brow lifted slightly, his head cocked to detect any noise coming from another room. When only the gentle breeze outside stirring up a rustling of leaves greeted him, he took a large bite of the bread and honey, picked up his cup and stood, crossing the room toward Edgar's. Standing in its archway, a frown deepened the lines in his brow. He was slightly surprised to find it vacant, but was certain the boy worked elsewhere in the house. He turned away and left the kitchen, calling out the youth's name as he crossed the foyer.

"Edgar!" he shouted again when the summons went unanswered. The scamp couldn't be in the study. He'd just come from there. He wasn't in his room or the kitchen. Maybe the parlor.

Stuffing the last bite of the biscuit in his mouth, Nicholas stepped into the sitting room doorway, a confused expression touching his face when he found no one. He turned back, deciding to check the bedchambers upstairs, swallowed the last sip of tea, and placed the cup on the long buffet. Taking the steps two at a time, he hurried up the long staircase and stopped outside the first room. Empty. He moved to the second, third and only after he had searched the entire lot did a dark scowl hood his eyes. He'd look in the stable, but intuition told him the result would be the same. Racing down the stairs, he went to the study to collect his papers and jacket. With luck, he'd find the boy walking the road into town.

"Will you be coming in tomorrow, Mr. Chandler?"

Nicholas looked up from his paperwork, a surprised expression wrinkling his brow. "Is it five o'clock already?"

"Yes, sir," Mathew nodded. "Did you wish for me to stay longer?"

Nicholas waved a hand. "No, no. I just didn't realize the time." He sighed. "Yes, I'll be in tomorrow morning. I would have come earlier today but I had problems at home."

Mathew stepped further into the office. "Mr. Chandler, my wife would be more than willing to help out with the cleaning and cooking."

"Oh, that wasn't my reason for being late. But I thank you for the offer." Nicholas fell back in his chair, elbows resting on the arms, his fingers toying with the feather of his quill. "Mathew, have you seen a young boy wandering about the docks? Claims to be eighteen, but I would guess about four less. He has blond hair and blue eyes and is in dire need of a bath and new set of clothes that fit properly."

"No, sir," Mathew replied. "There's a lot of young boys working the pier, but I know all of them. I would have remembered seeing someone like him. Why do you ask? Is he giving you trouble?"

That was an understatement, Nicholas mused. "No," he said aloud. "But if you should see him, let me know. And tell the others to keep an eye out for him. I'd like to talk to him."

"You want us to catch him if we can?"

Nicholas chuckled. "If you can. He's a slippery sort."

"Yes, sir," Mathew said. "Will there be anything else?"

Nicholas leaned forward and dropped the quill in the well. "Just one other thing. I'll be leaving Thursday for Raven Oaks to pay my grandmother a visit. I should be back in the office Monday."

"Very good, sir."

"And if you should find the boy while I'm gone, have someone follow him. Find out where he's staying. I'll take care of him when I return."

"Yes, sir. Good night, Mr. Chandler."

"Good night, Mathew. Give your wife my regards."

Mathew nodded, plopped his hat on his head, and left the office.

Nicholas remained seated behind the desk long after Mathew had gone, silently considering the events of the past three days. He really couldn't appreciate Edgar's reason for running away. Did he hate people of wealth so much? Did the thought of a bath and clean clothes displease him to such a degree that he would sacrifice a job? And where had he come from? Mathew had a vast knowledge of all the people living in the area for miles around, and yet the boy's description failed to spark any recognition. He thought of the tattered clothes, the dirty hair and pale blue eyes. For some unexplainable reason, he liked Edgar MacDonald, and he would miss their constant bickerings. He sighed, leaning back in the chair to rest his chin on the fist of his left hand. He hadn't really expected to find the scalawag walking the road leading into town. Edgar had had too much of a head start. And if he thought to flee, he wouldn't be foolish enough to travel an area where he could easily be spotted. No, chances were he'd seen the last of Edgar Mac-Donald. Absently, he closed the ledger, carelessly pushing it aside rather than locking it in his desk, and stood, oddly experiencing the sense that someone was watching him. He spun around to catch whomever it was staring in the window. Only the fading light of dusk filtered in. He shook his head. He must be tired. He was imagining things. Lifting his coat from the chair, he left the office, turned the key in the lock, and started down the pier toward the Chesterfield House. He'd eat dinner before he returned home.

Bright blue eyes watched him pass the stack of crates stored a few yards from the entrance to the Chandler Shipping Lines office, a mixture of anticipation and worry reflected in their clear depths. Amber did not move until Nicholas Chandler had crossed the street and traveled on for several minutes, his figure hardly more than a speck in the cluster of buildings at the far end. Peering out over the top of the crates, she glanced in both directions to guarantee her seclusion before guardedly leaving her haven. She had heard him lock the door, but if luck befell her she would find one window open, the chance she needed to climb inside and search his desk for any listings of shipments that might prove helpful.

The oversized shoes she wore clopped against the wooden sidewalk. She stopped, glanced about, then slipped from the noisy footgear and let them lie where they were. It would only be a minute before she could retrieve them and be on her way.

The first window she tried held steadfast. She moved to the next, the one where she had stood to spy on Nicholas while he worked. It, too, wouldn't budge. Irritated but determined, she rounded the corner of the building into the alleyway. Spying a smaller window higher than the rest, Amber's hopes soared when she noticed someone had left it open. Only a tiny slit, but enough to slip her fingers in between the sash and the frame. Now if she could find something on which to stand. Looking about, she decided on the only thing available, a single wooden box sitting several feet away. Though it looked as though it might not hold her weight, she paid it no heed as she placed the wooden object beneath the window and nimbly climbed up.

The window opened easily to her touch, and without hesitation Amber hoisted herself up to the sill and dropped noiselessly inside. The golden light of dusk streamed in across the office, a single shaft spotlighting Nicholas's desk. She quickly went to it and pulled open a drawer. A brief examination awarded her nothing. She tried the second and the third, her shoulders dropping in dismay when they too proved of no help. She straightened, one fist to her hip, the other cradling her chin as she fleetingly scanned the room for other possibilities. Then her gaze fell upon the dark leather book she had seen Nicholas with in the study. Urgently pulling it closer, she sat down in the chair and opened the ledger to study its pages. Her tawny brow lifted in silent admiration for the sum listed at the bottom of the first page, a slow satisfied grin spreading over her face. The amount she needed to pay her debts would only slightly alter this figure. With luck he would never miss it, and she could return home to Andrea to live out her life without anyone's knowing what she had done. Of course the trick would be to actually obtain the money, not merely to scribble in the book. She closed the volume and leaned back in the chair deep in thought, catching sight of a stack of papers on the counter across the room from her. Could this be what she sought? Leaving the chair, she hurried to them, noting the date listed on the first page as Thursday of this week. Outgoing shipments! Just the information she needed. Her smile returned. Soon, Nicholas Chandler, she grinned. Soon! The document held in one hand, she returned to the desk, where she copied down all the details on a blank piece of paper from one of the drawers. The humiliation she had endured at his hands now seemed well worth it. He would pay, and in a way a rich man would feel it most. His purse! Stuffing her treasure into her shirt, she replaced the original paper to its spot, looked about the room to make sure everything was in order, and sighed happily before she went to the window and quickly slipped outside.

Once her bare feet touched the sandy soil in the alleyway, Amber leaned back against the building to catch her breath and allow her heart to beat at a steadier pace. It had gone more easily than she had thought it would. Now her only problem was to find Paxton. And before Thursday. The letter she had sent him told him to dock at the port in Williamsburg and wait, that she would contact him rather than have him search for her. He wouldn't know whom to look for, anyway. She certainly didn't resemble Amber Courtney.

Her confidence restored, she straightened and set off after her shoes, planning to return to the room in the vacant warehouse she had found earlier to hide and wait for her partner. Stepping out of the alleyway, she glanced in both directions and hurriedly started off for the spot where she had left the footgear, a puzzled frown knotting her brow when she reached her destination. They were nowhere to be seen. Thinking she had mistaken where she had left them, she moved ahead, worry quickening her steps. Who could possibly want a worn-out pair of shoes? They would do no one any good, and she needed them. Although spring had warmed the days, the nights were still cool.

"Is this what you're looking for?"

Startled by the familiar voice behind her, Amber refused to turn around, knowing who spoke and what he held in his hands. Deciding it was more important to keep secret her reason for taking off her boots than to reclaim them, she bolted off down the sidewalk, stopped short by the painful entrapment of her short cropped hair in an unrelenting grip.

"Let go! You're hurtin' me," she howled as Nicholas spun her around.

"I ought to do more than that," he answered, a dark scowl kinking his brow. "I should turn you over to the magistrate for stealing."

"Stealin'? I didn't take nothin'."

"Only because you couldn't find anything. Do you think I'm foolish enough to leave money where an imp like you can find it?"

Her pale blue eyes glared up at him, the rebellious gleam confirming his statement.

"Well, I'm not. Now what were you doing in there?" he demanded, giving his captive a shake.

"Ouch!" Amber squawked. "You're pullin' out all my hair."

"I'll do worse than that. Now tell me."

"I—I was leavin' ya a note."

The muscle in Nicholas's cheek flexed in restrained anger. "I hope you'll understand when I say I don't believe you. I doubt you know how to hold a pen, let alone write."

"I don't care if ya do or not," Amber barked. "I was tellin' ya where ta send my pay and that I wasn't gonna work for ya no more."

"Oh, really?" Nicholas mocked. "Then let's take a look at your note." He tossed the shoes to the sidewalk. "Put them on."

Amber hesitated.

"Now!"

Slipping her feet into the shoes, afraid to move the slightest bit in the wrong direction and find herself minus a few more strands of hair, Amber quietly waited for Nicholas to lead the way. "You can let go of me now. I won't try to run," she said in a small voice.

"I wouldn't want to risk my life on it," Nicholas mumbled, trading the handful of hair for her arm. Dragging her beside him, he went to the warehouse door, unlocked it, and swung it open, pushing Amber in first. They walked down the short corridor and paused outside his office. "Now suppose you show me the note."

Knowing there was no such note, Amber forced a smile to her lips. "Well—ah—"

Nicholas leaned in, lifted the latch, and pushed the door open, extending a hand for her to lead the way. When she didn't move, Nicholas gave her a shove and followed her in, closing the door behind them. He stood barring the exit, feet apart, knotted fists resting on each hip. His dark scowl scanned the room for any damage his intruder may have caused before coming to rest on Amber again.

"Well?" he pursued.

Locking her hands behind her, Amber rocked to and fro on her heels, her gaze trained on the floor. "I didn't write it," she mumbled.

"Oh, really? I wonder why?"

Amber's narrow shoulders bounced up and down. "Couldn't find nothin' ta write on."

One dark brow lifted skeptically. "Did you look in the desk?"

Without thinking, Amber nodded.

"Then you're lying. I know there's paper to use—" He stopped abruptly, his gaze spotting the ledger lying on the desktop. His expression changed. Glancing first at the child, he rushed to the desk and opened the book, his back to Amber while he examined the pages. Even though he doubted the street urchin could read, the thought that anyone had pried into his personal affairs pricked his good nature. Deeply engrossed, he failed to see Amber move toward the small wooden stool near the counter. Nor did he hear her lift the item from the floor and quietly approach from behind. Only the dark shadow that crossed the yellow beam of sunset spilling in over the desk warned him of the oncoming attack—but not in time. A loud splintering of wood, then excruciating pain shooting through his shoulders, neck, and head preceded the explosion of tiny lights dotting his vision. His knees buckled. Unconscious, he fell against the desk, then rolled to the floor.

Amber stood over the unmoving form, two broken pieces of wood clamped in her hands, her body trembling. She hadn't meant to hit him so hard. Had she killed him? Oh, God, she hoped not. But he lay so still. Was he breathing? Bending down, Amber tossed away the remains of the stool and touched Nicholas's shoulder, gently turning him on his back. Her fine-boned, dirty hand reached out to lightly press against Nicholas's face. She was startled when he moaned. Bolting to her feet, Amber raced for the door and left the building as quickly as her steps would carry her, not once bothering to look back.

"Nicholas, I think you really ought to spend one more day in bed," Dr. Neely advised, a frown drawing his gray brows together. "You took an awful blow to your head."

"Thank you, doctor," Nicholas replied, an angry, dark look in his eyes as he left his bed and went to the armoire. Selecting a muslin shirt, he hurriedly slid it up over his arms and shoulders. "But I've already wasted one day lounging about. I don't intend to spend another."

"Nicholas, if Mathew hadn't come back to the office to work that night, you wouldn't have been found until morning. I don't need to tell you what lying on a cold floor all night would have done to you."

Nicholas stuffed his shirttail into his breeches and returned to the bed, where he sat down on the edge to put on his shoes. "Yes, I know," he said. "I was very lucky. And I thank you for caring. But I feel fine now," he added, standing. "And I have things to do. I'm leaving tomorrow for Raven Oaks, and we have a big shipment scheduled the same day." He ran the fingers of one hand through his hair. "That is, if Sean returns before then."

"Well, will you promise to take it easy? Use a carriage today.

You won't bounce around so much."

Nicholas glanced up and smiled. "Yes, I promise. But the carriage is out. I must get to the warehouse as soon as possible, and it only slows me up."

Dr. Neely chuckled. "You're just like your father. I could never talk any sense into him, either."

Nicholas grinned. "Then you know when to quit."

Doctor Neely sighed, feigning displeasure before a smile deepened the lines in his face. "Yes, I do." He went to the night table, returned his instruments to the case, and picked it up. "Do you have any idea what the boy was after?"

"You mean the one who hit me?"

The doctor nodded.

"Not really. That's why I want to go to the office. I caught him snooping around, but I didn't have the chance to find out what for. There's no money there, but maybe he didn't know it." Nicholas picked up his coat from the chair and eased into it. "I can promise you this. When I get my hands on that rascal, he'll regret the day he asked me for a job."

"Yes, I suppose he will." Dr. Neely moved toward the door. "Now remember not to exert yourself overmuch today. And if you can, lie down for half an hour."

"I can't promise, but if I get the chance, I will."

The doctor paused, shaking his head resignedly. "You young people," he muttered. "I don't suppose you'd stop by my office tomorrow morning before you go on to Raven Oaks."

Nicholas smiled, toying with the cuff of his jacket.

"I didn't think so," Dr. Neely said. "Well, at least tell your grandmother and sister that I send my regards."

"That much I will do." Nicholas hurried to catch up with the doctor's long strides when he started off again and walked with him to the front door, a hand resting on the older man's shoulder. When they reached the main entrance, they shook hands. "Thanks, Dr. Neely. I hope all your patients aren't like me."

"They're not!" the doctor replied with a chuckle. Lifting the latch, he opened the door and stepped outside, waving his final farewell before climbing into his carriage.

Nicholas stood on the veranda watching until the buggy had

109

wound its way down the road and disappeared from view. Warm rays of sunlight touched his face, reminding him that nearly half the morning had slipped away. His vague smile faded, transposed into a dark scowl.

Just wait, Edgar MacDonald, or whatever your name is. I'll see to it you don't sit down for a month! Turning abruptly, he headed toward the stable.

Amber's stomach rumbled with hunger. She had eaten the last piece of bread she had taken from the Chandler kitchen the night before, and as the sun rose higher with each passing hour she realized she must find another source of food. The undertaking would be difficult, since she hadn't a single coin with which to buy a loaf of bread, and she had no way of knowing how long she would have to wait for Paxton. Going home was out of the question. Her note had instructed him to meet her here, and with luck he would arrive in time to fulfill her plan on Thursday's shipment. Yet she knew the danger of walking the streets of the waterfront. Nicholas Chandler surely had people out looking for the street urchin who had attacked him. The gnawing and low rumblings of her stomach would have to wait. But then again, if she was careful . . .

"Mr. Chandler, are you sure you should be here?" Mathew asked, watching Nicholas sort through papers on his desk and in the drawers, then cross to the counter, where he continued to search.

"I'm fine, Mathew," he said, not pausing in his task. "Has anyone seen the boy?"

"No, sir. But they're still looking. I sent three of the men to search, since work is slow today. If he's here in the waterfront, they'll find him." Mathew cocked his head to one side. "What are you looking for? Maybe I can help."

Nicholas arrested his mission briefly to glance up at Mathew with a sigh, one hand to his hip, the elbow of his other arm lying on the stack of papers at his side. "I don't really know. But something in here interested that scalawag, and I would

110

like to know what."

"Don't you suppose he was looking for money? You said you hadn't paid him."

"I'd believe that if he hadn't clobbered me. However, he did have the opportunity to see my ledger and the amount the bank holds for me. It would be quite foolish of him to try and rob the bank, but I truly wouldn't put anything past him. Send one of the men to watch the bank for a few days, just in case." He frowned. "If it was all he wanted, why didn't he say so?"

"Maybe he was afraid."

Unexpected laughter exploded from Nicholas. "I truly doubt that imp fears anything." He glanced down at the papers beneath his arm, straightening slowly.

"What is it, sir?"

"The cargo list for Thursday's shipment."

"You don't think the boy was after that, do you?"

"I wouldn't know why, but it does raise another possibility. I only wish I had changed my mind about eating in town sooner. I might have seen what he was looking at. As it was I only caught him climbing through the window." The paper held in one hand while he examined it, Nicholas rubbed his thumbnail on his chin with the other. "No one knows who this boy is. He's never been seen around here before, and he shows up looking for a job. Not cleaning stables or washing dishes at a restaurant, but here, a shipping line."

"What are you getting at, sir?"

"Suppose it was part of a plan."

"A plan?" Mathew questioned, watching Nicholas return to his desk and sit down.

"Yes. The boy was sent here to get a job working for me only as a means to search this office."

"But why? What good would it do a child?"

Nicholas smiled. "None, if he's working alone. But let's suppose he isn't."

"You mean the shortage?"

"Yes," Nicholas grinned, laying down the document to lean back in his chair, elbows on its arms, fingertips tapping each other.

"But, sir, the shortage occurred before the boy started

working for you."

"Maybe one or two crates at a time wasn't enough."

Matthew's face mirrored his sudden understanding. "Oh, I see. So you think they plan to take the entire shipment and couldn't count on guesswork anymore."

"Yes. That's why Edgar was so upset when I told him he'd be working at my house. He knew he couldn't find any information there that would help."

"Why that little—What do you plan to do?"

"When do you expect Mr. Rafferty to dock?"

"Late this evening. Maybe tomorrow morning."

"Then I'll postpone my trip until he returns. I need to talk to him. I want his ship to be the one to carry this cargo."

The two men exchanged satisfied grins.

"Capt'n, ya think it's a good idea ta dock here?"

Barlow Paxton stood at the railing of the *Black Falcon*, looking out at the pier of Williamsburg's waterfront, his arms crossed behind this thin, wiry frame.

"Capt'n?"

Jolted from his thoughts, Paxton stumbled, catching himself with one hand clasping the balustrade. "How many times do I have to tell you, Dempsey? Don't sneak up on me."

Dempsey Rigg's brow furrowed, his lower lip protruding slightly. "I didn't sneak up on ya, capt'n. I called to ya."

Paxton hesitated, looking at his first mate, at the deck, and back at his companion. "Ya did?"

"Aye. I just wanted to tell ya that I don't think it's a good idea to dock here."

Paxton stiffened. "And why not? I do."

"Don't you remember?" Rigg argued. "The last time we were here they run us off."

"They didn't run us off. They just asked us to leave. There's a difference, ya know." Paxton turned back to the railing to gaze out across the sea, his shoulders squared, chin held high, one hand raised to shade his eyes and his other arm crossed in back of him. "If I hadn't wanted to set sail, we would have stayed longer."

Dempsey Rigg's eyes rolled back in his head. "Most certainly, capt'n," he agreed with a hint of sarcasm tingeing his voice.

Rigg had sailed with Barlow Paxton for nearly twenty years, five of them on their own ship, with Paxton as the captain. Prior to that they had worked on a British navy ship as deck hands, never earning more money than enough to feed themselves and supply their thirst with an adequate amount of rum. They had always dreamed of owning a ship of their own, to sail the seas freely and do as they pleased. But fate had never allowed it, until one day a pirate vessel attacked the British frigate and took them prisoners. Certain they were doomed to a life of slavery, their future looked bleak. Then one of the pirates had come down with the plague, and before a week had passed the entire crew had perished . . . except for Barlow Paxton and Dempsey Rigg. And the *Black Falcon* belonged to them.

It had been difficult at first, but as time went on Captain Paxton acquired a crew, by promising riches beyond their dreams. Unskilled in the management of a crew and ship, Paxton had hired the first men who offered their services and had wound up with the most unpolished, inept group of sailors ever to sail the Atlantic Ocean. Every frigate or brigantine they attacked outsailed them and left them no richer than before. Near starvation, they took to seizing fishing boats for food and finally went after a foe that could not sail away. They would anchor offshore, wait until night fell, and row inland in longboats to attack the shops of unsuspecting towns, then slip away to their ship and set sail before daybreak. Though they called themselves pirates, the townspeople along the eastern seacoast of America thought of the crew and captain of the *Black Falcon* as a nuisance.

"Have a longboat made ready, Dempsey," Paxton ordered, his high-pitched voice lacking authority. "I'm going ashore."

"Now? Don't you think you better wait till dark?" Rigg objected.

Barlow sent his first mate a disapproving scowl. "Who's captain here, Rigg?"

"You, sir," Dempsey mumbled.

"Very good. I'm going ashore to check out the stores. It will make our job much easier tonight. Don't you agree?"

Rigg shrugged.

"Now run along and do as you're told."

"Yes, sir," the first mate concurred, turning about and hurrying off.

Standing in the shadows of the alleyway, Amber studied the score of merchants bustling along the sidewalks, pushing carts full of fresh fish, cloths in a rainbow of colors, and fresh-baked loaves of bread. The last she watched intently. With so many people hurrying about, it would be simple to take what she needed without anyone's noticing. However, she must scan the crowd first for a dock worker who appeared uninterested in the wares of the others, rather as if he searched for some*one* instead. Amber doubted that Nicholas would undertake the job himself. If he had, it would have made Amber's job easier. She could spot him in an instant. The sweet aroma of bread drifted out to greet her, urging her to hurry when her stomach knotted as a reminder of why she had left the safety of her shelter.

A trio of men passed by the opening to the alleyway a few feet from Amber, then started across the street near the bakery cart. After one more quick survey of the crowd, Amber rushed to catch up with the men, stepping in stride just behind them. As the group passed the woman calling out her price for the goods she offered, her attention trained on the men, a dirty hand shot out to capture a loaf and quickly conceal it inside a baggy shirt before any of them had seen. Turning about, Amber raced back to the alleyway, her heart pounding as if it would explode. Once there, she collapsed against the wall, fighting for air and to calm her nerves, her treasure clutched to her chest. She closed her eyes, savoring the sweet smells of her next meal, when she heard someone coming down the alley. Her eyes flew open as she listened to shoes crunching the rocks beneath the intruder with each step. Panic threatening to rule, she decided she had stayed away from her hiding place long enough. The small room in the vacant warehouse located at the opposite end of the alley meant she must pass whomever approached, but maybe if she kept her head down, nibbled at a piece of bread and pretended it didn't matter that she shared the space with someone else, the stranger might pass by without a care to the young boy. Realizing there was no other way out of her predicament save risking the crowd of people in the street, Amber fumbled with the bread, tearing off a corner before she started on her journey.

"I think we'd be less noticeable if we went separate directions," Paxton told the sailor who had rowed them ashore. "You go that way." His thumb jutted southward. "I'll go this way." He started off without a backward glance or moment's time to allow the mate a chance to object. He didn't want the idiot tagging along. It would be much easier to steal some food for one rather than two. Let him find his own meal.

Although the sunshine warmed everything it touched, Paxton pulled his long black cape around him, giving him a sense of power, superiority that the victims of his rampage would cower at his feet by the mere sight of him. The people of Williamsburg would pay for ordering him out of town. How dare they! He was the feared pirate captain of the *Black Falcon*.

As he walked toward the center of town, he could hear the chatter of voices growing louder. The marketplace, a spot sure to be filled with all sorts of prizes for his simple taking. He hurried his step, the gnawing in his belly cramping his muscles. And just as soon as he ate, he would find himself a bottle of rum.

He passed several men, his chin held high, his chest out, failing to notice how they paused once he took several steps further to stare after him, an amused grin curling their lips. It had been a while since they had seen someone dressed as he was, in a long, flowing cape on a warm spring day. They shook their heads and continued on.

When the street grew more crowded, some of Paxton's courage faded. What if someone saw him take something while the owner's back was turned? They'd call the constable and he'd be thrown in prison. He walked on by the first cart in a hurry, certain everyone stared.

"Hey, you," someone called.

Paxton froze in his tracks, his Adam's apple bobbing up and down, sweat beading across his brow. He forced a smile to his lips and turned around.

"Wanta buy some fresh fish? They were caught this mornin'," the old woman asked, holding out a sample wrapped in brown paper.

"Ah—no," he replied, his voice cracking. "I'm on my way to the—ah—no, thank you." He spun around and dashed into a nearby alleyway, his heart pounding in his ears. Maybe this wasn't such a good idea, after all. In fact, he decided his stomach could wait. He'd return to the ship and wait until everyone was asleep. Then he could return and take whatever he wished.

Peering out at the gathering of merchants and customers, he elected to use the alley to return to the longboat. Pulling himself up, he started off toward his destination. The narrow passageway between the buildings took a sharp turn left, and once he cleared it he saw a young boy walking toward him, his head down as he nibbled on the crust of bread he held. Paxton's mouth watered.

Hell, this will be simple, he snickered to himself. I'll just take the brat's food for myself. First glancing back over his shoulder to make sure they were alone, he walked at a steady pace as though paying the youngster no heed, until they were side by side. Without warning, he lunged, grabbing at the boy's hand.

"Yeeeoooow," Paxton howled when the lad's shoe connected with his shin. Clutching the injured limb in his hands, he bounced up and down on one foot. "Ya didn't have ta do that!" He fell against the wall behind him and slid to the ground, slipping a finger beneath the edge of his stocking to pull it free of the wound. The skin had already glowed a bright red. "Looky there. Ya bruised me."

"Paxton? Is that you?"

Surprised anyone in Williamsburg knew his name, he looked up, moisture lining his eyes. A dirt-smudged face stared back. "Yeah. So who are you?"

116

The boy quickly crouched down beside him, forcing Paxton to retreat, certain the child intended to continue his attack.

"It's me, your cousin's daughter, Amber Courtney."

Paxton squinted his blue eyes, deepening the wrinkles on his weathered face. "You're a boy," he said, taking in the child's attire and short blond hair. "Amber's a girl."

"I am a girl," Amber replied impatiently. "Did you get my letter?"

Paxton looked her up and down once more. "Are ya sure? Ya don't look like Amber. What letter?"

Reaching out, Amber grabbed his arm and yanked him to his feet, an easy task, since the man stood no taller than she and weighed only a few pounds more.

"We can't talk here. It's too dangerous. I might be seen," Amber half whispered, her attention darting from one end of the alley to the other.

Paxton chuckled. "Nobody would know ya. I didn't." He frowned suddenly. "What ya doing dressed like that? Your father will whip you if he sees ya paradin' around in that getup."

"Papa's dead," she said flatly. "Now come on. I'll take you to where I'm hiding. I'll explain then."

"Hiding? What's happened? Where's Andrea?"

"Will you shut up and come with me? I have a plan that will make us both rich, and you won't have to resort to stealing from children."

Barlow's thin face wrinkled into a pout. "I wasn't exactly steal—"

"Oh, come on," Amber snapped, giving him a tug to start them off down the back way to her room.

It took them only a few minutes to arrive at the deserted warehouse. Once they were safely inside, with the door barred against intruders, Amber told Barlow Paxton her story, from the questionable way her father had died, to the baron's demands and the reason she had cut her hair. His chin sagged for the entire duration of the tale, his face paling when she mentioned her proposed attack on one of Nicholas Chandler's ships to acquire the needed money to pay off the evil baron.

117

"Oh—ah—I don't know, Amber. That's mighty dangerous," he mumbled, shaking his balding head.

Amber's smooth brow wrinkled. "But not any more than any other ship you attack. You wrote Papa several times about the battles you encountered at sea. Why should this be any different?"

Barlow turned away, hiding his worried expression. "'Cause we don't know anything about the shipment. Where—where it's going, how many men—how many guns." His final words came out in a whimper.

"Oh, but we do!" Amber sang out. Fumbling with the buttons of her shirt, she withdrew a piece of paper from inside. "That's what I was doing in Chandler's office. Here, look at this." She handed the document to him. "The ship sails for Boston on Thursday. It will be loaded with cotton and a minimal crew."

"Cotton?" Paxton echoed. "What do pirates want with cotton?"

Amber's shoulders slouched. "You resell it somewhere else, you fool." Throwing her hands in the air, she turned away. How could this halfwit be a relative? Or better still, a pirate? She had more courage and a lot quicker wit than he. No wonder her father rarely talked of him and seemed displeased when the man came to visit. She twirled back to face him. "Barlow, you've got to help us. You're our only chance. You wouldn't want to see Andrea wed to someone like Baron Von Buren, would you?"

His blue eyes fearfully glanced up at her before he shrugged, then shook his gray head.

"It will be simple. You'll outnumber them two to one."

Barlow looked up sheepishly. "Two to one?"

Amber nodded confidently. "Maybe even three to one."

"Well, I suppose we could," he said weakly.

"Good," Amber grinned, rushing over to crush his small frame in her embrace. She straightened suddenly. "Come to think of it, why are you here if you hadn't gotten my letter?"

"Ah—oh—well, a—business," he stammered. "And it ain't none of yours."

Fists to her hips, Amber raised one brow suspiciously, then

118

shrugged off her doubts as she said, "When you've sold the cotton, meet me here with my share. And do remember to hurry. I only have two weeks to pay off the baron."

"I will," he answered, heading for the warehouse door. "I better be going. We got a lot of plannin' ta do. Gotta load all our guns." He smiled, saluted, and walked out, leaving Amber to stare after him, a feeling of calamity pouring over her.

Chapter Six

Nicholas urged his team of chestnut mares into a trot. If he didn't hurry he would arrive at his grandmother's after dinner had been served and receive only an angry frown from the mistress of Raven Oaks for doing so. Not to mention the scolding his sister would deem necessary. He smiled in the protection of his carriage, certain they would forgive him once he explained his delay. Sean Rafferty had returned to Williamsburg early yesterday morning. They had spent the next two hours plotting out a scheme to catch whomever it was who worked with Edgar and how they would trick the thief into telling of the youth's whereabouts. Had Edgar not known of Nicholas's commitment to visit his grandmother, Nicholas would have sailed with Sean disguised as one of the crew. It had been a long time since Nicholas had experienced the thrill of a chase, but in order to make certain the plan went as agreed, he realized he must not do anything out of the ordinary should Edgar be watching him somehow and warn his conspirator. Besides, Sean had promised only to catch the thief, then he would send word to him at Raven Oaks and together they would question the man on how he had acquired the information needed to successfully attack one of Nicholas's ships. What fun it would be to find Edgar's hiding place and confront him. The palm of Nicholas's hand itched, impatient to connect with the seat of the rascal's breeches.

He had slept little the night past at the inn located halfway between Williamsburg and his grandmother's manor, lying awake wondering if Sean had encountered the corsair or if the attack would take place closer to Boston. He would have given almost anything to see the look on the enemy's face when they were met with more than twice the number of men scheduled to sail the merchant ship. But, unfortunately, it was not meant to be and he would have to be content with merely having out-foxed them.

The Chandler carriage neared the bend in the road that would open up to where the road divided, the lane at the right leading to Raven Oaks. His thoughts changed to the woman who waited there, a dark frown settling on his handsome face. Amber Courtney. A beauty such as he had never before seen. He had to admit the idea of spending an evening with her stirred a strange feeling in him. He would have enjoyed the time as nothing more than social had it not been for the fact that he didn't trust her. If the story she had told him was true, she would have raced for home to hide her shame and never chance meeting him again. But her acceptance of Alanna's offer to spend a few days at Raven Oaks confirmed his suspicions that she, too, merely sought to marry him and share in his wealth. The image of her long, flowing hair draped enticingly over her shoulders reared up to haunt him, and his pulse quickened. Her full breasts and soft skin burned vividly in his memory, the curves, the scent of her, and those beautiful, fearing blue eyes. He straightened in the carriage seat, silently rebuking himself for allowing her charms to invade his thoughts and weaken his defense. He snapped the reins to hurry the mares.

Expecting to find several coaches lining the drive, Nicholas frowned in surprise at not seeing a single one. He shook his head, a smile slowly spreading across his face. So that was his grandmother's plan. A weekend alone with one woman, one she liked, approved of, felt certain he would too, if given the chance.

Sorry, Grandmother, he thought, but it isn't going to work.

122

Even with all your help.

Long before his carriage had reached the end of the path leading to the house, a groomsman appeared, standing ready to see to the team. Obviously expected earlier, Nicholas assumed everyone was watching for his arrival, and was certain of the fact when the manor's butler stepped out onto the veranda and started down the stairs before the rig had come to a complete halt. Stepping easily from it, Nicholas handed the man his valise from the seat, straightened his attire, and followed him into the house. Instructed that his grandmother waited in the parlor, Nicholas set off in that direction, stopping in the archway when he found her alone.

"My apologies for being late," he announced, smiling when Alanna looked up from her knitting.

Her dark brown eyes, the beauty of her younger days still shining in them, failed to hide her pleasure at seeing him, although she spoke differently. "I'm not sure it's enough," she frowned, laying aside her work to come to her feet. She held out her arms. "But maybe a hug will help."

Nicholas laughed, quickly closing the distance between them. He held her frail form for a minute, then put her at arms' length. "You look lovely, as usual," he said, placing a gentle kiss on her brow.

"You must be tired from your journey. Why don't you sit down and I'll get you a glass of wine?" Alanna offered, smiling when he agreed. She gracefully moved to the buffet, her full skirts rustling about her ankles as she spoke. "Kate and Amber should be down soon. The poor child hadn't a suitable gown to wear, so Kate insisted they alter one of hers. They have been up in Kate's room for hours." Two glasses of wine in hand, Alanna returned to the sofa, handing one to her grandson before she took her place beside him. "Kate adores Amber. She is such a sweet, quiet thing."

"Quiet?" Nicholas chuckled after sipping his wine. "Quiet isn't the way I'd describe her."

"What do you mean?" Alanna asked.

Conniving, he mused, then thought better of it. After all, if he voiced his opinion to his grandmother, she would question why. "I'd call her hot-tempered," he answered instead.

"Oh, you're wrong, Nicholas. Amber is very shy, and I can't imagine her ever raising her voice."

Nicholas reached over to pat his grandmother's hand. "Never to you, I'm sure. But somehow I manage to provoke the worst in people."

"That's not true. You're a very wonderful, understanding young man. You wouldn't purposely anger someone."

He studied her for a long while, then grinned. "I wish everyone felt the same about me. I mean truly liked me."

"What makes you say that?"

He leaned back in the sofa, his legs stretched out before him while he twirled the contents of his glass. "I mean it's difficult to tell which women truly like Nicholas Chandler or his inheritance."

"Oh," Alanna whispered, "I guess it comes with the territory."

"Yes, it does. And it's also the reason I'm having such a difficult time finding a wife. Every woman I've known so far leaves me with the impression that she's summing me up, trying to decide how many ways she can spend my money, not how many ways she can please me, make me happy." He sighed heavily. "I'm not being obstinate, Grandmother. I simply want to marry a woman I can love. You understand, don't you?"

"More than you know. I almost married another man instead of your grandfather. I would have if he hadn't been killed. I adored Radford, but I truly doubt I would have ever loved him. Not the way I did Beau." Moisture glistened in her eyes.

"Now I'm making you unhappy," Nicholas apologized, leaning over to encircle her shoulders with a gentle squeeze.

"No, you're not," she assured him. "It's been twenty-six years since Beau was killed, and if I live twenty-six more, I'll still shed a tear for him, no matter what anyone says or does. I love him and miss him every day, that's all."

"The way my mother loved my father."

Alanna smiled. "Yes."

"I envy you both."

"It will come, my dear. Maybe not right away, but someday you'll find the right woman."

"I only wish it would happen within the next two weeks."
He chuckled. "Highly unlikely, don't you think?"

"Not really. I knew the minute I saw your grandfather that
there was something special about him. I admit it took me a
long while to voice my love for him, but we had a lot of
problems to overcome."

"Something special—" he murmured. Did it begin with a
stirring in the pit of your stomach? Did it cause your heart to
beat faster, your pulse to quicken, the privacy of your
thoughts to be intruded upon without warning? Yes, Amber
Courtney was special, for she and only she had done all that, if
that was what his grandmother meant.

Giddy laughter coming from the foyer interrupted their time
alone, growing in volume until the doorway filled with yards of
flowing silks and laces. Nicholas immediately came to his feet,
a satisfied smile curling his lips as he took in the view of two
very shapely, very beautiful women, as different as night and
day. Kate's dark hair bound up in curls on top of her head
accentuated her round dark eyes and glowing skin, comple-
mented by the soft shade of lavender she wore. Miss Courtney,
on the other hand, made a striking appearance in a pastel
green. The honey-blond hair falling in soft ringlets over her
shoulders seemed as smooth and silky as her pale skin, and a
light blush colored her cheeks. Several inches taller than her
companion, she held herself proudly, as beautifully as he
remembered, yet there was something different about her. He
cocked his head to one side to study her, wondering.

"Well? Aren't you going to say something?"

Nicholas straightened sharply when he realized Kate had
addressed him. "Forgive me," he teased. "But I was so
entranced by what I saw that I was struck mute."

"*That* will be the day," Kate chided. "I have never known
you at a loss for words."

"Now children," Alanna intervened, coming to her feet to
take Nicholas's arm, "let's not show bad manners in front of
our guest. Nicholas, you remember Miss Courtney."

A lazy smile kinked his lips. "Of course."

The pink hue of Andrea's cheeks darkened with his regard,
her gaze dropping to her hands folded in front of her. A long

silence hung in the room, as though everyone contemplated their next words. Finally Alanna broke the quiet when she suggested they adjourn to the dining hall, for the lavish meal awaiting them. Moving ahead of her grandson, she cunningly took Kate's arm to guide her away from Andrea and leave Nicholas to escort the woman from the parlor.

He waited until they were several steps apart before he offered his arm to Andrea. "An interesting ruse, Miss Courtney," he whispered. "But it won't work." He grinned victoriously at the sound of her rapid intake of breath. "You might be able to fool my grandmother, but not me. Enjoy your time here, but then I suggest you go home. I won't mention it to my grandmother or Kate, if you promise to keep still. Unfortunately, they want to see me married and are blind to people's tricks." He could feel her tremble.

"I told her it wouldn't work," Andrea whispered nervously.

For a fleeting instant, Nicholas wondered at the high pitch of her voice. He remembered it being much smoother. Mentally shrugging it off as unimportant, he asked, "Who?"

"My sister. I told her you'd know the minute you saw me."

Nicholas smiled politely, his gaze trained on the two women ahead of them. "I knew long before then."

Andrea's step faltered. "How?"

"Let's just say I have a good imagination. Now, if you promise not to let either Kate or my grandmother know what you're up to, I'll play along. But as soon as your little visit is over, I want you to go home and stay there. Understand?"

"Yes, sir," Andrea mumbled. But when they reached the entrance to the dining room, she pulled back. "What do you intend to do with my sister?"

Confusion wrinkled his brow. "Your sister? Why, nothing. I see no need." He held out a hand for her to take the lead and missed the surprised look on Andrea's face.

Nicholas seated the three women around the dining room table, then took his place next to Andrea, suddenly aware that he hadn't eaten since breakfast. His mouth watered with the warm aromas of roast duck, sweet potatoes, fresh corn, and cinnamon rolls coming from the kitchen. A moment later, a parade of servants trailed in, carrying covered dishes and a bottle of dark red wine for them to enjoy. They laughed and joked throughout the course of the dinner, and it wasn't until they had returned to the parlor for sherry that Nicholas realized Amber Courtney had spoken only a few words, and then in a quiet, shy manner. Oh well, he sighed inwardly. She had to keep up appearances. If she showed her true nature, Kate and his grandmother would wonder, and obviously Miss Courtney had taken his warning to heart.

The two younger women sat on the sofa, intently engaged in their conversation of the latest Paris fashions, something of which Andrea knew very little, while Alanna and Nicholas sat opposite them in a matching pair of wing chairs.

"Your sister really enjoys her," Alanna whispered, watching the two girls giggle over something Kate had said. "I didn't realize how lonely it must be for her living so far away from Williamsburg."

"I've been trying to tell you that for years. That's why I keep insisting the two of you move into town."

Alanna shook her head. "No, Nicholas. I've lived here most of my life. I'm not about to give it up now. Besides, it won't be long before Kate finds a husband and moves out."

"All the more reason to leave this big house. Then I could keep a better eye on you that way," he teased.

"Grandmother," Kate interrupted, "you'll never believe where Amber's older sister is."

"Where, my child?" she smiled.

"Boston." She looked back at her companion. "Do you know I've never been to Boston in my entire life?"

"What is she doing there, Amber?" Alanna asked.

The young girl's face suddenly seemed to pale, her gaze darting from Alanna to Kate and back. "Oh, she's—she's trying to locate a relative of Papa's."

"That's an awfully long journey for a woman alone. Wasn't she frightened about going?"

Andrea smiled. "No. Am—Andrea isn't afraid of anything."

"How much older is she than you?"

"Five—min—er—years," she quickly amended.

Nicholas smiled softly at the clever way Amber held to her story for their benefit, lifting his glass of sherry to his lips.

Then it struck him. "Older?" he asked aloud.

"Yes, older. Can't you hear?" Kate laughed.

Nicholas straightened in his chair. "I'm sorry, but I thought you told me you had a younger sister."

Her dark blue eyes, wide with confusion, stared back at him. If he knew the trick they were playing, why would he risk drawing attention to the fact by asking such a question? Although she couldn't pinpoint the reason, Andrea felt something was wrong. "Ah—yes, I meant older."

Suddenly it was as if Nicholas was seeing Amber Courtney for the first time in his life, as he recalled that the one thing that had attracted him most to her had been the color of her eyes. Or had he imagined it? He looked down at the brown circle of sherry in his glass. Had he drunk too much? Why did he have this feeling something was amiss?

Kate reached out to take Andrea's hand in hers and pull the young woman's attention back to her. "Oh, don't worry about it. I'm always telling everyone I have a *little* brother," she mocked, casting Nicholas a devilish glance. "What's the matter, Nicholas? Has your memory slipped away with your youth?"

"Kate, don't tease," her grandmother scolded. "Your brother is tired, that's all. Aren't you, dear?"

Nicholas downed the contents of his glass and set it aside. "I guess so," he replied.

"Maybe another drink would help," Alanna suggested.

"No, I've had enough, thank you. But if you like, I'll freshen yours."

Alanna nodded, handed him her goblet, and watched him leave the chair to walk casually to the buffet and the decanter, thinking how proud Dru would be of his son. What a shame they had never really got to know each other.

"How's Edgar?" she asked suddenly.

Laughter rumbled deep in his chest. "I have no idea."

"Why? What's happened?" Kate interjected, her curiosity aroused at the mention of the boy's name. She looked at Andrea. "Edgar's a young boy who works for Nicholas."

"Worked," he corrected. "The scalawag ran off the other day." He turned back to them, his humor fading when he saw the troubled look on Amber's face.

"Doesn't surprise me. You were so mean to him," Kate said.

"*I* was mean to him?" he laughed, his attention drawn to his sister. "I'll have you know, dear Kate, that little, sweet boy broke into my office to steal from me." Crossing the room to offer the stemware full of sherry to his grandmother, he failed to notice how their guest's mouth hung agape.

"Are you sure?" Alanna asked.

"Very sure. I caught him in the act. Then when my back was turned, he clobbered me with something."

"Oh, dear Lord," Alanna exclaimed. "How badly did he hurt you?"

"Knocked me unconscious. If Mathew hadn't come back to the office that night, I would have lain there till morning."

"But he seemed like such a nice boy. He must have had a good reason."

Nicholas smiled knowingly. "Oh, a very good one, I think."

"What do you mean?" Kate asked. "You never leave any money there."

"But he wouldn't know that," Alanna pointed out.

"True," Nicholas said, sitting down in the chair next to her. "But I don't think it's the reason he broke in."

"What?" Kate and her grandmother echoed.

"For the past two months, some of our shipments have been coming up short. It wasn't enough to worry about, but when I found Edgar in the office, it all fell into place."

"How?" Alanna asked.

"He wasn't looking for money. If he'd wanted to be paid, the little imp would have just asked me. He's brazen enough. I think he was there to find out what day would be our next big shipment."

"Whatever for?" Kate frowned, failing to notice the wide-eyed stare of her new friend.

"So his partner can attack the ship, steal the goods, and resell them. I believe the two of them were doing it all along and got greedy. One bale of cotton wouldn't bring as much of a price as thirty!"

"But you can't be sure. This is only speculation."

"Granted. That's why I've sent someone to the bank

to watch."

"The bank?" Alanna asked.

"Yes. I had left my ledger on the desk that night and I'm sure Edgar looked in it. He probably can't read, but I suspect his partner told him what to look for. If that's true, then the other possibility could be that they intend to rob the bank or finagle a way to get their hands on the money in my account. Either way, I've got myself protected."

Alanna fell back in her chair. "I can't believe it."

"Neither can I," Kate agreed strongly.

"Well, if my hunch is right, we'll know very soon."

"How?"

"Because if I'm right about the ship, they'll have a surprise coming. Sean and I set up a trap."

"A trap?" Alanna asked, looking from Nicholas to her granddaughter, then to Miss Courtney, suddenly aware of how pale the young woman seemed.

"Exactly," he continued with a smile. "Instead of the usual crew, I doubled it. They're hiding below decks. When Edgar's friend boards the ship they'll be outnumbered. And once he's caught, he'll tell us where to find my little housekeeper. I can hardly wait to get my hands on him."

"You won't hurt him, will you, Nicholas?" his grandmother asked worriedly.

"Only his bottomside." He grinned triumphantly. "I just might make him repay me by working it off. For, say, five years." He rested his elbows on the arms of the chair and tapped his fingertips together.

"If you'll excuse me," Andrea spoke in a weak voice, "I'd like to go to my room and lie down for a while."

Alarmed, Kate took the girl's hands in hers. "You're not ill, are you?"

"No, just tired." She looked from Kate to Alanna, carefully avoiding Nicholas's eyes. "I want to thank you for inviting me here. I truly enjoyed myself. But I'm afraid I must return home tomorrow, if it's not an inconvenience to anyone."

"Go home?" Kate moaned. "But you just got here."

Andrea looked to her hands. "I know it seems like that, but it's a two day ride and I really shouldn't be away from home any longer. A-Andrea might return and worry where I am. There was no way I could tell her that I'd come to spend some time with you, and she's rather—well—after all that's happened in the past few weeks, she may think the worst. I don't want to upset her unnecessarily. You understand, don't you?"

"Of course, we do," Alanna chimed in, giving Kate a warning shake of her head when she made to argue. "My granddaughter is disappointed, of course, but we'll have you back again for a longer visit."

A pout curled Kate's lower lip.

"Now be a good girl, my child," Alanna added, "and walk Amber to her room. I'll see the carriage is ready in the morning whenever she decides to go."

"Yes, Grandmother," Kate said quietly, coming to her feet to fulfill the woman's request.

It wasn't until after they had left the parlor and the sound of their footsteps faded in the distance that Alanna turned to her grandson. "Was it my imagination, or did your story seem to upset Miss Courtney?"

"Yes, I noticed it, too. I can't imagine why it should, but now that you mention it, there's something about her that bothers me."

"Why do you say that? I think she's perfectly charming."

Staring at the empty doorway, he remained quiet, pondering his skepticism, then said, "It's just that she seems different from—" He caught himself before he had gone too far.

"From what?"

"Well, she's so polite, childlike. She looks the same, but for some reason, she doesn't affect me the way she did that day she—she asked for a loan. And her eyes—"

"What about them?"

"I remember them being much bluer. Almost the color of the sky."

Alanna laughed. "How can someone change the color of their eyes?"

Standing next to her chair, Nicholas looked down and smiled. "They can't. I've just had a long day, and I guess my mind is playing tricks."

"Then why not retire and we'll get up early tomorrow and enjoy the day? Maybe you and Kate can go for a carriage ride."

"A very good idea," he agreed, holding out his arm to escort his grandmother from the parlor.

Having stripped himself of everything but his breeches, Nicholas paced the floor of his bedchambers. Although his body longed to rest, his mind raced with thoughts of Edgar's downfall. The little ruffian should be taught a lesson. That was if they could find him after all this was over. He should turn him in to the magistrate, but for some reason he didn't want to. He liked Edgar in his rough, unpolished way, and rather enjoyed the thoughts of transforming the young upstart into a respectable citizen. Obviously no one else had been able to, and locking him away wouldn't help. He grinned, envisioning the look on the boy's face when he confronted him, Edgar's partner at his side. *Should be well worth the wait.*

The distant pounding of hoofbeats filtered in through the closed windows. Hurriedly, Nicholas crossed the room to pull aside the curtains and peer out into the moonlit night. A lone rider approached at a gallop and disappeared around the corner of the house near the veranda before he could recognize the newcomer. But instinct claimed it to be the reason he had lost sleep the two nights past, and he smiled victoriously. Returning to his bed, he sat down and quickly donned his stockings and shoes, hearing the urgent rapping against the manor door. Lifting his shirt from the chair, he stretched into it as he ran from the room.

"Nicholas, what is it?" he heard his grandmother ask when he came into the hallway.

Looking back, he found her dressed in her nightgown and robe and standing in the doorway of her room.

"If I was right about my little friend, it should be Sean Rafferty," he smiled, turning for the stairs.

Before he had reached the front door, Kate and Andrea emerged from their bedrooms dressed like the older woman, and all three moved to the top of the stairs to watch and listen.

"Well?" Nicholas asked impatiently, closing the door

ehind Sean.

Stretching from the discomfort of riding for hours without
stopping to rest, Sean Rafferty's gaze fell on the trio of
onlookers. He came to attention quickly, smiled broadly at
hem, and bowed as he said, "Forgive the intrusion, Mistress
Remington."

"It's quite all right," Alanna answered. "Nicholas told us
hat you might come."

"Aye. And if it hadn't been a matter of urgency, ya wouldn't
be seein' me now." He rubbed a hand on one hip. "If I be livin'
ta see a hundred, I'll never be likin' ta ride a horse." He smiled
over at Nicholas, his mirth disappearing at the anxious, somewhat irritable look he received in return. He cleared his throat.
"Well—ah—I guess ya be wantin' ta know how things turned
out."

Nicholas's cheek twitched. "Uh-huh."

"Just like ya thought. We hadn't sailed an hour before we
came on a disabled ship. They called out to us and we moved in
alongside of her. 'Course we be suspectin' a trick, so the crew
was waitin' for me signal. Nicholas, me boy, ya wouldn't
believe the captain of this ship."

"Why?"

"I never saw such a stumblin', inept man in me life. Climbin'
from his ship ta ours, he tripped over a rope and fell flat on his
face. 'Twas all I could do ta keep from laughin' aloud."

"How did he tip his hand?"

"Well, I noticed how he kept lookin' around, like he was
countin' the crew. Then he motioned his mates ta come aboard
and they all pulled their pistols. Ya know, I even wondered if
the fool had his loaded. Anyway, he tells us he be takin' our
supplies. When I didn't argue, he looked sorta surprised, as if
he be expectin' more trouble than I gave him. Ya shoulda seen
him then. Acted like he thought he was Blackbeard, struttin'
around givin' orders. I waited until his back was turned and
nodded at McKenzie. As soon as the last of them was on board,
standin' all together, McKenzie dropped a net over them.
'Twas easier than scooping up fish in a barrel."

"Where is he now?"

"We sailed back ta Williamsburg and docked at the pier near

133

your warehouse. McKenzie's keepin' him in me cabin. The crew we tossed in the hold."

"Good job, Sean," Nicholas smiled, patting the man's shoulder. "Did you find out who he is?"

"Aye. His name is Barlow Paxton."

A commotion at the top of the stairs spun the men around in time to see Andrea fall to the floor.

"Good heavens," Alanna exclaimed, bending down to touch the woman's brow. "She's fainted."

For two days Amber stayed hidden in the vacant warehouse, sneaking out only at night to steal what food she could find. She watched them load the big ship with the supplies her father's cousin would take when the opportunity arose, telling herself everything would go as planned, while a glimmer of doubt gnawed at her conscience. Nicholas Chandler stood overseeing the work and remained at the dock until the ship with its handsome captain had sailed away. Crouched down behind some boxes in the alleyway, she stayed there until he climbed into the buggy outside his office and rode away, heading out of town. Only then did she feel safe enough to leave her shelter and return to the warehouse to wait. The single window in the building where she had found refuge afforded a full view of the Chandler Shipping Lines office, though some distance away and, for some unknown reason, she sat before it for the next two hours, her attention glued to the comings and goings of the men who worked there. She couldn't explain why, but she felt compelled to spy, to watch for signs of trouble. Or was she overreacting? Whatever the cause, she sat transfixed, praying Paxton would return in a few days with enough money to free her and her twin from the evil hold Baron Von Buren possessed. Then, just as she was about to give up her vigil at the window to seek a more comfortable spot to lie down for a while, she noticed the frantic movements of the workers at the pier. Within minutes, the huge ship that had left only hours before glided into view, ropes tossed to the men who awaited her docking. Surely Paxton hadn't attacked the ship so soon. And why didn't anyone come ashore? Something was wrong! She could feel it. She counted each second that passed with the pounding of her heart. Should she run? What if they had out-maneuvered her partner, trapped him? Having risen to her knees to better her view, she sat back on her heels while she nervously chewed on the nail of one thumb. Maybe there had been trouble with the ship, a mainsail had torn from its rig-ging, forcing them to return to repair it. No, wait! Someone hurried down the gangplank. Amber stiffened, her bright blue eyes wide with fear. The captain, alone. Why didn't the crew follow? Her fingers gripped to the windowsill, she pressed closer to the glass to watch his tall, lanky frame as he hurried down the pier. At the end, he stopped to exchange a few words with the man she had seen working in Nicholas Chandler's office. *Had* they been robbed and he was coming to inform him? A few more minutes ticked away before the captain turned abruptly and mounted a horse tied to the hitch-ing rail outside the office. Cruelly yanking on the reins, he spun the steed around and raced off down the street.

Amber fell back against the wall to catch her breath. It could mean Paxton had been successful. And then again, maybe he hadn't. Worry knotting her brow, she twisted back up to her knees, intent to study the frigate for any clues.

Evening came and still no one else left the ship. What could it mean? And where had its captain gone? With only one way to find out, Amber, still disguised as the young boy, cautiously left the warehouse and started for the ship. She would sneak on board to learn why they hadn't allowed the crew to leave.

Darkness her only ally, Amber darted from building to building, from crate to barrel, until she reached the pier. Knowing she couldn't simply walk up the gangplank, she decided on the only other method: climbing hand over hand up the mooring line at the aft of the ship. Kicking off her cumber-some shoes, she glanced in all directions to guarantee her solitude and grabbed hold of the rope. Hands clutched to its rough hemp, her ankles locked tightly around the stern fast, she began inching her way upward, a little at a time, keeping as quiet as possible. She had no idea what she planned to do once she reached the deck or what she might learn, but her curiosity and her trepidation urged her to continue. The muscles of her arms weakened, the blood pounding in her temples at the dizzying heights. She set her eyes on her goal, the chirping of crickets and the occasional moan of the ship her only companions. Then she heard them . . . voices coming from the captain's quarters. Hanging there, she moved closer, straining to peer in through the porthole. She didn't recognize the one who spoke nor could she see whom he addressed, only that the first seemed irritated with his companion by his warning tone and the forefinger he wagged in the other's direction. Her fingers numb, her left hand lost its grip, slipping from the rope. She squealed, latching on to it again with her arm wrapped around it. She decided to slide further up, closer to the ship. Grabbing a new hold, she pulled, her feet inching ahead a small measure. Her strength fading quickly, she dropped her head backward, hoping to renew her courage when she caught sight of the second man in the captain's quarters as he moved to look out the porthole. Her eyes widened in horror, for even upside down, the face unquestionably belonged to Barlow Paxton.

"Oh, no-o-o," she half moaned, half cried, all of her plans, her schemes, shattering before her eyes. Her lower lip quivering, she unknowingly loosened her hold, her weight pulling her from the rope. Without a sound, she fell headlong into the murky waters of the York River.

She pulled herself from the cold salt water and stumbled back to her hiding place in the warehouse, where she stayed, trying to sort out her problems. If they had captured Paxton, it meant the captain had gone to inform Nicholas Chandler. No doubt he would return here as quickly as possible to question the pirate, and Amber had no doubts her father's cousin would tell all if pressured into doing so. But would he only tell of the boy who had hired him, or would he reveal the youth's true identity? Surely he would not give her away. What reward could it possibly achieve? Now the second night crept over the city, and Amber still waited. For what? If Paxton told Nicholas Chandler of the boy, they would search the entire town until they found Edgar MacDonald. But how would they ever find him if he didn't exist? A new smile of confidence glowing in her eyes, Amber stood up, knowing the only safe place for her would be at home, dressed as a young woman. Yes, Amber Courtney would return to Jamestown to live with her sister. After one last glance at the ship and Nicholas Chandler's office, she left the warehouse, intent on finding a ride with someone along the way home.

Bright sunlight guided the way of the lone carriage rattling down the road toward Williamsburg at a breakneck speed, its occupants tossed about inside. It seemed the rig hit every pot-hole along the route, failing to irritate the driver, while his companion clung desperately to any handhold he could find.

"I not be knowin' why ya be in such a hurry, lad," Sean shouted over the noise of the coach and pounding hoofbeats of the mares. "He'll not be goin' anywhere. Slow it up a bit before ya throw me out and have ta waste time comin' back for me."

The thought of his father's cousin sprawled along the road-side brought a smile to Nicholas's lips and a surrendering tug on the reins. The expensively built carriage slowed to a comfortable pace.

"Thank ya, me boy. Ya almost had me wishin' I was ridin' me horse instead."

Nicholas laughed. "I apologize, Sean. It's just that my revenge on that young upstart burns an urgency in me. I know Paxton will still be there, I'm just impatient, that's all."

Sean twisted to a more relaxed position, brushing the dust from his sleeves. "Have ya given it much thought, lad, that your little friend might not be in on this?"

"I'd stake everything I own on it that he is," Nicholas replied quickly, hearing Sean chuckle in return.

"In two weeks, it won't be much."

Nicholas smiled at the gentle reminder, but refused to voice a comment.

"Ya know, when ya came ta meet me ship in such a hurry, I figured ya wanted ta tell me ya was gettin' married within the hour and didn't want me ta miss it." He grinned over at Nicholas. "Ya have found the lass, haven't ya?"

"Not yet," Nicholas answered, his mirth crinkling the corners of his mouth.

"What ya be waitin' for, lad?" Sean exploded, turning to

face his friend, one hand on the carriage frame and the other on the back of the seat. "Ya only be havin' two weeks. Ya will never be findin' someone in that amount of time."

"Why, Sean Rafferty," Nicholas scolded playfully. "I thought you found this whole situation amusing."

"Aye, that I did. Two years ago. I figured ya would be findin' someone long before now. Ya really don't intend ta let your inheritance slip through your fingers, do ya?"

"And would you have me marry just anyone?" Nicholas asked, his attention centered on the road ahead. "I must believe you never got married for the same reason."

"That's different," Sean barked, plopping back in the carriage seat.

"How so?"

"I didn't have nothin' ta lose."

"All right. I'll agree to that. But what if I marry a woman whom I don't love and find out afterwards what a shrew she can be? Would a life of torment be worth my father's shipping lines?" He sighed heavily. "And if worse comes to worst, I'll ask Heather."

"Ha!" Sean roared. "I'd rather be seein' ya wed a whore."

Nicholas burst into laughter. "I'm afraid Heather would find the comparison an insult."

"Not as long as ya soothed her over with a ruby trinket or two." He crossed his arms over his chest and rested one foot on the carriage frame, deep in thought. His lined, sun-darkened face, as handsome as twenty years ago, marked a displeasure rarely seen on it. Sean Rafferty took life as one continuous game to play, always finding humor in any situation. Only one other time had he seemed as troubled, and that had been the night he learned his cousin had died in the warehouse fire. "Come ta think of it, laddie," he said suddenly, straightening in the seat. "Who was the lass with Kate?"

Nicholas grinned. "Her name is Amber Courtney. And if you're thinking to match us up, don't. She's like all the rest."

"Nicholas, me boy, I wouldn't be thinkin' the sort. But she be the prettiest thing I've seen in a long time." He reached up to scratch his nose. "So if ya not be interested, why was she there?"

"Grandmother invited her. She has the same ideas as you."

"Me?" Sean wailed.

"Yes, you. Grandmother liked her and thought I would, too."

"Well, do ya?"

"As I said before, she's only after my money."

"And how would ya be knowin' that?"

"She came to me asking for a loan—"

"Oh, well, I guess ya be right. She did want your money. Did she ask ya ta marry her, too?" Sean mocked.

Nicholas couldn't refrain a chuckle. "No. But it was only a ploy. I'm sure she would have suggested it to repay the loan."

"Would have. Ya mean she didn't?"

"No. I didn't give her a chance," Nicholas said softly, suddenly disapproving of the direction in which their conversation was headed.

"Ya mean ya were rude ta her?"

"That's putting it mildly," Nicholas grumbled. "Look, let's change the subject, shall we?"

Sean twisted in the seat, one hand resting on the back, the other on his knee. "I be gettin' the feelin' there's somethin' wrong here, lad. Would ya be wantin' ta talk about it?"

"No!" Nicholas growled, then relaxed. "I'm sorry, Sean. I have no right to take out my troubles on you."

"Aye. But ya can be tellin' them ta me. I've always listened before."

Nicholas glanced up sheepishly. "I don't think you'll understand nor sympathize with me this time."

"Try me," Sean pressed, but when Nicholas remained quiet and refused to look at him, he added, "Somethin's troublin' ya, lad. Has been for a while. I knew it a couple of days ago when we talked of catchin' this pirate. And I not be meanin' Edgar. 'Tis somethin' else. If ya tell me, maybe I can be puttin' your mind ta rest."

"What makes you think it's anything else?"

"Ya lost the twinkle in your eye. I know ya be worryin' about your father's will, but that isn't the whole of it. Havin' your sister run the shippin' lines isn't your biggest concern. Ya will never hold a grudge because of that. 'Tis somethin' altogether different."

When Nicholas had first sought the high adventures of the sea at the age of seventeen, destined to explore the continents about which he had heard so much, he had left behind a friendship that had not fully developed between himself and his father. He had never shared any secrets with him, laughed about good times, cried about the bad, and when he had returned home to stay, to see his father buried, Nicholas painfully realized what he had missed, and that he would never be allowed to call on his father for advice, for comfort in his moments of need. Yet, here beside him now was a man whom he loved as deeply as Dru Chandler and offered support no matter what the problem might be. Oddly enough, Nicholas was tired of making his own decisions, and for once wanted someone else's opinion. "I've done something I'm ashamed of, Sean, something I've never done before and pray to God I will never do again."

"Nicholas, me boy, I be knowin' ya well and can't be thinkin' of anythin' as bad as all that."

"Oh, but there is. I'll tell you the whole story from the beginning, but you must promise to listen to it all before saying a word. Promise?" He waited for Sean to nod his head, then continued. "Miss Courtney came to my office that day, but I refused to see her, thinking she was just another woman wanting me to marry her. I had Mathew send her away before she even had a chance to explain.

"I was to meet Alanna and Kate for dinner and went home first to change. Miss Courtney followed me. When I found her standing at my doorstep uninvited, it made me angry. I asked her to leave, told her I wasn't interested in her problems, but she insisted, and I decided the only way to get rid of her was to hear her out, make my excuses, and send her on her way." He sighed heavily, leaning back in the carriage seat, the reins dangling from his hands. "I don't know what got into me. She told me her father had been killed and that one of the men he owed wanted his money or he would claim her sister's hand in marriage. I didn't believe her. In fact, I still don't. I thought it was just another approach to win me over. Anyway, when I asked her how she intended to pay off the loan, she said she

140

would work for me. I told her I didn't need the extra help, since I already had a housekeeper and cook."

The muscles in his throat tightened and he swallowed hard. "I must have been mad. I suggested she pay me back by spending the night with me. I figured it would scare her off. But it didn't." He fell silent, unable to finish.

"So ya made love ta the lass. 'Tis nothin' ta be ashamed of, Nicholas. Ya've done that before, I imagine."

"Not like this, I haven't. When I took her in my arms, she—she begged me to stop, that she had changed her mind. But—but I couldn't—"

"Oh," Sean nodded knowingly. He settled back in the seat.

"She was a virgin, Sean. I figured she had used this trick before, that I wouldn't be the first, or I never—I swear to God—I never would have gone through with it."

"And now ya be feelin' the guilt."

"Yes."

"Ya shouldn't. The guilt is hers. She must have known what she was gettin' into before she ever came ta ya."

"I thought so, too. I thought she was determined enough to do it just to trick me into marrying her. But after last night—"

Sean raised a questioning brow. "Last night? What happened last night ta change your mind?"

"Being with her, seeing her again. She isn't the same, Sean. It's like she's a whole new person."

"And what makes ya say that, me boy?"

"I don't know for sure. But she's gentle, not anything like the hot-tempered girl who dumped bread pudding in my lap. And why would she faint like that?"

"There could be a number of reasons why she fainted, but what is this about dumpin' puddin' in your lap?"

Nicholas laughed, recalling the incident in his mind. "I saw her later that night at the Chesterfield House. She was only having tea and I decided the least I could do was buy her something to eat. She thought otherwise and gave it back to me . . . all over my breeches."

Sean's shoulders began to shake, a chuckle rumbling in his belly until it exploded into merry laughter. "Ah, she be soundin' like your mother, God rest her soul."

"Yeah, I think my grandmother thought so, too. That's why she invited her to spend some time with us. Unfortunately, she saw the whole thing."

"Well, I wouldn't be worryin' about it, lad. Ya probably won't be seein' the wee lass anymore."

"I don't think so either. I told her that I knew her little plan and that she should go home and stay there."

"Then what be your problem?"

Nicholas shrugged. "That's what worries me. I can't say for sure, but there's something about this whole mess that doesn't seem right." He snapped the reins, calling out to the mares when the rooftops of Williamsburg came into view. "And right now I've got other things to think about."

"That ya do," Sean agreed, his hands clutched to the framework of the carriage as they bolted off once more.

The rest of their trip passed in silence as they rushed through the busy streets of town and headed out to the dock at the Chandler Shipping Lines. Before the carriage had come to a complete stop, Mathew Calloway stepped out of the office as if he had watched for them, reaching out to take the reins Nicholas offered and tying the mares securely to the hitching post. An invitational wave of his employer's hand to join the fun set the man's feet in motion without a second's hesitation, and the trio quickly headed down the pier, up the gangplank, and into the captain's quarters without bothering to knock.

"Good afternoon, Nicholas," Donovan McKenzie said, once the group had stepped inside and closed the door behind them. "Ya made good time."

Donovan had been lifelong friends with Nicholas's father and Sean Rafferty. They had all sailed away from Ireland in their own ship at the young age of eighteen, to share the excitement of the high seas and explore the world. When Dru married Victoria Remington and settled down in America, the bonds of friendship had pulled them even closer. If Dru Chandler had decided to settle down and asked his cousin to join him, it seemed only natural Donovan McKenzie would too. Snow-white hair trimmed the suntanned baldness of his head, marking his age, while his muscular build contested the fact. He radiated a quiet courage, a man who let no one push

142

him around and never once allowed his loyalty to the Chandler family to falter.

"Aye, that we did," Sean grumbled. "I be thinkin' he wanted ta set a record." He dusted off his clothes with brisk swipes to his sleeves and cotton breeches and moved toward the little man who sat huddled in the far corner of the cabin. "Nicholas, me boy, I'd like ta have ya meet Barlow Paxton, a man who foolishly thought ta steal from ya."

Paxton's thin frame quivered beneath the close scrutiny of his captors, his blue eyes trained on the youngest of the group as the man casually sat down at the desk. No one spoke, the quiet and tension in the air rapidly closing in on the pirate, who was certain he had met his doom, but unsure of the form it would take. He closed his eyes, praying it wouldn't hurt overmuch.

"Who gave you the information?"

The voice carried a warning not to dally, to speak the truth or find his tongue cut from him. He opened his eyes, a tremor of fear rattling his teeth. Tears lined his lower lids. "I—I didn't think this up. It wasn't my idea. I didn't even wanna do it." He gulped.

Nicholas's eyes glanced up at Sean, then back to Paxton. "Who supplied the information?"

Never having been one to practice valor, Barlow wondered if they would let him go if he merely told the truth. And what of his ship? Would they return it to him? His knees shook. He needed his ship. How else could he sail the coastline in search of food? His weathered face crimped in worry, a knot strangling the breath from him.

"Was it Edgar MacDonald?"

Barlow forcibly sucked in a breath, his hands trembling, their palms moist. "Edgar who?" he squeaked, the higher pitch of his voice revealing his apprehension.

Nicholas leaned forward against the desk, his arms folded in front of him. "It might go easier on you if you willingly tell us who helped you, rather than have my friend here," he looked at Donovan, "beat it from you."

"Oh-h-h," Barlow whimpered, his entire body convulsing with the threat. The man with whom he'd spent four days and nights took a step closer, reminding Paxton of the threats he'd made, beginning with a well-placed blow to his rib cage or breaking both knees for the mere sport of it. He forced his attention on the one who spoke.

"Now, was it Edgar MacDonald who told you which ship to attack?"

Paxton's mind raced. Who was Edgar MacDonald? Only he and his cousin's daughter had plotted out the venture. Where had they come up with the name . . . suddenly it hit him. That had been the name Amber had used. "Yes! Yes, it was Edgar MacDonald. He thought it all up." He grinned, certain they would turn him loose now.

"Where can I find him?" Nicholas asked.

"What?"

"Well, you must have agreed on a place to meet to divvy up the spoils of your thievery. Where were the two of you to meet?"

Barlow's eyes widened. Dear Lord, if he told where Amber hid—

"Mr. Paxton, I'm not interested in you. I only want the boy. But if you insist on not talking, I'll have to let Mr. McKenzie change your mind."

"No, wait!" he cried out when Donovan touched his shoulder. "You—you won't hurt the youngster, will you?"

"Why should you care? He's a thief and will be dealt with accordingly. If you cooperate, I just might let you go, since no real damage was done. But the boy must be taught a lesson. Now where is he?"

"What kind of a lesson?"

Nicholas frowned, wondering. "I haven't decided. Why are you so concerned? Is he a relative of yours, perhaps?"

"No, no! Never met the brat before the other day." He nervously twisted the ragged corner of the shirttail sticking out from his waistband, watching Nicholas Chandler lean back in the chair, his arms folded over his chest.

"You know something you're not telling, Mr. Paxton. What is it?"

"Nothing! Nothing! Look, the boy said to meet him—ah—in Yorktown. Yeah, that was it. Yorktown." Fearful blue eyes glanced from Nicholas to Sean to McKenzie and back.

"Why are you protecting him, Mr. Paxton?" Nicholas said after a while.

"I ain't!" he shouted, his tone hinting the contrary.

Nicholas studied the little man for several moments, a vague smile touching the corners of his mouth. "Very well. Then I guess we'll all go to Yorktown to find him. But if we don't, I'll have you gelded."

"What?" Barlow exploded, his voice shrill, his mind vividly depicting the scene. "No, you can't. You—"

Nicholas raised a hand to silence him. "If you're telling the truth, you have nothing to worry about." He nodded at McKenzie, who all but lifted the tiny shape from the floor with a steely hold of Barlow's shirt collar.

"No, please," he cried.

"Mr. Paxton, I told you before, I'm not interested in you. Only Edgar."

"But—but Edgar's too young to—"

"To what? Beat within an inch of his life? I think differently. Unless, of course, you'd rather take his place."

The cloth across his shoulders tightened. Maybe if this man knew that Edgar wasn't a boy, he'd show mercy. After all, Amber had only done it to save her sister. His eyes wide, he gulped, praying the young woman would forgive him. "He ain't who ya think he is," he said weakly.

The dark brown of Nicholas's eyes deepened. "Oh, and just who is he?"

"Put me down and I'll tell ya," Barlow choked when the fabric around his throat threatened to squeeze off his breath.

Nicholas nodded to McKenzie and Paxton stumbled to the floor. Rubbing his neck several times, tears blurring his vision, he swallowed repeatedly until the muscles in his throat relaxed. He looked up at Nicholas sheepishly. "Edgar Mac-Donald is a girl, a young woman," he said quietly.

His chin dropping slightly, Nicholas's eyes mirrored his surprise. He looked from Sean to McKenzie and back to Paxton. The child's strange behavior was suddenly quite clear. He hadn't wanted to take a bath for fear a shiny nose and fresh-washed hair would give him away. He hadn't wanted Nicholas to touch him simply because the gentle curves of womanhood could not be easily or completely disguised and he'd know in an instant the ruse the child played.

"A wench," he said, shaking his head. "I should have known." He recalled the youngster's claim. "How old is she? Eighteen?"

Paxton shrugged. "Close to, I guess. Mr. Chandler, ya won't beat her, will ya? She—she only did this because she needed the money."

"For what? To buy land and several slaves? The profit you two would have shared was more than any child could need. And it was dangerous. Why not continue stealing a loaf of bread or clothes to wear?"

Paxton's cheek twitched. "She didn't do it for herself."

"Oh, really? And I suppose you're going to tell me she did it to share with all the other people in need. It would make sense since she had such an obvious dislike for people of wealth. Her own sort of revenge."

"No, sir. She needed the money to pay off her father's debts."

"You mean her father knew of this?"

"No. He's dead, Mr. Chandler."

Nicholas leaned back in the chair, his attention still centered on his captive. "Why didn't she borrow the money?"

"She tried, but no one would help. Her father owed so many—please, Mr. Chandler, let her go. I'll talk to her, make her promise not to ever do it again."

"Oh, she'll be told, Paxton. Only I'll do the telling. Now, for the last time, tell me where to find her."

Barlow's chin trembled, and for the first time in his life he foresook his own safety to protect another. "You—you must promise me not to hurt her, or I won't tell you." He clasped his hands to stop their shaking, staring bravely at the man who held his future with one spoken word.

Nicholas raised a brow, admiring the man's courage. "She means a lot to you. A niece, perhaps?"

"No. My cousin's daughter."

"You'd risk your well-being for a cousin's daughter?"

His lips suddenly dry, Barlow's tongue shot out to moisten

them and ease the tightness in his throat. "Yes, sir. I owe Fletcher that much. He was killed unfairly in a duel, or he would have seen to his children's care. And if you have her put in prison, there'll be no one to take care of her sister."

"She has a sister?"

"Yes, sir. A twin."

Nicholas chuckled. "I pray she isn't of the same nature, or I'll have another to contend with." He smiled over at Sean.

Barlow shook his head. "Oh, no. Andrea is much too shy—"

The name seemed to pierce Nicholas's skull, to howl the deception in his head. "*Andrea?*" he exploded. "Courtney?"

The pirate fell back, his entire body quaking. "Y-yes."

Nicholas bolted from his chair. "And Amber is the one who thought up this whole thing?" he stated more than asked. But before Paxton could confirm the statement, Nicholas ranted on. "Of course, she is." He paced the small cabin, oblivious to all who shared the space. "It makes sense. Amber came to see me that day, to borrow money. She's the one who dumped the pudding in my lap, the one whom I made so angry because I wouldn't help. She cut her hair, dressed as a boy and returned looking for a job. She wanted access to the office, to find just what she needed, to *steal* what I wouldn't give her. Ha-ha!" he roared. "Then things got worse. My grandmother liked her, the woman from the restaurant. She invited Amber Courtney to spend a few days at Raven Oaks, only Amber couldn't go because she had no way to hide her hair. So she did the next best thing. She sent her twin sister, her shy, humble sister, the one whose eyes aren't the same color. I knew it! I *knew* she wasn't the same woman who came to my house."

Frowning, Sean stepped forward, for he suddenly wondered if Nicholas truly saw the humor of it or was beginning to act like a madman. "Nicholas, me boy—"

"Oh, Sean, don't you see it? It *wasn't* a trick. She told the truth! And Andrea swooned because she feared for her sister." Nicholas laughed loudly. "How frantic Amber must have been when I told her Edgar would be going along to my grandmother's. She couldn't be seen next to her sister. We'd all know in an instant! Oh, wait till I get my hands on her!" He rubbed the mentioned palms together as if feeling the slim form between them.

"Nicholas, lad, ya not be thinkin' ta hurt the wee lass, are ya?" Sean asked worriedly.

Nicholas spun around to face him, his eyes aglow with mischief, a broad smile enhancing his looks. "Hurt her? Heavens no! I intend to see she's repaid for this little scheme. And in a way I'm sure she'll find most unsatisfactory. I am going to marry her!"

Chapter Seven

"Amber, I knew this wouldn't work," Andrea sobbed. "And now we have more trouble than we did to begin with."

"Not if Paxton doesn't tell them who I am," Amber encouraged her as she cut a slice of bread and smoothed butter over it.

"But you can't be sure," Andrea moaned.

Setting aside her meager portion of food, Amber crossed the kitchen to sit down next to her sister at the table. "It's a chance I'll have to take. As soon as I've eaten, I'll bathe and shed these clothes." She reached up to touch the unkempt mop. "And wash my hair."

"But what if he does? And they come looking for you? Even if you claim it's a lie, they'll know. No woman wears her hair so short!" A renewal of tears flowed down Andrea's cheeks.

Amber studied her sister a moment, wishing she could find the words to ease her worry. "Look, Paxton may be a lot of things, but I don't think he'll give me away just to save his own neck."

"You think! You think! You don't know for certain." Frantic, Andrea seized her sister's hands. "You've got to go away until we're sure Paxton didn't tell. A week or two, maybe three."

"And go where?" Amber argued. "It was nearly impossible to find food while I was on my own, and stealing it just to survive while I wait can put me in greater danger. I might get caught and thrown into prison. I appreciate the concern, but I think I'm better off here. If what you suspect comes true, we'll simply watch for them. I'll slip out the back window and hide in the woods until they're gone. You can tell them I never came back—no, tell them you had no idea what I was up to. That way they'll leave you alone."

"I can't, Amber," Andrea cried. "Look at me. One word out of them and I'll start sobbing all over again. I nearly gave you away already. If he had said one more word to me, I would have."

"Don't worry about it. The two of you were obviously talking about two different things. You didn't hurt anything. Honestly," Amber assured her.

But Andrea was right, of course. Strength was not one of her greater virtues. Sighing, Amber left her and returned to the cupboard where she took down a tin of tea leaves and sprinkled a few in a cup. Maybe Paxton *had* told Nicholas Chandler the truth, but she would still be a lot safer here than running the hillsides. She would do as she had said, watch for him and hide in the woods should he come. How long would he search? After all, nothing was stolen and no real harm had been done. Of course, she *had* hit him over the head. A worried frown knitted her brow. But didn't he have more important things on his mind than some scalawag who clobbered him when he wasn't looking? Her delicate nose raised slightly. He had it coming anyway. Bending down to retrieve the kettle of hot water from the fireplace hook, every muscle in her slender frame tightened instantly with the rattling of a carriage outside the house.

"Oh, my God!" Andrea shrieked. "He's here already."

"Shhh!" Amber scowled, setting down her teacup. Racing to the window, she peered outside, a heavy sigh escaping her when she spotted Seth climbing from the buggy. "It's for you," she sighed, collapsing in a chair, beads of perspiration dampening her brow. If this is what it meant to wait, she doubted she would live through it.

"Good afternoon, Andrea," Amber heard Seth say once her

sister had opened the door and let him in. A moment of silence from the other room passed before he spoke again, concern mixed heavily in his tone. "Is something wrong? You've been crying."

Her head tilted back against the wall behind her, Amber closed her eyes and listened to the footsteps coming into the kitchen. Opening one eye at a time, she smiled up at the startled face staring back at her. "Good afternoon, Seth," she grinned.

"Good heavens, what's going on?" he asked, his brows furrowed as his gaze swept over the young woman dressed in rags.

"It's a long story," she replied.

"And what have you done to your hair?"

Oddly annoyed by his presence and the hunger knotting her stomach again, Amber stood up and returned to the fireplace. "Andrea can tell you. Right now I feel more like eating than explaining."

"Please do," he instructed, turning to the woman at his side. "I fear I will die of curiosity if you force me to wonder another minute."

Andrea guided him to a chair by the table and sat down next to him, reliving all that had happened in sob-choked words and telling him her reason for tears now that it had ended. Seth sat in awe, staring first at Andrea, then at her twin, who occasionally smiled back at him between mouthfuls of bread. Reduced to weeping, Andrea buried her face in her hands while Seth shook his head, unable to fathom that any woman would go to such lengths as Amber Courtney had.

"I don't believe it," he finally replied. "And Nicholas Chandler, of all people. Dear Lord, Amber, he's one of the wealthiest men around. He'll not rest until he sees you pay. How could you be so stupid?"

Her anger flared high, flashing blue sparks in the eyes glaring across the table at him. "What did you expect me to do? Sit by and watch Baron Von Buren claim Andrea?"

"No, of course not, but—"

"Do you have any money?"

Surprised by her question, he straightened, shifting his gaze from her to Andrea and back. "A couple of dollars."

"Well, that's more than we have. And Von Buren wants his money in two weeks."

"So borrow it!"

"I tried. No one will part with their money and give it to someone who obviously has no way to pay it back." She stuffed another biteful of bread in her mouth. "I couldn't even steal it," she mumbled.

"So now what do you plan to do? You're in more trouble than before."

"I don't know. But if worse comes to worst, Andrea and I shall leave."

Seth fell back in his chair, arms folded over his chest. "Oh, that's a wonderful idea. Then you'd have two men looking for you. Von Buren *and* Nicholas Chandler."

Swallowing her mouthful, followed by a sip of tea, Amber stood up, her lanky frame stiff with unrefuted anger. "Then why don't you marry Andrea? At least she would be out of danger. Von Buren can't claim something that belongs to another."

"Very true. It would only leave *you* to claim."

Amber sent him an icy glare and turned away. "I'll take my chances. And traveling alone would be simpler." Her gaze swept the length of her. "I fooled everyone before disguised this way. I can do it again."

"You really want to spend the rest of your life dressed like that?"

Amber spun around. "I'm only thinking about it! I simply meant I could if I had to."

Rising, Seth crossed to the hearth and fixed a cup of tea. "I hate to put a fly in the butter, Amber, but your disguise won't work with Mr. Chandler. He's already seen you this way. He'll know exactly who to look for."

Her body trembling with rage, fists clenched, Amber hissed, "You sound as if you want me to be caught!"

"I'm only trying to talk some sense into you," he shouted.

"Then you come up with a better idea!"

"Amber, please," her sister cried. "Arguing won't help."

Her tear-stained cheeks and swollen eyes, and the pleading look on Andrea's face quelled Amber's desire to dispute the topic further. But not enough to stop her from sending Seth a challenging glare before turning away. "I'm going to take a bath," she announced, stopped coldly by the trio of raps against the front door. Spinning about, she waved for her sister to answer the summons while she hurriedly fled to their bed-chambers to hide.

"I'll see who it is," Seth offered when Andrea left her chair to do as instructed. "If it's Mr. Chandler, he'll know Amber's here simply by looking at you."

Her lower lip quivering, Andrea pressed her fingertips to her mouth to still its trembling and stood beside the kitchen door just out of sight to listen.

"Good afternoon, sir. Is there something I can do for you?" she heard Seth ask once he'd opened the door.

"Yes, I'm looking for the Courtney residence. I was told this is it. My name is Nicholas Chandler."

Her body pressed back against the bedroom wall, Amber's knees gave way at the sound of his voice, and she slithered to the floor, her entire frame quaking. *Please, Seth*, she begged silently, *send him away*.

"Yes, this is, but I'm afraid no one is home right now. Maybe you should try later, Mr. Chandler."

"I've ridden a long way to speak with Miss Courtney. Do you have any idea what time you expect her, Mr.—?"

"Tyler, sir. Seth Tyler."

"Are you a relative of Miss Courtney?"

"No, sir. I've been courting Andrea. Someday I hope to marry her."

His declaration of love surprised Andrea as she listened from the kitchen. Never before had he told anyone of his future plans . . . not even her. Drying her eyes with the back of her hand, she pressed closer to listen. Maybe Seth's presence had been a blessing. He might be able to talk Mr. Chandler into leaving and give Amber time to escape.

"Oh? Amber never told me that her sister was courting."

"Amber?" Seth questioned, his voice tense.

"Yes, didn't she tell you? Miss Courtney was a guest at my grandmother's home a few days ago. We talked quite a bit."

"Ah—no, she didn't mention it."

A knuckle pressed against her lips, Andrea cursed her failure to include her visit to Mistress Remington's in her story to Seth. She could only pray now that he would go along with whatever Nicholas Chandler said.

"In fact, that's the reason I'm here . . . to apologize."

"Apologize?"

"Yes. I'm afraid our visit was cut short when I had to return home on business. I was hoping I could make up for it by inviting her to come to Williamsburg soon . . . possibly attend the theater with me."

A smile broke the worried lines on Andrea's mouth. He didn't know! Paxton hadn't told! Now all they had to do was keep Amber out of sight until her hair grew back. He'd never be the wiser, and Edgar MacDonald would simply disappear!

"You must miss her."

"Miss her, sir?"

"Andrea. How long has she been gone?"

A whimper lodged in Andrea's throat. Dear God! Seth didn't know she had told Nicholas Chandler that her sister was in Boston looking for a relative.

"Oh, a-about a week now."

"I understand Washington is beautiful this time of year."

Andrea's eyes flew open.

"Yes. Yes, it is. Andrea loves to visit there."

"Well, Mr. Tyler, I won't keep you. I have some business to take care of in Jamestown. When I'm finished, I'll stop by again on my way home. Maybe Miss Courtney will be here then."

"Yes, yes, she probably will be. Sorry you missed her."

Seth fell back against the door after he had closed it behind his visitor, a heavy, nervous sigh escaping him. Then his eyes caught sight of Andrea stumbling in from the kitchen.

"Andrea, what's wrong?" he asked, rushing over to catch her in his arms.

"It was Boston."

"What?"

"I told him Andrea went to Boston."

Seth's brow crimped. "Maybe he forgot."

"No, I didn't forget," a voice behind them proclaimed. They

154

spun around to find Nicholas haloed in the doorway. He smiled and walked further into the room. "And I assume I have the pleasure of addressing Andrea, not Amber Courtney, her twin sister?"

Andrea clung frantically to Seth, no words coming to her mind to explain the dire necessity of such a ruse.

"I must admit, you and your sister had me quite fooled. I never would have guessed if your father's cousin hadn't feared for Amber's safety. Now, I suggest you tell me where I might find her."

A loud crash thundered outside the cottage, followed by a scream and the sounds of a scuffle. Andrea gasped, tears beginning again as she clutched Seth's shirt front in her hands. Nicholas, however, smiled lazily and settled himself in a chair near the fireplace to wait. A moment later, two figures filled the front doorway.

"Just as ya be thinkin', Nicholas," Sean grunted, holding Amber's struggling form in his arms as he dragged her further into the cottage. "Caught the hellcat climbin' out the window."

"What—what are you going to do?" Andrea sobbed.

"What do you suggest?" he answered. "After all, she did try to steal from me."

Her bare heel found its mark on Sean's toe, her elbow to his ribs. He grunted but would not relinquish the hold clamped over her mouth, his other arm tightly encircling her slim waist. Unable to free herself, she reached up, grasped the hand silencing her, and soundly bit the fingers.

"Yeeeoow!" Sean bellowed, clutching his injured extremity.

Amber broke for the door, stopped abruptly by the painful yank of her hair in Nicholas's grasp. "I suggest, little Edgar, that you sit down somewhere and don't move, or so help me, I'll give you the thrashing you deserve."

Even her father's most ardent demands that she behave had never affected her the way Nicholas's did. Of course, she had known her father would never hurt her beyond a well-placed slap to her backside. This man, however, might easily lay her skull open. She relented, allowing him to spin her around and shove her into the chair he had so hurriedly vacated. She sat rigid, the muscle in her cheek flexed, nostrils flared. She stared at the floor, knowing his glare centered on her.

"That's better," he said. "Now I suggest the rest of you do the same, while I tell you what it is I've decided to do."

Seth ushered his weeping companion to the sofa and sat down quietly beside her, holding her tightly in his arms. All eyes focused on the man before them, his feet apart, arms folded over his chest . . . all except for Amber's.

"Since the man you sent to steal from me failed, I allowed him to leave with the promise he never return to Williamsburg, or he'll find himself in prison. However, Miss Courtney's punishment won't be as simple."

"Mr. Chandler, I beg of you," Andrea broke in. "Don't send her away. She only did it for me."

"Don't beg, Andrea," Amber snapped, "not of him."

A hidden smile twitched the corner of Nicholas's mouth. He straightened and stared down at her. "It would behoove you, Edgar," —he stressed the name— "to show a little humility yourself sometimes."

Her icy blue eyes glared up at him. "I did once. And you demanded I repay the loan with something you didn't deserve. I'm not a whore, Mr. Chandler."

"Only a thief," he finished.

"I can live with that," she sneered.

"Can you? In prison?"

Andrea gasped, and Amber studied the floor again.

"Well, I don't think you can," he continued. "And since I find myself in a bit of a predicament, I've come up with another solution. One which will benefit us all and free your sister from the baron."

Seth and Andrea exchanged puzzled glances. Amber glared suspiciously. "What?" she hissed.

"That you will return to Williamsburg with me, take a bath, and find a suitable gown to wear. As soon as I can summon the minister, you and I shall be married."

Stifling her gasp with fingertips pressed to her mouth, Andrea stared at her twin sitting stiffly in the chair before her. Had she heard? Or was she too numb to react? Then suddenly Amber burst into laughter.

"Do you think I jest?" Nicholas asked, unaffected by her glee.

"I see the humor, yes. Maybe you don't know it, but your sister told me why you hadn't wed before now. You're looking for the right woman."

"Yes, that's true. One who isn't after my money."

"There, you see? . . . the irony of it? I more than any other was after your money. I even tried to steal it."

A soft smile enhanced his dark features. "But for one very different reason. You wanted it, *needed* it for someone else . . . not yourself."

Set back on her heels at his declaration, Amber's amusement faded. "Then marry Heather and loan me the money. I'll work it off."

He bent down to stare into her eyes. "But I don't want to marry Heather. And I won't loan you a tuppence."

A frown creased the dirt smudges on her brow. "I fail to see where a union between us will benefit anyone but you."

Standing erect again, Nicholas strolled to the hearth and ran a finger over the wood carvings of the mantel clock. "When a man marries, his wife's debts become his. Therefore, I will pay Baron Von Buren what is owed him, thus freeing your sister."

"And entrapping me!" she howled, bolting from the chair. "I don't want to marry you!"

He looked casually at her. "I don't see where you have a choice."

"That's blackmail!" she screamed.

A wide grin stretched his lips. "Yes, it is. Become my wife or go to prison."

Panic coursing through her, Amber spun around and raced for the door, halted in her tracks by the huge Irishman who barred her exit.

"Now, Miss Courtney, I suggest you come along peaceably, or I'll have Mr. Rafferty tie and gag you. It's a long ride home, and I think you'd find it more comfortable riding on top of the horse rather than draped over him."

A chill ran up her spine. She must find another answer. She didn't want to marry, and certainly not this arrogant fool. She took a deep breath, let it out slowly, and turned to face him, a sweet smile forced to her lips. "Mr. Chandler—" she began, cut off when he interrupted.

"Nicholas. Call me Nicholas. After all, we are engaged."

She fought the urge to kick him. "Nicholas," she repeated, "let's talk this over. I'm sure we can come up with something a little more satisfactory for all concerned."

Slowly walking to her, he paused and leaned in, his face only inches from hers. "No," he said firmly, then extended his hand. "Shall we go?"

Amber hesitated. "But—but what about Andrea? I can't leave her alone."

"Oh, really? You did for nearly a week while you gallivanted around as a boy. And I'm sure Mr. Tyler will take care of her for now. Later if she wishes, she can live with us. My house is plenty big enough."

A flurry of ideas flashed through her mind. With Andrea, her *twin*, living under the same roof, Amber would be able to trick Nicholas into thinking his wife did exactly as he instructed, while, in fact, she had slipped away to live elsewhere before he discovered the ploy. Maybe marrying him to free Andrea wasn't such a bad idea, after all. Everyone would win, and in time she could shed the chains of wedlock. She glanced up, unaware of the smile on her lips.

"You might as well forget whatever you're thinking, sweet Amber. The color of your eyes gives you away."

Her hopes crumbled. Reluctantly, she allowed him to take her elbow and usher her from the cottage.

They traveled nearly all the distance to Williamsburg in silence, and Amber was forcibly held in the saddle in front of Nicholas, his strong arms encircling her as he guided the horse, the muscles of his chest and thighs molded against her.

How could she have gotten herself into such a mess? Three days ago she had thought everything would go as planned; she would have enough money to rid herself and her sister of Von Buren and live comfortably for a while. Now she was astride a horse on her way to get married! Her shoulders drooped, knowing of no way out. She was trapped. If she refused Nicholas Chandler, he would only throw her in prison, and Andrea would fall victim to the baron. Although she hated being a martyr, she knew she must surrender . . . at least until their debts were paid. A smile appeared at the corner of her mouth.

Nearing the edge of town, Nicholas waved at Sean as he rode off toward the church, instructing him to give the couple an hour or so before coming to the house with the minister. He felt it would take that long before he could scrub the dirt from his future wife and bring a luster to her hair. Thinking of her appearance, he leaned back to appraise her slight form.

"I think one of Kate's gowns will fit you," he said, remembering the three new dresses that had been delivered to his house. He was to have taken them with him when he visited Raven Oaks a few days ago, but in the excitement he had forgotten them. He smiled softly, satisfied with his lack of thought in regard to his sister's request.

"Is it white?"

Surprise curled his brow, "Why?"

"I want to be married in white. In fact, I want a big church wedding."

Laughter rumbled in his chest. "Stalling for time?"

Amber remained silent.

"If you're not careful, I'll have you wear what you've got on. Wouldn't you love telling our grandchildren what you wore on your wedding day?"

Amber suddenly twisted in the saddle to glare at him. "Let's get one thing straight, *Mr.* Chandler. This is a marriage of convenience, nothing more. There will be no children or grandchildren. So remove those lecherous thoughts from your mind."

"Only if you're barren."

"What?" she shrieked, nearly falling from the horse.

"I said there'll be no children only if you're barren." He snapped the reins to hurry the horse. "I intend to claim my husbandly rights whenever I want."

"Then it will be rape," she spat, each word slow and precise. "As it was before."

"Whatever you wish," he replied smoothly, hiding his grin until she turned away to concentrate on the road ahead. *Papa would be proud!*

The spectacle they made cantering down the center of town

turned everyone's head, for stories of the youth who had struck Nicholas Chandler had spread quickly among the townsfolk. A few applauded, and all wondered what he intended to do with the little beggar. And Amber noticed all the stares, how they stood there judging her, dressed in all their finery while she was reduced to rags. Well, let them watch. She didn't care. A tear pooled in the corner of her eye.

Instead of the wild ride down the path Nicholas had chosen the first time he brought Amber home, he guided the horse down the wide drive at a steady pace. The house loomed out in front of them and Amber suddenly knew what a condemned criminal must feel on his way to the gallows . . . the difference being that her sentence had just begun.

Reining the horse to a halt near the front steps, he slid down over the steed's rump and came to stand next to it, his hands raised to assist Amber to the ground. When she failed to move, he looked up sharply.

"Thank you, but I don't need any help," she said arrogantly and waited until he bowed slightly and moved away. She easily glided from the saddle and followed him inside.

"Hello, Mrs. Calloway," Nicholas smiled when the woman met them in the foyer. "I'd like you to meet the future Mistress Chandler, Amber Courtney. Amber, Martha Calloway, my bookkeeper's wife. Obviously, she's agreed to witness the ceremony. Is Mathew here?"

"Yes, sir. We heard you coming down the drive and he hurried to put a bucketful of hot water in the tub. He's upstairs." The small, auburn-haired woman turned to Amber. "I'm pleased to meet you, Miss Courtney."

Amber managed a weak smile. Apparently the woman knew all about her, for she didn't even flinch when she observed Amber's manner of dress, definitely unbecoming to a lady.

"Were you able to find one of Kate's gowns in the guest bedroom that would do for the occasion?"

"Yes, sir. It's all pressed and waiting. I also took the liberty of laying out a change of clothes for you," Martha replied. "And I'm fixing something for you to eat once you're all cleaned and changed."

"Thank you, Martha. It was very nice of you to help out on

such short notice."

"No need to thank me, Mr. Chandler. When Mathew told me why, you couldn't have kept me from coming. It's just a shame everyone else can't be here to see you get married. The whole town has been anxiously waiting for it to happen. Won't you even consider waiting for your grandmother? She'll be so disappointed."

"I'm sure she will be, but once I explain my reasons I'm certain she'll understand." He smiled at Amber. "Come, my dear, I want you all washed and pretty before the minister arrives."

"Would you like me to help, Mr. Chandler?" Martha asked.

"No, thank you. Amber already told me she didn't need any help." Placing his hand to the small of her back, he guided Amber toward the stairs. Once she had started up them, her back to him, he glanced over his shoulder at Mrs. Calloway and winked, bringing a bright smile to the older woman's face.

They traveled past Nicholas's room and entered through the second doorway to find Mathew bent over a brass tub, his shirt sleeves rolled up as he swished the water about. Hearing them step inside, he straightened with a smile.

"It's not exceptionally warm, Mr. Chandler, but it's the best we could do seein' as how we weren't sure when you'd arrive."

"It will do nicely, Mathew. Thank you." He turned to his companion. "Amber, this is Mathew Calloway. Mathew, Amber Courtney. You remember her, don't you?"

Mathew's pained expression swept over the dirty shape, lingering on the short-cropped, mud-caked hair. "Y-yes, sir."

"Don't worry, Mathew," Nicholas chimed in. "A bath will do wonders, and in time her hair will grow back. Now why don't you join your wife in the kitchen. We'll be down as soon as we've washed up and changed." He gently guided Mathew toward the door, one hand resting on the man's shoulder. "Sean will be arriving soon with the minister, and I'd appreciate it if you'd watch for them."

"Certainly, Mr. Chandler," Mathew said, stepping into the hallway.

When Nicholas was sure they were out of Amber's hearing range, he leaned closer and whispered, "and I'd be grateful if

161

you ignored any sounds coming from this room for the next half-hour."

Mathew glanced up, puzzlement crimping his brow until Nicholas smiled mischievously.

"Yes, *sir*," Mathew grinned knowingly. He glanced briefly at the woman who studied the tub full of suds, then turned and headed down the stairs, a slight chuckle bouncing his shoulders.

Entranced at the thought of soaking in lavender-scented bathwater, rinsing the grime from her skin and the dirt from her hair and shedding the awful clothes she wore, Amber failed to hear the door close or the key turn in the lock. Bending down, she scooped up a handful of suds, lost in the fragrance of them until she suddenly became acutely aware of the presence of another. Shaking the bubbles from her hands, she straightened and stepped back from the tub, her gaze darting across the room to find Nicholas casually leaning against the door, arms folded over his chest and a devilish smile curling his lips.

"If you wait much longer, the water will be cold," he said quietly.

"Then why don't you leave?" she sneered. "Or do you intend to watch?"

"Exactly what I planned, sweet Amber."

A chill raced down her spine, her face paling. "You can't," she exploded.

"Oh? And why not? This is my home and you, my dear, will be my wife before the hour is out. Besides I've already seen what you hide." He stood and strolled to the bed to examine the gown lying on it.

This has gone too far, Amber fumed, calculating the steps it would take her to reach the door. His attention drawn from her, Amber hesitated only a second before she raced toward her goal, certain she could outrun him and lose herself in the woods surrounding the house. Easily reaching the door long before he turned around, she seized the latch and yanked up on it. It wouldn't budge. Locked! The bloody cur had locked them in! Rage burning up within her, she spun back to glare at him, her chest heaving with her fury when she found him grinning in return, the key dangling from his thumb and forefinger.

"Wonderful little instrument, don't you think? In its minute way, it has the power to hold things one hundred times its size." He smiled again, dropping the key in his waistcoat pocket. "Now, as you already stated, you don't need any help. But if you dally a moment longer, I'll be inclined to think you lied and shall not hesitate to help you bathe." He crossed to the dressing table near the window while he removed his coat and sat down on the bench, his gaze never leaving her.

"Well, the least you can do is turn your head away," she snapped.

"And give you a chance to hit me again? I don't think so." He crossed his knees, draped one arm over them, and rested the other on the corner of the table, content to wait as long as it took.

"You ask too much!"

"I hardly agree, dear Amber. A minor price for all you owe me."

"Owe you? I'm marrying you to save your inheritance!"

"And in return, I'm paying your debts and freeing Andrea. I claim us equal there.'

"Yes! Equal. You have no right to demand more."

"Oh? What about the time you sought to embarrass me by dumping bread pudding in my lap?"

"You deserved it," she sneered.

"Took a job from me under false pretenses?"

"There was no harm done," she argued.

"Broke my mother's vase?"

She opened her mouth to argue, but he continued on.

"Entered my office without permission? Hit me over the head and left me there not knowing if I lived or died? And finally, hired a stumbling oaf to steal from me?" He folded his hands. "Do you really call that equal?"

"But—"

"Take off the clothes and get in that tub before I'm forced to help."

Amber's chin trembled. "Please, Mr. Chandler. I can't." She fell back against the door when he suddenly stood up. "All right! All right! I'll do it. But promise you'll stay where you are."

He chuckled. "Really, Amber, I hardly see where you're in a position to make conditions."

Her mixture of humiliation and fear fell second place to the anger she experienced. How dare he treat her like a slave, or, worse yet, a whore! *Damn you, Paxton*, she seethed inwardly. *If you hadn't been so inept, kept your mouth shut, I wouldn't be here now.* She glared heatedly at Nicholas, then turned her back on him, a stinging warmth settling in her cheeks. She knew he watched. She could sense it, *feel* his gaze raking over her as she unfastened the buttons of her shirt. Then her eyes caught sight of the fresh towel, folded and lying on the foot of the bed, and an idea struck her. Hurrying over to it, she quickly seized it and sent a sarcastic smile his way. He nodded in return.

Clamping the edge of the cloth in her teeth, its folds falling before her, she swiftly shed the dirty shirt and breeches, a light smile tugging at her lips, pleased with her ingenuity. Dressed only in her camisole, her gaze darted quickly to her silent audience, surprised to find the way his attention moved repeatedly from her face to the towel and then as if he looked past her, a satisfied grin brightening his eyes. Suspicious of his odd behavior, she cocked a brow and straightened, tucking one corner of the muslin under her arm to drape it across her chest as a curtain, certain she left nothing to observe. Sliding the straps of the remaining garment from her shoulders, she wiggled free of it, and hugged the towel to her knees with her other hand, smiling victoriously. It had been simpler than she imagined. Taking a tentative step forward, she paused, making sure he had no intentions of moving toward her, then quickly headed for the tub. The towel held out before her, she stepped into the sudsy water and slipped beneath the surface of bubbles. Sending him a triumphant leer and knowing the lather would hide any further chance of a glimpse, she allowed the white cloth to slip from her fingers and glide to the floor.

Nicholas sucked in a slow, calming breath, oddly thankful she had found the protection of the water to hide herself and give him a chance to still the burning in his loins. For, unknown to Amber, she had chosen to stand before the cheval mirror in one corner of the room, allowing him an unrestricted view as she undressed. His pulse had quickened at the mere sight of her in the camisole, but his heart had pounded as she slid it down past her narrow waist, so slim he felt certain he could encompass her with his hands. Blood drummed in his ears when the cloth fell to the floor and he saw the pale smooth flesh of her buttocks and thighs, the long, willowy legs and the gentle curvature of her spine. God, how he wanted to reach out to touch her! But he couldn't, he mustn't. He wanted to prolong her discomfort, to return all the feelings he had experienced at her hands.

When Barlow Paxton had revealed the true identity of Nicholas's houseboy, Nicholas had, at first, been angry to think a young woman could so easily deceive him. He had traveled in many foreign countries, dined with the King of England, saved the life of an Arab sheik, and had countless affairs. He prided himself on knowing women, understanding their moods, being astute enough to realize what drove them to do the unexpected. But this one had completely fooled him. Then his anger had faded when he considered the reason Amber Courtney had done what she did. He found it amusing, but more, he accepted the challenge to see she was repaid in the most fitting way. In the short time he had spent with her while she disguised herself as a boy, he had learned of her hatred for people of wealth. Exactly why she had such feelings, he could only guess. But if he could force her into being obligated to just such a person, she would be in a position she detested and yet be unable to change. And maybe, if his conscience would allow, he could set aside the guilt he felt for raping her.

And this, dear Amber, he thought, a faint smile wrinkling his cheek, *is only the beginning*. He bent down, snatched away the towel, and moved toward the bed.

"What are you doing?" Amber barked, dipping herself further into the foamy surface of water.

"Just moving it out of the way in case you splash. It's rather difficult to dry oneself on a wet towel," he replied, refolding the cloth.

Amber glared heatedly at him, knowing the error of her move and certain her pleas for modesty's sake would fall on deaf ears if she voiced them. This was one man she could not intimidate.

He strolled casually past her toward the bed, where he returned the towel to its place, straightened, and faced her once more, drawing her attention to him as she scooted around in the tub, not trusting him behind her. Then her eyes caught sight of the full-length standing mirror off to one side of him. Jerking her head around to judge the location of the dressing table and the spot where he had remained while she had disrobed in relation to the location of the mirror, she colored hotly when the realization that he had seen a full view of her backside all the while bolted through her. She moaned, squeezing her eyes closed as she sank further into the water.

"Don't forget to wash behind your ears," a soft, mocking voice instructed.

Knowing she could do nothing to alter the situation at the moment, she looked up at him, her lip curled, but refused any further recognition of his words. Capturing the tiny bar of soap in her hands, she vigorously worked up an ample amount of suds and covered her face, neck and arms with it, splashing away the dirt with a handful of water. It felt wonderful, and she delighted in the fragrance of the soap, something she had never before enjoyed, a bar of lye having been the most her family could afford. Resting her head back against the edge of the tub, her eyes closed again, she slid lower, her chin tickled by the numerous bubbles floating about her when of a sudden a huge hand grabbed her head and shoved her beneath the surface. She came up coughing and gasping for air, the soap burning her eyes.

"You—jackanape!" she choked, rubbing her eyes with her fists to clear her vision. "Are you trying to drown me?"

"No. Simply reminding you to wash your hair," Nicholas said, enjoying the sight of the full swell of breasts peeking out above the bubbles before he reached into the tub for the bar of soap.

Amber shrieked when his hand brushed her thigh, clutching her arms over her bosom. "I can manage on my own!" she barked, pulling back when he reached out for her.

"I'm well aware of that, my dear. But you might as well get used to it. I intend always to assist in your bath." He knelt on one knee, his other foot flat on the floor to brace him, and smiled to himself at the sight she made. Cowered in the far corner of the tub, submerged in suds, she glared balefully at him, water streaming down her face from the thick, matted crop of hair. Unable to contain his mirth any longer, he burst into laughter.

Her anger flaring high at his insensitive glee, Amber seized the sponge and flung it in his face, a spray of water droplets flying out in all directions before it fell against his chest, the knee of his breeches, and finally the floor.

His merriment shattered, Nicholas studied the damage the wet sponge had done, knowing he too must now have a change of clothes before returning to his guests. He dropped the soap back in the tub and stood, his eyes trained on the fearful woman staring back at him. With slow deliberation, he slid from his waistcoat, reaching up to unfasten the buttons of his shirt and pull it from his breeches, letting it fall to the floor. He kicked off his shoes and easily removed his stockings before he knelt down again, a determined gleam in his eyes as he retrieved the soap once more. A strong hand shot out, seized a fistful of Amber's hair, and yanked her closer, bringing a squeal of pain from her. Unaffected by her pleas to cease his inhuman treatment of her, he lathered up her blond curls, scrubbed vigorously, and promptly dunked her in the sudsy depths of the bathwater without so much as a moment's hesitation.

"You beast!" she sputtered when he repeated the process, baptizing her a third time.

Only after he was convinced that her hair glistened with cleanliness did he release his hold and come to his feet. "Now. Get out of the tub."

"No!" she wailed, tears clouding her vision. How could he expect her to shed all modesty and do as he commanded, as though standing naked before him had no effect on her whatsoever? She gulped and spoke softly, praying her words would sway him. "Listen, Mr. Chandler, I feel we must reach some sort of compromise—"

"In my house, I rule. There will be no compromises. Get out of the tub," he said again.

"Look, I'm sorry for throwing the sponge and getting you

167

all wet—"

"Out!"

Amber jumped at the loud command. "I can't!" she moaned pleadingly.

"Then I'll help you," he said firmly, bending down to grab her elbow in a strong yet painless grip.

"No!" she screamed, clawing at the fingers wrapped around her arm. "Anything . . . I'll do anything you say, just don't—"

"That's right, you'll do anything I say . . . without question!" Latching on to her other arm, he easily lifted her from the tub, kicking and screaming. "Stop! Do you hear? Stop!" he howled, giving her a bone-rattling shake that instantly subdued her.

Trembling, she stood before him, her eyes closed as if the act would hide her nudity from him, her arms clamped to her sides where he held them. Tears stole between her lashes.

"Look at me, Amber," he warned. "Open your eyes and look at me!"

A moment passed before she cast him a fearful, almost sheepish glance.

"I've suffered a great deal at your hands, young woman, and once the word is out that the *boy* I hired to work for me was actually a woman, I will be target for many jokes. The time for compromises passed long ago. You should have thought of them then instead of deciding to steal from me. You've made your own bed, as they say, and I'll see you sleep in it!"

Her pale blue eyes narrowed dangerously, the fear and humiliation of a moment before gone. "Not with you," she growled, lifting a foot to crush her heel to his bare toe.

Caught unawares, he yowled in pain when she connected, letting go of her to hobble about on one foot. In the same instant, Amber caught his wrist, yanked with all her strength, and sent him tumbling into the tub. A shower of bathwater splattered everywhere, but failed to cool the furor that erupted within Nicholas. He scrambled from the brass tub while Amber raced for the towel on the bed, quickly covering herself with it as she rushed to put the piece of furniture between them. They squared off, Nicholas dripping wet, Amber with a satisfied, mocking grin.

"You'll find the bed has many thorns, Mr. Chandler," she said challengingly.

Amber failed to realize the view she presented him. In her efforts to cover herself, she had crossed one arm over her chest to clutch the towel at one side, leaving a wide slit that exposed just enough flesh to melt his heated mood. Long, shapely limbs disappeared beneath the cloth, but the lean hip that defied protection seemed to dare him to claim what he observed. His anger faded, replaced by a burning sensation that spread wildly through him. He smiled triumphantly.

"But the rose will be well worth the prick to my finger," he replied in a half-whisper.

Amber experienced a chill not born of the air, the fatuousness of her threat quite apparent. She seized the towel in both hands, its size suddenly smaller than a moment before, watching him move to round the end of the bed. A whimper escaped her, and, in a desperate attempt to keep her distance, she agilely sprang to the center of the bed, ready to jump either direction from any advance he might make.

"Why prolong it, dear Amber?" he smiled. "Before this night is gone, I will have payment for all the tricks you played." His hands slipped to the button of his breeches.

"Tricks I played? Payment?" she howled. "I only sought revenge for what you did to me! I paid in advance, if that is what you wish to call it, you—you barbarian!"

A faint smile darkened his eyes. "Then you shall pay again," he said calmly, popping the first button loose.

"The first time is equal to a thousand tricks!" she argued loudly. "I *will* not pay again!"

The second button came unfastened, and Amber stared wide-eyed, a knot in her throat threatening to strangle her. The shadows of his room that night had prevented her from seeing more than his silhouette then. But now, in the brightness of day, she observed a narrow waist and flat belly. But what disturbed her to the greatest degree was the dark mass of curls that covered his chest and trailed to a narrow line that disappeared beneath his breeches. Then she heard him chuckle, and she forced her eyes to meet his.

He raised a finger and motioned her closer. "Come here."

"No," she shrieked, stumbling backward when he took a step. "Go away!"

"Now, Amber. Don't make me use force."

Tears burned her eyes. No man ever before had forced her to do something she didn't want to do, and usually a cross word had deterred him. But this man was different. And if she was to win, it would be a physical battle to the end. He moved closer. Startled, her courage fading fast, she jumped, catching her foot in the rumpled bedcovers that tumbled her to the mattress. She screamed when she saw him lunge for her and quickly rolled from his grasp. Landing on the floor, her towel still clamped around her, she bolted for his pile of clothes and the key hidden in the pocket, determined to free herself, her path blocked when Nicholas suddenly appeared before her.

"Give it up, my sweet. You don't stand a chance," he murmured, his hands slipping to his breeches. In one swift movement, before she could react, he slid the garment from him and kicked it away.

Amber's breath left her. She stood paralyzed at her first stark vision of a naked man, her eyes wide, mouth agape. Had he no shame? Suddenly a tremor quaked her entire body.

"I won't hurt you," he whispered, stepping closer. "I'll please you, teach you the art of love, make you yearn for my touch, my caress."

His words hit her like a blast of cold, winter air, snapping her back to her senses. "Like hell, you will," she growled, doubling up a fist and landing a blow to his stomach.

Taken by surprise, Nicholas staggered back, rubbing away the momentary stunning effects of the attack. He stared at her disbelievingly. Had she really hit him? He reached up, running his fingers through his hair, before the humor of the situation struck him and he threw back his head and roared with laughter.

"I find nothing funny," she hissed, her hand still clenched as if to launch a second assault.

"Not to you, I'm sure. But that is the first time a woman has ever struck me as you have," he chuckled.

"And it shan't be the last," she promised, pulling back to verify the pledge.

Expecting as much, Nicholas easily reached up, caught her wrist before any damage could occur, and slowly twisted her arm in back of her, pulling her closer. His other hand captured the dampened strands of hair at the nape of her neck, tilting her face to his. Without hesitation, his mouth covered her protests in a searing kiss, forcing her lips apart with his tongue as he sought the sweetness there.

Shocked by his boldness, her eyes flew open, and, without thinking of the consequences, she let go of her towel to push at him. Her arm trapped between them, it did little good until he lessened his hold slightly. And in that instant she realized her foolishness, as her only shield for modesty's sake slithered to the floor, leaving her naked body pressed tightly to his once more. Out of desperation to free herself from his branding touch, she heartlessly bit the tip of the tongue invading her mouth.

He jerked away instantly with a moan of pain, moisture glistening in his eyes, certain she had drawn blood. But when she stooped to retrieve the towel, his agony vanished at the sight she made, and he bent slightly to present her bare bottom with a stinging slap as he said, "If you intend to hurt me, I shall return the favor."

She straightened sharply with a squeal, her face burning with embarrassment. "How—how dare you!"

This time when he reached out to grab her, she ducked beneath his outstretched arms and raced across the room to hide in the numerous folds of the drapery. He caught only a glimpse of bare thigh and shapely backside before they were swallowed up by the yards of cloth, but it was enough to set his loins on fire. Heather might be beautiful, but Amber Courtney blossomed with the shapely curves of womanhood with one major difference. She was far from willing. It would be an interesting challenge to see how long it would take to tame this vixen. He smiled softly and strolled to the window, satisfied the battle drew near an end. But when he lifted a hand to pull the drapery away, he heard a rending tear of seams an instant before the velvet cloth cascaded earthward, encasing him within its clutches. Blinded in its darkness, he fought to free himself, certain the little minx had fled her cover and sought to

171

escape the room. Flinging the drapery from him, he found Amber frantically searching his clothes, a shapely profile leaving little for him to imagine.

"Surely you don't intend to run through the house as you are," he pointed out. "I would imagine the minister is here by now."

Her chin trembling, Amber ignored his observation, continuing her hunt for the key. He seemed content to watch, and in his moment of foolish pleasure Amber found the tiny object and raced for the bed, ripping the coverlet from it to twirl it around her, ready to defend herself when he advanced. A frown marred the smooth lines of her brow when he failed to move, and, deciding his motives made little difference, she bolted for the door. Her shaky fingers prevented the key from finding its place easily, and, much to her dismay, it slipped from her clutch to land with a clunk on the floor. Frantic, the numerous yards of cloth hampering her moves, she seized a handful of the quilt and tossed it over her shoulder. As she did this, the hem swept against the floor and with it the key scooted beneath the door and out into the hallway. Falling to her knees, Amber tried desperately to reach it, tears flooding her eyes when she failed.

"See what your foolishness has done?" his mocking voice above her asked.

"It's *your* fault," she snapped, choking back her tears and willing herself not to look at him. She collapsed to the floor, the coverlet tugged around her.

"It's just as well. If you escaped, your father's debts would go unpaid and your sister would marry Von Buren. Not to mention the fact that once I caught up with you again you would have gone to prison. Get up, Amber."

"No," she whimpered.

A strong hand reached down to claim her arm and haul her to her feet. She struggled briefly until he pushed her back against the wall to still her moves. She surrendered but refused to look at him.

"I do not intend to hurt you, Amber. I will be as gentle as you allow. But know this. I will take what I feel I deserve, whether you agree or not. And I will do so before we leave this room."

Her blue eyes flashed up at him. "Even though you know it's not what *I* want?"

He smiled warmly. "How do you know for certain?"

Her eyes narrowing, she spat, "You forget so soon. One other time a man held me in his arms, took me, hurt me. Why should I want that again?"

The painful memory darkened his eyes, a heavy sigh trembling his tall frame. "I thought you had lied to me then, and I wanted to teach you a lesson. For that I beg your forgiveness. I will never hurt you again. There will be no comparison. I will teach you the meaning of love." Pressing closer, his lips found hers in a gentle, warm kiss, his hand moving to cradle the slim line of her jaw.

Amber refused to close her eyes, denying him the sweetness of victory, for in her mind there would be none . . . not on his part, only hers. She did not believe him. Why should she? He was a man used to taking what he wanted, even if it meant twisting the truth to suit his needs. An apology would not weaken her tough reserve, melt her to his whims. But as she made these vows, a strange warmth began to grow in the depths of her being, her pulse quickening, and, without realizing it, her eyelids drifted shut.

The manly scent of him flooded over her, the taut muscles of his frame pressed against her through the cloth of the quilt. Logic begged her to push him away, but her heart forbid it, ravished by the tenderness, the unfamiliarity of a pleasure she had never dreamed existed. At first, as if testing her, his tongue lightly traced the outline of her lips before darting inside, and she found herself clasping him to her, yielding to the ardor of the embrace. But when his hand slipped beneath the protection of her cover to fondle her breast, she twisted away from his kiss, a startled gasp escaping her. She cried out for him to stop, but he paid her no heed, his searing kisses trailing down her throat, his thumb caressing the rose-hued peak of her breast. She fought in earnest and tried to break away, the folly of her act allowing the coverlet to slide from her shoulders and pool at their feet. She struggled furiously, but it seemed he had a thousand hands, all touching, exploring, igniting a wild fire

173

that raced through her with each caress. She sought to claw him, her intent easily deterred when he grabbed both wrists and twisted her arms in back of her, his ardent kisses covering her mouth and words of hatred. Her mind whirling, she vaguely felt him lift her in his arms and carry her to the bed, its feathery softness cushioning their fall. He curled her beneath him, his right hand sampling the voluptuous curves of her waist, hip, thigh. He kissed the corner of her mouth, her cheek, earlobe, and neck, then moved to capture the fullness of her breast, his tongue teasing its nipple and sending waves of fire through her. She arched her back to push away, only seeming to excite him more when their naked bodies touched full length.

"Nic-Nicholas, you—you mustn't," she begged, her words suffocated when his mouth returned to take hers, his long-stemmed passion soaring high.

With his manhood pressed against her thigh, Amber knew the game had ended. Yet his touch, through all, remained unhurting, guiding, and unfailing in his desire to fan the flames of passion within her. The body of a woman betrayed the pledge she spoke, the need to have him stop, for when he pressed his weight upon her, parting her thighs, she experienced no real want to fight him any longer. His manly hardness touching the soft flesh of her womanhood, Amber held her breath, awaiting his move as he teased, tormented, sharpened the will for her to have him freely take her. *Madness!* her mind called out. She didn't love him, yet she wanted him. *Is this the way it will be?*

Her arms encircled his neck, pulling him closer, the heat of his body sparking wanton desires foreign to her, an ache in her stomach. She moved to welcome his thrust, instinctively guiding him, hearing him moan when her hands slid caressingly down his spine to the small of his back and rested against his bare buttocks, her own pulse racing with a frenzy she wondered if she could endure. He came to her then in one quick move, taking her breath away. He started to withdraw at her muffled sob of pleasure, mistaking it for pain, until the desire to feel him deep inside her overruled all else and she raised up to meet him. She spoke his name in a whisper, his mouth covering hers in a passionate kiss, an urgency to do as she willed. A magic exploded within her, a tantalizing ecstasy coursing through every fiber of her being as their two bodies fused into one, moving in perfect harmony and soaring her to dizzying heights. Clasping him to her as though to draw them as one, Amber felt his heart beat wildly against her naked breast, his ragged breathing against her cheek. He moved faster, deeper, moaning her name deliriously, until, his passion spent, he fell exhausted at her side. She too lay breathless, glowing in the bliss of his caress as he stroked her breast, his teeth nibbling gently on her earlobe until the sudden reality of what she had done came crashing down on her. She had eagerly, lustfully, allowed him to take her, to claim the right she had saved to share with the man she loved. And why *this* man, one who stood for all the things she despised? A sob of shame knotted in her throat, and she squeezed her eyes shut to hide her tears, leaving his side quickly to find her clothes.

"Amber? What's wrong?" Nicholas spoke worriedly, rising up on one elbow. "Did I hurt you?"

Her pale blue eyes glared heatedly at him, the embers of their passion fading into memory.

Chapter Eight

The parlor of the Chandler house filled with the fragrance of flowers as Martha Calloway hurriedly gathered as many blossoms as she could to place about the room, waving off her husband's implication of their foolishness. The new Mistress Chandler deserved a wedding as close to tradition as possible, even on such short notice and in the absence of friends and relatives. Satisfied she had done her best, Martha set about entwining a flowery crown of bridal wreath for Amber's hair and a small bouquet of daisies resting on a leaf of fern for the bride to carry, ignoring the smiles of her husband and Sean Rafferty as they stood in one corner of the room watching and sharing a glass of wine while they waited.

"Where did you find Miss Courtney? You were gone quite a while," Mathew said. "Had Paxton lied about where she would be?"

Sean took a sip of wine and studied the minister, who sat at the small writing desk filling out the necessary documents. "No, Paxton was tellin' us the truth about the vacant warehouse. We just arrived too late, and Nicholas figured the lass went back home."

Mathew frowned curiously. "Why? She was supposed to meet her partner there."

Sean grinned and looked over at Mathew. "Remember the warehouse Argus Wilson owned?" he asked, waiting for the man to nod before continuing. "Well it be givin' the lass a clear view of the docks. Nicholas decided she had seen everythin' and feared we'd be comin' after her . . . or Edgar, anyway. Had ya been her, wouldn't ya have run home, too?"

"And that's where you found her?"

"Aye."

"Did she give you much trouble?"

Sean chuckled brightly. "If ya mean, did she willin'ly agree ta marry Nicholas, the answer is no. I'd be sayin' he blackmailed her into it."

"Oh, dear," Mathew moaned quietly. "Is Mr. Chandler sure this is what he wants? He always talked about loving the woman he asked to take his name."

Visions of Victoria Remington flooded Sean's mind, her stubbornness, her pride and spirit. And he recalled how his cousin had fallen in love with her almost immediately. Was Nicholas not of his father's blood and character? Crossing his arms, goblet dangling from his fingertips, he quietly considered Amber Courtney and noted the similarities between her and her future husband's mother, certain Nicholas had discovered them, too.

"Aye, Mr. Calloway," Sean said aloud, "Nicholas is quite sure. Ya will be seein' it for yourself before long."

Confused, Mathew's brow furrowed, his mouth open to question the man's meaning, when Martha interrupted with an excited wave of her hand.

"They're coming down, Mathew. Put aside your wine and get ready!"

"That woman," he muttered, doing as bade. "She thinks ya can't get married without all the frills." He looked up at Sean. "Well, are you ready, Mr. Rafferty?"

A lazy smile spread over the Irishman's face. "Aye. I've been ready for this for a long time."

The minister stood in the center of the room to await the bride and groom, his Bible in hand, spectacles perched on the end of his nose. Sean and Mathew moved to one side and Martha disappeared into the foyer, flowers in hand, only to return a moment later alone and seat herself at the delicate pianoforte. Her agile fingers stroked the keys and set the mood, the tinkling melody announcing the forthcoming union of two people. All eyes centered on the parlor doorway, and a moment later it was filled with the most handsome couple any of them had seen in a long while.

Amber's lean fingers were resting on the crook of Nicholas's arm and trapped beneath his hand. He led her further into the room, carefully watching for his friend's reaction. At first, Sean smiled brightly at him, a look of long-awaited satisfaction shining clearly in the blue depths of his eyes, until his gaze fell upon the woman at his side. Dressed in a vivid pastel green trimmed with a softer shade of mint lace along the decolletage of the gown, full skirts to accent her narrow waist, Amber was a striking beauty, one Nicholas could see obviously surprised and pleased Sean Rafferty. Chin sagging, his appraisal swept the length of her, from her slippered feet to her flower-adorned head, her short curls of honey-blond hue softly touching her cheeks and brow. His expression changed from awe to bewilderment, and Nicholas could only guess at the thoughts that raced through the man's head, for he, too, had wondered for a moment how a vision of loveliness such as this could be disguised so completely beneath a few rags. What seemed a long while passed before Sean closed his mouth again and forced his gaze to center on Nicholas once more. The younger of the two nodded a smile, at ease with his friend's apparent acceptance, for, though he seldom voiced it, Nicholas always sought Sean Rafferty's approval.

The couple crossed the short distance to the minister and stood reverently before him, the music of the pianoforte fading with the end of the song. Nicholas released his hold on Amber to fold his hands in front of him, his concentration centered on the preacher and the words he recited. Amber, however, studied the floor, vaguely aware of how the bouquet of flowers shook in her hands. Had not her need been so great, or had some other solution presented itself in that moment, she would have turned and raced for her freedom. What had happened only a few short minutes before in the bedchambers frightened her; she was certain that as soon as the guests left Nicholas would expect them to continue. Since it would be his right as her husband, she realized there would be little she could do to stop him. But what disturbed her more was the fact that she had not fought him for long, but had reveled in the fervor of his lovemaking. She felt the heat rising in her cheeks and fought to still the tremor that tingled her spine with the vision that exploded in her mind. She squeezed her eyes closed. He should not affect her in such a way. She hated him. She hated all he represented. If only she could escape. . . . She stood unmoving, listening to the man at her side pledge to honor, love, and cherish her, until death separated them.

Hearing the firm, unfaltering richness of his voice, Amber wondered what kind of man he could be, to force a woman he hardly knew into wedlock. Could his father's wealth be worth this much? *Of course*, she decided silently. *Money is all that matters to people like him. The wants and needs of a woman, his wife, are unimportant.* She raised her chin. *But once he sacrifices a little of his coin to pay my father's debts, we shall part company. Andrea and I shall sell what little we own and move north where he'll never find us. After all, this union is merely a convenience on both sides, and I think he would prefer his freedom to the chains of matrimony.* She glanced up at him from the corner of her eye to find him smiling, his concentration focused on the man before them. Knowing of nothing pleasant to lighten her mood, her gaze moved to the minister, who read from the Bible, then absently looked at the book in his hands. Cradled in the center, a tiny gold band lay nestled in its fold, a symbol of eternal love, no beginning, no end. Her breath grew labored as she fought to repeat the vows the minister was urging her to say, the mockery of the ceremony tasting bitter on her tongue. *I do this for Andrea*, her mind screamed, her eyes trained on the ring Nicholas reached out to take and slip on her finger. His touch, as well as the cold circle of precious metal, seemed to burn her hand, its falsehood searing her flesh as the final words were spoken.

"By the authority vested in me, I now pronounce you man and wife." The minister's voice rang clear, the finality of his words sending a chill racing down Amber's spine.

Nicholas turned her in his arms to bestow the nuptial kiss

180

and Amber found herself rigid in his embrace, allowing him the traditional kiss for appearance's sake only. But when his lips touched hers tenderly, she experienced a sudden rush of fever to her cheeks, a strange stirring in the pit of her stomach. *But any kiss from any man would affect me in the same manner*, she silently assured herself. She was the first to break away. She looked up into his eyes, oddly compelled to do so, until the small group of witnesses crowded around them to shake Nicholas's hand and voice their good wishes to his bride, while Sean Rafferty skillfully stole her away from the protective hold Nicholas claimed.

"Ya are a beauty, Mistress Chandler," he beamed, holding Amber at arm's length. "Ya'll do the former lady of this house an honor. And with your permission, I'd like ta be the first ta kiss the bride."

Although their former meeting had been unusual, to say the least, an experience she should have hated this man for, Amber found no malice in her heart toward him. In fact, she discovered she liked him, or at minimum, his manner and sparkling smile, the sincerity in the way he spoke and gently held her hand. Without realizing it, she nodded her consent, tilting her head back slightly to meet his gesture of good luck and prove her declaration to herself that this man, too, could spark an odd tremor of emotion in her. However, when they parted, an unwarranted disappointment spread over her, for his kiss had seemed nothing more than fatherly.

"If you'll excuse me," Martha's voice interrupted, "I'll see to our meal in the dining room." She turned to Amber. "You must be hungry after all that's happened."

Amber smiled weakly, thankful for a chance to break away from her new husband's presence and give herself a moment to consider where her observation of him fell short. "Yes, I am. And please, allow me to help."

"Oh, no, I wouldn't think of it. Besides, you and Mister Chandler have documents to sign," she argued, tugging at Mathew's sleeve. "My husband can assist me. By the time you're finished, the table will be set."

"Aye. 'Tis a good idea, Martha," Sean broke in, "and it will be givin' me a moment ta return ta me ship before we sit down."

"Your ship?" Nicholas questioned. "Whatever for?"

"Why ta fetch the bottle of champagne I bought in France a few years go. I've been savin' it for your weddin', lad," he grinned, bowing slightly to Amber. "If ya will be excusin' me, lass, I'll be returnin' before I'm missed." Turning away, he draped an arm along Mathew's shoulders, guiding the man and his wife from the room, adding, "I was fearin' maybe it would be goin' ta waste."

Once they reached the doorway, Sean glanced back over his shoulder at Nicholas and winked, bringing a chuckle from the younger man as he reached over to take his wife's elbow and draw her toward the writing desk and the minister.

"Had I asked Edgar this question, I'm sure the answer would be nay. But what of the lady I've married? Do you have the talents to pen your name, dear Amber?" he smiled.

"And read, Mr. Chandler," she sneered, her eyes averted.

He stopped suddenly and pulled her near. "Please, Amber, don't address me formally. The good Reverend Bauer will wonder why." He lifted a golden curl from her brow. "At least pretend to be the loving couple, if only for a few minutes."

Her cool, challenging eyes raised to meet his. "Do you think him a fool? As well as all of Williamsburg, *Mister* Chandler? There will be no question in anyone's mind why this union was made, and to pretend otherwise would be a mockery to their intelligence."

His soft smile revealed a sliver of white teeth. "Then consider it a way to humor me. I more than anyone know how you truly feel about me and merely wish a moment of your kindness." He took her hand and curled it over his arm, covering it with his own. "And you must remember, I haven't paid the baron yet. Until that's done, I suggest you not test me overmuch. I could forget my responsibilities." He held his laughter at her rapid intake of breath, nodding them toward their destination, the stiffness of her step marking her dissent.

Having placed his name to the certificate, Nicholas held the quill for his bride, his brows arching when she hesitated. A heated glare preceded the slim fingers that jerked the pen from his hand, and she bent to write her name, stopped abruptly when her gaze fell upon the words, "love, honor and obey." Obey, indeed, she fumed. But not for long.

The bonds of marriage sealed and recorded, the minister begged to take his leave, even with the offer of a meal, to return to his church and the matter of preparing for a funeral the following morning. Together the newlyweds escorted Reverend Bauer to the door, waved farewell, and watched him climb into the black carriage. A quick snap of the reins set the vehicle in motion and a moment later it rattled away, silhouetted against the glowing backdrop of the sunset.

Amber longed to ride away with him, to wake up to find the past few weeks had been a dream, a horrible nightmare, that Fletcher Courtney still lived, and, as usual, she and her sister waited supper for him. Absently, she thumbed the gold band on her left hand. But it wasn't a dream. She had lived every agonizing moment of it—her father's brutal murder, his death, the humiliation of asking for a loan, only to be turned away, the days and nights dressed in rags, and finally a marriage she wanted little to do with. Where would it all end? Would she have to pay for the injustice brought against her family for the rest of her life? Condemned to an unhappy existence for the remainder of her years? A feeling of hopelessness washed over her, tightening the muscles of her throat. She reached up to wipe away the tear. Well, she wouldn't accept this. Not for a moment longer than she had to. As soon as the debts were paid . . .

"Why don't we have a glass of wine while we wait for Sean?"

The deep richness of his voice startled Amber. Had he read her thoughts? She must be more careful in the future, lest she give herself away and spoil any chance she might have to escape. Without looking at him, she nodded and turned toward the parlor, hearing the manor door swing quietly shut behind them. Entering the room, she crossed to the velvet sofa and sat down, pulling aside her skirts to kick the slippers from her feet. Leaning back, she stretched out her legs before her, wiggling her toes to soothe their aching.

"Aren't you used to wearing shoes?" Nicholas commented from the buffet where he filled two goblets with wine.

She glanced up disdainfully. "Ones that fit, yes. These are

too small."

His attention drawn to the trim ankles, he looked up suddenly when Amber tossed the hem of her gown back over them, smiling at her cool aloofness. "Yes, I imagine they are. My sister favors her mother and grandmother, neither of them very tall." He came forward, handed her a glass, and sat down beside her, instantly aware of how she hurriedly slid away to avoid touching him. He grinned secretively. "Tomorrow we'll visit the dress shops and select a wardrobe for you."

"But what about Baron Von Buren? Shouldn't you send for him first? A pair of shoes can—"

"In good time, Amber," he said quietly, lifting his glass to sample the wine's bouquet.

"But there isn't much time—"

"Two weeks. Am I not correct?"

"Yes. But why wait?" she asked worriedly, sitting forward on the sofa to look at him.

He tasted the wine and settled more comfortably, his legs stretched out before him, ankles crossed. "To make sure this marriage will be what I expect," he answered, without looking her way, determined to play with her a while.

"Which is?"

His dark brown eyes glanced over at her. "That you are a loving wife."

Amber stiffened, her chin dropping. "You needed a wife in name only. I gave you that. You have no right to expect more!"

A flashing white smile challenged her statement.

"You can't!" she shrieked. "The papers are signed and witnessed."

"Witnessed by close friends who want nothing but my happiness, at any price. And a sizable donation to the church will see the papers disappear."

"You're a scoundrel, sir," she shouted, blue eyes flashing.

Nicholas shrugged. "So I've been told."

"Well, you've had all you shall get from me," she howled, leaping to her feet, wine spilling from the glass.

He sampled his drink once more, content to study the fine cut of crystal. "Then you call the marriage void?"

"Yes!" she barked, unthinking.

"And wish to return home?"

"Yes," she growled through clenched teeth.

"Tsk, tsk. What a shame. And I thought you wanted to free your sister from a cruel marriage."

Amber's face paled, her breath coming in ragged heaves, the stemware shaking in her hand. She glared at him, nostrils flared, recognizing the trap he had set. Suddenly needing the strength the wine could offer, she raised the glass to her lips and downed the contents in one quick swallow. It burned all the way, brought tears to her eyes, but fulfilled her need.

"You are the lowest of crawling vermin, Nicholas Chandler, my *husband*,"—she spat the title— "to force yourself on an unwilling woman. If there was no threat to hang over me, I would flee this house and you without a care. But as it is, I am trapped, as a hen before a wily fox. Gloat in your success, sir, but know this. I despise the very sight of you."

A hint of a smile crimped one corner of his mouth as he twirled the remaining drops of wine in his glass. "Then pray you can deceive me, my dear wife, for each time I call for you, I will expect you to come running." He set the glass on the end table and slowly rose to his full height. "Like now."

Amber jumped when he took a step forward and reached for her empty glass, a chill coursing through her.

"Kiss me as a bride would kiss her new husband," he said softly, setting the glass near his own.

"What?"

His brows arched questioningly. "Well, isn't that what everyone would expect from a newly wed couple? To steal a kiss at every available moment?"

Amber's lips parted to argue his words and he quickly raised a forefinger to silence her: "Remember, my bride, you're on trial . . . for two weeks."

Squaring her shoulders, her nose raised slightly, Amber asked, "And suppose I fail? Suppose you annul this marriage? I would not be the only one who suffers. You will lose your inheritance."

He smiled crookedly. "Not really. I'm sure Heather would be a most receptive bride."

"Then you should have married her in the first place!"

185

"But I didn't. I married you. And no one held a gun to your temple to force the vows of wedlock from you."

"Ha!" Amber exploded. "They might as well have. I had no choice."

"Oh, but you did."

Amber laughed cynically. "Most assuredly, Mr. Chandler. Marry you or go to prison. Weren't those your exact words?"

"But you did have a choice. As you have now." He moved closer, lifting his hand to lightly brush her cheek with the back of his fingers. "But don't tarry, my love. I might think you don't truly want to please me."

Her flesh burned where he touched her, setting ablaze that all too damning fire in the pit of her stomach, a sorcery that forced betrayal of her claim to have no need of any man. She started to pull away when he easily caught her chin in his hand, lifting her gaze to meet his.

"Why deny yourself the pleasure?" he whispered, his warm breath soft against her lips.

Amber could feel herself weaken. She closed her eyes, fighting off the desire to have his arms around her. She swallowed arduously and peeked through lowered lids to find him close. Praying it would be enough, she lifted her chin and lightly placed a dispassionate kiss on his cheek.

"Oh, Amber, do you really call that the kiss of a bride?" His brows lowered in concern. "You won't last out the week if this is how you intend to behave."

A lopsided smile answered him. "Would you rather I play the whore?" she asked sarcastically.

His features relaxed, as if he was contemplating her suggestion. "I don't really know, since I've never spent two weeks with one."

"Then let me offer a compromise. Spend your nights with one and leave me alone." She turned to walk away, stopped abruptly when he caught her wrist.

"Why should I pay for something I'm already entitled to have? No, my love, I'll be content to have you warm my bed. Now if you decide otherwise, I think we should tell Mr. Rafferty before he opens his bottle of champagne and it goes to waste on a marriage that's to be nullified."

She glared at him a moment, then spoke in forced politeness. "As you wish, good sir. But I'll never understand how you can accept affection from one who doesn't truly feel it."

"Does a whore?"

"But she is paid for it."

"As so are you."

Amber's face burned hotly. "And that is how you will think of me? A whore?"

"A high-priced one. I know of none other who will live as you will."

"You're deplorable," she spat.

"Only defining truth, my wife. And at such a cost, I merely seek something in return."

Amber's trembling lip belied the courage she fought to portray. Could he truly mean it? Did all men feel the same about their wives? Or only he? Only about her?

Nicholas tilted his dark head to study her face, wondering at her thoughts and hiding his smile. Amber Courtney was far from being a whore, and he doubted she could live long enough to become one. He spoke the words to snare her, set her on her heels, tame the wild nature of her tongue. He saw no other way to force her into his arms, but vowed that soon she would come to him on her own. And while he waited he would accept her touch whether honestly given or deceptively offered. *How long would it be*? he wondered, recalling the moments they had shared an hour before. She had fought him at first, then clung desperately to him, an unmistakably strong desire urging her onward. He had suddenly known what it meant to care about someone, to want to protect her, love her. Then she had turned cold, unreceptive, almost bitter toward him. What had extinguished the burning fire in her . . . turned a blossoming rosebud into the withering flower of autumn's first frost? Knowing spring would come again to place its kiss upon the earth, to breathe new life into all it touched, he too felt certain he could rekindle the flame of passion in her, given time. Turning her to him, he placed a knuckle beneath her chin, lifting her lips to his in a warm yet gentle kiss.

Amber's mind whirled with the embrace, every inch of her flesh tingling with his touch, his nearness. How long could she

187

play the maiden scorned when his mere presence set her heart pounding? What further demands would he make if he knew? But did it matter? He had taken the one most important thing she had, her virtue. What else he sought from her would seem less in comparison. But what of her pride? Had she not swallowed enough of it to consent to marriage? Must she abandon it completely to satisfy his whims? And what of him? Did he not see this as a game? A man of wealth takes pity on the poor. *To hell with him*! She stiffened, the warmth of their embrace vanishing.

Breaking his hold, he stood back to look at her, his hands still resting on her arms. "Ah, Amber, my love. Just when I thought you had yielded, you slice my ego with your blade." He sighed, releasing her, and glanced toward the parlor doorway. "But I suppose I must grant you a bride's modesty since we do have guests in the house. We'll try again later, after they're gone." He smiled, a hint of challenge in the curl of his lips, and extended a hand. "Shall we join them?"

Thankful for a moment's reprieve, Amber eagerly led the way, hurrying across the foyer to the dining hall lest he have a change of heart and call her back. But once her bare feet touched the cold marble of the floor, she stopped abruptly.

"I forgot my slippers," she whispered, turning to retrieve them.

Nicholas caught her elbow. "Don't bother. If they're uncomfortable, you shouldn't wear them. Besides, no one will notice."

Placing her hand in the crook of his arm, he directed them toward the dining hall, unaware of the effect of the courtesy when Amber felt the steady beating of his heart against her fingertips hugged to his chest.

The warm aromas of stewed chicken, boiled potatoes, and sweet rolls met the couple walking into the dining room. Amber's mouth watered in spite of herself, for it had been many days since she had partaken in such a feast. Putting aside her vexation, she set about to solve another, the rumbling of her stomach, easily allowing Nicholas to hold out a chair for her. He settled comfortably beside her to await the return of the Calloways from the kitchen and Sean with his bottle of champagne.

"Tell me about yourself, Amber," Nicholas asked, relaxing. He stretched out an arm across the back of her chair, the elbow of the other resting against the table's edge, his head tilted to watch her.

His nearness enveloping her, Amber forced her attention on the vase full of flowers sitting in the center of the table. "What is it you wish to know that you don't already?"

He shrugged. "Where did you learn to read and write?"

"My grandmother. She was a governess at one time."

"Oh?" Nicholas asked, his interest aroused. "For whom?"

The old hatred, and memories of the lonely, abandoned life her grandmother had led flashed their spiteful sneer in Amber's mind. "Nathaniel Cromwell," she said bitterly.

"Of Cromwell Manor, near Jamestown?"

"Yes," she said caustically.

"I've heard a lot about him. Quite the rogue, as I understand it." Nicholas leaned forward against the table to toy with the empty goblet sitting before him. "My father told me the man had many mistresses all the while he was married. And several children he made no claim to." He smiled in thought. "He certainly went through the nannies—" The realization of his words reached out to slap him. He stiffened and looked back at his wife, a helpless, apologetic twist on his handsome face. "Your grandmother wasn't . . . I mean . . ."

"Yes. She was. My mother was Nathaniel Cromwell's bastard child," Amber calmly finished. "You see, my grandmother foolishly thought her lover would come to claim his daughter. When he didn't, she felt certain he only waited for the right time. Then, when Andrea and I were born, she groomed us in the ways of the rich, preparing us for the day he would take us to live with him. Obviously, he never did. He didn't care about us. Not even my grandmother. She died alone, and with her last breath she swore he would still come for us." Amber looked away sharply. "The fool!"

A sadness tore at him. He reached out to lightly touch the hand lying in her lap. "Maybe he couldn't, Amber. Maybe he truly want—"

"Don't patronize, Nicholas Chandler," she exploded, jerking away. "You're all alike. You take whatever you want without a care to anyone else."

"You shouldn't judge us all by one man."

"I'm not! I grew up living next door to a plantation worked by slaves, watching the overseer whip them. Many of my childhood friends were the children of those slaves . . . until they disappeared. You know why? Because the rich owner *sold* them, like the merchant sells a bolt of cloth, for whatever price would fatten his purse." Her body trembled with her fury. "And then there was Baron Von Buren. He already had more money than he could spend and he wanted more. He married a rich spinster no one else would have. He cheated, lied, *murdered* to achieve higher gains."

"Not all wealthy men are like him," Nicholas argued softly.

"No, of course not. Only the ones I've met so far. Including you!"

Nicholas opened his mouth to debate the statement, his words failing him when he realized the mockery of his own wedding, or at least how it appeared to Amber.

"Won't you deny it? Correct my foolish claim if you can, Nicholas Chandler. Tell me you married me out of love and not to save your inheritance."

He stared at the angry face glaring back at him, daring him to set her straight. No, he honestly couldn't say he loved her. Lusted for her, yes, and hopefully in time love would fill his heart. And hers. But for now he would have to be content with the yearnings she aroused in him. He smiled softly.

"Would you believe me if I said I did love you?"

Amber laughed derisively. "And you think those of us who are poor are stupid as well."

He grinned, leaning back in his chair. "If money is all I think of, why would I be planning to buy you a new wardrobe? It would make more sense if I refused."

"Oh, quite the contrary, Mr. Chandler. We must keep up appearances. Everyone thinks so highly of you. You wouldn't want to endanger their respect by not dressing your wife accordingly."

His dark eyes danced with humor. "You have all the answers, don't you, Amber?"

"I only speak the truth."

He turned to face her. "Oh? Then consider this. If their respect and my money meant so much to me, why didn't I simply throw you in prison for the thief you are? Tongues will surely wag for the fool you made of me. And as for the inheritance, I could have married *any* woman to have it."

All logic and assuredness fled her.

He leaned forward, his head tilted to study her face. "Well? Have you a truthful answer for that?"

Amber's tawny brows lowered, creasing the smoothness of her brow. She looked to her hands, nervously playing with the nail of one finger.

Nicholas fell back in his chair. "I thought not," he stated confidently.

A searching need to find his profit in all this flooded Amber's thoughts. There must be a positive reason for his doings, yet none would come to mind. And love could certainly have nothing to do with it! She stole a secretive glance his way, silently appraising his fine profile. Slate-black hair curled thickly over the collar of his shirt and enhanced his sun-darkened face. A strong, square jaw, the muscle in his cheek that flexed while he contemplated a simple task, piqued her curiosity to peer into his thoughts, to know him fully. Yet the deep brown eyes seemed hooded, defying the possibility that anyone could. Had he no silver in his pockets, she granted the probability he could marry any of his choosing by his mere charm. Not her, of course. Flattery seldom interested her and more often than not warned her of a deeper ploy. Especially flattery of her, for she had no dowry to offer a marriage and always suspected any flatterer merely sought a night in the hayloft. *Then what drove this man*? she wondered. Why had he chosen her?

Suddenly she found the dark eyes smiling back at her, and she blinked, a flood of warmth stinging her face.

Amber chose the privacy the wing chair in the parlor offered, rather than the sofa where Nicholas might decide to sit next to her. The meal they shared with the Calloways and Sean

Rafferty had strained her nerves enough, and although she longed for it to end, she feared the time when their guests would take their leave, abandoning her to Nicholas. No doubt he intended to resume where they had left off following her bath, and his new conditions that she must prove herself before he would pay the baron left no question as to what he meant. If only she had some way to change his mind, to let him be the one who sought his bedchambers alone. . . . She stared into the black fireplace, deep in thought.

"An excellent meal, Martha," Nicholas complimented. "Especially on such short notice. I truly appreciate your help." He smiled warmly at Martha's soft blush, watching her husband guide her to a chair, then stand behind her.

"Thank you, Mr. Chandler," she replied. "I only wish it could have been more."

"Nonsense. It was perfect," Nicholas argued, his gaze wandering to the young woman sitting across the room from them, her chin resting against the fist propped up on the arm of the chair, her concentration elsewhere. His smile faded.

"Aye, that it was," Sean added. "And now we'll be havin' a taste of me champagne." He crossed to the buffet and set out five glasses before popping the cork on the bottle and filling each one. "I be preferrin' me fine Irish whiskey, but this calls for somethin' special. 'Tisn't every day me cousin's son gets married." He handed each person a goblet, lifted the last two, and walked across the room to Amber. "Here ya are, lass," he said, holding out the last. "And might I be offerin' a toast?" He frowned when she seemed not to hear him. "Mistress Chandler?"

Lost in thought, Amber felt more than heard Sean's presence. Snapping to attention, she glanced up. "I'm sorry. What did you say?"

"Are ya all right, lass? Ya look a wee bit worried."

Amber forced a smile, quickly glancing at the concerned faces staring back, but avoiding Nicholas's lest he read her thoughts. "No. Just tired, I guess."

"Well, have a sip of this. Will help ya relax and we'll not be stayin' much longer."

"Oh, I don't want you to leave—" She caught herself before

the urgency of her words rang clear. "I mean, don't feel you must go because you think I should rest." She took the glass he offered. "You may stay as long as you wish."

Sean studied her a moment, then set his gaze on her husband, knowing full well what she meant. Although it was customary for a bride to be nervous, he realized Amber was unusually so, and with justification, for obviously this little lass thought her husband was bent on revenge for her deeds. Sean enjoyed a good prank as much as anyone, certain it was all Nicholas intended, but for some reason her plight tugged at the soft spot in his heart. He cast Nicholas a warning frown and raised his glass.

"To the bride and groom. May they have a long and happy life." He lifted the goblet to his lips, staring out across its rim at the smiling eyes looking back. Nicholas nodded slightly with Sean's wish and joined in the toast.

"Will you be taking a few days off, Mr. Chandler?" Mathew asked, drawing Nicholas's attention away from Sean.

"Yes, several. I plan to take Amber to the dressmaker's tomorrow, and then we should visit my grandmother." He glanced back at Sean to find him relocating a chair next to Amber where he could sit down and talk privately with her. He smiled, knowing instantly that if any harm should come to his wife he would have to answer to this man, for although Sean Rafferty lived the life of an adventurer, he still harbored a tender side and would not allow his cousin's son to abuse a woman, especially this one.

"What do ya think of the champagne, lass?"

Amber looked up, startled. She had returned to her thoughts and failed to notice that Sean had settled himself beside her. She smiled weakly, observing the flaxen-colored drink, and wrinkled her nose. "I'm not sure."

Sean chuckled. "Aye, does take some gettin' used to. I prefer a cool mug of ale better meself." He lifted the glass to watch the draught swirl as he tipped the goblet side to side. "But it isn't the sort of thing ya sip with a lass." He swallowed the rest and set his gaze on her once more, relaxing in the chair. "How old might ya be?"

"Eighteen. Why do you ask?"

Sean shrugged. "Because I be seein' a sameness in ya as Nicholas's mother. She was only eighteen when me cousin met her." He laughed suddenly.

"And some humorous traits?" she said with a smile, oddly at ease in his presence.

"Not traits, lass. Just the similarity of situations."

"What do you mean?" she asked, her curiosity aroused.

Setting aside his glass, he crossed an ankle to one knee, his face an expression of pleasure with happy memories. "Victoria was sailin' ta Paris ta go to a finishin' school when pirates attacked her ship. She disguised herself as a cabin boy ta save herself from an awful fate. Well, a huge, obnoxious man named Kelsey claimed the child he mistook for a boy and brought Victoria on shore, an island called Barbados in the Atlantic. The minute me cousin saw Victoria he knew she wasn't a cabin boy."

"How?" Amber asked, thankful she had not tried to fool him if he could guess so quickly.

"By the way she walked, and her hands. She had no calluses like a seafarin' lad."

"What did he do?"

"Kelsey had a weakness for cards, only he'd met the master when he sat down across the table from Dru. Me cousin kept winnin', and when he had the man with only a few coins, he upped the wager beyond Kelsey's reach."

"Why did he do that?"

"So he could trick the pirate inta usin' Victoria as part of his wager."

"Did he?" Amber asked, smiling.

"Aye, that he did." Sean chuckled. "And the lass thought it a fate worse than death. She be havin' only one pirate ta outfox and found herself with two instead. Dru and meself."

"Pirate?" Amber repeated, realizing what the man had said. "You mean Nicholas's father and you were pirates?"

"Aye, lass. Didn't Nicholas tell ya?"

Amber looked away quickly. "No," she whispered.

"'Tisn't somethin' we be ashamed of, lass," Sean assured her. "We sailed the seas and stole from other ships, but they always be another pirate vessel. We never killed a man for the sport of it. If there be such a thin', lass, we be honest pirates."

He drifted off into thought a while, leaving Amber alone with her own confused reflections. So Nicholas's father had married into wealth, having been nothing more than a pirate, an ordinary seaman. But had he done so willingly? She longed to ask yet knew politeness forbid it. Maybe she could turn their conversation so he would be the one to say.

"Ya know, lass. I be thinkin' me cousin fell in love with Victoria the minute we found her in that tavern with Kelsey."

"That's ridiculous. No one can fall in love so quickly—" Silently she cursed her outspokenness, and was surprised to hear him laugh.

"Ah, but ya not be knowin' the two of them. It took Victoria a long time ta admit she not be wantin' ta live without Dru, but he knew right away. He told me so." Sean leaned back in his chair, arms folded across his chest. "He gave up a lot ta marry her."

A calculating curl appeared on Amber's lips. Just as she'd thought. He, too, had been trapped. Maybe Nicholas's father loved Mistress Chandler, but in order to marry her it had to be on her conditions. "Did he?" she asked aloud, feigning ignorance.

"Aye. He loved the sea and her ways, but gave it up to stay with Victoria."

"Oh. You mean Mistress Chandler refused to live the life of a sailor's wife."

Sean looked up sharply at her. "No, lass. Not at all me meanin'. In fact, Victoria didn't try to stop him when he sailed for home, thinkin' she'd never see him again."

Taken aback by her assumption proved wrong, Amber sat quietly for a moment, then asked, "You mean, she didn't force him into it?"

Sean chuckled with a shake of his head. "Why no, lass. What would be makin' ya think—" He stopped suddenly, as if finding his own answer written on the young woman's face. "Ya be thinkin' your husband follows his mother's ways."

Embarrassed to have him discover the truth so easily, Amber lifted the glass of champagne to her lips, looking past its rim as if gazing out the window.

"He be takin' on a lot of his father's traits, lass. If he hadn't he would have thrown ya in prison for stealin' and left your sister for the baron. He's not a heartless man and understood your trouble."

"I don't mean to sound ungrateful, Mr. Rafferty," Amber spoke in a low, sardonic tone, "but as I see it, this marriage, as far as he was concerned, was only for his benefit. You'll never convince me that he even once considered me because of my similar problems."

"Then why did he choose you?"

"I just told you," she snapped, her temper ruling.

"Aye, ya gave your opinion. But answer this, if ya can. Why didn't he ask Miss Branford, a lass who would be willin'? Why would he be askin' you when ya obviously wanted otherwise?"

Amber stared, lips parted, but no sensible answer came to still his argument.

"Ya be judgin' him wrongly, lass. Aye, he be needin' a wife ta save his inheritance, but any woman would have done. He be choosin' ya ta solve two problems. Yours and his."

"Why?" she asked, refusing to believe. "Why would he want to? He certainly had cause to want to send me away, to never see me again."

Sean smiled softly. "Because ya not be like any other woman he's known. Ya be one who fights for what ya want. Ya won't let anyone tell ya what ta do. Ya got spirit, lass . . . like his mother. What I be tryin' ta tell ya is simply that he likes ya."

"Ha!" Amber exploded. "I think not."

Sean cocked a brow. "How long ya be knowin' him?"

"Too long," she muttered acidly.

"A week? Two? Ya not even know his full Christian name. How can ya be sayin' whether the lad likes ya or not when ya've not spent enough time with him?"

Amber looked away, certain she had known Nicholas long enough to discover if there was anything about her that he liked.

"He's not a cruel man, lass," Sean half whispered encouragingly. "I wouldn't be lettin' him."

Her light blue eyes glanced over at him, and he smiled. Of a sudden, Amber wanted to tell him everything, to have a sym-

196

athetic friend. She needed to hear someone tell her that what she'd done was understandable, unselfish, the best regardless of the outcome. Ever since her mother had died, she had been the one to be strong, make decisions, keep the family together. She longed to be held in comforting arms, cradled against the turbulence of life. Would he listen, respond? She looked at the goblet in her hands and drew a breath. . . .

"Why is it I have the feeling I'm being talked about?" the deep voice intruded.

Amber glanced up, startled, her face warming instantly to find Nicholas standing beside them.

"And what would be makin' ya think that?" Sean said immediately. "Do ya consider me too old ta be able ta charm a lady without mentionin' your name? In fact I was just tellin' her how I be wishin' I was the one ta meet her first. Ya'd still be lookin' for a wife, laddie boy."

Nicholas smiled warmly. "No doubt. And had I not married her so quickly, you'd be set to steal her away while you still had the chance. Of course, no woman of sound mind would have you."

"Oh? And why would ya be sayin' that?" Sean rallied playfully.

"What do you have to offer? One day a week while she spends the others waiting for you to return to port?"

"Ah, but 'twould be well worth the wait," Sean grinned suggestively.

Nicholas's dark eyes twinkled mischievously. "Not from what I've heard."

"Ha! Ya just be jealous of me way with the lasses." He looked quickly at Amber and winked. "He always did want ta follow in me footsteps."

"And be a cranky old pirate run aground?"

Sean looked up, frowning, the gleam in his eye failing to stay hidden. "Ya may be a man full grown, laddie, but if ya not show me a little respect, I'll be forced ta remind ya."

Nicholas laughed gaily, bowing slightly at the waist to acknowledge the man's innocuous warning. "My apologies, sir. And if you'd be so kind as to allow me a moment with my wife, we should see the Calloways to the door. *They* don't intend to spend the whole night with the newlyweds."

Sean quickly came to his feet, holding out a hand to Amber. "Nor do I. But somehow I be thinkin' your lovely wife would be preferrin' me company ta yours." He waited for her to stand and placed a kiss on the back of her hand. "What lass wouldn't?" he grinned, wiggling his brows at Amber and bringing a smile to her lips.

"As my father always said, Sean Rafferty, you're full of the blarney," Nicholas laughed, reaching past his friend to steal Amber away. He pulled her close, entwining the fingers of her hand in his, and smiled warmly. "Of course, I can understand why he wants to keep you to himself. You are quite beautiful, Amber, my wife."

The nearness of him, his touch, his smell, pierced the defensive cocoon she had spun, nibbling at her reserve and sending a shiver down her spine, as she thought that in a few moments they would be alone.

"Are you cold?"

She glanced up to find his worried frown. "No," she whispered. "It's just been a long day." She fell into step with his leisurely stride toward the foyer, Sean close behind, not noticing the smile that spread over her husband's face.

"Am I to assume you are eager to return to our bedchambers?" he whispered, for her ears alone.

Amber stiffened, sucking in a long breath to harbor her angry retort. "Only to find peace in the solitude of *my* room." she answered in calm assuredness.

"*Your* room?" he questioned mockingly.

"Your house has several bedchambers. I see no reason why I can't be allowed the use of one."

"None at all," Nicholas quickly agreed, leaning closer. "I wouldn't make you sleep on the parlor's sofa when my bed is plenty big enough for both of us."

Her angry blue eyes flashed up at him, her mouth open to set the record straight, only to have him lift a fingertip to her chin, gently closing it again. "Hush now. This isn't something we should discuss in front of guests," he frowned playfully, with a nod toward the Calloways, who stood only a few feet away. He straightened, released his hold on her and extended a hand to

Mathew. "Thank you both for all your help. I really appreaiate it."

"Our pleasure, Mr. Chandler," Mathew said, accepting the handshake. "And don't worry about the office. Sean and I will take care of everything."

"I'm sure you will," he smiled, opening the front door and stepping to one side. They shook hands once more while Martha moved to Amber.

"I hope you're both going to be very happy, my dear," she smiled, gently patting Amber's hand.

I doubt I'll live that long, Amber thought, a false smile tilting the corners of her mouth upward. *I'd be happiest if you graciously offered me a ride in your carriage.* "Thank you," she replied instead, watching the couple turn and step out onto the veranda.

"Amber, me darlin'," she heard Sean call out before she felt him take her hand and lift her fingers to his lips, kissing them gently. "I be wishin' ya a world of good luck. And remember . . . if ya ever be in need ta talk with someone who can be givin' ya all the facts, please allow it ta be me." He looked over at Nicholas to discover the young man had followed the Calloways onto the veranda, his attention averted and out of earshot. He turned back to her, a serious expression deepening the lines of his face. "If ya ever have cause ta fear this man, lass, ya come ta me as fast as ya can. I made his father a pledge that should somethin' be happenin' ta me cousin, I would watch over his son as best I could. If he be doin' somethin' shameful, he be doin' it ta me too, and I'll be the one ta see he never does it again. I only be knowin' ya a short while, lass, but I be sure ya are the best thin' for Nicholas. And if ya be allowin' it, I'm certain too you'll find marriage ta this man can award ya some good times. Take care of yourself." Without a moment's hesitation and before she had a chance to thank him, he turned and left the house.

Amber stood alone in the foyer, oddly comforted by the Irishman's words. Without knowing it, he had eased some of her worries about marrying a stranger, and had offered a friendship she was sure would last a long while. She remained where she stood, watching the man talk and laugh with his cousin's son and wondered why a gentle soul such as he had never found a woman of his own. Or had the sea bound him in her arms, captured his heart, ruled his life? Lost in bewilderment, her gaze absently drifted downward to the soft shade of linen billowing out around her in a sea of pastel green. A pretty color, but she preferred blue or yellow. Her head snapping up with the realization of who owned the gown and why she wore it, she hastily regarded the two men on the porch, glancing at the long staircase leading to the second story and back outside. Satisfied they would not miss her since they appeared deeply absorbed in conversation, she turned and raced for the stairs, her bare feet noiselessly carrying her across the marble floor, multiple layers of linen and petticoats raised to clear her step.

"I don't want Amber to know," Nicholas whispered.

"Why, lad? As I be recallin', it was part of your agreement, take a bride and pay her debts," Sean asked, somewhat confused.

"I want her to squirm a while. That little lady got away with more than any *man* has tried with me, and I feel I deserve a chance to even the score. Will you do it for me?"

"On one condition."

Nicholas looked at his companion in surprised observation. "What?"

"That ya be promisin' me no harm will ever come ta her."

Nicholas fell back a step. "Sean Rafferty. What do you think I am? You've made it quite clear several times that you believe I'm going to beat her or starve her or heaven knows what. Why have you all of a sudden taken this little she cat under your wing? She isn't half as fragile as you think, I assure you."

The big, brawny Irishman suddenly fidgeted with the lace cuff of his shirt, clearing his throat and forcing his attention on the willow trees dotting the front lawn.

"Well?"

He shrugged one shoulder. "'Tisn't important," he mumbled, looking straight ahead.

"Oh, but it must be, or you wouldn't be worried about your appearance," Nicholas pointed out when he noticed how Sean rearranged his ascot, tugged at his jacket, then brushed a piece of lint from his breeches.

"Now you're the one who's kissed the blarney stone," Sean snapped, pulling at his collar, then jerking his hand away when Nicholas raised a brow to stress the issue.

"Tell me why and I'll decide."

"'Tisn't none of your business," Sean growled. "Now promise—"

Nicholas shook his head defiantly.

"What?"

"I won't promise until you tell me what it is you're hiding."

"I never even told me cousin about it," he stormed.

Nicholas studied the angry face a moment. "All right. You keep your secrets and I'll keep mine." He turned to reenter the house, stopped abruptly by the hand that clutched his sleeve.

"Ya are not ta tell McKenzie, ya understand?" Sean graveled. "If ya do, I'll be havin' your hide for me mainsail."

"Agreed," Nicholas said, walking to the porch railing to lean a hip against it, waiting for the man's confession.

Pacing in short, worried steps, several minutes passed before Sean paused beside Nicholas to stare out across the yard. "I be takin' a special likin' ta Amber because she be remindin' me of—of someone I knew."

Nicholas's mind raced in search of a woman, young or old, who had taken such a hold on this seemingly carefree man. When he failed, he gazed over at him. "Who, Sean?"

"Me daughter."

His chin sagging, Nicholas slowly stood up, speechless.

"The last time I saw her, she was Amber's age. I never married her mother, but the wee lass never hated me for it. I sailed back ta me homeland as often as I could ta see her, givin' her money and trinkets I collected along the way. I figured if I ever settled in one spot, I'd bring her ta live with me."

"Why didn't you?" Nicholas asked quietly.

"Just after your father married your mother and asked me ta work for him, I returned ta Ireland ta get her, but she was gone. Her mother told me Brenna had married and moved to Dublin. I figured she'd never come with me, but I had ta see her one last time." Sean stopped to clear his throat and rub a finger against the tip of his nose. He took a deep breath and Nicholas sensed the grief the man felt.

"If you'd rather not—"

"No, lad. I must be tellin' someone. I kept it hidden all these years, till it near eats me insides. I searched Dublin until I found someone who knew a lass named Brenna with long, blond hair, and a bright smile. I went ta the place he told me, an old, rundown shack, and knocked on the door. When no one answered, I went inside anyway. I never in me life saw a more awful place, with rats bigger than any I'd seen before. And from one corner of the room I heard a moan. Lyin' on the cot was a woman, her dead newborn babe in her arms. She'd tried ta deliver it all alone. Then I looked at the lass's face, all swollen and bruised, and me heart nearly stopped." Sean paused, his lip quivering. "'Papa,' she said ta me. Me God, Nicholas, it was Brenna!" Choking back his tears, Sean buried his face in his hands, gaining control once more. When he straightened, he looked at Nicholas. "She died a half-hour later, but not before she told me that her husband had beaten her and left her to have the babe alone." He gazed out at the fading embers of the day. "I lied ta Amber, Nicholas. I told her I never killed a man for the sport of it. But I did. I killed Brenna's murderer and enjoyed it."

A gentle hand touched Sean's shoulder, and the two men stared at the golden arc slowly descending upon the earth, its warmth and peace spilling out over them. A long while passed before Nicholas could find the words he felt.

"On my father's grave, Sean Rafferty, I swear I will never hurt my wife."

Sean's strong, lean hand covered Nicholas's, which still rested on the man's shoulder. "I know, laddie, I know," Sean whispered, then turned and walked down the stairs to his horse. Without a backward glance, he mounted, spurred the steed, and galloped off.

An hour passed, dark shadows encompassing all within their chilly arms, but, unaffected, Nicholas stayed on the veranda, slowly rocking in the white porch swing his mother had favored so much. How could life be so cruel? Had every man, rich or poor, committed a sin so great that he had to pay for it at the cost of someone he loved? Taken from him before he had the chance to say the things he felt in his heart? His eyes lifted to look at the wide doorway of the manor, as if seeing the woman it sheltered. Would she always hate him for that night he had raped her, had let his anger and mistrust rule? Had it been a mistake to force her to marry him? Would she remain unhappy all her years because of it? He sighed, gazing up at the sprinkling of stars. Only if she wanted it that way, for he vowed he would do everything in his power to make her forgive him, to love him as he now truly knew he loved her. Would others say it was too soon? Let them scorn him when he sang the words, for in his heart he knew of one who would believe him.

He closed his eyes, and visions of his father's sparkling smile and dimpled cheek flooded over him. "Even though you're gone, my father, I still learn from you," he whispered. "But will I ever be at peace?"

Slowly coming to his feet, Nicholas strolled across the veranda and into the house, letting the heavy door swing shut. Silently he climbed the stairs and entered his bedchambers, pulling up short when he discovered the room was empty, a platinum stream of moonlight flooding in from the window and across the well-made bed. Panic exploding in him, he spun around and hurried into the hallway, determined to search until he found her.

The first room awarded him nothing, only the vivid memories of their lovemaking when he spied the brass tub and the drapery torn from the window. A worried frown crossed his brow. Had he gone too far? Had she taken his name and then left his home? He anxiously moved to the next room, to find little more than darkness staring back. But when he lifted the latch of the third, the door wouldn't budge, as though something leaned against it. He smiled, knowing his wife hid inside. Pressing a shoulder to it, he pushed with all his strength, feeling the reward of his efforts as the door slowly swung inward. When the space was wide enough to squeeze through, Nicholas peeked inside, the pale glow of a single taper flittering its light in quiet serenity. A soft smile played on his lips when he saw her, for curled up in the wing chair near the fireplace Amber dozed peacefully, the iron poker from the hearth laid across her lap.

A shadow fell against the sleeping form, a hand reaching down to take the weapon and set it aside. Lifted in strong arms, she murmured, then snuggled closely, content in their protection as he carried her to the bed and gently laid her there. He pulled the quilt to cover her and chase away the bit of cool night air, then lingered a while, gazing upon the still face of slumber at rest with the world, golden curls surrounding it. Would she ever willingly accept her fate? Only time would answer it. Bending down, he placed a light kiss on her brow, straightened, and quietly left the room.

Chapter Nine

Amber stirred in the lingerings of sleep, the aroma of fried ham, eggs and biscuits flooding her senses and arousing her to wakefulness. She stretched, yawned, then sat straight up in bed, wide blue eyes scanning the room. When had she given up her vigil in the chair to find comfort in the feather mattress? Had Nicholas come looking for her? Her gaze darted worriedly to the door, a sigh of relief slipping from her to see it closed. Then she noticed the heavy trunk she had shoved in front of it sitting at an angle, pushed from the spot where she had left it. Tossing her legs over the edge of the bed, she crossed to the hearth, there to discover the iron poker hanging in its rack. She glanced back at the door. He must have come after she had fallen asleep, pushed his way in, and carried her to bed. Clutching the neckline of her gown, she let her gaze travel down the length of green linen wrinkles. Her brow furrowed. He had never touched her other than to carry her to bed. At least she didn't remember if he had. A sudden warmth spread over her face. Surely she wouldn't have slept right through . . .

The faint thuds of footsteps sounded on the stairs and grew louder as their owner approached Amber's room. Wishing for the key to lock him out, she heaved a disgusted sigh, knowing from the night before that there was none. Well, maybe the

205

trunk before the door hadn't kept him out, but if he intended to have what she had cheated him of by falling asleep, he would have to fight for it. She hurriedly lifted the poker from its stand, hearing the latch click as the door swung open.

"Good morning, my sweet," Nicholas grinned, stepping into the room with a tray full of food and a glass of buttermilk. "I'm glad to see you're already up. I really hated the thought of waking you." He went to the foot of the bed and set the tray down before smiling devilishly back at her. "And then again, your breakfast would have gotten cold if I'd found you sleeping all alone in that big wide bed."

The implication of his words rang clear and Amber's fingers clutched her weapon tighter, hiding it behind her in the many folds of her skirt. She watched him suspiciously when he stopped, cradled one elbow in his hand, the fingers of the other stroking his chin while he looked her up and down.

"I'd say that gown has seen the best of it for one day. Why don't you take it off?"

Amber's eyes glowed her disapproval. "Come near me and you'll find this smashed to your ear!" she warned, lifting the poker in front of her.

Resting his weight on one foot, his other knee bent, he folded his arms over his chest and appraised the slim beauty standing threateningly before him. "Really, Amber, do you think to scare me with that? If I wanted to tumble you in bed, I would have done so last night when I found you asleep in the chair. You posed less danger than you do now. I simply want to give the dress to Anna so she can press it."

"Anna?" Amber repeated, lowering the metal shaft.

"My cook. You didn't think I fixed breakfast, did you? If I knew how, I wouldn't have hired Edgar, and you wouldn't be here now." He chuckled. "A steep price to pay for a man's ineptness, don't you agree?"

She opened her mouth to add her thoughts on other areas where she found him lacking when he turned away.

"You should eat this before it gets cold," he said, returning to the tray of food and helping himself to a bite-sized piece of ham. "It's delicious. Would you care for a cup of tea? I can bring you one when I take the dress to Anna."

Anxious to have him gone, Amber shook her head and replaced her weapon in the rack. Hurriedly finding the buttons of her gown, she slid the garment from her shoulders and over her hips. The numerous layers of petticoats hid her shapely limbs, but Nicholas's keen eye instantly spotted the enticing view of firm, ripe breasts threatening to spill from the camisole when Amber bent to step from the gown. Even with her short blond curls there was no mistaking the womanly curves, and Nicholas shook his head, wondering how he could have been so blind as not to have discovered her ploy the moment he bumped into her that day at the pier. He stuffed the piece of ham in his mouth, hoping to swallow the knot that suddenly formed in his throat, his gaze devouring the trim ankles and bare feet peeking out beneath the edge of lace and ruffles as Amber approached. His attention slowly traveled up the length of her, lingering once more on the full swell of breasts that gently raised and lowered with each breath she took before he forced himself to look into her eyes. He gulped, a blank expression covering his face.

"You said Anna would press it," she said, answering his unspoken question with a shake of the gown she held out to him.

"Oh . . . yes, I did." He took the proffered article and moved toward the door, not trusting himself to stay at arm's length of her a moment longer. What he had in mind mustn't be spoiled too soon. Once he reached the doorway, he paused and looked back. "I sent word for Mrs. Garland to come later this morning with samples of cloth for you to pick from. She'll also take your measurements. She should have a couple of gowns ready for you by Wednesday. Then we can visit my grandmother and sister." He grinned, looking at the dress draped over his arm. "I wonder what Kate will think when she learns this was your wedding dress." He smiled back at Amber. "I imagine she'll be jealous. She thinks it's time she did the same." He turned and walked into the hallway, pulling the door closed behind him.

Exactly why she couldn't say, but Amber had the feeling she shouldn't trust Nicholas. Hurrying to the sealed portal, she pressed her ear to it, listening to the sound of his footfalls weaken as he descended the stairs and crossed the foyer. Only the delicious smells of breakfast pulled her away, certain he would return momentarily. She cautiously sat down on the bed, close enough to eat from the tray, but with a full view of the door should he return suddenly. She knew so very little about this man. Anything he might do would be a surprise, and she must stay alert at all times, not allow him to catch her at a disadvantage. She ate hungrily, devouring nearly the entire amount before she clumsily dropped the last bit of biscuit smeared with honey to her lap. A dark frown creased her brow at the stain it made on the lace of her white petticoat, and she quickly rose to go to the wash bowl sitting on the bedside table, hoping to clean she spot as best she could. But as she passed the dressing table mirror, she caught her reflection in it and was instantly aware of her scantily clad body. If she was to successfully keep Nicholas's thoughts anywhere but on his husbandly rights, she must cover herself properly. Standing in the center of the room, she hastily looked about, spotting the armoire and rushing over to it. Swinging the doors wide, her spirits sank, for only a dark, empty cubicle stared back. Not a single robe to drape across her shoulders or a blanket to pull around her. Then she remembered Nicholas's asking Mrs. Calloway if she had found *one* of Kate's gowns in the guest bedroom. A devious grin curled her lips and she headed for the door, a startled gasp escaping her when she pulled it open and found Nicholas standing before it in the hallway.

"I would have knocked, but you didn't give me an opportunity," he grinned. "Were you going somewhere?"

Amber retreated a step, glancing back around the room for an excuse of some kind, not wanting him to know the truth. Then, seeing the empty tray on the bed, she hurried to it and picked it up. "Ah . . . yes. I was about to return this to the kitchen," she smiled bravely, praying he wouldn't notice her trepidation.

Nicholas looked at the empty dishes she held. "No, need. I can do it later. And besides," he said, stepping into the room and pushing the door shut behind him, "you really shouldn't run around the house dressed like that." His gaze boldly swept the length of her, lingering on the full swell of breasts straining against the lace neckline of her camisole. "You never know who might come to pay a visit."

Feeling the fervor of his regard, Amber turned away to replace the tray on the bed, instantly wary of standing too near the four poster and arousing his desires, which already flared dangerously high. She moved instead to the dresser and set the dishes on it, carefully avoiding any favorable view of herself that he might enjoy when she refused to turn around. However, unknown to her, she presented an alluring profile for him to appraise in the reflection of the dressing table mirror.

"Yes, I know," she said softly. "That's why I wondered if Miss Chandler would mind terribly if I wore another of her gowns until I had one of my own."

"Kate," Nicholas replied.

Confused, Amber half turned to look at him. "What?"

"Her name is Kate. And I'm sure she'd want you to call her that. After all, you did marry her brother." He flashed a wide smile at her.

Her discomfort returning twofold when he stepped closer, she smiled weakly and presented her back to him once more. *In name only*, she thought. *A true wife wouldn't feel the way I do.* "Then possibly she wouldn't mind if I borrow another," she said aloud, jumping when she felt his hand touch her shoulder. Hurriedly, she moved away and went to the window to look outside. "A beautiful morning, don't you think?" she asked, hoping to divert his thoughts.

"If you like rain," he whispered in her ear, for suddenly he stood behind her, the heat of his body touching her everywhere, one hand raised to toy with a golden lock of her hair.

"Rain?" she asked timidly, her breath difficult to draw.

"Mmm," he breathed. "Dark clouds . . . over there." A long, lean finger pointed past her to the horizon on the right, then returned to stroke the velvety smoothness of her skin across one shoulder.

Her knees weakened but she forced her attention on the moisture-laden formations rapidly moving closer. She laughed uneasily. "Oh, yes. I guess I didn't see them." She took a deep breath, hoping to sound light. "It's been so dry lately, I think we could use a good downpour." His finger trailed down her arm, sending a shiver through her. "I—I rather enjoy the rain. I love to listen to it beat against the windows. Don't you?"

"Mmm." Leaning closer, he smelled the fragrance of her hair. "It always makes me want to return to bed, to lie beneath the covers and chase away the damp chill. Does it you?"

"Oh, no," Amber quickly answered. "I like watching it, the way the lightning races across the sky . . . in fact, I sometimes stand outside just to feel the raindrops on my face." She studied the darkening sky where black met blue, realizing that within the hour the storm would be upon them.

Of a sudden, Nicholas laughed, and Amber nearly strangled on the pounding heartbeats that seemed to thud in the base of her throat.

"I'm sorry," he chuckled after a moment, "but I envisioned such a picture of you standing on the lawn in your petticoats soaking wet. All I would need would be to have my grandmother pay me a visit at the same time and see you like that. I'd never hear the end of it." Much to Amber's relief, he stepped away. "Although I wouldn't doubt that she did the very same thing in her younger days. She's quite the lady, Alanna Remington. Hard to believe she was once an indentured servant to my grandfather."

Her fear and anxieties vanishing with his statement, Amber turned to face him. "What?" she asked, not able to fathom such a thought.

"Oh, yes," Nicholas assured her, sitting down on the bed and kicking off his shoes. Fluffing up the pillow against the headboard, he leaned back, folding his arms behind his head, his ankles crossed as he stretched out lazily to reminisce. "She came to Virginia from England with her father and stepmother. From what I've been told, her father couldn't afford passage for all three of them, so he sold my grandmother's service and didn't tell her. Just why, no one's certain. I don't think Grandmother even knows. Her father and stepmother died of fever on the ship before they docked and she first learned of it when the overseer from Raven Oaks came to claim her at the pier. She never had the chance to ask her father."

Totally entranced by the story, Amber slowly sat down on the dressing table stool. "What did she do?"

"Wasn't much she could do right then. She was alone in a new country, scared, and didn't know where she'd find her next meal. So she went with the overseer and decided to talk with my grandfather about the mistake she was sure someone had made. But once she arrived on Raven Oaks, she wasn't allowed to see him."

Amber's brow furrowed angrily. "I would have expected as much," she said more to herself than Nicholas. "If I'd been her, I'd have run away."

Nicholas glanced over and smiled. "She did."

"Good for her," Amber exclaimed, then the frown returned. "But if she fled, how did she wind up marrying him—"

"They found her and brought her back to be punished."

"What? How? What kind of punishment?"

Nicholas sighed and studied the brass footboard again. "She was flogged."

Amber bolted from the stool. "That's barbaric! You mean they actually whipped her?"

"Uh-huh."

She gasped for air, her hatred gleaming in her eyes.

"You're all alike," she stormed, arms akimbo. "You—you people with money. You'd beat us all if it suited you just because we have the strength to defy you."

"Not all," he said calmly.

"Oh? Name one," she spat.

"You were never beaten, were you?" He looked at her, one brow raised questioningly with a slight smile revealing a faint dimple in his cheek she had never noticed before.

"You would have beaten Edgar if you could have found him," she declared.

He shrugged and looked away. "Would I? We'll never know now."

"And besides, what you've done to me is the same thing," she continued irately.

"You mean making love to you?" he laughed.

"Yes!" she barked, coming to stand at the edge of the bed to glare down at him.

"Really, Amber. How can you call that punishment? I rather thought you enjoyed it."

211

"Well, I didn't! I hated it!"

"Maybe we should try again," he grinned, reaching out with lightning speed to grab her wrist and yank her down on top of him.

Amber knew her error in that instant powerful arms encircled her in a steely hold, crushing her to him, her arms pinned to her sides. All she could do was struggle, knowing her strength unequal to his, and only if *he* chose it to be would she find herself free of him.

"Let go of me," she groaned, her breath labored when he squeezed her in an effort to subdue her. "Please, Nicholas. Your—your cook—"

"Anna won't bother us," he teased.

"But—but the gown. She'll have it pressed—"

"I told her not to hurry, that we had things to discuss and I'd come down for it."

Panic flooding through her, Amber voiced her only other possible threat. "If you don't stop this instant, I'll—I'll scream."

"What good would that do?" he smiled, his face only inches from hers. When she stilled to enlighten his ignorance, his head shot up to steal a light kiss. She pulled back, outraged.

"What will Anna think . . . to hear a bride scream?"

A silly grin spread over his handsome features. "That we play games. I already told her you didn't want to leave this room for days. She understands."

"Ohhh!" she howled. "You're deplorable."

"Not really. Only a husband in love with his wife . . . one who wants to spend every moment with her."

"Ha!" she burst out, wiggling uselessly. "You're not capable of love."

"In my heart or of my loins?" he chaffed. "You can already attest to one."

She stilled her struggles and glared acidly at him. "I and Heather and God knows who else!" Suddenly Amber found herself beneath him when he rolled over unexpectedly, pinning her down with a knee on either side of her to rest back on his heels, her wrists caught in a firm yet painless grip.

"Why, Amber, my sweet. It sounds as if you're jealous,"

he mocked.

"Jealous?" she exploded. "Don't flatter yourself. What you do with other women doesn't interest me in the least. In fact, I'd prefer it if you satisfied your animal cravings with one of them and left me alone."

"Animal cravings?" he laughed, then gently slid down to brace his upper torso on his elbows, his face close to hers. Amber stared back, a mixture of fear and apprehension glowing in the pale blueness of her eyes. "No animal feels about its mate the way I do about my wife. What we share is a soft and gentle expression of love."

"Oh?" she asked bravely. "Then you love Heather, too?"

A warm smile parted his lips. "No. I doubt you'll believe anything I say, but she seduced me, just as she usually did."

A slight sneer twisted Amber's mouth. "You mean she raped you, took you by force, You fought her off all the while until your strength had faded and you were unable to do anything but let her have her way with you. How terrible."

A low rumble of laughter sounded in his chest, his eyes sparkling. "Not quite. I wouldn't be foolish enough to tell you Heather didn't excite me. But what I felt inside was not love, just a desire to satisfy my male needs. You can't deny me that, can you?" He pressed closer. "Besides, had I known the little ragamuffin waiting in the shadows was a beautiful young woman, I would have looked elsewhere for my pleasure."

"Then find another young woman, Nicholas Chandler," she hissed. "One who's willing!" Arching her back, she tried to push him away, discovering the task more than she could accomplish. "Get off me!"

A worried frown shadowed his dark eyes. "Are you afraid, Amber?" he spoke quietly.

"Afraid? Of what?"

"That you might learn to like what I can do to you." Clasping both her wrists in one hand, he pulled her arms above her head. "One kiss, one caress, Amber. Allow me that much, then judge for yourself."

"And if I do and tell you that I find it nothing more than that, will you allow me to go free?" she offered, certain his embrace would ignite nothing but a spark of displeasure.

He pushed up to better study her face. "Then you must agree not to fight me. It must be an honest test." He waited for the nod of her head before lifting from her, one hand caught in his to help her to her feet.

Once she stood before him, he raised a hand to her shoulder to draw her close, intent on feeling the full length of her against him. But instead of willingly accepting his move, she shrugged off his touch, leaned in and quickly kissed his cheek. His shoulders drooped.

"That isn't what I meant and you know it," he said, strangely amused by her reluctance. "*I* am to kiss *you*. *You* are to do nothing. Just stand there and force yourself to think you hate it. Understand?"

"I won't have to force myself," she mumbled, already certain she had trapped herself into something that might bring about her downfall. She tried another approach.

"Mr. Chandler—"

He raised a forefinger to stop her. "Nicholas," he corrected.

One corner of her mouth lifted disapprovingly. "Nicholas," she continued, "I know that when there is a marriage for convenience, such as ours," —she stressed the point— "that the husband takes a mistress and leaves his wife alone. Why can't you—"

The faint dimple appeared again. "Because I want a son to bear my name and carry on my heritage. A mistress can't very well offer that, can she?"

"I hate to disappoint you, sir, but I have no intention of having your brats and adding another of your kind to this earth."

"Oh?" he asked, brows raised. "Then consider this. The child will have your blood as well. If you raise him by your guidance, he will not be totally of 'my kind,' as you put it. You, my dear, have the opportunity to change all that."

Amber's temper flared. "By lying in bed with you? Do you think me ignorant? I know your tricks, and I choose not to have any of your children—for two reasons. I will not help in sustaining the Chandler name, nor will I give you pleasure whenever your 'male needs' require it."

"Ah," he grinned, beguiled by her anger, "we've come full

214

course and now return to the matter at hand. Whether or not you'll enjoy the desires I can stir in you."

"You conceited fool. What makes you think you can stir any emotion in me other than hatred? And *that* I will not deny. I enjoy despising you!"

"Shall we prove it?" he dared.

"Yes!" she snapped, her chin lifting haughtily.

Without further hesitation or delay, certain that if given the time to think she would change her mind, Nicholas quickly reached out, seized both her shoulders in his hands, and yanked her to him. His mouth covered hers in a searing kiss, his arms enveloping her slim form and crushing her to him.

The swiftness of his move took Amber's breath away. She hung limp in his arms, her mind whirling, his hands exploring as they slid to her spine, one pressed to the small of her back. The thinness of her camisole did little to veil the warmth of his body touching hers, inflaming that strange fire in the pit of her stomach. The manly smell of him filled her senses, dulling her reserve and causing her heart to pound. Surely another could affect her so. Nicholas Chandler couldn't be the only one. She felt the heat rise to her cheeks, her mind calling out to make him stop, her heart begging him to continue. Before she realized what she had done, she slipped her arms up around him, pulling him nearer, enjoying the masculine feel of his body against hers. His tongue darted out, and Amber willingly accepted its probing, matching his ardor with her own, wanting, needing to have him touch her, caress her. She clung frantically to him, feeling the petticoats slide from her hips, his fingers agilely undoing the strings of her camisole. Cool morning air poured over her, tingling her flesh and awakening the strange stirring in her loins. Her body ached to have him take her, but when he bent to sweep her in his arms and carry her to the bed, a remnant of pride surfaced.

"No," she wailed, wanting desperately to prove him wrong, that she didn't care, that he couldn't excite her, possess her.

Holding her tightly to his chest, Nicholas paused, looking into her eyes, and saw the passion flaring high in them. "No?" he questioned. "You truly want me to stop?"

Amber bit her quivering lower lip, blinking back tears of

frustration, and nodded.

"Why?"

"Because . . . because . . ."

"You're afraid."

Amber shook her head vigorously.

"Oh, but you are. You're afraid of falling in love with someone like me, someone who represents the kind of man you've always hated. It would go against all you've ever believed. Can't you, for once, look past the things a man owns and see him for what he truly is? A man, plain and simple, one who is capable of loving you as a man should love his wife? I am that man, Amber. And I can give you more. Patience, understanding, kindness." He let his arm slip from beneath her knees, allowing her feet to touch the floor while he still held her to him with his other hand pressed against her back. "And I shall prove that to you now." Placing a gentle kiss to her brow, he moved away, crossing to the table where he picked up the breakfast tray. Without a word, he went to the door, opened it and quietly stepped outside. He looked back only once, then closed the barrier between them.

Amber stood in his wake, her body trembling from the emptiness, the discovery of her own inadequacies. He mocked her. He couldn't mean the things he had said. It was too soon. He couldn't love her. Why should he? Tears found their way to her lower lashes, spilling down her cheeks and tasting salty in the corners of her mouth.

"Papa, why did you have to die?" she wept. Closing her eyes, she fought the wave of grief that swept over her, long held and destined to be expressed. She stumbled to the bed and threw herself upon it, burying her face in the pillow, her mournful sobs all that broke the quiet.

"You know, Mistress Chandler, you're one of the few women with your coloring who can wear almost any shade and look simply breathtaking in it. I think this one in particular is most becoming," Mrs. Garland said, holding out a bolt of mauve linen. "Trimmed in white eyelet around the sleeves, bodice and neckline, it will show off your complexion exquisitely. And to complete the outfit, I'll make your petticoats of the same lace, and a pair of gloves, too. You'll be the envy of every lady in Williamsburg. Mistress Chandler?"

Amber stood gazing out the window of the bedchambers at the yard below. The storm had passed an hour before, gently cleansing the earth in a light shower of silver raindrops, leaving in its wake a fresh, invigorating coolness in the air. Moisture glistened on every blade of grass, warm sunshine beckoning marigolds and daisies to lift their faces skyward . . . a quiet peace, yet Amber found no comfort in it as she stared outside. *Afraid*, he had called her . . . to fall in love with him. Was she? Was that her reason for making him stop? *No*, she argued inwardly. *Honor*. Her honor wouldn't allow it, not fear. She was free to love whomever she chose. It simply wasn't he. Her pale blue eyes darkened with a thought. Who then? And why had none other excited the response he had managed to arouse with a simple touch, a word, his mere presence in the room? Absently, she lifted her hand to her lips, recalling the warmth, the passion of his kiss, his tenderness. Visions of his masculine body gleaming with perspiration from their lovemaking emerged in her memory . . . strong, hard muscles, taut belly, wide shoulders, narrow hips, and those dark, unfathomable eyes. Truly he was the most handsome man she had ever known. . . .

"Mistress Chandler?"

Startled by the voice of a stranger, Amber blinked, straightening sharply. Silently, she chastised herself for her thoughts and turned around, an apologetic look on her face. "I'm sorry, Mrs. Garland. I'm afraid I was daydreaming. What did you say?"

The white-haired, robust woman smiled knowingly. "Most new brides do," she chimed. "It's to be expected. I merely wished to compliment you on your choice of colors. You'll look divine in all of them." Gathering several bolts of cloth in her chubby arms, she moved toward the door. "I think that will just about do it. Since Mr. Chandler instructed me to have as many gowns finished as possible by Wednesday, I better get started. I'll take these to the buggy and come back for the rest."

"I'll help you," Amber offered, picking up the remaining

few. "I can carry them as far as the door. I need to see Anna in the kitchen, anyway. She's pressing my gown."

The two women quietly descended the stairs. When they crossed the foyer, Mrs. Garland paused to smile up at Amber. "You're the envy of every young woman for miles around, Mistress Chandler. You're very fortunate to have a husband like Mr. Chandler. But then again, I think he's the one who's fortunate. You're very beautiful, my dear, and I'm sure your life together will be quite happy."

"Thank you, Mrs. Garland," Amber whispered, curious what the woman's definition of happy might be. She placed the extra bolts of fabric on the small table near them and opened the door for the dressmaker to exit.

"I'll return on Wednesday, Mistress Chandler," she called from the veranda steps, then hastened to her buggy.

Don't hurry, Amber wanted to tell her. *I'm in no rush to face my new husband's relatives.* A worried frown wrinkled her brow, wondering what their reaction would be when they learned the boy they called Edgar had married Nicholas Chandler. A devilish hint of a smile broke the straight line of her mouth. They'll be appalled to think a *lady* dressed in boy's clothing had spent several nights in the same house with a man unchaperoned. *Well, Mistress Remington and Miss Chandler, you're in for several other surprises*, she gloated, spinning around and heading for the kitchen.

Just as she reached the doorway of her destination, Amber pulled up short, realizing she hadn't seen Nicholas for the past two hours nor even heard him wandering about the house. Could he possibly be in the kitchen? Leaning in, she listened for any sounds coming from the room. She relaxed, hearing only the clunking of pans and a soft melody hummed by a woman's voice. She was certain the master of the house was elsewhere.

"Good morning, Anna," Amber said lightly, stepping into the kitchen. She smiled warmly at the startled face staring back at her. "I didn't mean to frighten you."

Anna Wilson had lived her entire life in Williamsburg, married the blacksmith, and borne him three strapping sons. Despite her tiny frame and frail looks, Anna had worked side by side with her husband in the shop until the day he died. She had grieved his passing a long while, refusing refuge in any of her married sons' homes, and only when the aching in her bones forbid her to continue managing and running the blacksmith shop did she turn to gentler methods to feed herself. She feared no one and very seldom held her tongue when she felt compelled to speak. Her red hair, untouched by silver through the years, proclaimed her fiery temper, and, though many cunningly avoided her well known tongue-lashings, Nicholas Chandler had not hesitated in hiring her services when she had offered them. If anything, he enjoyed the verbal battles in which they engaged as regularly as once a week. The well-suntanned face frowned back at her new mistress.

"Do you always run about half dressed, missy?" she spat, taking in Amber's attire. "And you didn't scare me. I'm just surprised, that's all." She returned to her task of dicing carrots for the stew, its aroma filling the small room as it bubbled in the pot over the fire. "Mr. Chandler told me you wouldn't be coming down."

Amber smiled lopsidedly, unaffected by the woman's gruffness, for her grandmother had always spoken in such a manner. Though fighting to present an authoritative front, Grandmother Forrester's threats had been harmless, and Amber sensed this woman's were the same. "I usually put on a robe, but since I don't have one and my dress was brought to you for pressing, I had little choice. Mr. Chandler was to bring it to me, but apparently he forgot."

Anna glanced up, frowning. "He didn't bring me no dress."

Grinning, Amber shook her head. "Oh, but he said—" The smile faded, replaced by a suspicious gleam in her eyes, the curl of her upper lip. "Where is Mr. Chandler?"

"Don't you pay no attention? He told me he was goin' to the office and said you understood his need. In fact, he said you suggested it, since you'd be with the dressmaker all morning." Anna attacked the vegetables with more zeal than before. "I was afraid he'd go off and marry some scatterbrain," she mumbled.

The woman's scorn went unheeded for Amber had already left the kitchen and headed for the stairs. Reaching the top, she hurried past Nicholas's bedchambers and entered the second room, only briefly noting that the tub had been removed and the drapery now hung where it belonged. Hastily crossing to the tall wardrobe, she pulled the doors open, a satisfied smile spreading over her face.

"Kate, dear sister-in-law, I hope you don't mind," she said, pulling a bright yellow gown from the hanger. "But you've lived with Nicholas longer than I and I'm sure you'll understand." Smiling happily, she slid the gown over her head and down her shoulders, watching it glide earthward, the skirt billowing out around her ankles as she quickly fastened the buttons up the bodice of the dress. "If only I had a pair of slippers . . ." she mused, looking at her bare toes peeking out from beneath the hem. Resignedly shaking her head, she left the room and stepped into the hallway, glancing over the banister at the front door. Reasonably certain she wouldn't be disturbed for a few moments anyway, she traveled the short distance to Nicholas's bedchambers and went inside.

Irritably Nicholas tossed the quill in its well, wadded up the piece of paper on which he had worked for nearly an hour, and tossed it in the basket near his desk, a haven for many other such failures. Heaving a disgusted sigh, he briskly rose from his chair and crossed to the window of his office to stare outside at the activity on the pier. He had shed his jacket and unfastened several buttons of his shirt to compromise with the early afternoon heat. His ruffled hair was a testimony to his discomfort, whether born of the day's warmth or the wanderings of his mind. For two years he had carried the burden of finding a wife as his father required he do, and had been awarded some relief from his anxieties by losing himself in the endless paperwork of the shipping lines. No matter how great his troubles at the time, the need to concentrate on the figures written in ink on the paper gave chase to any other thoughts. So why hadn't it worked this time? His dark brows knit in puzzlement and frustration, the muscle in his sun-darkened cheek flexing repeatedly. Had he traded one problem for another? If only his mother was still alive, he could seek her help. The lines in his brow disappeard, a slight smile parting his lips. Better yet, he'd talk with his grandmother. After all, she came from a background similar to Amber's. She could explain the hostilities his wife harbored. Anxious to solve his quandaries, he returned to his desk, put away the ledger, and locked the drawer. But first he would stop by Mrs. Garland's and double the price of his new wife's wardrobe on the condition that she finish three of the gowns by noon tomorrow. If anything, he never intended to leave Amber alone again. Not until he was certain she shared his feelings. Lifting his coat from the chair, he hastily left the office, mounted his horse, and galloped off toward the dressmaker's.

Having hunted through every drawer, trunk or coat pocket she could find in Nicholas's bedchambers, Amber moved on to the one final room she had yet to search, positive he had taken all the keys and hidden them in one spot. Since the trunk pushed against the door had failed to keep him out and the pieces of furniture had proved too heavy for her to move alone, her only other alternative was to lock him out. The strange yearnings he aroused in her forewarned her of the possibility that she might yield to him. And that was something she swore never to let happen. He was used to having things his own way, and she certainly didn't plan on being another conquest for his simple taking . . . not if she could do something to stop it.

Of the four bedchambers in the house, this proved the largest, and for one brief moment Amber wondered why Nicholas hadn't chosen it for his. Then she spotted the jeweled box sitting on the dresser and rushed over to it. In the short time she had spent in the manor disguised as Edgar, this room had been one of those she had not explored, simply because no one used it and therefore didn't warrant straightening. However, if she had, she probably would have experienced the same odd feeling she did now. She lifted the silver box in her hands and slowly raised the gem-studded lid. Amber's mouth fell open in awe of the treasure her eyes beheld. A diamond stickpin in a cluster of rubies, an emerald necklace and matching earrings, a gold watch and delicately carved bob, a strand of pearls unlike any she had ever imagined, and a silver locket etched with a "C" on its face, all sparkled back at her. Gently returning the box to its resting place, she carefully lifted the locket from inside and snapped open the lid. Steel blue eyes and a handsome face stared back at her in the miniature. An odd prickling of familiarity gnawed at her mind. She would have merely guessed the man's identity had it not been for the smile, heartfelt and warm, and the dimple showing in his cheek. Dru Chandler, Nicholas's father. Her gaze quickly scanned the surface of the dresser for clues to verify her hunch, finding a pearl-handled brush and a mirror, a shaving mug and a razor. Yes, this room had belonged to Victoria and Dru Chandler, and Nicholas apparently wished to see it remain as if they had only gone away for a visit, to return at any time, a quiet memorial to two people he loved very much.

Amber laid the silver locket with the rest of the keepsakes, a twinge of guilt for intruding pouring over her. Yet certain they would understand her need, she pulled open the first drawer of the dresser. Empty. The second was the same. And only after all had been examined did she turn her attention elsewhere. Standing rigidly tall and stately, the armoire in the far corner of the room beckoned her to it as if mutely announcing its importance. Without hesitating, she rushed to it and swung the double doors wide, her shoulders falling in dismay at finding nothing inside. Angrily, she slammed them shut again, but the force behind the act only bounced them open a second time, followed by a dull thud as if something fell to the floor of the wardrobe. Her irritation dissolving as quickly as her curiosity arose, she curled one finger around the finely crafted wooden plank and slowly pulled it outward, a stream of daylight falling on the object of her interest . . . a book. But where had it fallen from? Looking up, she noticed a small panel in one wall had jarred open with the abuse of a moment ago. Did Nicholas know of its existence, she wondered, stooping to pick it up. And why would a book, any book, be worth hiding? Lifting its cover in expectation of finding printed words, she found instead the markings of a pen with dates and figures. A log, perhaps? Or possibly a diary?

Suddenly a door slammed shut from somewhere in the

house. Fearing Nicholas had returned and might find her snooping in his parents' room, she quickly closed the text and returned it to its place, her fingers touching something else hidden in the cubicle. Startled by the unexpected contact, she quickly withdrew her hand, then cautiously reached in and lifted the item to examine it. A pistol!

Footsteps thudded on the stairs.

Frantic, no time to consider their purpose or reason for secrecy, Amber shoved both pistol and book into the tiny recess and slid the panel over them. Gently, but with haste, she secured the armoire's doors and raced noiselessly across the room to once again study the jeweled box a moment before she sensed someone's presence in the doorway. She turned, feigning surprise, and stared back at her husband. The absence of his jacket and his shirt opened to the breastbone, exposing the dark mass of curls over his muscular chest, set Amber's heart pounding. She silently cursed her vulnerability.

"I—I grew bored after Mrs. Garland left and thought to look about the house." Her excuse sounded weak in her own ears. "I didn't think you'd mind."

He smiled but said nothing, his gaze touching her everywhere, lingering on the bare toes sticking out from beneath the yellow cotton dress.

Wishing to draw his consuming stare away from her and give her pulse a moment to calm, she gestured toward the dresser and the articles lying on its surface. "I assume this room belonged to your parents," she said weakly.

He nodded.

"I—I didn't take anything. I only admired."

His grin widened. "As I," he said softly, relaxing against the door frame, his arms folded over the wide expanse of his chest. "I see you found another of my sister's gowns to wear."

Amber smiled feebly. "Yes. I pray she will understand my need of it."

"Of course." He observed the shortness of the skirt, the trim ankles that defied cover. "I hope Mrs. Garland took your measurements accurately, lest your feet get cold this winter."

She glanced down at the hemline, a slight blush rising in her cheeks. "If she didn't she shouldn't be paid. However, she was quite thorough, and I can assure you you will be pleased with the finished product."

He cocked his head to one side. "I'm pleased now. Rich cloth will only add to your beauty." He straightened and walked toward her. "As will my mother's jewels."

Amber's knees trembled when he drew near, certain he intended to touch her. But instead he reached past her for the box.

"As for the things in this room, or my house, for that matter, everything I own is yours." He lifted the emerald necklace from the case. "Whatever you wish to wear you may. When my mother died, my father set aside an equal share of her possessions for both Kate and me. I saved them to give to my wife." His brown eyes stared into hers. "They are yours, Amber. As you are mine." Several moments ticked away before he pulled his attention from her and returned the necklace to the box. Setting both aside, he looked back at her with a smile.

"I stopped by Mrs. Garland's on the way home. Some of your gowns will be finished by tomorrow noon."

"So soon? I thought—"

He moved away. "Yes. Enough to allow us to go away for a few days. I'm most anxious for my grandmother to meet you . . . as my wife, not the little scalawag who called herself Edgar. Grandmother will have quite a good laugh over that one."

"I rather doubt it," Amber speculated quietly.

"Oh?" he asked, turning to face her. "Why?"

"A woman of her standing would find fault with what I did."

"A woman of her standing? Amber, she's a woman, nothing more. Like you. And if you were to tell her the conditions of your situation and asked what she would do, I'd wager she'd have thought of the same idea. In fact, if you had asked her *before* you tried to steal from me, she probably would have helped. Grandmother may have lived many years, but in her heart she's still very young and full of the devil." He chuckled with a thought. "That day you came to our table in the Chesterfield House and graciously allowed me to wear the bread pudding, Kate was shocked. Grandmother laughed. Do you honestly think a 'woman of standing' would have reacted that way? She liked your spirit from the very first. That's why she invited you to her home."

"And got Andrea instead," she whispered.

Nicholas laughed. "Yes, so she did. Tell me, how did you manage to talk your sister into it? From the short time I spent with her, I found her courage for deceit lacking."

Amber lowered her eyes. "Her love for me is stronger. She feared I would be caught if she didn't do it."

"You managed that on your own," he pointed out. "And sending your sister in your place only raised suspicion."

Amber looked up in surprise. "How?"

"Several reasons," he answered, crossing to the fireplace where he sat down in one of the chairs before it. "Your voices aren't the same, for one. And she was much shyer than the saucy wench who begged for money."

"I didn't beg," she snapped, her temper flaring.

He smiled, the dimple appearing again to tease her.

"And stop grinning like that!"

"Like what?" he laughed. "I wasn't aware I smiled any differently than anyone else."

"Not always. Only when you think you've bested me. It shows in your cheek."

A lean, brown hand raised to touch the area. "My cheek?"

"Yes. The dimple," she spat, a shaky forefinger waved his direction.

"Oh, that. A characteristic of my father's, I'm afraid. My mother told me once it was what attracted her to my father. Does it affect you in the same manner?" He grinned widely, devilment sparkling in his eyes.

"No," she barked. "I find little about you that does."

Nicholas lifted doubtful brows. "Odd. I wouldn't have guessed that."

"What?"

Slowly, he rose from the chair and casually strolled toward her.

"Twice now I've proven that wrong. If not to you, certainly to me." He lovingly reached up to lift a yellow curl from her temple and sighed forlornly. "But, alas. I vowed patience. In time, my love, you will come to me."

"To satisfy my lust?" she questioned disdainfully. "I think not. The man I seek to hold me in his arms and whisper of his love will know I share the vow. You, sir, are not that man."

He nodded, admitting defeat, if only temporary. "Possibly. But since you are my wife and I am the possessive kind, you'll have no chance to search for such a love."

She glared triumphantly. "Then you shall have many cold nights, my husband, for I do not intend to share your bed."

He returned her threat with equal vivacity. "Nor will I allow you to warm another's." He smiled crookedly. "I know of no one who can spend their life without longing for another's touch or words of praise, or comfort when troubled thoughts plague their mind."

"Oh, but you do." Her quick wit rose to the occasion. "I stand before you."

He nodded. "But the question is, how long?"

"Forever," she sneered, turning to leave his company.

He caught her arm. "What were you really looking for?"

"What?" she asked, failing to understand.

"You lived in this house for several days before our marriage and had plenty of time to satisfy your curiosity. I propose you were searching for something. What was it? A key to lock me from your bedchambers?"

Amber wondered if the heat that rose in her cheeks glowed as warmly as it felt. "No . . . I . . ."

"Spare me the excuse, dear wife, and I'll spare you the useless search. I've taken all the keys and disposed of them. There will be no locks between us, and, starting tonight, you shall sleep in my bed as my wife should."

He raised a hand to silence her when she took a breath to argue.

"Remember, my love, the vows we spoke saved my inheritance, but I have yet to see Baron Von Buren."

A vocabulary of spiteful words surfaced but none found their way to her lips, each seeming more contemptible than the other, more fitting to be uttered than the one before it, and thus left her speechless, an affliction that had never before visited Amber Courtney. She stood in tacit frustration, glaring her hatred of him until he silently took her hand and led her from the room.

"If that will be all, Mr. Chandler, I'll be going home now."

Nicholas quickly came to his feet and crossed the study to greet Anna standing in the doorway. "Yes, that will be all for tonight. Dinner was superb as usual," he smiled, bending slightly to rest an arm gently across the woman's shoulders and guide her toward the front door.

"It weren't nothin' more than fillin', Mr. Chandler, and don't go trying to tell me otherwise," she grumbled.

"Anna, you do yourself an injustice," he laughed. "When will you learn to accept a compliment?"

"When I deserve it," she said firmly, then glanced over her shoulder at the study as they reached the main entrance to the house. "Are you sure you done the right thing?"

"About what?"

"Her." Her red curls bounced when she jerked her head to the left, indicating the woman they had left behind.

"Now why would you say a thing like that?" he chuckled.

"'Cause she seems a little addle-brained. She didn't even remember tellin' ya to go to the office while she was with Mrs. Garland."

Nicholas reached up to rub his lower lip and hide his smile. "Must have just slipped her mind. After all, a lot has happened to her in the past few days."

"Yeah, well, I still think you've asked for trouble with that one," she mumbled, lifting the latch. "See you in the morning."

"Good night, Anna," he called, watching her descend the veranda steps and head toward the stable and her buggy. *Trouble?* he thought. *Most assuredly. But something I can handle.* Closing the door again, he turned for the study.

Bathed in the glow of sunset, Amber stood near the window gazing out across the lawn, unaware of the vision she made for hungry eyes. Nicholas paused inside the doorway to feast upon her beauty, taking a moment to study the delicate lines of her

227

face without the usual scowl and cutting words. Yet even in her anger, her elegance shone clearly. In fact, the brows drawn together and the darkening of those pale blue eyes when she sought to remind him of her disapproval only added to her grace. He had known many women in his life, all of smaller stature than this one, but none more charming, more alluring.

And I vowed patience, he thought. *Curse me for being a gentleman and honoring my word.* A crooked grin curled one corner of his mouth. If only he had been a swarthy pirate, a man who gave his word to no woman, he would dash across the room and swoop her in his arms. Kicking and screaming, he'd carry her to his bed and throw her upon it to ravish her at his leisure for as long and as often as he wished. The passion of his daydream grew evident and he hurriedly returned to his desk and sat down behind it, hoping Amber wouldn't notice the discomfort he experienced. He concentrated on the figures of the paper lying there, but only a moment passed before his mind wandered back to the woman who shared the room, a space that grew smaller with every tick of the mantel clock. Oddly enough, he found himself wishing he hadn't ordered her to share his bed. For although he thought to prove to her that being so near to him without his hand raised to touch her would spark the desires he knew she had, he suddenly doubted the soundness of his ploy. Just sitting here thinking of her aroused his passion, and he would be hard pressed to slip into bed with the intention of sleep and nothing more.

The gentle movements of her skirts as she casually strolled to the bookcase awakened him from his thoughts. He forced his attention on the paper again, yet was keenly aware of each step she took. His eyes still averted, he sensed her purpose of finding a book to read and relaxed only slightly when she sat down in a chair near the fireplace. A moment passed before he lifted his eyes to peek at her, his heart pounding loudly in his ears when he observed the seductive manner in which she curled her legs beneath her. Totally absorbed in her book, Amber failed to notice how he fell back in his chair, his eyes closed, and sighed heavily. Yes, indeed, it would be a long night.

Amber tried a second time to reread the words before her,

each letter fused together in a blur. She had hoped to ease her mind of the thoughts of retiring later to his bedchambers by occupying her attention elsewhere. He had pledged to wait her out, to act the gentleman, but his oath came second place in her list of worries. What of herself? Could she in fact share the room, his bed, and ignore his presence, the warmth of him beside her, his manly scent? Amber looked out over the top of the book to find him adding yet another figure on the paper, and her pulse quickened. Without a doubt, he was the most handsome man she had ever seen, recklessly so, with exquisite black hair, thick and wildly tossed, equally dark brows drawn together now in thought, a thin, straight nose, and a strong, lean jaw. He radiated a quiet authority, a sternness with a hint of humor in the sparkle of those deep brown eyes and flashing white smile. Amber stared boldly, her gaze slowly caressing the wide shoulders and muscular arms before settling on the tan V his white shirt framed down his chest. Each time he penned a letter, the muscles there rippled enticingly, and she realized if she watched much longer her defenses would weaken and the weakness would grow evident in her eyes.

Her book snapped closed, instantly bringing Nicholas's attention to the woman sitting across from him, a lump forming in his throat as he watched the bare feet and slim ankles descend to the floor. He forced his eyes to meet hers.

"If you'll excuse me, I'd like to finish this in my room," she said, her tone flat. "And possibly retire early, if you don't mind."

Nicholas swallowed hard. "No, of course not. I have a few more things here to do anyway. You go on ahead." He set his gaze on his paperwork again, as if disinterested, but once she turned to leave he glanced up once more, watching the gentle swish of skirts as Amber made a quiet exit. He leaned back in his chair, praying she would be soundly asleep when he went to bed later.

The cool marble floor felt good against Amber's bare feet, and she hurriedly crossed it to the stairs, not hesitating to climb them in record speed. She paused outside his bed-chamber, longing to find escape in another room, but instinct warned her that if she tried it it would only provoke the man

working in the study. No, it would be best if she did as h
instructed and prayed he would keep his word once he foun
her in his bed.

Laying aside the book on the night table, she quickly she
her cotton dress and petticoats, carefully draping them over
chair to avoid further wrinkles, since she planned to wear then
on the morrow, and pulled back the covers on the bed. Sh
stood in the semidarkness of the room staring at the wid
feather mattress, praying sleep would claim her in an instant

A dark shadow crossed the stream of moonlight that fe
across the sleeping form. In quiet ambivalence, Nicholas too
the pillow from the bed and slowly walked to the chair in the fa
corner. Kicking off his shoes, his shirt falling to the floo
beside them, he settled as comfortably as he could in the stif
piece of furniture and closed his eyes, wondering how man
nights would find him seeking rest thus.

Chapter Ten

Golden rays of sunset kissed the treetops, filtering through the profusion of dark green foliage, casting warm shadows all about as day's finale drew near. The silhouette of a lone rider astride a prancing stallion disturbed the quiet peace. Seemingly unaware of the black eyes that followed his departure with great interest, Sean Rafferty spurred the horse into a canter, a satisfied smile on his handsome, suntanned face. Less than a week ago he had never even heard of Baron Kelzer Von Buren, but in that short period of time he had discovered in himself a prickling dislike for the man, long before he had met him face to face. But had he not been told of the baron's sordid past and his inexcusable threats to the Courtney twins, his contempt for the blackguard would not have been a degree less once he met Von Buren at the door of his manor, for the German radiated all things vile and corrupt. His mere bulk and manner proclaimed a desire to command everything he touched, and Sean found it difficult to simply fulfill his errand and be on his way without a word of advice. Doubtful that the baron would do as warned and never bother either of the twins again even though he had been threatened with a lead ball in each knee cap, Sean rode away from the Von Buren estates

231

feeling better for at least having voiced his disapproval of the man's tactics. Yet as horse and rider traveled further on, a small thorn of worry settled its sharp point in Sean's minor victory, for although Baron Kelzer Von Buren had been paid in full, Sean Rafferty suspected he would be seeing the man again.

"If you'd like, I could easily hit him from here," Von Buren offered, his voice low and threatening. He steadily observed the departing figure, his pistol drawn and ready.

"Don't be foolish," the voice behind him in the shadows growled. "It would only bring Chandler down around your ears. The man obviously sent him here, and if he didn't return you would be the first person he'd ask why. Besides, there's no need. If I wanted you to kill someone, it would be Chandler, and even then it would be too late. The Courtney twins are no longer in debt to you."

"Then you heard."

"Yes."

The baron's dark eyes glowed red with the burning sunset reflected in them. "I should never have given them a month to pay. If I hadn't, Andrea would be my wife, and our plan would have been that much closer to succeeding." Von Buren's left eyelid twitched. "Six months of scheming ruined because of that twit."

The pungent odor of smoke from the other man's cheroot filled the air. Staying in the shadows, he seemed more menacing than his tone or words implied. "Not ruined, Herr Von Buren." He took a long puff on the cigar, its orange glow momentarily and minutely lightening the darkness. "A setback, yes. But I think dear Amber might have helped us more than she knows."

"Helped?" the baron squawked, whirling around to face his cohort. "How did she help? Andrea will not marry me now."

"That's right, Kelzer. She won't. Not now, anyway. Nor will she marry anyone else. She's in love with Seth Tyler, and *he* won't ask her." An evil laughter filled the air. "That only leaves Miss Branford."

Frowning confusion, Von Buren watched his confederate

232

step onto the veranda and sit down on the porch swing. "I don't understand. If the Courtney twins are rightful heirs, why bother with Miss Branford?"

"Because I'm only guessing that the Courtney women were named in Cromwell's will. I have no real proof, since I wasn't allowed at the reading—only speculation. I do know, however, that Heather Branford is the old man's legitimate grand-daughter, and if the twins were not named Miss Branford will be the one to inherit."

"Well, she certainly doesn't act like a woman about to inherit so much money."

"That's because she doesn't know her grandfather died. Cromwell threw her and her mother out of his house years ago. In fact, he hadn't seen her since she was a baby."

"Then she doesn't know about the will, or that the twins are related to her."

"You catch on quickly, Herr Von Buren," the man in the shadows sneered, puffing on his cigar.

"So what do we do now?"

"I want you to marry Heather Branford."

"And do you have some intelligent method of achieving such an end? I'm not exactly a dashing swain who can sweep her off her feet."

Reaching into his coat pocket, the man pulled out several papers, which he tossed into the German's hands. "I've already taken care of it." He pressed back in the swing, allowing it to gently rock to and fro, the cheroot clamped in his teeth. "What you hold are receipts for all of Miss Branford's debts. I sent a man in your behalf to clear them up. It seems she is near ruin and stands to lose the plantation. Now if you suddenly appear on her doorstep, papers in hand, she'll be more than grateful. She will be our next pawn."

"All right. So I marry her. Then what?"

Even in the darkness, Von Buren could see the flash of the man's smile. "You'll arrange an accident and sadly find your-self a widower, as before. But try something more original this time. Falling down a staircase is so undramatic."

Von Buren pulled himself up, his chest heaving in anger.

"And what do you suggest? A carriage mishap?" He took a threatening step closer. "Remember, my friend, without me—"

The man's head snapped around, glaring portentously. "Without you, I would find someone else. Someone who listens rather than plays the strutting peacock. If you disapprove of my methods, Herr Von Buren, you are free to find some other means to fatten your purse."

The baron's eyelid twitched spasmodically. "I could kill you now and have the fortune for myself."

The figure in the shadows of the porch relaxed. "Oh? And how do you intend to enjoy your newfound wealth dangling on the end of a rope?" His ominous glower pierced the baron's challenge. "Remember, it is I who have your former wife's diary."

Quieted but far from subdued, Von Buren warned, "Hide it well, my friend, for if it finds itself in my hands, your life will end rather gruesomely."

The cheroot tip glared hotly. "A gauntlet of which I am most eager to discover the victor, Herr Von Buren, for there will, most assuredly, come a time when neither of us shall need the other." He set his gaze on the fiery sunset straining through the trees of the front lawn. "For now, I am master, and you shall do as I instruct without question."

His nostrils flared, the baron sucked in a slow, deep breath, the muscles of his cheek flexing repeatedly. "For now," he hissed.

"Then listen and listen well, my overzealous comrade. We mustn't waste any more time playing games. I want you to go to Miss Branford in the morning and see to it you're married before sunset."

"And then what?"

"We wait for the right time."

"For what?"

"Once you've disposed of your new bride, in a week or so, we'll find some reason to lure Amber away from her husband."

Watching the man cradle the stub of his cigar between his thumb and forefinger. Von Buren followed its flight when his companion flicked the cheroot into the air. It landed on the front lawn, where it smoldered into ashes. Lazily, the man stretched to full height and came to stand before the baron.

"With her sister at our mercy, Andrea will do anything we ask of her. Even marrying you."

The evil smile that curled Von Buren's lips faded quickly with a thought. "You certainly don't intend to tell Andrea, or Amber, for that matter, about the inheritance, do you? And if you just turn Amber loose once her sister consents to marriage, she'll run to her husband and he'll come looking for us."

A low rumble of laughter cut short Von Buren's tally of complications. "Every time you open your mouth, you prove again why you never thought of such a plan. Of course, she'll run to her husband. Even if we had someone else hold her captive, Chandler would know who was behind it the minute Andrea married you. And he wouldn't stop there. He'd keep searching until he found the real reason you're so intent on having Andrea as your wife."

Panic deepened the lines on Von Buren's face. "So what do we do?" he asked, watching the man walk past him and down the steps, pausing at the bottom to stare back up at him.

"We get rid of her, of course."

"You mean . . . kill her?" Visions of the fair-haired beauty lying motionless, her face ghostly white, magnificent blue eyes closed forever, rushed over him, and Kelzer wondered at his sudden, dubious sense of loss. He had killed before and planned to do so again. Why did this particular wench bother him? After all, women were only meant for a man's pleasure. Yes, that must be it. He would have to put an end to her life before he could sample the special treasures he suspected only she could offer. A pained expression crimped his rugged brow.

"Why, Herr Von Buren," the man growled satirically, "I do believe you find the idea of killing her more than you can manage. Have you gone soft?"

"I—I just think it a waste. Surely—"

"She *must* die!" The answer rallied loudly in his ears. "It will leave Andrea as sole heir, and, should she not be named at the settling of the will, Heather Branford will be. With you as Heather's widower, the fortune is ours either way. I will not share it with anyone else. One twin must be eliminated, and, since Amber is married and unobtainable, it must be she! We agreed!"

"Yes, sir," Von Buren mumbled, an idea of his own stirring in his mind. "I just thought—"

"You thought what? To keep her locked away in your house as some plaything, a secret mistress? You fool! How long did you think it would be before she escaped and told her husband?"

Unaccustomed to such verbal humiliation from anyone, his pride sorely injured, Von Buren's temper flared. "And how will you explain her disappearance to her husband? Have you thought of that?"

"*I* will explain nothing. Amber Courtney did not freely agree to marriage. He forced her into it. Now that her debt to you is paid and her sister is without worry, everyone will simply think she ran away. As will her husband. You don't know Amber Courtney like I do. Her pride always gets in the way. She will never accept anything she was forced into doing, and, even without our help, I'm sure she'll flee Nicholas Chandler at the first available moment." The man smiled confidently, a sinister twist to one corner of his mouth. "And we'll be there to help when she decides."

The exquisitely built carriage rolled to a stop outside the inn, the dying embers of sunset streaming through the trees and across the road in ribbons of gold and yellow. Nicholas Chandler easily stepped from inside and tied the reins to the hitching post before turning back to help his wife from the buggy, then retrieve two large satchels from the floor and escort Amber to the inn's door.

At the sound of someone's entering, everyone turned to watch the newcomers, smiling and voicing warm greetings when they recognized Nicholas, as this was his usual stopping place on his way to Raven Oaks. He returned their enthusiastic regards with his own and set the bags down beside the front desk to await Thomas Booker, the owner, and a chance to enter his name in the register. But no sooner had the inhabitants made their speculations on a good journey thus far, than all eyes centered on the beauty standing at Nicholas's side. A quiet hush fell over the group, and for a moment Nicholas worried that something was amiss. Then he noticed the gaping mouths and pleased looks on everyone's faces and knew the reason for their mute appraisal. He smiled and took his wife's elbow to present her to the patrons of Booker Inn.

"I would like you all to meet Amber, the new Mistress Chandler of Williamsburg. We were married two days ago," he boasted proudly.

A long moment passed while several patrons exchanged surprised glances, for the young man's plight had been a topic of conversation throughout the area for some time. Some had even wagered sizable amounts on whether or not he would take a bride in time or lose his father's shipping lines to his sister. It had been good sport to count down the days, and now that it had ended so abruptly, without any warning, they felt oddly cheated. And where had he found such a beautiful woman? She was clothed in a soft shade of pink cotton, white lace adorning the sleeves and low neckline, its color accenting the smooth blush of her cheeks, a hue that quickly rose under their close regard. The full skirts hid any minor flaw she might have had but the tight bodice proclaimed a trim figure and ample bosom. Nicholas Chandler had escorted many women on his arm, but this one was unmistakably perfection. Suddenly a cheer went up, and a band of wellwishers hurried over to crowd around the couple, offering to buy a drink and toast their good health and long life together.

Sensing Amber's uneasiness, Nicholas begged their understanding and the couple's need to rest after the long buggy ride, promising to join them later once his wife felt up to it. Reluctant to let them go but knowing Nicholas Chandler would have it no other way, they allowed him to sign his name in the register, pick up their bags, and lead his wife to the stairs and the many rooms on the second floor, calling their congratulations even after the couple had disappeared from view.

For Amber, the long walk down the hallway to their bedchamber rang with finality. If her husband chose this night to share her bed in the true sense, she could do little to stop him. Too many ears to hear her screams of protest and no place to run offered little solution. She had thought that by now they would be at Raven Oaks, and was stunned when Nicholas halted their buggy outside the inn and told her that they would be spending the night. Had she been informed of the distance between the Chandler house and his grandmother's estate, she would have sought to talk him out of visiting Alanna Remington so soon, allowing her time to figure out a safe way to travel alone with him for such a long while. Well, maybe she could think of something else. But what?

Opening the door to their room, Nicholas permitted her to enter first, her hopes for success slowly draining away when she was presented with the tiny space. She would have difficulty in simply turning around and not bumping into her husband . . . not even a place to change her clothes in privacy or tend her toiletries.

"'Tis the largest they have," Nicholas said, as if reading her thoughts. "But then again, newlyweds would prefer the closeness." He stepped into the room, closed the door, and sat the bags on the foot of the bed, turning to face her with a wide grin.

"Yes. If they enjoyed each other's company," she replied, her tone flat and denying the sweetness of her smile. Removing her gloves and bonnet, she casually strolled to the window and looked out. "Obviously you've been here many times. Did you and Heather share this room?"

Jealousy? Did her question mean disinterest, or that a spark of heartfelt emotion stirred in her at the possibility that he had been there with another? Whatever reason, he decided to give her the answer she expected to hear. "Yes. Several times." He noticed her chin raise slightly, and he grinned all the more. "But she never caused such a reaction from the guests as you."

She glanced back at him. "Only because they never expected someone like you to actually marry a woman he bedded."

His long, lean fingers reached up to scratch his chin thoughtfully. "Nor would they guess that once I did, I would become a monk."

238

She gazed outside again. "I don't imagine your celibacy will last long."

Fighting down the laughter that tightened the muscles of his throat, Nicholas moved closer. "No, as a matter of fact, it won't. I intended to give up my abstention tonight."

Amber whirled to face him, nearly stumbling over her own feet, her eyes wide pools of fear. "I didn't mean me. I meant you'd probably continue seeing Miss Branford."

Nicholas sadly shook his head and stepped nearer, taking the gloves and bonnet from her trembling hands. "Now that wouldn't be fair to you. You're my wife and you shouldn't be expected to share anything with another woman. Especially your husband."

"I—I don't mind," she stammered, shrinking away, the wall at her back forbidding further escape.

Tossing the items on the bed, he turned back to her, pressing in until the warmth of his breath when he spoke touched her face. "You don't have to lie to me, Amber. I can see how much you want me to hold you in my arms." His hand came up to brush away a curl from her temple. "To kiss you, tell you no other woman matters more to me than you, to protect you, pamper you, spoil you, if necessary."

Amber bit her quivering lower lip, swallowing hard. "N—no, I don't," she whispered.

Nicholas raised his other hand to brace himself against the wall near her shoulder, the fingers of the first tracing the delicate outline of her jaw. "Shall I prove it to you, my love?" he said softly, his eyes studying the pink, sensuous mouth only inches from his.

Her entire body seemed to convulse, her knees weak, a sudden tingling shooting up her spine. She closed her eyes, her head spinning with the manly scent of him, the strong muscles of his body much too near. The room seemed even smaller than before, and a nervous warmth flooded over her, her stomach knotting and giving her an idea.

"I'm hungry," she announced.

He pulled back in wonder and confusion, a frown marring his handsome features. "What?"

Drawing courage from his surprise, Amber opened her eyes and stared bravely. "I haven't eaten anything since we left Williamsburg. I'm hungry." When he straightened, his arms falling at his sides, she scooted past him and went to her valise lying on the bed. "If you'd be so kind as to order our dinner, I'll join you in the dining hall just as soon as I hang these up." Avoiding his bewildered stare, she lifted the new gowns Mrs. Garland had completed only hours before and walked to the armoire. "You don't mind, do you?"

When no answer came in return, she unthinkingly glanced over at him. Hooded dark eyes and a half-smile greeted her, sending a new wave of fear down her spine. Did he intend rape?

"No, I don't mind," he grinned. "I think it's a wonderful idea, to eat first. Only I'll have them bring it to our room. That way we won't have to share each other with strangers."

The gowns slipped from Amber's fingers and floated to the floor. Stooping quickly to retrieve them, she rose again to voice her preference to company, only to discover that he had already left the room, the creaking hinges and latch clicking into place roaring in her ears, a sense of doom prevailing.

"So, Mr. Chandler, you done found yourself a wife," Thomas Booker grinned, setting the mug of ale on the table. "And a right pretty one. Where she from?"

"Jamestown," Nicholas said, lifting the tankard to his lips.

The bald, rotund man with wire-rimmed glasses perched on the end of his nose chuckled, giving Nicholas a wink. "Can't say I blame you none for wanting to have dinner alone in your room. I'll bet she's got a temper."

Surprised by the man's ability to sense Amber's nature, Nicholas glanced up, half laughing. "Why do you say that?"

"How many times has Mistress Remington and your mother, God rest her soul, spent a night in this inn? And Williamsburg isn't that big a town for gossip not to spread. I've heard some of the things that went on in your house. Like the time your father decided to captain one of his ships to England and left your mother alone with a small baby to care for. The way it was told, she had the locksmith change all the locks in the house, and nearly a week passed before your father could sweet talk his way back in."

A wide grin stretched Nicholas's lips. "Not quite a week. And it wasn't sweet talk that gained his entrance. He kicked in the front door."

Thomas roared with laughter. "Now there's a man after my own heart. You've got to show these little fillies from the start who's master in his own home. Now mind ya, I don't mean laying a hand on them. I don't go for that." Booker tucked his thumbs in the pockets of his waistcoat and rocked back on his heels. "Been married thirty-one years myself and have eight daughters to show for it. And every time one of them got married, I gave their new husbands the same advice I'm giving you. It worked for me."

Suddenly a wave of remorse swept over Nicholas. Dru and Victoria Chandler had shared no more than ten and two years together before she had died giving birth to Kate, and even though Nicholas had been only a lad during that time, he had sensed the lasting love they felt for one another. It had showed in their eyes, their touch, or moments spent in silence as they walked hand in hand along the windswept shore of the ocean. Heated words had spiced their life together, a tiny fist in Dru's stomach or a slippered foot to his shin, but through it all the Irish pirate turned husband and friend had borne his wife's temper with a smile and a gentle hand. Yes, Alanna Remington could guide Nicholas's thoughts about reasons for his wife's behavior, but only his father could have explained a simple way to understand, to hold back and wait, to grant his bride the space she needed to sort out her emotions. A knot formed at the base of his throat. Now it could never be.

"Thank you, Mr. Booker," Nicholas said softly, before finishing his mug of ale. "I'll keep it in mind." He dug into his pocket, pulled out a coin, and started to lay it on the table.

"No, Mr. Chandler, I won't charge you for the ale. Or the advice. And I don't mean to sound like I'm sticking my nose in where it don't belong, I'm simply wishing you good luck." He turned away, calling back over his shoulder, "I'll see if your food is ready."

Nicholas watched the old man amble off, a faint smile parting his lips. *If only it were that easy, Mr. Booker,* Nicholas thought glumly. *If I only knew I could pull her into my arms instead of destroying any chance I might have to win her love through patience, I wouldn't hesitate to rush upstairs right now and . . .* His dark eyes clouded with the vision he conjured up—long, willowy limbs, slender hips, tiny waist, full, ripe breasts, and arms opened wide to receive him, to pull him into her willing embrace, sensuous lips parted, eagerly awaiting his kiss. He closed his eyes, his heart pounding wildly. *Patience,* he told himself. *You promised and it is the only way.* But how long must he wait? What if she never permitted herself to experience the joys married life could bring? If he ever touched her in the name of patience, gave her the freedom she wanted, how could he ever show her, prove to her that he wasn't as she thought him to be—a callous, heartless man? *Damn it,* he growled inwardly. *I do care. I feel for her as I've never felt for any other woman in my life!* He glanced up, spotting the innkeeper coming from the kitchen with a tray in his hands. *You're right, Thomas Booker,* he silently agreed, a confident smile twinkling in his eyes. *I must show her who is master. After all, if it worked for my father, it will work for me.* He hurriedly left his chair and started for the stairs.

"Mr. Chandler?" Booker called when Nicholas blindly raced past him. "What about your supper?"

"We'll eat later," Nicholas replied, not bothering to look back as he mounted the stairs two at a time. "Right now I have something to tell my wife!"

The old man's belly began to shake, a chuckle bursting forth before it grew to uproarious laughter. "That-a-boy!" he wailed, a stray tear cradled in the corner of his eye.

Determined in his cause, Nicholas sped past the man coming from one of the rooms, mumbling an apology for nearly bumping into him without losing stride, and stopped before his own. Squaring his shoulders and quickly combing his fingers through his tousled hair, Nicholas placed a hand to the latch and swung the door open. Soft shades of fading sunset filled the room and a worried frown flitted across his brow to find it empty. Then his gaze fell on the bed nestled in one corner, the covers in disarray and hiding the slight figure lying there. Concern wrinkled his brows, and he kicked the door shut with the heel of one shoe before hurriedly crossing the small space to stand beside the bed.

"Amber?" he whispered concernedly. "Is something wrong?"

A small-boned hand raised to touch her brow as she rolled onto her back to look up at him. She smiled weakly. "I don't know what happened. After you left, my head started pounding so badly I had to lie down."

Gently sitting on the edge of the feather mattress, he touched cool fingertips to her cheek, testing the warmth of her face. The frown continued. "You don't have a fever. Is your stomach upset?"

Her bright blue eyes blinked twice. "No. Only my head hurts."

He looked away, a thumb pressed to his lower lip, considering what he should do to ease her pain, and failed to see the anxious look on his wife's face.

"I'm sure I'll be all right in the morning after I've rested and had a good night's sleep," she vowed, closely studying him, her eyes quickly drooping shut when he turned his head toward her once more.

"Can I get you anything? Maybe you should eat." He rose from the bed, intent on carrying out his suggestion and returning for the tray he had left behind with Thomas Booker.

"No, no," she quickly blurted out, then eased back against the pillow. "I really just want to sleep. Why don't you go down and sup. I'll be fine, and there's no need for you to sit here and watch." She turned her face away, draping a bare arm over her eyes.

"Are you certain?"

The gentle nod of her head answered him, and Nicholas lingered indecisively for a moment. "All right. I'll be in the commons if you need me. And maybe I should ask Mr. Booker for another room. That way I won't disturb you when I come

243

to bed."

"That would be very kind of you." The answer came weak and pain-filled.

Frustration and helplessness washed over him, wanting to ease her discomfort but not knowing how. "If you're not feeling any better tomorrow, we'll stay until you do."

"Oh, I'm sure I'll be fine in the morning. Good night, Nicholas."

He watched her settle more comfortably and moved toward the door, mentally noting that he would ask his grandmother what she did to lessen such distress. Stepping into the hall, he quietly closed the bedchamber door behind him and headed downstairs.

Electing to occupy the table in the far corner of the room away from the few remaining guests, he crossed to it and sat down, unaware of the confused frown Thomas Booker gave him.

"Something wrong, son?"

Startled, Nicholas glanced up to find the innkeeper standing beside him, mug of ale in his hands. He smiled weakly and accepted the drink. "My wife isn't feeling well." He lifted the tankard to his lips and swallowed a long draught.

Booker settled back on his heels, arms folded and resting on his rounding belly. One brow raised suspiciously. "Let me guess. The little lady has a headache."

Nicholas sighed despondently. "Yes. It came on her all of a sudden." He took another swallow, pausing when he realized the man had easily diagnosed Amber's ailment, and glanced up with a frown. "How did you know?"

Booker quickly surveyed the area around them to make certain no one else might hear them, pulled out a chair beside his guest, and sat down. "My wife used to get them. But only when we were first married . . . until I straightened her around."

"What do you mean?" Nicholas asked, surprised.

"I simply told her that exercise would rid her of them." A wide smile pierced his chubby cheeks. "You know, she never had them again."

Nicholas's chin sagged, his dark features relaxing with the

realization of how easily he had been duped. "She's not ill at all," he declared, fighting down the grin that tugged at his lips until at last he threw back his head and roared with laughter. "And why not? That little lady has lied to me at every available moment. What makes me think she'll ever change?" He recalled her proclamation of good health that morning. "Fine, indeed." His dark eyes glanced up at the staircase leading to the second story. Without further comment, he stood up, slapped Booker on the shoulder, and raced for his room.

Pausing outside the door, Nicholas pressed in to listen for any sounds coming from within, certain Amber now enjoyed her freedom to do as she wished without worry of intrusion. A moment passed before he heard a window sash raised and he seized the opportunity to catch her out of bed. He hastily lifted the latch and opened the door. There before the window stood his wife dressed only in her camisole, her mouth agape, eyes wide.

"Nicholas—"

"Feeling better?"

A slight blush colored her cheeks. "I . . . ah . . . it grew stuffy in here and I thought to let in some cool air." Gathering her wits, she placed the back of her hand to her brow. "It's really pounding."

"Which?" he asked casually, stepping inside and swinging the door shut behind him. "Your head or your heart?"

Startled, she looked at him. "What?"

"Don't you think you'd be more comfortable sleeping in a nightgown rather than that?" He nodded toward her garment.

Glancing down, Amber realized the view she gave him, and hurriedly moved toward the bed, determined to hide beneath the covers. "No. This will be fine." She bent to grab the quilt, her wrist caught in the firm hold of his hand when Nicholas spoiled her plan. He drew her to him.

"I'll help you," he said, staring into her eyes.

A chill ran through her. "No, thank you. I'd prefer to—"

"To what? To be left alone?"

She swallowed hard. "Yes!" She tried to pull away, feeling his grip tighten. "Please, Nicholas, let go. I—I feel a little faint."

A soft smile played on his lips. "Maybe it's all the clothes you're wearing. Why not take them off?" His free hand came up to pull at the strings of the camisole. "After all, you did say it was a little warm in here. You'd be much cooler without these restrictions." The first loop fell free.

"Please, Nicholas," Amber begged, a hint of temper sharpening her tone, her hand clutching the fabric and lace cords. "If I wanted you to help, I'd ask you."

"Would you? And how long must I wait for the invitation? I only wish to be an adoring husband."

Unmindful of his trick, and fearing the worst should she allow him to go further, she leaned in, nose to nose. "Then find someone else to fuss over. I choose to be left alone."

"Is that why you sent me away?" He forced his lower lip to protrude in a silly pout. "You don't really have a headache. You only said it so I'd leave."

Wondering how this man had the ability to manage a big shipping line for the past two years and not send it into debt, she sighed disgustedly. "Yes, you idiot. But you were too stupid—"

Nicholas chuckled at her cloud of words, demeaning, angry, revealing, and suddenly Amber knew who lacked the sense to see the other's ploy. She jerked free of him, but he grabbed both arms above her elbows and crushed her to his chest. She squealed, fighting uselessly. Tears sprang up in her eyes.

"You promised—" She choked off the rest.

"Yes, I did. But only because I thought you had the modesties of a bride. Like all other times, you lied and played me the fool to suit your needs. I sympathized with your dilemma, knowing the hatred you've carried for men of wealth all your life. I held back to give you time, to let you discover for yourself how different I am from those you scorn. I would have waited forever. But not anymore. I will be the master in our house, and for once in your spoiled life you'll do as someone else tells you."

Her chin trembling, Amber stared bravely. "And be a slave."

"No," he whispered, all caution vanishing. "You'll be

my wife."

One hand slipped around her to hold her close, his other moving to the back of her head, his lips finding hers in a passionate kiss, searing, consuming, dissolving the hate-filled words she wished to shower on him. Though her body betrayed her, melting in his embrace, her mind would not. She brought up one knee, intent on crushing his toe with her heel, and struck him squarely in the groin. He released her instantly, groaning his pain, and for only a moment she wondered at the distress she had caused him before she seized her chance to make good her attack. With a healthy shove she sent him tumbling onto the bed, then raced to the nightstand and the water pitcher sitting there.

His need to see this vixen tamed greater than his discomfort, Nicholas flew from the bed and swooped her in his arms before the painted crockery was lifted from its bowl. He pulled her back into the circle of his arms.

"Yield to me, Amber, and know the pleasures I can give you," he whispered in her ear, the fragrance of her hair intoxicating. He held both wrists crossed in front of her, his forearms pressed beneath her bosom. "I am a man, not a beast to misuse you, discard you carelessly, heartlessly, but one to love you fully, of mind *and* body. Let me chase away your nightmares and fill your thoughts with happiness. Surrender this one time, my wife, and know in your heart I speak the truth."

His body was molded against hers, his arms enfolding her; she felt suffocated, a chill slithering up her spine, yet oddly warm. When he turned her in his arms, she closed her eyes, blocking out the sight of him and hiding the fervent desires she suspected glowed in them. Yes, he was a man, the only one who had ever fanned a flame of passion in her, set her nerves on edge, her heart racing, and it scared her. Not because of the wealth he had, but simply because of the power he possessed over her, the strength to melt her tough exterior and bend her to his will. She wanted him, to be comforted as a babe in its mother's arms, to reach the ecstasy of womanhood. But somehow she had thought she would be the one to do the

247

searching, not have it laid before her feet, to sample at her leisure as often or as many times as she wished.

Two hands, gentle and instructing, cupped her face, drawing her closer until his warm, moist lips found hers again. She moaned, wanting to call an end to the pleasurable torture, but instead lifted her arms to clasp him to her. His ardor grew. He twisted his mouth across hers, his tongue parting her lips as his fingers slid to the strings of her camisole and dropped the garment to the floor. Their lips sealed in a demanding kiss, Nicholas easily swept her up in his arms and carried her to the bed.

An odd sense of abandonment coursed through her when he laid her down and stepped away to shed his clothes. In the golden streams of the day's departure she watched him, boldly and unashamed, the muscles of his chest and arms flexing with each hurried move he made as if she feared he would have a change of heart and vanish, as her dreams so often did. Then he came to her, the warmth of his flesh against hers, a gentle caress as his hands explored the shapely length of her. He lowered his head to kiss the taut peak of one breast, his tongue tasting, teasing, then moved to sample the other. Long fingers traced the smoothness of her hips, of one thigh, and Amber felt the sudden urge to satisfy her own curiosity.

Timid at first, she ran her fingers through the thick, dark hair that curled upon his neck, roaming downward to the wide shoulders. He lifted up to gaze into her eyes, his breath catching when her hands slid over the muscles of his chest, his taut belly, and finally rested boldly on his manhood. His mind exploded. No other woman, practiced harlot or grand lady of the courts, had ever driven all sense from him as she did now. Impatient, his lascivious appetite obsessing him, he kissed her almost cruelly, his hand sliding beneath her to crush her to him, his knee parting her thighs.

She met his thrust with equal fervor, answering his moves with her own unspoken willingness. Passion soared, carrying them adrift in endless time to heights no mortal soul could reach alone. Clasped tightly, as if to draw her into himself, Amber felt the wild beating of his heart against her naked breasts, his ragged breathing in her ear, until at last he fell exhausted by her side.

No words were spoken, for none seemed important as they lay cradled in each other's arms, the distant piercing flashs of light in the darkened sky heralding the oncoming storm. Snuggling closer, Ambr wondered if its fierceness could match the tempest they had endured, smiling when she knew it couldn't.

Chapter Eleven

A thick haze settled over the countryside, a warm mixture of midday sun and damp earth combining to limit movement as humid air clung tightly to everything. The slightest effort was uncomfortable, but the heat of day seemed secondary to the occupants of the Chandler carriage that rolled easily down the road toward Raven oaks, its stateliness and nobility as serenely quiet as the two who rode inside. The blissful interlude they had shared the night past seemed forgotten as Nicholas studied the pathway the horses followed and Amber sat unspeaking on the far edge of the seat.

Since before his father's death, Nicholas had not slept as peacefully, his soul at rest, confident now that he had found true happiness, and, better still, within the limitations of his father's will. It seemed to him as if his father had blessed the marriage, that he could sense the smiling eyes shining down on him. Then he awoke to troublesome reality. Expecting to find the warmth of his wife next to him in bed, he quickly discovered that only he occupied the space, for Amber had already risen, dressed, and stood near the window gazing out in quiet petulance. Uncertain, yet painfully suspicious of her mood, he had quietly left their love nest and memories to don the breeches that still lay on the floor where he had discarded them hours before and had come to stand beside her. He raised loving fingertips to brush her cheek, only to have her pull away.

"Time, Nicholas," she had said. "I need time."

How much? he wondered, reining the horses down the long drive lined with black oak trees. *And why?*

Before the carriage had come to a complete stop outside the manor's front steps, the huge door sprang open and Kate raced from inside, calling her brother's name in joyful excitement. She scampered down the stairs and descended upon him as he began to tie the reins to the post.

"Grandmother and I have been so worried about you," she cried, flinging her arms around his neck and nearly spilling them both to the ground, "ever since you and Uncle Sean went back to confront the pirate. What happened?" Suddenly her gaze shot past him to the figure partly concealed in the buggy. She dropped her hold on him and curiously stepped nearer. "Who have you brought with you?"

Smiling at his sister's constant verbosity, he completed his task with the leather straps and brass ring, opening his mouth to satisfy her question, when he spotted their grandmother stepping out onto the veranda. Deciding to announce his wife's identity to both women rather than to one at a time, he moved to the bottom of the stairs and held out a hand to assist Alanna Remington down. Curling her arm around his, he guided the woman toward the carriage and his sister.

"Kate, Grandmother," he said calmly, releasing Alanna's arm to stand beside the buggy and offer a helping hand to his wife, "I'd like you to meet Amber."

A cheerful expression flooded over Kate's face, quickly replaced by a puzzled, somewhat irritated frown twisting her flawless brow. "But we've already met her—" The steel-blue eyes so much like her father's grew into wide circles when they suddenly fell on the young woman who climbed from the carriage. "Good heavens, Amber, what have you done to your hair?"

"Kate, if you'll allow us to go inside where we may sit comfortably, I'll explain everything," Nicholas smiled, envisioning the look on the young girl's face when she learned the whole story.

"Yes, of course. We mustn't be rude," Alanna interjected. "They've traveled a long way. Amos—" She looked back toward the house, only to find the black butler hurrying down the stairs. "Will you see that their things are brought inside?"

"Yes'm," he replied with a polite bow and moved past the group to do as bade.

His sister and grandmother led the way while Nicholas and the sullen woman at his side followed closely behind, and Nicholas found himself fighting the urge to laugh out loud each time Kate glanced back over her shoulder at them. Her perplexity formed wrinkles on her brow as she looked from him to Amber, then momentarily lingered on the crop of short blond curls. They crossed the foyer and entered the parlor, where Alanna and her granddaughter sat down on the sofa, watching Nicholas guide his companion to one of the chairs near the cold hearth, then stand beside her. Neither of the two women facing him spoke, but the anxiety shone clearly on their faces, and he braced himself for the storm of questions.

"Grandmother . . . Kate . . . I wanted to introduce Amber to you for two reasons," he began, resting one hand on the back of her chair. "First of all, you have never met *this* Amber Courtney. The one who stayed with you last week was Andrea, her twin sister."

Kate's mouth fell open. Alanna continued to watch, her expression unchanged.

"The second reason is because the last time you talked with this Amber, you knew her as Edgar MacDonald."

"What?" Kate exploded. "But Edgar was a boy—"

Nicholas grinned. "Yes, we *all* thought so. A very good disguise, and the reason for Amber's short hair."

"But why—"

"I think I can answer that," Alanna softly broke in, a smile of her own dancing in her brown eyes. "As I recall, Miss Courtney asked to borrow money from you, Nicholas, and you refused. Correct?"

He nodded.

"Now if I had been she and my need so great, I would have found another method, especially if my request was denied by

253

everyone." She looked at the silent girl sitting across from her, noticing how Amber continued to stare at her hands folded in her lap. "If no one would willingly part with a portion of their wealth, I would do it for them. But in order to be successful, it would have to be accomplished without throwing any suspicion on myself. And since I couldn't trust anyone to help, I would have to do it alone. So, the disguise. Who would ever guess the ragged little boy was truly a beautiful woman?" She cocked her head to wait for Amber to glance up. When she did, Alanna winked at her. "Now, since it's well known that Nicholas Chandler has more money than he knows what to do with, and he probably showed his irritable side in denying the request, I would choose to teach him a lesson. Am I right so far?"

A hint of a smile teased Amber's lips. She nodded and studied her hands again.

"Since I already know of the attack on one of Nicholas's ships, the plan is easy to guess. I simply don't know what drove you to such ends. Although the idea was a challenge, one which took great courage to see it fulfilled, you must admit it was rather foolish. Nicholas may be a little arrogant at times—"

"Grandmother!" he objected, laughing.

She raised a hand to quiet him. "He isn't stupid. He would have figured it out sooner or later. Of course, from the story I heard from Mr. Rafferty, your accomplice was your downfall."

Amber toyed with the lace trim on her skirt.

"A relative, perhaps? The only one you felt you could trust?"

"My father's cousin." The answer came weak and barely audible.

Alanna glanced up at her grandson. "And what have you done with this man, Nicholas?"

"In exchange for Amber's whereabouts, I turned him loose. I rather doubt he can be much trouble to anyone."

"And what do you intend to do with Miss Courtney?"

Nicholas smiled brightly. "We've made a deal." He glanced down at Amber. "Would you care to explain? I fear I may sound arrogant if I tell the story." Only his eyes moved to peer up at his grandmother, the humor of his jibe glowing in them.

"I think she'd better understand your dilemma if you told her."

Would she? Amber wondered. Did anyone know how trapped she felt? How confused? Would she understand and sympathize? It had been so easy at first. In trade for the payment of her father's debts, she would carry his name. No one had warned her of the consequences she would face living with this man, sharing his bed, reveling in his touch, his caress, his lovemaking. She felt the warmth rising in her cheeks and absently glanced up at Alanna Remington. The old woman's face marked no contempt, prejudice, or haughtiness, traits Amber had always webbed with ladies of culture. Instead her expression bore patience, kindness, even a glimmer of compassion. Maybe she would understand. After all, Nicholas had told her about Mistress Remington's past, how she had spent her early days as an indentured servant. She could hardly deny that Amber's predicament was anything less. She moistened her lips and took a deep breath.

"My father was a gambler, Mistress Remington. When he died, he owed many, one of whom was Baron Kelzer Von Buren."

"Oh, good Lord, not him," Alanna moaned.

"Yes. But unlike the others who showed a little leniency for our difficulties, he demanded payment in one month or he would claim my sister's hand in marriage."

"The swine," Alanna growled, her face knotted in a hateful glare. "No wonder you needed money enough to steal for it. I would have done the same." A dark brow raised, marking her contempt. "In fact I would have considered killing him if all else failed."

A bright smile spread over Amber's face. "I did. And would have if—" The smile faded. "If your grandson hadn't agreed to pay him."

Alanna's dark eyes moved from Amber to look up at the man at her side. "And what did he ask in return? No, let me guess. Since you are the first woman who needed his money for something other than herself, and he found you very attractive, he discovered a way to solve two problems."

"Grandmother, what are you saying?" Kate asked, confusion

255

distorting her face.

"That Miss Courtney must marry your brother as payment."

"What? He wouldn't!"

"I know my grandson quite well, Kate. I know how his mind works. That and the things we discussed the other day." Her steady regard of him never faltered even with the affirmative nod of his head. "Have I guessed it all?"

"With one exception. Amber and I were married three days ago."

"Oh, my!" Kate exclaimed, falling back in the sofa as she pulled a lace handkerchief from the bodice of her gown and fanned herself. "I don't know whether to laugh or cry."

"And I don't know if I should be pleased or angry with you, Nicholas. I'm certain your father and grandfather would say the former, but they would only see the man's side of it." Her gaze fell upon the silent new Mistress Chandler. "What of you, Amber? Are you pleased?"

Her pale blue eyes glistening with tears, she failed to look at Alanna. "I would do anything to save my sister, as I'm sure she would do for me."

Thoughtfully quiet a moment, Alanna studied her, then turned to her granddaughter. "Kate, take Amber to one of the guest bedrooms and see to her needs. Perhaps she'd like to take a bath and rest for a while."

"Yes, Grandmother," Kate answered, quickly coming to her feet. She crossed the short space to Amber, held out a hand for her to take, and eagerly pulled her up, not bothering to let go once the woman stood beside her. "Welcome to our family, Amber." She shot her brother an angry glare. "Even if it wasn't wholly by choice."

His dark brown eyes mirroring his amusement at his sister's words, he watched the pair leave the room before looking back at his grandmother. "I fear I shall have more trouble with Kate than my wife," Nicholas chuckled. He raised a questioning brow. "Or you, perhaps?"

"What is done is done, Nicholas. My liking or disliking it won't change anything."

"Except your feelings for me."

Alanna's angry frown softened. She patted the spot on the

sofa next to her. "Sit down and we'll discuss it."

Nodding agreement, he did as she suggested, stretching out his long legs with a heavy sigh. "What would you like to know?"

"That you love her," Alanna replied, her words strong and sure.

A grin settled on his handsome features, but he chose to look at the toes of his shoes. "I do."

"Have you told her?"

"Would she believe me? Or, for that matter, care?"

"It might help. I sense the young woman is scared."

"Scared?" Nicholas parroted. "Of what?"

"You, herself, her future. Nicholas," Alanna said, sitting forward in the sofa and placing her hand on his arm, "you must look at this from her side. When her father died, she was left all alone, except for her sister. And you've talked to Andrea enough to know she isn't strong enough to be of much help. Then this evil baron comes around and makes demands Amber can't fulfill. She runs into you, tries to steal from you, and what do you do? You force her into marriage. Think how frightening that must be."

Nicholas covered his grandmother's hand with his own, smiling into her eyes. "I knew you could explain it to me."

A frown deepened the wrinkles of her brow.

"Why she acts so . . . strange. One moment it seems as if she actually cares, then the next . . ." He shrugged and looked away.

"She's fighting with herself."

"How do you know that? How can you be so sure?"

"Simple, my dear boy . . . because I've been there. A long time ago, but I still remember. I loved a man who didn't have the courage to tell me he felt the same, and I wondered at my own feelings."

"I don't think that's her problem," he said softly.

"What is?"

"She's told me several times how she hates people with money."

"Could it be envy?"

Nicholas shook his head. "No, only hatred. You see, her

mother was the illegitimate child of Nathaniel Cromwell. He was already married at the time and would not, or could not, lay claim to the child. Apparently Amber's grandmother never gave up hope and constantly told her granddaughters that some day they would be rich. She died a lonely old woman. Then, of course, there is the baron and his wealth. Amber thinks he murdered her father."

"Does she have any proof?"

"No, only suspicion. Her father and the baron were playing cards. I'm only guessing, but I assume Von Buren accused him of cheating and they fought a duel."

"Mmmm. I've heard about the sort of duels Von Buren fights. Never quite fair, but no one has ever proven it." Alanna stood up unexpectedly. "She did the right thing in finding a way to keep her sister from marrying him. I have my own ideas about his first wife's death. The man is hungry for money *and* power." She moved to the buffet and poured two glasses of wine.

"Then why would he want Andrea Courtney? They have no money and no property, as his first wife did."

Alanna returned to the sofa and handed Nicholas a glass. "I don't know. He certainly wasn't doing it for love. I doubt the man is capable of such an emotion."

"It certainly does lead one to wonder," Nicholas frowned before taking a sip of wine. "Maybe I should have Sean ask a few questions."

Sitting down comfortably next to her grandson, Alanna warned, "But tell him to be very careful. If there's more to this than we know, Von Buren could be dangerous."

Nicholas chuckled. "And if I tell Sean Rafferty that, he'd enjoy every minute of it. I think he and McKenzie miss the excitement of the pirate's life."

A soft smile curled the older woman's lips. "I always thought your father would. But I guess his love for Victoria was stronger. Caring that much about someone can change your whole life. Look at me. I was nothing more than an indentured servant when I came to America, and now I'm one of the wealthiest women around. And probably the loneliest."

Nicholas studied the intricate details of the crystal goblet he held. "There's nothing I can do to bring my grandfather back to you. If there was, I would have done so long ago. But I hope to ease your loneliness, Grandmother, by presenting you with a dozen great-grandchildren."

Her thin hand, wrinkled with age, lovingly touched Nicholas's arm. "No one can bring Beau back to me, Nicholas. I know that. Nor can they return my daughter and her husband. And someday, I, too, will die. But my reward will be that I can join them once more." She patted his arm. "And as for the great-grandchildren, I'll take as many as you can offer."

Nicholas swirled the few remaining droplets of wine in his glass. "I hope you'll be patient enough to wait a while. I don't think my new wife is quite so anxious as we."

"Would you like for me to talk with her?" Alanna asked, her head tilted to draw his attention to her. "I don't mean about agreeing to a family, but to help ease her worries. Other than her sister, I don't think Amber has had a chance to talk heart to heart with another woman, and Kate is too young to understand. Besides, we have a lot in common."

Nicholas leaned over and kissed his grandmother's cheek. "Why do you think I brought her here?"

Laughing, Alanna slowly came to her feet. "I'll see to dinner first and then visit your bride." Setting aside her wine goblet, she walked to the doorway and paused, looking back. "Nicholas, everything will work out. I know it will."

The sun-darkened face wrinkled with his smile, but it failed to reflect in his eyes.

"Are you sure you want me to stay?" Kate asked, watching Amber slip from her gown and petticoats.

"Yes," Amber smiled. "I hate to let this warm bathwater go to waste and I feel I owe you an apology, one that mustn't be delayed."

"An apology? Me?" Kate's blue eyes widened in disagreement. "Whatever for?"

"For deceiving you."

"Oh, that," Kate laughed, taking Amber's gown from her to lay it on the bed. "Actually, I think it's funny." She straightened suddenly, turning back to look at her companion, the young face mirroring her worry. "I didn't say anything embarrassing, did I?"

"No," Amber smiled. "You only said what you felt." She centered her attention on the strings of her camisole.

"Like what? I don't remember."

"You told me about your parents, how you used to live in Nicholas's house . . . not much more, really. I do know you love your family very much."

A faint line creased Kate's brow. "Most of the time."

Amber looked up, surprised. "What do you mean, most of the time?"

"There are moments," she began, casually strolling to the windowsill, where she sat down on its edge and gazed outside, "when I truly disagree with what my brother does."

"We all feel that way sometimes about our families, Kate. But it doesn't mean we love them any less. If that were true, Andrea would hate me."

"Why?" Kate asked, looking back at her. "For doing something you believe in?"

"What has he done that displeases you?" Amber questioned, already suspecting the answer.

"Forcing you to marry him. You didn't really want to, did you?"

"No. But that's my point. He did it because he believed it was right."

"Only for him," Kate snapped.

A soft smile touched Amber's face. "I know you'll find it hard to believe that I'm defending him—I find it difficult to say, but I think he did it for me, too. I simply don't understand why he didn't use a different method. He could have loaned me the money I needed and married someone he loved."

"Ah, there lies the problem," Kate grinned. "There isn't a woman he loves."

"But what about Heather Branford? I thought—"

"So did she. But Nicholas told me a long while ago that he didn't love her."

"And that's why he didn't marry her?"

"Uh-huh."

"So why did he marry me?"

Kate sighed, shaking her dark head. "I don't know. In matters like this, he's so predictable, but this time he's completely caught me off guard."

"You maybe, but not your grandmother."

"What do you mean?"

"Remember how she speculated on the entire situation? Even to guessing Nicholas would force me to marry him?"

"Yes," Kate agreed, leaving the windowsill. "She said she knew how his mind worked. And if we're to know, we'll have to ask her."

"Oh, I don't think—" Amber frowned, turning away.

"Don't think what? That we should ask her?" Kate hurriedly moved to Amber's side, reaching out to take her hands. "We owe you that much, Amber. Grandmother will tell us. I know she will."

Amber's face wrinkled. "Owe me? You don't owe me anything."

"Well, maybe _we_ don't, but Nicholas does. And I'm going to see he explains his actions." She let go of her brother's wife and started for the door, calling back over her shoulder, "You take your bath and I'll find Grandmama." But once she reached it, she stopped and turned around. "I'm glad he married you, Amber. If I liked Edgar, I liked you. And what you did to Nicholas was what he deserved. Just like Grandmama said, he's arrogant sometimes, and it's nice to see a _woman_ put him in his place." She smiled brightly, turned, and hurried from the bedchambers, her step light and enthusiastic.

Amber stood alone in the room, staring at the closed door, and wondered if by chance she had finally found peace. Yet the stirrings in her mind about the man they called her husband kinked the smooth line of her brow. To find true peace and happiness, she must find love, too. Was it such an emotion she felt for him? Or only the unleashed desires of womanhood? Would she ever truly know?

The fragrance of rosewater drifted up to steal her thoughts away and she quickly shed her camisole to revel in the luxury of the bath. A multitude of bubbles surrounded her, and she scrubbed vigorously, concentrating on her knees, elbows, and

261

face, hoping to wash away visions of the last bath she had take and not wishing to linger in the water too long in case *he* shoul chance coming to her room. Her short blond curls rinsed clea of soap, Amber seized the towel lying on the chair next to th tub and stood, briskly wiping the moisture from her skin befor wrapping her hair in the white square of cloth.

Donning a clean camisole, she covered herself with a rob and sat down at the small dressing table to brush the tangle from her hair. The image staring back at her when she glance up at the mirror took her breath away. What had happened t the innocent face of maidenhood? Her gaze moved to the pearl handled brush, the exquisitely crafted furniture before her velvet draperies, porcelain tub, massive four poster bed appraising all the wealth in the large room. She didn't belon, here. She had done nothing to earn such lavishness. Sham suddenly washed over her, for she felt no better than a high priced whore, that sharing a man's bed had rewarded her wit these gifts. Her lip trembled and she pressed a fingertip to th tear that raced down her cheek. She belonged with her sister with someone who loved her, needed her, wanted her. And jus as soon as Nicholas paid the baron, secured her sister's safety she would return to the tiny cottage outside Jamestown.

A knock at the bedchambers door spun Amber around, he heart pounding, certain whoever it was had discovered he intentions. She stood transfixed, praying they would go away One look at her and her secret would be known.

"Amber?" came the gentle voice filtering in through th door. "It's Alanna, my dear. May I come in?"

Knowing of no way out of the room unseen save through th window, Amber took a deep breath to calm her jittery nerves stood, and went to the door.

"I—I just finished my bath, Mistress Remington," Ambe explained, once she stood before her in the doorway. "I'm no dressed. I hope you'll excuse me."

"It is I who should offer an apology for intruding, but wanted to talk with you alone," the older woman smiled. "An please call me Alanna. I never really liked being addressed s formally. Would you care for some tea? I can have Amos brin us some."

"No. Thank you. Won't you come in?" Amber replied, stepping aside to allow her guest to enter. She watched the mistress of Raven Oaks slowly make her way across the room and sit down in one of the wing chairs by the fireplace, noticing for the first time how their upholstery matched the heavy draperies adorning the two windows of the room as well as the quilt on the bed. Infinite care had been taken in designing the bedchambers, and Amber grimaced slightly at the thought of all the wasted money it must have taken to create such a look, wondering at its importance or need. She dismissed the thought until she looked back at the doorlatch to make certain it had caught and noticed how it was made of brass with a pearl thumb rest. Surely the dollars could have been put to better use. She turned a smiling face on Nicholas's grandmother.

"Did Kate send you here?"

A slight frown marred Alanna's brow. "No. Should she have?"

Amber felt a sudden need to hold secret the conversation the two of them had had. If Kate wanted to ask her grandmother about Nicholas, it should be in her own time and not forced on her. She pulled her robe snugly around her and tugged at the sash, an embarrassed laugh trailing from her lips. "I guess not," she responded weakly. "We were only playing games and I feared she sent you here unnecessarily. "She quickly crossed the room and sat down in the chair opposite Alanna. "What was it you wished to talk about?"

"First of all, I want to welcome you to my home and my family, Amber. You might not believe this, but I knew you were special the first time I saw you and hoped, somehow, Nicholas would see it, too."

"The first time?" Amber reflected, tilting her head to one side, for the memory of their meeting evaded her.

"Yes. At the Chesterfield House . . . when you dumped the pudding in Nicholas's lap, and I tried so hard not to laugh."

Amber felt the heat rush to her face. "Oh, that," she mumbled, smoothing the wrinkles from her robe.

"I don't know what brought it on, but I'm sure it was well deserved." Alanna eased back in her chair, eyes lifted upward, reminiscing. "It seems to me, the men of this family have always tangled with wildcats when they chose their women. I remember the first time I met my husband. I didn't know who he was . . . actually, I don't think it would have mattered if I had . . . but he had the misfortune of knocking a bowl of flour from my hands and spilling it all over both of us. I was so angry, I doubled up a fist and struck him in the face. Can you imagine?'"

Her curiosity aroused, Amber sat forward in the chair. "What did he do?"

"He couldn't do anything. I left before he had a chance. Just as you did." She giggled, her eyes clouding with memories. "I remember a time when Dru came home late one night and full of the spirits. He gave up a lot for Victoria, but never his ale. Anyway, Victoria was furious with him. She had waited up for him and heard his carriage coming down the drive. So she hurried downstairs and waited at the front door for him. After his third attempt with the key at the evasive lock, she flung the door open and in he fell, right on his face. He had the biggest black eye you ever saw, and it didn't go away for weeks. I never could get the whole story out of either of them, but from what I gather he slept on the floor in the foyer that night."

"Wasn't he angry?"

"Dru?" Alanna laughed. "I can count on one hand the times I saw him angry. I think he realized he got what he asked for most of the time." She glanced over at Amber. "Nicholas is a lot like his father, with a little of his grandfather's serious side."

"I've never seen his humor," Amber grumbled, falling back in the chair, one elbow on its arm to cradle her chin in her hand.

"I know, Amber, and that's the other reason for my visit, to offer a sympathetic ear if and whenever you need one. I wanted you to know that I understand what you're going through."

"I don't see how you could," Amber mumbled, her gaze absently sweeping the furnishings of the room again.

Alanna smiled secretively, noting where the young woman's eyes had wandered. "More than you know, Amber. I was raised by my father and stepmother with only enough money to feed us and buy material for a new dress once a year. My father dreamed of being rich one day and decided his only chance would be in America. He sold everything we had to book passage on a ship, but it wasn't enough for all of us. So he sold my services to a total stranger in exchange for my passage here."

Amber glanced up. "Nicholas told me."

"But did he tell you everything? That I never knew what my father had done? That he died before he could explain and I found myself an indentured servant to a man who showed no pity, who didn't seem to care if I had feelings?"

"He told me you ran away and were caught and flogged."

"Yes. And I still carry the scars."

"But eventually you married the man responsible . . . of your own free will. How can you possibly think you understand how I feel?"

"It took nearly a year before we admitted our love for each other, Amber. And until that time, that very minute he said those three magical words, I was filled with doubt, anxiety, fear, and at times even loathing. I didn't belong here. I wanted to go home."

A knot suddenly formed in Amber's throat. "Why didn't you?"

"I had no way to get there. And only an aunt waiting for me if I did. I wasn't even sure she would take me in, so I decided to make the best of what I had."

"And that's what you think I should do?"

Alanna ignored the bitterness of Amber's tone, toying with the gold band on her left hand. "Things have a funny way of working out. What I'm trying to say is don't judge Nicholas by what he owns. Give yourself time to know him as a man. I've watched him grow up, Amber, with an adoring father to guide him. He would never purposely hurt you. He can be a good husband if you'll let him."

Amber stood up and went to the window, pulling aside the lace undercurtain to look outside. Several moments passed in silence. "Did you love your husband when you married him?"

"Yes . . . very much."

"Then this is one difference that makes my problem greater. I didn't and still don't."

"But who's to say you can't, given time?" Alanna left the chair to stand beside her grandson's bride. "Amber, my child, I can't tell you the things your husband should say to you, but I can promise you happiness if you'll look for it. And, at the risk of sounding vain, you could have done much worse." She reached up to brush a stray curl from Amber's cheek. "You rest now, my dear. Think of what I've told you and try to be fair, for your sake as well as Nicholas's."

Amber continued to stare outside at the activity near the mill, hearing the click of the latch to mark Mistress Remington's departure. "I will," she whispered, a single tear gliding down her cheek, "but I doubt my conclusions will be what you want."

Morning dawned clear and bright, only a sprinkling of white, fluffy clouds set adrift in the sea of blue sky. A gentle breeze billowed the lace curtains of Amber's room and found her seated before the dressing table brushing her hair. She had not been able to nap as Mistress Remington had suggested the afternoon before, and had spent a quiet meal with her husband, Kate, and their grandmother before begging her leave to the privacy of her bedchambers. No one had objected, and Amber wondered if she had been their topic of conversation that afternoon, agreeing to allow her space to sort out her thoughts. Whatever reason, she had silently thanked them and disappeared upstairs.

But once she had closed herself in and shed her gown for the comfort of her robe, Amber discovered a second door to her room, one she had not seen earlier, nor had either of her hostesses pointed out. Cautiously, she approached it and lifted the latch, opening the door only a crack to peek through. To her dismay, she found that it led to another bedchamber, and, sitting on the wide feather mattress, she recognized Nicholas's valise and jacket. *His* room! Next to hers! She slammed the door shut and hurried to one of the wing chairs, straining to shove the large piece of furniture into position. She stood back, appraising her work, and realized it wouldn't keep him out if he wished otherwise, but at least it would warn her of his coming.

Her nerves aflutter, too apprehensive to sleep, Amber had chosen to sit in the second wing chair a while, until she had heard him retire, certain he had elected not to pay her a visit. An hour had ticked away, and before she knew it, she had fallen asleep in the chair.

Now Amber's mouth twisted in an angry pout as she irritably yanked the brush through her hair. She had awakened an hour earlier, in bed and dressed in her nightgown.

"Damn him," she muttered, glancing past her reflection to glare at the pair of wing chairs sitting before the fireplace. What else had he done while she slept? "It's only a matter of time," she hissed into the mirror, "you know that, don't you, Amber dear?"

Tossing her brush aside with a nettled flip of her hand, she stood up and crossed the room, praying he still slept in the early hours of morning, giving her time to breakfast alone. She stepped into the hallway and started down the long staircase, heading in the direction of the dining room, the fresh aroma of fried ham and biscuits floating out to guide her steps. Pausing outside the doorway, she hoped her prayers were answered and that she would find only the mistress of the house and possibly Kate. She took a deep breath and entered the room.

"Good morning, Amber," Alanna smiled cheerfully once she had seen her. "Do join me. I hate to have breakfast alone, and neither of my grandchildren are early risers." She watched the young woman round the long table and pull out a chair next to her. "Did you sleep well?"

"Yes, thank you. I'm sorry I wasn't much company last night."

"Oh, don't worry about it," Alanna assured her, pouring a second cup of tea and pushing it toward Amber. She lifted the silver bell sitting near her plate and shook it gently, its staccato notes ringing in the air. "You are hungry, aren't you?"

Amber grinned. "I may have a poor appetite for conversation, but never food. I fear someday there will be enough of me for two to love."

Alanna laughed, then bent nearer, as if to keep a secret from being heard. "You should see my cook. Cinnamon has been at

Raven Oaks longer than I, and each year she grows a little heavier. But I love her dearly. In fact, she is the only true friend I've had my entire life. She and I used to share a cabin."

"You mean she's an indentured servant?" Amber's brows knitted, unable to imagine that the length of servitude would last so long.

"Not any more. She had served out her time before I came, but loved Raven Oaks so much she decided to stay." Alanna looked up at the creaking of the door. "Oh, Amos. Bring some breakfast for Mistress Amber, will you?"

"Yes'm," he nodded, then turned to do as instructed.

Amber followed his departure with mixed interest. She had never had the morning meal served to her and felt restless at allowing it to be done, especially when she experienced no illness that preventing her from doing it herself. Pushing the twinge of guilt to the back of her mind, she lifted the teacup and sampled the brew.

"I asked Cinnamon many times to move in here with me and let others do her work, but she absolutely won't stand for it," Alanna continued. "Says she won't have others talking about her behind her back. She's such a dear. How's the tea?"

"Very good," Amber smiled.

"I used to drink it with a little lemon, but over the years, with the scarcity of it, I learned to use sugar instead. It's not quite as good, but it will have to do."

"Have you tried honey?"

"No. And I can't imagine why. It sounds delicious. When Amos returns I'll have him fetch us some." She tore apart a biscuit and spread butter over it. "How's Andrea?"

The mention of her sister's name brought a tightening to Amber's chest. "Fine, I guess. I haven't talked to her since— since Nicholas came for me that day."

"I have an idea. If you and Nicholas plan to stay here for a while, I could send a carriage for her. Kate enjoyed her so, I'm sure the three of you would have a pleasant visit. Does she intend to continue to live in Jamestown?"

"I don't know. Nicholas said she could live with us, and to be quite frank I'd worry about her if she lived alone in the cottage. For some reason, I still don't trust Von Buren. If he

268

wanted her before, I don't think repaying our debts will stop him."

"All the more reason to have her come here. She can stay with us until a room is ready for her at your home. What do you say?"

Amber looked up at the smiling face. "I'd say that's very kind of you. You're—you're a very generous lady."

"Thank you. I want to be fair to everyone I deal with, whether they are family, friend, or business acquaintances. There's so little love spread around these days, I try to give as much as I can."

Amber smiled crookedly, watching the older woman sip her tea. "Alanna," she said after a while, "how did you know you loved your husband? I mean what did it feel like?"

"That's a hard question to answer," Alanna replied thoughtfully, setting aside her cup. "It didn't hit me all at once. I mean I didn't wake up one morning and say, 'Alanna, you love Beau.' It was a gradual process. He did a lot of things that hurt me, and for a long time I wondered if what I felt could possibly be love."

"Like what?"

Alanna's dark eyes glanced up at Amber, the troubles of her past mirrored in them. "I've never told another single person this, Amber, and you must promise never to tell Kate. If the time ever comes when I should, then I will, but *I* must be the one to decide. Promise?"

Certain she had overstepped her boundaries, Amber pulled back. "Then don't tell me, Alanna. I didn't mean to pry."

A thin, wrinkled hand reached over to pat Amber's arm. "You're not. If I didn't want you to know, I would have avoided it. But I think it's important and will help you."

Amber looked down at the aged hand resting on her arm and covered it with her own. "Then I promise."

"Beau never trusted women, because of his mother. She shunned him from the day he was born, and he constantly thought to get even by hurting any woman who got too close to him. When I found out I carried his child, I decided to leave him before he discovered it for himself. You see, we weren't married, and his closest friend agreed to give our child a name. I thought Beau hated me. I thought so because he could never

269

bring himself to tell me otherwise. What happened next is a long story, and one I won't go into now, but, because of our foolishness, stubbornness, if you will, his good friend was killed and I lost our baby because of a fall." Alanna's words caught in her throat. She looked away and swallowed hard before continuing. "If I had told him the feelings I carried in my heart, that baby might have lived. If he had said the words I longed to hear, his . . . *our* dear Radford might still be living at Briarwood Manor." She turned in her chair to face Amber, taking both of her hands in hers. "How do you know if you love someone? You feel it in your heart, you worship the sight of him, long to be held in his arms, know you can't bear to live without him. Is that how you feel, Amber?" Tears glistened in the old woman's eyes.

Her own sorrow, the grief of the recent days tightened the muscles in Amber's throat. "I don't know," she whispered. "It's too soon."

"Then take the time to find out, my dear. You will never be at peace if you don't. Return home to your sister, walk the paths of your father's land, and listen to your heart. Feel the emptiness those days will bring without your husband near, then decide if only he can fill that void."

"Nicholas would never permit it."

"Then he won't know. Spend the day with him, enjoy him, learn about him, and tonight, while he sleeps, I'll have a carriage made ready for you if you so decide."

Amber's blue eyes, tears shining in them, stared deeply into the dark brown pools of sympathy, searching. "Why, Alanna? Why would you do this?"

"Because I understand, my child. I wish to see you profit from my mistakes. I want you to be happy." She released her hold and straightened. "And I want my grandson to learn something, too."

Amber tilted her head to one side, waiting.

"He must learn that just because he wants something, he isn't always allowed to have it. Dru spoiled his children, Kate more than Nicholas, I think all parents do, but Nicholas has to realize some things are earned, not taken."

"But what if I decide I don't love him? What will you

tell him?"

Alanna looked over at the beautiful woman who posed the possibility. "That it wasn't meant to be."

They stared at each other for a long while, an unspoken friendship bonding them, a kindred feeling destined to last until their final days. No other vows imperative, Amber leaned in, put her arms around the frail form, and held her close, a strange, unfamiliar emotion coursing through her. Then the sound of footsteps in the hall broke the trance and Amber pulled away.

"There you are, my wife," Nicholas grinned from the doorway, his shoulder leaning against the frame, arms folded over his wide chest. He had donned only breeches, shoes, and stockings, his white ruffled shirt opened to the breastbone, and when Amber glanced up at him, her pulse suddenly beat faster. No matter what time of day or night, bright sunlight or silvery shadows, he presented a most striking figure, whether scowling or grinning as he did now. The mere sight of him sparked strange feelings in her and seemed to set her blood on fire. She chose to return her attention to the cup of tea before her.

"I didn't think you were awake, or I would have waited." Did the tone of her voice reveal the falsehood of her words?

His grin became lopsided. "Yes, I'm sure you would have." He dropped his pose and strolled recklessly into the room. "Good morning, Grandmother. Sleep well?" He pulled out a chair opposite them and sat down.

"I was about to ask you the same," Alanna answered, her concentration turned in the direction of the doorway where the butler had gone. "I wonder what happened to Amos." She lifted the bell and briskly shook it, vaguely aware of how Nicholas stared at Amber, his gaze devouring, touching her everywhere.

"I slept well, but not nearly as soundly as my wife." He leaned forward, his elbows pressed against the table's edge. "I don't think you even heard me come to bed, did you?"

The sudden desire to dull his obvious delight at provoking her, Amber met his challenge with a question of her own. "Yours or mine?"

A playful smirk settled on his face. "The latter, I'm sure of. I

271

simply wondered how long you had sat up in the chair."

"Not long enough, apparently."

His lips stretched into a wide sparkling grin followed by a low rumble of laughter, the dimple making a slight appearance. "And had I not come in to check on you, you might have slept there all night."

"I wouldn't have minded." She lifted the teacup to her lips and peered over the edge at him. "But thank you, anyway."

He nodded. "Anytime."

Feeling as though she intruded upon a private conversation and thinking that perhaps they had forgotten her presence, Alanna cleared her throat. "Well, Nicholas, what do you plan to do today?" she asked, hoping Amos's appearance would ease the tension she felt. Then, as if entering on cue, the portly butler pushed the swinging door open with an elbow and stepped into the room carrying a tray. "There you are, Amos. I thought perhaps you'd forgotten us."

"Oh, no, madam. But when I told Miss Cinnamon who this was for, she wanted to make it extra special." He set the tray on the buffet and hurried to serve their guest. When he finished, he turned to Nicholas. "Good morning, sir. Shall I bring your breakfast now?"

"Good morning, Amos. And yes, please do."

"Very good, sir," Amos replied and turned quickly to exit the room and fulfill his errand.

"You know, Grandmother," Nicholas chuckled, looking at the wide assortment of foods set before his wife, "I do believe Cinnamon wants to see every beautiful woman as plump as she. She never served me so heartily." He reached over and took one of the three sweet rolls covered with a sticky syrup. "There's enough ham to feed all of us." He bit into the biscuit and muttered, "Feel honored, Amber. Cinnamon has never treated anyone so royally."

Amber stared at the feast for several minutes, thinking how breakfast in the cottage consisted of tea, a slice of bread, and, on rare occasions, a fried egg. Knowing she could never possibly eat it all, she shook her head and covered a giggle with her hand. "I hope Kate comes down soon. Between the two of us, we might be able to eat half of this."

Alanna joined in the laughter. "Well, don't worry. Knowing Cinnamon as I do, if any of it is returned to the kitchen, she'll eat what's left."

"That's probably why she gave you so much," Nicholas chortled. "She's hoping you can't finish."

"Poor Cinnamon," Alanna smiled, holding back her glee. "If she only knew how we talked about her—"

"And she's worried what others would say, when there's more danger here," Amber snickered.

Alanna glanced over at her, and the two women burst into laughter.

Settling back in his chair, Nicholas watched his grandmother and wife, confused, knowing they shared a secret. He swallowed the rest of the sweet roll and poured himself a cup of tea. "I think I missed something," he half mumbled, half laughed.

"Well, what did you expect when you leave two women alone for a while?" Alanna smiled. "Maybe next time you won't sleep so late."

"Agreed," he proclaimed. "That's why I intend to steal my wife away just as soon as we've eaten."

"Oh? And where, may I ask, do you plan to take her?"

"I thought she might enjoy seeing how a plantation this size works. And if you don't mind, I'd like to show her the other house."

"I don't mind at all," Alanna insisted. "I'll have Cinnamon pack a basket for you and you can spend the whole day touring Raven Oaks."

Amber surveyed the food before her once more. "Why not just have her pack up what's left here. I'm sure there'll be enough for another meal." She looked up at Nicholas, then at Alanna, and all three broke into joyful guffaws.

"Oh, Amber," Alanna sighed, wiping a tear from the corner of her eye, "I don't know when a meal has been more enjoyable. I hope it's the beginning of many more to come. Now hurry and eat before Kate comes down. She might look like a young lady but if she learns what you've planned for the day, she'll want to tag along."

"Grandmother is right. Sometimes I think I would have married sooner if I hadn't had to take my little sister along whenever I courted a lady."

"Nicholas, that's not true," Alanna laughed. "You never married because of your reluctance to settle down."

He took a sip of tea, then settled his gaze on Amber. "Not really, Grandmother. I just hadn't found the right girl until now."

Suddenly the humor of the morning vanished and Amber lifted a knife to cut the ham into bite-sized pieces, forcing her eyes to remain trained on the plate. It was a simple enough statement, one that, if spoken by another, could ring of truth, but instead only raised doubts in Amber's mind.

The rest of the meal passed quickly, and before Amber realized it, Nicholas had left the two women to see about a carriage. Amber returned to her room for a bonnet to shade her face from the hot sunshine and found Alanna waiting at the front door when she returned.

"Now remember, my dear. If you'd like to have some time alone for a while, just let me know. I'll take care of everything. And if you decide not, then I'll have Andrea brought here. Either way you can spend a few days with her." She slipped an arm around her companion and led her out onto the veranda. "But I hope spending today with Nicholas will convince you that only good times lie ahead for you."

"Thank you, Alanna. You've helped to make things much easier for me already. I wish I had met you sooner."

Alanna gave her a gentle squeeze. "Don't go wasting a moment on cursing the past. You can't change it. Simply look ahead," she grinned, hearing the rattle of the carriage as it rolled to a stop at the end of the long pathway. "Now have fun, and we'll talk more later."

Without hesitation, Amber leaned to place a kiss on the old woman's cheek before starting down the steps. Although her life hadn't turned out the way she had hoped it would, her future didn't seem as bleak as before. Alanna Remington had offered her the chance to make a choice, and whether that choice was right or wrong she would always be thankful that someone had cared enough to give her the opportunity to decide. With the help of her husband, Amber climbed into the small, four-wheeled buggy and waved back at the elegant woman standing on the veranda. Nicholas cracked the reins to set the rig in motion. She settled back to enjoy the day, vowing to do as her newfound friend had suggested—to learn all she could about Nicholas Chandler.

"I wish I had my grandmother's charm," Nicholas sighed as the buggy made the first bend in the drive. It led down the road past the long line of log cabins.

"Her charm?" Amber repeated with a half laugh.

"Yes. Maybe you'd kiss me without any urging." He concentrated on the road ahead, trying to conceal his smile, which only caused the corners of his mouth to twitch.

"Well, someday when you truly deserve it, maybe I will."

"Oh, please, dear wife, tell me what it is I must do to deserve the honor," he mocked, turning sorrowful eyes her way.

"Stop acting like a buffoon, for one."

"Is that how you see me? I, a man who only behaves as a man in love would do."

"Love," she snorted. "Do you know the true definition of love?"

Nicholas pressed his lips together, voiding the smile. "No. But I imagine you're going to tell me."

Turning in the seat to face him, she said ardently, "Yes, I am. When I was a child, before my mother died, I found an injured fawn too small to take care of itself. I brought it home, nursed it back to health, and kept it in the stable where it couldn't run away. Then one day my mother came to me while I played with the fawn and said, 'Amber, if you truly love your little friend, set her free. If she comes back to you, she is yours. If she doesn't, she never was.' I sat there for a long while deciding what my mother really meant. Then I understood. I kept the fawn locked up to make *me* happy. It was a creature of the wild and would die if I didn't turn it loose. It took a lot of courage but I finally did as she said."

"And what happened?"

"It lingered for a while. Then it lifted its nose in the air smelling freedom, discovering what life should be for her and she ran off. I never saw her again."

"Were you sorry?"

"At first, yes. But then I realized that the fawn would be

275

happier with its own kind."

"Interesting. But I don't think it applies to us." He glanced over at her. "That is why you told me, isn't it?"

Amber shrugged and sat back in the carriage seat. "Maybe."

"You feel that I've locked you up against your will and will never be happy until I set you free. Is there a young man somewhere who has stolen your heart, Amber?"

Her head snapped around to stare at him. "No. Why do you ask?"

"Because I see no other reason for your wanting to be free of me."

"You conceited lout. If I'm not in love with someone else, you think I should be content with you," she snapped. "What arrogance."

Nicholas chuckled. "Well, it isn't exactly what I meant. And besides, who's to say you can't love me one day?"

"Because you have too many faults to overlook."

He threw back his head and roared with laugher, bringing a startled expression to Amber's face. "That's one of the things I liked about Edgar. He never held back when he thought I had it coming. Tell me, my dear wife, can't you find one attribute about me that pleases you?"

"If Edgar couldn't, how do you expect me to?" she rallied, oddly enjoying the sting of her words.

"Edgar," he chuckled. "A dirty little snot-nosed brat who should have had the seat of his pants warmed." As if struck with an idea, Nicholas hauled back on the reins, stopping the carriage near a grove of trees some distance from the manor and out of sight from any workers. "And since you and Edgar are one and the same, I see no reason not to carry out the punishment he should have received."

"What?" Amber shrieked. "Nicholas, you can't."

"Oh, really?" he sneered, his eyes aglow with mischief. "And why not?"

"Y-you wouldn't hit a lady, would you?" she stammered, scooting as far away as the seat would allow.

"A lady who would cut her hair and dress in boy's clothes should expect any kind of treatment. And since I'm your husband," he moved closer, "I can do anything I wish. Consider it

276

one of my faults." But when he shot out a hand to grab her, she slapped it away and scrambled from the carriage before he could guess her intent.

Seeking protection from the trees, Amber raced toward them, hearing his deep-throated laughter grow in volume as he dashed after her. She rounded the first and lost herself in the low-hanging branches of the willow, her heart pounding and her breath coming in ragged heaves. She didn't bother looking back, knowing he followed close behind and praying she could hide in the thicket before he caught up to her. Her skirts lifted high to clear her step, she ran left, then cut right, thinking to outmaneuver him and gain some distance. Ahead she spotted a fallen tree, and, knowing he would have the advantage if she wasted time trying to climb over it with all the skirts and petticoats hampering her moves, she darted to the right once more. From out of nowhere, Nicholas stepped from behind the huge trunk of an oak tree and Amber collided head-on with him. The impact caught him off balance and unaware as she hit full against his chest. Unable to catch himself, or save her from the same fate, he grabbed her arms, pulled her to him, and tumbled to the ground. He took the bone-crunching blow in stride as he connected with the hard earth, the frailer body of his wife on top of him, ignoring the tremor of pain that shot through him to enjoy the softer curves pressed against him.

"Really, Amber," he chided, "what will others think to see you throwing yourself at me? I realize we've only been married a few days. . . ."

Before the sentence reached its conclusion, Amber rolled from the cushion he made, unaffected by the fall, and scrambled to her feet. He had only time enough to see the lace trim of petticoats before she disappeared in the profusion of trees, bushes, and wild flowers growing all around them. He laughed heartily and sprang to his feet, haphazardly dusting off his clothes as he rushed after her.

Certain of his determination to see his verdict carried through, Amber fled as if her very life depended on it. This time, however, she glanced back over her shoulder periodically to warn herself of his whereabouts. His long strides cut the distance in half after only a few moments, and she decided that if she was to save herself, she must reach the carriage first and race for the manor. Surely he wouldn't dare beat her in front of his grandmother, nor would Mistress Remington permit it.

The muscles of her legs cried out for rest. Her lungs burning and the pain in her side unbearable, Amber longed to stop but knew she mustn't. She darted left, planning to circle back in a wide arc, positive the carriage stood a few yards away and she would reach it in a few more minutes. She glanced over her shoulder, afraid Nicholas rapidly closed the space between them, and slowed her step when she discovered him nowhere to be seen. She stopped, gasping for breath, her gaze darting from tree to bush, bush to rock. She couldn't have outrun him. Had he tripped and fallen? She gulped, hoping to silence her ragged breathing and enable herself to hear every sound in the woodlet. Only the rustling of leaves in the gentle breeze filled the void, and Amber's pulse began to quicken again. He played tricks! He sought to fool her, to entice her into coming back to look for him while he hid behind a tree! She wouldn't search. He wouldn't beguile her. Yet, what if he lay injured, a twisted ankle or knocked unconscious, perhaps? Could she just leave him? A devious knot formed on her brow. Of course, she could.

Tossing her blond, curled head, nose raised loftily, she grabbed two handfuls of skirt and marched victoriously toward the carriage, unmindful of the dark, smiling eyes that observed her trek. She walked for several minutes, dodging low-hanging tree branches, stepping over decayed stumps and broken limbs, carefully avoiding harm to a clump of bluebells in her path, and all the while grinning widely as some soldier on his way to claim the spoils of his conquest. But as her steps grew in number, the smile faded, concern twisting the smooth lines of her face. Somehow she hadn't thought the carriage was this far away. She stopped and glanced up at the treetops overhead, hoping to spot the sun and know in which direction she ventured. A tangled web of leaves and branches formed the canopy, with a tiny square or two of blue intruding on perfect green. One cheek crimped in a disgusted scowl. Maybe she could recognize a tree or a formation of rocks she had passed earlier. Or the fallen log she had chosen not to climb. She looked around, every tree seeming the same and none of them familiar. Her attention moved to survey the ground, anticipating the discovery of footprints in any direction but the one from which she came. Panic stirred in the pit of her stomach, for she found not only those that had brought her to this spot but many more among them. She moved closer, reluctant to test their size with her own slippered foot for measure. The same! Each and every one belonged to her! Circles, she had traveled in circles! Now what would she do? With no sun peeking through the leafy overhead to guide her and a path marred with several passes of her own making, how would she find her way out? How long must she wait before someone came looking for her? The foolishness of her folly hit full force, and tears burned in her eyes.

"Nicholas?" The name, spoken weakly yet urgently, filled the air and quickly floated away, exchanged for the stillness of the woods. "Nicholas." The encore rang louder, tinged with fear. "Nicholas, where are you?"

Her lower lip quivering, Amber stepped forward, the silence closing in and pounding in her ears. She must find him. Surely he knew the way to the carriage. She walked faster, the snapping of twigs frightening a pair of blackbirds from their lofty perch to wing away in a frantic duet toward the sky.

She thought again of the possibility that he lay hurt, unconscious. What would she do if she found him thus? She concentrated on the marks left in the tall grass, put there by her passing, and stopped suddenly when larger ones trailed off alone. A smile fought to curl her mouth upward, mixed with tears of relief. She hurried to follow them, continuing several yards before a trio of large rocks crossed their path. She hastened to the other side, certain to find them again. But to her dismay they had disappeared. . . . As if the owner had vanished into thin air. She circled the rocks twice more, positive she had only overlooked them, before she plopped down on the largest piece of granite in total frustration. A mixture of worry, fear and helplessness washed over her and she tilted her head back to call out his name in louder volume. "Nic—" But as her gaze lifted skyward, her voice caught in her throat, for there, sitting comfortably in the large crook of the tree above her, Nicholas grinned down at her.

"Hello," he said cheerfully. "Did you get lost?"

Her tears dried instantly. Her nostrils flared. Her chest heaved in anger. Quickly scanning the ground around her feet, Amber bent to retrieve a handful of pebbles. Bolting from her resting place, she drew back her hand and let go of the rocks, sailing them through the air to shower painfully on her husband.

"You lousy . . . contemptible boor!" She stooped to arm herself again.

Fearing the worst, Nicholas fled for safety just as another assault was launched, the stones rifling off the trunk of the tree to ricochet harmlessly to the ground. Dissatisfied with the results, Amber scooped up another ration of ammunition.

"Come out from behind that tree, Nicholas Chandler, and get what you deserve!" she screamed, hand held high, her eye trained on her target.

"But Amber, I simply climbed the tree to rest," he argued, sneaking a quick peek only to duck back out of the way when she hurled more stones.

"You liar, you jackanapes! You must have heard me calling for you. Why didn't you answer?" Spying a broken tree limb to use as a club, she traded the pebbles for it, her skirts held in one hand, the bat in the other as she circled the barrier protecting him.

"I'm sorry, but I must have dozed off. I didn't hear you. You know I would have come to you if I had." His back against the tree, he leaned slightly to the right, hoping to catch a glimpse of her, dropping his guard when he discovered she had gone. A frown chased away the amused gleam in his eye until a crack behind him spun him around in time to see Amber swing her club. With artful dexterity, he sidestepped the affront, her weapon missing him by inches but connecting soundly with the tree trunk. The blow jarred her teeth and she let out a howl of pain, the thick wooden shaft dropping to the ground, her fingers and hands numb from the shock.

"Tsk, tsk," Nicholas mocked, shaking his head, fists resting on each hip. "Now aren't you ashamed? Trying to hurt me only caused your own grief."

Tears brimming over the edge of her lower lashes, she glared up at him. "Only that I missed. Before I met you there were few I couldn't best." She rubbed her hands together to stop the stinging.

"A good point, dear wife. At last you have met your equal. Or is it your better?"

"Ha!" she rallied. "You've won a battle but not the war, sir knight."

"Is that how you view our marriage? A war to win?" His dark brows raised questioningly. "Are you a damsel in distress?"

Her eyes narrowing, she shot blue sparks at him. "Not for you to rescue. I still await the knight of my dreams to ride into my life on his handsome white charger. You, sir, belong on a mule. After all, you are a braying ass."

His sparkling smile had little affect on her.

"Why not find yourself some doxy with whom to play your games, for I see little humor in them." Her stare dropped from his grinning face to the dark mass of curls covering the muscles of his chest where his shirt fell open. Why didn't he take more care in his manner of dress? She concentrated on brushing the dried leaves from her gown.

"And what makes you think it's games I play? As I recall, this all came about because I sought to teach you a lesson and deal out the punishment you deserve." He crossed his arms over his chest, one knee bent, and waited, watching her with close curiosity.

Her round blue eyes stared up at him. "You don't intend to strike me?"

His smile grew lopsided. "And why not? You tried the same."

"But that's different."

"How so?"

Befuddled, Amber absently glanced down at the ground as if the words lay at her feet for her choosing. "B-because a gentleman wouldn't hit a lady."

"Ah, yes," he nodded. "And therein lies the dissimilarity. A gentleman wouldn't, but a husband can." With lightning speed he jerked forward and caught her wrist, crushing her to his chest. "A husband can do anything he wishes."

Her arms were pinned against him, his encircling her, his entire body molded the length of her. Amber felt suffocated, but even more she felt the need to set him straight. "Except force his wife to love him."

The mischievous gleam returned to his eyes. "Truer words I've yet to hear, my sweet. But given time, *I* can claim that, too."

"Don't wager all you own on it, Nicholas," she jeered.

"Only the condition of my heart."

Her brow wrinkled.

"It's quite simple, Amber. You've stolen my heart and have in your power the ability to cast it aside or cherish it as I would yours, given the chance. In other words, my pet, I've fallen deeply and hopelessly in love with you."

Pulling back as far as his hold would allow, she stared dubiously. "I don't believe that. How could you? You've known me too short a time."

All mockery vanished from his handsome face. "How do you measure time? In seconds, minutes, years? Or by instinct, a gut feeling, the calling one hears in his heart? Whether a day or a lifetime, Amber, no more will come to pass to change my mind. I've searched many countries, sailed the seas looking for you. Don't you think I'd know it the minute I saw you?"

Amber's heart beat erratically, a sorrow weighing heavy in her mind. She turned her head away. "But to know true love, it must be returned. I—I don't love—"

He raised long, lean fingers to silence her vow. "Not yet, Amber," he whispered. "Wait before you speak such an oath. Be sure." He loosened his grip. "Now I suggest we be on our way lest those who saw us stop here think I took you for a tumble in the woods." He spun her around in the direction of the carriage and soundly slapped her bottom, delighting in the pained squeal it produced.

Fearing more of the same, Amber hurried onward, one hand rubbing the injured spot and his laughter ringing in her ears.

"As much of a spanking as Edgar will get from me," he called after her, his eyes glowing with devilment. But as he watched her go, yanking her skirts from side to side with her agitated steps, a sadness touched him. *I've said the words, Grandmother,* he sighed inwardly. *I've bared my soul and laid my future at her feet. And if she tells me nay, what then? Though I boast of winning her heart and her love, I find a gnawing ache of worry that I won't. Is true love meant to be so painful?* He raised the hand that had struck her, studying the wide palm, wondering when, if ever, he would caress her cheek, her breast, and know she welcomed it.

Chapter Twelve

The boundaries of Raven Oaks spread further than Amber's imagination. Fields of tobacco, cotton, wheat, orchards of fruit trees rambled on for miles in all directions, dotted with hundreds of workers, wagons, and teams of horses. Groups of children played in the road while their parents worked, and, as hard as she tried, Amber failed to see where any of them had cause to complain. The workers, men and women side by side, thinned weeds from the endless rows of tobacco, humming cheerful tunes and laughing all the while. Huge flat bed wagons sat waiting with barrels of fresh water and baskets filled with foods. The men had stripped themselves of their shirts and the women wore bonnets to ease the discomfort of the noonday heat. If anything, they seemed content as they worked for the profit of another. No overseers hovered near with long black whips gripped in their hands, and for the first time in Amber's life she saw a plantation operated by slaves and indentured servants in a new light. This freedom from a threatening hand puzzled her and formed the troubled frown on her face.

"Nicholas," she asked, sitting forward in the carriage seat, "if all this belongs to your grandmother, won't it one day be yours?"

"And Kate's," he corrected.

"But if you own the shipping lines, what will you do with both?"

Nicholas chuckled. "Somehow I've never thought much about it. I suppose I'll simply let Kate run it with her husband . . . if and when she ever marries." He paused a moment to look at her. "I suppose you think I should let everyone go free and sell the land at a third its value to those who aren't so fortunate."

Although the thought had flitted across her mind, Amber resented his mocking tone. She slid back in the seat and stared straight ahead. "What you do with your property,"—the insinuation rang clear— "is your business, not mine. I'm sure you wouldn't do what I ask, anyway."

"You're wrong on two counts. First of all, my property is now yours, and any decisions that have to be made concerning it will be done by both of us. Secondly, as to whether or not I'll do what you ask . . . try me. You might be surprised."

One finely arched brow raised as she tilted her head to peer over at him. "Oh? Then have our marriage annulled and lend me the money I need to pay the baron."

Dark brown eyes sparkled into blue eyes. "Within reason," he grinned.

Amber studied the road ahead, her nose raised triumphantly. "As I thought," she sighed.

Giving in to his desire to provoke her, Nicholas snapped the carriage reins to hurry them along and said, "Even if I consented, you could possibly regret it."

Amber glanced briefly at him from the corner of her eye, her tone sarcastic. "Your conceit is showing again."

"My conceit has nothing to do with it. I simply meant there is a chance you carry my child, and you know what people think of a woman in that condition without benefit of marriage." He bit the inside of his lip to stifle his laughter when he heard her gasp. "Obviously, you've not thought of that. I would suggest you wait a while to be sure before you make such a request."

Suddenly the warmth, the serenity of the day faded into anxiety, a blanket of doom, of entrapment, enshrouding Amber. Had he planned it all along? Had he suspected she might leave him when their bargain reached completion and plotted such a scheme? Visions of Sarah Forrester flooded her consciousness, a young frightened woman, alone and with child, destined to raise the babe without a father's guiding hand. Although Amber's mother had never mentioned Nathaniel Cromwell, the sense of abandonment must have ridden high throughout her life. Could she do the same to her own child, if that was the case? No, she couldn't. And she wouldn't stay with Nicholas. Her lower lip trembling, Amber bravely raised her chin higher. She would do as Alanna Remington offered and return to her sister in Jamestown. She would wait out the time necessary to make certain his seed had not taken, then seek an annulment. And above all else, she would never let him hold her in his arms again.

The road twisted and turned down the rows of majestic oaks and willow trees before it curled sharply to the left and opened up to display the most elegant manor house Amber had seen. Tall and stately against the backdrop of vivid blue, it emanated wealth and beauty, a quiet peace, a sense of returning home.

"Nicholas, who lives here?" Amber questioned, awed by the imposing structure, with the numerous windows and white colonnades adorning the mammoth veranda. Thick flower beds spread on either side of the brick pathway leading to its door and along the circular drive they traveled.

"Only a few of my grandmother's servants."

"Servants?"

"Yes. This house belonged to Radford Chamberlain. He was—"

"I know who he was. She told me. But I didn't know she owned his house."

"And his property. He had left it to her in his will. She lived here before she married my grandfather and wouldn't sell it. She wanted to keep it as a memorial to his name."

"But it seems like such a waste. Does she always intend to leave it like this?"

Their carriage rounded the curve of the drive and rolled to a stop at the end of the pathway. Nicholas set the brake and climbed down to tie off the reins before answering.

"I imagine she plans to give it to Kate and her husband,

although she's never really said." He held out a hand for his wife. "I'm sure she'd give it to us if we wanted it."

A devilish smile crept over Amber's face. "What a wonderful idea. Why don't you ask her? Then I could live here with my sister and you could stay in Williamsburg." She slid across the seat, lifted her skirts, and took his hand as she climbed from the carriage. Safely on the ground, she smoothed her gown and smiled up at him. "Then we'd all be happy."

"Would we? For how long, I wonder?" he asked, his eyes sparkling. He bowed properly and held out a directive hand for her to lead the way, grinning broadly after she had stepped past him.

"The housekeeper's name is Feodora. She's the granddaughter of Radford's first housekeeper and thinks of Briarwood Manor as her own," Nicholas advised as they walked across the veranda and stood before the huge front door. "The place is always spotless, as if she expects company at any minute. In fact, I think she prays for it. It gives her a chance to take care of someone. I'm sure you'll like her, and I know she'll hover over you like a grizzly over her cub." He lifted the latch and swung the door open, calling out the woman's name.

Amber's first view of Nicholas's house had been breathtaking, but sorely lacking in comparison to what she saw now. The foyer circled out before her to lead to several doors, while in the center the wide staircase opposite her graciously flowed upward, dividing at the top to trail off in separate directions. Its banisters, further apart at the base of the steps, gave an illusion of huge arms opened wide to welcome all into its bosom, and Amber felt drawn to them. Overhead hung a mammoth chandelier with thousands of tiny crystal teardrops and candles in multiple rows of highly polished brass. The marble floor at her feet sparkled as brightly as an icy pond on an early winter morning, the only furniture that dared touch being the high-back arm chairs sitting rigidly tall beneath the gold-framed portraits hanging on every available space. One in particular drew her attention and without a word, Amber slowly crossed the foyer to get a better view. Warm blue eyes smiled back, the strong, lean jaw set in a devilish grin. The man's blond hair, pulled back into a knot at the nape of his neck, revealed a high forehead and wide cheekbones, a thin nose and a square chin. Even the clothes he wore spoke of wealth.

"He's rather handsome," Amber whispered, as though visiting a shrine. "Who is he?"

Nicholas strolled to take a place beside her. "A man who, if he hadn't died so young, might have changed my grandmother's life. This is Radford Chamberlain."

It seemed as if the painting took on new form when Amber looked at it again. All the pain, frustration, turmoil the youthful Alanna must have experienced, surfaced in the gentle features of the face Amber observed. And had he lived, would the woman-child have found the happiness she so obviously had found with Beau Remington? A chill ran through her, for the question posed another. Destiny had worked its magic to comfort one who searched. Had it already decided Amber's future?

"Why are you frowning?"

His question startled Amber and she half laughed to cover her embarrassment and hopefully hide any clue of what she really thought. "I just wondered if your grandfather was the jealous sort."

"Jealous? Of what?"

Amber stepped away, her hands spread outward to indicate the room and its contents. "This . . . that his wife would care so much for another that she would see his house preserved."

Nicholas smiled knowingly. "Apparently my grandmother didn't tell you everything. Radford and my grandfather grew up together, thought of each other as brothers. If my grandmother hadn't done this, I'm sure he would have." The creaking of a door drew his attention away from his wife. "Feodora," he exclaimed when the short, round figure of the black housekeeper suddenly appeared before them.

"Mister Nicholas," she returned, equally exuberant, rushing over to him to crush him in her chubby arms. "Why didn't nobody tell me you was coming? Is you planning to stay a while?" She set him at arm's length, her dark eyes traveling from his booted feet to his black tousled hair. "Let me look at you. How long it been? Two months? Three? Did Mistress

Alanna come?"

Nicholas burst into laughter at her shower of questions. "And what shall I answer first? Or all at one time?" He pulled the rotund shape into the circle of one arm and turned to face them toward Amber. "No one told you that we'd be here because we didn't know until this morning. Feodora, I'd like to present Amber, my wife. Amber, this is—"

"Your wife?" The question exploded with surprise. "Nobody tells me nothin'. When did you all get married, Mister Nicholas?" She broke free of his hold and hurried over to Amber. "And such a pretty young thing. Lordy, Mister Nicholas, where was you hidin' her all this time?"

Overcome by the woman's merriment and enthusiasm, Amber's lips twisted into a smile, her gaze darting from the housekeeper to Nicholas and back again, unsure of which words would satisfy the woman and in what order.

"Oh, don't matter none, I guess," Feodora continued, "only that you all is here. You must be tired. And hungry." She seized Amber's hand and gently pushed her toward one set of doors. "You and Mister Nicholas go in the parlor. I'll have tea and some tarts brought right out to ya." She stopped suddenly and looked back at Nicholas. "You all will spend the night, won't you?"

"Feodora, if you'll just give one of us a chance to answer—"

"Oh, I is sorry. I do tend to run on a bit."

"A bit," Nicholas grinned. "Amber and I are simply spending the day riding about Raven Oaks. I wanted to show her this house, and Cinnamon already packed us a picnic basket. If we're to see everything, we won't have time to stop for lunch or tarts or even tea for that matter."

"Why, you mean you all will be leaving right away?" Feodora's ebony skin wrinkled into a disappointed frown.

"Afraid so," Nicholas nodded. "But I do promise you this. Very soon we'll all come to spend several days here . . . Kate, my grandmother, and Amber and I. We really only stopped to see the house and introduce Amber to you."

"Well, I is sure glad you did that much." She turned to face Amber. "Honey, I is real thrilled you married Mr. Chandler. It's about time he settled down and got hisself a family. I hope it will be a big one. Say, you all wouldn't wanna move in here, would ya? Why, we's got plenty of room for youngins. Why that first room facin' east would make a right pretty nursery, mornin' sun and all—"

"Feodora," Nicholas interrupted. "Amber and I have only been married a few days. We haven't even discussed a family yet. And until it becomes too large, we'll be living in Williamsburg."

"Oh, yes, of course," she mumbled. "But it seems like such a waste. A big house like this with no youngins running about." She heaved a sigh, then smiled brightly once more. "You all want me to show ya around?"

"No, thank you," Nicholas grinned, moving forward to wrap his arm around Feodora's shoulders. "I'm sure you have other things to do, and that way we won't disturb you. When we're ready to leave we'll stop to say good-bye. All right?"

"But—"

Nicholas raised a hand to silence her. "Newlyweds, remember?" he whispered, then glanced back at Amber.

A sudden dawning lit up Feodora's eyes. "Why sure, Mister Nicholas, I gets it," she giggled, slipping out of his hold to head for the door from which she had entered. Reaching it, she paused, looking back. "I is really glad to meet you, Mistress Amber. And try real hard to talk Mister Nicholas into livin' here. It's much bigger than his place."

"Feodora . . ." he warned.

"Yes, sir . . . yes, sir . . . I is goin'," she surrendered, throwing both hands in the air as she spun around and exited the room.

"You'll have to excuse her, Amber," Nicholas chuckled, "but without someone here to remind her that she's only a servant, she sometimes gets a little out of hand. I think she's decided to become Kate's and my substitute mother."

"Actually, I found her charming. And you were right. I do like her, even though I never got to say a word."

"What's really amusing is to see her and Kate together. I swear they try to outtalk each other." He took Amber's elbow and led her toward the parlor. "Shall we get started?"

The rest of the morning passed in a blur for Amber. The size

291

of Briarwood Manor at times overwhelmed her, leaving her breathless and without comment. In her childhood dreams she had envisioned a faraway castle where kings and queens lived, and she was certain any member of royalty would be pleased to claim this house as theirs. They toured the gardens, the stables, and the kitchen, stopping often to talk with the servants, and again Amber learned that being a slave wasn't always as horrible as she had thought. These people appeared content and genuinely happy to meet her and renew their acquaintances with Nicholas Chandler. And not once did her husband shun them. He truly wanted to hear what they had to say and even exchanged a joke or two with some of the men.

The sun had begun the final half of its arc by the time they boarded the carriage again and left the manor behind them. They traveled down the road until it divided, the left leading to Raven Oaks. Nicholas reined the mare to the right.

"But isn't your grandmother's house the other way?" Amber asked, concerned. "I realize I've only ridden this way once, but I would swear you took the wrong turn."

"It is and I did. Sort of," Nicholas smiled. "There's a spot not far from here that I wanted you to see and I thought maybe we could have our picnic there."

"Not another house, I pray . . . bigger than the last?" Amber giggled. "If I live to be a hundred, I know I'll never see another quite as elegant. And huge! Mr. Chamberlain must have been very rich."

"Actually, he wasn't. From the stories Grandmother tells, he gave away most of his money and was near ruin when he died. He loved being with people and having many friends and he thought if he spent his money on them, they would like him."

"That's awful," Amber moaned. "I never realized someone like that could be so lonely."

"You mean because he had wealth?"

"Yes."

"I'm afraid he and I were a lot alike in that respect. We didn't know what true happiness was until we found the woman we wanted to spend the rest of our lives with."

Amber's heart pounded, but she chose to pretend his words

had no effect. "But your grandmother told me she didn't truly love him."

Nicholas grinned over at her. "Another similarity."

This time Amber could feel the heat rising in her cheeks. From the seat next to her, she picked up the bonnet she had elected not to wear and flipped it from side to side, hoping the small puff of air might help. "Rather warm today, don't you think?" Her question seemed even more trite than it was. She touched the back of her hand to her brow and tried again. "How much further?" The words nearly caught in her throat and she wanted to pull them back, not sound like a child anxious to get home. Frustrated, she decided silence would be her best ally.

Sensing her uneasiness, thinking he knew the cause, Nicholas smiled to himself and reined the carriage off the road through a field of tall grass and wild flowers, their vivid purples, reds, and yellows dotted against the dark green like a painter's palette smeared with oils. Birds sang in delightful chorus all around them, and a quiet serenity captured the moment. Ahead hovered a stand of willow trees, the thick, delicate branches swaying in the gentle breeze, their tips raised enticingly as if in invitation to explore all they hid from view.

"Where are we?" Amber asked quietly once Nicholas had stopped the carriage and climbed down to tie off the horse.

"It's a place my grandfather use to spend a lot of time whenever he wanted to be alone," Nicholas replied, reaching into the carriage for the picnic basket and a blanket. "On the other side of the willows is a stream. It's probably more private than any single room in my grandmother's house." He held out his hand for her. "Shall we see?"

Wondering if she wished for such solitude, fearing her own weakness should he sit too near or brush her cheek with his fingertips, Amber hesitated.

"You are hungry, aren't you?"

To deny the fact would only raise another question, and Amber grudgingly accepted his help in aiding her to the ground, determined to eat something if only to hide the reason for her uncertainty.

His description of privacy proved accurate, for once they

made their way through the tangled mesh of leafy tendrils, the cove offered complete seclusion in the curtain of willow branches on three sides and the narrow stream flowing rapidly by on the fourth. Amber paused beneath the protection of the last willow, oddly experiencing the comfort Beau Remington must have felt whenever he visited this sanctuary. As though sheltered from all the turmoil and evils of the world, this haven volunteered a space in which to sort out one's thoughts, a peace not many other spots could equal. The gurgling of the brook as it raced for the sea drew Amber's attention, and while Nicholas spread out the blanket on the bed of grass she ventured near the water's edge to watch it curl and stumble over rocks along the way. Compelled to sample its coolness, she quickly found a fallen tree on which to sit and removed her shoes and stockings, then dangled her bare toes in the brisk current. It sent a chill through her and she giggled, never having felt quite so alive, so impetuous as she did at this moment. Raising her chin in the air, she closed her eyes and sucked in a long, slow breath, savoring its rousing crispness.

A narrow shaft of sunlight filtered through the trees, as though guided by some celestial being, to fall gently on the shapely figure by the stream. Lying down on the blanket, Nicholas stretched out on one hip, his elbow propped to support his head on his fist. He watched her, smiling, knowing his decision to bring her here had been wise. He had suspected she would enjoy this retreat, and, with any amount of luck, he could move on to more pleasurable ideas. Of course, he would have to advance slowly. Amber was by no means agreeable to accepting his caresses without putting up some sort of resistance. If good fortune chose to fall on him, he could entice her into his way of thinking, and, deciding it was best to be prepared, he sat up and slipped off his jacket, then his shoes.

"What are you doing?"

Startled, he glanced up. "What?"

She nodded at his pile of clothes.

With a weak attempt at a smile, he shrugged to cover his near fatal mistake and said, "Just getting comfortable . . . like you. Would you care for something to eat?" Avoiding her stare, he reached for the basket, opened the lid, and peered inside. "Bless her. Cinnamon thinks of everything." He lifted two goblets and a bottle of wine, and held them up for Amber to see. "How about a drink first? Ah . . . er . . . before we eat, I mean."

Only Amber's innocence of courting allowed the statement to go unchallenged. "I guess," she replied, pulling her feet from the water. She left the tree trunk and walked toward him, unaware of how the simple act sparked a flame in Nicholas's loins.

"Easy boy," he warned softly through clenched teeth and set about popping the cork and filling both glasses. Keeping his gaze on anything but the trim ankles and bare feet that moved closer, peering out in perfect rhythm, as if tempting him to forget about the wine or lunch for that matter, proved nearly impossible. The flame grew, and he absently unhooked another button on his shirt front, perspiration of another breed dotting his brow. He waited for her to sit down, hoping she would curl her feet beneath the layers of skirts before he spoiled everything and tossed away the glasses and . . .

"Are you all right?"

Certain his face reflected his innermost yearnings, he forced a laugh and handed her a glass, his eyes averted. "Fine. Why do you ask?"

"You look flushed." Unexpectedly, she touched his cheek with her hand. "You're warm."

Hot is more like it, he moaned silently, then grinned one-sidedly. "Just the day's heat. I'll be all right." He took a sip of wine.

"I know the perfect cure."

The liquid lodged in his throat, cutting off his breath. He coughed. "What?"

"Take off your stockings and put your feet in the stream. It's quite refreshing."

"Oh," he whispered.

"Now don't say it like that," Amber insisted with a smile. "I guarantee it will help." She took his glass, set it beside her own on the ground, and bounced to her feet. "Come one, we'll both do it." She held out her hands for him.

Nicholas's gaze slowly traveled upward, past the full skirts, the slim waistline, the bodice that clung much too tightly to the swell of her breasts, the long column of her neck, and finally to the smiling face. Never, in all his years, among the tens of women he had courted, made love to, had any of them ever affected him, aroused his male needs so easily as the woman he now called his wife, a woman who preferred an annulment, to have nothing to do with him. Was this justice? Must he pay for all the broken hearts he'd caused by sacrificing his own? One side of his mouth twitched in a feeble grin and, unwillingly, he hooked a finger in the top of his stockings to slide them free. He sighed heavily, accepted her help in standing, and sullenly followed her to the creek.

"Sit here," she instructed happily, with a pat to the log she had used.

"And where will you sit?"

She took his hand and pulled him nearer. "Right next to you," she said, guiding the way. Perched comfortably on their makeshift bench, Amber lifted her skirts slightly and allowed the cool waters of the stream to caress her feet. She giggled. "Come on, Nicholas. Do it. It feels wonderful."

It looks wonderful, he thought, staring at the slender ankles peeking out from beneath the hem of her gown. His breath caught in his throat when she raised the skirts higher, the shapely calves of creamy, smooth skin exposed for his pleasure. He looked skyward, letting out a sigh. Why didn't he have the same effect on her? He shrugged, resigning himself to the inevitable, and feebly sat down beside her.

"Go on, put your feet in," she urged, smiling cheerfully when Nicholas chose to crimp his legs, his knees touching his chin.

Somehow the idea of wading in a stream belonged more to childhood than to the life of a full-grown man, and Nicholas suddenly decided he wanted no part of it. "I think I'll just splash water on my face," he said aridly, staring at the small whirlpools in front of him.

"What? Why? Nicholas, this is heaven. In fact, I'd like to take off my clothes and go swimming," Amber said excitedly. Her smile faded and she twisted on the log to look directly at him. "Don't tell me you're too pompous to want to do the same."

"I'm not pompous," he barked. "I'm just too old to play these games. And a lady certainly wouldn't remove her clothes and swim in a stream."

"Oh," she rallied, one tawny brow lifted, "what would she do? Sit in the parlor and sip tea? Maybe sew a quilt and gossip about her neighbors? Lord knows she certainly wouldn't want to muss her hair." She shook her head. "Really, Nicholas, you've never enjoyed life if you always do what's expected of you." She glanced back at the blanket. "Come to think of it, how many of your lady friends would eat sitting on the ground? Heaven forbid." She batted her eyelashes, playing the temperamental snob. "Oh, my, imagine the explaining little o' me would have to do if I came home all wet or had grass stains on my petticoats. Why, it would be unthinkable." She grinned up at him. "I'll wager your grandmother has done it."

"Leave my grandmother out of this," he warned, oddly ruffled by her deftness to pinpoint fact.

She shrugged. "All right. Then how about your father? Mr. Rafferty told me he was a pirate. I can't envision him sitting around smoking a pipe and talking about the weather."

"Amber . . ."

"No, I want to say this, Nicholas . . . high and mighty . . . Chandler." Her mood turned challenging. "You sit there and condemn the things I do and like, and not a breath ago you choose to tell me how wrong I am about the way you live. Who's right? You or I? Well, I've got a surprise for you. Neither of us. There are good and bad points in both, and what makes it right is what makes us happiest. We're from two very different worlds, and I doubt there's any chance we'll agree on one."

Nicholas sat by tolerating her reprimand and recognizing the logic behind it. However, he wasn't about to swear surrender and let her go her own way. "A valid point, my dear," he said with a smile, "but as you've already mentioned, my father was a pirate and my mother a lady. Couldn't get more different than that, and they married and found happiness anyway."

"Probably because they each gave up something in their life to please the other," she gritted out, leaning closer until her nose nearly touched his.

He stared at her a moment, then shrugged. "Probably," he agreed. "Does that mean we'll be just as content by giving in a little?"

"I doubt it. They loved each other," she sneered.

His handsome features brightened with his smile. "Then we're halfway there."

Amber pulled back, confused.

"Because I already love you."

A disgusted frown knotted her brow. "You haven't been listening. Love is only part of it."

"Yes, I have. Not just emotions but giving of one's self. Isn't that what you said?"

"Yes."

"Then consider it done." He unbuttoned his shirt, pulled the tail from his breeches, and tossed the garment away. Sticking a toe in the water to test its crisp bite, a chill ran through him, but he decided a dip in the stream might be invigorating. He slipped off the log, sank knee deep and suddenly dove beneath the surface.

Shocked by his abrupt change in temper, Amber watched mutely, wondering how long he could hold his breath when he didn't emerge immediately. She straightened, craning to see him in the clear, briskly flowing current. Worry set in when several more seconds ticked away, and Amber instantly regretted provoking him. What if he drowned because of her? Alanna and Kate would never forgive her. Tears sprang to her eyes. She bit the first knuckle of her hand, panic squeezing the muscles in her throat. Hoping for a better view, she awkwardly scrambled to her feet, her toes digging into the bark of the log to balance her. The sun sparkled against the water's surface, bright and vibrant, as if laughing at her, and the chance the swift movement of the creek had taken his life. Her stomach knotted, and Amber knew the reason, She didn't want him to die.

Frantic, she began unfastening the hooks of her gown, her gaze scanning the stream for any sign of him. Dear God, had he been swept downriver? She shimmied out of the dress, followed by her petticoats. Without wasting a moment more, she stepped into the water, calling his name with each step she took, the strong current tugging at her and threatening to pull her into its chilly clutches. She had waded out to where she had last seen him when suddenly something grabbed her ankle from behind. She screamed just as she was jerked from her feet and dragged into the water. Fearing some monster from the bowels of the earth had come to claim her, Amber fought with all her strength as powerful arms came up around her. In that instant she knew the demon's name. She wiggled free of him and surfaced quickly, gasping for air. She spun around, pushing wet strands of hair from her face.

"Damn you, Nicholas," she screamed. "How dare you play such a horrible trick! I thought you had drowned."

"But Amber, you just said a minute ago you wanted to go swimming. I only thought . . ."

"I wish you had drowned, you insufferable cur," she shouted, turning away to trudge toward shallow water. Her anger ruling, Amber failed to choose her steps carefully, the toes of one foot entangling with a thick net of greens, tripping her. Fighting to catch her balance and free its hold on her, the instep of her other foot came down hard on the jagged edge of a rock. She squealed in pain and promptly sat down with a splash, the crystal waters swirling around her and playfully lapping against her bosom. She presented a rather delightful vision, one Nicholas thoroughly enjoyed, and he wasted no time in coming to her aid.

"Let me look at it," he ordered, stooping beside her. A small gash oozed several drops of blood, but had already lessened its flow. He splashed water over the wound and noticed how the area around it had turned a bright red. "I think you'll have a nasty bruise, but nothing more."

"It hurts," she pouted prettily.

"I imagine it does. You should be more careful."

"I should . . . this is all your fault. If you hadn't . . ."

He smiled up at her. "If I hadn't what? Done as you wanted?" Without further comment or seeking her permission, he slid an arm beneath her knees, the other under her arms, and stood. With little effort he carried her to the bank amidst squeals of protest. "Stop fighting me, Amber, or you'll find us both back in the water."

She surrendered reluctantly, preferring the prospect of a soft bed of grass beneath her to the one of stone she had been sitting on. Not wishing to touch him, she dourly placed an arm around his neck and allowed them both to easily climb from the stream. Although the distance they covered was only a few steps, it seemed an eternity to Amber, for with each move he made she could feel the strong muscles of his chest and arms flex. The heady, manly scent of him clouded around her, intoxicating, and, oddly enough, she found herself relaxing in his arms. He took his light burden to the blanket spread out in the center of the clearing and gently laid her on it. He stood, returned to the log by the water's edge, and gathered their clothes.

"I'm afraid our foolishness has a price," he grinned, holding up the garments. His shirt as well as her gown dripped with moisture. Strolling to a nearby bush bathed in sunshine, he draped the articles over it to dry and started toward her once more.

Wet breeches clung tightly to the hard, well-proportioned thighs that rippled with each step he took. But what bothered her more was the revealing tightness of the cloth across his manhood, leaving little to the imagination and a scarlet hue on her cheeks. She tried to pull her eyes away, only to have them drawn to the wide expanse of his chest covered in a dark mass of curls. Tiny droplets of water remained, sparkling in the sunlight, and she noticed how the soft furring tapered to a narrow line down his belly and disappeared beneath the waistband of his breeches. She swallowed the lump in her throat and looked up at his face. He had raised both hands to shake the moisture from his hair, the muscles of his forearms tightened in reflex action, strong, sleek, powerful. Amber wondered if he could crush her in his embrace if he so desired. She jerked her head away, suddenly needing the glass of wine she had discarded earlier.

"I don't think it will be long before they're dry," Nicholas said, stooping on one knee. "Are you cold?"

She glanced up nervously. He nodded at the goose flesh on her arms.

"A little." She picked up the goblet and drank nearly all of the wine.

"Here, wear this," he instructed, leaning over to pick up his jacket and cover her shoulders with it. "Maybe we should move to a sunny spot so your hair will dry."

"No, I'm all right. The wine helped. Thank you," she mumbled, before taking a second long swallow.

Sitting down near her, his arm draped over his knee, Nicholas studied her a moment. "Why must you fear me, Amber?"

Startled by his ability to read her thoughts, she forced a sweet smile and handed him her glass. "Don't be silly. I have no reason to fear you. Would you pour me another?"

His long, lean fingers covered hers wrapped around the goblet. "Then why are you trembling?"

She jerked her hand away. "Just a chill. If you'll give me another drink, I'll be fine." Her words had a sharp edge, something she hoped he wouldn't notice, for it gave them a tone of defensiveness. She smiled weakly again and lifted her chin to smell the air. "It's beautiful here. I can understand why your grandfather chose it."

Nicholas admired the delicate lines of her cheek, jaw, and the smooth flesh of her neck before settling on the gentle rise and fall of her bosom peeking out from beneath his jacket. "Yes, it is. He and my grandmother often came here to be alone. I imagine they made love in this very spot."

His statement set every inch of her on fire, starting at her toes and rapidly spreading upward to tingle hotly in her cheeks. She knocked the jacket from her and awkwardly found her feet.

"Where are you going?"

"My petticoats are still dry, aren't they?" She started toward the bank and the place where she had left them.

"Petticoats?" he echoed, standing up to follow her. "Come to think of it, I didn't see them."

Amber stopped, looked back at him, then spun around and ran to the river's edge. Frantically searching the ground near where she had disrobed, Amber felt her chin tremble. Nothing! They were gone! She moved a few steps to look further. A flash of white caught her eye and glancing up she spied the lace trim and yards of cloth slowly floating downriver in the steady current, too far away to reach without swimming a good distance.

"Oh, no!" she moaned, hurriedly stepping into the water, intent on retrieving them. She traveled knee deep before Nicholas could catch her, grabbing her arm and pulling her back.

"Let them go, Amber. I can always replace them," he said.

"No. You don't understand," she argued, tugging at his steely grip. "I can't go back without them. What will Alanna and Kate think?"

Nicholas grinned playfully. "I can't say for sure about Kate, but my grandmother will think we had a good time."

Without warning, Amber drew back her hand and presented a stinging slap to his face. Stunned, Nicholas released her, shaking his head. He opened his mouth to question the act, for in his mind the declaration rang true, and snapped it shut again when he saw her raise the other hand to continue the attack. Surprise slowed his reflexes and he took the blow gracefully but in muted awe. However, when the third round seemed imminent, his anger flared. With lightning speed, he reached up to seize her wrist only inches from her goal.

"I gave both cheeks, dear wife, before I had the chance to offer. Now calm yourself and tell me what it is that disturbs you so."

"Disturbs me?" she shrieked. "You . . . you dimwitted cad . . . you disturb me."

One dark brow raised derisively. "That much I figured out on my own. The cause is what I question."

Amber struggled to free herself, frustrated when she failed. "There aren't enough hours left in the day to list them."

Not wanting to discuss it any further, and wishing to be rid of him, she turned sideways, her wrist still trapped in his vise-like grip, and rammed her shoulder into his chest, thinking the surprise of such a move would catch him off balance and plunge him into the water. However, she figured he would let go first. Instead, she found herself crushed to his chest as they both tumbled into the stream.

302

Water surged around her and Amber grew acutely aware of the hands that freely touched her buttocks and the small of her back. She fought to get away, pushing at his chest, her legs entwined with his. Then, much to her surprise, his arms slipped up under hers and with little effort he lifted them both from the water. She struggled, her feet dangling in the air, the thin, wet camisole doing little to pamper her modesty, for, pressed against his chest as she was, she could feel every muscle of his broad, hard body. And when his lips suddenly came down hard on hers, she knew there would be no turning him away. She was his wife, and if this was what he wanted, he would take it. However, the warmth of his kiss dulled any desire she had to bring an end to it, though her mind demanded otherwise. She hung limp in his arms at first until his mouth twisted across hers, his teeth nibbling, his tongue tasting the sweetness of their kiss that sent wild sparks of fire through her. Much against her will, as if they had thoughts of their own, her arms came up to encircle his neck, returning his ardor with her own. Her earlier pledge to see that this never happened again faded to the far recesses of her mind as he gently slid one arm beneath her knees, their lips still clinging passionately.

He easily carried her from the water and returned to the blanket in the clearing. He lowered himself to one knee and tenderly laid her down, his fingers quickly finding the strings of her camisole. Stripping the garment from her, he then touched the buttons of his breeches, a slight frown flitting across his brow when Amber pushed aside his hands to do the task herself. His naked body pressed to hers, they lay there touching, exploring, feeling emotions no other had ever aroused.

"Oh, Amber. Amber . . ." he whispered, bending low to kiss her temple, the bridge of her nose, and finally the corner of her mouth. "I love you."

Capturing her lips in an ardent expression of desire, his hand roamed freely down her neck and across her shoulder to softly caress the full swell of one breast, his thumb stroking its peak. She moaned, her own caresses playing with the muscles of his back, her nails lightly clawing. She wanted him to take her, to feel him inside her, and time played the enemy. An urgency prevailed, as if a single word, a moment delayed would steal him from her and leave her alone with her stubborn pride. She opened her mouth to voice the words of her heart when she felt him rise above her, a knee parting her thighs, and the vows she wanted to proclaim fled as swiftly as a rabbit in the thicket. She welcomed him, arching her hips, urging his first thrust, and wondered if heaven could make so sweet a claim.

Chapter Thirteen

Night descended upon the countryside in unearthly quiet. The dying oranges of sunset mixed with ebony shadows cast an eerie curtain of gloom on all who ventured out this night. Owls, perched high in treetops, craned their necks, round gold eyes searching, watching for a tasty morsel scurrying below to be swooped down upon and devoured as silently as the night's passing.

Set amidst this stage of isolation, the dark silhouette of a carriage moved steadily onward, destined for the inn a few miles ahead and a haven for the night. The driver, cloaked in black, skillfully urged the team of dapple grays to hurry, wishing to seek shelter and safety for his passenger.

Amber pressed back into the plush velvet seats of the coach, bracing herself for the next lurch of the rig racing along in frenzied flight as if a demon from hell chased after them. Dressed in a like manner to the coachman, Amber had pulled the hood of her cloak to shadow her face and hide her identity, feeling somewhat more secure that no one would recognize her should they be stopped along the way. Although Mistress Remington had guaranteed her Nicholas would not follow, Amber feared at any moment he would appear, the violence of his rage at finding her gone twisting his handsome face. She remembered the numerous letters she had begun to write, wadding up each one and tossing it away, none quite fitting and all lacking in depth. Now she wished she had selected one to ease the explaining she had forced on his grandmother. But could Alanna simplify Amber's feelings? Could she easily say Amber must have a moment alone to sort out her thoughts? What did Amber feel? Was it love? Desire? Need? A frown darkened her eyes. Alanna was right. She must search for the answers on her own, in whatever length of time it took. She closed her eyes, hoping to block out all thoughts for a while, but in the darkness behind her lowered lids a flashing white smile, a strong, lean jaw, and deep brown eyes loomed out to haunt her. She stifled a gasp with fingertips pressed to her mouth, straightened and pulled aside the leather window covering to concentrate on the fading embers of sunset. How could she decide if he continued to invade her mind?

The driver hurled a command, hauling back on the reins, and within moments the carriage came to a sliding halt outside the inn. An instant later he stood by the open door of the coach, his hand held out for her.

"We'll spend the night here, Mistress Chandler. It's too far yet to reach your place before daybreak. You must be tired, and the horses need food and rest."

"Thank you, Gibbens," Amber said, accepting his help in descending the carriage.

They had left Raven Oaks shortly after midnight, traveling hurriedly toward Jamestown and stopping only to rest the horses and eat from the basket of food Alanna had thoughtfully sent along. Amber had managed to sleep a little in the carriage as they jostled through the countryside, but Gibbens had not, and she wondered how much more he could take. She was glad he had chosen to stop for the night, but not so much for herself as for him.

Together they went into the inn, where Gibbens sought out the keeper and instructed two rooms be made ready. Silver coins exchanged hands before the coachman returned to his mistress.

"If you'd prefer, you may sup in your room. Or I'd be very willing to remain in the commons near you so that you won't be disturbed."

"Thank you, Gibbens. I'd like that. But first I wish to freshen up a bit before I eat."

"Very good, madam," he nodded courteously. "That will give me time to see to your bags and stable the horses." He turned back toward the innkeeper, waved his hand, and beckoned the man near. "Please show Mistress Chandler to her rooms while I get her things from the carriage."

"Yes, sir," the man replied, nervously wiping his hands on the towel tied around his belly as an apron. "This way, madam." He held out a directive hand, allowing Amber to take the lead and climb the staircase to the rooms above.

"I hope you'll find the chambers to your liking, Mistress Chandler," the gray-haired innkeeper said, once they had stepped inside and he had lit a lamp, the pungent odor of burning oil filling the space.

"Yes, they're fine, thank you," Amber said softly. In fact, this room was much more than she had expected. A small velvet sofa sat before the fireplace, large paintings hung on the walls, and double french doors led to the balcony of the sitting room. She stepped further inside and spied the huge four poster bed and elegantly crafted armoire in the bedchambers.

"If you'd like, I could send my daughter, Linette, to attend you. She could fetch hot water for a bath."

Amber dropped the hood of her cape from her head and untied the strings. "That won't be necessary. I'd simply like to eat and retire as soon as possible."

"Yes, madam. Will you be dining in the commons?"

Pulling the cloak from her shoulders, Amber tossed it carelessly over the back of the sofa and removed her gloves. "Yes."

"Very good, Mistress Chandler." He started for the door, pausing when a thought struck him. "Oh, and my congratulations on your wedding."

Amber didn't know why his knowledge of the ceremony should surprise her, but it did. She glanced up and forced a smile. "Thank you." At the moment she felt no explanation for her husband's absence was needed, and she turned away to inspect the bedchambers, hoping the man would not press the issue. She heard the click of the door latch and stopped, letting

307

out a long sigh.

In all the time she had spent dressed as Edgar, roaming the streets and hiding in warehouses or stealing food to eat, she had never felt as scared, as alone as she did at this moment. And yet if questioned why, she knew she could not explain the emotions, justify them, or accept them. She wanted the moments of solitude, away from pressures, obligations, worry. She wanted to be free. She wished she was a child of ten again, that her mother still lived, that her father had the responsibility of caring for her and Andrea, that she could play in the yard surrounding their cottage, laughing, enjoying life as each day presented itself. Standing in the doorway of the bedchambers, she leaned back against the frame. But what was it that truly plagued her thoughts, stirred the ache in her heart and brought tears to her eyes? To compare her future with what could have been? Why was she running away? And from what?

Anger seizing her, she yanked herself up and brushed the moisture from her eyes.

I will not think of it now, she vowed silently. *I will decide tomorrow.*

"I have a table all ready for you, Mistress Chandler," Gabriel Penrose smiled when Amber had entered the dining hall. "It's near the fire and away from everyone else."

"Thank you," she answered weakly, allowing him to lead her to it. Unconscious of the many stares that followed her, she sat down in the chair the innkeeper held out for her and glanced up to find Gibbens sitting alone in the opposite corner of the room. She smiled in response to his nod.

Although night had claimed a chilly hold on all it touched, the warm, crackling fire in the hearth near Amber spread its comfort throughout the room, and she turned in her chair to watch its dancing flames, unaware of two men who studied her instead.

"That's gotta be her," the heavier of the duo said. "Didn't ya hear the innkeeper? He called her Mistress Chandler, and we've been followin' the carriage ever since it left Raven Oaks."

"*Oui*, but we didn't stay close enough to see it all ze time," the other argued in a heavy French accent, his words tinged with sarcasm. "Maybe it turned off somewhere and we followed ze wrong one, *mon ami*."

The first lifted his mug of ale to his lips, whispering, "Don't be an idiot. Ain't no chance of two carriages having the same-looking mares, same driver, and going the same way."

A worried frown pierced the other's brow. "I guess you're right. I just want to be sure, that's all. You know what they'll do to us if we bring ze wrong woman." He concentrated on the bowl of stew before him.

"Whatsa matter, Pierre, my little French pastry-head, you scared?"

A thin face haloed with slate-black curls glared back at his partner. "I'd be a fool if I wasn't. You know what Von Buren ees capable of."

The heavy-set man grunted. "Don't worry me none. I can handle myself."

Pierre Duehr's lip curled. "Ees that what you want on your gravestone? 'Here lies David Allison. He handled his own problems.' If you know so much, how are we going to take ze woman without anyone getting suspicious?"

"We'll climb up to the balcony of her room and hide inside until she comes."

Duehr stuffed a forkful of meat in his mouth and mumbled. "*C'est bon*, but how will you find out what room ees hers?"

"I already have, stupid! I heard the innkeeper tellin' her man where to take her things when we walked in. It oughta be easy enough."

"Easy," Duehr mocked. "Do you think she will come with us without any trouble, *monsieur*?"

"Yeah. After I tell her we got her sister holed up somewhere and our men will kill her if we don't show up in time."

Duehr shrugged one shoulder. "It might work."

"Might? Of course it will. Now finish that slop you're eatin' and let's go."

Duehr opened his mouth to add a few of his own observations on Allison's past schemes, clamping it shut when he noticed a young woman pass their table, a tray full of steaming dishes held in her hands. He watched her approach Mistress Chandler, set down the tray, and begin serving the wide assortment of foods, wondering why only people with a high and mighty air about them received better service than someone like himself. His gray-green eyes narrowed, appraising the arrogant way the woman ignored the serving maid.

"Mistress Chandler?"

Amber blinked at hearing another's voice, oddly embarrassed at the fact she had been summoned and failed to recognize the title. She glanced up from studying the fire. "'Yes?"

"May I get you anything else?"

Her gaze quickly viewed the feast spread out before her. A tin of fresh-baked bread, a jar of raspberry jam, a bowl of potatoes oozing with butter, a thick slice of roast, wild rice, and peas in white sauce, nestled on a large plate. Nearly every available space on the table was covered. She looked up at the young girl who sought perfection, her lips parted in awe, and failed to respond.

"Is something wrong, Mistress Chandler?"

Amber shook her head, another such extravagant meal coming to mind. She laughed and said, "I'm sorry. Everything is fine. It's just that everyone seems to think I eat like a man. I'll never be able to finish all this."

The girl shrugged. "Don't matter. Papa said to bring it all, and I did."

Amber couldn't help noticing the sharp edge to the girl's words. "Linette, isn't it?" she asked, recalling her conversation with the innkeeper.

"Yes, ma'am."

"Well, I thank you and your father for your trouble. I didn't mean to cause such a stir."

"Kinda hard not to," Linette said brusquely, "you being married to Nicholas and all."

"Nicholas?" Amber repeated, taken aback by the girl's familiar use of her husband's name.

"Yes, Nicholas," Linette sneered. "You don't think you're the only one who tried to catch him, do you?"

Mouth agape, appalled by such impertinence, Amber quickly took in the girl's appearance. She was pretty enough,

310

with light brown hair accenting the oval face and dark eyes. But Amber noticed the slim shape and flat bosom, wondering if the child had yet to see her fifteenth birthday.

"Tell me," Linette continued when Amber failed to speak, leaning closer so only she would hear, "How did you manage to trick him? Did you tell him you carried his child? Yes, that must be it. That would explain why you're traveling alone. He found out it wasn't true and sent you packing." She straightened and toyed with a long curl resting over her shoulder. "At least my idea took a little imagination. I told him I was young enough to bear him many sons to carry on his name."

Her icy blue eyes glaring, Amber's temper rose to the challenge. "Obviously he did not agree. I imagine he did not wish to have to wait for you to reach the childbearing age."

Linette's spine stiffened at Amber's well-aimed retort, her narrow chin dropping as she opened her mouth to argue.

"I wouldn't if I were you," Amber warned, her voice held to a whisper, "lest your father wonders what held us in conversation so long. I don't imagine he would find favor in knowing you angered Nicholas Chandler's wife. Now be on your way before I decide to tell him just for the mere sport of it."

Her chin trembling in rage, silenced by the fear of her father's stern hand, Linette turned sharply and hurried away, leaving Amber to stare after her.

The little chit, Amber fumed silently. *What does she know about pleasing a man? Especially Nicholas Chandler. A toss in a hayloft could hardly satisfy him for long. He isn't a simple lad, content to herd sheep or make candles all day. He searches for more in his life, and the love of a woman is one of them. He . . .*

Amber's breath caught in her throat. Dear God, what had made her think of that? Her appetite for food suddenly gone, she quickly stood up and blindly headed for her room.

"Ya dumb Frenchman, be quiet," Allison growled when the man's boots thumped against the floor of the balcony.

"Madame Chandler ees not here," Duehr argued in a harsh whisper. "She ees still in ze commons talking with *le femme-soldat*."

"I know that, but you don't have to warn everybody else."
Allison lifted the latch of the french doors, praying it would
move with his touch. He sighed inwardly when it proved
unlocked and he easily opened the door.

"Where are we going to hide," Duehr asked, glancing over
the balcony's railing to guarantee no one had seen them.

"In the bedchambers," Allison said. "Ain't enough room
out here for both of us if she decides to get some fresh air.
We'll wait till she goes to bed. Come on." He motioned for his
partner to follow and together they felt their way into the other
room, darkness hampering their moves.

"How long must we wait?" Duehr asked, crouching down
beside the bedchambers doorway.

"How would I know?" Allison snapped. "Ya want me to go
ask her?"

In the blackness of the room Duehr's sneer went unseen.
"And what are we going to do with her coachman? They told us
we were to make it look like she decided to go away on her own,
not like she was kidnapped."

"I already figured that out. We'll leave him a note."

"A note?"

"Yeah. You know how to write don't ya?"

"*Oui*, but—"

"She's gonna tell him she decided to go away and be alone
for a while where no one can find her. And they ain't to look,
either." Allison tilted his head to one side, listening. "Shhh! I
think I hear somebody coming."

Duehr scrambled to his feet, and both men pressed against
the wall on either side of the bedchambers doorway, waiting
and hearing the latch of the sitting room door click open. A
yellow stream of candlelight flooded into the room, and a
moment later they could smell the burning of lamp oil. Each
man slipped back into the shadows.

Nicholas sat resting one hip on the windowsill of his bedchambers, looking out at the darkening shadows of evening, a
wrinkled piece of paper in his hand. He had read the discarded
note over and over again, wondering what Amber would have

312

written if she had finished it. Could she have explained her departure better than his grandmother had? Could she have chased away the worry that crimped his brow and brought a stinging to his eyes, or the emptiness he felt tugging at his heart? Had he driven her to this? Did she truly hate him? No, he couldn't believe that. They had made love in the clearing near the stream, an unrestrained, joyful giving on both parts. She hadn't pulled away, begged him to stop. And it had been he who suggested they dress before being intruded upon by some unsuspecting visitor sent looking for them. He studied the perfectly penned words once more.

Nicholas,
   I hope you'll understand

Understand? he thought. I've tried but I don't. I thought I had won. I thought you had finally given in, accepted your fate, my love, our destiny. Has it all been a game to catch me off guard so that while I slept you would slip quietly from our bed and disappear into the night, return home before I knew? Well, I won't accept this! And I won't sit here a moment longer waiting, praying you'll change your mind and come back to me.

He bolted to his feet, a gesture mixed with anger, pain, pride. Stuffing the tattered letter in his pocket, he hurried to the armoire to pack his clothes. He would bid his grandmother and Kate farewell and return to Williamsburg. If Amber wanted to come home, to be his wife, she would have to do it on his terms. He would not go after her.

Amber crossed to the opened french doors and stepped outside onto the balcony to feel the cool bite of the night breeze and study the sprinkling of stars overhead. Although her body longed for sleep, her mind raced on. *He knows by now*, she thought. He knows I'm not coming back for a while . . . if I ever do. I wonder what he's thinking. Had he become angry when Alanna told him? Did he blame her for it? She hoped not. Alanna had nothing to do with her choosing to leave. She had only supplied the means and a chance for Amber to decide on her own about the way her life should be. She simply had to be alone for a while. Surely he would understand, give her that much.

A gentle wisp of air sent a shiver up her spine and she turned back for the warmth of her room, quietly closing the doors behind her. She paused a moment, a slight frown marring her brow, thinking that she had left them barred when she went downstairs. Shrugging it off as unimportant, she extinguished the lamp light and moved toward the bedchambers, her tired limbs aching for the comfort of the feather mattress. If only she could find peace for her mind and her heart. Stepping through the archway, she unfastened the first button of her dress, a shadowed movement to her right distracting her. She glanced up, a scream lodging in her throat when two huge arms flew at her, one clamping painfully around her waist, her body crushed against her assailant, her spine nearly cracking while the man's other hand stifled any chance for her to call out as his fingers dug cruelly into the flesh of her cheeks, the powerful hold covering her mouth.

"Don't fight me, Mistress Chandler," the deep voice threatened. "It won't go good for Andrea."

Amber echoed the name, but it came as a muffled sob. She stilled her struggles when he squeezed harder, cutting off her breath.

"You hear me? We have your sister, and all I have to do is send word and she's dead. Now either you cooperate or I send my man here with a message."

Some logic returned to her, and Amber held still as the second man tied her wrists in back of her, the rough hemp cutting into her flesh. If these henchmen sought only to kidnap her for ransom from her husband, why would they bother with Andrea? Or, more simply, why not kidnap Andrea and send a ransom note? Their reason had to be something else. They wanted her, not her sister. They only used Andrea to get her to do as they wished.

A foul-smelling rag was jammed into her mouth, nearly gagging her, followed by a second strip of cloth tied behind her head. The man who had spoken clamped onto her elbow and heedlessly ushered her into the sitting room, where he shoved her onto the sofa.

"Light the lamp and get the note written," he ordered. "I wanna get out of here."

A warm golden brightness filled the room and Amber quickly took in the appearances of the two men. As different as night and day, the one who seemed to be the leader stood nearly a head taller than his companion with gray hair and deep lines in his face, thick jowls, and a protruding belly that hung over his belt. The other, skinny in comparison, moved swiftly, his thin nose and narrow face almost birdlike. He quickly found a piece of paper and sat down at the small desk. His partner moved to stand next to him, peering over the smaller man's shoulder.

"Please don't follow me or try to find me," he began reciting, pausing while his cohort dabbed the quill in the well again. "I don't want to live with Mr. Chandler—"

"*Mon Dieu*, she would call her husband Nicholas," Duehr pointed out irritably.

"All right . . . all right . . . Nicholas," Allison growled. "Just shut up and write. And try to make it look pretty . . . like the wench wrote it."

Annoyed, Duehr held up the paper for Allison to examine.

"Yeah, that's good. You do that real nice," Allison grinned.

"*Faible d'esprit*," Duehr mumbled beneath his breath, bending over the paper to complete his work. Once he had finished, he returned the quill to its resting place and propped the letter against the lamp's base. "It ees done, *mon ami*."

"Good," Allison smiled. "Now let's get going."

"*Oui*," Duehr agreed, hurriedly crossing to the french doors and swinging them wide. Silently, and with agile grace, he slipped over the railing of the balcony and climbed down the trellis to wait.

"Ya don't look like ya weigh much more than a keg of gunpowder, but ya better not squirm too much. Otherwise, I might drop ya," Allison warned, bending down to seize Amber's arm. He jerked her to her feet, put his shoulder in her stomach, and straightened, one arm clamped tightly behind her knees. As if she posed no difficulty at all, he stepped out onto the balcony and awkwardly climbed over the railing.

315

Amber squeezed her eyes closed, blocking out the sight of the perilous journey down the trellis. Although her abductor's muscles seemed cushioned with more weight than needed, she could feel their strength, and she found she feared less that he might grow weary of the extra weight he carried than that the wooden latticework would break and send them both tumbling to the ground. But after what seemed an eternity, he settled comfortably on the ground and set off after his companion. A few yards away, hidden among the trees, their horses whinnied softly at their approach, and Amber was roughly hoisted into the saddle of the first.

"You ride with the wench, Pierre," Allison ordered. "My horse has enough to carry, and we have a long way to go."

Without comment, Duehr easily swung up behind Amber, took the reins in his hands, and spurred the horse into a gallop.

She glanced back at the inn only once as its yellow lights began to fade in the distance, a silent prayer on her lips that Gibbens would think her departure strange and send word to Nicholas.

Chapter Fourteen

Lyle Gibbens pulled his gold watch from the pocket of his waistcoat, took note of the time, and snapped the lid shut, a troubled frown piercing his brow. He had risen two hours ago, certain he would find Mistress Chandler already dining in the commons, anxious to start their journey again. But with each customer that walked past his table, ate breakfast, and appeared before him once more on his way out, his concern grew. He waved off Linette's offer of more tea and stood up, fishing several coins from his jacket to toss on the table. Spotting the innkeeper engaged in conversation with several patrons at the front door, he hurried over to him and waited for the man to look up.

"Excuse me," he said, "but has Mistress Chandler sent word that she's ill?"

"Why, no," Gabriel Penrose replied. "Is something wrong?"

"Probably not," Gibbens answered, glancing back at the stairs. He remained quiet a moment, then turned back to the innkeeper. "Do you have another key to her room?"

"Yes. To all of the rooms."

"Then would you be kind enough to accompany me to Mistress Chandler's? I'm responsible for her safekeeping and I would like to be certain that she only elected to sleep late."

"Of course," Penrose agreed. He excused himself from his guests, asked Gibbens to wait, and disappeared through a doorway a few feet away. A moment later he returned with a ring of keys clenched in his fist and guided his companion up the stairs. They traveled the distance down the hallway in silence and paused outside Amber's room.

"Would you like for me to unlock it now?" Penrose asked.

"No," Gibbens said. "She might be dressing, and I wouldn't want to frighten her. I'll knock first."

But when the third summons went unanswered, Gibbens put a hand to the latch, finding the way locked. He called out to her, his voice full of urgency. Again, no reply. Stepping back, he motioned for Penrose to open the door. Both men hurried inside.

Soft shades of morning light flooded in through the open french doors, and Gibbens instantly felt the chill in the room. He glanced at the dark fireplace, saw her cloak lying on the sofa, and rushed into the bedchambers calling Mistress Chandler's name again, pulling up short when he found the huge four poster bed hadn't been slept in. Spinning around, he raced for the balcony and peered over the edge, heaving a sigh of relief when he didn't find what he feared he would; the twisted, mangled body of Mistress Chandler on the cobblestones below.

"Where do you suppose she is?" Penrose asked. "I haven't seen her since she left the commons last night. I thought it was odd then and even more so now."

"What do you mean?" Gibbens frowned, anxiously walking back to examine the bedchambers once more. He spotted the two valises untouched and still sitting on the floor at the end of the bed where he had put them last night.

"Well, she obviously came down to sup but left without touching her food. I never saw her talking to anyone, but she seemed upset."

"She was upset before we arrived," Gibbens mumbled, not willing to explain further. He stood in the center of the sitting room, one fist resting on his hip, his other hand stroking his brow as he contemplated the mysterious disappearance of his mistress. Then he spied the piece of paper leaning against the lamp on the writing desk and hurried over to it, discovering the second key to the room lying beside it.

"What is it?" Penrose asked, coming to stand next to Gibbens as the man unfolded the note and began to read.

"Nothing that concerns you," Gibbens answered gruffly, tucking the letter in his pocket. He turned and went into the bedchambers, where he gathered his mistress's things, then headed for the door. "I'll be going now."

"But what about Mistress Chandler?" Gabriel Penrose called, following the man into the hallway.

Gibbens stopped at the top of the stairs and set down one valise to dig in his pocket. Finding a silver dollar, he tossed it to the innkeeper. "I'll be returning to Raven Oaks. I doubt you'll hear from her, but should Mistress Chandler send word or should anyone ask about her, send a message to Mistress Remington. Your effort will be well paid for."

"Yes, sir," Penrose nodded, his weathered face wrinkled in confusion.

Lifting the bag from the floor, Gibbens turned away and rushed down the stairs, well aware of the long, hard ride he had ahead of him.

A thin stream of daylight filtered in through the crack in the closed doors of the root cellar. Amber had watched it brighten for the last three hours, the narrow band slowly moving across the floor as the sun gradually rose in the eastern sky. She could only guess the hour but felt certain Gibbens had found her room empty by now. Crouched in one corner of the dark, damp cubicle, she silently prayed he would find her departure questionable and send word to Nicholas. She had no idea who these men were or what they really wanted with her, but she feared for her safety should she be forced to stay with them for very long.

They had traveled the entire night at a steady pace, heading southwest along the road to Jamestown until they veered to the right and made their way to a cabin nestled in a small clearing. Amber wondered why they hadn't covered her eyes with a blindfold to confuse her and hide the location of their retreat.

It would be quite simple to lead Nicholas and the sheriff to the bandit's lodging once this was all over. And she had gotten a good look at both men. Their only hope for survival would be to flee the state, for Amber knew Nicholas would search for however long it might take until he found them.

Nicholas. The name rang clear and sweet in her troubled mind and brought the lump to her throat. She had made the decision to hate him, to seek her freedom of him, and to find the man who was truly meant to share her life. Someone she would choose, not have forced upon her, a gentle man of her upbringing and station. She couldn't love someone who practiced all the things she despised. So why did he fill her thoughts? Why did her heart ache just thinking of him? Why did she long to have him hold her, soothe her worries, and kiss her trembling mouth?

Her stomach rumbled, bringing a disgusted curl to her lip. And how could she think of food at a time like this? Every muscle in her body was stiff, tired. She should be more concerned with sleep than satisfying her hunger. But then again this was a root cellar, and when they had thrown her into it she had seen the straw-covered bins partly filled with fruits and vegetables before they had closed out the light from the lantern. She would eat something first and then maybe find a comfortable spot to lie down and sleep. Since she had no way of knowing what to expect, she decided it would be best to renew her strength in any small way she could, for, given the opportunity, she would escape these men and return to Nicholas. On foot it would be a long journey, and once they discovered her exodus she knew they would hunt her down with great speed. She would need every ounce of energy she could muster to succeed.

The small shaft of light acted as a beacon, singling out the fruit bins on the opposite side of the room. Awkwardly finding her feet, Amber crossed the short distance to stand before them. Brushing aside the thick bed of straw, she uncovered a crib filled with apples. Her mouth watered at the sight, and she quickly plucked the largest, wiped its dust against the skirt of her gown, and ate hungrily. Within minutes, the meager feast eased the knot in her stomach and her mind wandered to the men who had sentenced her to such an existence. Selecting a second bright red apple to devour as quickly as the first, she slowly made her way to the steps leading upward, barred by the old wooden planks of the doors. She settled on the one nearest the top and peeked out between the slits to catch sight of anything outside her prison that might offer a ray of hope.

About thirty feet away, she spotted the split rail fence of the corral and two horses idly standing near its gate, their heads down and their eyes closed as they sought a moment's rest. The pungent odor of burning wood drifted in, and she wondered if the men had started a fire to heat water for tea and to cook their breakfast. She imagined the smells of frying ham, eggs, and even a sweet roll dripping with a glazed frosting. Suddenly her apple didn't seem worth eating, and she irritably tossed it away.

"The least they could do is bring tea," she muttered in the semidarkness of her cell.

The wild chirping of two robins engaged in battle drew Amber's attention. They attacked in midair, wings flapping wildly as they fought to wound each other. Amber shifted positions to watch, a tangled meshwork of silvery cobwebs capturing her hair when she leaned into them. Moaning her displeasure, she hurriedly brushed them away with her fingers, her desire to observe the duel gone, her own temper flaring. She too would be victorious, but sitting by, simply waiting for something to happen, was not the way. With her hands pressed against the rickety doors, she pushed outward, hearing only the rotted wood groaning from the strain and feeling her single reward, a splinter in her palm.

"Damn," she growled, holding the injured extremity before the light. Though a tiny splinter, the pain it caused seemed unbearable, and she quickly pulled the sliver from her flesh.

Angered, but far from defeated, she realized she must use something as a lever if she was to budge the doors. Quickly surveying her surroundings, she spied the latticework of the fruit bins. With luck and a little strength she might be able to pull a board loose. Scrambling to her feet, she hurried over to them, intent on fulfilling her plan, when the pounding of hoofbeats thundered outside as if the horse and rider meant to trample the root cellar beneath their advance. Amber froze in her tracks.

Nicholas? her mind called out. Could he have found her so soon? A tiny glimmer of hope pierced the darkness of her world and she raced to her spot on the stairs and the chance to see who had arrived. Her face inches from the crack in the doors, she strained to observe the newcomer through the limited slit, spotting only the horse's rump and the tail that swished spiritedly, but no more. Then she heard the stranger call out to the men who had kidnapped her.

"Where's the girl?" his menacing voice demanded.

Amber pressed closer, hoping to identify the man, but the horse pranced nervously and put them both out of sight. She had to be content to listen.

"In the root cellar," Allison replied.

"What about Chandler?"

"He wasn't with her."

"Were you followed?"

"No, sir. We took her when she came to her chambers after supper, and I doubt anyone would come looking for her until morning."

"Good," the deep voice of the stranger replied. "You're to keep her here until I send word. It shouldn't be more than a day or two. Did she give you any trouble?"

"No, sir."

"I must warn you, Allison, she is not to be trusted. She's a clever young woman, with the spirit of a wildcat. You give her an inch and before you know it, she'll be gone. I needn't tell you what the consequences will be."

"Yes, sir. You can count on me not to let her get away."

"Think of it more as insuring your long life," the stranger warned.

A moment of silence passed before the horse whinnied loudly, spun around on his hind legs, and raced off at a wild speed. Amber sat quietly, unmoving in the shadows of her dungeon, with an unsettled look in her eyes. Although she couldn't put a name to the stranger, the voice seemed coldly familiar.

* * *

Mournful weeping penetrated the stillness of the room. Heavy draperies covered the windows, disallowing any light to filter in and chase away the gloom. From somewhere in the house a slamming door echoed loudly and brought about a renewal of tears. In the center of the huge four poster bed, the new Baroness Von Buren sobbed, the quilt pulled up to hide the blackened eye and swollen lip. As had been the custom since their hasty marriage, Kelzer Von Buren had beaten his wife before claiming his husbandly rights, and no amount of pleading on Heather's part had swayed him.

"A wife must know her place," he had howled, lifting a meaty fist to crash against Heather's cheek.

Time and time again he had torn her clothes from her, forced her to parade before him, make her crawl on her hands and knees, then kicked a booted foot into her rib cage. Grabbing a handful of her auburn hair, he would yank her cruelly to her feet and throw her on the bed, ordering her to watch as he removed only his breeches, his mammoth hardness a staunch reminder of the pain she would endure. Mounting her as some wild boar would its mate, he forsook all words of tenderness, for none were felt, and rammed his manhood deeply inside her, his lust raging high with her screams of terror and suffering.

A week had nearly passed since he had trapped her into marrying him, waving the papers of the debts he had paid in her face, and each day exhausted itself in the same manner. Heather seldom left the bedchambers, finding it too painful to move about a great deal, and wondered how long her abused body could withstand such torture. But even more she sought the comfort of the feather mattress out of fear, for Von Buren had threatened to whip her should she try to escape and tell tales of their lovemaking. *He* was the master of this house, and she owed him too much ever to think she could just walk away.

Whenever business took the baron from the room they shared, Heather pulled herself from the bed and dressed. With shaky hands she brushed and styled her hair, selecting a brightly colored ribbon to bind it. Her face dusted with powder to hide the signs of Von Buren's cruelty, she ventured to the room several doors down the hallway from her own. Inside it, her mother lay near death, and Heather treasured this time alone with the only person who had ever shown her mercy and love. She sat for hours by her mother's side, holding the unconscious woman's hand in hers, pleading with her to find a form of escape from this living hell. Reduced to weeping at the lack of response, Heather finally staggered to her feet and went numbly back to her room, there to stare out the window until her husband returned and her nightmare began again.

The aroma of cooking ham and hot breads drifted up to seep into Heather's semiconscious state and bring a rumbling to her stomach, the first in many days. The heavy guilt slipped beneath her chin and she rolled onto her back to peer over at the dainty mantel clock. Past noon already? She must have dozed off again. *Where had the baron gone?* She lay quietly, listening for any sounds coming from another part of the house to warn her of his whereabouts. Silence prevailing, she prayed he had been called away for the afternoon to allow her some time alone.

Flipping the covers from her, she swung her legs over the edge of the bed and sat up. Her head began to spin immediately and she cradled her brow in one hand to still the motion. The cool air of the room chilled her, and Heather painfully remembered the baron had forbid her to dress again after he had had his way with her earlier. One eye opened a slit to examine the soreness of her right leg. A dark, ugly bruise discolored the ivory skin of her thigh. She shuddered, recalling the brutal manner in which Von Buren had struck her with the brass candlestick. At the time she was certain he had broken the bone, and she wondered now if she would be able to walk on it.

Again the warm smells from the kitchen floated up to tempt her, and some logic surfaced in her mind. If she was to survive she must eat, build up her strength to continue. Surely there would come a time when she could free herself from this torture. Visions of her mother clouded her mind. *When she's gone, I'll be free to leave, find a new place to live, far, far from here.*

Heather struggled to her feet, stumbling to the dressing table and her robe lying over the bench. Slipping the silken fabric over her shoulders, she pulled the garment tightly around her narrow waist and sat down to fix her face and hair. The image that stared back at her brought a tearful frown. One eye was nearly swollen shut, the skin black and puffy. Her lower lip was cracked and oozing blood. She steeled herself against the sight and lifted a brush to her hair, stroking the long auburn strands into shiny curls. Selecting a mint-green ribbon from the wide assortment on the dressing table, she bound back her hair, tying the bow just above one ear, then reached for the rice powder and dusted her face with it. Satisfied with the results, she stood and crossed to the armoire where she chose a gown of the same hue as her ribbon, then returned to her dresser to find a clean camisole to wear.

Several awkward minutes passed before Heather was fully dressed and left the room, heading for the long staircase on her way to the kitchen and something to eat. But when she reached the first tread, she froze, the angry voices in the study frightening her. The deepest, most menacing belonged to her husband, and for a moment Heather's feet would not move, certain any sound she might make would bring him thundering down upon her. Her body convulsed, and, knowing the only safety she might find away from him would be in her bedchambers until later that night, she forced her trembling legs to turn her around. Then she heard the second man's voice raised in volume over Von Buren's and her name upon his lips. Suddenly her fear melted, overtaken by the foolish notion that a stranger had come to save her. Hands clasped tightly around the staircase railing, she willed herself down the steps and across the foyer. She stopped a few feet from the study's closed door to listen, hearing only parts of their conversation, as the rest came out muffled through the thick wooden portal. Again her name was spoken, and she recognized the stranger's voice. He was a business partner of the baron's. She had seen him on many occasions and still did not know his name. Heather had thought her husband took orders from no one, but this man always appeared to be the one in command. She cowered by the side of the study doorway, knowing the baron's associate would care very little what happened to her. And, if they found her standing here listening to everything they said, she felt absolutely certain that if Von Buren wouldn't beat her for it, his companion would. She began inching away.

"I'm telling you, Kelzer, it must be done now and done

quickly," his cohort bellowed. "We mustn't run the risk of Chandler's getting suspicious about his wife's disappearance."

"Nicholas?" Heather whimpered, the sound of his name stopping her departure. She paused, straining to hear.

"But if we kill her now, before her sister agrees to marry me, it could prove difficult," Von Buren argued. "Maybe Andrea won't believe that we've kidnapped her sister. She might even demand to see her. Then what?"

Kill her? Heather's mind shrieked. *Nicholas's wife?* And how could the baron marry Andrea Courtney when he was already married to— The muscles in her chest tightened. *Dear God, they're insane.*

A long silence dominated the tense moments as Heather heard one man move about the room. "I rather doubt it," the other replied. "Andrea hasn't that kind of courage. But there is always the chance she might surprise me." Quiet prevailed for a moment, as the man considered the possibility. "All right, we'll wait. But only until you've talked to Andrea. And you must dispose of your wife as soon as possible."

Heather's hands flew to her mouth, a rush of tears welling up in her terror-stricken eyes.

"And have you any suggestions, since you didn't approve of my previous method?"

Heather forced her legs to carry her closer to the study door. She must know the scheme if she was to save herself.

"Pour a few drops of this into her tea at breakfast tomorrow. Then go for a buggy ride. It will take a while to work, but it isn't a pretty sight when it does. It's better that there are no witnesses."

Poison! They planned to poison her!

"It will appear that poor, sweet Heather's heart failed," he added callously.

"And am I to use it on Amber, too?" The baron asked calmly.

"However you rid us of Mistress Chandler is up to you," his partner replied, his tone unmerciful. "Just be quick about it. And I suggest you visit your future wife just as soon as you've become a widower."

Heather scrambled from her place before the door to hide in the shadows of the highboy when she heard the man laugh sadistically and walk across the room toward the exit. Pressed back against the wall, she listened as someone lifted the latch and both men stepped into the foyer.

"I must leave now and take care of some matters of my own," the other man announced. "Good day, Baron Von Buren."

Kelzer followed the man to the front door and stood in the archway watching his companion walk the short distance to the horse tethered in the front yard. He mounted easily, presented the baron with a mocking salute, and yanked his steed around to gallop off down the lane.

A dark, threatening scowl settled over Von Buren's face, his eyes trained on the figure of the one rider appearing to grow steadily smaller in the distance. Flipping the bottle the man had given him in the air, he caught it in one huge fist, as if he wished to strangle from it what life it might possess. Turning on his heels, he went back inside, slamming the door behind him. He would take care of Heather as planned, but he had different ideas for the hot-tempered beauty he held captive. And no man would tell him otherwise. Marching back into the study, he swung the door closed with a bang, turned the key in the lock, and crossed to the wine decanter sitting on the corner of his desk. Right now he needed a drink.

Heather's chin trembled violently and she feared her rattling teeth would give away her hiding place. She had heard her husband and his partner plot out her demise, but the frown that crimped her brow came from the confusion she experienced listening to them plan the murder of a second woman, Nicholas Chandler's wife. And how did Andrea Courtney fit into their scenario? Knowing of only one man who could solve the puzzle and save her life, Heather quietly moved to the doorway leading out of the back of the house, her gaze affixed to the entrance of the study. If she only had the strength to hitch up the carriage without anyone's seeing her . . .

*　　　*　　　*

Nicholas returned home to an empty house around noon after riding the distance from Raven Oaks nonstop. His body longed for rest, but his mind raced on, clouded with images of the woman who had declined his companionship, who held his love, his heart. Unconsciously he unsaddled the horse, led him to a stall, and tossed him a pitchfork full of hay. He lingered a moment, watching the animal munch contentedly, before he wandered slowly to the house. Once inside, he went directly to his study and poured himself a glass of sherry, swallowing the entire amount without stopping for a single breath. It burned going down, but gave his weary body a spark of life. He poured a second and rounded the desk to settle in the high-back chair. His elbows propped on the arms, he lifted his feet to rest on the edge of the dark piece of furniture, ankles crossed, his chin lowered on his chest. His deep brown eyes stared off into nothingness, his mouth twisted in an angry grimace. The ticking of the hall clock grew louder with each beat, hammering in his head until he thought he would explode. A deep-throated growl burst from him, and he bolted from the chair, whirling about to glare outside at the front lawn. Remembering his drink, he raised the glass to his lips, threw back his head, and finished it off quickly. Deciding on another, he turned back to his desk, straightening sharply when a vision flashed into his mind. How many nights had faded into sunlight since the first moment he had seen Amber Courtney standing haloed in the study doorway, the candle's soft glow bathing her face and golden hair in warmth? Recalling the time as though it was only yesterday, he felt the quickening of his pulse that her presence had aroused. Had he loved her even then? Fond memories softened his features, of the thing she had done to try and get the better of him. She had cut those beautiful yellow curls, discarded the rustling skirts for baggy breeches, the manner of a lady for a rough-necked boy, suffered his foul temper at every turn when he had thought of her as only a street urchin. He smiled gently, remembering how many times he had threatened to redden her backside and the sassy way she had dared him without saying a word.

I wonder what she thought of Heather Branford, he silently

grinned, the smile vanishing as he remembered that Amber had been in the house the night he took Heather to his room. "Damn," he growled, slamming down his glass. He stalked from the study and started up the long staircase, pausing to look back at the portrait of Victoria.

"Mother, how do I manage to always do the wrong thing?" he moaned, gradually easing down to sit on the third step. "I ran away when father needed me, lived recklessly, and only came home because he had died. Is this my punishment?" He sighed heavily, running his fingers through the dark, thick hair. "Was it any easier for him? Once he proclaimed his love, did you run to him with open arms? What must I do to have the same results?"

Glancing up at the smiling face once more, he dismissed his queries, knowing that nothing short of a miracle could will her lips to move in answer. He grabbed the railing with one hand, pulled himself up, and skipped down the steps, crossing the foyer on his way to the stable. Maybe a ride along the beach would help.

Heather wondered if the horse's hooves raced nearly as fast as her heart. Since harnessing the mare and leading her out the back of the barn, Heather knew every second counted. If the baron went to their bedchambers and found her gone, he would check her mother's room before sending out the alarm. He was a highly intelligent man and it wouldn't take him long to figure out why she needed a horse and buggy and where she was headed. She prayed God had given her enough of a head start to make it to Nicholas's before he caught up to her.

The road divided. To the left lay Williamsburg, but Heather reined the mare onto the second avenue, one not as well traveled as the first, a lane that led directly to Nicholas Chandler's house. *Dear God*, she cried inwardly, *let him be there*. She snapped the reins again, willing the horse to run faster if possible. Only one half-mile more.

Although her mind was filled with the urgency of saving her life, Heather's thoughts returned to the day she had heard of

Nicholas's wedding. Panic, a sense of hopelessness had washed over her, for she thought herself in love with him and had assumed he felt the same and only a matter of time would pass before he would ask her to marry him. Her estate near ruin, her mother dying, a union between them would brighten her future and allow her to live out her life in peace and serenity with the companionship of a man for whom she cared a great deal. She had cried the night away, certain that morning would bring nothing but doom. Then Baron Kelzer Von Buren had appeared on her doorstep. She remembered the unexplainable tension she had felt, an odd fear that this stranger, a man of whom she had heard, but had never met, had not come out of compassion but a selfish need, to satisfy himself. She had invited him in for tea more out of curiosity than politeness, merely to discover his reason for calling on her. He had remained courteous, his manner soft, even after Heather had broken out in laughter at his proposal of marriage to save her estate from bill collectors.

He had tried to reason with her, to point out her necessity to wed if only to give her mother the things money would buy to make her passing easier. But Heather had grown angry at his mention of her mother, offended that he would pry into her private affairs, and his mood suddenly changed. He had pulled several documents from his coat and waved them in her face, paid debts for which he had taken responsibility. *He* owned the estate, he owned *her*, and if she did not wish to spend the rest of her days in debtors' prison, her mother thrown out into the street, she would marry him without delay. Heather shivered at the memories, cursing herself for not having been stronger, for not having refused him. Now she was paying the price. And the only one who could save her lived in the house that suddenly appeared before her now.

She waited until the carriage had nearly reached the front steps before hauling back sharply on the reins. The wheels slid in the soft earth, jerking to a stop. She climbed awkwardly from the rig, calling out Nicholas's name repeatedly. Hurrying up the stairs, she crossed the veranda and fell against the front door, tears flowing freely down her face.

"Nicholas!" she screamed, pounding frantically on the wooden surface.

Several moments of silence passed. Certain he was in another part of the house too far away to hear her summons, she fumbled with the doorlatch and swung the door wide. Tears blurred her vision. She stumbled into the foyer, calling out to him again. When no answer came, she swallowed hard, biting her lip to calm her panic, and brushed the moisture from her eyes.

She must get hold of herself . . . think this out logically. The baron's partner had said they had kidnapped Nicholas's wife. How long ago? She shook her head, realizing she didn't know. It could have been days ago or just this morning. Maybe Nicholas wasn't aware of it yet. In that case, where would he be? And if he did know about the baron's devious plot, Nicholas would surely seek out the help of the magistrate. Either way, he would be in Williamsburg. A fistful of skirts clutched in both hands, Heather spun around and raced back outside, leaving the front door wide open. She scurried down the steps with a new surge of strength and determination, and quickly boarded her carriage. Shouting a command to the mare, she bolted off toward town, a provocation born of fear, but more so the will to see Von Buren's plan spoiled hastening her onward.

Heather's carriage blindly galloped past three others on the road into town, veering off the path to thunder through the grass at the side of the lane when the rigs failed to give her free passage. The inhabitants of each jerked back hard on the reins, fighting to keep their teams at bay, their eyes wide with surprise to discover the offender was a woman. Reins held tightly in her hands, she yelled repeatedly, and although the mare was lathered from its exercise, the animal raced heedlessly, as if mindful of the danger her mistress faced. Nose held high, nostrils flared, the mare stretched long and sure, cutting the distance in record speed. Yet when they neared the edge of town, the rig failed to slow, dashing through the streets toward the waterfront as if some demon held the reins, an opaque gathering of dust billowing skyward to mark their passing.

As the office of the Chandler Shipping Lines came into view, Heather yanked back on the reins, bringing the carriage to a stop just outside the entrance. Scrambling from the rig, she hurried across the wooden sidewalk and seized the doorlatch, a look of alarm distorting her face when she found the way locked. Frantic, she moved to the window of the room where Nicholas usually worked. Shading her eyes with one hand to her brow she pressed forward, peering inside. But the space held darkness, the void telling her that she would not find Nicholas here. Her chin began to tremble, tears welling in her eyes, and she stiffened bravely, steeling herself to remain composed. Looking left, then right, she decided that he might be working on the dock, or, at least, there might be someone who would know of his whereabouts. Squaring her shoulders, she took a deep breath and started down the long pier.

Only one ship was anchored there and at first glance it appeared to be deserted. But as she neared the huge vessel she heard the voices of several men on board, one of which unmistakably belonged to Sean Rafferty.

"Hello there . . ." she called, hoping not to sound too distraught, ". . . on the ship. Would one of you be Sean Rafferty?" She came to stand at the edge of the pier near the end of the gangplank. "It's Heather, Mr. Rafferty. I must speak with you."

A moment passed, one which seemed to stretch into infinity for Heather, before the tall figure of a man stepped into view. "Aye, lass, 'tis Sean Rafferty. What is it I can be doin' for ya?"

Heather had always liked Dru Chandler's cousin. She had sensed long ago that he did not share the feeling, but it mattered little to her. She had forgiven him and actually understood his hesitation, since she was sure he thought that she only sought out Nicholas's affection because of his inheritance. It was partly true, but she had hoped to prove to Mr. Rafferty that love had an equal part in her interest in Nicholas. She glanced down at her hands, knowing now that she would never be able to prove it to him. Her sigh trembled her delicate frame.

"I'm looking for Nicholas. It's important. Do you know

where I can find him?"

"He's on his honeymoon, lass."

Had she imagined it or did his voice hold a tone of tenderness? "I know of his marriage, Mr. Rafferty. Possibly you don't know of mine."

Sean's head tilted to one side. "Nay, lass. I had not heard. Who might the lucky lad be?"

Suddenly filled with grief, Heather wanted to run to him, throw herself in his arms, and tell him of all the horror she endured. For once in her life she wanted the comfort of a man holding her gently, stroking her hair, whispering words of sympathy, something she had never enjoyed. The only man who had ever cared that much for her had been her father, and he had died when Heather was a small child. But unsure of this man's reaction to such boldness, she pushed aside the desire and glanced nervously around.

"I only mentioned it, Mr. Rafferty, so you wouldn't think that I had come to cause Nicholas trouble. It's just the opposite. When do you expect them to return?"

When he failed to answer, she looked back up at him, discovering he had started down the gangplank toward her.

"Are ya all right, lass?" he frowned.

Suddenly remembering the bruises on her face, she backed away. She didn't wish to explain, nor take the time. "Yes, fine. Please, Mr. Rafferty,"—the words came pleadingly—"tell me where I can find him."

"Heather—"

"Please!" she half sobbed, half screamed.

"Raven Oaks, lass," Sean said quietly, a hand raised to calm her. He stopped some distance away from her, sensing her anxiety. "They went ta visit Mistress Remington."

Whirling around without a word of thanks, she raced off down the pier, unaware of the worried frown on Sean's face. He stayed unmoving, watching her hurriedly climb into her carriage, jerk the reins to pull the horse around, and bolt off down the road. Several minutes passed before the dust settled again and only Sean's memory could bear witness to her visit. He started back up the gangplank, then paused and looked at

333

the road again. He had seen the blackened, puffy eye, and had detected her reluctance to stand too close, as if she preferred avoiding a discussion on how she had acquired it. Heather was a gentle sort and he suspected the injuries were not accidental, yet he could think of no just cause for their existence. Could her wounds have something to do with her new husband? And who was he? Sean shook his head resignedly. They were questions he couldn't answer by himself. He would have to ask Mathew Calloway. He would surely know who Heather had married so hastily, and possibly why. And maybe then he would understand more clearly. Although he truly didn't care for the young woman, he felt a twinge of compassion for her. He glanced back up at the ship. Yes, Mathew would help.

The quiet peace of the countryside fulminated with the wild pace of a carriage racing down the twisted, bumpy road in frenzied flight. Birds scattered from their lofty perches, squawking disapproval, while rabbits hurried out from underfoot, the thundering hooves of the mare invading their domain. Hazel eyes, darkened with pain and worry, steadily watched the path the horse traveled, hands clamped tightly to the reins and unaware of the labored breaths the animal took. Heather vowed to put many miles between her and her husband, if it meant traveling all night.

If what she had overheard was true, that the baron and his partner had kidnapped Nicholas's wife and planned to kill her, she would do whatever was necessary to see the men brought to justice. A faint, almost evil smile twisted Heather's lips, the fear and panic disappearing from her eyes. She relaxed slightly with a thought, her narrow fingers raised to lightly touch her swollen lip. *You will pay for this Kelzer, my husband,* she sneered silently, *for when Nicholas learns of what you've done, he'll kill you, and I will be set free! You've paid my debts and I now share your name and wealth.*

The laughter of a madwoman pierced the late afternoon air as the carriage rattled onward.

What irony, good baron. You thought to trap me and have brought about your own downfall. When you're dead, I'll see you buried in a pauper's grave. And I shall spit upon it!

Her mind full of various plots to seek revenge, Heather failed to see the huge pothole in the road ahead. The mare stumbled, then lurched forward, dragging the carriage over the rut. The first wheel hit hard, the second cracked, then shattered, throwing the rig off balance. It bounced once, the axle digging into the soft earth. Out of control, the weight of the carriage pulled it and the horse to the edge of the road and a ravine filled with rocks. Heather screamed only once before the vehicle veered off the road, toppled to one side, and began a turbulent fall to the bottom, the mare unable to break free of the harness. The desperate cries of the animal ended abruptly when she mercifully crashed against a large boulder, her heart bursting from the impact.

Heather had clung frantically to the broken framework of the carriage until the first jolt tore her fingers from their hold. Thrown clear, she fell upon a soft bed of dried leaves. Stunned, too slow to react quickly, she looked up in time to witness the rig hurling toward her. She rolled to her knees, wildly clawing the earth to pull herself out of the way. She slipped, slid backward, and glanced around screaming as the broken remains of the buggy crashed down on top of her.

The silvery moonlight streamed earthward, falling softly on the quiet earth and singling out the deserted ruins of a house, its windows broken and its rooftop hanging at a slant. Lyle Gibbens reined the horses off the main road and headed toward the secluded spot. He still had several hours more to travel before reaching Raven Oaks, and though he sensed his arrival was most urgent, he knew the horses must rest and graze a while.

A rotted fence of logs surrounded the cottage, and Gibbens climbed from the rig to lead the mares closer. He unharnessed the pair and took them to the corral. Overgrown with weeds and grass, the small circle offered enough to fill their bellies for the night, and Gibbens turned them loose to sate their hunger, replacing the rail to guarantee they wouldn't wander off. Satisfied of their safety, he turned and entered the dilapidated house, brushing away the cobwebs that hung in his path. Filtered light from the windows illuminated the cold stone fireplace, and Gibbens immediately crossed to it, finding a small stack of firewood sitting off to one side. Within minutes he had a hearty blaze cracking in the hearth, and he settled down on the floor next to it, leaning back against the stone wall to savor the warmth of the fire and rest his weary body.

He hadn't expected to be seeking lodgings in such a place two nights ago. He was to have stayed in Jamestown, make certain Mistress Chandler was safe at home, and then return to Raven Oaks. He should have spent this night at the roadhouse, not sleeping on the floor in a rundown cottage. Recalling the reason for his change of plans, he fumbled in his pocket and withdrew the note he had found in Mistress Chandler's room. Tilting it toward the dancing light of the fire, he read it again, a suspicious frown furrowing his brow. Something was wrong. He could sense it, and as soon as he had rested a while, he would take this note and his story to Mistress Remington.

An eerie stillness gripped the wooded area. No deer moved about, no fox in the hollow searching for food. Not even the usual night sounds cheered the gloom as even crickets quieted their song. Moonlight bathed the road but failed to reveal the place where Heather Von Buren lay injured and dying. Nearly seven hours had passed since her fateful flight down the road, and with the coming of darkness she had lost all hope of anyone's finding her.

Blood trickled from her mouth and nose, her body shivering from the cold. A tear escaped the rim of her lashes and disappeared into the matted hair near her cheek. Her breathing became more difficult with each passing hour, the pain increased, and she soon realized one or several ribs were broken and pressed against her lungs. Her right arm lay grotesquely twisted, and she suddenly prayed death would take her and end her misery.

Her throat dry and parched, Heather spoke in a whisper,

though she knew no one would hear. "If only I could have warned you, Nicholas. I could have told you . . . where to look." Her tears flowed more rapidly. "You could have helped us . . . both. And . . . I could have told you . . . just one more time, so you would believe . . . I love you, Nicholas."

A sharp pain shook her entire body. She gasped for air. Then, as if her prayers had been heard, Heather looked up at the heavens, her gaze locked in an unseeing stare.

Chapter Fifteen

Early morning sunlight streamed in the windows of the dining room and fell warmly across the table. Scowling, Kelzer Von Buren poured his third cup of tea and added two teaspoons of sugar before staring off in quiet frustration once more. He had discovered his wife's disappearance around midnight when he had gone to bed and had summoned two of his men to search for her. He had little doubt that they wouldn't find her, but the worry that knotted his stomach came from a different reason. His superior had warned him not to abuse the woman as he had, for given the opportunity he felt certain she would flee the baron's house and seek help, thus ruining their chances for success in a well-thought-out plan. But had Heather only run away because she sought freedom from his cruelty, or had she learned the secrets Kelzer had kept hidden all these years? He took a sip of tea, wincing when it burned his tongue. How could she have acquired the information needed to link him with the gunrunners supplying the Shawnee? Had she discovered the title he was known by? Von Buren frowned. *Scalp Hunter.* The words burned in his memory, a smile creeping over his face. He had loved the danger, the mystery involved in buying guns from England, shipping them to America in crates marked "tea," and then selling them to the Indians. It gave him a sense of power, superiority. He enjoyed killing for money, just as he had done when the colonies fought for independence and England had hired him to fight their war. Now they were fighting again, and although he lived in America he had no loyalty to her, knowing he could return to his homeland if he was ever discovered.

Von Buren slammed the fragile teacup onto its saucer, nearly breaking it, and stood, marching to the window of the room to glare outside. He had been so careful to hide his moves, his treason against the States. He had even managed to cover up the murder of his first wife. It had been so easy. He was gaining wealth, property. But the little bitch had left a diary! She had recorded everything.

"And now *he* has it," Von Buren growled, recalling the first time he had been made aware of the diary's existence. The man who now held rein on him had suddenly appeared on his doorstep, only one week after Baroness Von Buren's funeral, threatening to turn him over to the authorities if the baron didn't agree to help in his fight to win the Cromwell estate. The bastard son of Nathaniel Cromwell, the man had no claim and had devised another method. But he needed the assistance of someone like Baron Kelzer Von Buren. Fearing the loss of everything for which he had worked so hard, Von Buren had agreed, but only until this venture was accomplished. Then he would demand the diary as payment for his aid. Kelzer grinned viciously. "Then you shall die, my friend, for ever thinking you could blackmail me."

A sudden clamor of racing hooves pulled Von Buren's attention to the front lawn. He glowered when he saw his men returning alone. They had failed and he would see them whipped for it. Turning sharply on his heels, he stormed from the room, across the foyer, and out onto the veranda before the pair had dismounted.

"Well?" he demanded loudly, arms folded over his mammoth chest, his dark eyes glowly hotly.

"We found her, sir," the first of the two men answered, climbing down. He tied the horse's reins to a post and came to stand before the baron. "I'm afraid she's dead."

"Dead?" Von Buren echoed, straightening abruptly.

"Yes, sir. From the looks of things she was heading north out of Williamsburg when her carriage hit a rut and overturned. She was crushed beneath it."

Von Buren turned to hide his satisfied grin. "What did you do with the body?" he asked quietly.

"We weren't the first to find her, sir. Some people on their way to church this morning arrived ahead of us. They had already contacted the authorities in Williamsburg and were waiting for someone to come with a wagon. We thought it better if we got back here right away to tell you." The man glanced up at his companion, then studied the ground at his feet. "We're sorry, Baron Von Buren."

Kelzer waved a hand dismissingly. "Yes, yes. I understand. You did the right thing." He moved toward the door. "Now if you'll excuse me, I'd like to be alone for a while." He hurried inside, barely hearing the men thank him, and started for the study, a wide grin wrinkling his face. "It is I who should be thanking you, my dear, dead wife. You've saved me a lot of inconvenience. And within the hour, I plan to strike a deal with the most beautiful, lively wench I've ever known." Slapping his hands together, he rubbed the palms vigorously, feeling triumph near.

Amber sat huddled in the shadows of the root cellar near the closed doors, the piece of wood she had managed to break off the apple bin clenched in her hands. An hour ago the men who held her captive had brought her a crust of bread, a cold piece of meat she discovered to be squirrel left over from their dinner the night before, and a cup of lukewarm tea. It wasn't much of a breakfast, but it had served to quiet the rumblings of her stomach and sharpen her desire to free herself. Her initial fear of the men had faded with the sunlight and thoughts of spending another night in this damp, musty cellar sparked her anger. She would use this piece of wood to club the first man who dared enter and with luck he would come alone, allowing her the advantage to surprise the other. With both men knocked unconscious, their hands and feet bound, she would have more time to find safety. But should she try to reach

Nicholas or return to Jamestown? Which direction would the men think she had taken? Or would they split up? Maybe she should cut across country and head for Williamsburg. A devilish smile crimped one corner of her mouth. What had their visitor said? He had warned them that if she escaped they would die. That would certainly make it easier, with only one man following her. The odds of success would be in her favor. She shifted positions when the muscles in her left leg began to ache.

Deep inside the earthen prison, her pale blue eyes widened at the sound of hurried hoofbeats drawing nearer, and Amber moved to peer outside through the crack in the doors, hoping to catch a glimpse of the newcomer. She prayed he had come to rescue her, but knew in her heart that his presence only meant a delay in her plans. The horse and rider raced by, leaving only a billowing of gray particles to mark their arrival, and Amber returned to her hiding place to wait, no more cognizant of the visitor's identity than a moment before. Testing the weight of the club in her hand, Amber relaxed slightly, hoping the stranger would not stay long. She was tired of sharing this space with spiders and mice.

A few minutes of silence passed, and Amber leaned back against the wall, her thoughts wandering to Nicholas again. Had he remained at Raven Oaks or elected to go home? By her calculations, Gibbens probably hadn't returned to the plantation yet, although it wouldn't be long before he had, and if Nicholas had decided to wait there for her, it would save a lot of time. Gibbens wouldn't have to chase after him. She closed her eyes in supplication for good fortune, since something deep inside her forewarned her of the failure of her own scheme.

The snapping of a twig near the cellar doors startled Amber. She scrambled up, bracing herself for her attack when she heard the wooden bar being slid from its place. *Dear God, let him be alone,* she moaned silently, just as the double doors were swung wide.

"Come on out, Mistress Chandler," Allison ordered gruffly. "Somebody's here ta see ya." He tilted his head to one side when silence seemed to be his only answer and guardedly studied the area where sunlight reigned. "You hear me? Don't

342

make me come down there. I guarantee ya won't like it."

Worry crimped his brow. He glanced nervously toward the cabin, then surveyed the woods surrounding the clearing. There was no possible way the chit could have gotten out of the cellar. So why had perspiration started to bead across his upper lip? She was playing games. He was sure of it. His face twisting into an angry frown, he started down the stairs, his instinct failing to guide him carefully. As his foot left the last tread, a movement to his right pulled his eyes to it in time to see the thick wooden timber descend upon him. The blow caught him in the bridge of his nose and a shower of tiny lights exploded in his vision. But before the pain had time to register, blackness overcame him and he crumpled to the ground.

Amber stared down at the unconscious man, her body trembling, and she felt a wave of nausea wash over her. She had never hit a human being so viciously before, and, although she knew he would not hesitate to kill her, she couldn't shake the feeling of guilt, until she remembered the two men who waited inside the cabin for their partner's return.

Her heart pounding wildly, Amber started up the stairs, dismissing her earlier plan to surprise the man in the cabin. Instead she would steal the visitor's horse and turn the other stallions loose, leaving the men afoot while she raced for Jamestown. But she must hurry. Allison would be missed soon, and someone was sure to come looking for him.

Pausing once she reached the top of the stairs, she studied the grounds around her. The stranger's horse had been tied to the porch rail about ten yards away, and she suddenly couldn't decide whether to turn the others free first then chance running to the third or secure her own means of escape before attempting to scatter theirs. It meant approaching the house when she wasn't quite ready to flee and since she was not a practiced horsewoman, she knew they would easily catch her if they had horses to ride. But it was a better chance than none at all, and she bravely started out toward the cabin.

Moving slowly, she waved a hand to attract the stallion's eyes, hoping it would be enough to keep him from being startled and whinnying in alarm. He watched complacently, his long tail swishing away a pesty fly before he lowered his head to scratch his nose against his foreleg. She moved closer, hearing the muted voices of the men inside the cabin, the beating of her heart echoing in her ears. Near enough to touch the animal, she reached out to gently pat his rump and run her hand along the steed's side and down his shoulder to soothe him as she leaned forward to pull the reins from the rail. Within a few moments, she would swing herself up to straddle him and race for her very life . . . just as soon as she saw to the other horses.

Leading the stallion away from the cabin, Amber held her breath, for she feared the noise of the horse's hooves crushing the rock beneath him would carry the warning to the unsuspecting men. She glanced over her shoulder at the door to ease her concern and reached the rough corral in a few hurried strides. Flipping the horse's reins around the top of a post, she quickly moved to the gate and slid the first rail from its resting place. The second proved more difficult, but after a brief struggle it too fell to the ground, and she hastily scooped up a handful of rocks to hurl at the horses prancing nervously inside. They reared, snorted frantically, then dashed off through the opening in the fence.

Victory within her reach, Amber spun around, yanked the reins loose, and lifted her skirts to clear her step to the stirrup. With a handful of the horse's mane in one hand, the edge of the saddle in the other, she awkwardly pulled herself up, swinging one leg over the animal's rump as they bolted off away from the cabin.

Tears sprang to her eyes, tears of joy, relief. She was free, and before the sun's disappearance this day she would be in Nicholas's arms once more. But before she had ridden a hundred feet the thunderous volley of pistol fire exploded behind her and she instantly felt the horse beneath her stumble, then plunge headlong to the ground, throwing her clear. She hit the hard earth and rolled several times. Dazed, she lay unmoving for a moment, then pushed herself up on her elbows and shook her head, unable to comprehend what had happened until she spied the magnificent stallion lying still a few feet from her. Bright red blood oozed from the wound in his side, and Amber stifled a cry of anguish with the back of her hand to her mouth. How could anyone be so heartless as to shoot a defenseless animal? She glanced up at the cabin and instantly knew the answer. Standing on the porch, his huge frame seeming to overpower the tiny house, Baron Kelzer Von Buren glared back at her, tapping the muzzle of his gun in the palm of his hand.

"You slimy vermin," Amber hissed, hardly aware of the Frenchman who took her elbow and yanked her to her feet. "I should have known you were behind this."

"Bring her inside, Duehr," Von Buren ordered, unaffected by her words. "Then see what she's done with Allison and find those horses."

"*Oui, monsieur,*" Duehr replied quickly, pulling Amber along.

"You'll never get away with this," Amber continued hotly. "Nicholas will hunt you down. You'll die for kidnapping his wife." She stumbled when Duehr shoved her up the steps. She jerked free of him and bravely stood before the baron. "What have you done with Andrea?"

A slow, menacing smile crossed Von Buren's face. "Nothing . . . yet, Mistress Chandler. But then that's up to you to see it remains that way." He bowed slightly and held out a hand, indicating the cabin door. "Shall we discuss it inside where it will be more private?"

Wanting more to spit in his face than talk one moment with him, Amber realized the consequences and begrudgingly entered the cabin while Von Buren waved Duehr on to fulfill his commands. She crossed to the far side of the room and turned back to face him, watching as he closed the door and stuck the pistol in the waistband of his breeches. He moved to the table in the center of the small room and sat down in one of the chairs, holding out a hand.

"Won't you make yourself more comfortable?"

Amber glared back at him. "I'd prefer not being any closer to you than I have to, Baron Von Buren," she sneered, bringing an amused chuckle from the man.

"I think you may change your mind after I've explained your choices," he grinned, pulling a tin filled with cheroots from his pocket. He popped the lid open, withdrew one long, thin cigar and stuck it in his mouth without bothering to light it. "I've been told to kill you."

Amber experienced a chill through every fiber of her being. Her heart pounded, but she willed herself to stand still as if his declaration had no effect on her at all. "Then why haven't you?"

He stuffed the box into his coat pocket again and took the cheroot from his mouth to roll between his fingers and thumb. "Because it would be such a waste. And I don't think you're ready to die just yet, are you? He smiled when she simply glowered at him. "So I've a better idea. In return for your life, you shall become my mistress. I can—" A loud, piercing laughter cut him short, and his gaiety turned to anger. "I see no humor, Mistress Chandler," he raged, slamming a huge fist on the table.

"Oh, don't you?" she asked mockingly. "I was forced to marry Nicholas because I wouldn't allow you to have my sister. Do you think I feel any differently about myself? If I'm allowed a choice, Baron Von Buren, I will take death without hesitation, for having you touch me is far worse than that!"

Kelzer bolted to his feet, knocking the chair from under him. He doubled up his fists and leaned forward on his knuckles against the table. "You're right on one point, Mistress Chandler, you will have no choice," he grated out. "And what I have in mind for you will be far more evil an existence than you can imagine, for not only will you suffer, but your husband and sister will, as well." Sliding his hands under the edge of the table, Von Buren hurled the piece of furniture aside and rushed toward her, cruelly grabbing a fistful of her hair when she started to run past him. One wrist caught in his steely hold, he twisted her arm in back of her, causing her to cry out in pain. "This is only the beginning, my proud whore," he growled, nearly lifting her from her feet as he shoved her toward the door.

"No, wait!" she screamed, clawing at the fingers that entrapped her hair. "What are you going to do to Nicholas and Andrea?"

Once they neared the door, he lifted a booted foot and kicked it open, knocking the hinges from the frame to send the wooden slab crashing to the floor of the porch. Without answering, he dragged her across it, down the steps, and toward the root cellar, calling out to his men.

"Please, Baron, don't hurt Nicholas and my sister," she pleaded, tears burning in her eyes.

"I won't even have to touch them," he sneered, shoving her into the waiting arms of his henchmen. "Tie her up and leave her that way. I don't want her getting loose. Do you understand? I'll slit your throats if you're this careless again!"

He stepped back to supervise their efforts, his nostrils flaring with each angry breath he took and motioned for them to put her in the cellar once she had been securely bound. Both men clamping onto her arms, they escorted her down the rotted wooden steps and threw her to the ground. Unable to scramble to her feet, Amber twisted around on her knees to look back up at Von Buren while the men hurried outside once more to stand on either side of him. He seemed to dwarf even the largest of the duo.

"Please, Von Buren, promise you won't hurt them," she begged.

The evil smile returned to his lips. "Promise? You're hardly in a position to ask anything of me, little Amber. But I see no reason why I can't tell you what I've planned." He crossed his arms over his chest and glared down his nose at her. "I have an acquaintance in Boston who deals in slavery. With all the uproar concerning such practices, it's grown increasingly difficult and expensive to buy slaves from Africa. But you, my dear, will lower the cost. I plan to sell you to him, and he, in turn, will take you to Casablanca, to the marketplace. The price you bring should buy many slaves. There's always a sheik or two roaming about looking for a new wife to add to his harem. Who knows? Maybe you'll wind up in a sultan's tent. But the best part is that your husband and sister won't have any idea where you've gone. You'll spend your last days in a country halfway around the world, with no hope of ever returning home." He nodded at his men and they quickly closed the doors over the square shaft of light, blocking out the sun and filling Amber with despair.

* * *

347

"Grandmama!" Kate shouted, bursting into the room, her skirts raised to hasten her step. "Come quickly."

Alanna Remington glanced up in alarm, absently laying aside her knitting. "Calm down, child, and tell me what all the excitement is about."

"It's Gibbens," her granddaughter answered breathlessly.

"Gibbens?" Alanna repeated, coming to her feet. "So soon? I didn't think he'd return for another day or two. Is something wrong?"

"I don't know. He wouldn't tell me." Kate rushed to her grandmother's side and took the woman's elbow to urge her along. "He wants to talk to you."

"Where is he?"

"In the parlor. Please hurry, Grandmama. I'm worried about Amber."

"All right, all right," Alanna soothed her, patting Kate's hand as they rushed from the bedchambers. Neither spoke as they quickly descended the stairs and entered the first room off the foyer.

Alanna wondered at the sudden, unexpected presence of her coachman. Gibbens had worked for her for over twenty years and never had he once burdened the mistress of Raven Oaks with problems that were unimportant. Something troubled him now, and Alanna feared he would be right again. Only this time it concerned a member of her family, someone she had grown to love in only a few short days, the wife of her grandson.

"Gibbens, did you wish to see me?" Alanna asked, pulling the man's attention away from something outside the window, where he stood looking out. He promptly came to stand before her.

"Yes, madam. It's probably nothing but I wanted you to decide."

"Decide what?" she pressed, a strange disquiet seeping into her consciousness.

"Maybe you should sit down while I explain," he offered, guiding her to the sofa. He waited until she seemed comfortable, then continued. "Mistress Chandler and I stopped at the inn on the road to Jamestown just as you instructed we do. She had dinner in the commons, then retired. I assumed she wanted to get an early start."

"Assumed . . . Gibbens, you make it sound as if something terrible has happened," Kate broke in, her eyes suddenly glistening with unshed tears.

"Katherine, come sit down and give him a chance to finish," Alanna said softly, forcing a smile as she extended a hand toward the vacant seat next to her. She waited until the young woman had done as she suggested and looked back at the man standing before them. "Go on, Gibbens."

"Yes, madam." He took a deep breath. "I arose early the next morning . . . yesterday . . . and had the horses hitched up to the carriage. I then went back inside the inn to wait. After two hours, I asked the innkeeper to bring a key and go with me to Mistress Chandler's room. I can't explain why, but I had a feeling something wasn't quite right. When she didn't answer my knock, the innkeeper let us in."

"And what did you find?" Alanna asked quietly, hoping to sound at ease for Kate's sake.

"Nothing, madam. She was gone."

"Gone?" Kate exploded. "Where would she have gone?"

He shrugged. "Maybe this will help," he added, pulling the letter he had found from his pocket. "It was on the desk in her room." He handed the paper to Alanna and the two women read it carefully.

"Don't try to find me . . ." Alanna recited quietly, a frown deepening the wrinkle in her brow. "I don't understand."

"What, Grandmother? What don't you understand?" Kate urged. "Do you know something?"

Rising slowly, Alanna walked to the window of the room and stared outside, the letter clenched in her thin hand. "Only what Amber and I discussed before she left. I was under the impression she wanted to go to her sister. She specifically told me that talking with Andrea would help. And from whom is she running away? I promised her, gave my word Nicholas wouldn't follow her." She turned back to Gibbens. "Did she say anything to you? Anything out of the ordinary?"

"No, madam. And that's why I find her leaving a little mysterious."

"Oh?" Alanna replied, one brow lifted questioningly.

"Well, not that she would have hinted at it to me. After all, I'm only a coachman . . . hardly her closest friend . . . but it's the manner in which she left that raised my curiosity and the need to talk with you."

"Please . . . continue."

"First of all, the room was locked. I found her key on the table, which means she had to have left out the balcony. There are no steps, so she would have had to climb down the trellis. If she didn't wish to be seen, she could have simply waited until everyone in the inn was asleep.

"Then there is the fact that she left all of her things behind. Her bags hadn't been unpacked and her cloak still lay on the sofa." He sighed, frowning. "She must have realized the danger she'd be in traveling without escort and on foot."

"On foot?" Alanna parroted.

"Yes, madam. When I went for the carriage I asked the stableboy if anyone had hired a rig. When he said no, I asked if any of his horses were missing." Gibbens shook his head. "It's not my place to say, madam, but I think it should be looked into."

"Grandmama, what does it mean?" Kate asked worriedly.

Alanna glanced at the paper again, then folded it carefully and held it out to Gibbens. "It means I have to ask my faithful servant to take this to Nicholas right away. He should decide. I want you to tell him everything, just as you've told me."

"Yes madam," Gibbens nodded, tucking the letter in his pocket again.

"He's returned to his home in Williamsburg. You'll find him there or at the shipping lines. Take the fastest horse we have and don't waste any time. My instincts tell me that Mistress Chandler is in danger. God speed, Gibbens."

"Thank you, madam," Gibbens bowed slightly, turned on his heel and quickly exited the room.

"Grandmama," Kate whispered, her chin trembling. "What kind of danger?"

Alanna had continued to stare at the empty doorway after Gibbens had gone, too encased in her own thoughts to remember her granddaughter's presence until the tiny voice penetrated her concern. She blinked and glanced over at the young woman, who had risen from the sofa. A wave of beautiful memories flooded over her for an instant as she observed the long black hair and steel-blue eyes staring back at her. A mixture of both of her parents' traits, Kate's worried frown reminded Alanna of the day Dru Chandler stood in that same spot looking just as lost, as pained. It had been the day he had buried his wife, her daughter. She had gone to him then as she now went to Katherine, and had held him in her arms, whispering words of comfort when her own heart felt as if it would break.

"Don't worry, Katherine," she forced herself to say, though she had the same fears. "Nicholas will find her."

They stayed enveloped in each other's embrace for a long while.

Andrea Courtney stood in the doorway of her cottage watching Seth's rented buggy rattle off down the lane, a troubled look on her beautiful face. His visit had been so unexpected and welcome, filling her with happiness once she opened the door and found him standing there. They had spent the better part of the morning talking about unimportant things; the weather, Jacobson's new baby, his job at the general store, until their conversation drifted to her sister's somewhat unusual marriage. He had asked if she had talked with Amber since that day Nicholas Chandler had pulled her from the cottage, or heard any rumors about their stormy relationship. She quickly assured him that she hadn't, sensing something worried the young man and it concerned her sister. Only when she insisted, demanded he tell her what was wrong, did Seth move from the chair next to her to settle beside her on the straight-backed Deacon's bench.

"I've heard rumors," he stated softly. "Mind you, they're only rumors. But some of the people in town say Amber has left her husband."

"You mean run away?" Andrea asked.

"Yes."

She looked down at her hands folded in her lap. "It doesn't

surprise me. He forced her into marrying him, and she did it only to spare me. I suspected she would leave him sooner or later. How long ago did you hear this?"

"Two days."

"Then I imagine she'll be home soon." She shook her head, sighing. "Poor Amber. Life has been so cruel for her. I wonder if she'll ever find happiness."

"Like you?" he asked, with a onesided smile that made her blush.

"I'm content, Seth. I don't have a score to settle, like Amber."

He leaned over and took her hands, drawing her gaze to his. "Some day I'll be able to offer you happiness, Andrea. When I have enough money to buy you the things you deserve, we'll be married. I promise."

"Oh, Seth," she argued, "don't you know that money isn't important to me?"

"It is to me."

Andrea tilted her head to one side, studying him as though it was the first time they had met. In her eyes he was the most handsome, kind man she had ever known, and the time they spent, no, *wasted*, being apart tore at her. Didn't he realize that simply sharing their lives was all she truly wanted? Not the silks and jewels, mansion or house full of servants that only wealth would bring? If she had all that and failed to hold his love, it would all be meaningless.

"Being your wife and bearing your children are all I want, Seth," she said tenderly.

"Then you're a fool," he shouted, jumping to his feet. "Our children deserve more than this." His outstretched hands indicated the humble dwelling Andrea called home.

"Seth—" she pleaded, totally caught off balance by his outburst.

"No! I mean it. I will not raise my family under conditions like this." He stormed the door, yanked it open, and looked back. "If you can't wait until I've fulfilled my dream, then marry someone else!" He had given her no chance to reply, but stomped off to the buggy and angrily climbed in. Hurling an oath at the horse, he jerked the rig forward and set off down the lane, leaving Andrea to stare after him in total confusion.

"Oh, Seth," she whispered, her head resting against the door frame, "Won't you ever understand that I love *you* and not what you can offer?" A tear spilled over her lower lashes and fell to her cheek. She brushed it away and went back inside the cottage, slowly closing the door behind her. They had never argued before, and she wondered why they had now. In fact, they had never discussed marriage so openly until today. She went into the kitchen to heat wash water for the breakfast dishes and have a second cup of tea while she waited, hoping Amber would come home soon. Although they seldom agreed on major issues, her sister always managed to make Andrea feel better simply by showing both sides. Maybe she could help her understand Seth.

The blaze in the hearth warmed the room. Mixed with the steady rays of sunshine coming through the window, it brought perspiration to Andrea's face and neck. She unfastened the top button of her dress, then lifted the heavy mass of curls from her shoulders, deciding to tie back her hair with a ribbon. Postponing her chores for a moment, she left the kitchen for the bedroom, nearly having reached it when she heard a carriage pull up outside. A smile brightened her eyes, thinking Seth had returned to apologize for his flare of temper, and she hurried to the door before he had a chance to knock. Lifting the latch, she pulled the door open, her smile vanishing, her heart seeming to stop when she found Baron Kelzer Von Buren descending from his landau.

"Good afternoon, Andrea," he grinned sardonically, with a tug to his waistcoat.

"W-what are you doing here? What do you want?" Andrea forced the words to come, each as trembling, as fearful as the emotions that coursed through her body. She stood transfixed, watching the man who had played such a sinister part in the lives of her family come nearer.

"I think we have a matter to discuss," he said calmly, taking her elbow to escort her into the cottage.

Too numb, too horrified to object, she allowed him to direct her to the chair near the fireplace. Aware of how her legs trembled, she willingly sat down, hoping for a moment to calm herself. Whatever the baron wanted, she knew she would have no one on whom to rely for help. She must do it alone, and, for once in her life, she had to be strong.

"What do you want?" she bravely asked again. He had moved no further than the mantel, resting one elbow against it, the fingers of both hands interlaced and a knee bent as his booted foot found the stone slab of the hearth. His huge size seemed to overpower the tiny room, and she suddenly imagined herself as the small, fearful rabbit cowering before the hungry, relentless mountain lion. She clenched her hands, hoping to still their quaking.

"I want what I've always wanted. You as the Baroness Von Buren," he answered prosaically.

She stiffened. "I have heard you are already married. I know you have few morals, but that, sir, is against the laws of the church."

He raised one brow, a sinister smile curling one corner of his mouth. "As of this morning, I'm a widower," he responded coolly, pausing to nod his head at Andrea's surprised look, then continued, "and since I have always preferred to have you as my wife, I have come to discuss the details of the ceremony."

Andrea was surprised by her own laughter. "You assume a great deal, baron. What makes you think I would ever marry you? You have no hold over me anymore, and it would be the only way you would have my consent."

"Oh, but I do, and after I've explained I'm sure you'll not hesitate in becoming my wife."

She opened her mouth to insist that the possibility had not even the slightest chance, only to be cut off with a wave of his hand.

"Don't bother arguing. Just listen." He dropped his pose and crossed to the Deacon's bench she had shared with Seth only minutes before. He sat down in the center and spread out each arm along its back, his thick, muscular legs stretched out before him, ankles crossed. "When your foolish sister married Nicholas Chandler, she thought to sacrifice herself for you. Now you may return the favor."

A worried frown creased the smooth flesh of Andrea's brow,

her dark blue eyes fearful. "What do you mean?"

"I mean simply that if you wish to see your sister live out a full life, you will agree to our marriage before the sun sets this day." He laughed viciously at the confused expression marring the young woman's lovely features. "You see, my dear, two of my men are holding your sister at my orders and will not hesitate to kill her if I so command it."

"But Seth said—" The words caught in her throat. What had he said? He had admitted they were only rumors, but that he had heard Amber had left Nicholas. Maybe Von Buren had heard the rumors too, and only wished to use the information to scare her. "I don't believe you," she whispered.

He cocked his head to one side, unaffected by her refusal. "Are you willing to take that chance?"

Perspiration beaded across her brow, and she slowly came to her feet, her knees weak. "I—I need proof."

Von Buren sat up, slapping his hands against his thighs to push himself to his feet. "I'm a patient man, and the request is a small one. What kind of proof?"

Andrea touched shaky fingertips to her temple, her mind whirling with possibilities, something the baron had no way of knowing unless Amber told him. Her hand slid down the side of her face to her mouth and she chewed nervously on the knuckle of her forefinger as she aimlessly paced the room. Then an idea struck her. "Ask her how our father got the scar he carried on his cheek."

If the question offered difficulty for Von Buren to answer, Andrea saw no trace of it in his eyes. He merely bowed and moved toward the door, stopping to look back at her when he reached it. "I'll return within a few hours with the proof you request and a minister. Don't try to seek anyone's help, Fräulein Courtney. Your sister is well hidden, and I would not hesitate to kill her if I think someone has followed me because of you." His dark brown eyes glowed a demonic red, the black spirit of his evil electrified in his glare as though Satan himself reached out his arms to envelop her. Then, as if by the powers of darkness, before her mind could register it, he vanished from the room.

Chapter Sixteen

A trio of lonely mornings had dawned since his wife had left him, a bright, cold reminder of how the day would continue. Nicholas's ride along the windswept shores had done little to cheer him or chase away the pain that twisted his insides and left him empty, hurting. No solutions had come to mind, no simple path to take to win her love. He felt defeated, a failure, and wondered if fate had willed his life to be this way for eternity.

With the third day's coming he vowed to fill his thoughts with other things, to busy himself and occupy his mind with work, to forbid a sorrowful moment to invade his sanity. He rose, dressed hurriedly, and left the house to fetch his horse from the stable before Anna had a chance to question his wife's absence.

He arrived at the warehouse without anyone's seeing him and locked the door behind him. His unexpected presence would draw questions, ones he truly wished to avoid. He settled himself behind the desk in his office, withdrew a stack of papers from the drawer, and lost himself in the endless rows of numbers.

The afternoon passed quickly, and only the stiffened muscles in his back and neck forced Nicholas to lay aside his quill and stretch, his gaze falling on the clock on the opposite wall. Almost time for the evening meal. He frowned when his thoughts wandered to the cottage outside Jamestown. Would Amber and her sister be preparing their dinner? Or might she be packing . . . no, he mustn't think that, he mustn't hope. She wasn't coming back. Why should she? What had he ever done to make her want to? Angry with himself for allowing his will to weaken, he carelessly grabbed the papers from his desk and shoved them back in the drawer, slamming it shut with such force that the lamp sitting on top rattled and threatened to topple over. His curiosity piqued, he straightened, observing the sway of the glass piece until it settled once more, wondering if the same thing had happened to his father. If the base had shattered and spilled oil over the desk and onto the floor, it was very possible that it had ignited instantly and quickly set the wood structure ablaze. But even so, he refused to believe his father wouldn't at least have felt the heat of the flames, if not heard the noise of breaking glass, surely enough to awaken him from the sleep the authorities claimed he had been in.

What good was it to keep going over the accident in his mind? It had happened two years ago, and if they hadn't found proof to the contrary by now they never would. He stood up, lifted his jacket from the back of his chair and headed for the door. He hated the thought of going home to an empty house, but unless he wanted to be bombarded with questions and raised eyebrows from the patrons of the Chesterfield House, he knew he would have to dine alone . . . at home.

He stepped out onto the sidewalk and turned to lock the door behind him, startled when someone called his name. He glanced up to find Sean Rafferty walking toward him.

"What are ya doin' here, lad?" Sean asked, noticing the skittish manner in which Nicholas centered his attention on the key in his hand, then stuffed it in a pocket and looked around without meeting Sean's eyes. "When did ya get back?"

"Ah . . . yesterday." He smoothed a wrinkle from his jacket.

"The honeymoon over so soon that ya came ta spend time here?" The question seemed playful enough but hinted at a truer meaning.

"Yeah, something like that," Nicholas replied softly. "Look,

358

I've got to get home now. I'll see you tomorrow." He started past his friend, his eyes lifted abruptly when Sean stepped in the way.

"I needn't be tellin' ya how well I know ya, lad. Ya not be havin' ta say a word and I can sense ya are unhappy. Would ya care ta be talkin' about it?"

Nicholas let out a long, troubled sigh, his shoulders slumping. "I've done nothing but talk about it for three days and still haven't come up with an answer."

"And who might ya have been talkin' with?"

"Me. Who else knows me better?"

Sean grinned. "At the risk of soundin' a wee bit stuck on meself, I'd have ta say one other. And ya be lookin' at him."

Nicholas smiled halfheartedly. "Maybe. But this time I doubt even you can help. Talking me into something isn't the problem. It's Amber."

"Oh? And what might ya be wantin' ta talk her inta doin', lad?"

Nicholas looked up at him. "Into loving me."

Sean straightened. "Oh. I guess ya be right. No one can be talkin' her inta that if she doesn't feel it in her heart." He saw the pained expression on his companion's face and quickly put an arm around Nicholas's shoulders. "I've a fine bottle of Irish whiskey in me cabin. How about sharin' a little with an old friend. I won't keep ya long enough ta make the lass worry about your whereabouts." He gently set them off in the direction of the ship, his big hand moving to the nape of Nicholas's neck, a gesture he had always displayed when he sought to comfort the young man.

"I'm sure it wouldn't bother her if I didn't come home at all."

"Now, lad, ya can't be meanin' that. Of course, she'd worry."

"Not if she doesn't know."

Sean stopped, confusion twisting his face. "And how wouldn't she be knowin'? Are ya meanin' ta tell me ya don't share the same bed?"

"Or house, at the moment," Nicholas added.

Sean moved to stand in front of him. "House? Ya mean the

359

lass didn't come home with ya?"

Nicholas smiled lopsidedly. "That's right. In fact, she packed up her things and left Thursday night."

"Ta go where? Why?"

Nicholas started off down the dock in a casual stride. "She decided to go home to her sister. She told my grandmother that she needed time to think, to be alone for a while."

"Ta think about what?"

Nicholas shrugged. "Whether or not she'll agree to live with me, as husband and wife."

"But there's no thinkin' ta do. She is your wife," Sean argued fervently. "Did ya try ta stop her?"

They reached the end of the pier and Nicholas elected to sit on a crate near the gangplank rather than board the ship. Sean stopped beside him.

"She slipped away before I found out. And my grandmother made a lot of sense."

Sean chuckled, bending down to pick up a piece of twine to curl around his finger. "She usually does. If it hadn't been for her, I don't know how your father would have managed after Victoria died."

"She told me to be patient, that she was certain Amber would come back. She said Amber was scared, mixed up about her feelings toward me, my way of life." He laughed. "And she reminded me that the way I proposed to Amber was a little unusual. It wasn't as if she really wanted to marry me. Besides, I want Amber to live with me only if she wants to. I'd never be happy knowing I forced her into it."

"Then it be soundin' ta me that ya already made up your mind."

"Yes, I have, I guess. It's just this infernal waiting. And not knowing. I can't imagine what I'll do if she decides not to return."

"Can I be makin' a suggestion?" Sean asked, flipping the string into the water.

Nicholas grinned resignedly. "I'm always willing to listen to you, my big, Irish friend."

"Then I'll be tellin' ya an easy way ta win her over."

"Easy? Are we talking about the same woman?"

"Aye. It's easy because ya've done it time and time again."
Nicholas frowned, the smile lingering.

"Court her, just like ya did all the women in your life. With your charm, you'll have her home before ya know it."

"Ohhh . . . I don't think . . ." He stood, shaking his head and walked a few steps away to gaze out across the shoreline.

"A fine-lookin' lad like you?" Sean argued. "Of course ya can. How do ya think your father won Victoria? He didn't wait for her ta come runnin'. He chased her. And Amber is no different. Look," he moved to stand before his friend, "if ya aren't there ta remind Amber what she's missin', how will she know? Send the lass flowers, or a pair of ruby earrings." Sean grinned devilishly. "It always worked on Heather."

Nicholas's dark brown eyes gleamed at the man who offered such a solution. "Maybe," he answered quietly.

"No maybe about it, lad. Mark me words, you'll woo Amber right back into your arms." He lifted his brows mischievously, then sobered. "When did ya say ya got home?"

"Yesterday around noon, why?" Nicholas asked, shading his eyes with one hand to watch a pair of sea gulls soar skyward.

"Have ya talked ta anyone?"

Nicholas grinned, recalling the way he had refused to open the study door for Anna when she brought his supper the night before. "My cook would have liked it otherwise, but no, I didn't."

"Then I be thinkin' we should go ta me cabin and have that drink. I've got somethin' ta tell ya."

Puzzled by his friend's sudden change in mood, Nicholas hesitated a moment before holding out his hand for Sean to lead the way. They ascended the gangplank and Nicholas nodded his thanks to the mate who offered congratulations on his wedding when they met him at the ship's railing. They crossed the deck in silence and entered the captain's quarters, where Sean set about pouring two glasses of whiskey while Nicholas sat down in the desk side chair. He took the drink Sean held out to him and watched the long, lanky frame of his companion slowly move to the opposite side of the room, where he gazed out the numerous portholes at the sea.

"Heather was here yesterday lookin' for ya."

"Me?" Nicholas echoed in surprise. "Do you know why?"

Sean shook his head. "She didn't seem ta want ta tell me."

"What did she say?"

"Nothin' much." He turned back to look at Nicholas. "She'd been beaten."

"What?" Nicholas exploded.

"Aye. She wouldn't let me get too close, but there's no hidin' a swollen lip. And when I started toward her, she kept backin' away, like she didn't want ta have ta explain. She asked where ya were and since I thought ya was still at Raven Oaks, I told her she could find ya there. Nicholas, lad," he began, walking closer, "someone found her body this mornin' on the road headin' north."

"Oh, my God," Nicholas moaned, leaning forward in the chair, his drink cradled in both hands. He had known months ago that he had never loved Heather and never would, but he had cared for her a great deal, and learning of her death left a dull ache in his chest. "What happened?"

"The lass's carriage overturned. The magistrate thinks it happened late yesterday, and since she was travelin' the road ta Raven Oaks, I be thinkin' it was just after I talked ta her. Nicholas, if I hadn't seen the bruises on her face, I would be thinkin' it an accident but—"

Nicholas glanced up suspiciously. "But what, Sean?"

Sean came forward to rest a hip on the edge of the desk. "She told me she was married."

"Married? I hadn't heard—"

"Aye. And that in itself is not reason ta be thinkin' anythin' out of the ordinary, but it's who she married."

"For God's sake who? What cur would strike a woman if that's what you're saying."

"Baron Kelzer Von Buren."

"What?" Nicholas rallied. "In all that's holy, why would Heather marry him?"

"I wondered the same thin', so I did some checkin' around. Were ya aware that Heather owed nearly every merchant in Williamsburg? And a few in Jamestown?"

"No, I wasn't. So?"

"It seems the baron found out, too, and paid all her

debts . . . *before* they were married."

"Blackmail?"

"Aye. That's what I be thinkin'."

Nicholas set aside his glass untouched and stood to pace the floor. "Then you think Heather's death wasn't accidental?"

Sean shrugged. "It does raise a few questions."

"Yes, it does," Nicholas agreed. "Like why did he blackmail her into marrying him? Why was she beaten?" He spun around to look at his friend. "And why did she come searching for me? Damn! Why couldn't I have been where she could have found me?"

"Now don't go blamin' yourself, lad. I'm just as guilty. I should have kept her here and sent someone for ya."

Nicholas sighed heavily. "I suppose. But it all seems so senseless."

"Aye, that it is."

"I think we should pay Von Buren a visit," Nicholas growled.

"Ya won't learn anythin' from him, lad. If he's hidin' somethin', he'll simply tell ya they had argued and the lass went for a ride. As for the bruises, I'm sure he'll say she fell or somethin' just as safe."

Nicholas returned to the desk and lifted the glass of whiskey to swallow in one gulp. He stood quietly a moment, studying the crystal cylinder in his hand. "Poor Heather," he whispered. "She never hurt anyone."

"I know, lad," Sean agreed, reaching over to touch Nicholas's shoulder.

"What about the carriage?" Nicholas asked suddenly. "Maybe if we examined it, we—"

Sean shook his head. "Ya'll find no clues there, me boy. It fell into a ravine. Nothin' left but splinters."

Angered, Nicholas jerked away and resumed his pacing. "Am I just to stand by and let him get away with it? You know as well as I that in one way or another he's responsible for Heather's death!"

"Aye, lad, but without proof—"

"I don't care about proof," he raged.

"Nicholas, calm down a wee bit. Ya be lettin' this get the

363

better of ya."

"Oh, Sean," he groaned, "don't you see? It's my father's death all over again. We know he was murdered, that Heather was too, but we can't prove anything! Where's the justice?"

A knock at the cabin door interrupted and Sean quickly rose to answer it while Nicholas poured himself another drink.

"Excuse me, capt'n, but there's a man here to see Mr. Chandler," the mate said once Sean had opened the door. Both men glanced over at Nicholas.

"Who is it?" he asked, his tone sharp.

"Lyle Gibbens, sir. Says you'd know him."

Nicholas stiffened. Lyle Gibbens was his grandmother's coachman and the one who had taken Amber home. He silently prayed the man had been sent to tell him that his wife had returned to Raven Oaks . . . better yet to Williamsburg. "Send him in," he said quietly, hopefully.

The mate stepped aside and a moment later the stocky frame of the coachman filled the doorway. The man's usually neat suit was covered with dust, his hair was ruffled, and there was no mistaking the tired look in his eyes.

"What is it, Gibbens?" Nicholas asked, sensing trouble.

"Mistress Remington sent me, sir," Gibbens said, walking further into the room. "She asked that I tell you what happened and give you this." He held out the letter he had guarded carefully for the last thirty-four hours.

Setting down his glass, Nicholas took the note and unfolded it to read. His heart sank as if weighed with lead. *I don't want to live with Nicholas any longer.* The words screamed in his ears, and he folded the paper to block out the message. "I know all of this already, Gibbens," he said quietly, handing the letter to Sean. "Grandmother told me the night Amber left. Why did she think I should have it? It doesn't make any more sense than she did at the time."

"Excuse me, sir, but you've misunderstood. The note was meant for me."

"You? Where did you get it?"

"Please, allow me to explain. Mistress Chandler and I stopped at a roadhouse along the way to Jamestown that night. She had dinner, then retired. I did the same. In the morning when she failed to come down for breakfast, the innkeeper and I went to her room. The door was locked, sir, and when she didn't answer my summons, I had the innkeeper let us in with a second key."

The hair on the back of Nicholas's neck stood on end. "Well, good Lord man, what did you find?"

Gibbens swallowed hard. "Nothing, sir. Mistress Chandler wasn't there."

"Then where did you get this letter?"

"I found it on the table in her room."

"Sounds ta me like the lass changed her mind about goin' home," Sean observed after studying the note. He handed it back to Nicholas.

"Yes, sir," Gibbens agreed. "It appeared to be that way."

"What do you mean appeared? Is there more to it than that?"

"Well, I thought so. And so did your grandmother. That's why she sent me to find you."

"Go on," Nicholas urged.

"As I said before, the door was locked. I found *her* key next to the note on the table."

"So?"

"It means, sir, that Mistress Chandler left the room through the balcony, a second story. Since there were no steps, I assume she climbed down the trellis. A difficult feat for a lady. And then there were her bags. They were still packed and sitting where I put them the night before. Her cloak was laying on the sofa, and her bed hadn't been slept in."

"What are you saying?" Nicholas demanded.

"That if it weren't for that note," he nodded at the paper in Nicholas's hand, "I would think she left against her will."

"Why? Were there signs of a struggle?"

"No, sir."

"Then—"

"Just a gut feeling, I have, sir. That and what I found out from the stableboy. Mistress Chandler did not hire a rig or take a horse, sir."

A worried frown pierced Nicholas's brow.

"I would have looked for her, but from the appearance of the room, I figured she had a full night's head start, and there were so many tracks in the dirt, I didn't know which way to go. So I decided it was better to talk with you, that you might be able to figure it out. But you had already gone home, sir."

Nicholas crossed to the desk and sat down behind it, his mind clouded with a hundred questions. He spread the letter out in front of him. "If someone kidnapped her, why would they leave a note like this?" he said more to himself.

"Aye, lad," Sean concurred. "'Twould make more sense for them ta leave ransom instructions. And why would they be makin' the lass write it if that be the case?" He moved quickly to stand by Nicholas and peer over his shoulder. "Read it again, me boy. Maybe ya missed somethin'."

Each man studied the words again. *Please don't follow me or try to find me. I don't want to live with Nicholas any longer.* After several minutes passed, Nicholas fell back in the chair.

"I have to agree with Gibbens, Sean. If Amber meant to spend some time alone, why wouldn't she take her things with her? And why sneak out like that? She could have sent Gibbens home and waited until after he had gone to leave. And for God's sake, she surely would have hired a coach. No, if she has indeed been kidnapped, they obviously wanted to throw us off the track. The question is why? Surely they're after money, and this would only delay payment."

"Aye, I agree, lad," Sean sighed, resting a hip on the edge of the desk, his gaze still locked on the wrinkled piece of paper. Then his brow furrowed. "Is Amber French?"

"French?" Nicholas half laughed. "Why do you ask?"

"I knew a French lass who spelled her name like that," he said, pointing to the signature.

Nicholas glanced at it only briefly, then back up at Sean. "No, she isn't French. She—" His face lost the hint of amusement and he quickly grabbed the piece of paper to see it clearly and make certain his eyes hadn't deceived him. "That's it, Sean! The name! It's spelled A-m-b-e-r, not A-m-b-r-e. And now that I think about it, the slanting of the letters is wrong. Here . . ." He fumbled through his coat pocket and pulled out a second paper, which he unfolded and laid beside the first. "I found this note in my grandmother's study the morning after

Amber left. She had tried to write down her reasons for leaving but couldn't. Look," he added, comparing the two, "the styles aren't quite the same. She didn't write this, Sean!"

"Then she was taken by force. But why?"

"Well, whoever took her didn't do it for money or they would have left word on how much it would take to get her back, just as you suggested. So what other reason would they have?"

Sean lifted a finger to scratch his temple. "I haven't an idea. Do you?"

"She must have known something . . . about someone," Nicholas proposed, leaving his chair to trek across the cabin, "something that could be dangerous to him. But who? Who does Amber know that might be guilty of something so great they must dispose of her?"

"Ohhh, I don't like it Nicholas, me boy. I'm gettin' a funny feelin' in the pit of me stomach."

Nicholas spun around to look at him. "What, Sean? Anything! Any ideas will help."

"The baron."

"Von Buren?"

"Aye. Haven't ya noticed that every time somethin' evil happens, he's right in the middle of it?"

"You mean Heather?"

"And your wife. After all, the lass said he killed her father."

"Ha-ha, Sean! You've got it. Amber finally has proof!"

"And the baron has ta stop her," Sean added. "So what do we do now?"

"We pay him a visit," Nicholas said, moving toward the door. "And on the way we'll stop by Andrea's just in case we're wrong and she's had word from Amber. But somehow I don't think we will be." He paused, remembering the coachman's presence, and turned back. "Thank you, Gibbens. Without your help . . . well, you just might have saved Amber's life. I'll see you're repaid handsomely."

"All I want, sir, is to know she's safe again. I feel kinda responsible."

"Don't. It would have happened no matter what you could have done. And do one more thing, will you?" He waited for

367

Gibbens to nod, then continued. "Find the constable and tell him everything. Tell him where we've gone. We might need his help,"

"Yes, sir."

He opened the door, Sean close behind, and called back over his shoulder. "And tell Mistress Remington everything will be all right."

Warm aromas from the cooking pot filled the tiny kitchen, the dancing flames of the fire casting odd shadows in the room when the dying sunlight failed to spill inside. In the corner of the room, a lone figure sat huddled in a chair, blue eyes darkened with despair, staring blindly ahead. A tear escaped the rim of her black lashes and trailed down the smooth ivory skin to her trembling mouth, and Andrea swallowed again to stop the burst of weeping that threatened to overcome her. She had spent the time since the baron's visit pacing the floor, her mind awhirl with various schemes to save her sister and change their destiny. But what could one woman alone do to free his captive? He had promised to kill Amber if such an attempt was made, and Andrea painfully realized she was too weak, too stupid to devise a method on her own that would succeed in one try.

Disheartened, she had absently gone to the kitchen to prepare a small kettle of stew with the rabbit she had caught that morning. It seemed the natural thing to do until the smells penetrated her troubled state and hunger fled for more important things. Maybe Seth could help. But how? What if they failed and Amber died because of it? Her chin quivered, and she sat down in the chair to think. She owed Amber. After all, hadn't Amber married someone to save her, as the baron had so heartlessly pointed out? Now it was her turn. But Kelzer Von Buren could hardly compare to Nicholas Chandler. The man who sought to trap her into wedlock had been responsible for Fletcher Courtney's death. What she had heard of Amber's husband had only been that he had fine, upstanding qualities.

Her tears starting anew, Andrea rose and went to the narrow

window of the room to look outside, brushing away the salty moisture from the corner of her mouth. How did Von Buren find himself a widower again? What had happened to Heather Branford? And more, why had she married him? Why did he want Andrea? She had nothing . . . no property, no money. Surely love had not softened his heart of stone. Only Seth loved her.

"Seth," she sobbed. His name upon her lips brought a flooding of tears. Now she would never know the bliss of his husbandly embrace. She would never feel his tenderness nor carry his child in her womb as she had dreamed. Yes, she would agree to marry the baron, but only to free her sister. And once that was done, Andrea would free herself. A life without Seth would not be worth living.

The loud clamor of racing hooves outside the cottage startled Andrea into awareness. Had the baron acquired his proof as he had claimed he would and returned now with the minister? Her gaze traveled the length of the faded cotton gown she wore, thinking how she had planned on white lace for her wedding day. She raised her chin, bravely holding back her tears. But then she had never planned to marry someone like Von Buren either, and the ceremony would be a mockery no matter what gown she chose. Forcing her feet to move, she left the kitchen and had nearly reached the front door before the first knock sounded.

Remember, she silently told herself, *he must have proof.* Tears pooled in the corner of her eyes again. *For you, Amber. Only for you.*

The rapping came again, and with great effort Andrea put a hand to the latch, slowly pulling the door open. Her eyes averted, she failed to look at the visitors, bidding them to enter. But when no one moved, she glanced up, her chin sagging, her breath catching.

"Are you all right, Andrea?" Nicholas asked worriedly.

Her gaze darted from him to his companion and back. "I—I was expecting someone else." Remembering her appearance and wanting desperately to hide the obvious signs of despair, she forced a laugh and quickly wiped a knuckle to her eyes.

"Come—in, won't you?"

"You've been crying," Nicholas continued, his frown deepening.

She smiled sadly and turned away, hoping they would follow and allow her a moment to collect her thoughts. She musn't let him know about Amber. "It's . . . it's nothing. I was cutting onions. You know how they burn your eyes when you work with them for too long. Please sit down, won't you? I'll get some tea."

Nicholas exchanged a suspicious look with Sean, then said, "We haven't time for tea just now, thank you. But we would like to ask you something."

Andrea's heart pounded harder. "All right." She moved toward the fireplace and took a long taper from the mantel. "I'll light the lamp first," she offered, forcing herself not to look at the men. The wick caught fire instantly and she cupped a hand around the flame to protect it as she crossed to the small chair side table. A moment later a yellow glow flooded the room and mixed with the light of the hearth. She extinguished the taper and returned it to its place. "Would you care for something to eat? I have some stew—"

"Andrea," Nicholas interrupted, stepping further into the room, Sean shadowing his move and allowing the door to swing quietly shut behind them.

Unthinkingly, she glanced up. His face mirrored concern and she quickly turned away, fidgeting with the corner of her apron. She walked to the darkest part of the room and began rearranging the items on the table before her.

"Andrea, who were you expecting? Amber, perhaps?"

Her hand quavered at the mention of her sister and she knocked over the small sewing basket sitting there. Its contents spilled to the floor. Fighting back a rush of tears, she stooped to gather the scissors, spools of threads, and needles, hearing the sounds of Nicholas's boots against the floor as he came to kneel beside her.

"Andrea, my wife's life may be in danger," Nicholas whispered, capturing her hands in his to pull her to her feet when she chose to ignore him, refusing even to look his way. "Andrea, you and Amber may be twins, but the similarity stops

370

with your appearances. I can tell by looking at you that you're hiding something. What is it?"

"Nothing!" she snapped, jerking free of him. "I was expecting Seth and you surprised me, that's all. And I was cutting onions like I said. Now, please tell me what you want to know and be on your way."

He glanced over at Sean, then sighed. "All right. But I want you near the fire's glow where I can see your face."

"Why?" she retorted.

"So I can tell if you're lying."

Panic distorting her features, she sucked in a nervous breath and let it out just as quickly. Without prompting, she crossed to the chair before the fire and sat down. "What would I have to lie about?" she asked crisply, staring into the flames. She listened to him approach, then stand near the open hearth, an elbow resting on the mantel, one foot on the stone slab. An uncontrollable shiver raced through her at the thought of the last man who had stood in the very same spot.

"I doubt the two of you will ever stop protecting the other, even if it means hurting someone else."

Andrea continued to stare.

"*I'm* hurting, Andrea. Right now. My heart aches with worry for my wife. Three nights ago, she decided to leave me. She told my grandmother that she had to come home, to you, to sort out her feelings. She didn't know if she could live with me, love me, as I love her."

The anger and stubbornness disappeared from Andrea's face and she glanced up at him, at his expression, veiled in the shadows. "You love her?" she whispered disbelievingly.

"With all my heart. Do you find that so impossible?"

Embarrassed that the thought had crossed her mind, she elected to study her hands folded in her lap. "I guess not."

"Then maybe you can understand why I'm here. Something happened, something that has me a little frightened, and I must know that Amber's safe. I'm not asking you to tell me where she is, if you know, but that you've seen her, talked to her, or in some other way know that she's all right. I haven't come to drag her home if she's hiding in the bedroom. I realize she needs time and I want her to take all she needs." He tilted his head to one side, trying to see Andrea's face. "Can you ease my worries?"

"No," came the choked reply. "I—I haven't seen her."

Nicholas glanced up at Sean, who shrugged in return. Bending his knees, Nicholas crouched down, elbows to his thighs, his hands dangling between them. "Then tell me why it didn't come as a surprise to you to learn Amber had left me?"

"Seth told me."

"Seth?" Nicholas's face crimped in confusion.

"Yes. There are rumors all over Jamestown about it. He came to see if I had heard."

"Then no one has seen her?"

One narrow shoulder lifted slightly.

Nicholas's eyes moved to gaze down at the floor. "I don't mean to frighten you, Andrea, but I must tell you the real reason I'm here. But before I do, I want you to promise me that if Amber comes home that you'll send a message to me. I won't come after her, I give you my word, but I must find her and know no harm has come to her. Will you promise?"

How Andrea longed to run to him, bury herself in his embrace, cry, tell him of the baron's plan, and hear Nicholas guarantee that he would find Amber before Von Buren could hurt her. But the only words that screamed in her mind were the evil threats the baron had made, the pledge to murder her sister if anyone came to rescue her. To send Nicholas was too great a risk. Amber would be left unharmed if Andrea agreed to marriage. A simple remedy. No one would suffer. Not even her.

"If Amber comes home to me, I promise I will send a message." It wasn't really a lie.

Nicholas smiled tenderly. "I do believe you love her as much as I."

Only her eyes moved to look at him. "More," she whispered.

"Then I will tell you something that will lay your suspicions to rest."

"Suspicions?"

"Yes. About your father's death."

Andrea stiffened slightly. "What do you mean?"

"Sean and I feel that the reason Amber has not arrived yet is because she's unable to," Nicholas said grimly.

A nervous qualm seized the muscles of Andrea's stomach. She glanced up fearfully at Sean Rafferty, then back at Nicholas.

"We think she has proof about your father's death and doesn't realize it. But his murderer fears she will discover it and turn him in."

"W-why do you say that?"

"Because she disappeared on her way here. The last time she was seen was at an inn on the Southwest Road about fifteen miles away. She didn't take her things with her and she didn't hire a rig, which tells us that she had some other means of travel."

My God, they suspected! But did they know who? She forced a smile. "She probably decided to walk."

"Fifteen miles?"

"Certainly. Amber's always been unpredictable." She stood up quickly. "I'm sure there's nothing to worry about, Mr. Chandler. Why don't you and Mr. Rafferty just go home. She'll probably show up here before morning and make us all look foolish."

Nicholas slowly came to his feet, an incredulous stare darkening his eyes as he focused his attention on the young woman. Andrea began to squirm under his penetrating glare, feeling as though he had bared her to the soul.

"Really!" she stressed. "Amber's fine. I know it."

"How? Have you talked to her?" Nicholas asked, his voice calm, quiet.

"No, but I'm sure she is."

"Well, I'm not, Andrea. And I won't be until after I've talked with Baron Von Buren." He started for the door.

"No! You mustn't!" Andrea blurted out, instantly wishing to retract her outburst. A clenched fist covered her mouth, tears welling in her eyes. "Please. Just go home."

Nicholas and Sean traded knowing glances before Nicholas unhurriedly came back to face her. "Why, Andrea? Why don't you want us to visit Baron Von Buren? Do you know something?"

Andrea vigorously shook her head, a tear breaking free to run down her cheek.

"Amber was kidnapped, Andrea. We're sure of it. And if you know where she is, you must tell us."

Her frightened eyes stared back at him and Nicholas was suddenly filled with compassion. "Andrea, you must realize that no matter what demands are made, they will kill Amber whether or not they're met. If they were to let her go, she would inform the authorities. If they didn't punish the scoundrels, I would. It's a chance these men won't take. Please tell me, Andrea, for your sister's sake."

"I—I can't. He promised—" Her voice cracked.

"Who? Von Buren? What did he promise?" He gently took hold of her arms. "Andrea, I love my wife. I'd never do anything to harm her. But if I don't try to find her before it's too late, her life isn't worth a tuppence."

"He . . . he said he would . . . kill her. . . ." Her tears fell freely. "He promised to let her go if . . ."

"If what, Andrea? Tell me," Nicholas asked, forcing himself to remain calm.

"Oh, my God!" Andrea screamed, heart-rending sobs quaking her body. She clung frantically to him. "I was so scared."

"You don't have to be anymore. Sean and I will take care of you." He wrapped an arm around her narrow shoulders and led her to the wooden bench, pulling her down onto it. Sean quickly moved to crouch before them, reaching out to hold one of her hands.

"Aye, lass. Ya will be safe with us. Just be tellin' us all ya know so we can be helpin' your sister."

The fearful eyes of a child looked back at him, and he smiled.

"I wouldn't be lyin' ta ya, lass. Take a deep breath and tell us everythin' that happened."

A moment passed while Andrea fought to still her quivering chin. "He . . . he came here earlier. He said he had Amber hidden away where no one could find her and if I sent someone to look he would . . . kill her."

"What did he want for her return?" Nicholas asked quietly, wiping away her tears with the thumb of one hand.

"He . . . he said I would have to . . . to marry him if I wanted her to live out the day. Oh, Mr. Chandler . . ." She

374

buried her face in his neck, weeping sorrowfully.

"Marry him?" Sean repeated with a frown. "Why would he . . ." He shook his head. "Nicholas, me boy, I don't understand. The man has gone ta great lengths ta have this lass as his wife, and I can't be believin' it's because of love."

"Neither can I, Sean. But I guess I won't know until I ask him." he stood, bringing the crying woman with him. "I want you to take Andrea to my place. Anna will take care of her. And she is not to be left alone. Either you stay with her or have one of your men there."

"Aye, lad. But ya not be meanin' ta go ta see the baron alone, are ya? It could be dangerous."

"I have to. I can't waste another minute." Tenderly, he placed a knuckle beneath Andrea's chin and lifted her gaze to meet his. "How long did he give you to decide?"

"I—I told him that he would have to prove to me that he . . . he had Amber. I told him to ask her how Papa got the scar on his cheek. Only she would know that."

"And what did he say?"

"He said he'd be back with the answer and a minister in a few hours. *He* was the one I was expecting. Oh, Mr. Chandler, please find her. If she's killed because of—"

"Hush, my dear," Nicholas whispered, hugging her to him. "I'll find her and everything will be all right. And I'll see to it that Von Buren is put in prison where he belongs." He held her closely as the trio walked from the house, helping her up on the horse behind Sean before he took the reins of his own steed in one hand.

"I be wishin' ya luck, lad," Sean smiled down at him. "And for God's sake, be careful. A man like that won't hesitate ta put a bullet in your heart before askin' why ya came ta visit."

"I know," Nicholas grinned, reaching up to pat Sean's thigh. "All I ask is that you take care of Andrea until I bring Amber home."

"'Tis a deal, lad." Sean pulled back on the reins, spun the animal around, and raced off down the road.

Nicholas stood quietly a moment, his dark brows knotted together, his mounting rage blackening his scowl. "You'll pay for this, Von Buren. So help me, God, you'll pay." Jamming a foot in the stirrup, he skillfully swung into the saddle, kicking his heels in the stallion's sides. They bolted off, their thunderous departure scattering the tiniest of creatures from their path.

Von Buren paced the floor of his study, impatiently waiting for one of his men to return with the answer he needed, and cursing himself for letting his temper get in the way. If the little she-cat hadn't struck a blow to his ego, he wouldn't have ordered Duehr and Allison to take Amber to Boston this morning. He could simply have asked her what Andrea wanted to know and been on his way to fetch the minister. As it was, he was forced to send word to his accomplice, praying that he knew how Fletcher Courtney had gotten the scar on his cheek.

"Damn you, you tramp! You've caused me more trouble than anyone else in my life." He kicked at the wicker basket sitting on the floor near his desk. "Well, no more! Within the week you'll be on a ship sailing to Casablanca and your sister will be my wife!" He rounded the mahogany piece of furniture and threw himself into the chair behind it. "And I will be rid of my partner. Just as soon as I have that diary."

Spotting the wine decanter on the corner of the desk, he jerked forward and seized the bottle by the neck. He filled one goblet to the rim, jammed the stopper back in place, and banged the container down on the wooden surface again while raising the glass to his lips. He took a hearty swallow, feeling it burn all the way down and spread a fiery warmth throughout him. It soothed his taut muscles but not the anger that glowed hotly in his dark eyes. He took a second drink, more at ease after the first, and lost himself in his plans for Andrea Courtney and his partner as well, failing to hear a rider approach outside the front of the house. Only the loud banging on the study door brought him back to the present, and one corner of his lip twisted into a sneer, certain his man had returned with the answer he needed.

"Come!" he bellowed, rising from the chair and setting his glass aside. He reached the center of the room as the door swung open.

"Well, Thorne? Do you have the answer?" he demanded of the man trembling before him.

"Yes, sir, but . . ." Thorne gulped, his breaths coming in ragged heaves.

"But what?"

"It's . . . it's . . . Nicholas Chandler. He's . . ."

Von Buren stiffened. "What about him?"

Thorne collapsed forward, bracing his hands on his knees in an effort to catch his breath.

"Damn it, man! Tell me," the baron roared, grabbing the collar of Thorne's shirt to yank him up.

The smaller man swallowed hard, fear nearly strangling him. "He's . . . he's coming. I—I saw him on the road—"

"Are you sure?" Von Buren growled.

"Y-yes, sir. And he's riding hard."

The baron's face distorted in an evil grimace and he roughly shoved the man away. Had Andrea shown the courage his partner claimed she lacked? Had she sent for Nicholas Chandler and told him about the baron's scheme? Or did Chandler come for another reason? What? To share a cup of tea? A menacing growl erupted from Von Buren and he swung around to storm his desk. He yanked open a top drawer and withdrew a pistol, checking it to be sure it was loaded before he thrust it in the belt of his breeches, keeping it from view beneath the edge of his coat.

"Sir?" Thorne dared ask. "Is there someting I can—"

"Get out!" Von Buren shouted. He blindly watched the man make a hasty departure. He moved to the window of the room and looked out, almost instantly seeing the distant figure of horse and rider bearing down on the Von Buren estate. "You had better be coming here to express your sympathy on my wife's death, Herr Chandler," he whispered dangerously. "Or you shall never leave." He continued to watch until the horse slowed to a canter at the end of the drive. Kelzer's eyes narrowed to fine slits, a spark of evil augury shining in their depths. Absently he rested a hand on the butt of his pistol, a strange forewarning of tragedy prickling the hairs on the back of his neck. An odd panic, a fear that he would not reign victorious once more, commanded his feet to move, and he hurriedly left the study to find Thorne.

Nicholas reined his stallion to a trot once Von Buren's house loomed out before him, a mansion of red brick, black shutters and roof, and a single willow tree in the front yard, its long, twisted limbs swaying slightly in the breeze, like giant, icy fingers waiting to entrap anyone who ventured near. Nicholas shook off the chill that had settled in his spine, forcing his attention on the house. It appeared deserted, as though no mortal creature moved about and he wondered if he would find Amber hidden in one of the rooms upstairs, her eyes filled with terror at the abuse she had surely endured. He forced the vision from his mind, knowing blind panic would not save her. He must be calm, rational, outguess the baron's moves, or most assuredly he too would face a similar fate.

His gaze quickly surveyed the grounds surrounding the huge building, and though no one showed himself, he could feel eyes upon him. He reached in back of him beneath his coat and pulled the pistol from his waistband. He checked the load and powder, realizing one bullet would be worthless against the baron's army. Smiling to himself, he returned the weapon to its place, vowing the one shot would find Von Buren's heart if all else failed and he had to rely on his other skills to free his wife. The smile faded as he concentrated on his plan. He would request privacy, a moment alone to speak with the baron on the premise a bargain could be met. Then at the right moment he would draw his gun. Nicholas was certain that the only thing of great importance to the baron was money, and, since holding Amber to force Andrea into marriage promised none, Nicholas felt confident he could offer Von Buren's life in exchange for Amber's. One or a dozen men with firearms would not assure the baron he could win when Nicholas pressed the cold black cylinder to the man's temple. No man had that kind of courage. He could only hope that Amber was somewhere near.

He guided the horse down the stone path toward the house and stopped near the front steps. Dismounting, he tied off the reins and guardedly studied the windows facing him, the bushes surrounding the structure, before climbing the stairs to the main entrance. He slowly approached the finely crafted wooden portal, painted in the same ebony color as the shutters. He lifted a hand, caution guiding his moves. The brass door knocker resounded its announcement throughout the house, its resonance hammering in Nicholas's ears before all fell quiet again. A long moment passed. He glanced around. Had they fled? Should he check the back of the house? Or was that part of a trick they hoped to implement? No, he would wait. He would knock one more time. . . . Suddenly the door-latch rattled, and Nicholas felt his muscles tighten.

Part Two

Chapter Seventeen

July 20, 1806

Somewhere in the world the sun shone clearly, its golden fingers stretching earthward to caress the morning into wakefulness, while in the bowels of the merchant ship time held no meaning, each day passing like the night, a dark, ominous void. A great many weeks had passed since the vessel had set sail, its treasure locked below and all but forgotten. It guarded and protected its precious cargo against the turbulent storms at sea, but even more it held its victim prisoner. The single ray of sanity appeared at three sparse moments each day, an obscure reminder that life still continued, plodded onward, that somewhere above decks men roamed about caring for the ship, laughing, drinking, and filling their bellies with food, a meager sampling brought to the hold once they had finished.

Amber accepted the simple offering weak-heartedly, for, though she felt her life had ended, the rumblings of her stomach forbade her to let it slip away. She ate in darkness, never positive of what she was eating, only tasting the salty blandness of it washed down with water. She guessed a week had passed before she had managed to swallow a morsel without her stomach's retching. The rolling pitch of the wooden planks beneath her grew less intense, and she could only assume she had become accustomed to it.

In the blackness that seemed her vale of hopelessness and tears, she had stumbled about curiously, seeking comfort to ease her weary body and numb her soul. One of numerous bales of cotton that crowded the hold served as her bed, where she remained a great deal of the time, since moving about blindly gave no reward except a bruised shin. During one of her few ventures about the cramped space and its enormous cargo, she had discovered a crate of cloths. She was reasonably certain they were only discarded burlap bags from their rough texture, but she envisioned one to be a bright vivid green silk and tore off a strip of it with which to bind up her hair. She had taught herself how to braid the shoulder-length curls in an effort to avoid tangles, since she knew a brush would be a luxury she would not see for many weeks, if ever again.

Hours stretched into days, days into countless score, and with their passing Amber's rebellious nature, her strong will to survive, returned little by little. She knew that unless she fought back her sanity would flee, and she would spend her final days locked away in solitude, unable to revenge herself. Thus, she set her goal, though seemingly futile, on gaining her freedom to return home and see the baron brought to justice. She plotted ways to escape, yet realized it would be a minor victory if the ship was still at sea. She must wait until they docked to take on supplies or to deliver the cargo that had become her sanctuary. She would hide among the crates to await the moment when backs were turned and she could run from the space, jump overboard and swim to shore, if necessary. She had heard two mates discuss their destination, and she knew in England there would be understanding ears to listen to her plight. If only her chance would come soon. She deemed the waiting terminal.

Though hard to estimate, Amber concluded the noon meal had been delayed when it seemed her stomach rubbed against her backbone. Wondering what the reason was, she fumbled her way to the portal leading topside, pressing an ear against it to listen for any part of a conversation that would give her a clue, her heart pounding hopefully at the excited shouts of the men on deck. Land had been sighted, and within the hour the merchant ship would dock. Tears burned her eyes, and she felt glee, certain she was about to end her agony. She moved away from the barrier, close enough to dash through it when her time came, and crouched down to serve out the remainder of her sentence.

An hour passed, and all the while she listened to the sounds of the ship dropping anchor, the shower of footfalls above her on the deck. She closed her eyes, praying God would grant her her one minor request. Then it came. The chatter of voices outside the door. But with it, a frown crimped Amber's grime-smudged brow, for mingled with the joyful verbiage of the men rang the clear soprano tones of a woman sobbing.

A key rattled in the lock a moment before the door swung open, filling the black cavity with a blinding light. Amber heard more than witnessed the woman being thrown inside and squinted in the brightness for an indication of the new prisoner's whereabouts. Then someone grabbed her arms and shoved her further back into the hold.

"Stand there and don't move," a deep voice warned.

But Amber feared her chance to escape would slip through her fingers if she did as he instructed, and she suddenly broke for the door. She had traveled only two steps when strong fingers dug painfully into her shoulder, spinning her around, and before her eyes could focus on the obscure figure standing before her, the sailor raised a huge fist and landed a blow to her temple. A thousand tiny lights exploded in her head, all swirling, blending, and she stumbled backward, her eyelids drooping before dark overcame her and she fell unconscious to the deck.

The heavy wooden door banged shut again, closing out the light, and the turning of the key in the lock stirred Amber into wakefulness once more. She pushed herself up to her knees, her head pounding, and she wondered how much time had elapsed since the ruffian had struck her until she heard the pitiful weeping of another. Her own sorrow fled, knowing someone else needed comforting.

"Please don't cry," she whispered, hoping not to startle her new companion. "My name is Amber."

"I—I . . ." came the reply before a renewal of tears robbed her words.

Amber moved toward the sound, her own throat tightening with each sob, for although it had been weeks since she had first been abandoned in this black existence, she remembered the panic, fear, the lunacy, as if it was only yesterday. Awkwardly crawling across the deck, one hand held out before her, the other tugging periodically at the skirts trapped beneath her knees, she groped her way closer, wanting desperately to hold the woman in her arms, to share this madness and calm her own terrors.

"Please," she begged, her throat tight when the journey seemed too far, "reach out to me. I want to touch you. I *need* to touch you."

"Here," came the tiny answer. "I'm here."

Their fingers met, and, as if clinging to life, pulled toward each other into an embrace. Amber knew in that moment that she cradled a child, a woman half-grown, and her heart ached for the horror this delicate creature suffered. She pressed the other's head to her shoulder, stroking the long thick curls and rocking gently on her knees, a soothing method her own mother had often used to chase away a bad dream. And, if anything, this was truly a nightmare. Amber let the girl's tears run their course, and, when she seemed to quiet, Amber wiped the moisture from the face she could not see.

"Now tell me your name and what port we're in," she coached softly.

"H-Holly. My name is Holly Clark. We're . . . we're in the port of Cardiff. In England."

England. The word exploded in Amber's mind. "Will the men be coming back to unload the cargo here?" She could feel the girl tremble.

"But—but they already have. Amber, why are we being held here?" Holly's voice rose in pitch, near panic threatening to overcome her.

"Shhh," Amber comforted, hugging her closer. "We mustn't waste our energies on why, but on how to get out of here." Amber realized with Holly's words that her plan had failed before she'd had a chance to try. She stiffened courageously, knowing she would think of another way. "Did someone mention how long the ship would be in port?" she asked hopefully.

"It's . . . it's so dark . . ."

"Concentrate, Holly," Amber guided. "I'm here with you. You'll be all right. Just close your eyes and pretend you're anyplace but where you are. It will help."

A moment of silence passed, and Amber wondered if Holly had done as she suggested.

"My father is a—a shipping merchant. I had come to the dock to ask him to dine with me when—" Holly's voice cracked and she fell quiet. Several minutes ground out before she could continue, all the while held tightly in a stranger's embrace. "Two men took me. I tried to struggle, but they were too strong. One of them said that if they could get a lot of money for the sale of one woman, two would bring twice as much. What did they mean?"

Amber remained quiet a moment. Obviously the men had gotten greedy when they decided to kidnap Holly. But did they intend to sell her, too, as Von Buren had promised her fate to be? She could only hope they had other ideas, yet in her heart she knew they didn't. "Do you suppose they will contact your father about ransom?"

"I—I don't know how. I wasn't with my father when they took me, and they don't know who I am. Amber . . ." the young girl pleaded, twisting in Amber's arms as if she wished to see her face. "Where are you being taken?"

Amber knew the name, Von Buren had told her, but she had no idea exactly how far away from England Casablanca really was. And she certainly wouldn't tell this young frightened child. "It doesn't matter where, Holly, only that we remain strong and brave. We must always think of escape, no matter how bleak the circumstances. And we *will* escape, Holly. I promise you that."

Suddenly Holly broke free of Amber's embrace. "But we must get out of here now," she screamed. "I don't like it here. It's too dark. My father will be looking for me. I want to go home!"

"Hush, Holly, you'll be all right," Amber soothed, searching the darkness with outstretched hands for her new companion. "Come to me—"

"No!" Holly shrieked. *"I want out!"* Stumbling forward, she fell against the portal. "Let me out of here!" she shouted, near hysteria cracking her voice as she pounded her fists against the door. "Papa! Papa, save me. Dear God, someone help me!"

Hurrying as best she could in the darkness, Amber fumbled her way to the panic-stricken girl, an arm raised to protect herself when Holly violently swung out at her.

"No! No, I won't stay here!"

"Holly, please . . ." Amber begged, clamping her arms around the girl and tumbling them both to the deck. "If we are to free ourselves, I'll need your help." She clung frantically to the struggling form. "Do you hear me, Holly? Stop! I need you, Holly," she half cried, her own tears stinging her eyes. Several moments passed before the young woman quieted and Amber could relax her hold. "That's better. Now try to get some rest, all right?"

Holly didn't answer and Amber shifted to sit up beside her new prisonmate, allowing the girl to lay her head in her lap. Closing her eyes, Amber prayed Holly would fall into an exhausted sleep and not hear the rattling of the chain as the ship weighed anchor once more.

"Amber, how old are you?"

The question seemed to loom out at her in the vacancy of her world, and Amber oddly found herself grateful for the absence of light, for she knew the sadness she felt pulling at her heart shone clearly on her face. "Nineteen," she half whispered.

A moment of quiet passed before Holly moved to touch her new friend. "Why does it make you sad?" she asked worriedly.

Amber forced a laugh. "Sad? What makes you think I'm sad?"

Holly squeezed the hand she sought in the darkness. "We've shared this . . . this place for nearly a week now. You've told me all about yourself, as I have you. I've never seen your face,

388

but I can tell what's written on it by the sound of your voice. You've helped me more than anyone else has ever done in my life, Amber, and if I can return the favor, I will. Please share your sadness with me."

Amber brushed away the single tear from her cheek. "Andrea and I turned nineteen on June ninth. I—I spent it here . . . alone, and I wasn't even sure which day it really was."

"Oh, Amber," Holly moaned, putting her arms around the tall, shapely frame of her companion. "I'm so sorry. Do you think Andrea knows you're all right by now?"

Amber shrugged, accepting the comfort of the young woman. "I don't have any idea. But I rather doubt she does. I imagine Von Buren didn't tell anyone what he'd done."

"But what about your husband? You told me he loves you. Surely he will figure out what happened."

Amber bit her lower lip to hold back her tears. "I don't think he'll try. I—I ran away from him, remember? I told his grandmother I needed time to think, that I didn't love Nicholas. And she promised to make him wait, not to let him come looking for me. By now, he's sure I don't want to ever see him again."

"Amber, that's not true." Holly objected strongly. "He would have waited a week, maybe, but not two months! You must believe that. You must tell yourself that he's already on a ship sailing here. He's coming for you, Amber. He'll find you."

"How could he, Holly? Only Von Buren knew where I was taken, and he would never tell. I doubt Nicholas could beat it from him. In fact, I'm sure if Nicholas went to see Van Buren, the baron would try to kill him just for the pleasure of it. No, Holly, I won't give myself false hope. He isn't coming, and what happens to me from now on is of my own doing. I'll survive. *We'll* survive." She turned to clasp both of Holly's hands in hers. "We'll show these men that we're not just simple-minded women they're dealing with, but sharp-witted, cunning foxes, hell-cats! We'll beat them, and when we have, I'll return home to see Baron Kelzer Von Buren pays for everything!"

Amber hugged her friend tightly to her, tears streaming down her face. She believed the words she spoke, that somehow she would live through all this wretchedness and return home. But a seed of fear had planted itself in her mind, and it was gestating into a full-grown anxiety that things would be different when she returned, that Nicholas would no longer love her. Did it matter? Hadn't that been what she truly wanted all along? To be free of him?

Their last meal of the day had been served an hour earlier. Knowing that one more night would pass as so many had before, each girl blindly found her makeshift bed, willing sleep to triumph and rid her troubled mind of all the horror they endured. Yet, Amber found a worry of a different sort when sleep would not come. She thought of her sister, frightened and alone, not knowing what had become of her twin. She envisioned Baron Kelzer Von Buren laughing at the sordid trick he'd played, and remembered Nicholas's warm, loving eyes staring at her, smiling, teasing, daring her at every turn. Although the details of his handsome face had faded in her memory as if a thousand years had passed, she still relived the gentle touch of his hand, his soft, tender kiss, and the passionate embrace she'd only found in *his* arms. She may have screamed her hatred of him, his wealth and power, but now, trapped in this black hell, she knew she would never forget him nor find another to fill the void she felt in her heart.

"Oh, Nicholas," she whispered, sliding from her bed to huddle on the floor. "I pray you never figured out what truly happened, that you never went to see Von Buren." A tear fell from the corner of her eye and glided quickly to her chin. "I know he's killed you if you did." Grief and long-held fears overcame her, and Amber pulled up her knees to rest her brow against her tattered skirts, quietly sobbing, uncertain if she cried for herself or for the thought that she would never see her husband again.

A long while passed before her tears were spent and she leaned back against the wall, exhausted sleep coming quickly. She dreamed of sunshine, fresh air, wild flowers in the meadow, and the moments she had spent along the riverbank, making love in the tall grass with Nicholas. The vision, blurred with the passing of time, played upon her mind. Dark hair and eyes, wide shoulders and flashing white smile, the scowl that crimped his brow when something angered him—each feature took shape briefly, then faded into memory. Amber stirred, uncomfortable in her slumber, jolted awake with the shouts of men on the decks above her prison. She sat upright, listening to the sounds.

"Amber?" came the frightened voice several feet away.

"Yes, Holly, I hear them," she answered.

"What does it mean?"

"I'm not sure." She struggled to her feet. "Stay where you are. I'm going to try to find the door. Maybe I can hear what they're saying from there." Hands stretched out before her, Amber slowly made her way across the wide area, her knee bumping into something and nearly tumbling her to the deck. But the determination to discover the purpose of the men's activity kept her on her feet, and a few moments later her hand found the doorlatch. She pressed forward to listen.

"Holly," she whispered excitedly after a while. "We're dropping anchor!"

"Where? Did someone say where?"

Leaning in again in an effort to overhear even the slightest clue, Amber jumped nervously when the clamor of footsteps grew in volume, marking the approach of several men to the hold.

"Quickly, Holly, come here! Someone's coming and we must be ready for them."

"W—what do you plan to do?" her young friend asked, tripping over a box and falling into Amber's arms.

"We'll stand beside the door, and once they've opened it we'll run out after they've come in looking for us. Do you know how to swim?"

"N—not very well."

"Then stay close beside me. We're going to jump overboard and swim for shore. There has to be someone there who will help us." She hugged Holly to her and moved away from the door just as one of the men slid the bolt free. But Amber's high hopes plummeted earthward when he held out a lantern in front of him, its bright yellow glow flooding the room and blinding both women.

"All right, me ladies," he mocked, "show yourselves. I know you're in here."

Amber frantically rubbed her eyes, willing them to adjust to the light, knowing every moment wasted lessened their chance of escape. But the weeks in total darkness had taken their toll. The pain was almost unbearable, and she could only pray that the men entered the room before any of them turned back to find her and Holly standing near the door. Squinting, she could vaguely see three figures move about, and, deciding they could wait no longer, she seized Holly's hands and dashed through the open doorway.

"Stop them!" someone shouted, followed by the thunder of racing footfalls.

Above decks the sun shone brightly as morning had dawned clear and lustrous, a single beam filling the passageway where Amber and Holly raced for freedom, their eyes shaded by one hand raised above their brows. For weeks Amber had dreamed of basking in the golden glow of day, but now she only found it a troublesome burden when its brilliance deprived her of clear vision. She stumbled, nearly fell, yet pulled her companion onward, suddenly jerked off balance when Holly's hand seemed to be wrenched from her grip. The young girl screamed, and Amber spun around to discover the men had wrestled her to the deck. She struggled frantically, calling out for Amber to run, to seek help, but Amber's feet would not move. Holly Clark, the young English girl she had grown to admire, bore a striking, startling resemblance to Katherine Chandler. Long black hair, matted and tangled, fell in disarray over her shoulders, but the gray-blue eyes that stared back at Amber sent a chill through her, and she knew she could never leave this young woman behind. In the next instant, a hand cruelly squeezed Amber's arm, dragging her toward the ladder and topside, her eyes still affixed to the terror-stricken face of a half-grown woman who didn't deserve such a horrifying fate.

Hauled into the full light of day, Amber squinted in the sunshine, its blinding rays now less painful, and she quickly took in the scene around her. The sailors on board hurriedly secured the ship, and she could only assume they had dropped anchor in the port of Casablanca, their destination, and that within a few minutes she and Holly would be taken to the marketplace and sold. The muscles in her throat tightened, fighting off the rush of tears that threatened to shatter her tough reserve, and she glanced back over her shoulder at Holly for strength. Knowing the young woman was more frightened than she, Amber rekindled her courage simply by looking at her, silently pledging to take care of her new friend with a reassuring smile. She prayed whoever bought them would take them both, for Amber doubted Holly would survive on her own.

The gangplank had been lowered and the women were hastily ushered down it to the pier. It was teeming with other sailors and merchants, and they found themselves jostled and shoved about, steadily moving toward the marketplace amid loud chatter of the natives, a language Amber could not understand. Her hopes for a sympathetic ear dwindled with their chant, for even if she were able to get free of her captors, she realized no one in the village would comprehend a word she spoke. And hiding among these people would prove difficult for their appearance differed greatly from her own. Sundarkened skin, deep brown eyes, and black hair described them all, in vivid contrast to her own fair coloring, and she noticed how a large number of the village men already watched her closely. The women, however, paid little attention, their heads and faces covered with cloth draped around them. Only their eyes showed, and Amber prayed that somehow she and Holly could obtain such garb. Maybe then if they kept their eyes averted, they could move about the town unheeded. That was, of course, if they managed to escape.

The caravan left the docks and headed further inland, the crowds growing more profuse. Amber considered breaking loose of the man who clamped tightly to her elbow, but she dismissed the idea just as quickly. She would not go without Holly. They traveled down the narrow path leading to a monstrously tall stone wall, in the center of which a beautifully carved opening allowed people to enter. On each side large pillars had been built adjoining the gate, and Amber could see men with guns standing at the top manning the stations, as if the structure was a castle from long ago. On either side of the road the merchants had erected small tents or lean-tos in which to display their wares—from baskets full of dates, olives, grapes, and nuts, to blankets woven from wool and bins filled with fresh fish. Small burros carried heavy loads of cloth, goatskins filled with water and often their owners as well. Amber wondered how such tiny creatures could uphold such weight.

As they neared the huge stone gate, Amber glanced off to her right at the landscape. In the far distance she could see the hazy outline of a mountain range thick with the dark foliage of trees, the plains leading up to it covered in scrub brush and alfalfa grass. Warm breezes billowed her skirts and teased the stray tendrils of her hair that had pulled loose of the braid. It smelled fresh and clean and she longed to find a place to bathe.

Suddenly an unearthly howl overrode the volubility of the throng of marketgoers, though none seemed to notice, and Amber jumped fearfully at the noise, quickly finding the source of the uproar. Standing only a few feet from her, she saw the strangest animal she had ever seen in her life, and she was certain it had to be a messenger of Satan. It reached a height nearly twice her own, with short brown fur covering its bony frame. It had the feet of a deer, yet was ten times its size, a long, thin tail with an abundance of hair at the tip, a large protruding jaw and wide-set eyes shadowed by extremely long lashes. It seemed to be all legs, but what captured her attention more was the large deformity on the beast's back. She stared wide-eyed when they were forced to pause at the gate, amazed that the man who held the creature's reins seemed quite at ease, not the least affected by the animal's foul temper as it stubbornly tugged at the restraint. Then, as if singling her out among the lot, the behemoth glared down at her, curled its large lips back over yellowing teeth, and snorted loudly. Startled out of her wits, Amber jumped backward, colliding with the man who held Holly and followed close behind.

"Stand still, wench," the sailor spat, "or I'll let the beast have ya for breakfast."

Fearing he might do as he promised, Amber forced herself not to move, thankful when the camel herder turned and guided his animal away, leaving her to wonder how many more odd denizens she would meet before her journey came to an end.

The crowd pressed onward, and soon Amber and her party

found themselves inside the huge stone wall, mingling in the bustle of the marketplace. All around them, large tents in a rainbow of colors dotted the area, their silky cloth flapping in the breeze. As they passed by them, Amber could see the interior of several. Large pillows were scattered around the floor, small tables in the center were covered with trays of fruit and brass urns. But one in particular caught her eye, for, standing outside the opening, two men guarded its entrance, feet spread apart, arms folded over their bare bronze chests. The only things they wore other than the full-length breeches ballooning to their knees were the brightly colored turbans on their heads, and the long swords tucked in the sashes around their waists. For a fleeting moment she wondered if this tent belonged to the sultan of whom Von Buren had talked. She jerked her attention away, forcing herself to think of other things rather than what might transpire inside if a man like that bought her.

When it seemed they had walked the entire length of the hot, dusty village, the man who had steadily guided her onward stopped near a small wooden platform built higher than the ground, as though a stage for all prospective buyers to better see the merchandise for sale. He looked around for several moments, then motioned his companion to bring Holly closer.

"Put them in there," he instructed, pointing to a large cage made of thin wooden poles and tied with leather straps at the joints.

Without comment, the second sailor did as bade, shutting the women inside and securing the crude door with a chain and lock intertwined between the posts. Amber and Holly quickly hugged each other, watching the two sailors talk with a man dressed in the usual garb of the merchants.

"What's going to happen now?" Holly asked, her voice quivering.

"I don't know," Amber replied quietly, her gaze fixed on the three men, "but let's be ready in case we get the chance to run."

"Run?" Holly echoed, her eyes wide as she glanced around at the horde of faces staring back. "Where would we run? To what? These people don't even speak English. How will we make them understand?" She sidestepped a hand shoved between the bars at her.

Twirling Holly behind her, Amber slapped away the intruding hand, frowning back at the man who clutched his injured fingers to his chest. "There must be *one* person among them who does," she offered, wondering briefly how great the possibility might be. "It's a chance we must take."

Holly shrieked when the nimble fingers of another marketgoer pinched her backside through the narrow shafts of the cage, bringing a roar of laughter from the crowd who steadily gathered around the women. Clutching the young girl to her, Amber moved them to the center of the small space, out of reach.

"God, this place smells awful," Holly said, wrinkling her nose. "Is it always like this, do you suppose?"

Amber guardedly watched the faces of those closest to her, a chill creeping up her spine. All of the men seemed old, with deeply tanned, weathered skin, several teeth missing when they smiled or chattered inanely to a companion, their hair greasy and their clothes covered with dust. Von Buren had said she would be sold. Did he mean to one of these simpletons? Was this to be her fate? Would she live out her life in servitude to one of these cretins? Her courage threatened to elude her.

"Holly," she said quietly, her attention glued to the creatures standing all around them, the small cubicle that separated them seeming to grow narrower, "I want you to promise me something."

Holly retreated a step when one old man jabbed a stick through the bars. "What? That I won't go mad before all of this is over?"

"I want you to promise that if the chance comes for you to escape, with or without me, that you will."

"No, Amber—"

"You must, Holly," Amber interrupted, jerking the hem of her tattered skirts free of an imposing hand clenched around them. "You're to find help, return home, and send word to Nicholas's grandmother, Alanna Remington. Alanna will help me, and she has enough money to send an army if she has to. I'll just wait." She glanced up at the bars overhead, noticing how brightly the sun shone. She wished they hadn't put them in this cage.

"Then you must promise the same or I won't agree," Holly said bravely, her face contorting disdainfully when one of the men grinned toothlessly at her.

"I can't promise you that," Amber frowned, wondering why these horrible men didn't go home to their wives.

"Why? Both of us shouldn't have to suffer if there's the slightest chance." She slapped out at the hand that tried to touch her.

"You're only fifteen, Holly. You've never known a man. I have."

Holly's fearful eyes looked at her companion. "W-what do you mean?"

Drawing in a breath, Amber took Holly's hands in hers, forcing herself to ignore the crowd and their noise. "If we're sold into bondage, we'll be expected to . . . to ease our master's needs . . . lie with him."

The color drained from Holly's face.

"I don't mean to frighten you, only show you the importance of your getting away. I've lived a tougher life than you. I will survive." Amber reached up to touch Holly's cheek and bring her attention back when the young woman worriedly glanced at the hostile stares of the group. "Promise?"

Holly's chin trembled. "Yes. But I promise more." She continued to face Amber, but her eyes wildly scanned the crowd. "I promise we won't have to send word to Mistress Remington—that my father will return here with his own army."

Amber smiled softly for the first time in a long while, still holding the young woman's hands in hers. "If I could change any of this, I would have you dining with your father right now. But since I can't, I must admit I'm glad I didn't have to go through all of it alone. You've helped me, Holly, more than you realize." She lifted a hand to push Holly's dark hair from her face, a dull ache stabbing at her heart when she stared into the gray-blue eyes so much like Katherine's, and she silently thanked God that Nicholas's sister was safe.

Nicholas. His image came to haunt her again. How could she have been so foolish? He had never intended to hurt her, only love her, share his life with her. Why had she run away? He had aroused in her feelings she had never thought existed, a wild abandonment, a bliss, a pleasure she enjoyed in both body and soul. She looked away from Holly, not really seeing anything else as her mind drifted to more pleasant memories. She closed her eyes, shutting out the foreign sounds around her, and let her thoughts whisk her away to the clearing near the stream, to the last time she had seen Nicholas. She could almost smell the manly scent of him, feel the thickness of his hair, the strong muscles of his shoulders. A tear stole between her lashes and slowly trailed a moist path to the corner of her mouth, and, without realizing it, she spoke his name in a choked whisper.

"Forgive me, my husband," she wept, all the trials of the weeks past closing in on her.

"Amber!"

Startled back to reality by Holly's summons, Amber brushed away her tears and opened her eyes. Holly's face reflected horror, a deeper fear than any either girl had felt so far. She nodded past her, and Amber followed her lead, afraid yet wanting to know what had disturbed the fragile young woman to such a degree.

The sailors who had brought them to this place had gone and a crowd had gathered in their wake, but, standing in the center of them all, towered the obese shape of a man, feet spread apart, arms folded over his mammoth chest. Amber trembled instantly, for though she doubted she had seen a man more huge, more threatening, his size had little to do with the tremor of revulsion she felt race through her. He was dressed in bright colored linens and a cape was draped over his rotund frame, but his clothing failed to pull her attention away from his face. One dark brown eye glared back at her, radiating his contempt, while a long, grotesque scar seemed to divide his ugly features in half. It ran from beneath the turban he wore to his temple, across the left side of his brow, the bridge of his nose and the opposite cheek, leaving his second eye a white, cloudy orb. He stood rock still, only the slight movement of his chest marking the fact that he was a living man and not a figment of Amber's imagination. On either side of him stood men dressed in similar garb and posed in the same fashion, and she wondered why he required their protection. Surely no one of sound mind would cross him.

"Amber, why is he staring at you?" Holly whispered nervously, her fingers clamped tightly around Amber's arm.

"I don't know. But he makes my skin clammy."

"My God, Amber, you don't suppose he's . . ."

"I don't know," Amber said, noticing how the crowd had grown and begun pushing toward the platform. "But I think we're going to find out who makes the highest offer very soon."

The marketer who had met with their captors shoved his way through the gathering of people toward the stage, climbed the pair of steps, and raised his hands in an effort to quiet them. Once they had stilled, he spoke loudly, waving his arms and laughing, then pointing toward the cage that held Amber and Holly. Both women trembled when all eyes seemed to focus on them.

"W-what did he say?" Holly asked, her gray-blue eyes wide with fear.

"I imagine he's telling what great prizes we are to bring up the price," Amber frowned, studying the various faces staring at them. "If we have a choice, let me go first."

"Why?"

"Even if they don't speak our language, I might be able to get whomever buys me to purchase you too."

"How will you do that?"

Amber smiled reassuringly and patted Holly's arm. "I'll think of something."

The noise of the crowd grew in volume, but Amber really didn't notice. Her attention was concentrated on the barbarian with one eye who continually stared at her. He hadn't moved, yet no one had stepped in front of him. It was as if everyone in the marketplace feared him, and whatever he wanted he would have. What formed the furrowing of her brow came from her failure to understand why he would be interested in her. She didn't have to see her image in a mirror to know how matted and dull her hair had become or to be aware of the dirt that seemed to cover every inch of her. Her once beautiful lavender gown trimmed in lace hung in rags from her thinning frame, the same grime that was on her face covering its soft hue and turning it a dull gray. Amber's heart pounded in her chest as she stared at the horrifying man, and she found herself preferring Von Buren over this menacing hulk. Maybe it was because she had never feared the baron. Her lip curled disdainfully. And if it hadn't been for Von Buren, Holly and she wouldn't be here now.

I must thank you for one thing, baron, she thought bitterly, if my hatred for you hadn't been so strong, I would have died on the ship. I lived through that, and I will live to see you dead.

Suddenly the door of the cage was thrown open, and Holly frantically clung to the woman at her side, tears streaming down her face. The marketer motioned for Amber to step out, and she turned to comfort Holly.

"Be brave, Holly. I swear I won't let anyone hurt you." Without further delay, she pulled the frightened girl's hands from her and left the wooden cell, courageously walking to the stage where her fate would be decided.

The buzz of the observers grew more intense and quieted only when the marketer shouted something at them. Then he turned toward Amber, waving his hands and spewing alien words as he walked a complete circle around her. He touched her hair, his nose wrinkled unpleasantly and she jerked away. He pulled back, feigning surprise, and the onlookers guffawed their delight at his pranks. But when he bent to lift her skirts and expose the shapely limbs hidden beneath the tattered cloth, Amber angrily slapped his hand away, bringing a roar of laughter from the crowd. Obviously displeased with her rebellion and the fact that she had made a fool of him in front of so many, he stiffened instantly. He glared at her a moment before his hands went to the rope belt around his waist. Watching him pull it free, Amber wondered fearfully if he intended to whip her with it, but her anxiety turned to wonder when she observed him tie one end into a loop. He took a step toward her and she retreated, unsure of his intention, planning to continue if he advanced further. Suddenly he shot out a hand to grab the braid of her hair. She squealed at the painful tug as he forced her to her knees, slipping the rough cord over her head and pulling it tightly around her neck. Tears came to her eyes when the hemp cut into her flesh, and she stayed perfectly still, certain he would strangle the breath from her if she didn't.

The marketer boasted loudly, bringing a cheer from the spectators. He called out again, only this time someone in the group responded, and Amber assumed the auction had begun. Without moving her head, she scanned the crowd for the one-eyed man and found him watching, a slight smile curling one corner of his mouth. The man standing next to her called out a second time, and the great hulk unfolded his arms and shoved his fists into the flab of each hip. His thunderous voice answered the marketer's question, and all eyes widened at the sum he offered.

Amber's heart thumped loudly, her certainty of overcoming all her trials now sorely tested, for it seemed the barbarian would outbid any price the others might submit. She glanced over at Holly to find her sobbing and silently said her good-byes. She had vowed to keep them together, but if this brute was to be her master she would not allow Holly to endure the same tortures she was sure to have forced on her. No, it was best if Holly was purchased by someone else. She bowed her head, her tears trickling down her face, and prayed God would give her the strength to continue.

With her head down, Amber failed to see the mass of market-goers scramble out of the way of three horsemen riding toward the platform until the buzzing of the people caught her attention. She looked up, spying the most magnificent Arabian stallions she had ever seen in her life, but her gaze was immediately drawn to the proud figure of the man leading the trio. Bright green flowing silks nearly covered his entire frame, leaving little for her to appraise. The turban he wore hid the color of his hair, and a cloth draped across his face allowed only a narrow slit for his eyes, the bridge of his nose, and a portion of his high-set cheekbones. He glanced at her only briefly before settling his attention on the one-eyed man who glared dangerously at him.

"Yaakob," the newcomer nodded at the man, his baritone voice raspy as if he found it difficult to speak.

Her interest aroused, Amber stared openly, wondering at the sudden increase of her pulse, and watched in awe as the long, lean frame unfolded to dismount. The silk of his garb billowed softly in the warm breezes, then clung to his muscular body, to the wide shoulders, the broad curve of his chest and the well-proportioned thighs as he stood feet apart, one fist to his hip, the other resting on the stallion's mane. His companions followed his lead but stayed close by his side, and Amber sensed a great hatred between by the two men who stood facing each other.

"Ronen," Yaakob growled through clenched teeth, before turning away to summon the marketer to continue.

But when the little man who still held on to the rope around Amber's throat raised his hand to declare the auction done, the man called Ronen interrupted. The crowd gasped at what he said, and Amber wondered if by chance this stranger had out-bid Yaakob. She glanced quickly at the hulk, seeing his face contort in rage. He raised four fingers in the air. Before the marketer could respond, Ronen bid again and was countered by Yaakob. The group of observers pressed closer. Several more rounds were voiced, and at each addition Yaakob's face darkened.

The group's attention drawn away from her, Amber looked over at Holly. She had dried her tears and was watching intently. Apparently she felt the same small hope Amber did, that the one-eyed man would not win, for although they would have preferred to be set free, bondage to the new stranger seemed more tolerable than to Yaakob. She glanced back at the duo to find the Ronen had not moved, in fact appeared quite at ease, while Yaakob glowered his hatred. All had fallen quiet, and when it seemed no one would speak again, the marketer called out weakly, his gaze centered on Yaakob, and Amber could almost feel the little man tremble. One brown, one white orb shifted to look at him. He spoke again, gasping when Yaakob straightened. But instead of answering or approaching the platform, Yaakob turned and strode angrily away, the roar of the crowd drowning out the sounds of his footsteps.

Amber's long-held breath escaped her in a rush and she rested back on her heels, her eyes closed. How many more such adversities must she face—and would she always be spared the harshest of possibilities? Of course, now she must figure out a way to have the stranger buy Holly, too. That might prove rather difficult, since she doubted he intended to purchase two slaves, and, with Yaakob's absence, there would be no game to play against his enemy. If only he spoke English, she could explain the rewards his investment could offer. But certain her luck had run out long ago, she decided she would have to try some other sort of venture to convince him. She opened her eyes, her breath catching when she found Ronen had moved to stand directly in front of her. Even though he stood on the ground and she knelt on the platform, she had to look up into his eyes. Her pulse quickened again, and for a fleeting moment she wondered if she would be any safer with this man than with Yaakob, for there was little mistaking the gleam in his dark brown eyes. She forced down the knot in her throat and waited, oddly fearing he might strip her here for all to see and have the profits she felt certain he thought he deserved. Several moments passed before he nodded at the marketer, and the man quickly took the rope from around Amber's neck. She longed to rub the bruised flesh but remained motionless, not trusting the man should he catch her off guard. Without looking away from her, he motioned his men to bring the horses. Once they reached him, Ronen held out a hand for her to take. She trembled, took a deep breath, and steadied herself to voice her request, knowing he would not understand her words.

"Ronen?" she questioned and paused, waiting for him to acknowledge the name. "I know you don't speak my language, none of these savages do," her outstretched hands encompassed all who watched, "but maybe you will understand if I show you." Slowly coming to her feet, she moved toward the end of the platform and walked down the steps toward the cage and Holly. Reaching through the bars, she took the girl's hand and looked back at him. "This is my sister. Sister," she repeated, pointing first at Holly, then herself.

Ronen didn't move.

"He doesn't know what you mean, Amber," Holly whispered. "Try something else."

Amber thought a moment, then pretended to pull a knife from the make-believe sash at her waist. She drew the imaginary blade across the inside of her wrist, repeated the demonstration with Holly, then pressed the fake wounds together. "Sisters," she said again, both women staring hopefully at the man garbed in bright silks.

Ronen tilted his head to one side, watching, then glanced back at his companions. They exchanged a few words that neither Holly nor Amber could hear before they broke out in heartfelt laughter. Amber's temper flared, positive they had shared a vile joke. She stiffened, her earlier fears of the man forgotten, and stomped angrily toward him. Once she reached him, she doubled up a fist and waited for his laughter to die.

"I will not go anywhere without her," she stormed, landing a blow to his stomach and bringing an excited shriek from the onlookers.

His breath left him in a painful *whoosh*, and he clutched his belly, shock darkening his eyes. The crowd stilled, awaiting his next move, certain he would strike the rebellious, foolhardy woman. Then his brows came together in an ill-humored scowl, and with lightning speed he grabbed her arm just above the elbow, crushing her to him. But Amber would not cower beneath his strength. She glared back at him, raised a slippered foot and brought it down hard upon his. He winced but steeled his hold. Unaffected by his stubbornness, Amber yanked back, breaking free of him, and raced for the cage where Holly looked on in horror. The crowd stepped aside to watch.

If his muscular build had seemed overpowering before, he appeared to magnify in size as he straightened to full height and started toward her.

"She goes with me or I won't go," Amber screamed, backing around the corner of the wood structure.

"Amber, you've made him angry," Holly cried, her voice quivering. "It's not worth it. Please go with him. I don't want you hurt because of me."

"I don't expect my life with this . . . cold-blooded viper to be pleasant," Amber argued, continuing around the cage several steps out of reach. "So why give in just to postpone it? You're coming with me."

"But he doesn't want me. And you can't make him understand." Holly moved closer to her friend until only the width of the bars separated them. Without warning, her hand shot out and firmly clasped Amber's tattered skirts, holding her fast and not allowing her to run.

"What are you doing?" Amber shouted, pulling at the fingers grasping her dress, her eyes widening when she saw Ronen quicken his steps. "Let go, Holly! He's—"

But before her words were finished, Ronen's wide hand descended on her, squeezing her wrist and jerking her forward. He shoved her ahead of him and paused to stare at Holly, a confused expression crinkling the corners of his dark eyes. Holly returned the look, her fear receding when she thought she saw a glimmer of compassion race through their ebony depths. But it disappeared when Amber brought her free hand around, intent on striking his face. He easily caught it, too, in an unrelenting grip only inches from her goal, pulling her against his chest. He stared down at her, and Amber wished the cloth didn't hide his face, for she felt certain he smiled.

"Amber, don't fight him," Holly whispered when she saw Amber struggle to push away. "I sense he'll not hurt you if you behave."

How could Amber tell this poor, young innocent girl that she struggled to free herself from the contact she endured? Her flesh seemed to burn wherever he touched her and if Holly sensed something about him, so did Amber. As soon as night fell and he took her to his tent, Amber knew she would have to fight in earnest, that before the sun rose again, this man would have her in his bed.

"Holly, please," she begged, her eyes trained on the masked face, "pull his hand from mine. I—I can't go with him."

But before Holly had the chance to help or even respond, Ronen spun Amber around and shoved her into the waiting arms of one of his men. He crushed her to him and nearly lifted her from her feet as he dragged her to the horses. In one effortless sweep, he sat her on the steed's back, and swung himself up behind her.

Holly watched the procedure in tears, praying she had done the right thing, and failed to notice Ronen approach the marketer. They exchanged a few words before Ronen withdrew a small pouch from the folds of his garb and handed it to the man. He then motioned his other companion to unlock the cage. When the door swung wide in front of her, Holly stood transfixed, unable to comprehend the purpose until Ronen stepped inside, gently took her arm, and escorted her out. He guided her to one of the stallions, waited for his man to mount, then helped Holly up behind him. He nodded at her smile, turned, and strode to his horse where he agilely swung himself into the saddle.

A cheer from the crowd who had watched it all accompanied the band of misfits as they made their way through the marketplace and out the gate, heading for the mountains in the distance.

Chapter Eighteen

A warm, bright sun shone overhead, guiding the way to a narrow path in the foothills of the Atlas Mountains. Evergreen, fir, and spruce trees dotted the landscape, and gentle sea breezes filled the air with a fresh, sweet aroma, in startling contrast to the weeks she had spent locked below decks in the foul-smelling hold. Amber closed her eyes, sucking in a breath. She would have preferred to be standing at the rail of a huge English ship sailing for America—but that would come in time. She was sure of it.

The cortege had traveled nearly an hour, but to Amber's abused backside it seemed an eternity. She wanted to stretch, to shift her weight, and would have if she thought she would not come into further contact with the man riding behind her. It was bad enough that his arms encircled her to hold the reins, but she realized the slightest move one way or another would touch their bodies full length. She gritted her teeth, not wishing to arouse him in the least, whether it be in lustful interest or short-tempered annoyance.

Having gone without breakfast or a drop of water, her stomach growled its protest and her lips became quite dry. Yet she would have gladly traded both food and drink for a hot bath and clean clothes. Thinking of her appearance, she looked down at the soiled remains of her lavender skirts smudged with dirt and torn in several places. Would the man called Ronen allow her something else to wear? Or would she be forced to repair this garment and wash it each evening before she retired? A sudden chill raced through her when she thought of the probable sleeping arrangements. From lowered lashes, she guardedly studied the leader of their group. He rode to one side of them and ahead several paces. He hadn't spoken to either of his men since leaving the marketplace or looked her way a single time. Maybe, just maybe, with luck—did she have any left?—he had purchased her and Holly only as servants to bring his food, wash his clothes, and do other menial chores expected of their women. Dear Lord, she hoped so. Being outnumbered as they were, Holly and she would be defenseless in stopping any of the men from doing as they wished. Lifting her chin a little, she appraised him openly, drawing courage from the fact that he seemed more interested in the rough terrain than his companions. His gaze constantly surveyed the shadows and bluffs, as if he anticipated trouble. The dark silk cloth covered a great deal of his face, leaving her to imagine what lay beneath. She had already noticed how his complexion was paler than that of most of the other men at the marketplace, yet much darker than her own. He sat ramrod straight in the saddle and rode with a practiced grace, the firm muscles of his thighs absorbing the jolt of each step his horse took. Even in silence, he commanded power and respect, and although she would have much preferred to be home fighting off Nicholas's advances, she somehow sensed a safety with this man. And at the first available moment, she would tell Holly how she felt.

Thinking of the young woman again, Amber twisted slightly in the saddle to look at her friend. Her face reflected her surprise when she noticed how Holly contentedly studied their surroundings, almost appearing as if she enjoyed the ride. Caught up in the beauty of the scenery, Holly failed to notice that Amber watched her, and Amber frowned when she saw how willingly the girl wrapped her arms around the man sitting in front of her. Amber concluded that the young English-woman had no knowledge of or skill in riding horseback, but she had assumed Holly would find it distasteful to touch a man with such familiarity. Was there more to Holly Clark than she realized?

Several more hours dragged by, each step the horse took reminding Amber how much she favored traveling in a carriage to this method. Especially astraddle the beast! Every muscle in her body ached, and she longed to stop, dismount, and stretch her legs, and give her tender backside a few moments to recover. And what about eating? Judging from the location of the sun in the cloudless blue sky, it must be approaching midafternoon. Surely these men were hungry, too. She ran her tongue over her lips. They were so dry. She glanced over at Ronen, who still traveled a short distance ahead of them, spying a goatskin pouch hanging from his saddle. She had not seen him drink from it, but from its odd shape, full at the bottom and narrowing to a point with some sort of stopper in it, she could guess it held water. The longer she stared at it, the thirstier she became. *Hang the consequences,* she thought. She needed a drink too badly to worry about angering him.

"Ronen," she said with a smile, a chill running through her when he turned dark brown eyes upon her. "I'm . . . thirsty. Do you carry water with you?"

He continued to stare at her as if he didn't understand.

The smile broadened. "I'm sorry. I forgot you're too stupid to know what I'm saying." She nodded toward the pouch. "Drink. I'd like a drink, you clod." The tone of her voice denied the insult.

Glancing first at the goatskin, then back at Amber, Ronen slowed his horse with a jerk of the reins, allowing her mount to catch up to him. He untied the pouch from the leather straps holding it to the saddle and handed it to her.

"You're too kind," she nodded, the implication of her words most clear, and eagerly accepted the article.

The leather bag, its bottom heavy, seemed to elude her grasp, rapidly oozing from one hand to the other, until, out of fear that she would drop it and spill the contents on the ground, she was finally forced to cradle the object on her lap. She didn't have to look at Ronen to know he enjoyed her dilemma. She could feel his amused appraisal.

The buffoon knew what would happen before he had handed it to her, she thought irritably. *Well, he's had his fun.*

Pulling the cork loose, she wrapped one arm around the water bag and held the open end to her mouth. She squeezed, only a trickle moistening her parched lips. She pressed harder. A rush of clear liquid squirted out, covered her entire face, and dripped down the front of her gown. The trio of men exploded into laughter.

Anger raged up in Amber at the trick he'd played, and before any of the group could react she pointed the goatskin at Ronen and lifted the opposite end high in the air. A long stream of water flowed outward, hitting Ronen in the chest. She heard Holly gasp at her boldness and the laughter of the men die immediately, and she smiled. Planning to soak his entire body, she lifted the end higher. However, before she could succeed, the man sitting behind her grabbed the water pouch and jerked it from her hands, splashing a good quantity on himself.

"Oh, excuse me," Amber mocked, staring at Ronen, who did not move in the slightest, his brown eyes glaring back at her, "but no one showed me how to hold the pouch. Besides, you got what you deserved, you heathen." Her face glowed apologetically while the twinkle in her eye disproved all sincerity.

Several moments passed. Neither Amber nor Ronen looked away, and although by all rights Amber should have feared this stranger's reaction to her attack, she didn't. In fact, she drew courage from his stillness. She even contemplated slipping from the horse to stretch her legs, since it appeared they were not going to stop for a while longer. But just as she had about decided to do exactly that, Ronen leaned forward, took the goatskin from his companion, and spurred his horse onward, the others instantly following his lead. A frown flitted across Amber's brow, for she wondered how far she could push this silent man before she truly angered him, and what sort of punishment he might then deem appropriate. Curiosity replaced the weariness of her body, and she fixed her attention on the man who rode ahead of her.

Sunset had turned the sky to their right a vivid orange before the group reined the horses to a stop in a small clearing several yards from the path they had followed for the greater part of the day. The men quickly dismounted, tied off the horses, and unfastened several bundles from their saddles. By all appearances, it seemed they had decided to set up camp. Amber glanced back at Holly with a smile, certain they would soon be allowed to ease the gnawing in their stomachs, and frowned when she saw the third member of the group assist Holly from the horse and gently set her on the ground. Annoyed that no one offered any aid to her in dismounting, she irritably swung one leg over the stallion's neck and slid to the ground. Her tight muscles forbid her to descend gracefully, and once her feet touched the earth she stumbled and fell. Tiny pebbles cut into her knees and she cried out in pain. Rolling to her backside, she lifted her skirts to examine the wounds. Several dots of blood marred her flesh, and she gingerly brushed away the dirt. Selecting one small section of clean petticoat, she moistened the spot with her tongue and washed the area. No real damage had been done, the cuts would heal, but Amber's temper smoldered. Looking up, intent on finding someone on whom to vent her dissatisfaction, her chin sagged when she discovered no one paid her any heed. Ronen had already taken a musket from his horse and started off toward the woods surrounding them, the man with whom she had shared the horse ride was gathering dried sticks for a fire, and Holly and her companion were spreading out blankets on the ground. Her pride ruffled at being so neglected, Amber awkwardly stood up, fists knotted on her hips and glared at the three remaining in camp. When no one seemed to care or take notice, an idea struck her.

Carefully watching the two men, she hurriedly examined the baggage on the stallion for any kind of weapon, a smile brightening her eyes when she found a dagger in one of the pouches. With the knife held tightly in her hand, she moved toward Holly and the man who had his back turned. Close enough to touch her friend, Amber reached out, grabbed Holly's arm, and jerked her away from him, instantly bringing everyone's attention to her.

"All right, you barbarians," she hissed, waving her weapon at them, "just stay where you are. We enjoyed our visit, but it's time Holly and I were going home." She began inching her way backward toward the stallion, Holly at her side. "Can you mount alone?" she asked, her eyes trained on the two men who followed their every step.

"I—I think so," Holly answered. "But you know this won't work, don't you?"

"Can you think of anything better? We're moving further away from the seaport. How will we get home if we don't stay near the ships?"

"But what about Ronen? He'll come after us," Holly warned, clumsily hooking one toe in the stirrup. Clamping onto the horse's mane with one hand, the back of the saddle with the other, she tried unsuccessfully to pull herself up. "I'm—I'm not strong enough," she confessed, letting go.

"All right, then you hold the knife on them while I mount," Amber instructed, shoving the weapon in the frightened girl's hand. Without giving Holly a chance to object, Amber traded her places and easily swung herself up into the saddle. "Give it to me," she nodded toward the dagger, her hand extended.

But as Holly reached up to do as Amber wanted, a shot rang out from somewhere in the woods, startling the horse. The beast sidestepped nervously, its broad shoulder bumping into Holly and knocking her to the ground, the knife flying from her hand. The men reacted quickly, one rushing to grab Holly by the arm before she could scramble to her feet, the other seizing the horse's reins. However, Amber was determined to be free. She kicked out, catching the man in the side and knocking the wind from him. Clutching his belly, he let go of the bridle, and Amber jerked back on the reins, spinning the horse around.

"I'll come back for you, Holly," she shouted, whipping the horse to set them off in the direction in which they had come. She never bothered to look upon the group again, destined to put a safe distance between herself and the barbarians before she would slow the animal. She must be safe first, then decide how to rescue Holly. Maybe later, when everyone was asleep, she could sneak into camp, steal Ronen's musket, and hold them all at bay while she and Holly took their horses.

The horses! Amber's heart pounded in her temples, instantly aware of the foolishness of her scheme. She should have chased away the extra stallions first, before ever trying to run. It would only take a few minutes to catch her when she left them easy access to a speedy method. Glancing over her shoulder as the beast galloped down the narrow path, low-hanging branches reaching out to hit her, she felt a moment of relief to see that no one followed as yet. If she could only find a place large enough to hide both her and the horse. . . .

Concentrating on the path ahead of her, Amber spurred the stallion on, praying her skill with a horse would grant her sufficient time to locate a hideout. Up ahead she spied an assemblage of huge rocks and trees off to one side. Since the men couldn't understand what she had said to Holly as she raced off, she doubted they would ever expect to see her again or that she would stop running after such a short distance, if they elected to follow. Thus she felt secure in reining the steed from the trail and into the protection of the boulders. Winded after their frantic ride, the stallion eagerly halted at her command and stood contentedly catching its breath.

A gentle breeze whistled through the trees, stirring up dead leaves and particles of sand and dirt. Amber watched their chaotic flight unconsciously, listening for any sounds that would mean one of the men had followed. When several minutes passed, a short space that dragged on, her curiosity urged her to dismount and climb atop one of the rocks to get a full view of the trail. After tying the horse's reins to a tree branch, she began her perilous journey and had climbed half-way up when she heard the clamor of racing hooves. Flattened against the rocks, she glanced down at the stallion, praying the scent of another creature would not make him whinny. But her luck held as the intruder raced on by and her horse merely shook his large head to chase away an insect perched on his nose.

How long would they search? she wondered. Darkness would come soon, and they would never be able to find her then. And in all the excitement, she had forgotten about food. Disheartened but not discouraged, she twisted around to sit down on the rock ledge. Her stomach would have to wait. She couldn't chance starting a fire with them so near, and she didn't have anything to cook if she did. She let out a long, disgusted sigh, hoping the night would not become too chilly for her, her gaze falling on the animal that munched happily on the leaves dangling before him and spotting a large bundle still tied to the saddle. With everything happening so fast, no one had had time to unfasten the blankets and pouches from the steed, and Amber relaxed a degree, knowing at least that she would be warm. She waited a moment longer, listening for any evidence that the rider had stopped and turned around. When silence prevailed, she inched her way back down the rock toward the horse and the supplies. Standing safely on the ground once more, she loosened the leather straps holding the goods and quickly examined the contents of the packs. A frown marred her brow for a second as she lifted a small, sticky piece of fruit from inside. Dark brown, it smelled sweet, and her stomach rumbled approval for her to sample it. Taking only a nibble, her mouth watered instantly at its aroma and delicious flavor. Whatever it was, it tasted good, and she didn't hesitate finishing it off, carefully spitting out the pit. She reached for another, when of a sudden the stallion reared back his head and snorted loudly. Dropping the bag of fruit, Amber quickly grabbed the animal's bridle in an effort to soothe the creature. But the more she tried, the more he fought her, tugging at her hold until he had nearly spun her around. And in that instant, she saw the reason for the steed's behavior. Standing on the rock ledge, the spot she had vacated only minutes before, Ronen glared down at her.

How had he managed to find her? To sneak up on her? Hadn't she heard him—or someone—ride on by? Panic tingling the hairs on the back of her neck, she silently measured the distance between them, praying she could untie the horse, mount, and race off before he could get to her. But did it matter? She must try. She had no way of knowing what punishment his anger would deal out to her for having eluded his men and making them all look like fools. Sucking in a breath to ease the pain in her chest, she continued to watch him, one hand reaching up to free the reins from the tree branch. He didn't move. If only the damn horse would stand still! Knowing he would lunge for her at any second, Amber spun around, hooked a toe in the stirrup, and pulled herself up into the saddle, kicking the horse's sides without the slightest glance Ronen's way. If she had looked in his direction she would have known his plan, for as she raced back for the trail Ronen climbed to the highest rock overlooking the path, a spot she must pass beneath if she intended to return to the village.

A triumphant smile curled her lips, thinking she had won, had outfoxed him, and she quickly looked back at where he had been, only to find the place where he had stood empty, and a shadow falling on her from somewhere above. She had little time to react or scream before Ronen came sailing through the air, his arms outstretched to envelop her as he knocked her from the horse. He twisted in midair to shield her frailer form and take the brunt of the fall as they fell together on the ground cushioned by a bed of pine needles, grass, and dried leaves. The jolt startled Amber into awareness that she had not been victorious but had played right into his hands and that now she was at his mercy. But her stubborn pride would not allow him an easy win and she kicked out wildly, her nails digging into the flesh of his arms as he held her tightly to him. She could feel the rock-hard muscles of his entire body pressed against her own weaker ones, but refused to be intimidated by his strength. She would do damage to the fine physique if only with a bruise or two, or long, bloody furrows where her nails found their mark. She struggled harder against his unwavering grip, and the slow realization that her efforts failed brought tears to her eyes, for when he had dragged her from the horse he had caught her around the waist, her back pressed against his chest, and made it nearly impossible for her to strike his face. Left with no other alternative, she sought to kick his shins, but he spoiled that affront by merely wrapping his legs around hers.

"Let go of me, you cowardly whoreson," she howled, her breath nearly squeezed from her. "I'll see you're hanged for this."

A low rumble of laughter sounded in her ear, and for a fleeting moment Amber wondered if he understood her words or simply mocked her futile scuffle, only second-guessing her meaning. Then, without warning, he shoved her away, forcing her to sprawl facedown on the hard earth. Recovering quickly, she pushed herself up to her knees, glaring at the tall figure that now stood over her, his fists knotted on each hip. The green silks hid his face, but Amber could see the twinkle in his dark brown eyes. He nodded for her to get up, and she slowly obliged, her upper lip curled in an unflattering snarl. She wanted to strike him, but from the ungentlemanly manner by which he had merely postponed her escape, she figured he would be uncivil enough to return the gesture. She would have to be satisfied to seek revenge some other way, at a better time. And it wouldn't be a mere slap to his face.

The horse had only wandered a short way after losing its rider, and it was an easy task to claim his bridle again. Ronen quickly guided the stallion back to his companion. He mounted agilely, then extended a hand to assist Amber onto the animal's wide back behind him. She stared at the lean, sun-darkened fingers held out to her, wishing for another way to bestraddle the steed than by touching this dark, mysterious stranger. She longed to return to her home, to Williamsburg, and vowed to do so someday soon, but standing here now in a strange country with a man who couldn't even speak her language she somehow sensed that he would become a vivid part of her future. It frightened her, and at the same time gave her an odd feeling of safety. Looking up into his eyes, she saw a glimmer of compassion before it disappeared, replaced by an impatient scowl. She took his hand and awkwardly climbed up, vowing to find a better time to escape him, an opportunity where both she and Holly would succeed.

The two men who had been left in camp at Ronen's orders hurriedly came to meet their leader and the woman who sat rigidly behind him when they returned. They exchanged a few words before Ronen swung a long leg over the animal's neck and slid to the ground. Handing the reins to his companion, he turned back to help Amber from the horse, his head tilting to one side in bewilderment when she smiled sarcastically down at him. Without comment, she too tossed a leg over the animal's back and glided to the ground unassisted. They stared at each other for several moments, one testing the other, and Ronen finally made the first move. Gently but unprovoked, he took hold of her wrist and guided her toward the fire in the center of the camp, unaware of the frightening effect his touch of steel had on Amber. Her heart fluttered, a mist of nervous perspiration veiling her brow, and she wondered if the time had come to pay her dues for all the trouble she had caused. She relaxed only slightly when he forced her down on the blanket and stood silently observing her for a while before he turned and strode away.

"Amber," Holly beckoned, quickly coming to kneel beside her, "did he hurt you?"

Amber continued to observe the man as he returned to the stallion and his men, pulling the bundles and blankets from the steed before he spoke quietly to one of them. He turned slightly toward the path they had traveled and pointed its direction, then stepped aside to allow the man to mount. Spinning the horse around, he galloped off down the trail.

"No, he didn't hurt me," Amber finally answered. "And that's what scares me."

"What do you mean?"

As Ronen approached them, he seemed distracted as he bent to spread out the blanket near the fire and discarded the other sacks. When he had finished, he crouched a few feet away to clean the rabbit he had shot before his wild ride to catch his stubborn, determined property, ignoring the two pairs of eyes watching his every move, but close enough to hear the women's conversation, though he could not understand them.

"I expected these men to be . . . abusive. Yet they're not." She noticed how the muscles of his forearms flexed as he skillfully gutted, then skinned the animal. "I can't imagine someone like him buying a woman, two, in fact, without demanding his rights before now." She frowned irritably when she heard Holly's rapid intake of breath, but refused to take her eyes from Ronen. "You'll have to face the truth, Holly. Sooner or later one of us will find ourselves warming his bed, if we don't escape very soon."

"You're not going to try again, are you?" Holly asked worriedly.

"Well, of course," Amber snapped. "I don't have any intention of becoming this lecher's whore. Do you?"

"No, but—"

"Then we'll try again tonight when everyone's asleep."

Holly quickly sat down next to her, moving closer so that Ronen wouldn't hear their plan, even though he couldn't understand. "All right, we'll try again. But don't talk so loud. He will hear us."

"What if he does? This vile guttersnipe doesn't understand a word." Amber smiled with her insult as Ronen proceeded in his preparation of their meal, securing the rabbit to a stick that he hung over the fire, and seeming uninterested in anything the women said. "See what I mean? Why this buffoon probably doesn't even know who his father is."

Holly's hands flew to her mouth to stifle her gasp, her eyes wide as she stared at the man, certain that at any moment he would turn his wrath on her foolish friend. But when he simply added another stick to the blaze without the slightest look their way, her mouth twisted into a smile and she bit her lip to keep from giggling out loud. "You're right, Amber. He doesn't know what we're saying." She straightened bravely. "I'll wager his mother slept with many," Holly added, grinning widely when he continued to work, her face burning with her boldness.

Amber chuckled, looking over at her companion. "Well, let's not tax our luck. He might grow suspicious by our tone." Slipping her hand in Holly's, she sighed happily. "So listen carefully and I'll tell you what to do. If these clods are as stupid as I suspect, we'll have no trouble getting away."

The pale blueness of Amber's eyes darkened as she glowered at the group gathered around the fire, the small rabbit long since devoured, shared in equal portions, except by her. Ordered to sit several yards away, she had been forced to watch them all, including Holly, sample the tender meat and sate their hunger, accompanied by crusts of bread and fruits from the pouches and washed down with wine. Her mouth watered at the sight, her lips parched, since none would offer her a drink.

So, she thought acidly, this was her punishment for running away. No supper, as if she was a child. She shifted, uncurling one leg from beneath her to bring back the circulation, and realized she hadn't moved since Ronen had escorted her to the spot. At first, when she had discovered his motives for secluding her from the rest, she had defiantly claimed no need for food. But the longer she had watched the others eat, the warm, tempting aroma of cooked rabbit attacking her senses, the louder her stomach had seemed to growl. Her stubbornness had turned to self-pity, feeling that the sentence for her misdeeds was too harsh, and tears had sprung to her eyes. Did he mean to have her beg? Crawl on bended knee and ask forgiveness, pledge to behave? Then, as if sensing her thoughts, Ronen had turned a questioning gaze upon her and her rebellious nature had ruled. She would not let this ruffian, this uneducated lout trick her into doing as he wished. She had lifted her nose in the air and glared back, the soundness of her rebuttal tested when he merely shrugged and returned to his meal.

You shall pay, Ronen, she seethed inwardly, *and you shall pay dearly. At first chance, I will slit your throat.*

Darkness had settled on the camp, a cold chill filling the air. The other men, Ehud and Nasser she had heard Ronen call them, moved from the fire to see the horses fed, watered, and secured for the night. Holly remained next to Ronen, though her sorrowful eyes never broke their hold on Amber, until Ronen stood up suddenly. Lifting a bag from the ground beside where he had sat, he motioned Holly to come with him, and a few moments later the pair disappeared into the woods.

Amber stiffened, her eyes wide and alert, listening for Holly's screams, which were sure to follow. The poor fool hadn't even given him a fight. Didn't she know what he intended to do once he got her alone? She raised up on her knees, straining to hear a clue to the direction they had taken after leaving the clearing, her gaze quickly surveying the whereabouts of Nasser and Ehud. Both men busily cleared away the remains of their meal, tidied up the campsite, and found places where they planned to bed down for the night, a position that put them in a direct line with the spot where Ronen had taken Holly and the point from where Amber observed it all. Should she stay still or chance running past the men? Should she wait until Holly screamed or try to postpone the inevitable? Would Nasser and Ehud allow her the chance or stop her before she traveled two feet? Her mind whirled with alternatives, and her anger flared when she noticed how indifferent the men appeared to be to the whole situation, removing their shoes and settling down on their blankets as if the violation of a young girl was commonplace and quite acceptable.

"Well, aren't you going to stop him?" she demanded loudly, startling the men upright.

Propped up on their elbows they exchanged puzzled glances.

"Ronen," she growled at their stupidity. "Stop Ronen!"

Ehud mumbled to his partner, shrugged, and lay back down. Nasser stared at her.

"You miserable cretins. You halfwit, spineless vermin. Do something about Ronen!" She waved an agitated finger toward the shadows of the woods.

"Ronen?" Nasser repeated, glancing over his shoulder at the darkness, then back at Amber, and nodding. "Ronen." He dismissed her then and settled comfortably in his blanket.

"Ohhh," Amber hissed, struggling up to her feet. But before she had taken a step, a movement in the shadows caught her eye. Looking up, she saw Holly walk from the protection of the trees, a smile on her lips and her damp hair clinging to her freshly scrubbed face and neck. Amber's mouth fell open. Ronen had taken Holly to a stream to bathe! "H-Holly," she crooned, the desire to do as her friend had done willing her feet to move before she knew it. But she pulled up short when the tall figure behind Holly stepped into the firelight. The golden glow of the flames danced in his dark eyes when he returned her stare, and, certain he would not allow her the same luxury, she slithered to her knees.

With downcast eyes, she listened to them move about and finally found courage to look. Ronen had given Holly a blanket of her own near the fire, but away from Nasser and Ehud. She smiled up at him when he handed her a hairbrush, and Amber thought she would go mad with envy. Imagine after all these weeks, months, she was so close to washing her matted hair and brushing the tangles from it. So close . . . tears burned her eyes and she squeezed them tightly closed, not wanting anyone to see her cry. Such a minor thing to desire so greatly. It seemed foolish, selfish, to want to wash her hair when what she truly should be thinking of was getting home. What did it matter how she looked? Only that she was safe. A noise before her jolted her attention to it, and she glanced up to find Ronen standing there, his tall, muscular frame blocking the firelight. In the shadows he seemed more menacing, and she wondered briefly what cruel sport he had decided on for her now.

"Leave me alone," she whispered, a tear stealing from the corner of her eye. She briskly wiped it away, all the frustrations, fears, worries of the days gone by draining what strength she had. She wanted to curl up in a tiny ball and sleep away her misery, wake up to find a clear, blue dawning and the troubles of her world departed. But this stranger, whose presence clouded her mind, stifled her breath, presented the reality that no number of dreams would rid her of this nightmare. "Oh, damn you, Nicholas," she choked in muttered words, "how could you have forsaken me so?"

His face veiled in the shadows and the silks he wore, Ronen's curious frown went unseen. He lingered a moment longer, then bent to take Amber's wrist. She wiggled out of the way.

"Where am I to sleep," she spat, "with the horses?" She kicked out at him when he reached for her a second time. "I won't sleep with you!"

His silence, his unquestionable authority, piqued her disobedience. She had suffered enough. She had been degraded, misused, manhandled for the last time, and when he tried again to capture her wrist, she twisted away from him and sprang to her feet.

"Can't you understand?" she shouted, tears flowing down her face. "I don't want you!" Her gaze took them all in. "I don't want *any* of you. I want to go home!"

"Amber—" Holly soothed, her breath catching when Ronen turned sharply to scowl at her. She swallowed hard, her eyes locked on his stormy glare, and bravely continued. "You told me countless times to have courage. You said no matter what, we would survive. I believed you, Amber. Now you must believe. Please don't fight him. He won't hurt you."

Amber's lip curled in a sarcastic smile. "Not now, maybe. But he will. It's just a matter of time. All men are the same once you get to know them. Women aren't important to them. Except for one thing."

Holly opened her mouth to argue, then snapped it shut when she caught Ronen's warning frown. She turned back to the fire without a word and finished brushing the dampness from her hair.

"I wish you understood, you heartless reprobate," Amber continued, taking a step backward when he advanced. "'I'd tell you how disgusting you are. You buy women for pleasure. Just like Nic—"—the name caught in her throat—"someone else I knew a long time ago. Well, I wouldn't give in to him and I won't give in to you!"

She glared at him, daring him to touch her. But when he remained motionless, she carelessly dropped her guard, glancing triumphantly at Holly. In the next instant, with the stealth of a mountain lion, a wide hand shot out, took her wrist, and yanked her forward. Before she could react or even open her mouth to scream, Ronen bent, placed a shoulder in her stomach, and stood, lifting her from her feet.

"Put me down, you imbecile," she demanded, pounding on his wide back as he carried her along. "I'll fight you to the death, so help me God."

Ronen seemed unaffected by her threat, steadily walking toward the woods, his steps sure and unhindered by the slight weight he carried. He followed a narrow path for several yards before the stand of fir trees separated to reveal a small pond fed by a thin mountain stream, all the while enduring the constant beating of tiny fists to his back. At the water's edge, he paused. Without warning he let go of the woman draped over his shoulder and dropped her to the ground.

"Ohhh!" Amber cried out when her backside landed hard against the earth. She glared up at him, chest heaving. "He won't hurt you, Amber," she mimicked, remembering Holly's pledge of a few minutes before as she scrambled to her feet. "What's next, oh great master? Do you plan to strike me in return? Or just rip my clothes from me?" They stood eye to eye, Amber's thin frame trembling with rage, Ronen quite relaxed. In the darkness that surrounded them and because of the silky cloth that covered his face, Amber could not read the expression on his features, but she felt certain he mocked her. "Do you treat all women the same, you beggarly coward, you cur, you whoreson?"

Before she could react, Ronen's hands shot out to grab her shoulders and spin her around. Agile fingers found the fastenings of her gown, trailing down the long, slim back before she could guess his intent. Cool night air touched her bare flesh, the last button free, bringing her the stark realization of what he was doing. Her elbow raised, she brought it around to jab his midsection, only to find it caught in his iron grip, the sleeve of her dress quickly slipped from her arm. She opened her mouth to scream her hatred, to demand an end, but gasped instead when he pulled the garment from her. It fell unrestricted to the ground. Shocked by his agility in disrobing her so easily, she stood mouth agape, eyes wide, watching numbly when he undid the hook at the waist of her petticoats. They, too, pooled at her feet. Surprise turned to rage, and her lovely face crimped into an ugly sneer.

"Come one step closer and I'll scratch your eyes out," she hissed, head bent to glower at him.

Unaffected, Ronen grabbed her elbow and started toward the water.

"What are you doing?" Panic mixed heavily with her demand. "Do you plan to drown me? Why bother to take off my clothes if you do? You leave the evidence behind, you fool."

Struggling to stay on dry ground, Amber pulled back against his restraint, her slippered feet sliding in the muddy soil.

"Wait! Ronen, don't—"

Before her plea had reached its finale, Ronen stopped, bent, and scooped her into his strong arms. Twisting, he swung her around in midair and let go, hurling her screaming form into the pond. A loud splash followed, and several moments passed before Amber came to the surface. She was dressed only in her camisole, the whiteness of the cloth contrasting brightly with the dark water, and a pale shaft of moonlight illuminated the place where she coughed and sputtered for air. Her honey-blond hair matted against her face, the braid having come loose, and the creamy smoothness of her breasts heaved with her indignation.

"You're more stupid than I thought," she snapped, the crisp bite of the cold water chilling her. "How c-can you drown me when I k-know how to s-swim?" She shivered. "Or do you plan to let m-me freeze to death?"

Ronan surveyed his work in silence, arms akimbo, then crouched to retrieve the bag he had left behind when escorting Holly to the same place. After searching inside, he withdrew a bar of soap, stood, and moved to the edge of the pond. Holding it out to her for her to recognize the treasure he offered, he stooped to wait. If she wanted the luxury, she would have to come and take it from him. A few moments passed while Amber eyed him suspiciously, Ronen content to outlast her, before she cautiously swam closer. Near enough to easily touch the soap, she hesitated, her pale blue eyes staring into his dark brown ones. Then, slowly at first, her delicate hand moved to take the proffered item, snatching it from his grasp without delay, and she quickly swam beyond his reach, her gaze locked on him. Curious as to his sudden change in nature, she watched him as she lathered her arms with the soap until she was certain he would stay where he was, and proceeded to the enjoyment of washing her hair.

Ronen's eyes never wandered from the vision he appraised. Long, slender arms moved in graceful motion as the beauty before him scrubbed the ivory skin of her face, neck, and shoulders. Rich lather bubbled in her once dull, dirt-caked hair, and when she dove beneath the water to rinse it clean, his pulse quickened at the momentary glimpse of her willowy legs and the voluptuous curve of her backside. She surfaced again, the fabric of her camisole clinging tightly to the well-shaped breasts beneath it, and he forced himself to look away, the desire in his loins threatening to shatter his self-proclaimed celibacy.

The soiled, tattered gown and petticoats lay a few feet away from him, and without hesitation he crossed to them and picked them up. Returning to the pond, he knelt and shoved the garments into the water, washing them as clean as possible. When he had finished, he squeezed the moisture from them, stood, and started back toward the camp.

The cool, fresh water of the mountain spring revitalized Amber's spirits as she floated lazily on her back, savoring the pleasure of feeling clean again. Overhead, the sky sparkled with a million tiny stars, and she stared contentedly up at them, ignoring how her teeth chattered. She had not been able to bathe for weeks, months, and somehow she feared if she left the luxury of her bath now, she would not be allowed its pleasantness again for quite some time. Rolling to her stomach, she dove once more and emerged near the edge of the pond where Ronen had stood observing.

A frown wrinkled her brow when she discovered the place empty. Where had he gone? She glanced quickly to the right, straining to see his figure in the shadows of the trees. Did he hide to trick her? She looked left. *But why?*

"Ronen?" The name hung heavily in the quietness of her haven. "Where are you, Ronen?"

She listened more intently, and when no other sound than the gentle stirring of leaves in the soft breeze answered, a devious smile touched her lips. Studying the shadows once more for any sign of movement, Amber climbed from the water when she felt certain he was nowhere around. The light air chilled her damp flesh, and she hurried toward the spot where Ronen had dropped her clothes, longing for the warmth they were sure to offer.

A puzzled frown distorted her face. This was where he had left them. She was sure of it. But the gown and petticoats were gone. Over here, perhaps? She moved a few steps. Nothing. Panic tingled in the pit of her stomach. Surely he wouldn't hide them. She looked again. But how could she escape with only her camisole to wear?

"Damn him," she fumed outwardly.

She decided to look again. Maybe she had just missed them or forgotten exactly where they lay. She moved to search again when the snapping of a twig spun her around. Standing before her in the silvery strips of moonlight filtering through the trees, Ronen stared back at her, a blanket draped over his arm.

"What have you done with my clothes?" she demanded, stumbling backward when he unfolded the coverlet and moved toward her. "Did y-you hear me? Where are m-my clothes?"

Her teeth chattered fiercely, and she yearned for the warmth of the cloth he held out to her but feared the price she must pay to acquire it. Her knees trembled from the cold, her fingers numb, and she only slightly objected when he stepped close enough to twirl the blanket around her shoulders. Drawing her into the circle of his arm, he led her quietly back to the campsite.

The others had retired, and at first Holly's sleeping face angered Amber, that she could so easily dismiss her friend's dilemma after seeing her carried off to the woods by some barbarian. But once she saw her freshly washed gown and petticoats hanging on a nearby tree branch to dry, Amber realized Holly had been right in her prediction that Ronen wouldn't hurt her. *For now anyway*, Amber stubbornly concluded, wearily allowing him to guide her to the fire. Another blanket had been spread out there, and she sat down upon it to welcome the heat of the blaze and chase away the chill to her bones.

The crackling flames and pungent odor of smoke lulled her defensive mood, and within minutes Amber felt the exhaustion of her eventful day close in on her. Removing her damp slippers and stockings, she laid them by the fire to dry and settled back to enjoy the firelight. She yawned, snuggling into the cocoon of her blanket, and glanced around for Ronen. He had gone to the horses, and when he turned back to face her she noticed a long strip of cord in his hand. Her curiosity aroused, she watched him suspiciously as he came toward her and knelt down. Without looking at her, he grabbed her wrist and proceeded to tie one end of the rope around it.

"What are you doing," she snapped, trying to jerk free. His grip tightened. "I'm too tired to run away, you fool, and I won't go anywhere without my clothes."

Ignoring her, as it seemed he always did, he proceeded to fasten the other end in a slip knot, then slide the loop over his own hand to his wrist. Amber straightened in surprise.

"But how do you intend to let me sleep?" she asked with raised brows. "The rope is too short—"

Ronen answered her by his moves. Without giving her time to voice the question, he stretched out on the blanket beside her, his arms folded over his chest, his eyes closed. Amber stared disbelievingly for a long while, realizing his plan. The slightest move in any direction would tug on the rope and wake him. A simple method to insure that she would remain in the camp, and at the same time force her to lie down next to him. The idea sent a rush of blood to her face, burning her cheeks. Well, she wouldn't lie next to him. She'd sit up all night! Drawing her knees to her chest, she rested her chin against them and concentrated on the orange glow of the fire.

Dark brown eyes sparkled with mischief.

Chapter Nineteen

Yellow sunlight stole between the tree branches and warmed the early morning with its rays, chasing away the night's chill and the dew upon the grass. In her dreamy state, Amber snuggled closer to the body next to hers, content to sleep a while longer, one arm draped intimately over the wide, muscular chest and completely unaware of how she lay nestled against the broad shoulder. Birds chattered gaily overhead, their merry song awakening her from peaceful slumber. One eye opened slightly, then both widened in alarm when a bright, vivid green filled her vision. Jolting upright, her face burning with embarrassment when her foggy mind recalled the happenings of the night before, she forgot the cord tied around her wrist, the small measure of hemp linking her to him, and jerked back in horror. The sudden jar brought Ronen full awake and he sat up instantly, the confused frown that twisted his brow fading slowly when he found pale blue eyes staring back fearfully. The smile beneath the *yashmak* went unseen.

Relaxing once he discovered she had not intended to run but only to set herself apart from him, he rubbed away the stiffness in his left shoulder and openly studied the shapely form now curled upon her knees, hands clutched to her bosom, trembling lips parted as if it was difficult for her to breathe.

More than an hour had passed after he had bound her wrist to his and she fought to stay awake, determined to keep her distance. He had watched her through half-closed eyes until her head began to bob, her body slouching, and when he thought she might tumble forward into the fire, he had quietly raised up on one elbow, gently touched her shoulder, and pulled her down upon his blanket. She had mumbled someone's name before drifting off in quiescent slumber, bringing a frown to his brow when he failed to understand. But his curiosity had quickly disappeared as he gazed upon the sleeping face. He remembered now the softness of her curves, the smoothness of her skin, and the fragrance of her freshly washed hair, wanting to touch a golden strand as he had done then, but knew he mustn't. She still didn't trust him, in fact, she feared him, and he vowed to wait her out, that she must come to him willingly. This time it would be different.

A rustling in the trees snapped Ronen's attention to their surroundings. The others in camp still slept, but at the loud click of his fingers, Ehud and Nasser opened their eyes instantly, their gazes locked on their leader. A quick nod of his head toward the horses sent the men rushing from their beds, gathering the blankets and supplies to load upon the animals once more, while Ronen untied the cord from around his wrist and stood up. Hurrying to the tree where he had hung Amber's clothes, he carelessly jerked them free of the branch and returned to her. The furrowing of his brow warned her to remain quiet, and, for some odd reason, she sensed danger. Maybe not for her, but if trouble encompassed the camp, it meant both she and Holly would be innocent victims. It would be better if she went along with whatever Ronen wanted. For now, anyway. Her time would come. Taking the clothes he held out to her, she quickly donned them, watching Ronen move to where Holly lay. Crouching low, he gently shook her shoulder to awaken her, a fingertip pressed to his lips to silence any question she might voice when her eyes flew open and she sat upright in a hurry, the blanket clutched tightly beneath her chin.

The group hastily abandoned camp, leaving behind only the cold ashes of the fire to mark their passing. Ehud assisted Holly up behind him on his horse and waited quietly for the rest. Nasser mounted, too, but when Amber started to approach to take her customary place before him, he shook his head and nodded past her. A prickling of worry knotted her brow, for instinct told her his meaning. Turning slowly, she found Ronen astride the chestnut stallion, foot slipped from the stirrup and hand extended to her, dark brown eyes watching her closely. If she chose not to ride with him, would they leave her behind? She glanced over at Holly. The young girl frowned in return, a silent plea to do as asked, and Amber once again told herself that she would not run without Holly. And judging by her prior failure, she would have to exercise careful planning where Ronen was concerned. This was one man not easily duped. The vision of Nicholas raced through her mind.

Preferring to mount the huge animal without help but knowing it was impossible, Amber forced herself to take his outstretched hand after placing a slender foot in the stirrup. He easily swung her up behind him, ready to lead his group further through the foothills, but paused when Amber refused to hang on. Twisting slightly in the saddle, he reached back, grabbed her wrist, and firmly placed it on the silk cloth of his shirt. He kicked his heels into the stallion's sides and the steed bolted off, Amber's fingers frantically clamped to the folds of Ronen's garb.

The narrow path took many twists and turns, winding higher with each step they traveled until it seemed to disappear and the caravan was forced to slow their pace, the horses allowed to pick their own trail. Tall bluffs thick with evergreens hovered near them on the left, a thirty-foot drop on the right. Fear sent Amber's heart pounding, that the horse might stumble and send them all crashing down the side of the mountain. Without thinking, she closed her eyes and encircled Ronen's wide chest with her arms. If she slipped from the saddle, she was taking him with her. Several moments passed as they were jostled about before Amber realized how tightly she clutched the firm body molded against her own. Her hands nearly met in front, her head pressing to his muscular shoulder, and with shocking suddenness she felt every inch of his broad back touching her. She straightened abruptly, unaware of the smile that danced in

431

his eyes at her act, and forced her gaze upon the course they took, willing herself to be brave, unaffected by their perilous journey. However, her fingers still held tightly to the silk cloth around his waist until the path widened and she could relax a degree.

They traveled most of the morning, pausing only once to refresh themselves, and Amber begrudgingly mounted the Arabian once more. Ronen had not allowed her to speak with Holly, something she failed to understand, nor would he spare her the embarrassment when she sought privacy in the woods. He had followed her, and only after her stubborn refusal to move had he graciously turned his back, all the while cursed for his ill-breeding and lack of compassion. When she had finished and started back toward the others, he had taken her arm to guide her. But Amber had jerked free of him and glowered her dissatisfaction, stomping off ahead of him. The corners of his eyes had wrinkled with his amusement as he bowed consent for her to walk alone.

The sun high overhead, Amber's stomach rumbled again, as it seemed to do with growing regularity. Though the others appeared unaffected by skipping breakfast, Amber's hunger grew. She hadn't eaten in over a day, and with each growl of neglect, her patience wore thin.

"Ronen," she said, holding her irritation to a minimum. "Ronen, I'm hungry." She studied the back of his head a moment, noticing the dark hair curling gently beneath the edge of his turban. "Ro-o-nen."

Twisting slightly, he looked back at her over his shoulder.

"Food," she said, pointing to her open mouth.

He returned his attention to the narrow mountain pass several hundred yards ahead without so much as a grunt or blink of an eye to verify that he understood.

"You beast," Amber snarled at his back. "When Alanna sends men to find me, I'll see you're repaid for the way you've treated me." One corner of her mouth crimping with annoyance, she decided to solve her problem by herself. Studying the packs tied to the saddle, she selected the smallest in hopes it contained a sampling of the fruit she had tasted the day before. Shifting her weight to one side, she let go of Ronen and began

432

unweaving the cords that held the bag. Unaccustomed to the extra load, and now offbalance, the Arabian began to sidestep nervously, brushing into the dense branches of evergreen trees growing on both sides of the trail. Ronen tugged on the reins to gain control once more, only to have the horse swing his hind-quarters around abruptly and back into the massive limb of a fir tree, sweeping Amber from his rump. A frightened squeal ended sharply when she landed on the sandy soil only inches from the animal's hooves, and the quick horsemanship of Ronen saved the foolish woman from being trod upon when he yanked the steed away.

Amber sat unmoving, her eyes wide, breath coming in painful heaves, and silently thanked the angel watching over her that no greater injury had befallen her than a bruised hip. Then she spotted Ronen. Dark, stormy eyes glared down at her, and a sudden chill bolted through her thin frame as she watched him dismount slowly, his gaze locked on her. Did he mean to beat her? But why? It wasn't as if it were her fault that he couldn't handle the beast. She glanced back at the others, who had watched in alarm, Ehud and Nasser smiling now as if aware of what Ronen intended and approving wholeheartedly. Holly could only stare, one hand raised to her mouth as she chewed on the nail of her thumb.

Looking back at the man stalking her, a lump wedged in Amber's throat, stealing her breath away. She gulped, wondering if she should just sit there or entertain the thought of running for her life. Even if he could speak English, she doubted she could get him to agree that this whole incident wasn't entirely her doing. Maybe she should try.

"Look, Ronen," she began, drawing back when he continued, his steps quickening, "this isn't really all my fault. If you knew how to control that stupid piece of horse flesh—" He came within two strides. "I was only looking for something to eat."

He bent to grab her wrist and she kicked out at him.

"I'm hungry!"

His eyes darkened.

"You imbecile. Can't you understand? I—"

With a swiftness she could not detect quickly enough,

Ronen swooped down, seized her elbows, and hauled her to her feet. Crushing her to his chest, his veiled face inches from hers, he glared at her for what seemed a lifetime. And in those moments, Amber felt an unexplainable familiarity in his touch, his anger. She studied the deep brown eyes, searching for a cause, yielding to his rage while caught up in her own curiosity. But when she raised a hand to strip away the silk covering his face, he jerked her around and irritably led her toward the stallion. Her wonder deepened. Until this moment she hadn't really thought much about it, but neither Ehud nor Nasser wore veils. Why did Ronen? Was it possible that custom dictated it? That the chief of the tribe was forbidden to show his face? Mentally she shrugged off the desire to know, since she felt certain she would never be able to find out. He didn't even understand that she was hungry. How could she ask about the veil and get an intelligent answer? Maybe he was so grotesquely ugly that he wanted to hide his face. A devilish smile twitched the corner of her mouth and disappeared. Tonight, while he slept, she would see for herself. She would pull the cloth free and discover his reason for wearing it.

That must be it, she thought. He was homelier than the wrong end of a donkey. She looked at him from the corner of her eye as he pulled her along. Yet how could he be? He had a strong brow and a deep tan, dark, handsome eyes, and thick black lashes, and there was no disguising the well-proportioned, muscular frame beneath the garb he wore. It must be something else. Studying the profile of his face, she noticed for the first time that the line of his jaw seemed misshapen. A beard, perhaps? Or something else? Oh, well, she'd find out tonight.

Standing beside the stallion, Amber waited, expecting Ronen to mount and help her up. Instead, he continued to hold on to her arm while he searched through one of the pouches hanging from the saddle. Had he understood after all? Was he searching for something to give her to eat? She grinned triumphantly. Maybe her little display of temper had worked. And if it had, she would use it time and time again to get whatever she wanted. She'd show this oafish baboon what it meant to tangle with a woman who wouldn't cower at his every whim.

Finding what he wanted in the leather pouch, Ronen turned

to face her, a long, thin rope held in one hand. Amber's brow knotted.

"What's that for?" she demanded when he started to loop one end around her wrist. She pulled loose of him. "You're not going to tie me up."

Ronen stiffened, his eyes flashing his annoyance with her.

"Listen, you overgrown viper, it wasn't my fault the horse got skittish. No!" She yanked back when he tried to grab her again. "I won't let you tie me up. What if I should be thrown off? I wouldn't be able to catch myself with my hands tied."

Amber noticed how dark his eyes became, his growing ire reflected in them. He lowered his chin slightly, took a deep breath that expanded his wide chest, and slowly let it out. Amber knew he was angry, but then again, so was she. And she had more reason. She raised one finger to stress the words she meant to speak, only to have Ronen instantly grab her arm just below the elbow. She struggled, digging the nails of her free hand into the fingers clamped securely around her wrist. He seized it, too, twisting her arms until he forced her to kneel before him. The pain he inflicted was minimal, but the humiliation he aroused brought tears to her eyes. She stared up at him without a word, while he easily bound her wrists together, knowing her strength was no match for his. Bending slightly, he caught her arm and yanked her to her feet. One arm around her waist, he slipped his other behind her knees and agilely lifted her from the ground, swinging her up into the saddle. Grabbing the reins of the Arabian, he hooked one toe into the stirrup and mounted the animal behind Amber. A kick to the stallion's ribs started the caravan down the trail toward the gathering of buildings nestled in the side of the mountain, a destination Amber prayed would end her imprisonment.

Although it took less than an hour to reach the village, Amber lived every agonizing minute of it trapped within the muscular arms draped around her. She sat stiffly, not wanting to brush against him, but as the trail became rougher, with rocks, brush and the decayed remains of fallen evergreen in their path, the horse stumbled repeatedly, jostling its passengers until, out of worry his companion would be bounced off, Ronen slipped an arm around her narrow waist.

435

Had it been her father or even Nicholas who held her thus, she would eagerly have accepted the aid, but Amber feared such close contact would only spark a flame of interest in her that could only be inimical to her well-being. His body seemed molded around hers, the strong chest pressed against her back, his muscular thighs curved beneath her own, flexing with each move he made to guide the stallion. But what disturbed her to the greatest degree was the manliness of him touching intimately to her backside, the thinness of her well-worn gown doing little to cushion the unintentional caress. Her mind whirled, a flush rising in her cheeks, and Amber had to fight to breathe. Her only consolation for his proximity was her thought that once the band arrived in town she would be free of him, never forced to sit so close to him again.

As the town spread out before them, Amber noticed the simplicity of the villagers' dwellings. Flat-topped houses made of stone and mud, an absence of windows, and single openings serving as doors. Amber wondered how a family found any privacy with each building huddled so closely to the next.

Children filled the dusty streets, playing and laughing happily, while several women drapped in dark-colored fabric from head to toe balanced large baskets on their shoulders, rushing from one point to another, dodging a flock of sheep and goats one man herded out to pasture. The arrival of the newcomers seemed unimportant, until from somewhere in the village a shout rang out and the streets suddenly crowded with men and women of all ages, each calling excitedly and waving as if they welcomed the chieftain of their clan.

Amber watched in awe as everyone abandoned their tasks to rush toward her group, smiling faces and enthusiastic chatter greeting her. The reins of the stallion were taken from Ronen and he quickly slid to the ground, taking the cheers of the people in stride, while his huge hand tousled the hair of a young boy standing next to him with great familiarity. His son? Amber wondered. Could this be Ronen's village? The people his followers? She hoped not. She would find no sympathy here. And most assuredly not if Ronen had a wife tucked away somewhere. After all, how would she have reacted if Nicholas had brought a woman home with him? She smiled halfheartedly. She would have wanted it at first. In fact she had begged him to find another. But now? She concentrated on the movements of the crowd pressing closer.

Suddenly the mass of village people moved aside, opening the way to Ronen. At the opposite end, Amber noticed the tired, slightly crippled shape of an old man, snow-white hair showing beneath the edge of his turban, equally fluffy brows knotted in a frown. Looking at the young man facing him, Amber sensed a feeling of love between the two, and again her imagination took hold. His father? Or perhaps his grandfather? Was the old man angry with Ronen? Why? Would she find help from him? She sighed, discouraged. Maybe. But only if she learned to speak their language. Her shoulders slumped. She didn't have that much time. She wouldn't stay here long enough to learn it. She was going home, and soon.

The onlookers quieted, watching Ronen walk the distance to the other man, his arms extended to clasp the frail form when he reached him. Several moments passed while they held each other, and Amber wished she knew what all of it meant. Where was she? Would this be the place Ronen intended for her to stay? Would the villagers resent her? If she escaped, would she and Holly ever find their way back to Casablanca? Thinking of her friend again, Amber twisted around to look at her, a rush of panic quickening her heartbeat, for Ehud had already dismounted and helped Holly to the ground. Her hand held in his, he guided her through the crowd toward Ronen and the old man.

The distance between them was too great for Amber to hear the words they spoke, and she could only sit by quietly observing. It appeared Ronen was explaining how they had come to have two women in their midst, by the way he nodded toward Holly and then back at her. Dark, tired eyes followed where Ronen directed, and Amber suddenly felt uncomfortable when everyone turned their gazes upon her. But of them all, the old man's radiated compassion rather than curiosity. She forced herself to smile weakly in return, vainly hoping for a method of communicating with this man.

Ronen turned back to draw the white-haired gentleman into conversation once more, and Amber took the opportunity to

437

study the rope tied tightly around her wrists. No amount of twisting or yanking would free her, and she examined the knots in hopes of finding one end, one loop, that she could unfasten with her teeth. The corner of her mouth curled disdainfully when she found the piece she sought was too tight to budge, and she quickly surrendered to her fate when the slight movement rubbed her flesh raw beneath the cord. Irritably she glanced up at Ronen, her brow smoothing in surprise to discover that both he and the old man had started toward her. But what of Holly? Looking about quickly, she spotted the girl with Ehud as they walked further away, heading toward one of the dwellings. Surely they didn't intend to separate them? But of course! It would make it that much more difficult for her to escape if she had to take the time to find Holly first. She turned a hate-filled glare on the man who approached, waiting until he was close enough to execute her plan.

"Stay away from me," she growled. Lifting a foot to plant squarely in his chest, her hands clutched to the saddle for support, she kicked forward, knocking Ronen off balance. He would have fallen to the ground had it not been for the quick hands of several village men standing behind him, and the crowd observing gasped in unison.

Once more Amber realized that no other man in the village wore a veil when she saw the vague smile on the old man's face. It puzzled her, for she thought her actions would have done anything but please him. Was that why he smiled? Or did he know the punishment Ronen would bestow upon her? Something torturous, no doubt. She glared back at Ronen, ready for whatever he chose to do.

"I want to talk with Holly," she demanded, knowing the words were lost on him.

He stepped closer.

"Holly," she repeated, lifting her foot slightly. "I want Holly."

The villagers stared wide-eyed, expectant.

Of a sudden, Ronen's hand shot out, caught the trim ankle raised to strike him, and yanked down hard, spilling Amber from the stallion before the scream had time to form in her throat. She landed painfully on the ground, spitting particles of sand and dirt from her mouth. The crowd roared approval. Amber's temper raged. Pushing up on her knees, she glared at him, her chest heaving with her fury.

"You bastardly cur—"

Again Ronen's hand claimed her. This time he seized a fistful of golden hair, pulling her to her feet as she screamed defiance and forced back her tears of pain and frustration. He half dragged, half shoved her along, the volume of cheerful cries growing as every member of the village followed the display of her hardheadedness. From somewhere in the crowd, a pair of pale blue eyes, their corners wrinkled with age, watched the goings on with a mixture of amusement and pity.

Ronen took his struggling captive to a stone building set apart from and bigger than the rest. He never paused when they reached it. Ronen simply swung her around in front of him and pushed her inside. The furnishings of the room went unseen by Amber, for Ronen continued on to another doorway, propelling her through it with a tug on her yellow locks. Spinning her around, he knocked her backward with a slap on her shoulder and sent her tumbling onto a mountain of pillows. Before she could scramble to her feet again, he turned and left the room, slamming the door shut behind him. Grabbing the nearest thing to her, Amber tossed the multicolored rectangular bolster at the sealed portal, watching it bounce and fall harmlessly to the floor and listening to the key turn in the lock.

Tears of humiliation flooded her eyes and raced down her dirt-smudged cheeks. There had been only one other person in her lifetime who could make her feel so helpless, so inept, so much a weaker gender. But an ocean separated them, and she knew in her heart she would never see him again. Bound hands raised to wipe her face, she realized her foolishness with Nicholas had put her in this godforsaken country. Could it be that she found herself thrown in this room, wrists tied together, for the same reason? That if she curbed her show of temper, behaved herself as Holly begged her to do, this man Ronen would treat her honorably? Her lips curled into an unflattering sneer. Not likely. Chances were he'd mistake her meaning and think she'd given in. And she knew what that

439

would mean. He'd expect her to come to his bed every night. No, it was best, she decided to continue on the way she had. No man would remain interested in a woman for long if it meant fighting off her attacks just to be in the same room with her.

Sighing happily with her resolution, she fell back on the cushion of pillows surrounding her and stared up at the ceiling, her tired body welcoming the rest. Only a few minutes passed before her eyelids fluttered shut and she drifted off into quiet slumber.

Amber sat straight up when the key rattled in the lock and chased away her need to sleep. She had no idea how long she had closed her eyes, but her body still ached. And it seemed her stomach rubbed her backbone. Did he intend to starve her to death? Well, the minute he opened that door, she'd demand to be fed. She struggled to her feet. *And* have the rope taken from her wrists. Readying herself for their next confrontation, she took a deep breath and glared at the doorway.

Several moments passed while Amber watched the entrance to the room, a suspicious frown wrinkling her smooth brow, wondering if he played a game when it seemed he did not intend to step inside. If he thought to worry her, he was wrong. She would not be goaded into weakening with a useless show of strategy. Marching across the small room, she seized the doorlatch and swung the portal wide, startling not only the young girl standing on the other side but herself when she discovered the tiny creature standing there trying to balance a tray of food in her hands. Round brown eyes set in a tan oval face stared back at Amber, and Amber scowled with a mixture of emotions. Embarrassment, surprise, and finally suspicion surfaced. He *was* playing tricks to catch her off guard. Vowing not to be so easily taken in, she leaned forward to inspect the outer room, to find the spot where he hid. It was sparsely furnished, with only a wide assortment of pillows, a chest on one wall and a fireplace opposite it, and Amber realized that only the girl shared the place with her. Thinking of the child again, she turned her attention to her.

"You know, this wasn't my fault," she told the wide-eyed

stranger. "Your master," she sneered the word, "enjoys testing me at every turn. I wouldn't have reacted so if he treated me as a lady." She looked at the girl as if expecting a reply, then, remembering they spoke two different tongues, Amber nodded for her to enter the room.

Watching the youngster set the tray on a short-legged table in the center of the room, Amber contemplated spinning on her heels and running off. But the sweet smells of bread and roasted meats changed her mind, and she decided to eat first. She wouldn't get very far if she didn't fill her belly soon. She already felt weak, and it would take all the strength she had just to free herself of Ronen and his men, let alone travel all the way down the mountain. Crossing to the table, Amber clumsily sat down on the floor, her eyes drawn to the quantity of food before her, and she failed to notice the knife the young girl held in her hands until the sharp blade cut the ropes from Amber's wrists. She smiled, looking up to offer thanks, but the child had already left the room.

Amber truly had no idea what she ate, only that it tasted good and eased the knot in her stomach. A small brass pitcher accompanied the feast, and once she had finished with the rest she poured its contents into a tiny cup, grinning appreciatively when she discovered it was wine. Cool and very tart, it soothed the tired muscles of her arms and legs and brought a warm glow to her face, and she wondered if Holly had enjoyed the same banquet.

Holly, Amber thought, taking another sip of wine. Was she being treated kindly? She hoped so. Holly was such a fragile thing. She wouldn't last long if someone abused her. Worry for the girl's safety brought Amber to her feet. Drink in hand, she started toward the door, planning to sneak a glimpse of the village outside the house and possibly her friend. But the chatter of voices growing louder and coming toward her froze Amber's feet to the spot where she stood. Seconds later a caravan of women filled the tiny house and forced Amber back into the room where Ronen had taken her. She stared in awe as a round wooden tub replaced the table and the remains of her meal, each woman pouring a bucket of steaming water into it before two of the giggling crew approached her. They set aside her cup of wine and began unfastening the buttons of her gown, stripping away her garments before Amber had a chance to react. Guiding her gently toward the bath, they helped her climb in and proceeded to wash her hair and lather her arms and face. Amber had never been treated in such a fashion and to her surprise found that she thoroughly enjoyed the luxury, the infectious laughter of the women turning the corners of her mouth upward.

When they had finished, rinsing her shoulder-length hair to a shiny brilliance, they urged her from the tub and vigorously patted her dry with a mammoth white towel. Still giggling, they presented her with the most stunning, shimmering piece of blue silk cloth Amber had ever seen. Mouth agape, she stood there numbly, allowing them to cover her slender shape beneath its many folds, a strip in a lighter hue adorning her head and hiding her hair. A hush fell over the women as they observed the rewards of their work, and, although no one spoke, Amber sensed they were pleased with what they saw. She smiled back at them, a silent appreciation for their efforts shining in her eyes. It felt wonderful to be clean, warm, and fed. She wished she could repay them and suddenly realized they were probably only doing as instructed. Her smile disappeared.

Again the procession moved about, now clearing away the tub and other items from her bath. The women prattled on, smiling up at Amber, then giggling all the more. She thought they would leave her then, but as the final two passed her they each took hold of Amber's arms and led her from the room and outside the house into the street. They appeared excited about their journey, and their constant gibberish and laughter, hidden behind raised hands, animated Amber's own enthusiasm. They traveled down the narrow dirt road and paused outside another stone house while one of the women rapped softly on the door. A moment later it opened and a man stepped outside. They exchanged a few words, and, just as quickly as the group had appeared on Amber's doorstep, they hurried away, leaving her to stand alone with the man, who was dressed solely in white. Worry tingled the flesh across her arms, yet the man himself seemed to be of no immediate threat as he

442

nodded politely, extended a hand toward the house, and waited.

Amber bit her lower lip, wondering who might be inside. Ronen, perchance? Or maybe Holly. Praying it to be the latter, she slowly moved past the stranger and entered the building.

In comparison to the place where Ronen had left her, and in view of the fact that the village was hidden high in the foothills of the Atlas Mountains, the interior of the house was magnificent. Multicolored rugs with thick fringe along the edges covered the wood floor. An array of pillows in all sizes were sprinkled about, several scattered in front of the huge marble fireplace covering one entire wall. Above it hung a gold-framed mirror, and on each side were richly polished chests with brass handles, and urns and bowls of fruit on top. Opposite was a long bench filled with an assortment of figurines and even a musket, which seemed out of place. Overhead Amber spied a simple but exquisite chandelier. How odd that a place so primitive would house such luxuries. Then her gaze fell on the old man sitting on the floor in the center of the room behind a low table covered with more fruits and a pitcher that Amber guessed held wine.

"Come in, Amber," he smiled warmly, his words flowing in perfect English.

A bright golden orb claimed the clear blue sky, warm rays flooding earthward to caress the white sands that spread for miles in all directions. No fowl or creature of the wilds roamed about in the solitude of ghostly magnitude. The air was still, the heat rising languidly upward, reaching for the heavens, the illusion of a transparent curtain of rain. Suddenly a horse and rider appeared atop the tallest peak, the steed's hooves spraying a shower of tan particles in the air as they raced laboriously through the ever changing surface of the desert, intent on reaching the oasis and the chief of the tribe. The rider traveled over another mound of sand, and in the distance he could see the gathering of brightly colored tents sprinkled on the hillside, like the spots on a leopard, and clustered around a small pond of crystal-clear water, which was shaded from the burning rays of sunlight by several palms. He urged the horse to hurry, hauling back sharply on the reins when they reached the largest of the tents. Dismounting in a rush, he entered the dwelling without forewarning, as his mission demanded haste, and pulled up breathlessly before the obese figure of a man lounging on a stack of pillows that were flattened beneath his weight. Wineskin held high in one hand, the dark red liquid spilled from his jowls and dribbled down his chin to stain the yellow silk of his shirtfront. As though disinterested in the rider's presence, one eye slowly raised to stare, a thick brow lifted expectantly.

"I have learned the information you desire, Yaakob," the man panted, hands pressed together in church-steeple fashion as he presented his leader with a curt bow.

Laying the wineskin aside, Yaakob reached for a handful of figs, popping several in his huge mouth. His thick lips smacking as he chewed lazily, Yaakob eyed the messenger once more. "And?" he asked, a thin brown stream trickling from the corner of his mouth.

"They have gone to his village in the foothills."

Wiping the saliva and sticky fruit from his chin with the back of one hand, Yaakob pushed himself up with great effort. "Did they know you followed?"

"No."

"And the woman?"

"She was taken to his dwellings. She will be his, not a slave to the old man."

Yaakob gazed off in thought, one meaty finger rubbing the stubble on his multilayered chin. "What language does she speak?"

"I have heard it before, Yaakob. I believe she is English."

"English," he hummed. "And Ronen thinks she is his." Struggling to his feet, Yaakob paced the wide floor of the tent, the flap of his belly bouncing with each step. "I will enjoy the battle. I will teach him who is strongest. And I will have my revenge." He waved the man off, dismissing him without a word, and returned to his bed of pillows. "Yes, Ronen, our paths have crossed too many times. I will take what is yours and claim the village for my own. And I will take your woman as my slave."

He settled back comfortably, lifting a jeweled dagger from the table at his side, and began picking the dirt from his nails with its tip. An evil grin separated his thick lips to reveal broken, uneven teeth, the snarl of a lion, which chilled the very bones of his closest friend. Studying the wide scar across the back of his left hand, he recalled it had not always been this way, for as a young man Yaakob had been strong of mind and body, and as fit as any warrior of the Algerian army in their fight for freedom from Turkey. He had ridden with the best, and had won high rank and favor with his superiors, finally turning to piracy against the Christian European nations. He had acquired great wealth and a ship of his own, sailing the Mediterranean and attacking vessels at his leisure. A frown curled the folds of his brow, his one good eye flashing hatred. It had been on one of those ships that he had met Linnea, a beautiful Swiss woman of wealth. He had fallen in love with her the minute he saw the long locks of golden hair, had melted when she cast her blue eyes upon him, her smile pure and sweet. He pushed the vision from his mind, tossing aside the dagger to seize the wineskin and drink a hearty swig. It burned going down, but he needed the pain to ease his haunting memories. He tipped the skin once more, spilling more down his chin than in his mouth, the image of his woman surfacing. He had hated and loved her equally, and he had sworn revenge for her cruelty. But time had played his enemy, for the fair Linnea had died some years ago, leaving the wound of his heart to fester and grow with twisted logic, blinding him to everything. His skills as a ship captain had suffered when he thought of nothing else, and one night, while they lay anchored off the shore of Tangiers, an American ship had fired on them, its cannonball burying itself deeply in the prow of his ship. Within minutes, Yaakob's vessel and most of his crew had sunk to the bottom of the sea. Barely escaping with his life, the defeated warrior had fled to the Atlas Mountains to heal his wounds and plot out ways to repay the Americans. He took to besieging helpless villages, building his wealth and the number of his followers. Thinking of Rashid, Yaakob rolled to his knees and pushed himself up.

Rashid, he thought, *my loyal friend when all others deserted me.*

Crossing to the small three-drawer chest against one wall of the tent, he gazed down upon the jeweled box sitting on top. His body stiffened as he stared at it, thinking of what lay inside. Slowly, one beefy hand reached out to lift the lid, a venomous curl distorting his upper lip as he devoured the sight of the small, plain knife hidden there.

I had planned to slit your throat with this, my sweet Linnea, he thought acidly, picking the weapon from its velvet cushion. He rolled it from side to side in his wide palm, appraising its simplicity; a wooden handle, a narrow blade. *I had planned to watch, just as you did when they castrated me at your command.* His throat tightened at the thought and almost viciously he jammed the knife back into the box and slammed the lid shut over it. Turning away, he went back to stand beside his bed of pillows, seizing the wineskin to raise it high and drown his sorrow.

Five years had passed since the day he had declared his love to her and she had laughed at his proposal. No Swiss royalty would marry a commoner. Especially a foreigner. And he had relived the nightmare of her scorn in his dreams and in each waking hour. He closed his eyes now, choking back his tears, the muscles of his throat constricting as visions of that horrible night exploded in his mind, the humiliation of being stripped of his clothes and forcibly held down while two of Linnea's men took the simple blade and severed the cords, leaving him useless as a man. Huge hands flew to his ears as the shrieking sounds of Linnea's laughter rang loudly in his head.

"I loved you," he cried, tears streaming down his face. "I always will love you. Damn you for dying!"

Anger raged up in the huge, hollowed-out figure of a man. His eyes flew open, hands twisting into fists, his tears gone.

Laugh at me, will you, he seethed inwardly, a fiery glow illuminating the brown eye. *You'll pay. I'll take you from Ronen and you will be my slave.* Pudgy lips curled into a sinister smile, kinking the scar on his cheek as sanity fled, hardening the

446

features of the beast who ravished the countryside.

"My name is Yasir. I am the leader of this village," the old man smiled, extending a hand toward the pillow on the floor next to him. "Please sit down."

Amber's breath seemed to elude her, every muscle in her thin body frozen. She stared, then gulped. "Y-you speak English," she breathed. "Dear God—"

"Please," he urged. "Rest yourself and we will talk while we share a drink. You do like wine, don't you?"

Tears moistened her eyes, hands trembling as she touched her fingertips to her mouth to fight back her sobs of joy. She smiled, her chin quivering, and eagerly took her place beside the gentle old man dressed in white. She waited patiently for him to pour two cups full of wine from a brass pitcher and offer one to her. Holding it with both hands for fear she would drop it, she stared at him until he cast warm brown eyes upon her.

"You can't imagine how relieved I am to find someone who speaks my language," she said happily, watching him sample the drink. "I have so much to tell."

"Yes, I know what it is like to be among strangers with no way to communicate. I have traveled in many countries and always find the experience a bit . . . unnerving." He leaned forward, picked up a bowl of fruit from the table, and held it out for her. "Try one of the dates. They are most delicious."

Amber glanced briefly at the appetizing array, recognizing the proffered food as what she had found in the pouch of Nasser's horse the day before. She shook her head, declining his offer. "Thank you, no. I've been well fed already. And clothed," she added, one hand sweeping the outline of her garments. She smiled up at him, noticing how white his hair seemed curled against the dark skin of his face. "And what I propose will more than repay your generosity."

A tiny line appeared between his brows when he drew them together. "Not mine, child. Ronen's. It was he who fed you and gave you the silks you wear."

"But—but you said you were the leader here," she argued.

He nodded. "But you belong to Ronen. Anything you are

given to wear or eat comes from him."

"Then . . . then perhaps you will speak to him for me." She fought the urge to tell this man how horribly one of his people had treated her. But then again, he should already know. After all, he had seen how Ronen knocked her from the horse and dragged her away with him. Setting aside her cup of wine untouched, she cleared her throat, folded her hands in her lap and looked up at Yasir. "I was unable to tell Ronen," —the name seemed to lodge in her throat—"that I had been kidnapped from my home in America and brought here against my will. If you—or Ronen—would send word to Alanna Remington in Williamsburg, Virginia, she will see you're repaid for all your trouble and will send a ship to escort me home. And—and Holly, the young girl who arrived with me. She was taken from her father when the ship I was on docked in England to unload its cargo. Oh, you must see the travesty of injustice brought down upon me."

During her recital, Amber had absently leaned closer to Yasir, her hand touching his in an expression of her sincerity and longing. The old man, sensing the turbulence that filled her, covered the slender fingers with his own gnarled and aged ones, patting them gently.

"I wish I could help, my dear," he said softly. "But you belong to Ronen—"

"I belong to no one!" she stormed, snatching her hand away and settling her troubled gaze on the table before them.

Tilting his head to one side, his white brows knotted, Yasir bent to see her face. "Please allow me to explain," he said, hoping she would look at him. But when she continued to study the brass objects, he sighed and stood up slowly to pace the floor.

"A long time ago, a mountain warrior attacked this village, killed many of our men, and took what food we had. Each season after harvest when his supplies ran low he would come again. We were helpless to stop him, and many of our children died because we could not feed them. He would attack in the middle of the night while we slept and catch us off guard, unprepared. We never knew when to expect them.

"Then Ronen came to our village."

Amber's eyes moved to watch Yasir when she heard the pain in his voice and he paused to draw a breath. He had crossed to the open doorway and stood staring out. Small of stature, he still possessed an air of worldliness in his rounding shoulders and loose-fitting clothes, the illusion of a priest about to give his own confessions. Amber sensed the anxiety he felt and vowed to hear him out without a word.

"Ronen had never been here before, never met any of our people, but when he saw the destruction, the starving children, he seemed filled with rage. I thanked him for his concern, but told him there was nothing he could do against so many. I remember the way he smiled after I said it, and the next day he was gone.

"Nearly a week passed before we saw him again." Yasir slowly shook his head. "I'll never forget it. He rode in here with twenty armed men. I still don't know where he got them, but those men are still here." He turned back, smiling. "Some have even married our village women." He laughed softly and looked outside again. "They trained every day, like an army. They set up guards to watch during the night, and when the mountain warrior and his men came two months later, they were beaten for the animals they were.

"A month passed before they came again, prepared to fight, but Ronen and his men easily sent them away. I've seen the warrior in the hills from time to time, watching, waiting for our army to leave. But they never have, and Yaakob has not attacked in over three years."

Amber's head shot up. "Yaakob?" she echoed.

Yasir turned to look at her. "Yes, my child, the man who bid against Ronen to own you. So you see, even though you dislike Ronen and what he's done to you, it was for your own good. Although I do not agree with his plans, I will not interfere. I owe him the life of my village and I respect him. It is not in his heart to hurt you, so you should not fear him and should do whatever he asks of you."

Foreboding tingled the hairs of the back of her neck. "What kind of plans?" she asked.

Yasir smiled softly, moving back to sit down next to her and refill his cup with wine. "I have said too much already. In

449

time, you will learn what he wants."

"In time?" Amber exploded. "How much time? I do not intend to stay here for long. My home is in America. I have a husband and a sister who need me." She leaned forward to draw Yasir's attention to her. "If it's the money he spent, I will see he's more than repaid."

Yasir shook his head and took a drink of wine.

"Then what about Holly? Dear God, she's only fifteen. You must send her home." She wiggled around to better see him. "Yasir, I appeal to your sense of compassion. At least free her of this damnation. She's frightened."

"What Ronen decides is how it will be."

Amber stiffened and looked straight ahead defiantly. "For you maybe, but not me."

Setting aside his cup, Yasir took one of her hands in his. "Trust me, Amber. Things will turn out for the best. You'll see."

"No!" she snapped, jerking free of him. Scrambling to her feet, she stomped to the door and stopped, looking back. "Thank you for the wine and hospitality, sir, but I shan't be back." Her nose raised slightly, she turned around and walked out into the street, ignoring the man who suddenly appeared at her side. Chin set, shoulders squared, she marched determinedly toward the lodgings where she had left her tattered gown and petticoats. She would change her clothes, find Holly, and leave this awful place before the sun set, even if it meant getting lost in their travels down the mountain. No one would own her, no matter what price he paid. She would be a slave to no man!

Entering the coarsely built dwelling, she slammed the door shut behind her before her companion had a chance to follow and continued on into the second room where she had taken her bath. But once she started through the doorway, she pulled up short, her chin sagging, eyes wide. The entire space had been cleaned, and all that remained was the mountain of pillows in the center of the room.

Damn them, she fumed inwardly. *I will not wear the clothes he gave me.*

Spinning around, she headed for the door, set on finding the garments they had taken from her. As soon as she had changed into them she would look for Holly and be on her way, whether they liked it or not. She would not stay a minute longer. Seizing the latch in her hand, she swung the portal wide, frozen where she stood when her blue eyes met brown ones above a pastel-green silk veil. Her pledge of the moment before forgotten, Amber nervously backed into the room when Ronen advanced, her breath labored, a knot of fear in her throat. For some odd reason, she sensed he knew what she was about and had come to bind her hands and feet, a sure method to keep her where he wanted her.

Watching him close the door and turn the key in the lock, Amber swallowed hard, forcing the words from her mouth. "I—I was going to look for Holly," she said, stepping out of his way as he crossed the room. "Holly—my friend. I want to see Holly."

Warily, she followed when he continued into the next room, pausing in the archway a safe distance from him and watching him stoop to straighten the pillows as if he intended to lie down. Satisfied with their placement, Ronen knelt, then rolled to his hips to remove his knee-high suede boots and toss them aside. He stretched, ignoring her, and settled down on the cushions, arms folded behind his head, eyes closed, ankles crossed. To all appearances, he had drifted off to sleep in record time.

Her fear of his wrath quickly ebbed and her own irritation rose. How could he dismiss her so easily, so completely, as if she didn't even exist? She straightened and cleared her throat to gain his attention. "I want to see my friend!" she demanded loudly.

One brown eye opened to peer over at her. "I thought Holly was your sister," came the raspy reply.

"Oh . . . ah . . . yes," she began, a light flush to her cheeks when she realized her mistake. "That's what I meant. My sis . . ." Amber's breath left her in a rush, for it hadn't been his question that shocked her, or the strange huskiness of his voice, but the fact that he had spoken in flawless English. Speechless, she gasped, not really certain if she had heard him speak or only imagined it. Her mind raced back to their first

451

meeting and the things she had said, the names she had called him. Dear God, she had thrown every insult she could think of, and not once had he reacted as if it made a difference. Why? Why had he chosen not to speak? Her confusion turned to rage. He had played her the fool. He had done it to humiliate her, the beggarly cur! Her body trembling with fury, she advanced a step, jerking the blue cloth from her head and tossing it aside. Ronen quickly sat up.

"Why didn't you tell me you understood? Why did you let me go on thinking . . . Oh, you—you—" The many insults that had flowed so easily before now evaded her, and Amber's mouth opened and closed repeatedly in frustration at her failure to find the one most suitable. "I wouldn't be here now if you had given me a chance to explain. And Holly *isn't* my sister. She's a poor frightened child who should be sent home. I only told you that so we could stay together. I wanted to protect her." She stood within arm's reach of him, glaring down at him as he settled comfortably on one elbow.

"And who will protect you?" the hoarse voice asked lazily.

Her blue eyes widened, the angry flush of her cheeks vanishing, and Amber moved to step away. A brown, lean hand shot up, caught her own, and yanked her to the pillows before she could dodge out of the way. Ronen curled her beneath him, pinning her down in the soft cushion of his bed and stilling her struggles instantly when he pressed his weight full against her. The contact of their bodies burned every inch of her flesh, her golden tresses falling in disarray. She stared fearfully, certain her doom had encased her and praying it would end quickly. But the gleam in his eyes seemed more amusement than lust.

"I—I think I must w-warn you," she panted, her breath difficult to draw when he chose to stay put. "I—I'm married. M-my husband will shoot you for your very thoughts."

Her hands entrapped by his own and raised beside her head, Ronen easily lifted himself up slightly and scanned the small interior of the room. Amber's brow furrowed.

"What are you looking for?" she asked nervously, wondering if he sought a whip with which to beat her.

"Your husband," his voice graveled out.

"What?"

"You said he would shoot me. I merely wish to know from which direction." Warm, twinkling eyes returned to gaze down at her, and Amber felt the gibe of his statement.

"Well . . . well, he will when he comes for me," she retorted bravely, though the tone of her words refuted the strength of her promise.

"And you think he will?"

"Of course," Amber snapped, a twinge of doubt stabbing her heart. "H—he loves me."

"And do you love him?"

A knot moved to her throat. "What difference does that make? He wants me back. H—he'll come."

"How will he find you?"

Amber's body stiffened in outrage to hear this stranger attack Nicholas's talents. "He is not stupid like you. It won't take him long." She wiggled, attempting to push him away, but failed when he pressed harder. "I—I suggest you watch over y-your shoulder. Before . . . before you realize it, Nicholas will be holding a gun on you."

Shifting her hands above her head in order to hold them both with one of his, he eased from her to lie at her side, one leg twisted around hers to spoil her efforts to kick out at him. "I don't think he'll come, Amber," he said softly, tracing a finger-tip along the delicate line of her jaw.

She jerked away from the caress. "And why not? He loves me."

"But if you don't love him, he will think the journey too far with no promise of reward."

"I didn't say I didn't love him," she snapped, struggling briefly to free her hands. His grip tightened.

"Then you do?"

"It's none of your business."

The low rumble of his laughter mocked her and she opened her mouth to retaliate, cut short when his hand gently encompassed her throat and she feared he would strangle the breath from her.

"Maybe you will grow to love me," he rasped, his gaze moving to the swell of her bosom heaving in frustrated anger.

"You?" she jeered. "Never!"

He shrugged. "We shall see."

"You shan't live long enough to see. I intend to escape. To stop me, you'll have to tie me up. How do you plan to win my love by treating me like that?" Her voice raised in pitch. "And why would you want my love?"

His eyes moved back to stare at her. "I want a wife and I want her love. If she hates me, how could she bear my children?"

"Wife? Children?" The words choked her. "Are you deaf as well? I already have a husband."

Ronen leaned back, his hand resting much too familiarly on Amber's waist as he stared off in thought. Had her anger not occupied her mind, she would have worried more about the present rather than his proclaimed future, but instead she waited for him to answer. Only a moment passed before his brows lifted with an idea. He glanced back at her.

"Holly, then. She isn't married."

"No!" Amber screamed, fighting with all her strength to be free of him, surprised when he willingly released her. She flew from his side, scooted off the pillows, and moved far enough away that he couldn't reach her without getting up. Spinning around to face him, she glared disdainfully, straightening immediately when she found him lounging casually on the bed, propped up on one elbow, fingers interlaced over his belly and ankles crossed. The silken mask hid his smile, but Amber sensed it from the sparkle in his eyes. "You—you can't do that to her. She's too young. She belongs with her father."

Ronen shrugged. "I could give her all she wants."

Old hatreds surfaced. "Money and riches have nothing to do with the heart."

"No, they don't. They just ease the living. And many times are an expression of love."

"No, they aren't," she argued hotly.

"Sharing everything one has with another is *not* an expression of love? Why?"

"Because . . . because . . ." All reason abandoned her. Frantic for a suitable answer, Amber fell quiet, drawing in a breath when one seemed near, expelling it in a rush when she failed.

"Maybe you would prefer wearing your torn dress and going hungry."

Her blue eyes brightened. "That's it! You share out of compassion, not love."

"How do you know that?"

"That it's compassion, not love?" she rallied and waited for his nod. "Because you can't love me. You've only known me for one day."

Ronen didn't answer, creating a silence that grated on her nerves. He continued to stare, then rolled to his back and studied the ceiling overhead, hands locked behind his neck. "It matters not. I sold Holly a few hours ago."

The impact of his words hit her like a bolt of lightning, rocking her back on her heels, knees weak. "What?" she cried out, tears instantly burning her eyes. "Oh, God, you couldn't! She . . ."

Ronen's head jerked around to glare at her. "I can do whatever I wish. She belonged to me and I had the right to sell her."

"Right? What right? Who gave you such a thing? Who do you think you are, God?" Amber's heart pounded, envisioning all the cruel debasements Holly would surely endure. "Please, Ronen, don't do this." She moved forward and fell to her knees. "I'll do anything you ask, just don't send her away."

His dark brown eyes raked over her. "Yes, you will, and it's too late. She's already gone."

The blood drained from her face, her heart aching, and she collapsed to one hip, tears of worry and pain streaming down her face. "But . . . but I promised her . . ." The words came in a choked whisper.

"Promised her what?"

The gravelly sound of his voice penetrated her fog, but she couldn't bring herself to look at him. "To care for her, that no one would hurt her."

Ronen sat up and swung his legs off the pillows. He leaned forward, elbows resting on his knees, hands dangling between them. "And you think because I sold her that she will be abused? Are you assuming I sold her to someone like Yaakob?"

Tears glistening brightly, Amber turned hopeful eyes upon him. "You didn't?" she asked weakly.

"No. I didn't. So you see, your promise was kept."

She looked away. "No, it wasn't. I also promised to take her home."

A long silence surrounded her, and Amber studied the blue cloth covering her knees. How could her life have changed so drastically in just a few short months? She had gone from living with Andrea and her father in their cottage outside Jamestown to marriage with Nicholas after Fletcher Courtney was murdered, to being kidnapped by Baron Kelzer Von Buren and sent to Casablanca, and she now faced spending the rest of her days in this strange, hot country with a man whose face she hadn't even been allowed to see. Where would it all end? Why must innocent victims like Holly be forced to pay? And what of her twin? Had Von Buren's plan succeeded? Had he tricked Andrea into marriage? She squeezed her eyes closed, a single tear dropping on her folded hands. If he had, Andrea would soon die because of him. She could never endure his cruelty. Amber swallowed the lump in her throat, knowing there was nothing she could do for her sister now. Suddenly her eyes flew open, an idea coming to her mind. And she might be able to help Holly and herself if Ronen agreed. Twisting around to face him, Amber bravely lifted her chin and stared at him.

"I have a proposition I think you might be interested in," she said, her voice strong.

Ronen returned her gaze equally, unblinking.

"I will marry you, bear your children if I must, on one condition. You will send Holly home." Blue eyes round with anticipation, Amber waited, knowing that if this barbarian fell for her scheme, Holly would tell her father what had happened and send word to Alanna Remington. All she would have to do was sit by patiently. She fought to hide her deceptive smile. And who said that once Holly was safely sent to England Amber would have to meet her part of the deal? It was perfect. This fool would lose them both—

"No."

The word seemed to hang in midair, ricochet inside her head, and shatter her hopes. But even more it ignited her anger.

"Why not?" she shouted, jumping to her feet. "You said you wanted a wife and I've offered you that. The price is small."

"To you, perhaps," Ronen pointed out hoarsely. "I suspect the cost will be greater."

A prickling of worry that he had outguessed her slithered up her spine. "I don't know what you mean," she argued, damning the cursed veil that hid his face.

He lay back down on the pillows, blatantly ignoring her.

"I will be true to my word, if that is what you fear," she assured him, her ire growing.

His laughter set her nerves on edge. "What I fear, dear woman, is what Holly will tell her father. Then I will not only have to fight off Yaakob, but an outraged husband, as well." He glanced over at her. "I'm not stupid, Amber. Holly is gone, and you shall be my wife whether you like it or not." He settled back and closed his eyes. "Now find a place to sit down. I need to rest, and all your threats and promises weary me."

Amber rallied to the cause. "Then you will find no willing woman as your bride." Her slim nose elevated slightly. "Tell me, sir, do you enjoy rape? For that is what it will be if you intend to have me bear your children."

The green silk outlined his face and a strong jaw, and Amber saw it move as if he smiled.

"Well?" she demanded.

"I don't know. I've never raped anyone. But if that's the way it must be . . ."

Amber stumbled back. "I want to talk with Yasir."

"No."

"I *demand* to talk with Yasir."

"Be quiet, Amber. I wish to sleep now."

"I don't care what you wish to do. I want to talk with Yasir!"

The *yashmak* covering his face moved slightly with his sigh. He rolled to his side, rested his head on one clenched fist, and stared at her. "If you don't want to find out now whether or not I enjoy rape, I suggest you find some place to sit down where I won't be bothered. Then after I've rested, we'll begin our lessons."

Amber's heart pounded in her ears, her knees suddenly weak, and she glided to the floor, her round blue eyes watching him.

"That's better," he said calmly. "By morning you'll know what's expected of the women in this village." He lay down again. "And if you learn quickly, we can be married within the week."

A flood of emotions washed over her as she sat dejectedly in the center of the room. But amid them all, Amber shuddered with hopelessness.

Chapter Twenty

Sleep played heavily on Amber's eyelids. She stirred, the cold hardness of the tile floor chilling her. Her muscles ached, her body longing for rest, and she shifted to find a more comfortable position. She moaned when it seemed the new spot was even more objectionable, and a dull awareness of her surroundings began to seep into the folds of her brain. She awoke with a start, her eyes dartingly scanning the room. The door was closed and Ronen no longer lay on the pillows. A single candle flickered in the sconce hanging on the wall, spreading a yellow glow about her. The air held a crisp bite and she sat up, hugging her arms to her and wondering how long she had slept. Glancing at the door, she assumed he had locked it until a noise sounded from somewhere inside the small dwelling and his promise of lessons came rushing back to mind. Were they to begin tonight? Did he intend to be the teacher or to summon one of the village women, since he had proclaimed her need to learn their duties? Twisting, she stretched the cramp from her back, some spirit returning.

If you learn quickly we'll be married within the week. She recited his pledge in her mind. *A fatal mistake, Ronen,* she thought devilishly. *You never should have given me such a reward for being quick. It will take me a month to learn a simple task.*

Another noise from the other room broke the quiet, and she nervously looked toward the door, noticing the orange flickering light beneath it as if a fire had been started in the hearth. She longed to warm herself by it but feared his presence there. Rising, she went to the pillows and sat down to escape the chill of the floor, and discovered for the first time that his suede boots were gone. She had never seen Nicholas in such apparel, but she thought how much better he would look in them than Ronen. Mentally, she compared the two. Though she found little difference in their overall builds, she considered them quite opposite, but a frown creased her lovely brow when she couldn't distinguish exactly what made it so. Of course, Nicholas wasn't some barbarian who bought his women—The conditions of their marriage surfaced, and her face paled when she remembered he had needed a wife to save his inheritance, not because he wanted one. And she had been unfortunate enough to share the same needs. Their union had been a facade, for neither had proclaimed love in the beginning.

Amber wiggled, tucking her cold feet beneath her, and studied the closed door. But Ronen didn't need a wife, he *wanted* one. He had stated simply that to have a wife, he must have her love as well. Confusion wrinkled the smooth lines of her face. Although he had purchased the woman he wanted to wed, he had implied that he intended to woo her, court her into marriage. Nicholas certainly hadn't done that. Her gaze took in the meager interior of the room. And this did not compare to Nicholas's home. If Ronen had wealth, he spent it on other things. And what he had he willingly wished to share with her. She recalled their earlier conversation.

"Sharing everything one has is an expression of love," he had said.

Her face reflected the possibility. Maybe. But why had Nicholas's wealth offended her if that was the case? She shook her head. This was too much to figure out at one time. Why did it matter anyway? She was already married to Nicholas and she belonged back home, not in this remote, isolated corner of

460

the world. A sarcastic smile kinked one corner of her mouth. And that was the irony of the whole situation. She was wed to a man who *needed* a wife, and desired by another who *wanted* a wife. If she had the choice and times were different, with both suitors calling on her at the doorstep of her cottage, she could have easily decided. A low growl erupted from her and she tossed herself backward on the bed, staring up at the ceiling. Love would come with the passing of days, had both men started equally. Maybe she had grown to that with Nicholas. But so many things stood in the way, challenged her ideals of the perfect husband. She wanted to say she didn't love him, yet she could not deny the ache in her heart whenever she thought of him. She rolled to her stomach, her ankles crossed and swaying to and fro, her chin resting on one fist. And what of this man called Ronen? This mysterious messenger, her savior from a terrifying fate. She had to admit she found him attractive. Or was it merely because she knew nothing of him? Even Yasir had little knowledge of the man's past. She sat up suddenly. And why did he wear that aggravating mask over his face when no one else did? Hearing the rattle of dishes beyond the door, she decided to ask. After all, what could it hurt? She obviously was going to spend several days with the man, and if she could learn a few secrets she might find a way of convincing him to let her return home. Crossing to the door, she hesitated only a moment before she noiselessly pulled it open.

As she had suspected, Ronen was there, kneeling before the hearth and stoking the fire beneath a large kettle that hung there. A warm aroma of cooking meat filled the air and made Amber's mouth water instantly, though she couldn't understand why, since she had eaten only a short while before. Looking at the front entrance of the small dwelling, its door standing open, her eyes widened when she discovered the sun no longer spread its golden wings and warmed the earth. Night had descended quietly and without warning, allowing her to sleep the afternoon away and bringing a chill to the air. Such a stark difference from the hot daylight hours.

Several candles adorned the room, and mingled their lights with the ruddy glow of the fireplace, an illusion of peace and contentment, a feeling that quickly washed over her. She relaxed, returning her gaze to the man by the fire. He crouched on one knee, his right arm dangling over the other, and busily rearranged the stack of burning logs. He was unaware of her presence and thus granted her a moment to appraise him without his knowing. The thick muscles of his shoulders flexed with each move he made, straining the seams of his shirt sleeves. His wide back narrowed to slender hips and accentuated the width of his thighs. But to admire further proved useless, since the headpiece covered his hair and the *yashmak* forbid a view of his face. His task completed, he made to rise, Amber's breath catching as she watched the long, lean frame unfold to full height. He moved gracefully, yet with a sureness of which not many men his size could boast. He appeared as slick and powerful as the huge steed he rode, a strength ready to explode at the slightest command, held in rein but ever present. Could his gentleness be described the same way? She pondered the thought, then jumped when she discovered the warm brown gaze upon her. He smiled beneath the veil, and Amber saw its reflection in his eyes. She cast her own away, ashamed that she could look upon any other than her husband with such favorable sensitivity. She should find the sight of him annoying. He knew she belonged to another yet would not allow her to leave.

"Are you hungry?" he asked, his voice raspy.

Amber nodded, afraid to speak and reveal the turmoil she endured.

"Then sit by the fire and warm yourself." He touched her arm in a gentle almost loving fashion and guided her to the stack of pillows by the hearth. He waited for her to sit down before offering her a glass of wine. "You slept a long time," he said, watching her sample the dark red liquid as he sat down next to her. "Are you rested now?"

Her eyes trained on the goblet in her hand, she nodded.

"Good. You'll need the strength for what I have in mind."

Amber's head shot up. "What?"

He glanced sideways at her and rested back on his elbows to enjoy the beauty of her. "It has been a long while since this place was cleaned properly. After you clear away and wash the

462

dishes, I would like these walls scrubbed and the floor shiny again." He looked away to pick a speck of lint from his breeches and hide the mischief in his eyes.

"But 'tis night!" Amber exploded. "And we traveled nearly two days. The nap I took will hardly give me that much strength. Surely it can wait until tomorrow."

Ronen shrugged. "Yes, it could. But I supposed you would want to lessen the amount of tomorrow's work by finishing some tonight."

The glass shook in her hand, her irritation mounting. "Have you set such an amount for each day and plan to see it finished before I rest?"

"Before you eat," he corrected calmly.

Amber's mouth flew open in heated retaliation, snapped closed again when he raised a hand.

"It is the custom of our women to work until all is finished, seeing their men fed and comforted before they take their own meal. You will catch on quickly."

"Catch on—" the words burst forth. "And what if I don't follow custom?" Sitting up straight, she turned to confront him. "What if I decide not to wait? Maybe I'll do my chores, all I'm capable of in a full day, and elect to have my meal whenever I choose and leave the rest of the work for the next day. What then, ol' lord and master?"

Ronen examined the calluses on one hand almost casually before he said, "Then you'll be beaten for your failure." The husky tone sounded even more threatening. "That too is custom."

"Custom?" Amber screamed, jumping to her feet. "You beat women and call it custom? That's—that's barbaric!"

"Sit down, woman," the hoarse voice commanded.

"Or what? You'll beat me for disobeying?" she challenged, blue eyes flashing.

Lazily, he looked up at her. "Yes."

Amber's lips parted as if she wished to test his claim, thought better of it, and slowly returned to the pillow. A man who would buy and sell another human being would not be beyond striking her. She clamped her teeth together, but the flare of her nostrils warned Ronen she was far from being subdued.

"That's better," he said. "Now I suggest you eat so you can begin your work without delay. It grows late already, and you have a lot to do."

Watching him rise, Amber chewed on the inside of her lip, fighting back the angry retort she felt he deserved yet certain he would carry through with his threat if she voiced a complaint. He picked up a clay bowl from the stone slab of the hearth, filled it with stew from the kettle, and handed it to her before sitting down once more. Amber ate in silence, although she constantly watched him from the corner of her eye. He chose not to dine, and her temper quickly ebbed, wondering if he had already eaten or intended to do so later when he was alone. Again her curiosity was aroused. Did he deem himself too ugly for others to see and elect to find seclusion for his meal, or was this, too, one of their customs?

When she had finished, he took the bowl from her and set it aside, stretching out on the pillows to watch the flames in the fireplace. Its warmth and her full stomach dulled some of Amber's earlier hostilities, and within minutes she too studied the flickering light before her, relaxing in their solitude. It seemed almost natural for them to be there, sharing a meal, each other's company, and she pushed the sudden spark of guilt from her thoughts. She hadn't truly abandoned Nicholas. She was simply enjoying the first moments of sanity she'd experienced since being kidnapped over two months ago.

"Ronen," she said suddenly, surprised by her own boldness.

He grunted but continued to watch the fire.

"Since I'm to learn the customs of your village, may I ask something?"

He nodded but would not look at her.

"I have noticed no other men here wears a veil but you. Why?"

Reaching for the brass pitcher beside him, he refilled her glass of wine and gave it to her, resuming his observation of the dancing blaze. A long moment passed before he spoke, his voice raspy, low. "I was wounded in battle a long time ago and nearly killed. It left me with a grotesque scar and a voice that would chill the soul of any man. I grew a beard, but it wasn't enough. I

464

simply choose to avoid pitiful stares." He glanced over at her, his eyes smiling. "I would have seemed even less appealing to you than Yaakob otherwise."

Amber couldn't restrain the smile that separated her lips. "No one could be less appealing than he." She shrugged, studying the glass in her hand. "Except maybe Baron Von Buren."

"Someone from your past?" he questioned, shifting to one hip so that he could look directly at her.

"Yes. The baron is an evil man. He uses anyone to satisfy his needs." She looked up at Ronen, a frown marring the flawless brow. "It's been said he killed his first wife. And I'm sure he killed my father just to have my sister."

"Holly?" Ronen teased, his eyes sparkling.

Amber stared a moment, a light blush darkening her cheeks, then laughed. "No, not Holly. I really do have a sister. A twin, in fact. Her name is Andrea."

"A twin," he whispered hoarsely. "Then there are two beautiful women in the world. Not just one."

Amber smiled modestly, averting her eyes. "Thank you."

"My pleasure, I assure you."

He rolled to his back again, legs crossed and fingers interlaced to support the back of his head. He watched the fire, and Amber openly studied him. Surely no scar could be as disfiguring as he assumed it to be. And with all his other handsome features, it would only add a touch of intrigue to his character. Amber sipped her wine, forcing her attention away from the exquisite profile bathed in the glow of the fire. She truly could not understand why, maybe it was his manner or the stories Yasir had told her about him, but she found she actually liked him, and wished they had met under different circumstances. The soft line of her brow wrinkled. If only she could understand how he could have sold Holly without the slightest twinge of regret or conscience. She decided she would have to learn more about him to come to any honest conclusions.

"Haven't you ever been married before, Ronen?" she asked, quietly.

He chuckled huskily. "Yes. But my wife ran away."

"Ran away? Whatever for?" A thought struck her and she laughed before he could answer. "Maybe you beat her too often."

His dark, handsome eyes glanced over at her and then away. "Not enough perhaps."

"I was only teasing," she gasped. Resting on one hand, she turned to face him, her glass dangling from the other draped across her thighs. "You can't really think someone will continue to love you if you constantly abuse them."

"Then what should I have done? Given her everything she wanted without expecting something in return?"

"No. Just love, Ronen. It would have been enough."

He frowned up at her. "I did. But apparently she wanted something else."

"Such as?"

He grew quiet for a long while. "If I had known, she never would have had cause to leave me."

Amber sensed the pain he felt and suddenly thought of Nicholas. Hadn't she played the coward and left Alanna to interpret her motives to him? She couldn't explain why, but she felt compelled to narrate her story to this stranger. Maybe, somehow, she would ease his conscience as well as her own.

"Ronen," she began quietly, pushing herself up. She set down her glass and wrapped her arms around her legs, hugging her knees to her chest. "Maybe I can help you understand." She sighed heavily, wondering if she truly could, since her reasons for leaving Nicholas were still quite unclear even to herself. "My marriage to Nicholas was a union of compromise. He needed a wife to save his inheritance. I needed a husband to pay my debts and save my sister from a fateful existence. I would have preferred finding some other way of acquiring the money I needed, but time had run out and I had no choice.

"I hated Nicholas at first. He stood for everything I despised in life; money, power, selfishness. But as time went on, I soon realized I had misjudged him, that just because he had money and power, he was far from selfish. I couldn't bring myself to admit it, and when he declared his love, I ran away." A tear pooled in the corner of her eye. "I guess I was too proud, but I could not let myself fall in love with him, and I didn't want to believe he could really love me. I had always thought of wealthy people as heartless." She reached up to catch the tear before it fell to her cheek. "I suppose I ran hoping he would follow me, prove me wrong, that no matter what I did to him he would bear it and come to me time and time again." A sob shook her body, and she looked up at the ceiling overhead. "I didn't get the chance to find out, and I'm sure after all this time, he's given up trying to find me."

"I rather doubt it," came the hoarse reply.

Amber looked over at him, surprised. "Why?"

"If he loved you as much as you say, he'll never rest until he finds you."

She shook her head, embracing her knees again. "His grandmother promised me that she would not let him. You see, I was supposed to take all the time I needed to decide if I loved him, and he would have to wait. Since I've not returned after such a long while, he can only assume I've wanted it this way."

"So you do love him after all."

"I'm not sure. I miss him . . . but I'm not sure I love him."

Several moments of silence passed, each quiet with his own thoughts, and Amber was the first to speak.

"Did you ever try to find your wife? Maybe her situation is similar to mine. Maybe she can't come back to you, and she's praying you'll find her."

Before answering, Ronen pushed himself up from the pillows and went to the door. "I don't have to look for her. I've found you." His brown eyes raked over her, and Amber felt a chill dash up her spine.

"Ronen, wait," she called when he turned to leave. "I can't stay here. I don't want to stay. I want to go home, and you should be eager to find your wife." She quickly came to her feet and crossed the room, stopping a short distance from him. "I have an idea that will help us both." She swallowed nervously when his eyes seemed to darken with his suspicious stare. "Send word to Nicholas. He has plenty of money and will pay you well for taking care of me. And if I asked him, I'm sure he would help you find your wife."

"No," came the sharp reply.

"But—but why?"

"I don't want money. If I did, I would steal all I need."

A slight wrinkling on her brow formed as she asked, "Then what is it you need?"

His gaze softened as he reached out a sun-darkened hand to gently caress her cheek. "Love," he whispered.

Suddenly Amber sensed the pain this man felt, the longing, the desire to be loved, and she thought how very much like Nicholas he was. She looked away, truly sorry she could not help either one.

The click of the doorlatch intruded into her thoughts. Glancing up, she discovered he had left her as quietly as a breath of air. Moving closer, she listened at the door for the sound of his footsteps. When they had faded, she noiselessly opened the portal a crack, peering out into the night for some clue to his travels. At the end of the narrow, dusty road, she saw his tall, silken figure stride, a quickness to his step, then pause before the last of the dwellings, the light spilling out of the open doorway to silhouette his broad frame against the ebony backdrop of night. Then, the tall, lean profile moved, disappearing inside the rough-built lodging, as mysterious as life itself.

Amber continued to watch, though only memory conjured up the vision of him standing there, and she wondered whose place he had chosen to visit. There was so much about the man that remained a secret to her and she felt an unexplainable need to learn more. She stepped back, closed the door, and leaned a shoulder against it, her gaze drifting to the fireplace and the single bowl and wine glass sitting there. He had shared what he had with her and offered himself as well.

"Why?" she whispered. When there were so many women in the world from whom to choose, why her? Deciding it was a question she would likely never answer, she straightened with a sigh and set her goals of the moment on cleaning his house.

Amber stood back to appraise her work, noticing the sparkle to the tile and the dust-free surfaces on the few pieces of furniture. She had even fluffed up the pillows before the hearth and stoked the fire against the night chill. She took pride in her work and suddenly realized she had done it to please Ronen. She smiled at the thought, then stiffened when the twinge of guilt surfaced once more to haunt her. She had never done anything to please Nicholas. She had fought him at every turn, deceived him, tried to steal from him, screamed her hatred, and finally deserted him. A troubled almost angry frown kinked her brow and twisted her lovely face unflatteringly. How could she abandon him so easily and willingly do for another, without the slightest care? The lines of frustration disappeared. Sighing, she slid to her knees and closed her eyes, hands folded over her lap. She was simply tired of fighting; with Nicholas, herself, Ronen. The last months of her life had been a constant struggle. Everything had happened so fast that it had all seemed unreal, and she considered the thought that God had planned it this way. Could He have charted out her life, brought her to this point for a reason? Was it possible that He wanted her to have the time away from Nicholas to decide without influence from anyone? If so, why had He allowed Ronen to step into her world? Was it to discover the other side of loving, to present the gentler way, and bring about a reckoning?

Nicholas. Suddenly his handsome face, his sparkling smile, the devilish twinkle in his eyes flashed into her mind. She recalled the pond surrounded by giant willows where they had last made love, his gentleness, caress, warm kisses, and burning desire. She felt his warmth, his touch, his nakedness, and relived the way he had held her close, his lips brushing hers, the cool flesh of her neck, her breast. And in his passion he had called her name, declared his love for all eternity. A tear stole between the thick lashes and slowly fell to her chin. Why had she been so stubborn? Why had she forbidden him to capture her heart?

"Oh, Nicholas," she whispered tenderly. "I truly do love . . ."

Amber jumped at the sound of the doorlatch clicking open, hurriedly brushing away her tears, her memories shattered. She scrambled to her feet as the door opened and Ronen stepped inside. She chose not to look at him and went to the hearth instead, kneeling to rearrange the cooking pot and spoon as she had already done before. She needed a moment to compose herself. She knew so little of this man, she feared his anger if he discovered she cried for another. Blinking away the moisture from her eyes, she took a deep breath and stood, forcing a smile to her lips as she turned to look at him. Standing before the fire in the hearth, her profile cast a shadow across the room and masked the expression in Ronen's eyes, but from the silent way he stood, Amber worried he already knew. Looking down, she smoothed the wrinkles from her garment and laughed.

"I had hoped to be finished before you returned." She prayed her statement sounded more convincing to him than it did to her. "Would you care for some wine before you retire?"

When he failed to answer, she glanced up. He had remained near the door, his broad frame relaxed, his head tilted to one side, studying her.

"Do you cry for yourself or your husband?" he asked quietly after a moment.

She smiled weakly. "Cry? Whatever makes you think—"

"Amber," he interrupted, "you have talked with Yasir, and I know he told you that I would never hurt you. He speaks the truth, so don't hide your feelings for fear I will punish you for them." He stepped closer. "You are a very brave woman, the strongest-willed I have ever known. But even they must let down their barriers now and then. There is no shame in shedding a tear because of the ache in your heart." He stood before her. "But more, don't deny yourself the need."

Although the voice was raspy, the words he spoke were gentle, consoling, and Amber fought the urge to have him hold her in his arms. Yes, she needed to cry, for her father, her sister, Holly, Nicholas, for herself, for all the wretchedness she had endured, the times she had had to stand tall when she had really wanted to fall to her knees and weep until her tears were spent. She longed to have someone else take the burden from her shoulders, cradle her, and soothe the troubles from her mind. But not now, not Ronen. It would be too easy, he was too willing. Given a chance, her mind would rule her heart, and Nicholas, her husband, would become a memory. Mentally she hardened herself and smiled courageously up at him.

"When I cry, *if* I cry, I will seek my privacy to do so. I have never depended on anyone in my whole life, and I will not change. If I let down my barriers, as you suggest, someone will find my weakness and then control my life." A sigh tremored her thin frame. "I will never allow that to happen. *I* will choose the path I take and let destiny have its way."

"And renounce the love only a man can give?" His dark brown eyes softened. "To live your life alone is only half of living. The days are cold without companionship, the nights dark, but love will fan a spark of warmth, a light for better things to come, a chance to grow. There is no greater joy than giving of oneself to another."

His declaration rang of truth but ignited a sliver of doubt. "And what if one allows another this gift and finds a falsehood there? To give one's heart is a dangerous thing if done so foolishly. How can he be certain that the one chosen is sincere, willing to give equally, with no other reason but love?"

"You will feel it," he said quietly, one fist raised to his chest, "in here."

Amber studied the suntanned hand resting against the broad chest, appraising its strength and gentleness, certain that if raised in anger it could deal a death blow, and yet could tenderly hold a fragile blossom without harm to its delicate petals. "Yes, I suppose I will." Her pale blue eyes lifted to meet his. "But that time has not come, and I'm not sure it ever will."

The warmth of his gaze held hers, and for the first time in a long while, Amber felt safe, and, oddly enough, loved. His manner radiated compassion, kindness, a sincerity to chase away all her fears, hatreds, to soothe her troubled state. Without thinking, she raised a hand to pull away the folds of silk covering his face.

"No," he said quietly, the wide hand catching hers before it reached the veil. "'Tis too soon."

Confusion marred the fairness of her face.

"What you feel in your heart must be spoken. You must not hide from the truth and seek another way to deny it." He continued to hold her, his free hand lifted to brush his fingertips against her cheek. "It will come. Give it time."

He turned away abruptly, and Amber wondered at his mood.

471

Did he sense the admission that had nearly spilled from her lips, and was he asking that she consider it a while longer, take the chance, perhaps, to know another kind of love? She watched him curiously as he crossed the room and knelt before the hearth. What sort of man, this stranger? Any other would have played upon her weakness of the moment, but not he, not Ronen, this man who sought companionship and love. Must love come first for him? She smiled softly. How different he was from Nicholas. She looked away. Or was he, really?

Chapter Twenty-One

Platinum streams of moonlight played upon the branches of the pine tripping lightly through long green needles to caress the earth and set the stage of night aglow in silver rhapsody. Warm breezes, filled with the fragrance of evergreen, rustled the tree tops and soothed the wild beast to sleep. Admist the quiet pageant, one figure moved about, his step sure and quick as he traveled the dusty road bathed in ashen beams, while, unbeknownst to him, a pair of light blue eyes secretly observed his journey.

From within the archway of their dwelling, Amber hid among the shadows, a puzzled frown upon her face as she quietly watched Ronen walk further away, Nearly a week had passed since they had come to terms, the days and nights passing in friendship. They had shared secrets and feelings, laughed and worked together, Ronen showing her how to prepare the wild game he hunted with herbs and spices, a feast common to their village. Not once had he touched a hand to her with lust in his eyes, only with tender compassion. They slept in separate beds, and Amber grew to enjoy their time alone by the fire after they had finished their evening meal. He had not, however, allowed her to leave the dwelling unless escorted by him, for her safety, he said, but Amber wondered if there was another reason. She never questioned his motives, for she felt certain he would only avoid the answer, but she suspected he did not trust her, that he thought that given the chance she would run. And he was right to some degree. Amber *had* plotted out a way to return home and Ronen would be the one to help her. She would win his affection and gradually convince him that she would be happiest living in America. If he cared for her in the slightest, he would understand and, in time, agree. Each night that passed, he stole from their lodgings when he thought she slept and walked to the dwelling at the end of the village. Several hours elapsed before he returned, and Amber wondered if her plan would work after all. Could it be he visited a village woman each night to ease his male needs? Was it possible that he had changed his mind about taking Amber as his wife?

Stepping back inside, she slowly closed the door, her frown deepening. But was she worried about her scheme or the possibility that Ronen found someone else more appealing? She tossed her head arrogantly, her blond curls bouncing about her shoulders. He could spend his time with anyone he wished. It didn't matter to her. In fact, she welcomed it. After all hadn't she spent every evening before retiring worrying that he might decide that this would be the night he would take her? A pleased grin lit up her pale blue eyes. Maybe that was the reason he sought out another. He fought with himself and knew she would never allow him more than a tranquil moment of conversation. Yet something inside her gnawed at her. Did he find her too undesirable to even attempt pursuit? Could the woman who so obviously captured his attention possess such beauty that Ronen thought of Amber only as a requirement for marriage? But what of his declaration of love? Amber's mouth pursed uncomplimentarily. He had told her that he wanted children. Was he so stupid that he thought by simply marrying a woman children would follow because the documents had been signed? Amber exploded into heartfelt laughter, quickly covering her outburst with hands pressed against her mouth should someone be near and think her mad.

Crossing the room, she entered the next and lay down on the neatly stacked pillows she used as a bed, covering herself with the thin quilt. Though the nights were chilly, the single hearth spread enough warmth throughout the small building that Amber slept comfortably. But this night offered no rest. She closed her eyes, and faint visions of a shapely woman floated through her head. She was draped in silks in a rainbow of color, and Amber fought to see the image's face, certain that dark hair and eyes would materialize on any native of this faraway land.

She must be very beautiful, Amber mused, a hint of jealousy surfacing, Her eyes flew open. So what if she was? Let her be a damned Venus for all she cared! She raised up on one elbow to punch a pillow into a knot and plopped back down, squeezing her eyes shut and demanding sleep to overcome her. Several minutes ticked by, and her mood relaxed. Her gaze suddenly fell upon the bed where Ronen slept. She imagined him there, lying on his side, the muscular body outlined beneath the cover. She had never managed to stay awake until he retired, and he was always gone when she awoke, thus leaving her to wonder if he slept at all, and if he did, had he worn that cursed veil? A devilish smile crept over her face. Tonight she would find out. She would wait up for him.

Rolling onto her back, she gazed up at the ceiling, watching the disfigured golden shapes dancing about the room, the light of the fireplace spilling in. She thought of Andrea and wondered if her twin was safe or trapped into marriage, as Von Buren had promised. No, she decided mentally, Seth would never allow that to happen. He loved Andrea. . . . Amber blinked away her tears, forcing herself to think of other things, and Holly's cherubic face flashed into her mind. What fate had made its mark on her? Had Ronen spoken truth when he had said no harm would come to the girl? The lines of Amber's mouth hardened. Such an arrogant statement. Did he honestly think Holly would be happy with anyone other than her father, living in a different land?

I make my promise to you again, Holly, she silently declared. *I will see you're taken home. Just as soon as Nicholas—*

Amber closed her eyes, willing herself not to think of him. Or the chance he would not come. She forced the image of the village to mind, the group of laughing children who played outside her dwelling, the women at the stream where Ronen had taken her to wash clothes, and she thought of Yasir. She studied the figures overhead again. She hadn't seen Yasir since the day they had talked in his house. Did Ronen purposely keep her from him? The old man had said he didn't agree with the younger man's plans, and perhaps Ronen felt threatened that she would be able to sway Yasir into helping her. Or might he be ill? A faint frown drew the softly arched brows together. She prayed not. Even though they had talked only a short while, she had liked the old man, felt a safety with him. She sighed, her eyes drifting shut again. Maybe Ronen would permit her to speak with his leader if she asked. Yes, tomorrow she would voice the request. She yawned, shifting to a more comfortable spot, her breathing relaxed. Her pledge to wait for Ronen faded, and within a moment Amber fell into a peaceful slumber.

"Damn," Amber muttered, sitting upright on the bed, her angry glare surveying the empty room.

Morning light flooded in through the open doorway and she knew Ronen had already risen and gone. She looked at the bed opposite hers. Or had he? Could it be he never returned at all, that he really spent each and every night in the same place? Cloudy visions of a raven-haired beauty flashed before her eyes and she shook her head, chasing them away. Glancing toward the door, she lifted one tawny brow artfully. Maybe that was the reason she had never caught him sleeping. Or for that matter, even in his bed. A mischievous grin curled the corners of her mouth upward. And if it was still early, she just might find out for sure. Slipping the cotton shift from her slender figure, a garment she used to sleep in, she donned the shapeless attire of the village women, covered it with a heavy cotton robe, and concealed her hair beneath an equally unflattering headdress, flipping one end across her face. If she kept her head down, she stood a chance that no one could recognize her. Gathering a basket filled with dirty linen, she hoisted it to her hip and guardedly left the building. To all appearances, it would seem to anyone who observed her travels that she was one of the village women on her way to the stream to begin her

476

day's work.

A quiet serenity surrounded Amber once she stepped out into the street. The sun had barely made its showing, casting a diffused warm light all around her, and she smiled beneath her guise, knowing few others were awake. Setting her goal on the square, flat-roofed structure at the end of the road, she hurried her pace, determined to find Ronen still sleeping. Her grin faded when she imagined what she might see. Two bodies entwined within the blissfulness of slumber, his arm draped intimately about the woman's waist. She stiffened, casting aside the picture, and quickened her step.

The distance grew shorter, and when she had nearly cut the stretch in half, a trio of laughter filled the air. Forcing herself not to turn around, she recognized the sound as the gaiety of children and knew she must hasten the execution of her plan, for if the youth of the village had risen, Ronen would soon follow. She passed another crude shelter, a narrow alleyway, and a stone dwelling larger than the last, nearly startled out of her wits when a mongrel dashed outside, barking and nipping at her heels.

"Go away," she hissed, tugging at her skirts to free the mutt's hold on its hem. Finally, out of desperation, she kicked out at the dog, sending him yelping off down the dusty street. Watching his departure, she covertly glanced around, making certain the display had not drawn any attention, and relaxed a bit to find that only they shared the pastel lights of dawn.

Her destination within a few yards, Amber slowed her stride, wondering exactly what she should do next. But her decision was made for her when of a sudden the front door of the small house opened and she heard Ronen's deep laugh. She knew she must hide, for of all the other inhabitants of the town, Ronen was sure to suspect the identity of the woman in the road. Spying a two-wheel cart near the side of the house, she dashed toward it, crouching down in its shadow to wait until he had gone. She could only pray he had other duties to perform before returning to their shelter, lest he sound the alarm of her disappearance and have the village down upon her head. She squeezed her eyes shut, envisioning the punishment he might bestow upon her, and listened to the rocks crunch beneath his step as he moved away.

Several lengthy, agonizing minutes passed before she drew up the courage to open her eyes. The long, narrow road stretched out in both directions and Amber's face mirrored her surprise to find it empty. Where had he gone? He hadn't had the time to return to their dwelling. Still crouching low, she moved toward the front of the cart, peeking left, then right to make certain he had not lingered or sensed her presence and hidden in a doorway to catch her. From somewhere down the street a doorlatch clicked shut, and she let out a long, comforted sigh. Now all she had to do was get a glimpse of the woman—

Suddenly the door opened again. Amber scurried from view and collapsed against the wall of the building, praying whoever stepped outside would not see her. The steady rhythm of footsteps moved away from her and she relaxed slightly, knowing she had been granted a reprieve. She took a deep breath to calm her nerves and quietly moved out from the protection of the building, glancing in the direction the stranger had gone, and she stiffened in surprise to discover that it wasn't the woman she had expected to see but a man dressed in garb similar to Ronen's. He was headed for the pond located a good distance from the edge of the village, and Amber frowned as she watched him. Maybe he was the woman's brother and she still waited inside. Well, there was only one way to find out. After a quick inspection of the street to make certain no one observed her, she noiselessly tiptoed to the door of the house and looked inside, her frown returning when she found the small dwelling had but one room and it was empty. Straightening, she glanced back down the road at the man.

If it hadn't been a woman who attracted Ronen's presence every night, it must have been the man. But why? Who was he? She decided to find out. Retrieving her basket of laundry, she started off toward the pond.

She kept to the side of the road, ready to duck out of sight should he turn around unexpectedly. He walked steadily, sure of stride, and Amber noticed for the first time that he appeared much taller than the rest of the men in the village, as tall as Ronen. And Ronen was much bigger in build than anyone else.

She cocked her head to one side, curiosity hurrying her step.

He left the road and cut through a stand of pine. Amber hurried to catch up. His figure, clad in bright blue, contrasted brightly with the evergreen, and she found no difficulty in keeping an eye on him, but when he neared the pond she stopped, and Amber had to hide among the trees. Setting aside her basket she moved closer, wondering if he spoke English. If he did, maybe she could talk with him. Standing in the shadow of the last pine, she hesitated, wondering what sort of response she might receive from him if she called out, her breath catching when she witnessed him unfasten the sash around his waist. Dear Lord, he intended to bathe! A hot flush rose to her cheeks, and she quickly turned her back. Should she wait? Would time allow it, or had Ronen already begun his search for her? Was there really any importance in speaking with this man? What could she possibly learn from him to warrant the risk? Suddenly a splash of water reverberated in her ears and the stark image of a naked man flashed before her eyes. She gasped, falling to her knees, and quickly crawled behind the evergreen, her heart pounding in the base of her throat. She hadn't meant to spy. She had only followed out of curiosity. Should she leave? What if he saw her? A mixture of worry and fear quaked her whole body. Could she manage to be quiet enough, or would the bed of pine needles give away her presence? Without thinking, she glanced back at the man in hopes of learning that he was too absorbed in his bath to notice, and she stiffened instantly, her mouth sagging. There, spotlighted in the glow of morning sunshine, she watched him swim lazily about, blond curls glistening in the golden rays. But more—she recognized the face. Her breath seemed to leave her. Tears sprang to her eyes. Dear God, she had been saved! Sean Rafferty had come to take her home! Both hands raised to her mouth, she stifled her sobs, wanting so desperately to run to him, have him hold her, tell her everything would be all right. How long had he been here? Had Nicholas come too?

"Nicholas," she whispered, her throat tightening. Oh, God, how she longed to see him, to tell him how sorry she was for running away, beg him to forgive her. Twisting around, she sat down, wiping her tears from her face. Would he understand?

Could he convince Ronen that she belonged with her husband? Ronen's dark image flashed into her mind, and for an instant she felt a twinge of regret. After all, he had saved her from Yaakob and treated her kindly. He searched for a wife and had offered all he had, and only to have the woman he had chosen taken from him. A smile lit up her eyes as she remembered how she had foolishly thought he sought out another with whom to share his nights. And all this time it had been Sean. The smile disappeared. *All this time?* A whirlwind of questions consumed her. If Ronen spoke with Sean, then Sean knew she was here. If he did, why hadn't he come to her? He wasn't a prisoner, or he wouldn't be bathing so freely now. And why did he dress like all the other villagers? It was as if he *wanted* to mask his identity from her. But why? What purpose would it serve? Was he waiting for Nicholas? Did Nicholas hide in the foothills, plotting out a scheme to overrun the village and steal her away when Ronen least expected it? That didn't make any sense. Why would he have sent Sean on ahead? Dear Lord, his blond hair and blue eyes would give him away if Nicholas had thought Sean could mingle among the rest without discovery. Why, Nicholas stood a better chance to fool them all. *He* was just as dark as Ronen . . . *Nicholas? Just as dark, as tall, just as forceful? Ronen . . . Nicholas. Nicholas . . . Ronen.*

The shocking revelation of his ploy hit Amber with as much force as a gale wind, leaving her breathless, no single word coming to mind. Her mouth agape, she sat paralyzed, a slow rage boiling up within her. Why? How could he let her go on thinking she would live her life in this place, never certain whether her sister had escaped the baron, or if he, in fact, had survived Von Buren's plans? How could he? Amber bolted to her feet, spinning around to glare at the man still swimming in the pond without a care.

And what of you, Sean Rafferty? What is your excuse? Are you too spineless to go against your cousin's son? Blue eyes flashed sparks of vengeance. *You shall pay, you gutless Irishman. You and all your promises to care for me should my husband fail. Ha!* Twirling, she stomped off through the pines. But before she had traveled three steps, she stopped abruptly, a wicked grin kinking her lovely face. Turning back slowly, she centered her attention on the garments lying on the ground.

You wish to hide beneath the silks so no one will know who you are? she sneered in silence. *Well, all shall see you now, Sean Rafferty, in all your glory!*

Watching him swim about, diving deep beneath the surface to emerge again on the far side of the pond, Amber quietly left the covering of trees and approached with feline stealth, her movements sleek and unseen by her prey. He dove a second time and before he showed again she had snatched his clothes from the ground and disappeared into the woods.

I would love to stay and learn how you manage to return to your house without anyone seeing you, she thought sarcastically, *but I have someone else to visit before I speak with Ronen.* Her lip curled at the mention of his name.

Tossing the stolen garments in with the soiled laundry, she lifted her basket to her hip and headed back toward the village and the old man who knew all the answers and had decided not to share them.

"Amber, my child," Yasir frowned when he found her standing in the doorway of his house. "I . . . does Ronen know you're here?" His nervous gaze looked past her before settling on her once more.

"No, he doesn't," she replied, holding her anger at bay. "And I'm sure he'd not like it if he knew. But I will not tell him, and neither will you." She stepped further into the room, set down her basket, and closed the door, blocking out the bright sunlight. "I just came from the pond, where I made a startling discovery."

"The—the pond?" Yasir questioned, his wrinkled hand rubbing his chin. "What did you find at the pond? You didn't go alone, did you? It isn't safe for you to roam about alone."

Amber smiled grimly. "So Ronen has told me. I had thought it was because he feared Yaakob hid in the hills. But I have learned otherwise."

His white fluffy brows raised sharply. "No one hurt you, did they?"

"In a manner of speaking, yes." She held out a slim hand,

indicating the stack of pillows near the fireplace. "But please sit down first and I will explain." She watched him reluctantly do as she suggested, then added, "and after I'm through, you will have your chance."

"My chance? For what?"

"To explain," she answered casually, plumping up a pillow next to him. Lifting her cotton skirts slightly, she sat down cross-legged, tucking the hem beneath her ankles. She interlaced her fingers, balanced her clasped hands on one knee, and stared over at him. "Or would you care to start?"

The lines of his brow deepened. "I don't know what you mean," he said worriedly.

"Oh, don't you?" she asked sweetly, yet her words were razor sharp. "Then allow me to give you a clue." She stood up again and went to the basket of clothes. Lifting the pale blue silks from the top of the pile, she turned back to add, "I saw a man swimming in the pond just now."

"A . . . a man?" Yasir repeated, his voice weak.

"Yes, a man, one from the village. Or so I was supposed to think. But the funny thing is, he didn't look at all like be belonged here."

Crossing to the table before Yasir, she dumped the garments haphazardly on top. His worried gaze studied them in silence.

"You see, he had blond hair," she continued, taking her place beside him again. "I couldn't see his eyes, but I just know they're blue. And unless my mind was playing tricks . . . like you and Ronen have . . . I would say his name is Sean Rafferty. Do you know him?"

Yasir swallowed hard, then nodded weakly.

"I thought you might, since he's been living across the road from you. How long has he been here? A week? Two? A month, perhaps?" She raised her head to stare at the ceiling, one finger tapping her chin. "Let me see if I can be more accurate. If a ship sailed from Virginia directly to Casablanca, fortunate enough not to encounter any storms . . . yes, I think it could have arrived a week or two ahead of mine." She cast him a sideways glance. "After all, the ship I was on dropped anchor in England first. That delayed it some."

Yasir sighed resignedly and turned to face her. "Yes, Amber, they arrived nearly two weeks ahead of you."

"They?" she mocked, feigning ignorance.

Yasir's brow furrowed. "Must we continue the games?" he yielded.

"But I thought you liked games. Everyone in this village has played except me. I think it only fair."

Yasir reached out and took Amber's hand in his. "He had his reasons, Amber."

"Did he?" she interrupted before he could continue. She pulled free of him and stood to pace the floor. "And what were they? To make a fool of me? To pay me back for running away?" Tears glistened in her eyes. "Had he no idea how scared I was? I lived in the hold of a ship for over a month, never sure if I would live to see another day, then I was taken to a marketplace and *sold*!" She whirled on him. "Have you any idea how that feels? I was *sold*, like a plot of land, to the highest bidder! And did it stop there? No. I was told I would never go home, that I would wed a stranger." She laughed almost hysterically. "A stranger indeed. My own husband . . . Nicholas-the bastard-Chandler." She stared at him, her chin trembling, and suddenly burst into heart-rending sobs. "How . . . how could he do that to me?"

Yasir quickly came to his feet and rushed to her, enveloping her delicate frame in his arms. He held her tightly, allowing her tears to flow and not daring a word until he knew she would listen. When finally her weeping eased, he guided her back to the pillows and gently pushed her down upon them. He filled a glass with wine and forced her to drink, waiting until she calmed before he sat next to her, one aged hand stroking the shoulder-length yellow curls.

"The story I told you of Ronen was true. Our village was attacked and this stranger saved us. I owed the man or I never would have agreed to his plan, even after he explained the need. Now I will tell you why and hope you will understand." He smiled softly when she looked at him. "And maybe you won't hate us both so much." He took a deep breath and settled more comfortably, wondering where he should begin.

"The man I know as Ronen, a name given him by the people

483

of my village, had not returned here in over two years. We were told his father had died and he felt his duty lay in his homeland. Two weeks ago, he suddenly appeared, he and his friend, Sean Rafferty. They told me about you, how you and Ronen . . . Nicholas . . . had come to marry and that you had been kidnapped. I offered the aid of my men to help in rescuing you, but he said no, that he had his own plan."

Yasir fell quiet a moment, toying with the nail of one thumb before he turned to look at her. His tanned face reflected his pain, and Amber wondered at the cause.

"You may not believe this, my child, but he did this out of love."

"Love?" she exploded.

"Yes, love," Yasir hurriedly interjected. "He knew the troubles that plagued your mind, that he stood for all the things you despised, and only wanted to show you that it was the *man* who made the difference, not what he owned."

"By lying to me?"

Yasir looked away, his shoulders drooping. "I said as much when he told me how he wanted to prove his devotion to you. I disliked his method, but I would not go against him as long as he promised no real harm would come to you."

Suddenly Amber laughed and Yasir glanced up confused. He had seen no humor there.

"Doesn't he realize his own trap? If I had fallen in love with Ronen, he could never be certain which man had stolen my heart." She stood up slowly, a calculating smile parting her lips. "And what better way to pay him back?"

Yasir stood in the doorway long after Amber had gone, wondering if he had done the right thing.

Nicholas's frown deepened as he left Nasser's home and headed back toward his own. He had sought out the man's advice after talking with Sean, and both men had confirmed his suspicions. Yaakob's men watched the village and had done so for three days. It could only mean that Yaakob had not accepted Ronen's purchase of the girl, that he intended to attack and steal her from him. Nicholas hurried his step, covertly studying the hillside filled with pine and shrub. Although Nasser had assured him that several of their own men constantly guarded, guns ready, Nicholas worried for his wife's safety. He should take her home, reveal his ruse, and pay the consequences, but his determination to see the game played out held him back. He had come too far to let one man ruin his happiness. And he was sure that Amber would soon realize that her place was beside her husband, to love, honor, and obey.

For the past week they had spent the time in friendship, laughing, sharing, enjoying each other. And at every available moment he would cunningly bring up her husband's name. At first she would smile, remembering something pleasant, then frown, her temper short. It seemed she fought with herself, and he knew he could change her mind if given the time. He sighed and continued on, his gaze locked on the small dwelling they shared. Had she awakened yet or did she still lie sleeping peacefully, the beautiful face haloed in golden curls?

Absently, he rubbed the stiffness from his shoulder, a dull ache that even now, after two months, reminded him of the terrifying fear he had experienced the day he had gone to see Baron Kelzer Von Buren. The baron had met him at the door, smiling as if he welcomed a friend into his home. He had offered Nicholas a glass of sherry in his study and Nicholas had accepted, guardedly surveying the room for any sign of a trap and marveling at the casual way Von Buren talked of Heather's death. He truly felt no sorrow for his wife's gruesome accident and resulting demise, and Nicholas soon realized that he dealt with a madman. The conversation had turned to Fletcher Courtney and the way Von Buren had tricked the old man into fighting a duel. He had openly admitted that he had turned on Courtney before full count and had shot the man down without giving him a chance to cock the pistol. Nicholas had sat by quietly, wondering why the baron so freely admitted everything to him, a prickling of horror kinking up his spine. And then it came. Von Buren had gone to his desk, set down his glass, and leisurely pulled a gun from beneath his coat, aiming it at Nicholas's chest. He further explained in quiet calm how he had kidnapped Amber and had already sent her to Casablanca, and that within the hour he would marry Andrea. Of course, Nicholas would have to die. If he was to inherit the full estate of Nathaniel Cromwell, Andrea would have to be the only living heir. A shot had rung out from somewhere in the house, distracting Kelzer and giving Nicholas the needed second to draw the pistol tucked in the belt of his breeches behind his back. But Von Buren had seen him move and had fired upon him before Nicholas could level his aim. The lead ball tore into Nicholas's shoulder, throwing him from the chair. The pain nearly blinded him, but he knew he must act fast if he was to save himself. Rolling, he came to his knees, pistol cocked and ready, watching Von Buren lunge for the top drawer of his desk and a second pistol lying there. Another shot exploded and Von Buren was hurled backwards, crashing into the multipaned window behind the desk. Its fragile glass shattered, and Baron Kelzer Von Buren fell through it, tiny fragments catapulting in all directions.

His head spinning, Nicholas had fallen forward, catching himself on one hand, his gun falling to the floor. Weak, he struggled to his feet. He had to make certain Von Buren was dead. Staggering, he made his way across the room and collapsed against the wall near the broken remains of the window. There on the ground outside lay the twisted, lifeless form of the evil baron.

"For you, Amber," Nicholas had whispered. "For you and your father and Heather." His head fell back against the wall and his vision blurred, and he clasped the limp arm with his hand, blood staining his coat and trailing a steady stream down its sleeve. He mustn't faint. He had to find Sean. They had to sail for Morocco right away.

He had pulled himself up and started for the door when of a sudden it had burst open. Haloed in its frame had stood Sean Rafferty, a pistol in each hand, and Nicholas had smiled before blackness claimed him and he crumpled to a heap on the floor.

As he studied the crude house where they had spent the last several days, Nicholas longed to tell Amber that he had killed Von Buren and that her sister was all right. The day he and Sean had set sail for northern Africa, he had waved farewell to the young woman held lovingly in Seth's arms. He smiled to

486

himself. It wouldn't surprise him any to learn of their marriage once he and Amber returned home. He sighed forlornly. Sometimes he wished Amber was more like her sister. But then again, he wouldn't have fallen in love with her if she was. Readjusting the *yashmak* over his face, he lifted the doorlatch and stepped inside the dwelling.

Nicholas paused in the archway, warm, mouth-watering aromas from the cooking pot floating up to greet him. His dark brow twisted as he studied the place. In the center of the room sat a small table with a setting of dishes for two and a single candleholder with a flickering taper, and he half expected a quartet of violinists to appear. Had Amber suddenly gone mad or had he, perhaps, gotten the wrong house? He had turned slightly to make sure of his location when he heard the doorlatch rattle to the other room, and looked back. Beneath the veil his bearded jaw sagged.

"Oh, there you are, Ronen," Amber smiled sweetly, a brass tray with two goblets and a pitcher of wine in her hands.

She had disgarded the cotton gown and robe she had worn earlier and donned the sheerest of silk imaginable. Ivory in color, it blended with the fairness of her flesh, and Nicholas blinked twice before he realized she had anything on at all. It clung intimately to her full, ripe bosom, her nipples taut and pressed against the fabric, drawing Nicholas's eyes almost immediately. He gulped, but his feet wouldn't move. It shimmered down her bodice, hugging the trim waist in delicate folds, to fall gently over her narrow hips, over the smooth outline of her willowy legs to sway temptingly at her bare feet. She had washed her hair, and it curled in soft strands about her shoulders. The vision of a dirty-faced boy flashed through his mind. How could he ever have mistaken this lovely creature for a snot-nosed urchin?

"I hope you haven't eaten," she murmured, snapping him back to reality.

He shook his head, for no words would come to his lips, and he knew he would only babble if he tried.

"Then sit down. I've prepared a feast for you," she instructed, crossing to the table. She stooped to place the tray there, a lean hip outlined in silk.

For my palate or my eyes? he wondered, his pulse quickening. He took a deep breath, let it out slowly, and numbly approached the spot she indicated with an outstretched hand.

Seated opposite her, Nicholas doubted Amber realized the view she presented. The cloth of her dress had been loosely gathered and tossed over one shoulder, and with every move she made the neckline slipped lower. Only when it threatened to expose the treasure hidden beneath would she halfheartedly push it back in place. His heart pounded in his throat and he swallowed arduously before speaking, his voice barely a whisper.

"Where did you find that?"

Blue, innocent eyes glanced up at him. "What?"

He nodded at the silk inching its way from her shoulder.

"Oh, this," she laughed. "I found it in the chest." She concentrated on pouring two glasses full of wine.

"What chest?" he graveled, recalling none.

She paused in her duty and looked at him in surprise. "Why the one Yasir sent." She finished filling the second goblet. "He said I might enjoy them."

"Them?"

She smiled brightly. "Oh, yes. There were several in the chest. I guess he figured I was tired of wearing the others." She crossed her arms against the edge of the table and leaned in, nearly spilling her breasts from the elusive cloth. "You know, I really prefer wearing these garments to my gowns. I have more room to breathe." She giggled. "And I rather like not wearing anything underneath."

Nicholas's breath seemed to leave him. He reached for the glass of wine, remembered the *yashmak* and the difficulty it would present if he tried to drink and pulled back, frowning.

"Why don't you take it off?"

His dark brown eyes glanced up in shock. "What?" he asked, amazed at her calm suggestion that he disrobe her.

"The veil," she said softly.

The flesh of his cheeks burned at his misguided assumption, and, rather than have her notice, he picked up the wine, stood, and turned his back on her. Pulling the cloth aside, he downed his drink in one gulp.

"You shouldn't be ashamed, Ronen. And we're friends, aren't we? Friends should share their secrets."

Suddenly she stood behind him, much too close, and Nicholas could almost feel the delicate shape of her pressed against him.

"N-no," he coughed.

"Ronen," she continued, her voice soft, alluring. "I've bared my soul to you. Why not do the same? After all, we'll be married soon."

The glass trembled in his hand. "What did you say?" he asked over his shoulder, afraid to turn around.

"I've come to a decision, one you'll like, since it was your plan all along." She moved away and Nicholas watched her out of the corner of his eye. "I've grown rather fond of living here." Her hands encompassed the small room. "It sort of reminds me of home. I've decided to stay and be your wife, if you still want me."

Nicholas felt as if his heart had been torn from him. "But . . . but what about your real husband? And your sister?"

"I thought I'd send a letter to Andrea, if you don't mind, and tell her I'm all right and won't be coming back. As for Nicholas . . ." She paused to stare into the fire of the hearth, and when she did he turned to watch her. "Apparently he doesn't truly love me, or he would have come for me by now. I would never be happy living with a man who didn't love me or I him." She glanced over at him. "You understand, don't you?"

Suddenly Nicholas's knees weakened, his head beginning to pound. Where had it all gone wrong? Not two minutes ago he had been convinced she truly loved him, that with a little more time she would admit it to herself. Now this. Now she asked to live with someone else. He returned to the pillow and sat down.

"But I said you must love me first," he pointed out dismally, grasping for one last shred of hope.

"Yes. And that's the best part," she smiled, quickly kneeling at his side. "I've learned in the last few days that I do."

His angry brown eyes glared up at her. "No, you don't," he snapped, quickly coming to his feet. "You couldn't possibly. You . . . you haven't known me long enough. This . . . this place isn't where you belong. You should be with your husband."

"But I don't love him," she argued, her pretty face twisted with his rejection. "I love you."

"Stop saying that," he shouted, jumping to his feet. "You weren't meant to love me. You're supposed to love your husband."

"But why?" she asked beseechingly.

Of a sudden, Nicholas realized his voice had lost its raspiness. He stared at her, wondering if she had noticed, then decided it was best if he left her. He needed time to sort things out, figure a way to change her mind about the man she knew as Ronen. Whirling, he crossed the room and quickly made his exit, missing the smile that curled the rose-colored lips upward.

Chapter Twenty-Two

Nicholas hurriedly walked the distance to Sean's small dwelling, glancing back over his shoulder repeatedly toward the place where he had left his wife. He needed to talk with his friend, to tell him of Amber's sudden change. Together they would unravel the tangled shreds of his plan. Good God, if she didn't love Nicholas and chose Ronen instead, must he live out his life dressed in this outfit? He tore the *yashmak* from his face. *The woman was fickle!* How could she speak so tenderly of her husband one day, then turn around the next and declare undying devotion to a man she hardly knew? A new thought came to mind and his step faltered. What if he hadn't arrived at the marketplace when he had? What if someone else had bought her . . . not Yaakob, but a real man? Would she have fallen in love with him if he vowed allegiance? He shook his head. No, of course not. She loved Ronen, and *he* was Ronen! All he had to do was show her. He stopped in the middle of the street near Sean's front door, staring at the crumpled silk in his hand. Was that what he should do, show her who he really was? One side of his mouth crimped. *And have her wrath down upon my head? No.* He'd think of something else. But what? Folding one arm over his wide chest, he clasped the elbow of the other, his hand raised to stroke his bearded chin in thought.

"Nicholas!" a desperate voice called out in a hush.

Blinking, he straightened and glanced all around, knowing the voice had to belong to Sean, for none other in the village used his Christian name.

"Over here, lad."

Following the direction from where the plea came, Nicholas spotted the damp golden curls sprinkled with silver partially hidden in the low-hanging branch of a pine several yards away. He started toward him.

"What are you hiding from?" Nicholas asked.

"Come closer and ya will see!" Sean snapped. "But if ya value your life, ya'll not be laughin'."

"Laughing? Why would I . . ." Nicholas stopped abruptly discovering the reason for the man's warning. Artfully arranged, the wide, spreading evergreen covered most of Sean's muscular build but failed to completely hide a long, lean hip or bare feet. "What the—"

"I was takin' me bath and someone stole me clothes," Sean growled. "Now would ya be kind enough to be findin' me somethin' ta wear?"

The corners of Nicholas's mouth twitched beneath his beard. "Certainly, Sean," he said quickly, forcing himself not to reveal the amusement that played upon his lips. "I don't want you catching a chill."

"Just be keepin' your comments ta yourself and hurry up before someone sees me," Sean warned through clenched teeth.

"Yes, sir," Nicholas nodded curtly. He started off toward the dwelling, then paused abruptly to look back over his shoulder. "Did you have a certain preference to attire or would anything do?" Laughter rumbled in his chest for only a moment before he agilely ducked out of the way of an angrily thrown pinecone.

Fully clothed once more, Sean led the way back inside his small house, going directly to the bottle of Irish whiskey he had carefully hidden in a wicker basket. Raising it high, he took a long swallow before he visibly relaxed. Crossing to the hearth he stoked the fire to chase away the chill of his early morning

492

adventure, his hands held out before him, the bottle tucked beneath his arm.

"Ya know, laddie, I'm gettin' damned tired of this masquerade," he grumbled, his attention held on the flames. "If it wasn't so important, I'd be tellin' ya to give it up and take Amber home."

Dropping to the stack of pillows Sean used as a bed, Nicholas stretched out, his ankles crossed, clasped hands holding the back of his head. "Up until a few minutes ago, I would have thought we could do just that in another day or two. But now I'm not too sure." He studied the toes of his suede boots.

Sean shifted positions, turning to warm his backside, and look straight at his companion. "And what happened to change your mind, me boy?"

Nicholas sighed heavily. "Amber."

"I suppose you're gonna be tellin' me she's decided she likes livin' here?"

A half smile appeared on Nicholas's face. "Not only that, but she told me just now that she loves Ronen."

Clutching the whiskey bottle by its neck, Sean slowly stepped closer, easing himself to the floor near Nicholas. "Ya not be serious, lad."

"Afraid so, my friend. My little scheme has backfired. If I was to tell her who Ronen really is, she'd never forgive me and I'd lose her forever."

"Then what do ya plan ta do?"

Nicholas shrugged one shoulder. "I'm not sure. I'd like to take the time to convince her that she really belongs with her husband, but with Yaakob's men roaming about, I fear for her safety."

"Aye. I be thinkin' the same as you, lad. It's been a long time since he attacked this village, and I'm afraid this time he's after the lass Ronen took from him."

Suddenly, Nicholas bolted upright with a snap of his fingers. "I've got it."

"What? A way ta change her mind?"

Nicholas smiled confidently, his dark eyes gleaming. "Yes. I've been doing this all wrong. How could I expect her to miss her husband when I gave her a substitute?"

Sean frowned, shaking his head. "I'm not followin' your meanin, lad."

"From the day we rescued her, I've been nothing but kind to her, telling her how she must love me before I'd ever touch her *or* marry her. That was Nicholas talking, wanting to correct the wrongs he'd done. But it was a fatal mistake. In trying to change, I made Ronen ideal in her eyes . . . nothing like her husband."

"Now, be waitin' just a minute, me boy. You're not plannin' ta get rough with her, are ya?"

Grinning, Nicholas slapped his thigh and stood. "I promise not to bruise anything but her ego." He headed for the door.

"It won't work," Sean warned.

Pausing, one hand raised to the door frame, Nicholas looked back with a frown. "Why not?"

"Sooner or later you'll have ta be tellin' her who Ronen is. If ya force yourself on her, in the end it's still Nicholas Chandler."

The smile returned. "Ah, but you're wrong. She'll never know we're one and the same. The minute she admits she wants her husband, you shall come riding out of the hills, take her from Ronen's arms, and return her to her husband."

One knee raised to brace his arm, Sean looked up at his young friend almost casually, a slight twinkle beaming in his blue eyes. "Somehow I suspect you've underestimated the lass. Ya are diggin' a hole and before long you'll be fallin' in."

His assuredness shaken a might, Nicholas's brows came together briefly. Shaking it off, he straightened with new conviction. "Not a chance, my friend. Not a chance." He turned, stepped outside in the growing light of morning, and started toward his dwelling.

Nicholas's pace quickened as he thought of ways to turn Amber's affections away from Ronen, a smile brightening the dark depths of his eyes, the faint dimple in his cheek masked beneath the beard. It wouldn't be long before they all sailed home on his father's ship, the *Defiance*, a proud vessel Sean Rafferty had cared for and maintained for over forty years. Visions of his father's handsome face came to his mind. *Andrew Michael Chandler, you'd be very proud of me.* His grin

494

widening into a devilish smirk as he reached the front door of the house, he paused, fastened the veil in place, and touched the latch.

As he stepped through the archway, Nicholas opened his mouth to call out to her, frozen to his spot when the narrow shaft of sunlight stealing in around him fell alluringly on the wooden tub in the center of the room and the beauty bathing in it. A knot lodged in his throat. His heart pounded wildly, and his long-starved passion grew evident almost immediately. Candlelight flickered about the room, casting a warm glow on the creamy white flesh of her bare shoulders and the golden strands of hair curled atop Amber's head. With her back to him, Nicholas could only imagine the way the soap bubbles clung to her breasts or the long, slim column of her neck as she leisurely washed each area. He longed to take the sponge from her and finish the task himself but knew he mustn't if he intended to fulfill his plans successfully. He gulped, forced himself to step further into the room, and closed the door with a thud. His eyes never left the figure in the tub, and when he opened his mouth to speak, no words flowed from his lips. He straightened sharply when Amber twisted around to look at him.

"I didn't expect you back so soon," she smiled softly, bath-water and suds lapping dangerously low against her bosom.

He pulled his gaze away from the delicious temptation and went to the fireplace to stare into the flames. "A little late in the morning to be taking a bath, don't you think?" he rasped. The slight edge to his words came not intentionally but rather from the uneasiness he experienced being so close to her while she was in a state of undress. He quickly shut his eyes, hoping to block out the image, and only made it worse when the trickle of water penetrated his thoughts.

"Yes, I suppose so," she agreed, lifting her other arm to squeeze water from the sponge down its length and rinse away the thick lather. "But since I had finished my other work and had nothing to do, I thought I'd take a bath now, instead of this evening."

A moment of silence passed and Nicholas entertained the thought of making a hasty exit. But when he commanded his feet to move, it was as if they had a mind of their own, determined to stay where they were. He reached up to brace himself against the stone face of the hearth, his knees suddenly weak.

"If you'd like, I could heat water for you."

The soft tones of her question forced an involuntary shudder to run through him. He cleared his throat in an effort to mask the effect. "Ah, no. I—I have things to do." He turned, praying his feet would carry him, his eyes averted, and stopped short when the honey-smooth melody of her inquiry hit him full force.

"Would you mind scrubbing my back? I can't reach it."

Without thinking, wondering if he had heard correctly, he glanced over at her, his breath catching at the lovely sight she presented. The aching in his loins quickly spread upward, knotting the muscles in his belly, for draped seductively against the edge of the tub, Amber displayed a tantalizing view of womanly curves partially hidden beneath soap and the wooden planks of the bath. In one hand, she held out the sponge for him, and his eyes devoured the sight of her silky-smooth skin glistening with water, the gentle curves of her slender arm, and the alluring manner in which she smiled pleadingly up at him. She had pulled the blond curls into a knot upon her head, but several defiant tendrils fell in spiraling coils against her brow and neck, now wet and dripping tiny droplets down her face. He watched the journey of one silver bead follow the contour of her cheekbone, jaw, and throat before it disappeared between the valley of her breasts, and he longed to trace its path with a fingertip.

"Please?"

The question shattered his daydream and he blinked, his gaze returning to her face.

"It will only take a moment. Surely you can spare me that," she coaxed enticingly.

He shook his head with great effort, for he truly longed to do as bade yet knew the danger there. For weeks he had visualized this moment, a time when he could hold her in his arms, kiss her, make love to her. But as her husband—not as a hill warrior of the Atlas Mountains! "We are not married, and I

496

should not be here with you now," he replied hoarsely, the energy to mask his voice almost more than he could muster.

Amber frowned as if hurt, a pretty pout distorting her mouth. "I only ask you to wash my back, Ronen. Nothing more. And if no one knows, what will it hurt? Besides, we'll wed soon enough that one day or two won't matter." She held the sponge higher. "Please?"

Nicholas listened to the pounding of his heart in his ears and wondered if she could hear it, too. He shook his head again.

"Oh, don't be such a prude," she chaffed, pulling back her arm to let go of the sponge and send it sailing across the tiny room at him.

It caught him squarely in the chest, splattering tiny droplets of water in the air, bounced against his knee, and landed on the toe of his suede boots, yet the soggy damage to his clothes was not the reason his brow furrowed. Without comment, he whirled and left the dwelling.

Amber sat in the tub for several minutes after Nicholas had gone, staring at the closed door, a vengeful grimace distorting her lovely face. *Now what will you do, my husband, thinking I've abandoned you for someone else?* she thought acidly. *I would say you fled to keep the hurt from shining in your eyes and giving away your secret. Well, you wasted your effort. I already know.* She twisted back to resume her bathing, slipping down until the soap bubbles touched her chin and her teeth began to chatter. Heaving herself upright, she quickly stepped from the icy water and covered herself with a towel, vigorously rubbing her arms and legs for warmth. She had elected to torture Nicholas with the bath after he had stormed from the house earlier. Knowing the sight of her bare arms and shoulders and the promise of more intimate treasures would put a great strain on his good intentions, she had heated the water, filled the tub, and stripped herself of the silk cloth. Submerged to her neck, she had waited, not certain when he would return yet positive he would. Nearly an hour had passed, the cool water becoming nearly more than she could tolerate, when she heard him outside the door and hurriedly lathered up her face and neck and splashed them clean to secure the guise. And it had worked. She was sure of it. She moved to the hearth to capture the heat of the blaze within the towel held open in front of her, mentally plotting out her next step.

Nicholas hastily walked past the lodging where he had left Sean, hoping not to be seen. He wasn't in the mood to lie to the man, and he certainly didn't want to admit he had failed in his plans to cure Amber's infatuation. If anything, they had gone downhill. A pained expression darkened his eyes, and he concentrated on the road that led to the pond. What he needed now was a moment alone and a lot of time to think. He cut through the grove of pine and walked out to the edge of the sparkling pool of water, sitting down on the largest of three rocks.

The men of the small village had joined together to dam up the narrow mountain stream just enough to form a pond where all could bathe and still allow the water to flow across the rocks and course tirelessly on toward the sea. Thick pine encompassed the area, shielding the spot from view, except near its bank. The waterfall glistened in the sunshine and soothed the most troubled minds, yet Nicholas found no peace as he listened. Bright rays of sunlight warmed him, and he absently touched a dark hand to his damp shirtfront, remembering how it had gotten wet. He recalled, too, another moment when Amber had flung a wet sponge at him. It had been the day they had been wed. Only then she had done so out of anger, as a desperate way to ward off his advance, to protect her vulnerability. Today she shamelessly played the aggressor, first with the meal, then the bath. What could he expect next, and how could he fight her off when his own desires threatened to shatter his scheme?

Bending, he picked up several stones, tossing them one at a time into the pond, watching the ripples circle out and slowly disappear before he threw another. Maybe Sean had been right. He should have just sailed to Casablanca, found his wife, and taken her home. He sighed, heartsick, his gaze lifting skyward to the endless blue plane speckled with a few white fluffy clouds drifting aimlessly above him. He should call an end to the ruse, return to Williamsburg, and put everyone's minds to

498

rest. Visions of his grandmother loomed out at him. Especially Alanna's. The day he had killed Baron Von Buren and Sean had taken him home, Alanna and his sister had arrived just ahead of them. Katherine was hysterical, their grandmother quiet, withdrawn. But the wound to his shoulder had been clean, the lead ball having passed through the fleshy part, and no surgeon had been called. His color had returned, and by the next day Nicholas had sent Sean to ready the *Defiance* for their voyage to Morocco. Katherine had begged him not to go, to send someone else, that his injury was too fresh and might fester under such abuse. But Nicholas had been adamant until he had seen Alanna Remington's worried look. Pulling her aside to question the obvious pain she suffered, he had learned that his delicate grandmother had taken the blame for everything: Amber's kidnapping, Nicholas's wound, and the necessity of the ocean voyage. She was certain Nicholas would never find his wife, and that the innocent young woman would spend the rest of her life in a place she should never have been sent to.

Slipping off his suede boots, Nicholas put his feet in the clear, crisp water, letting its brisk chill run through him, and remembered how he had assured his grandmother that everything would turn out all right. He didn't intend to let the only woman he had ever loved get away from him. His dark brows drew together, hooding the troubled look in his handsome eyes. Even Yasir had warned him of the problems that might arise in trying to trick the young woman. Had they all seen what he couldn't? Had he been wrong in wanting to prove she really loved her husband and belonged with no one else? A lump formed in his throat, the cold reality of reason striking out at him. Maybe the simple truth was Amber *didn't* love him, that she never would, and that no amount of persuasion would ever change the feelings in her heart for him.

Almost angrily, he lifted his feet from the water to shed the rest of his clothes. Right now he needed a swim in the pond.

Nicholas awoke with a start, pushing himself up on his elbows to survey his surroundings. The warm light of day's end had faded, and night had claimed the land within its silvery embrace. He had spent the afternoon visiting several of the village men, helping with odd jobs, repairing fences and herding sheep into the newly built corral, anything to occupy his mind and keep his thoughts away from the golden-haired beauty living in his small house. When the rest had returned to their lodgings for the evening meal, he had gone back to the pond to consider what he might do next where his wife was concerned. If he came right out and told her who Ronen was, he felt certain he could expect her fury, and justly so. But if, as Ronen, he allowed her to return home without a word of explanation, he might stand a better chance as Nicholas to win her love once she was surrounded by those who cared a great deal for her. And when should he tell her? This evening or in the morning? Exhausted from his day's labors and mental suffering, he had lain back against the soft grass, his arms cradling his head, and had studied the bright orange of the sky overhead as the sun fought for one more moment of life. His eyelids heavy, he had fallen asleep almost immediately.

"Well," he mumbled to himself, "I might as well get it over with." Coming to his feet, he brushed the dirt from his clothes and headed back toward the village.

The narrow road before him seemed to stretch on for miles, yet he covered the distance much too quickly to satisfy him, and before he realized it he stood at the front door of the small dwelling. He truly didn't wish to step inside, for he knew that once he had and had told Amber of his decision to send her home in the morning, he would have brought a termination to his dreams of conquering her affections. He sighed, disheartened. Hadn't someone said one time, "'Tis better to have loved and lost than never to have loved at all?" He found a small measure of comfort at the thought, for indeed he had loved and knew the joy it could bring, would always bring, for even if he lost her, he would always love her. He touched the latch and opened the door, his pulse quickening when he saw Amber sitting by the fire, her blond tousled head bent over her task. And when she glanced up at him and smiled, he thought he would perish from the aching in his heart.

"We must talk," he half whispered, half mumbled in the

raspy voice, pushing aside his grief as he stepped further into the room and closed the door behind him. When he turned back, he found she still looked at him.

"Would you like something to eat first?" she asked quietly.

He shook his head, knowing he needed a drink of Sean's whiskey more. "I've come to a decision today."

Amber laid aside her mending, relocated a large pillow on the floor next to her, and patted its surface invitingly. "Then sit down and tell me what it is."

Her blue eyes stared up at him, and for a moment Nicholas forgot all else, longing to cup the beautiful face in his hands and kiss each closed eyelid. He tore his gaze away from the tempting red lips and elected to stand near the hearth where he could watch the flames instead. "I'm sending you home," he said abruptly. He braced himself for her exuberance at the prospect of seeing Andrea again. Or was it her arguments he expected? After all, she had already declared her decision to stay. The muscles in his jaw flexed. To stay with Ronen, however.

"Why?" The question hung in the air.

Why? he laughed sarcastically to himself. *Because I've decided to set you free, my love.* He turned to face her and said aloud, "I need no reasons. Nor must I explain anything to you."

He watched the long, slender form stretch up to full height, his heart pounding in his ears, for she wore the same silk as earlier, and its shimmery cloth clung to every curve. She moved closer, and Nicholas dug his nails into the palms of his hands to keep from touching her,

"I thought you wanted a wife, Ronen," she said softly. "And her love."

Nicholas wants a wife and her love, he argued silently.

"I can be that wife, and I already admitted my love." She reached up, a fingertip playing with the folds of his shirt across his chest. "Let me prove it."

God, how he had longed to hear those words! But they had been spoken for another. He seized her wrist and put her from him.

"I will have one of my men take you to Casablanca in the

501

morning. From there you'll board a ship sailing to America."

"Would it matter if I told you I didn't want to go?" She gazed up at him, pale blue eyes soft and warm. "I could change your mind, perhaps."

Nicholas's pulse quickened, his breath short. "No. There is nothing you could do to change my mind." He stepped away. "Nothing!"

"Are you afraid to let me try?" The words floated out enticingly.

His male ego pricked, Nicholas turned back with a chuckle. "Afraid? Of a wisp of a girl, half my strength? What could you do that could possibly arouse such an emotion?" Confident, he stood arms akimbo.

Amber smiled, her tawny brow raised. *You arrogant fool. I have you where I want you, and you will bend as easily as a willow in the wind.* One hand raised to the cloth draped over her shoulder. *Ronen may fight to send me home, and Nicholas will feel the loser, but the man in you will melt at a simple touch. I will brand you this night as my own and cast you aside in the morning for the schemer that you are. All three will fail, and you will live out your days regretting the trick you played, for in your heart you will never know who I held in my arms this night.* The ivory silk glided from her fingertips.

Nicholas's grin vanished, every muscle in his tall frame rigid. He fought to breathe, gulping down the knot in his throat as he thought to voice his wishes that she desist in disrobing. But no sound came from his lips as he watched her unfold the multilayers from around her trim waist, the creamy fabric floating effortlessly to the floor. The long-held fire in his loins exploded, rapidly engulfing him, and he forced his eyes closed to block out the magnificent vision standing proudly before him. But even in the darkness of lowered lids he could see the smooth flesh of her body bathed in the glow of the firelight, her long, shapely legs, narrow hips, flat belly, and those exquisite breasts, their peaks taut, inviting his touch. In his wildest of dreams he had never imagined she would willingly offer herself to him without any prompting on his part. Then the irony struck him. She hadn't. She offered herself to Ronen. Drawing in every ounce of composure he could, he took a deep

502

breath and opened his eyes. He would tell her to dress, to behave like a married woman. . . . His knees suddenly grew weak, for during his moment of thoughtful unrest Amber had ventured closer and now stood only inches from him. He forgot his purpose, drinking in the splendor of the lovely face staring up at him. Without realizing it, he reached out to smooth the yellow strands of hair, then moved to cup her face and lift her eyes to meet his.

"You belong to another," he stated, yearning to discard his veil and place a tender kiss upon her mouth.

"I belong to you," she whispered. A slim hand came up to take his.

Without a word, she guided him to the adjoining room, the diffused glow of the hearth showing the way. Stepping into the shadows, she turned to face him, not hesitating to pull away the thin cloth that hid his identity. Tossing it aside, she searched the darkness for a glimpse of his handsome features, a sight she had once longed to see. Suddenly, unexplainably, she felt a strong need to have him hold her, and she lifted one tiny hand to touch his face, surprised when her fingers met the softness of his beard. Her frown went unseen in the obscurity of the room. Did it flatter his appearance or hide the rugged, appealing lines of his jaw? Or the haunting dimple in his cheek? She smiled, remembering how it never showed except when he teased, and her amusement faded, for she doubted she would ever see it again.

Nicholas wondered at her hesitation. Had she suddenly realized this wasn't what she wanted? He prayed she had, yet wanted desperately at that moment to hold her, no matter what her reasons.

"Amber," his raspy voice implored, uncertain for what he asked.

"Hush," she whispered, a fingertip pressed to his mouth. Her arms suddenly encircled his neck, drawing him to her. Lifting her chin, she gently kissed the parted, waiting lips.

His passion flared again, and though he wanted to fight he couldn't. He had wanted to kiss her from the moment he had seen her on the auction block nearly two weeks ago, to tell her how he loved her, that she would be safe now and always by his side. Torn between the desires of his body and the logic of his mind, her intoxicating scent and her nearness made his choice. Swooping her into his arms, he returned the kiss tenfold, hungrily, eagerly, one hand entwined within the golden locks of hair at the back of her head, the other clinging frantically to the small of her back. Her naked body pressed against him sent his mind reeling, reliving the joy, the bliss he experienced only with her. His kisses moved to her chin, the long, slender neck, her ear, and each eyelid before capturing her lips once more, his tongue darting inside to taste the sweetness of her mouth, and he moaned. She did not resist him, as she had always done before, and he forgot that it was because he was Ronen.

Lifting her easily in his arms, he took her to the cushion of pillows and laid her upon them, quickly shedding his attire, his eyes never leaving the pale form watching him. And when he knelt, she opened her arms to him, and he thought his heart would explode. Their bodies touching full length, he rolled to his back, taking her with him, his hands wildly exploring every curve of her; the trim back, the tiny waist, the fullness of her buttocks, and, finally, the smoothness of her thighs. Amber raised up, bracing herself on her elbows on either side of him, allowing her full, ripe breasts to press against his chest while she smiled seductively down at him, her expression lost in the shadows of the room. But the heady scent of her compelled him to bury his face in her neck, kissing her hungrily. His hands beneath her arms, he lifted her slightly to free the firm mounds of flesh and allow his mouth to trail hot paths to one rose-hued peak, his tongue eagerly caressing, teasing, his teeth nibbling gently. His lips found hers again, her ardor matching his, and, to his surprise, her tongue lightly caressed the outline of his mouth and his teeth before darting inside. He moaned, wondering if he could endure such bliss. Falling to her side, she pulled him with her, their legs entwined, their naked bodies touching, and, with practiced grace, her slender hands roamed lovingly across the wide expanse of his shoulders, waist, and lean hips, then moved to cup his face and bring his mouth to hers once more. They kissed tenderly, warmly, then with fierce urgency, hugging the other as if to draw themselves into one. She felt his heart beat wildly against her breast, the warmth of

504

his desire, and the manly boldness of him pressed to her thigh. Without any urging, truly wanting him to take her, Amber shifted her hips, opening her thighs to welcome him.

At first, he hesitated, wanting this moment to go on forever, to experience her willingness with slow anticipation. But his long-denied passion surged within him, consumed him, and he breathlessly slid his hands to her narrow waist, lifting her hips to meet his first thrust. He moved slowly, tenderly, feeling her arch beneath him. Whispering her name, his arms moved to clutch her to him, his breathing growing rapid. He kissed her mouth, her neck, and as his desire overcame him, moving him faster, deeper, Amber hugged him to her, her nails raking the broadness of his back as she moaned her pleasure. They moved as one, soaring higher, bodies fused together in the rhapsody of love, the time for lies and deceit gone. Nothing else mattered, for in that moment they knew they belonged together.

A long while passed before Nicholas raised his head, his eyes searching the darkness that encased them for the beauty of her smile. He wanted to speak, to tell her of the trick he'd played and why. But something held him back. He didn't want to spoil this beautiful sharing they had experienced. Not now. He eased himself to lie at her side, cradling her within his arms.

Snuggling happily within his embrace, Amber laid her head on his shoulder, breathing in the scent of him while she entwined one dark curl of hair on his chest around her fingertip and listened to the steady rhythm of his heart. She heard him gasp when she lowered her caress to his flat belly, then rested intimately on his thigh as if it were a natural thing to do, and she smiled, confident with the knowledge that he would surrender easily at a mere touch of her hand, or a sweet promise from her lips. It had been her plan, yet she realized with some bewilderment that the pleasure had not been all his. Caught up in the rapture of his tenderness, his love, she had disturbingly felt her barriers crumble, her anger at him vanish. She had returned his ardency with her own, equaling his passion out of her need, and felt contentment even now as she lay in his arms. Could it be that she truly loved this man and unconsciously forgave him for only wanting to win her affections any way he could? One dark hand came up to smooth her rumpled hair, and she absently brushed her cheek against it. But could it be so simple? In the morning light, would she still feel the same? When she looked into those handsome, sparkling eyes, would she remember the lies and hate him for them? Her sigh trembled her body.

"Are you cold, my love?" his deep voice asked.

Smiling, she cuddled closer, her arm draped across his wide naked chest. "No," she whispered, knowing that as long as he held her the embrace would radiate a warmth from deep inside her, one stemming from her very soul.

He placed a gentle kiss to her temple, breathing in the sweet fragrance of her hair and skin. One hand leisurely caressed her shoulder and traced the gentle curve of her waist and hip, lingering there before he took her hand and pressed the fingertips to his lips. Pulling the coverlet over them, he closed his eyes, satisfied with the few hours they would spend this way, for while she slept he would dress and leave her. Tomorrow he would tell her the truth.

Chapter Twenty-Three

The aromatic scent of burning pine and the warmth of the fire drifted in to arouse Nicholas from a peaceful slumber. He stirred, rolled to his stomach, and buried his head in the pillows, willing sleep to return, The satiny coolness of his haven refreshed him and called for him to linger a while longer. He had never slept so comfortably, and not more contentedly in a long while, images of the home he'd shared with his parents and Katherine drifting into his mind. He had never been allowed to sleep late, even as a child, had been dragged out of bed by his adoring father, one foot held playfully in Dru's hand as he pulled the boy nearer the edge and the possibility he would let young Nicholas fall to the floor. When it seemed inevitable, the youth would scream defeat and his father would seize him in his arms and tumble onto the blankets with him, laughing and tickling until his son cried for mercy. They were good times, fond memories Nicholas had often recalled. Turning onto his back, he stared up at the ceiling overhead, a sadness darkening the handsome brown eyes. He had wasted those last years of his father's life, living in Europe, sailing the seas. If nothing else, he vowed to find his father's murderer before his own life ended. He owed him that much.

507

The crackling of the blaze intruded upon his musings. He crossed his wrists and placed them behind his head, the quilt covering his lower torso as he relaxed in the yellow glow of the firelight. The fire created odd shapes against the ceiling, and he admired how each one was different and never repeated. There was something about dancing flames in a hearth that always soothed him no matter how distressing his thoughts. And he certainly had a lot to worry about lately. Of a sudden, memories of the night past exploded in his head. Not daring to move, certain Amber slept peacefully beside him, he knew he must dress before she awoke and discovered who he was. He needed a bit more time to decide just how to tell her. He didn't want her to find out on her own. Easing his hands from behind his neck, he slowly raised up, glancing at the space beside him from the corner of his eye. To his dismay, he found it empty. Dear God, she had already risen! Had she seen his face? No, it wasn't possible. She would have had to rekindle the fire first. He worriedly looked at the door, spying the intensity of the blaze's reflection framed in its archway, knowing instantly that she had already done just that. But had she returned to the room, found him sleeping and discovered his ploy, then run from the place in a fit of rage? No, she would have stayed to have it out with him. He shook his head. Knowing Amber, she would simply run a blade through him before asking why. Absently he touched a hand to his bare chest, half expecting to find the knife buried deeply between his ribs already. Maybe she had just awakened and hadn't had time to return. Yes, that had to be it. His frantic gaze surveyed the floor for the location of his clothes and veil, his mouth crimping ruefully beneath the heavy growth of beard when the garments were nowhere to be seen.

"Are you looking for these?"

The honey-smooth tones of her voice loomed out at him from the shadowed corner of the room, and he froze, feeling his doom close in on him. Only his eyes moved in the direction of her voice, and he nervously watched her step into the light, his silks held in one hand, the *yashmak* in the other.

"I will explain," he stated simply.

Amber had not fallen asleep after their lovemaking, too filled with confused thoughts to rest as guiltlessly as he. When morning had brought the faint chirping of birds to mark its arrival, she had slipped from beneath his arm draped over her hip and risen to dress. She had stoked the fire, gathered up his clothes, and taken her place in the far corner of the room, where she could observe him in slumber without his knowledge should he wake. Only a few minutes had passed before he stirred and rolled to his stomach, his handsome face hidden from view. She elected to study the wide shoulders, the sinewy curve of his arms, and the powerful muscles along his spine that disappeared beneath the coverlet. Then he turned once more, hands behind his head, and Amber's breath caught in her throat as she hungrily appraised the divine shape of his bronze chest, darkened by the mass of curls that narrowed to a straight line down his taut belly and vanished beneath the quilt. How she longed to trace a fingertip along their path. She closed her eyes for a moment to draw a deep breath and calm her rapid pulse. It had been such a long time since she had been able to feast her eyes upon his handsomeness unrestricted. Looking at him again, she had to bite her lower lip to keep it from trembling. The sleek, muscular arms framed his face, slightly flexed as they cushioned his head, and Amber rediscovered the perfection of his devastating features. She had been right when she thought the beard might complement the strong line of his jaw. If anything it enhanced his countenance, added an air of nobility, a hint of quiet strength. Yet with all its qualities, it failed to detract from the exquisite brown eyes outlined in magnificently thick black lashes. What seemed a hundred days and nights had passed since she had last looked fondly at him, and not one had passed without his superb likeness clouding her vision. And even now as she stood before him, her anger held in check, she wanted to run to him with open arms and find her comfort there. She fought the urge. She would hear his excuses first.

"More lies no doubt," she answered quietly with a slight nod of her head. She crossed to the door and entered the adjoining room without a backward glance, the garments still clutched in

509

her hands and dragging on the floor behind her.

Nicholas quickly scrambled to his feet, draping the thin coverlet around his waist, and followed her through the doorway, pulling up short when he witnessed her toss the veil and then his clothes into the fire. He opened his mouth to object and clamped it shut again when she turned to face him. His eyes roamed freely, approvingly, over her slight form, for standing between him and the flames she presented a most sensuous picture. The thinness of her garb failed to disguise the narrow waist and the long, shapely legs. His pulse quickened and he forced his mind onto the problems at hand.

"I intended to tell you the truth this morning," he said, watching her move away from the hearth.

She went to the front door and opened it, bright morning light flowing into the room. Studying the crystal clearness of the blue sky, she mocked, "Did you?"

"Yes, Amber," he answered hurriedly. Clutching the evasive cloth back to his hips, he started toward her, stopping abruptly when she turned around and raised a warning hand that he should not trespass further.

"Then suppose you tell me now. I am most anxious to hear why you let me go on thinking I would never see my family again. It must have been quite fun to watch your wife fight for her life and that of a young stranger." Her mouth twisted into a sarcastic smile. "I suppose when you told me you had sold Holly, you actually sent her home to England." She waited for his slight nod, then continued, her arms crossed over her chest. "You must have had a good laugh over that."

"Amber, please. . . ." he appealed,

"No, Nicholas, I do not please!"' she shouted, tears springing to her eyes, clenched fists dropping to her sides. "Did you hope to have me hate you for it? If you wished to have revenge for all the tricks I'd played on you, why didn't you take the easy way? You didn't have to come. You could have left me here. Or was that your justice . . . to watch me pay?"

"Let me explain, please?" He moved closer, only to have her whirl away from him and return to the hearth.

"Is Andrea all right?" she asked, staring into the flames.

His heart aching, Nicholas took a deep breath to ease the pain. "She's fine. I left her with Seth."

Amber laughed bitterly. "At least one of us is happy." A moment of silence passed before she turned back to look at him. "Everyone in this village knows, don't they? *Everyone* knew. Even Holly. You told her. That's why she was so sure you wouldn't hurt me. Ha! If she only knew how much."

"I love you, Amber."

"Liar!" she screamed, tears flowing down her face. "Liar! You gutless, conniving, heartless . . . bastard! You took another's name and thought to play me the fool."

"I thought to convince you that you loved your husband."

Clasping her elbows, she hugged her arms to her, fighting for control. "Well, it didn't work, did it? I fell in love with Ronen." Amber felt little pleasure now watching the pained expression cross his dark face before he chose to look at the floor at his feet, and she wondered at the feeling.

"No. It didn't." He remained quiet a moment, then cast warm, loving eyes on her. "It's why I decided to send you home."

"Really?" she spat. "How gallant. I suppose then my husband would have been there ready to begin where Ronen left off."

Nicholas shook his dark head, a stray curl resting against his brow. "I intended to tell you the truth. *All* of it. Before you left this village, you would have known Ronen and your husband were one and the same."

Amber stiffened arrogantly, her finely chiseled nose raised high. "And chance the possibility of my hating both of you?"

He nodded. "'Tis what I deserve. Everyone told me of the foolishness of my scheme, and I wouldn't listen. I was sure you loved me and in time would admit it to yourself."

"By hiding behind a veil? Why the disguise?"

"I had to know you were safe and trusted no one enough to have you stay with them."

"Not even Yasir?"

Nicholas raked his fingers through his thick, tousled hair. "Yasir wouldn't have done it if I asked. In fact, he was strongly against it and only agreed because he felt he owed me." His eyes found hers again, noting the hint of doubt shining in them. He frowned, realizing she was far from convinced.

"If all you say is true, why did Ronen make love to me?" she asked coldly, one brow raised.

"Ronen didn't. I did. I knew that once I told you the truth, I would never be allowed to hold you in my arms again. I was being selfish, but I needed that one last time to help me endure the void losing you would bring. I only regret you found out the way you did."

Enjoying the power she had over him, Amber began to sashay about the room, pausing periodically to glance over at him, a wicked smile parting her lips. She stopped at the door, one hand resting on the latch. "Then let's pretend I don't know."

His dark brows came together.

"I want you to go outside, knock on my door, and ask to speak with me. I want to hear how you would have explained this to me."

Nicholas hiked the quilt higher. "Amber, I'm not dressed. . . ."

"Do it, Nicholas. You owe me that much."

"But I wouldn't have come here half clothed. . . ."

"We're pretending, remember?"

Suddenly Nicholas had had enough. The muscle in his cheek flexed beneath the beard. "There's no need," he said quietly, starting for the bedroom and the chest that held his remaining wardrobe.

"Oh?" she asked, delaying his exit. "Had you ever stopped to think that maybe, just maybe, I would have understood? Don't you agree it's worth the try?"

Nicholas's wide chest expanded his slow intake of breath, his nostrils flaring when he expelled it in a noiseless sigh. Dropping his chin a degree, he looked over at her through lowered brows. "No, I don't. And I won't have you making a mockery of my love and my attempts to prove something to you. Apparently, you don't share the feeling."

She put her hand on her hip. "Oh? And how do you know that? Did you ever ask me?"

"If you did, we wouldn't be standing here like this now." He jerked his dark head toward the other room. "We'd still be in there."

"You conceited lout!" she exploded, slamming the door shut. "Do you honestly think I would have forgiven your trickery so easily? In case you didn't know it, I lived in the dark, foul-smelling hold of a ship for six or seven weeks, never permitted topside for a breath of fresh air or warm sunshine on my face, fed poorly, never allowed to bathe, and never sure if I'd live another day. But thoughts of *you* kept me going. I wanted to explain why I ran, as I should have done instead of forcing your grandmother to do it. Then the ship anchored in England. I thought to escape, but instead I was knocked unconscious and when I woke I found Holly, a poor frightened child who reminded me of Katherine. I vowed to take care of her, send her home if it meant my life." Amber's eyes blazed her fury.

"We dropped anchor again and we were taken to the marketplace and put on an auction block and sold! *We were sold!* And all the while the man I feared would rape me was *you*! My sweet, adoring, *loving* husband, trying to prove something. What, Nicholas? What were you trying to prove? That you could drive me mad?" Her body trembled with her rage. "And what did you do? You told me you sold Holly to someone else." Knotted fists raised to her temples, she squeezed her eyes closed. "God, how I hated you at that moment."

Tears threatening to steal her words, Amber blinked them away and crossed to the hearth, swallowing repeatedly to calm herself. "I hated you and yet felt safe with you, emotions that constantly plagued my mind, and before long it was cluttered with guilt. Instead of trying to escape, I accepted living in this village, your promise of marriage, and actually thought what had happened to me had been for the best." She laughed ill-humoredly. "And then I saw Sean swimming . . ."

"What?" The question cut through the air like an icy wind in December.

Glancing up at him, Amber frowned, surprised to see the anger gleaming in his dark eyes. She studied the flames once

513

more. "What does it matter?"

"It matters a great deal, Amber. I will know when you saw Sean," he ordered loudly. The coverlet seized in one hand, he came to stand next to her. "Did you steal his clothes?"

A light smile flitted across her face and disappeared, but she refused to answer.

"You knew yesterday, didn't you?" He glared down at her. "Didn't you?"

Her angry blue eyes flashed up at him. "Yes, I knew!" she shouted.

"And you made love to me knowing who I really was. Why?"

"Because I wanted you to suffer! Just as you made me suffer! I wanted you to think Ronen had won my love away from my husband."

Suddenly Nicholas threw back his head and roared with heartfelt laughter. "Well, you succeeded. I certainly did think that." Wiping the moisture from the corner of his eye with one knuckle, he fell upon the stack of pillows near the hearth. "And I suppose the dinner and bath were for the same purpose?"

His merriment was infectious, and Amber turned her head to hide her grin and shrugged one shoulder.

"And had you been more careful with your secrets, you would have let me live out all my days wondering."

"'Twas the least I could do," she confessed, running a fingertip along the minutely carved wood of the mantel to avoid looking at those captivating eyes.

"I love you, Amber."

A mixture of pain and yearning washed over her. She wanted to repeat the vow, to declare her love for him, and she wondered why she couldn't. Turning slowly, she looked at him, that strange sensation of a few hours ago erupting in the pit of her stomach, and again appraised his wide chest and the dark mass of curls gracing the shape of his upper torso. Unable to endure a moment more, she closed her eyes, damning that powerful attraction he radiated without the slightest move or blink of an eye.

"I have trouble believing that, after all that's happened,"

she answered quietly.

Nicholas pushed himself up, the quilt wrapped discreetly about his hips. "Then hear me out. Let me tell you my side. Maybe then you will understand what drove me to do what I did."

Looking at him once more, Amber saw the pleading in his dark eyes and felt her own need to listen. Without a word, she gave her consent by sitting down quietly on the stone slab of the hearth, one shoulder resting against its face, her hands folded in her lap, and fixed her gaze on his. He could not hide a falsehood in his eyes.

Smiling in vain, he took a deep breath to begin. This would be his only chance, and he prayed he would not spoil it by a careless slip of the tongue. He must tell her everything, not delete a single detail lest his case seem insincere.

"I have known a lot of women in my life, some titled, some of royalty, but until I met you, none seemed worth the trouble. I think I fell in love with you the first moment I saw you there in my house." He frowned, sighing heavily, and ran lean fingers through his hair. "Unfortunately, I mistakenly thought you were like all the others, conniving a way to have me marry you." He chuckled. "How wrong I was." Lifting his chin in the air, he studied the ceiling overhead. "So I thought I would teach you a lesson. I was angry. I figured your request to borrow money was only a new scheme to trap me somehow, and suggested you pay it back by spending the night. You'll never know how shocked I was when you agreed."

His memory of that encounter brought pain, and he looked over at the quiet figure near the fire for even a slight show of forgiveness. But Amber remained silent.

"I truly didn't think you were that kind of woman, and I knew for sure when I touched you and you pulled away. You begged me to stop, but I couldn't, and I've regretted it every moment since. I hate myself for what I did even now. I deserved your revenge."

Unable to sit still, Nicholas came to his feet, tucking one corner of the quilt in the folds around his waist and tossing the other over his shoulder, and Amber felt a shudder run through

515

her. He looked like any Greek god she had ever imagined.

"You disappeared after that, and I shoved the horrible thoughts from my mind. I tried, yet the vision of your beautiful face would come to haunt me from time to time. Then I learned that the ragamuffin I had taken under my wing was in reality the woman who plagued my very soul." He stopped his pacing and faced her. "I know you'll never believe me, but I married you because I wanted you, *needed* you, but *not* to save my inheritance. I would gladly live out my life here with the few things we have if you would agree to stay with me as my wife."

Her unreadable blue eyes returned his stare, and Nicholas felt an aching in his heart. But he would not surrender, not yet, not until he had told everything. After that . . .

"Those few days we spent as man and wife were the most beautiful, fulfilling times of my life. I had never been happier and vowed to have you share those feelings." He began his aimless trek once more. "I thought I had succeeded until I awoke that morning and found you gone. Then my world came crashing down around me. I had been blind, selfish, thinking you would want the same things I wanted.

"Several days passed, and when I didn't hear from you I figured I had lost you. Then Gibbens came with the note the kidnappers had left. I knew you were in danger, but at the same time, I felt as if a great burden had been lifted from me as I realized you couldn't have come back to me if you'd wanted to. It had to be the only reason you didn't."

Crossing the room, Nicholas stooped down before her. "But after I talked with Andrea, I began to understand how you felt. I sympathized with your views on people of wealth and decided then to change your mind. In your eyes, I seemed no different than the rest. But as Ronen, I planned to guide your thoughts and have you make your own discoveries about your husband."

His dark brows moved together at her vague smile.

"Didn't work, did it?" she teased, a twinkling in her eyes.

Nicholas hadn't realized it, but he had held his breath waiting for her answer. Letting it out with a low chuckle, he grinned. "No. But if you'd like, I'll adopt the name of my conspirator and court you as I should have done before."

Amber's gaze took in his stunning features bathed in the firelight—his ruffled hair, dark eyes, high cheekbones, full, almost sensuous mouth, his lean jaw covered with the flattering growth of beard, the wide, strong shoulders . . . without thinking she lightly touched the scar on his left side, which was partially hidden by the thick, dark curls on his chest.

"I don't remember . . ."

Nicholas covered her hand with his, lifting the open palm to his lips. "A trophy of my battles," he whispered, his brown sparkling eyes gazing warmly into hers.

"When did you get it?" she asked curiously, ignoring the flutter of her heart at his kiss.

"Just before Sean and I set sail to find you," he breathed, the back of his fingertips tracing the smooth line of her jaw.

"But this looks like a pistol wound, Nicholas. How did . . ."

The sound of his name upon her lips warmed him, clouded his thoughts with the yearnings he had had those many weeks they had been separated. He smiled, brushing a golden curl from her brow. "Von Buren," he answered dreamily, unaware of the impact his confession would have.

"What?"

He blinked, hearing the surprise and astonishment in her voice. He opened his mouth to explain, only to be shoved aside as she quickly came to her feet and circled behind him, examining his back.

"There's a scar here, too. It must have been a terrible wound. How did it happen?" she demanded crossly.

Nicholas fell to one hip, thoroughly enjoying the sight of her face twisted with her anger. Even in her rage, she was beautiful. "He was quite mad, you know."

Crouching beside him, the lines between her brows disappeared. "Was?"

"Yes. He's dead."

Dead! Her lips formed the word, but no sound escaped them. Could it be? Could Baron Kelzer Von Buren, Satan in mortal form, be dead? Amber closed her eyes, sucking in a breath, and felt as if a heavy chain had been lifted from around her neck, somehow knowing it was true. When she spoke, her voice came out in hardly more than a whisper. "Did you kill him? Is that how you got the scar?"

He nodded. "I went to see him after Andrea told me he had paid her a visit. I knew he was responsible for your kidnapping but had no real proof until then. He let me in his house, offered me a drink, and calmly told me how he'd killed your father, and his first wife, and how he felt no sorrow for Heather's death, and how he'd kidnapped you. He even confessed to having you sent to Casablanca. If he hadn't, I'm afraid I wouldn't have found you as quickly as I did."

Amber's blue eyes widened. "My God. I didn't know Heather . . ."

Nicholas quickly patted the hand resting on her knee. "I'm sorry, my love. There's a lot you don't know and I'd forgotten. Would you like a glass of wine while I tell you what happened?"

She nodded and Nicholas quickly fulfilled her request. As she sat sipping the wine before the fire, Nicholas took his place on the stone slab where he could watch her.

"Von Buren blackmailed Heather into marrying him," he began, cut short when she interrupted.

"But he wanted to marry Andrea!"

"I know. I was as surprised as you when I heard. Anyway, Heather must have known of his plans for kidnapping you and came to Williamsburg to tell me. But her carriage overturned and she was killed before she could find me."

"How awful," Amber whispered, the glass trembling in her hand.

Nicholas watched her take another drink, using the moment to select his next words. "Amber, Von Buren said something else that day that confused me. Maybe you can help."

She glanced up. "What?"

"Since Heather was dead, he intended to use you to get Andrea to marry him. He said she was the only heir to the Cromwell estate. Do you know what he meant?"

"Nathaniel Cromwell?"

Nicholas shrugged.

"My mother was his illegitimate daughter, but Cromwell never claimed her. According to my mother, he never once came to see her. Andrea and I would be heirs, but he had his own children and grandchildren. He would leave his estate to them, not us." She shook her head. "No. I don't understand either. And I guess we'll never know now that Von Buren's dead." Lifting the glass to her lips once more, her eyes caught sight of Nicholas's smile over the rim. She paused. "What do you find amusing?"

Nicholas rubbed the corner of his mouth with one finger. "Oh, nothing really. I was just thinking that if Cromwell really did leave his estate to you and Andrea, your share alone would nearly equal my wealth, from what I've heard about the man."

"So?" she asked suspiciously.

"I was just wondering . . . well, would your attitude toward the rich change then? I mean it would be rather difficult hating something you yourself had become without sounding like a hypocrite."

Amber's eyes narrowed, but a hint of mischief glowed in them. "What I would do, my husband, is hire a lawyer and post the bonds of divorce." She cast him a devilish grin, stood, and went to the small table that held the brass pitcher of wine.

"Oh," Nicholas mumbled, studying the floor. "I guess I deserved that."

"But," she continued, pouring another drink, "I might then allow the good Nicholas Chandler of Williamsburg to call on me as a gentleman would." She glanced demurely over her shoulder at him. "Of course, I can't promise what might result."

Knowing she teased him, Nicholas rose to the occasion. His head shot up and he smiled broadly. "Then let's not waste your money."

"Waste money?" she repeated, watching him unfold his exquisitely muscular frame and start toward her.

"Allow me the honor first and then decide. Who knows? Maybe you'll find one appealing quality about me and elect to stay my wife." He stood before her and reached out to take her glass. But Amber held him off with the nail of one fingertip pressed to his breastbone where the quilt had fallen away.

"Not until you're fully clothed," she said firmly.

He shrugged. "If I must. But I also see a waste there, too."

Amber cocked her blond head to one side. "How so?" she asked warily.

The dimple went unseen beneath the beard, but there was no mistaking the suggestive gleam in his eyes.

Unable to hold back her smile at his improper notion, her pulse shamelessly quickening at the idea, she fought off the urge to agree, twisting one lock of hair on his chest around her finger and heartlessly jerking her hand away, taking several strands with her, "Do you always court women in your bed?" she asked through lowered lashes, as she walked past him and went back to the fireplace. Turning to watch him, she lifted the glass to her lips and slowly drank from it, her pale blue eyes never leaving his.

Rubbing the injured spot on his chest, he said, "I don't believe in wasting time, either."

Raising a delicate chin in the air, Amber playfully looked down her nose at him. "And what makes you so sure it's what I would want foremost? Maybe I'd enjoy a single rose blossom first or sweet words upon your lips."

Looking at his feet, Nicholas strolled toward her. "Correct me if I'm wrong, but didn't the woman who made love to me last night know who I was?"

Amber coyly shrugged one shoulder and looked away. "Maybe," she mocked.

"Ah, but you did, by your own admission." He stood next to her now, hands clutched behind his back, allowing his nearness without a touch to unnerve her as he had seen it do many times before. "And maybe she played a game at first, but I doubt the woman who clawed my back did so for fun."

A light blush rose in her cheeks. "That's something you'll never know for sure, will you?" she answered nervously, feeling the trap he'd set.

"I will if you'll look at me and tell me it's so."

520

Amber toyed with the glass in her hands, refusing his request.

"Look at me and tell me that in that moment you hadn't forgiven this foolish man for the tricks he'd played, possibly even understood."

She glanced briefly up at him from the corner of her eye, then studied the glass again. "Maybe in the heat of passion I did. But we will not spend every moment in bed. What about the daylight hours, when doubt begins to creep into my mind—"

"Doubt? What doubt? That I love you more than life itself? Amber, I've followed you across an ocean and would do it a hundred times if it would prove to you how much living without you pains me." He pressed a hand to the wall behind her. "I can say the words, feel them in my heart, but if you refuse to believe, what more can I do? I can never erase the conditions of our marriage from your mind, but I swear on bended knee for all to witness that it was not my sole need. I loved you then as I love you now and only wish for you to feel that love, accept it, grow in it, and, by the grace of God, return it." Placing a knuckle beneath her chin, he brought her eyes around to meet his. "Can you say in all honesty, to yourself and to me, that you hate me, that there isn't a spark of tenderness in you for me?"

The orange glow of the fire sparkled golden depths in his eyes as he stood there waiting, all hint of mockery gone. She *had* forgiven him, she *had* understood, but did she truly love him? The yearnings of her body declared a tenderness, but had they surfaced out of lust and not love?

"I do not hate you," she whispered, "but—"

"Say no more," he interrupted, fingertips pressed to her mouth. "The rest will come in time. And I will give you all you need. I can be a very patient man when so much is at stake." His fingers moved to cup her chin and draw her close, his lips gently finding hers.

And Amber knew in that moment, with that kiss, that no matter what she had thought of Nicholas Chandler in the beginning it had all changed. She returned the kiss with equal desire, her arms encircling his neck, the wine glass dangling

521

from her fingertips, and enjoyed the bliss such an embrace allowed. Her heart fluttered, her pulse quickening, and even though she had not admitted love, the bonds of marriage dissolved her momentary twinge of shamefulness for the urgings of her womanly body. A slow awareness that he failed to slip his arms around her spoiled the longing, and she pulled back to look into his eyes, wondering.

"Why do you hesitate?"

Glancing down, his answer came soft, unsure. "I would know first that it's what you truly desire."

"And if it isn't, how long would you wait? Forever?" she asked.

His sigh shook him. "If I must," he answered. "It would be a time of torture, not knowing to what depths you care, but one sweetened by the mere sight of you. A true test of my endurance, yet worth the effort if on occasion you gave a hint of rich reward."

She grinned impishly. "That much I will give you. But only a hint."

His brown eyes raked over her, his smile shining in them. "Enough for now," he surrendered lightheartedly, relaxing in their momentary truce.

Her arms still draped about his shoulders, she moved one hand to trace the softness of his beard. "I rather like the way you look. It hides the fact that you are a man of wealth. Most would be clean shaven."

"If it will help to sway your heart, I will always wear it," he firmly stated, presenting a flash of white teeth.

Her gaze took in the rest of him. "And garb yourself thus?"

"If it be your want."

Stepping back, she set aside her glass to appraise him from head to toe, one fingertip tapping her chin. "I fear you would draw too much attention from the maids of this village if you swaggered about half dressed. I think you should take it off."

Bowing from the waist, he said, "As you wish." Straightening, he took the cloth from his shoulder, and before she could object and make her meaning clear, he dropped the quilt to the floor.

"Nicholas!" she gasped, a rush of blood darkening her cheeks.

"But I only wish to do whatever makes you happy," he argued, feigning innocence.

Turning away, she closed her eyes. "I meant you should wear something else, not disrobe."

"But I haven't anything to wear now. You burned them, remember?"

"That's not true," she rallied, glancing back at him. "You . . . you have more . . . in the other . . ." Suddenly Amber burst into laughter, hiding her face with her hands. "You . . . you look so funny standing there like that." Peeking through her fingers at him once more, she fought her mirth but failed to overcome it, hit with a surge of giggles.

"Funny?" he objected loudly. "I know of a few who wouldn't agree."

"Oh, do you?" she laughed. "And had you proclaimed your love and set the mood with romantic words, only to drop your clothes and strut about as a rooster before the hen house?"

"I'm not strutting," he argued. "I'm standing perfectly still." One corner of his mouth twisted upward. "But if you'd like, I could—"

"No, no, that's all right," she assured him, one hand raised to stop him. Her smile lingered and she bit her lower lip, hoping to still her glee. She swallowed twice, then said, "Why don't you cover yourself before I damage your pride further?"

"Damage my pride?" he repeated. "How so? Do you honestly see anything to criticize?"

Amber's chin sagged at his pomposity. "Maybe the others you spoke of couldn't, but I know you better than most and could name a few things."

"Such as?" he challenged.

She opened her mouth to set him straight only to discover that no flaws in either his character or his physique would come to mind. Her gaze took in the sight of him standing before the fire, and their joyful bantering of a moment past disappeared. The golden glow of the flames bathed his long, lean frame and cast the illusion of a bronze statue, with one major difference. This was no man made of stone, but a living, breathing specimen of perfection, and suddenly Amber lost the desire to mock him.

She moved with graceful beauty to him, her arms slowly encircling his neck to draw his mouth to hers, and he eagerly welcomed the advance, one hand placed behind her head, the other resting familiarly on the small of her back. He pulled her closer, the coolness of the cloth she wore pressed against his bare chest as they partook of the sweetness of the kiss. He twisted his opened mouth across hers, his tongue darting inside, and he thought his mind would explode when he found no resistance there. With smooth mastery, his hands untwined the knot of fabric at her neck and let it glide softly to the floor at their feet, his hot, eager mouth trailing kisses to her bare shoulder while his thumb found the peak of one breast.

Her anger at his trickery vanished with the caress, and Amber's head fell back with her moan, inviting him to sample the silky flesh of her throat, her hands raised to frame his face and guide him there. Memories of the treasures they had shared the night past blossomed to awareness and Amber's pulse raced in anticipation. He lowered his head to the valley between her breasts, his tongue tasting the velvety skin, and her breath caught, waiting for the moment he would claim the taut peak. But instead, he pulled away, his hungry gaze studying the simple beauty of her nakedness, and all modesty fled beneath his loving regard.

Impatient to have him, Amber slowly knelt upon the pillows before the hearth, her alluring gaze silently prompting him to follow. One knee upon the cushion, he encompassed her delicate form in his arms, his mouth capturing hers in a fierce urgent kiss, their naked bodies touching. He held her to him, his fingers entwined in the golden locks of her hair, reveling in the sweet fragrance of her, his heart racing with each gentle caress of her hands as they moved along his back and lingered on the bareness of his hips. His passion soaring, he fell with her to the bed of pillows, kissing the corner of her mouth, her neck, the pulse beating wildly in the hollow of her throat, and finally the aroused tip of her breast. She called his name huskily, arching her hips against him, a pleading to fuse their bodies, their souls, as one, and he lifted up, one knee parting her thighs.

A magic exploded within them when he came to her, spiraling them to heights neither wanted to end. They moved together, a merging of love, hearts, passion, coupled for eternity, all pain, frustrations, doubts gone forever.

"I love you, Nicholas," Amber whispered.

Chapter Twenty-Four

Stretched out on the soft cushion of pillows, hands tucked behind his head for support, Nicholas lovingly watched his wife slip into her clothes, silently cursing the muted light of the dying fire for not allowing a better view. A soft blush from their lovemaking darkened the fairness of her face, golden strands of hair rumpled, and he concluded he would see to it that she always rose in the morning looking much the same.

"I truly see no need to be in such a hurry," he sighed contentedly. "I'd much prefer to linger here a while longer."

Tucking the last corner of the silk wrap into place, she tossed the thick mane of yellow locks, running her fingers through them for some sort of order. "As much as he deserved the theft of his clothes for his part in this charade, I think your father's cousin has suffered long enough," she said firmly, turning to look at him, her fists resting on her hips. "And I don't know about you, but I'd like to go home, and I'm sure Sean feels much the same.

Nicholas chuckled. "Yes, he does. He told me so just yesterday."

"And what of you?" she asked with a smile, bending down to rest one hip on the pillow next to him. "Don't you want to go home?"

Pushing himself up on one elbow, he traced the delicate outline of her face with a fingertip. "I do, and yet I worry things will change."

Surprise wrinkled her brow. "What things?"

"The way you feel about me," he confessed sadly. "I'd rather live out my life right here in this house, if it would guarantee your love. There are a lot of memories in Virginia."

Taking his hand from her cheek, she kissed each finger bent around her own and cast him a warm look. "I'm afraid you're trapped, my husband. I've declared my love for you, and no matter where we find ourselves my feelings will never change. You're stuck with me and better pray your desires for me never fade."

"Have no fear of that, my love," he grinned happily. "Even when your hair is touched with gray and living shows its mark around the corners of your eyes, my passion will live on." He wiggled his brows. "I plan to die in bed with you beneath me."

"Nicholas!" she gasped, sitting upright. "You're shameless!" She made to rise and he caught her wrist, pulling her to him to rest against his chest.

"Yes, I know. And I intend to constantly remind you."

His lips found hers in a warm and tender kiss, as his hands roamed freely down her back to her buttocks. Amber responded eagerly until his opened mouth twisted across hers and his tongue darted inside. Hands pressed against his chest, she broke the embrace abruptly and stood.

"Then cool your lust, for we have more important things to do just now."

He grinned at the slight coloring in her cheeks and knew it had taken great resolve for her to calm her own desires. "And what could be more important?" he teased.

"Your grandmother," she stated.

Nicholas's brows lifted in surprise. "My grandmother?"

"Yes. She doesn't know you found me, does she? Or for that matter whether or not your ship arrived safely here."

Sitting up with a nod, he agreed. "You're right, she doesn't, And I would suppose your sister would be grateful to learn you're all right."

"Then get dressed, you randy knave, and let's visit Sean."

They left the small dwelling a few minutes later, hand in hand, and unaware of anything or anyone around them. Several villagers paused in their work, surprised to see Ronen without the veil and the woman from whom he sought to hide his identity talking and smiling happily with him. They could only shrug their shoulders in confusion and step aside to allow them to pass, knowing that if this was what Ronen wanted, they would not question it.

When they reached the door of Sean's lodging, Amber grinned mischievously at Nicholas, pressed a fingertip to her lips, and motioned for him to wait outside. Rapping three times on the portal, she paused, listening for Sean's consent to enter, and when it came, she smiled once more at her husband and lifted the latch.

Bright sunlight fell into the room and spotlighted the tall Irishman kneeling before the fireplace. "If I be livin' ta be a hundred, Nicholas me boy, I'll never be gettin' the hang of startin' a fire that will stay," he grumbled, not bothering to look up. "Do ya suppose ya could be helpin' me? I haven't had me breakfast and can't hear meself think for the rumblin' in me stomach."

His concentration still centered on his work, he failed to notice the slender form move away from the door and approach. It wasn't until Amber knelt beside him and took the stick he held from him that the sudden realization of whom he had invited in to join him hit full force, for no man in the village had such a delicately boned hand, nor were the women as fair. He froze, uncertain what to say or even if he dared to move.

"Well, aren't you going to ask me how I am, Sean Rafferty?"

Gulping, he slowly raised his blue eyes to look at her, wondering at the sweet smile she gave him. "H—How are ya, lass?" he asked weakly.

"I'm fine, thank you. And you?"

His breath painful to draw, he worried exactly how much longer he had to live. He had spent enough years with his cousin and Victoria Chandler to know that when a woman was truly angry, she often times masked it with a facade of pleasantry before nailing her victim with a merciless blow. And the new Mistress Chandler certainly had more than enough reason to be angry with him. Nervously, he glanced at the opened doorway.

"I—I . . . would be explainin', lass, if ya be allowin' me a moment." Damn if he didn't feel like a young lad standing before his mother with cherry pie stains on his chin. Of course, with Kyna Rafferty, taking a piece of dessert without asking wasn't the same as lying.

"Explaining what, Sean?" Amber asked lightly, stoking the fire to a healthy blaze. Dusting off her hands, she stood, watching the man slowly come to his feet.

"Has Ronen talked with ya yet?" His silvery brows knotted.

"About what?" she goaded. She raised a hand to brush back a curl from her frown, and Sean jumped apprehensively. "Is something wrong?"

"Ya have me puzzled, 'tis all," he responded feebly.

"Puzzled? How so?"

His gaze quickly darted between her and the front door. "I can't be understandin' how ya would calmly stand there and talk ta me as if we were at the docks in Virginia."

"And why not? We're friends, aren't we?" She smiled innocently up at him, and in that instant Sean's suspicion mounted, guiding his words.

"How did ya know I was here?"

Amber shrugged. "Ronen told me."

One wrinkled blue eye squinted down at her. "And so ya thought ta pay me a visit? Ya aren't mad or anythin', just thought ta talk with an old friend. Somehow I don't think I be needin' ta explain. Ya already know, don't ya?" Suddenly he straightened up. "Ya wouldn't happen ta have an extra pair of men's clothes, now would ya?"

Amber opened her mouth to respond, cut short by the laughter in the doorway, and both Sean and she turned to face Nicholas. Amber smiled in return, but Sean's mouth curled disapprovingly.

"I told you he's too smart to fool for long," Nicholas grinned.

"And if I wasn't, ya both would have tormented me until me final breath, now wouldn't ya have?" His face flushed with his annoyance, then slowly faded when he realized the humor of his plight and watched the loving way Nicholas approached his wife and possessively slipped an arm around her waist with no resistance on her part. He relaxed, a smile settling on his handsome face. "Am I ta assume ya both have forgiven each other and have finally agreed ta go home?"

Amber snuggled closer in Nicholas's embrace and smiled up at him. "Yes, Sean, we have."

"Thank the Lord and all the Saints watchin' over us," he shouted, hands held high, his eyes looking toward the heavens. Focusing his attention on the couple once more, he added, "Now mind ya, it isn't that I don't enjoy livin' here, but as I was tellin' your hardheaded husband, he could have persuaded ya ta his way of thinkin' on the ship as we sailed for home and not had ta spend even a night in this . . . this . . . barbaric wasteland."

"You'll have to forgive him, Amber," Nicholas laughed, "but Sean's always been more comfortable on a ship than having dirt beneath his feet."

"I would be settlin' for that," he argued hotly, "but there isn't nothin' here except sand! I've had it in me shoes, me food and even in me bed." Thinking of the pesty substance, he bent forward and briskly ran his fingers through his hair, shaking the tiny particles free. "See what I mean? I'm plagued." He straightened. "If we leave right now, I would be more than grateful."

"Then I won't be the cause of your grief any longer, Mr. Rafferty," Amber grinned. "We may leave as soon as you wish."

The thought of seeing his ship again soothed Sean into a lighthearted mood. He smiled and came forward to take Amber's hand in a gentle grasp. "I would have stayed as long as it took, lass, ta get ya ta come home as Nicholas's wife. So don't go thinkin' I truly suffered." He placed a kiss to the back of her fingers, then stood. "'Tis good ta see ya smile again."

"Thank you," she whispered, and he nodded.

A moment of quiet passed as Sean appraisingly studied the beautiful young woman, knowing his cousin would have approved of his son's choice of a wife. His face reflected his momentary pang of sadness that Dru hadn't lived long enough to meet her, then disappeared with his sigh.

"Now," he grinned, clapping his hands together, "I best be findin' some men willin' ta ride back ta Casablanca with us."

Looking first at Sean, then Nicholas, Amber frowned, "Why would we need anyone to go with us?"

His arm still draped around her waist, Nicholas gave her a gentle squeeze, his gaze resting on their companion. "Just a precaution, my love."

"For what?"

Not wishing to upset her, yet knowing she would not let the matter die without an answer, Nicholas glanced down at the floor at his feet. "Yaakob's men were watching the village a few days ago. They haven't been around lately, but we must be sure they aren't hiding somewhere near just waiting for a chance to catch some of us alone."

"Yaakob? But Yasir told me that he had not bothered the village for years. What do you suppose he wants?"

Sean quickly looked away and returned to the fireplace and his preparation of breakfast. Nicholas stood quietly for a moment.

"We're not sure, Amber," he said softly, turning her in his arms, "but we fear he may want you."

Her face paled instantly. "Oh, dear God, why?"

"Remember our first meeting at the marketplace?"

She nodded.

"If I hadn't come when I had, he would have bought you. Many men fear Yaakob and none would have interfered with his getting what he wanted. But I did. I took you from him and he will never forget it. I have shamed him in front of too many too often, and I think he seeks revenge this time."

"By taking me?"

"Yes, my love," he whispered, pulling her into his embrace. "That's why you must promise me that you will never leave the village alone."

Visions of the one-eyed image of Satan flashed into her thoughts. "You don't need my promise, Nicholas. I would rather die than do anything that might allow him to come

532

within a mile of me." Snuggling closer, she laid her head against his chest, listening to the steady rhythm of his heart and feeling safe within the circle of his arms.

Placing a kiss to the top of her head, Nicholas centered his attention on his friend once more. "Since there's a chance that Yaakob and his men are still around, I suggest we leave first thing in the morning. I don't want to spend more than one night on the road if it's possible."

"Aye, lad, I agree. I'll find the men we need and be ready ta go before first light."

"Thank you, Sean," Nicholas smiled, tucking Amber into the protection of his arm around her shoulders. "I just found my wife again, and I don't intend to let anything happen to separate us. Whether she likes it or not, she's stuck with me."

Grinning playfully, Amber glanced over at Sean. "The poor fool. He truly thinks he did all the chasing."

The two men exchanged a look of confusion, then burst into laughter.

"If that had really been the case, lass, I would have been likin' it better if ya'd done it back home," Sean chuckled. "I always enjoy an ocean voyage, but not so long a stay on land."

"Then rest easy, Mr. Rafferty," she assured him. "I have no intention of ever leaving this stubborn man again." Standing on tiptoes, she kissed the tip of Nicholas's nose. "Now I suggest we make our apologies to Yasir. He had to endure much at our hands."

Bowing from the waist, Nicholas extended a hand for her to lead the way, straightened after she had passed, and winked at Sean before he followed Amber outside, leaving the Irishman to stand in the doorway watching, a smile on his lips and a satisfied look on his face.

From behind a single cloud in the velvety-black sky the moon fought to show its face and cast its platinum rays of light upon the earth. The air still and breathless, a serenity encased the tiny village on the mountainside, sweetened by the overture of crickets and the occasional hoot of an owl perched high atop a tree. All seemed content, protected against any foe that hovered about as the people of the remote town settled down to rest.

Along the narrow road that wound its way toward the pond, two figures walked leisurely, arms entwined, smiles upon their faces. At peace with the world, they had shoved aside their thoughts of all the adversities that had plagued their lives. Bathed in the warm glow of moonlight guiding their steps, the pastels of their garb contrasted brightly with the ebony backdrop and gave the illusion of two lost souls in search of their destiny.

Amber and Nicholas had walked the distance in silence, each caught up in his own thoughts. They had visited Yasir after leaving Sean and had spent the greater part of the afternoon with him, laughing and sharing wine, reliving the events that found them in such an unlikely spot. It had been a joyous time and it hadn't taken Amber long to realize she would miss the old man a great deal. She had never known the benefit of a grandfather, and in her heart she vainly wished to convince him to return to Williamsburg with them, but sadly dismissed the idea without voicing it, for she knew he would never agree.

The rush of the waterfall a short distance ahead set the mood, and Amber took a deep breath, reveling in the smells of the forest surrounding them. Wild flowers, pine, and fresh air relaxed her, and she felt an inner warmth of well-being, at ease with her husband's presence. Hugging him tighter about the waist, she rested against the strength of his muscular frame, one hand touching his broad chest.

"You know, I'll always remember this village and its people with kindness," she said dreamily. "It's been a very special time in my life."

Hiding his smile, Nicholas asked, "Then you don't hate any of us overmuch?"

"I don't hate anyone," she strongly objected, harmlessly slapping the taut muscles of his belly. "No one here was to blame for your tricks."

"The truth be spoken," he concurred with a chuckle. "And I doubt you will ever let me forget it."

She stopped abruptly and turned to look at him. "And why should I? I think it's the only way I will keep you in line." Her eyes sparkled in the silvery beams of the moonlight. "I even plan to tell your grandmother what went on here. Between the two of us, we'll soon teach you how to behave."

Nicholas threw back his dark head and laughed loudly. "And Katherine too, I suppose?"

"Of course," she agreed, fighting with the smile that tugged at the corners of her own mouth. "She's not too young to learn how to handle men."

Shaking his head in defeat, white teeth flashing his amusement, Nicholas again draped an arm around his wife's neck in a gentle hold and pulled her to him as he guided them to the edge of the pond. "As long as it means you'll always be there to remind me, I think the cost well worth it."

He stood watching the sparkling water cascade over the small group of rocks opposite them, listening to its hypnotic sounds, its steady flow inviting, then suddenly dropped his arm from Amber's shoulder. Without comment, he began to pull his shirttail from the waistband of his silk breeches.

"What are you doing?" Amber gasped, her gaze darting in all directions for anyone who might see.

"I'm going for a swim," he stated matter-of-factly, hopping on one foot while he tugged off a suede boot. "Come on. It may be our last chance to do something so scandalous."

Amber could feel the heat rise in her cheeks as she watched him disrobe and wondered what had happened to the pompous man she had once known who was unwilling to simply dangle his feet in a pond. Were there a lot of things about Nicholas Chandler that she had yet to learn? Deciding that there probably were, she shook her head at his blatant disregard for proper behavior and calmly stepped aside as he dashed by her and dove into the pond. Laughter threatened to overcome her at his buffoonery until a spray of clear water splashed up to attack her and she squealed, attempting to dodge the assault only to be showered from head to toe, cold, stinging droplets instantly taking her breath away. She stood perfectly still, her teeth clamped together to stop their chattering, and heard his

535

merry laughter.

"You should have moved a little faster," Nicholas guffawed, bobbing in the glittering surface of the pool, mischief glowing in his dark eyes.

Turning around slowly, Amber peered out at him through wet strands of hair plastered to her face. The comical sight she presented brought a heartier round of chuckles than before, and she straightened to full height, a well-deserved payment for his pranks coming to her mind. Swooping the heavy locks of hair from her eyes, she bent, briskly picked up each piece of Nicholas's attire, and stood once more. Lifting her nose haughtily in the air, she spun around and started off for the road.

"No! Amber! Don't!" Nicholas shouted, frantically swimming to the grassy bank, his playful mood shattered. "Oh, Amber, I only teased."

She continued on as if she hadn't heard, the corners of her mouth turned upward.

"Amber, stop where you are or so help me . . ."

"So help you what?" she threw back over her shoulder, her step never faltering. She intended only to torment him, to worry him that he might have to hide among the trees, as she was sure Sean had had to do, and had planned to stop a safe distance away, make him beg for his clothes, plead forgiveness. But with the sudden splash of water, she stopped and turned around, chin sagging, her breath lodged in her throat, for there running toward her in the shadowed edge of the woods, Amber caught a glimpse of the naked man rapidly closing in on her.

"Oh, my . . ." she breathed, absently dropping his garments, her eyes wide. Stumbling backward, her mind could not react quickly enough, and before she had traveled a step Nicholas was upon her. Swinging her up in his arms, he headed back to the pond.

"What are you going to do?" Her fearful blue eyes calculated the distance to the pool's edge. "You're not . . . oh, Nicholas, don't!" She wiggled, attempting to free herself, but when the distance diminished to three steps she fought in earnest. "Put me do-o-own!" she wailed.

"My pleasure, madam," he chaffed, twirling her away from him.

His strong hands let go, and Amber found herself sailing through midair. She opened her mouth to scream but took a deep breath instead just as she hit water and plunged beneath its surface. The chill of it dampened her desire to see justice done, certain as she was that the contest would simply be one-sided anyway, and she fought to emerge and declare surrender. But as she neared the top, two muscular arms entrapped her, pulling her to him, and as they sprang from the chilly depths of the pond, Nicholas's mouth claimed hers in a hungry, urgent kiss. The rock-hard muscles of his chest pressed against her breasts, Amber's desires for play changed abruptly, and she returned the embrace with as much fierceness as he. They clung to each other, the warmth of their passion chasing away the crisp bite of the water. Together, in silent understanding, they swam to the shallow side of the pool, where Nicholas swept her in his arms and carried her to a secluded spot. Nearly hidden from view by the low-hanging branches of a pine, he laid his slight burden upon the ground cushioned by a bed of pine needles and rested on one hip to unwind the heavy, wet fabric of her silk wrap from around her. Soft shades of moonlight flitted in to warm them and bathe the pale beauty of his wife in a most alluring manner.

Nicholas's heart beat faster as he looked at her, the desires of her body shining brightly in the blue depths of her eyes. With one fingertip touching the delicate line of her jaw, he followed the contour of the long, slim neck, the silky smoothness of her shoulder, and circled one breast before continuing on to the velvety softness of the flat, lean belly. Leaning in, his kisses retraced the path his caress had made, and Amber moaned in the delight of it. Slipping his arm beneath her, he raised her up, his opened warm mouth covering the peak of one breast, his tongue sampling the tender flesh and taut nipple. Her skin was sweetened by cool droplets of water, and he tasted each one as they trailed the valley between the firm mounds of her bosom, licking each playfully in the prelude to their symphony.

Her hands framing his face, Amber guided his lips to hers,

wanting desperately to feel his muscular body molded against her own and savor the rich nectar of their kiss. He pulled them both to their knees, his touch roaming freely down the slender back to rest intimately against her buttocks, drawing her within his embrace, the manly boldness of him pressed against her naked thigh.

The kiss, at first tender, grew with mounting passion, a hungry need to draw the other closer, become as one, and Amber felt the rapid beat of his heart against her breast, his body stiffen with desire. He buried his face in her neck, nibbling at her earlobe, and she arched against him, her head falling back with a moan. His kisses moved across her throat and to the swell of her bosom, his tongue teasing the delicious peak before sucking greedily upon it, and Amber felt the exquisite tingling his lovemaking aroused burst within her, stealing her breath away.

Impatient to sate the cravings of their bodies, they fell together on the bed of dried leaves and pine needles blanketed by the silk of her garb, lost in the delirium of their world. Breathless and panting, Amber moved to welcome him, parting her thighs when he lowered his weight upon her. But instead of the first thrust she expected, wanted, he held back, his manly hardness teasing, tempting the soft flesh of her womanhood. Pleadingly, she looked at him, his lust aflame in his dark eyes, and she knew he wanted this moment to last forever. Locking her fingers in the damp, thick mass of hair at the nape of his neck, she drew his mouth to hers, her tongue lightly touching his, and she felt the tremor that shook him, destroying his will to suspend the time for even a moment longer.

He came to her then, the thunderous beating of his heart matching hers. They moved together, answering the blissful, raging heat of their desires, soaring toward the heavens on wings of ecstasy. A fierce enchantment encased them, cradled them within its arms, until both thought wildly that they would perish from the rapture of their love, and a long while passed before they lay exhausted in each other's embrace.

Nestled in the crook of his arm, Amber lovingly traced the hard muscles of his chest. An impish gleam appeared in her eyes when she rasped a long nail over the male nipple and saw it respond, his body tensing from her play. A lean, brown hand shot out to capture hers and draw it to his lips.

"Unless you wish to spend the night here and chance the people of the village finding us in the morning light, I suggest you tread lightly, my love," he warned softly. "I am not too modest to oblige."

Amber giggled and moved up to nibble on his earlobe.

"Ouch!" he cried out when her sharp teeth found their mark. "Pray tell, have I mistaken a vixen for the adoring, gentle wife I thought to have escorted here?"

Lifting up, she braced herself against his chest and smiled into his eyes. "I only wish to make certain you know I'm here," she teased.

Chuckling, he pushed a damp curl from her brow. "Have no fear of that, my sweet. I'm forever aware of your presence, even though sometimes it's only in my dreams."

"And will you always want me there?"

His dark eyes glowed lovingly. "Always," he whispered, tenderly placing a light kiss on the delicate mouth only inches from his.

Rolling from him, she snuggled closer, suddenly realizing the warmth of their passion no longer chased away the chill of the night air. She shivered.

"I suppose we should get dressed before my chattering teeth awaken the village and all the sleeping creatures we forced to share their haven," she sighed, sitting up, her arms hugged to her. Lazily, she looked out across the pond and spotted her husband's clothes where she had dropped them. She giggled.

"And what do you find so amusing now?" he asked, rising up on one elbow.

Her slender finger pointed toward the cause.

"Mmmm," he replied, the corner of his mouth twisting resignedly. "I don't suppose I could talk you into getting them for me, since you are the reason they are so far away?"

Her blond curls shook in the silvery moonlight.

"I didn't think so," he sighed, coming to his feet. "Well, I never really got the swim I wanted anyway." Without the slightest hesitation, he walked knee deep into the water, then dove beneath the surface, emerging several moments later on the far side. Spinning around, he waved back at Amber and dove again.

Laughing, she waved in return, knowing he hadn't seen, and watched him splash about until another chill shook her body. Deciding this sort of sport was better left for sunny times, she quickly stood and lifted the damp gown from the place where they had made love. A soft smile touched her lips as the cloth fell into place around her trim figure, and, although the wet fabric did little to warm her, she ran her hands over it, thinking that, in a way, Nicholas surrounded her. Wondering if he might think the same, she turned back to watch him dress, a slight frown wrinkling her brow when she found the pond empty, only the ripples of the waterfall marring its smooth surface. Had he already clothed himself and denied her the pleasure of observing? Her eyes quickly looked to the spot, and her frown deepened, for in the muted light she could see the suede boots still lying on the ground.

You tease, she thought, the gleam returning to her eyes. *Well, I can play, too.* Lifting the heavy skirts, she walked to the edge of the pond where it narrowed to a thin stream, carefully stepping on the rocks protruding from it, and crossed to the other side, her eyes constantly looking to the trees surrounding her for any sign of his presence. When she reached the boots, she stooped to retrieve them and started back toward the pond.

"If you don't come out right now, I'll toss these in and you'll never be able to wear them again," she called, stopping abruptly at the snapping of a twig behind her. Grinning, she turned around slowly. "I thought you'd see it my way. . . ."

Although partly hidden in the shadow of the trees, the size of the figure standing there instantly told Amber that Nicholas and she had not been the only ones seeking the privacy of the pond. Her heart thumped, fear instinctively prickling the hairs on the back of her neck, and she guardedly surveyed the area for any hint of her husband's whereabouts. Had he seen the intruder too and taken refuge in the woods to allow himself the advantage? She could only pray he had.

"W-what do you want?" she asked, straining in the darkness to see the trespasser's face. "W-who are you?"

The immense form moved forward a step, his white-clad body illuminated in the glow of the moon, and before he ventured into full light, a shock of recognition bolted through her.

"Yaakob!" The name trembled from her lips.

Knees weak, Amber fought to stay upright. Had he come alone? Or were there others lurking about? The question had barely formed in her thoughts before the dark green of the forest was dotted with other figures, none nearly as huge as the man she faced, but just as threatening.

Fearing for her life, she stumbled backward. Knowing she had to escape, she spun around and raced off toward the road, brought to a painful, abrupt halt when one of the bandits seized a fistful of her hair and yanked back. Tears instantly sprang to her eyes, and she frantically fought to grab hold of the hand dragging her toward the circle of men, caught off balance when he twirled her around and threw her to the ground at Yaakob's feet. Tiny rocks gouged her hands and knees, but she willed herself not to let him see her cry and bravely lifted her chin to stare up at him, praying Nicholas had gone for help.

"Y-you can't expect to get away," she said courageously. "The village is well guarded. Even now our men surround you." She shook but not from the cold night air, rather from unholy terror.

A thick arm raised to motion one of his men forward, and in the next instant, the lifeless form of another was hurled to the ground beside her. Amber's stomach convulsed and she quickly clamped her hands over her mouth to keep from retching, for there, close enough to reach out to, lay the body of one of the village men, his throat cut and his chest covered with bright red blood. She squeezed her eyes shut, blocking out the sight, but the image burned vividly in her mind. Blindly, she inched away, forcing herself to think about her survival and Nicholas.

"W-what do you want?" she half whispered, half choked.

When he didn't answer, she willed herself to look up at him, cringing at the evil smile he bestowed upon her. He squinted down at her, the brown eye shadowed by his brows, the glassy white orb sightless and unmoving.

"You," his gravelly voice droned out. "Yaakob want you."

Amber's body shook uncontrollably. "But . . . but Ronen won't . . ."

His throaty, roaring laughter crescendoed in her ears, striking every nerve, and Amber felt a horror she had never imagined to experience in her wildest of nightmares. She covered her ears with her hands to stifle the sound, her fearful eyes watching as he jerked a hand forward again in silent command. Several men stepped aside while two others dragged the motionless body of her husband from the protection of the thick pine trees.

Nicholas. His name caught in her throat, tears returning to burn her eyes, and she sat unmoving, certain they had killed him.

Held by his arms, his head fell forward and she could see the oozing gash at the base of his skull. And when they tossed him down, he rolled enough so that she could watch the gentle rise and fall of his chest. He lived! But for how long? Many thoughts raced through her head, all whirling and consuming, until she felt she would explode from sheer confusion. Brushing back the hair from her brow, she continued to watch the unconscious body of her husband, a selfless compromise surfacing in her troubled mind.

"Leave him here, untouched, and I will do whatever you want," she proposed, her voice weak in her own ears, and barely more than a whisper.

"No."

His answer cut through her as sharply as if he'd run a blade through her heart.

"He come," the voice thundered. "He will pay for shaming Yaakob. Then he die!"

"No, you mustn't," Amber screamed, lunging forward to crawl on hands and knees toward Nicholas. But before she had traveled very far, Yaakob's boot caught her shoulder, painfully

542

knocking her back to the ground. Tears flowing down her face, she fought to rise again, a frightened moan tearing from her throat when the barbarian bent, locked a huge fist in the thick mass of her blond hair, and hauled her to her feet. Her eyes failed to focus before the broad, meaty knuckles of his hand crashed against her temple, snapping her head to one side. Blackness claimed her instantly, and she crumpled to the ground.

High above the desert floor, the bright, glowing orange of the midday sun cast its blistering rays earthward. An ocean of blue sky met the sand-swept horizon, blanketing the rolling hills of barren wasteland with an eerie stillness. Nestled in the endless sea of arid terrain, a single oasis broke the monotonous void. Clustered around the small pool of water and palms, a dozen brightly colored tents stood protectively guarding the rare treasure in an otherwise bleak expanse. From beneath the shaded canopy of the largest tent, pale blue eyes filled with tears and helplessness continually watched the still figure of a man staked out in the sand and left there to die a slow, agonizing death. Her wrists tied with leather straps and fastened to a pole at the opening of Yaakob's lodgings, Amber sat rigidly, praying that each breath Nicholas took would not be his last.

A tear spilled over her black lashes and fell to her chin as she recalled the journey that had brought them to this place, The band had traveled throughout the night, leaving the foothills of the Atlas Mountains at daybreak and continuing on into the desert in the full light of the piercing sun. She had regained consciousness only a few minutes after Yaakob had struck her when she was roughly hoisted to the broad rump of a stallion, her arms tied behind her, a gag stifling any chance for her to call out a warning to the villagers. Her head pounded from the attack, her left cheek swollen and trickling blood, but she soon forgot her own pain when she saw Yaakob's men heartlessly throw the limp body of her husband across the back of one of their horses and secure his feet and hands beneath the belly of the animal. The caravan had not stopped to rest a single time during the entire trip, and Amber worried frantically that the blow to Nicholas's head had shortened Yaakob's wish to see his foe suffer longer. But when the group had dismounted in the center of the camp and untied Nicholas to pull him from the saddle, he had suddenly come to life, bracing himself against the steed to kick out with both feet to send his captors sprawling on the ground. Two more joined the fracas, landing blows to Nicholas's stomach, rallied by a stinging punch to their jaws. They too stumbled back, surprised by the man's agility after such a grueling ride. But their admiration had been only momentary, for together the small team of men then spread out, surrounding their attacker. The struggle had lasted only a few short minutes, for, being outnumbered as he was, Nicholas was quickly subdued and brought to his knees, his arms twisted cruelly behind his back.

Yaakob had remained on his horse, watching with quiet interest, never doubting this man's strong will to survive, and silently wondered how many days would pass before this stranger to his land would surrender to a spirit more powerful than any of them. Dispassionately, he had glanced over at the stunningly beautiful woman who had witnessed it all, taken note of the misery reflected in her eyes, and then waved his men off to carry out his sentence.

The hill warrior had purposely chosen a spot for Nicholas to lie where Amber could see him, yet far enough away to prevent any chance for them to speak with each other. She had stubbornly refused a drink of water or their offering of food, for in her heart she had decided to die with her husband rather than live a moment without him. But as the sun reached its summit, it became more difficult for her to swallow, the heat of the desert draining what strength she had. Even now, when she wanted to cry, no tears would moisten her eyes, and she could only imagine the agony Nicholas endured.

An hour had passed since the last time he had looked at her, and she forced her eyes to watch for the labored movement of his chest. He had been stripped of his shirt, and Amber could see the bruises beneath his right arm. Perspiration glistened over his entire body and the leather straps around his wrists

544

and ankles cut into his flesh. Her own skin burned where she had absently tugged at the restraints, wanting desperately to free herself and go to him.

Lifting her gaze toward the heavens, she silently prayed that his death would come quickly, vowing that her own life would end by her own hand. She closed her eyes, resting her brow against the wooden pole that forbid her escape. It would take too long for Sean to find them.

"He is strong man."

Amber jumped at the sound of Yaakob's voice behind her, but refused to look at him.

"He will die slowly, Yaakob think. He not want to leave you." A sinister laugh bounced off each vertebra of Amber's spine. "He is fool. He should know Yaakob would not let him have you. You are mine."

Her eyes still clamped shut, she could feel his mammoth presence standing beside her.

"She is mine, Ronen!" he shouted, then laughed again and turned to crouch at her side. Catching her chin in a cruel grip he lifted her face toward him, squeezing her jaw until she opened her eyes. "You not laugh at Yaakob," he sneered. "Yaakob not like that."

Terror shaking her, Amber forced the words from her lips. "I didn't. I never laughed—"

"You did!" he roared, angrily bringing the back of his opened right hand across her cheek. She fell away, dangling from the short piece of rope tied to the pole above her head. He seized a fistful of her tangled hair and jerked her back, squinting his good eye at her. "You lie. You always lie to Yaakob. You take lovers and laugh at Yaakob."

Fear and confusion darkened her eyes. "I have no lovers."

A smile kinked the grotesque scar on his face. "No more. Yaakob kill them all, one . . . by . . . one." Shoving her from him, he arduously pushed his massive frame to his feet and stood glaring out at the proud figure of his enemy, now motionless and bound by ropes in the hot, burning sand.

*   *   *

The roaring blaze of the camp's fire cast dancing images against Amber's closed eyelids, the hearty laughter of the men testing her sanity. The long torrid hours of the afternoon had finally exhausted themselves, bringing with day's end a cold, black night, and she shivered, certain Nicholas suffered more. Slowly, she looked out to where she knew he lay, but in the darkness she could not distinguish his shape. In the dying embers of sunset she had imagined the blisters already formed on his lips and brow, knowing full well that the sweltering heat of the sun's rays had burned the flesh across his chest and belly. It had to be pure torture now, his body feverish and lying in the cold night air, and she wondered how he managed not to call out or simply moan deliriously. Again she fought with the ropes tied tightly around her wrists, tears blurring her vision when her efforts awarded her nothing.

Uproarious guffaws from the band surrounding the fire drew her attention and she absently ran a moist tongue over her parched lips as she watched the group share a wineskin, spilling more of the dark red liquid down their chins than into their mouths. Weak from exhaustion, she sagged against her bonds, her head bobbing, and sleep overcame her instantly.

"Wake up, woman!"

Amber bolted upright at the startling command, the bright rays of morning light blinding her. Raising her bound hands to shade her eyes, she squinted in the direction of the voice, her head throbbing, her body weary from a lack of food and water and a comfortable night's rest. For a moment nothing made sense, her foggy mind reacting slowly until her gaze rested on the menacing face staring back at her. A devious smile twisted Yaakob's mouth, and with stark reality Amber jerked her head around to look at her husband, certain his life had drained away during the night. A lump knotted her throat, her heart aching, and with great effort she kept from crying out. He lay so perfectly still, the wide muscular chest unmoving, his eyes closed and his head rested to one side.

"Come," Yaakob jeered, pulling a dagger from his waistband. Effortlessly, he sliced the cord from the post, returned the knife to its scabbard, and wound the end of the leather strap around his hand, yanking Amber to her feet. "Yaakob want you to see him."

Her wobbly legs buckled beneath her when the monstrous beast tugged on the rope, and Amber tumbled to the ground, particles of sand clinging to her damp skin and scraping the tender flesh of her elbows and knees. An involuntary whimper escaped her and she fought hard not to let the tears stream down her face. This savage wanted her to suffer, to beg for his pity, to beg him to have mercy on her, but she had willfully decided long ago that she would never give him the satisfaction. If he intended to murder her husband, he would find no weak-spirited woman groveling at his feet. With every ounce of strength she had, she awkwardly pushed herself up, stumbling forward when he pulled on the restraint once more.

Moving from the protection of the canopy, Amber flinched when the hot sun hit the exposed skin of her shoulders and arms, the fiery sand burning her bare feet. Until that moment, she hadn't truly realized how horribly Nicholas must have suffered. Locking her gaze on him, tears glistening in her eyes, she failed to notice the wineskin Yaakob retrieved from the cold campsite of the night before.

Dragging Amber with him, they climbed the huge mound of sand where her husband lay, halfway up. The climb took great effort for Yaakob, his opened mouth sucking in each breath and his linen attire instantly soaked with sweat. Each step became more difficult as his mammoth weight shoved him ankle deep in the sand, and he had to pause several times to still the rapid beat of his heart. But the sight of his longtime enemy lying bare chested and spread-eagle in the hot, blazing sun drove him on, twisting his pudgy features into an evil grimace. His discomfort seemed to vanish as the distance grew shorter, his strides quickening, and when they stood at Nicholas's feet, Yaakob yanked hard on the rope, spinning his captive around to fall facedown in the sand.

Numbly, Amber pushed herself up, brushing the particles from her mouth and cheek against her shoulder, forcing herself not to look at her husband. She would rather remember the way he had looked that night at the pond after they had made love. Squeezing her eyes shut, the image played upon her mind, and she withdrew into her own little world, unaware of the man who moved closer to Nicholas.

Brutally, Yaakob kicked out a large boot at Nicholas's thigh. "Yaakob think you not dead, Ronen," he laughed menacingly, then stood back to watch.

The still form lay motionless, unaffected by Yaakob's attack, and the warrior's thick brow wrinkled disapprovingly. Seizing the wineskin by the neck, he popped the cork free and stepped in, one foot between Nicholas's parted knees, the other near his waist. Leaning slightly, Yaakob tipped the pouch and allowed only a trickle of the liquid to drain out and fall on the man's dry, blistered mouth.

From somewhere in the black void of Nicholas's oblivion, he heard the laughter of a woman, the vision of her shining face and pale blue eyes illuminated in his dreams. He smiled in return, reaching out in the hazy glow of his subconscious to draw her near. Golden locks cascaded over the silken skin of her bare shoulders and rested invitingly against the full bosom. He placed a fingertip to her chin, lifting her mouth to his, but she giggled and eluded his embrace. The white satin of her gown floated breathlessly around her as she twirled and danced before him, a slender finger raised to beckon him to follow. Laughter trailing from his own lips, he chased after her, running effortlessly through the gray spiraling fog that encased them. Swooping her in his arms, he lifted her high in the air, his love for her glowing in his eyes.

"I love you, Nicholas," he heard her whisper. "I love you."

Moaning, he opened his mouth to speak when suddenly she was taken from him. Frantic, he searched the swirling mist closing in on him, darkness threatening to separate them. Hands raised to fight off the attack, he felt himself falling, tumbling deeper and deeper. Then, when all hope seemed lost, he saw a light, faint and distant, heralding the way. He began to climb, the orange ball glowing brighter, hotter. His strength fading, he willed his body to continue, stretching up to touch the yellow orb, jolted back when it burned his fingertips, and he hung suspended. Uncertain of which path to take, for one promised eternal rest, the other pain and suffering, he suddenly felt drawn, knowing where Amber waited, and he turned his face to the sun once more. The steady rays blinded him, scorched his brow and cheeks. His mouth became dry, his lips blistered, but he continued to struggle. *Amber, where are you?* his inner voice called out. *I'm thirsty, so terribly thirsty.* Suddenly she appeared before him, a wine goblet held in one hand. Kneeling, she touched the glass to his unmoving lips.

Nicholas's eyes fluttered open. His vision blurred, he fought to focus on the figure standing over him.

"So, you are not dead," the deep voice boomed, and reality came crashing down around him.

His body weakened to the point of near collapse, Nicholas forced himself to stay awake. His tongue thick, he wanted to speak but couldn't, and instead he slowly turned his head to gaze through half-closed lids at the tent where his wife had been held prisoner. Though difficult to distinguish at first, he soon realized Amber was no longer there. Had Yaakob killed her? Dear God, he couldn't stand the thoughts that he had not been able to help her, protect her. A spark of anger surged through him and he tried to lift one hand, to tear the leather straps loose, but the effort only quivered his fingers.

"You look for this?" Yaakob laughed sinisterly.

His dark brown eyes dulled with pain found his enemy once more, and a hint of relief flashed through them when Nicholas saw the frail beauty slumped against the enormous man. Yaakob had nearly lifted Amber from her feet with one arm wrapped around her waist, a fistful of her hair caught in his hand, cruelly pulling her head back.

"See? He not dead," Yaakob mocked, glaring into her face. Grabbing her chin, he jerked her face around to look at her husband.

Nicholas's heart lurched once he saw the bruised and swollen cheek of his wife. Her eyes glistened with tears, her beautiful golden hair was dull and matted, and he sensed from the dryness of her lips that she had not been given water. But what surprised and worried him more was that the spark of stubbornness, that unwavering spunk, no longer shone in her eyes. It seemed as if she had given up, and he couldn't understand why. Had Yaakob or his men abused her beyond endurance? Broken her strong will to survive no matter what the crisis? God, he hoped not. He needed her now more than ever, for if they were to come out of this alive, she would have to be clearheaded, as fiery as the first day he had met her. He closed his eyes to moisten them and struggled to open them once more. *I love you, Amber,* his mind declared, but no sound escaped his parched tongue.

Amber felt her body tense when her gaze fell upon her husband. Every ounce of exposed flesh was burned by the sun's intense rays, his lips were dry and cracked, and blisters covered his brow and one cheek. Particles of sand clung to his beard, and at one corner of his mouth she could see the dried blood of a wound inflicted during the men's attempt to subdue him. The straps around his wrists and ankles had cut into the skin, and she could see where he had rubbed the flesh raw in his struggles to free himself. His eyes lacked their usual twinkle, but even in his weakened state she could read his love for her in them. Her chin quivered. She didn't want him to die, but she didn't want him to suffer. The roughness of Yaakob's attire scratched her tender skin as he held her to him, and it gave Amber a sudden ray of hope, her spirit returning.

"Yaakob," she said softly, and silently prayed God would give her the strength to see this through. "May we go back to your tent now? I grow weary in the sun and have a matter I wish to discuss with you."

The brown eye closed tightly. "Yaakob thought you wanted to see Ronen."

"I did and I have," she replied, forcing a smile. "But not for the reasons you assumed." She paused, wondering if he would believe her. "Put me down and I'll explain."

The nomad shifted his gaze to his prisoner stretched out helplessly before him. "You not care if he die?"

Hoping the barbarian could not sense the truth mirrored in her eyes, she quickly lowered her lids. "No," she responded

550

quietly. "And it's the reason I wish to speak privately with you."

The woman's answer not only surprised Yaakob, but disappointed him. Half of the pleasure in watching Ronen die had come from the thought that she would scream for mercy to spare her lover's life, and he had played the scene over and over in his mind. She would fall to her knees, wrap her arms around his legs, and beg. After all these years, Linnea would be humbled before him, and he would taste sweet revenge. His thick brow wrinkled sourly, and without warning he let go of the slender form dangling in his hold. His evil glare settled on the woman struggling to rise.

"Why? Why you not care?" he demanded, his booted foot knocking her back to the hot sand.

Amber had executed many schemes in her life, most of which had been brilliantly handled, but none had meant the immediate saving of another's life, and she knew every word she spoke had to be the best performance she had ever given. Pushing the thick mass of hair from her face, she smiled up at the man who held her husband's mere existence in his hands.

"This man, Ronen, bought me to be his slave. He took me from you. I didn't want to go with him and fought many times to escape him but always failed. He abused me, Yaakob, and I prayed someone would save me." She clasped her hands together and held them to her bosom, as if thanking the Supreme Being. "Then you came and I knew I was finally free. I don't care if he dies, because it is what he deserves."

Yaakob folded his heavy arms over his chest, staring down at her over pudgy cheeks and the thick jowls resting on his neck. "And what you want from Yaakob?"

"Nothing," she answered quickly, "only to serve you."

The sightless white eye sent an instant chill through Amber when he continued to study her quietly, but she masked the emotion with another smile.

"I will be *your* slave."

Suddenly the monstrous form threw back his head and roared with laughter, the thundering vibrations echoing loudly in her ears, and Amber wondered at the soundness of her ploy. She jumped with a start when he leaned to seize her wrist and haul her to her feet, uncertain if she should fight him or go willingly. But her answer came when he grinned victoriously down at Nicholas.

"You hear, Ronen? She is mine!"

Turning laboriously on his heels, Yaakob jerked Amber with him and started back toward his tent, unaware of the pleading look she bestowed on the pitiful face of her husband, a silent expression of her hope that he understood her intent.

Amber's gaze quickly took in the interior of the warrior's tent when he cruelly shoved her through the opening and onto the carpeted floor. Elegant rugs in a rainbow of color cushioned the sand beneath it and felt cool to the touch. In the center of the large room lay a huge bed of fur pelts and silk pillows, and on either side small tables held an assortment of daggers, swords, pistols, and numerous muskets—a small arsenal of weaponry, and Amber prayed her chance would come soon. She had hoped Yaakob would allow her the freedom of his camp with her pledge to serve him, and thus permit her a moment to arm herself when his back was turned. Although the band of cutthroats outnumbered them ten to one, Amber knew it was her only hope of saving Nicholas. Curling her feet beneath her, she sat perfectly still, watching Yaakob cross to one of the tables and toss down his dagger.

"Why you want to be my slave?" he asked, before turning back to stare at her.

Amber swallowed the knot in her throat. "Because—because you are a great warrior. A man among men." She wondered at the strange look that came over the obese man's face, but bravely continued, deciding for the moment that it was best to play on his ego. "I have heard many men fear you and women long to be in your company. I only wish—"

"Enough!" he bellowed, his sudden fury quaking his rotund body. "You lie!"

Amber fearfully shrank away, her blue eyes wide.

"Yaakob no man," he raged on. "Linnea make sure. She laugh at Yaakob's love for her. You laugh!"

Amber shook her head. "No, no, Yaakob. I don't. I think you are a great man, and any woman would be honored to have your love."

"Not Linnea," he stormed, pacing the floor of the wide tent.

Amber had no idea what troubled this man so greatly, but she sensed he harbored a pain no blade could have inflicted. Drawing up the courage to go on, she slowly came to her feet and crossed to a small table that held a brass tray, three goblets, and a pitcher. Assuming the latter contained wine, she hurriedly filled one glass and extended it to Yaakob.

"Tell me about her," she coaxed softly.

Yaakob stopped his lumbersome trek and glanced up at her in surprise. His gaze took in the beauty of her face and the offering she held. She could see the hurt he felt in the twisted expression on his mouth and suspected his tough exterior had to do with the treason of a woman called Linnea. Her hand trembled slightly when he took the glass from her.

Crossing to the opening of the tent, Yaakob stared out at the endless hills of sand. "Yaakob loved Linnea, but she hated Yaakob. She play him for fool, let him chase her until she grow tired of him. She was cruel. She had no heart. She had Yaakob gelded like dog."

Amber stifled her gasp with a hand pressed to her mouth. How could anyone be so ruthless?

"She said Yaakob would learn to leave her alone. But he only wanted to show love. He did not mean to hurt anyone."

"Who, Yaakob? Who did you hurt?"

His huge frame shook, and Amber wondered if he was crying.

"Yaakob did not know the boy who protected Linnea's door was brother. He pulled sword and Yaakob shot him down. She ordered her men to do the evil deed, then cast him off to die in the mountains." He paused and lifted the goblet to his mouth, swallowing its contents in one gulp. "But Yaakob not die," he continued in a calmer voice. "He live. And now, Linnea, you will pay for making Yaakob less than a man." He turned then to face her, and Amber felt a bolt of terrifying fear jar through her, for instead of the sadness she had seen a moment before, his face was twisted into that of a madman.

The long daylight hours slowly faded into a star-filled night
its beauty breathtaking. But for Amber it only brought the pai
of knowing that her husband would continue to suffer, hi
body raked with chills. Surely he would die before the sun ros
again.

Crouched in the far corner of the tent where she ha
remained the entire day, Amber steadily watched Yaakob pac
the floor, her hand clutching the small dagger hidden amon
the folds of her skirts. He had left her for only a brief momen
when he stepped outside into the shade of the canopy and sum
moned one of his men to bring more wine and something t
sate his hunger. But it had been long enough for her to steal th
tiny knife from the table filled with many knives and return t
her place unobserved. He had all but forgotten her presence
and she could only pray he would soon fall asleep from hi
overindulgence of wine, leaving her free to sneak from th
tent, cut the straps from Nicholas, and, with luck, secure
horse for them to ride.

Bile rose in her throat when she heard Yaakob belch loudly
his huge belly shaking, and she squeezed her eyes shut
wondering how much wine one man could drink before he fe
victim to its power. Her answer came quickly, when a lou
crash jolted her nerves and she looked up in time to see hin
stumble once more and fall headlong upon the bed of furs, th
table that had held the brass pitcher and goblets overturned, it
contents scattered about the floor. Facedown, he remaine
motionless, and Amber willed herself to stay where she was
waiting for any sign that he might still be awake. Several lon
minutes passed, and once his sonorous breathing filled the ten
Amber felt her tense muscles relax a degree. Now all she had t
do was to get to Nicholas without anyone's seeing her.

Crawling on hands and knees, she moved toward the openin
in the canvas, her gaze darting from the obese form on the be
to her goal and back again. But when Yaakob grunted an
rolled to his back Amber froze, until his mouth fell open and h
resumed his snoring even more strongly, and her heart seeme
to pound more noisily than his recital. Deciding not to wast

nother moment, she scooted through the slit in the tent and uickly surveyed her surroundings.

A fire had been started and several of the bandits hovered ear it for warmth, while others wobbled back to their lodgings oo drunk to notice anything amiss. Hastily, Amber rounded he corner of the tent to hide and gather her wits. The horses ad been tied to a rope strung up between two palms and pposite the campsite, Obtaining a steed would be difficult, nce the men sat much too near them, but she vowed she ould do it. She would free her husband, steal a horse, and by orning they would be far away from Yaakob and his band of uffians.

Keeping to the shadows, Amber half ran, half crawled hrough the thick mounds of sand toward the place where 'icholas lay. The dagger's blade clamped between her teeth to nable herself to claw her way more quickly and lessen the anger of dropping the knife in the darkness where she ouldn't find it, she fixed her eyes on her destination. Seconds eemed like hours before she had climbed the hill, falling to her nees to catch her breath and clear her thoughts, for she was ure this was the spot where Nicholas had been bound help- ssly to die. Worriedly, she glanced back down at the camp, ffirming her conviction, and tears came to her eyes. Surely hey hadn't moved him! It made no sense. Twisting, she sat own hard, taking the knife from her mouth and stretched out o brace herself on one hand, her fingers touching a protrud- g object in the sand. Her gaze flew to it immediately, already ensing that it must be one of the wooden stakes that had held er husband prisoner, and she bit her lower lip to stifle her utcry. She was too late. He had already died, and they had uried him!

"Oh, Nicholas," she moaned, long-held tears welling in her yes, blinding her. Had God chosen this to be her lot, pre- estined her love to be taken from her just when she had found ? Sobs raked her body, and she wept uncontrollably, unaware f the figure of a man starting toward her. A tear dropped from er face and fell upon the blade of the knife she held, and she tared at it for a long while. If He meant for them not to share a life together on earth, surely He would not deny their union in heaven. Both hands gripping the weapon, its sharp point held inward, she pulled it toward her breast, her tears suddenly gone.

"I love you, Nicholas," she whispered, a promise of inner peace guiding her, and she closed her eyes, her face lifted skyward. Bemused, she neither heard nor felt the presence of another until the knife was kicked from her hands and someone seized her arms, dragging her to her feet. "No!" she screamed. "I must. I *want* to die." She fought with what strength she had left, reaching up in an effort to scratch the face with her nails, her tears renewing. "I want to be with Nicholas!"

Suddenly a stinging slap to her cheek jolted Amber to awareness, and she looked up into the worried face of Sean Rafferty.

"Oh, God!" she howled, her grief overcoming her, and she collapsed in his arms, weeping deliriously.

Hugging the frail form to him, Sean silently motioned the men waiting at the top of the hill to descend upon the quiet camp and stood by to watch as his pledge of vengeance was fulfilled. One by one, the village men slit the throats of their sleeping enemy, then set fires to their tents, and seized their horses. All but Yaakob's went up in rapid flame, and Sean's mouth grew into a hard line as he glared down upon it.

"Ya will be left ta wander the desert, ya beggarly cur," Sean growled softly, "and when you're crazed with thirst, ya will know who put an end ta your murderous life."

Their task completed, the villagers gathered together, staring up at their leader to await his command. At a sharp wave of his fist, they converged on Yaakob's dwelling, and Sean turned away satisfied, swooping the young woman clutched to him in his arms.

Amber's moist cheek snuggled against his neck, Sean's hatred of the moment vanished with the need to comfort her. "Be dryin' your eyes, lass," he murmured. "I've somethin' I want ya ta see."

Her arms draped around him, she squeezed harder. "No. I don't want to see anything. I want to die. I want to be with Nicholas."

Reaching the crest of the hill, he paused, slipping one arm from beneath her knees. "And that ya will, lass," he concurred, pulling her from him.

Confused, she frowned up at him, the silver light of the moon shining in her eyes. He nodded past her, and, with great effort, fearing what he meant, she turned. There, stretched out in the sand and covered with blankets lay her husband, his eyes open and looking at her. Suddenly her head swirled, her breath left her, and Amber gave way to the darkness that claimed her mind.

Chapter Twenty-Five

Amber stood at the railing of the *Defiance*, looking out at the horizon where the blue sky met the opaque green of the sea, her face bathed in the dying glow of evening sunlight, a soft breeze playing with the long yellow curls cascading over her shoulders. By morning, if Sean was correct and the winds held steady, they would dock on the shores of Virginia and bring an end to their long journey. It was nearly four months since she had been thrown on board the ship that had taken her to a distant land, and now it plagued her only as a stubborn nightmare refusing to die. Lifting her face, she breathed in the fresh smell of salt air, the quiet peace of the ocean soothing her as she listened to the flap of the sails overhead and the splash of water as the ship's prow cut through the choppy surface of the sea. She longed to return home, to see Andrea again, yet worried her life would not be as she had prayed it would. Absently, she touched a slender hand to her flat stomach.

"Have ya told him yet, lass?"

Startled from her musings, she glanced up with a nervous smile. "Told him what, Sean?" she asked innocently, as she watched his long, lanky figure stride toward her.

His blue eyes, their corners lined with age, looked in all directions to make certain no one heard, then settled their approving gaze on the beauty standing alone at the railing. "About the babe," he said, casually drawing up at her side. He grinned when Amber's mouth fell open. "Did ya think no one would notice? Only a husband is blind to his wife's secrets."

"If you know, how can it be a secret?" she laughed, truly glad she had someone with whom to share it. She had suspected for some time, but now that the second month had come and gone without her curse, she could give no other cause.

Bending slightly, he leaned an elbow on the balustrade, hands clasped, and studied her a moment. "I may not have married meself, but I lived with me cousin and his wife long enough to know when a lass has a secret. It shows in her eyes. I saw it in Victoria's twice . . . when she carried Nicholas, and again with Katherine."

Amber tilted her head playfully. "And you knew *before* her husband?"

"Aye," he nodded quickly, then paused. "Why is it ya feel ya shouldn't tell Nicholas?"

Amber's memory clouded instantly with visions of that night she had climbed the hill of sand to free her husband and had found only the four wooden poles used to bind his hands and feet. She had thought him dead, that she would never see him again, and she had known a sorrow greater than she could bear. She had wept for him as for no other in her life, and the tiny dagger clutched in her hand had offered an end to her misery. She would never forget the look on Sean's face after he had knocked it away.

Sean Rafferty and a virtual army of villagers had followed the tracks Yaakob's group had left, surrounding the camp in the late afternoon of the second day. It had taken all the strength Sean had not to storm the enemy and free his cousin's son once he saw Nicholas bound so helplessly in the hot, blistering sand, but he had worried that such an assault would endanger the young woman tied outside Yaakob's tent. They had waited until dark, and for the men around the fire to fall drunk before they silently climbed over the dune separating them from Nicholas. He was unconscious, but Sean soon realized that he would survive given proper treatment and time to rest. Gently and in haste, they freed Nicholas of his bonds and carried him to safety.

It had been decided that Nasser would sneak into the encampment, posing as one of Yaakob's warriors, and locate himself near Amber to wait for the right moment to free her. But when he set out to execute the plan they had seen a shadowed figure moving toward them, crouched as if to remain unseen by those near the tents. It only took them a second to recognize her, and they had fallen back to wait until she was near enough to call out to her and reveal their presence. Many times Sean had shoved the memory of that night from his thoughts, for he knew that if he had lingered only a moment longer, Amber would have run the blade through her heart.

It had taken over a week for Nicholas to regain his strength and be declared well enough for the long ocean voyage home, the only evidence of his gruesome ordeal being a small scar over his right brow, left there by the blazing sun. Amber had remained by his side the entire time, and her love for him glowed in the sparkling depths of her eyes. But now, as the ship neared the shoreline of Virginia, a new worry beset her.

Taking a deep breath, Amber cast her gaze out to sea. "He said once that he feared going home, that there were a lot of memories there."

"And did he happen ta say if they were good or bad?" Sean asked, taking in the quiet beauty of her profile.

"No. But our time together there was based on deceit. I want him to learn first if his love for me is as strong as Ronen's—then about the child."

Sean tilted his head to better see her. "And what if he decides he doesn't love ya? Ya will still carry his child no matter what his feelin's for ya."

Amber looked down at her hands resting on the thick wooden railing before her. "I know. But if I tell him about the child first, I will never truly learn if he loved me or simply the mother of his child."

"'Tis no difference, I think," Sean argued, pushing himself up. "Lass, how many times must the man prove his love for ya?"

Amber blinked back a tear that suddenly filled one corner of her eye. "Don't scold, Sean. I need a friend right now."

"And ya have it," he replied softly, reaching out to cover one of her hands with his. "And this friend is tellin' ya the truth. He does love ya. I know him better'n anyone, lass. He loved ya from the first and will carry that love until his last breath. Believe me."

"I want to," she answered quietly. "But I guess I must see it for myself rather than have someone tell me."

He studied her a moment, glanced down at the deck, and sighed. "Aye, I can be understandin' your need." He looked back at her, a twinkle glowing in his blue eyes. "But I hope ya discover it soon. Otherwise the babe will spoil it for ya."

Amber smiled surrenderingly up at him. "Sean Rafferty, if your cousin was half the man you are, it would have been an honor to know him."

"Ho-ho!" Sean laughed, his face lighting up with the compliment. "I be wishin' Dru could hear ya say that. I always walked in his shadow, wantin' to be just like him, and ta know someone is thinkin' his little cousin might outdo him would have given me great pleasure. I never would have let him live it down." His smile faded, his eyes sad as he thought about the past. "Of course, me cousin would have said there was never any doubt. He was a selfless man." Turning, he leaned against the railing and stared out to sea. "I miss him, and someday I'll see his murderer pay."

What had been said to please the old Irishman had turned to grief, and Amber suddenly regretted being the cause. Quietly she slipped her arm into his. "Tell me about him, how he lived, loved, and . . ."

"Died?" Sean finished. He patted the hand resting on his arm reassuringly and hugged it to his broad chest, casting his gaze out to the whitecapped waters once more. "He took life as it came, one day at a time, enjoyin' it, makin' life miserable for all of us." He winked down at her. "That was, of course, until he met Victoria. She was his match, and hardly a day went by that they didn't test each other. Those were good times. Then Victoria died givin' birth ta their daughter. Dru changed after that. He became more serious. But he didn't change enough to be careless. That's why Nicholas and I think he was murdered."

"Why, Sean? What happened?"

"There was a fire at the warehouse. The authorities said Dru had fallen asleep at his desk and knocked over a lamp. But I never believed it. And when Nicholas came home, he didn't either. We just could never be provin' it." He sighed heavily. "That was over two years ago."

"Had there been trouble at the warehouse before it happened?"

He shrugged. "Not directly. But there was word of gunrunners in the area, men who sold guns to the Indians. I can't put me finger on it, but I suspect it had somethin' ta do with Dru's reason for bein' at the warehouse that night. I had sailed ta Boston the week before, but we had talked about it earlier." His tawny brows knit. "Damn, I wish I had never gone."

"Sean, you can't take on the responsibility for what happened," Amber argued compassionately, a small hand squeezing the larger.

"Aye, but 'tis a guilt your husband carries too," he returned. "The lad blames himself for not bein' there when his father needed him."

Amber shook her head in obvious disagreement. "When someone we love dies, we all take on some guilt for something we should have done. It's only natural. But we shouldn't let it eat at us. They wouldn't have wanted those they left behind to live out our lives regretting the past."

A long while elapsed before Sean turned to look at her. "A rare treasure ya are, lass, with the wisdom of a scholar. So why is it ya can't see the answers ta your own problems?"

A smile teased the corners of her mouth until, unable to hold it back, Amber burst into laughter. "Because I'm as stubborn as any Irishman I know," she bantered. "Have you anything to say to that?"

One shoulder jutted upward. "So ya have one minor flaw. 'Tis somethin' I can be overlookin'." He pulled her into the circle of his arms, and they studied the fiery glow of the sunset, unaware of the figure in the shadow that approached them from behind.

"Somehow I knew the minute my back was turned that someone else would try to steal my wife away," came the low, accusing voice.

Amber started to turn, smiling, but Sean held her steady. "Just ignore him, lass. Maybe he'll go away."

"Never, you scoundrel," Nicholas chaffed. "I've saved her from the hands of more foolish men before, and I see little challenge now."

Sean glanced down at his companion with a secretive smile. "Listen ta who he be callin' foolish. On me worst day, I could be pinnin' back his ears."

"On your best, you'd have trouble finding them," Nicholas rallied.

Sean squinted playfully. "Now he's gone and done it, lass. He's called me out." Turning with Amber still held tightly in his arms, he added, "but suppose we let your wife decide and save ya from an awful beatin'."

Although he teased, Sean had little doubt who his young, beautiful partner would choose, just as he had never questioned his cousin's decision to return to America and ask Victoria's hand in marriage. The love of both couples had been unwavering, strong enough to withstand any trials thrown in their way. Unobserved, he raised his eyes toward the heavens, certain Dru and Victoria watched approvingly.

Amber's eyes softened with a loving grace when her gaze fell upon the man who had come to claim her, and she hesitated a moment to allow herself the pleasure of appraising his handsomeness. The warmth of fading sunlight fell across his face, enhancing his rugged features and lacing his dark hair with threads of gold. He had donned a collarless white shirt, its sleeves full and billowing to his wrists, cut low over his breastbone to expose the dark mass of curls beneath. Tan-colored breeches clung to his well-proportioned thighs, with beige stockings and brown shoes completing his attire. At her insistence he had kept the beard, its thick richness failing to hide the strong line of his jaw, while constantly reminding them both of their time of discovery. But it was the sparkle in his brown eyes that held her, the unspoken pledge of commitment, and she suddenly wondered how she could ever have doubted him. His arms opened to welcome her, and Amber quickly obliged, snuggling closer against his broad chest as they turned to watch the blazing orange ball slowly descend into the sea, setting the water's surface aflame and spreading a quiet peace throughout the stillness of their world.

The *Defiance* had been spotted long before the huge vessel dropped several of her sails to bring the ship to compromise and skim effortlessly toward the docks near Williamsburg. A crowd had gathered, anxiously awaiting their arrival and word on the fate of Amber Chandler, a cheer going up when one observer spotted the delicate beauty at the railing wrapped within the protective arm of her husband.

The crew set to work securing the brigantine once it neared the docks, tossing off guide lines to men waiting on the pier, all sails dropped and tied with lanyards. After what seemed an eternity to all who watched impatiently, the gangplank was lowered and the passengers on board excitedly departed to a hearty round of applause and the shouts of good wishes from the gathering of townsfolk.

The first to reach Amber and Nicholas were the smiling Mathew Calloway and his wife, tears of relief streaming down the woman's face and glistening in Mathew's eyes.

"Oh, Mr. Chandler, we're so glad to see you're all right," he said enthusiastically amidst the shouts of a dozen others, shaking Nicholas's hand and bringing a wide grin to the younger man's face when it appeared Mathew would never let go. "And we prayed every day you would find your wife." He smiled over at Amber, who returned it with one of her own.

"Thank you, Mathew," Nicholas nodded. "But I'm afraid neither of us would be here if it wasn't for Sean." He gave Amber a gentle squeeze.

"Mr. Rafferty?" the man echoed, then caught sight of the Irishman descending the gangplank toward them.

Nicholas leaned to whisper. "Yes, and I'll tell you about it later, but whatever you do, don't let on to him that I feel that way. I'd never live it down." He turned slightly to acknowledge the greetings of several merchant friends and their wives,

Amber still held possessively to him.

Mathew punched his wire-rimmed glasses back on his nose, his lined brow furrowing. "Yes, sir," he replied, glancing over at Martha for a clue to his employer's meaning. But his wife only shrugged.

Of a sudden a squeal crescendoed above the hum of the crowd, and Nicholas and Amber turned their attention in its direction, instantly spotting the slender, blond-haired woman fighting her way toward them.

"Andrea!" Amber screamed, breaking away from Nicholas. Her eyes clouded with tears of joy, Amber frantically pushed through the tangled web of people separating them. Suddenly the way opened up, and the two women ran to the outstretched arms of the other, hugging and crying and chattering in unison until they both burst into laughter.

"Oh, Amber, I was so afraid I'd never see you again," Andrea moaned, wiping the tears from her face with the back of her gloved hand.

"There were many times I doubted it myself," Amber laughed, absently tucking a stray curl back beneath her sister's bonnet. "If I could have found a way, I would have sent word."

"I know," Andrea nodded, staring at her twin a moment. Relief flooding over her again, she quickly pulled her sister to her once more and squeezed as if she feared her mind played tricks and she held a stranger in her arms. "I missed you," she whispered with a new rush of tears.

"And I you," Amber guaranteed.

They remained clutched in the embrace until the trance was broken by a polite clearing of the throat. They parted to find the approving smile of Amber's husband, their mirror-image likeness breathtaking to all who watched.

"Oh, Mr. Chandler," Andrea cried, rushing to him to throw her arms around his neck and present him with a bold kiss on his mouth.

Stunned, yet pleased, Nicholas drew back slowly, a wider grin separating his lips. "If we're to be so intimate, shouldn't you at least call me Nicholas?" he teased, bringing an instant flush to the young woman's face and hearty guffaws from those standing near the trio.

Her gaze darted from him to her sister, then to the strings of her purse held in her hands, fighting to ignore the smiling faces of so many strangers. "I don't mean to seem too forward . . . Nicholas . . . but I promised myself I would do that if you brought my sister back to me."

Winking at Amber, he tenderly placed a lean arm around Andrea's shoulders. "Then you were too quick to comply, my sweet sister-in-law."

Andrea glanced up worriedly.

"I brought her back, but I'm afraid she's decided to live with *me*."

The crowd cheered wildly, but Andrea's chin sagged, failing to recognize his jest. "Oh, I didn't mean—" She looked helplessly at Amber. "You know I never—" She stared up at Nicholas again, her mouth open, but no words escaped her.

Coming to the rescue, Amber quickly pulled her sister away from her tormenter. "Pay him no mind, Andrea," she declared, sending him a disapproving curl of one lip. "Living with barbarians has left him a little touched." She tapped a fingertip to her temple and a ripple of laughter floated through the group of listeners before most turned away to allow the sisters a little privacy.

"Barbarians?" Andrea gasped. "What do you mean?"

"I'll explain later. Right now, I'd like to go home. You'll come too, won't you?" she begged.

"I'd love to, but I promised Seth I'd come home just as soon as I found out you were safe. I've been staying at the Chesterfield House for over a month now."

Amber straightened in surprise, glanced up at Nicholas, then turned back, truly seeing her twin for the first time. The light pink cotton of her gown added color to her usually pale complexion, and she wore a bonnet of the same hue. She wore white lace gloves of the same fabric that trimmed the sleeves of the dress, and Amber realized that it would have taken their father a year of scrimping and saving to afford such fine clothes. And they certainly couldn't have paid for even a single night in Williamsburg's finest inn. She frowned.

"What's wrong?" Andrea implored, noticing Amber's dismay.

"Where . . . how . . ." Her hand swept the length of the full-skirted gown, and Andrea's eyes brightened immediately.

"Seth bought it for me."

"Seth?" Amber's frown deepened. He more than anyone lacked the funds.

"Yes," Andrea nodded, then grinned devilishly over at Nicholas. "And you may call me Mistress Tyler."

Amber's mouth fell open instantly. "Oh, Andrea!" she exclaimed, quickly pulling her sister to her. "I'm so happy for you." Releasing her, Amber stepped back to slip an arm around her husband's waist. "We both are."

"Somehow this announcement doesn't surprise me," Nicholas smiled warmly, resting his arm across Amber's shoulders. "How long has it been?"

"Almost four months now," Andrea declared proudly, then her smile faded. "He asked me shortly after you were kidnapped, Amber. He said he couldn't bear the thought of anything happening to me. And you know what?" she continued excitedly, in a sudden change of mood. "You and I were named in Nathaniel Cromwell's will. We have enough money to support our husbands now."

Amber felt as if every ounce of strength had been drained from her, and she sagged against her husband, recalling the conversation they had had about Von Buren and his reasons for wanting Andrea as his wife. "Then the baron told the truth about Cromwell's will," she whispered.

"It appears so," Nicholas replied, his dark brows drawn together. "But I'd like to know how he came by such knowledge before anyone else."

"Who?" Andrea broke in, failing to understand why her news brought such a strange exchange of words.

"It's not important right now," Amber smiled, avoiding the subject, and gave Nicholas a secret squeeze, hoping he understood that she preferred not to trouble her sister with such information. Holding out a hand toward Andrea, Amber pulled her sister within her loving hold, her husband still clasped in her other arm, and pointed them toward the main street in town. "If you and Seth have come into so much wealth, where are you living now?"

"Oh, you'll never believe it, Amber," Andrea giggled. "On the Cromwell plantation."

"What?" Amber rallied, stopping abruptly.

"Yes. He left us everything. His land, money, slaves . . . everything." Andrea pulled away to stand before her sister, her pretty face wrinkled in worry. "You don't mind, do you? I mean half of it is yours."

"Of course not," Amber quickly assured her. "I have my own home now . . . with my husband."

Andrea grinned happily. "I told Seth you'd feel that way. I think we argued about it for a week." She looked down at her hands. "It's the only fight we've had. Listen," she beamed, smiling up at the couple again, "I know you're both very tired from your voyage, and I must get home, so let's agree to have dinner at my house in a couple of days. I'm sure Seth would like to talk with Nicholas." She laughed. "He's never run a plantation before, you know, and I think he could use some advice." She paused, her head tilted to one side as she studied her twin and the handsome man at her side. "I'm so happy you're back, Amber. But I'm happier still that you've finally found someone to love." She leaned to place a kiss on Amber's cheek, then straightened. "I'll send a carriage for you in two days. All right?"

But when Amber took a breath to agree, Andrea cut her off. "No excuses, you hear?" She waved a gloved hand, whirled in a rustle of petticoats and cotton, and hurried through the crowd, which had begun to disperse.

"I guess everything turned out for the best," Nicholas said quietly, his gaze locked on the trim figure of his wife's sister. "And before we go, I really should talk with Mathew and Sean a moment. Someone should send word to Grandmother that we've arrived safely. You don't mind, do you?"

Amber shook her head, tilting her cheek upward to accept his kiss on the corner of her mouth. But her eyes remained trained on the well-dressed shape of her sister. She couldn't really say why, but something seemed amiss.

A quiet darkness settled over the stately mansion nestled in the woods at the edge of town, a full moon casting silver light through the profusion of trees and bathing the earth in an unspoken air of peace. The occupants of the Chandler house had retired to their bedchambers an hour before, exhausted from the day filled with visits by friends and acquaintances wishing them luck and expressing their delight and relief to find the couple safe and at home once more. But in the shadows of a huge oak tree fifty feet from the manor lurked the dark figure of a man cloaked in a black cape, his gaze locked on the activity inside. One by one the lights in the house fell dark, until only one window glowed yellow, and he moved quietly closer, the sound of his footfalls nothing more than the rustling of leaves in the soft night breeze.

Clad only in his breeches, Nicholas stooped before the hearth to bank the fire for the night, its ruddy glow dancing about the room. In the wide four poster bed, Amber sat propped up against several pillows, golden hair falling about her face as she read the letter she held in her hands, and when Nicholas stood to request her approval on his task, he paused to study her. The white nightdress she wore brought a pleased grin to his lips, for, gathered at the wrists with lace trim, full across her bosom and high, concealing neckline, it gave the illusion that an innocent child had sought the comfort of his bed and his protection from the evils of a terrifying nightmare. His eyes sparkled, for this was no fearful little girl but his wife in name, and now in body and soul. A soft smile played upon his features as he watched her unobserved, knowing that if he lived forever his love for her would never die, and he blinked when he felt her warm gaze upon him.

"Do you plan to stand there all night or share the bed with me and keep the chill away?" she asked invitingly, her hand patting a spot next to her.

He grinned. "I will always share your bed, madam, even when I'm old and need help getting in."

Amber giggled. "Then come and share it now. I want to read Holly's letter to you."

With no further coaxing, he shed his breeches and slipped

beneath the covers, snuggling his cool body next to the warmer one. He frowned suddenly. "Must there always be something between us?" he asked, tugging at the skirts of her nightgown.

She slapped his hand away when he pulled the cloth up to her thigh, his fingers boldly searching for the softness hidden there. "Cool your lust, you rutting knave. Right now I have other things in mind."

Brown eyes flashed disappointment and he shifted his weight, nearly crushing her beneath him. "Then let me change your mind," he murmured.

"No," Amber declared, fighting the smile that tugged at the corners of her mouth. "And unless you wish to find yourself rolled to the floor, you had better behave."

His lower lip protruded in a boyish pout. "Then grant me, at least, a kiss to tide me over."

Her blue eyes danced with mischief. "Most certainly." Her head shot up and she briskly kissed the tip of his nose, giggling when she saw him scowl. But when he began to lower his mouth, determined to have what he truly wanted, her eyes widened and she quickly shoved Holly's letter between them, hiding her face and avoiding the embrace. Several seconds ticked away, and when he didn't move or say a word Amber's curiosity got the better of her. She lowered the parchment an inch until she could peer up at him over the edge. Dark brown eyes stared back at her.

"Well, you didn't say what kind you wanted," she teased, exploding into laughter when his hands moved to her ribs and found each ticklish spot with quick fingers. "Oh, Nicholas! Stop!" she begged through her tears, her sides aching from his tormenting play.

"Not until you kiss me the way you should," he demanded roguishly.

"All right! All right!" she cried out, collapsing on the pillow when he yielded. She stared up at him a moment, wondering how she ever could have denied him, and slid her arms around his neck, pulling his mouth to hers.

The warmth of the kiss sent a flood of contentment through her and sparked the ever present embers of her passion, her mind whirling from its heady brew. She relaxed, savoring the embrace, and flipped the letter from her fingers to send it floating to the bed. She wiggled to get closer, but in the same instant Nicholas lifted his head and stared down at her.

"That's all I wanted," he grinned impishly, having felt her respond, and fell to the mattress beside her, tucking the quilt beneath him, hands locked behind his head. "Now you may read to me."

The heat of her desire darkening her face, she bolted upright in the bed at his sudden claim of disinterest, her lips pressed tightly together. Glaring at him, she opened her mouth to curse him when he raised a forefinger.

"Ah-ah," he said, a smile glowing in his eyes. "You started it."

"Oo-h-h-h," she howled, grabbing a pillow. Determined to suffocate him with it, she raised it above his face, but Nicholas guessed her intent and easily knocked it from her hands, grabbing her arms and pulling her to his chest.

"You can't rid yourself of me so easily," he laughed.

Amber struggled briefly as if truly vexed, then gave way to their gaiety with laughter of her own. "And what makes you think I want to be rid of you?"

"Did you not just a minute ago try to smother the breath from me?" he objected.

"I only wished to teach you a lesson."

His brows lifted. "As I recall, you were constantly teaching me lessons when I wasn't even aware of it."

"What lessons?" she asked, as she braced herself on his chest and toyed with the dark mass of curls beneath her fingers.

"Well, for one, to never trust a snot-nosed brat begging for a job."

Of a sudden, Amber bounced from the coziness of their bed, the thick mane of golden locks flying about her shoulders as she swung her legs to the floor and stood. She went directly to the hearth, took down a taper from the mantelpiece, and touched the end to the flame of the fire. Without a look in her husband's direction she started for the door, one cupped hand shielding the candle.

"Where are you going?" Nicholas asked, supported on one

572

elbow to watch her, befuddled.

Undaunted in her mission, she continued across the room. "I just remembered something I should have given you a long time ago."

"Couldn't it wait? I thought you wanted to read Holly's letter to me."

Reaching the doorway, she stopped and smiled back at him. "It's waited too long now. And in an odd way, I'd like it to be my wedding gift to you." She tilted her head demurely. "Keep my side of the bed warm. I'll be right back." In a whirl, she made her exit, the soft light of her candle fading slowly as she descended the stairs.

Nicholas settled back in the comfort of the feather mattress, pillows stacked behind his upper torso, and reached for the parchment lying near his feet. *Would he ever understand the moods of a woman?* he wondered. A smile played across his face. *And what fun would be left if he did?* Unfolding the paper he held, he began to read, pleased to learn that Amber's adopted sister had reached England and her father safely, and begged them to visit someday. He could almost see the look on the young girl's face as she wrote asking Amber's forgiveness for not telling her of Ronen's identity, but that once he had explained the need for the disguise she understood and knew no real harm would come to her while in her husband's protection. *If she only knew*, he mused, scratching the thick growth of beard on his chin and recalling the torture they both had suffered at Yaakob's hands. But that was a part of their past now, and he silently vowed no one would ever hurt his wife again, even if it meant laying down his life for her.

Nicholas glanced up toward the hallway outside their bedchambers when he heard the familiar moan of one stair step, remembering how many times it had given away his presence when he tried to sneak downstairs for an extra sampling of his mother's blueberry pie. He had often wondered if his parents had lain awake at night just waiting for their young son to steal back to the kitchen after they had told him to go to sleep, for they never failed to hear him, no matter how careful he had been. Grinning, he decided Amber had attempted to succeed where he had not, and he rose quietly to slip into his plum-colored floor-length robe, hurriedly pulling the sash tightly around his waist as he crossed the room and hid beside the door. He would give her just enough time to reach the entrance of the bedchambers, then jump out at her and catch her in his arms. He would soon teach her that he was no fool.

"Ouch!" Amber mumbled when her bare toe connected with a chair leg in the kitchen. She had carelessly allowed the flame of her candle to go out when she hurried into the room and now found herself with only the muted light of the moon streaming in through the windows to guide her way. Yet she felt certain she could reach her destination even with her eyes closed and awkwardly continued on. A pleased smile parted her lips once she reached the second doorway leading into the small bedchamber where she had lived a short while as Edgar, and her gaze quickly went to the bed on the opposite wall. She could only hope now that Anna hadn't found what the urchin had hidden beneath it so long ago.

On her knees, Amber leaned over and stretched in the darkness, her fingers fumbling about for the treasure she sought. An excited squeal accompanied its discovery, and she hastily seized the bundle in both hands, twisting to sit down on the floor and cradle the cloth-covered item in her lap. Tenderly she unfolded the material that had protected her prize and smiled warmly when her gaze fell upon the vase she had stolen from Nicholas. Maybe its return would help erase all the trouble she had caused him. Tossing aside the tattered piece of cloth, she stood and started back through the kitchen.

The way grew lighter once she entered the foyer, for the flames of the hearth in their bedchambers cast a steady beam out into the hallway above her and to the left. She opened her mouth to call out to her husband as she headed for the stairs, too excited to wait until she returned to their room, and looked up, spying a shadowed movement on the landing. Certain it couldn't be Nicholas, for the man wore a long dark cape and appeared much smaller than he, Amber felt a sudden alarming chill bolt through her.

"Nicholas!" she screamed, "there's someone—"

But before she could complete her warning, the figure turned with raised pistol and fired. In the darkness his aim fell short, and the ball whizzed past Amber's head, burrowing into the wall behind her. Instantly dropping to her knees, the vase clutched in the crook of one arm, she scrambled across the floor and hid beside the tallboy located against the wall beneath the stairway. Her heart pounded rapidly, and she quickly realized how helpless both she and Nicholas were, for she imagined the only guns in the house would be in the study. Nicholas certainly couldn't go for them, and it meant she would have to cross the foyer again and put herself in the open. And by now the man was surely reloading his pistol.

"Amber!"

She could hear the terror in her husband's voice. "I'm all right," she yelled. "He's on the stairs."

Trapped between the two, the assailant quickly realized who posed more threat. And once he had killed Chandler, it would be easy to overpower the woman. He would have plenty of time to reload then. Pulling the second pistol from his belt, he laid the first aside and started up the remaining steps toward the room from where he had heard his victim call to his wife. He moved slowly, his back pressed against the wall, and inched his way closer. He would wait outside the door and listen for any indication of where Chandler stood, then jump into the archway, gun ready, and kill the man before he could react. Sweat beaded across his brow, for though it seemed simple enough, he knew he was not dealing with an ordinary man. He passed the darkened doorway of the first bedchambers, silently drawing up beside the next where firelight glowed. His heart pounding wildly, he waited. Several minutes ticked by. No sound came from the room. He leaned forward slightly, seeing only one corner of the bedchambers through the open door. He gulped, taking a deep breath, ready to spring. Suddenly an object sailed through the air and crashed loudly against the stair's railing. Carelessly he turned toward it just as Nicholas catapulted from the room, arms held out wide to envelop the foe, a growl much like an angered mountain lion erupting from him. Both men crashed to the floor, the intruder's hand clamped tightly around his weapon. In a duel of sheer strength, one fighting for his life, the other seeking revenge for the invasion of his home and an attack against his wife, they struggled for possession of the pistol.

Jolted from her hiding place by the sound of battle, Amber rounded the balustrade and started up the stairs, her gaze affixed to the wrestling forms. She gasped when they rolled and the stranger straddled her husband, twisting the gun toward Nicholas's head. The skirts of her nightdress held in one hand, she raced up the remaining steps intent on striking the man with the vase she held in the other. But in a flash of rationality, she realized the tiny piece of crockery would not cause much pain or render him unconscious, and she roughly set it down on the small hall table, spinning about to return to the study for a gun of her own, when she suddenly remembered the pistol she had found so many months ago. Dashing into the darkened bedchambers, she ran directly to the armoire and flung the doors wide. Frantic, she clawed at the secret panel, tears burning her eyes when she thought her time would run out before she could save her husband.

The black bore of death inched closer. Nicholas's muscles strained, a fine mist of perspiration veiling his body. His attacker had unhuman strength, and Nicholas realized the man would not stop with killing him. He would murder Amber, too. Filled with rage at the thought, Nicholas heaved upward, his brow smashing against the other's chin, hurling him backward, and followed the attack with his fist to the man's jaw. The assailant rolled from him, but just as quickly came to his feet, the pistol still clutched threateningly in his hand. In the yellow glow of the firelight, Nicholas could see the victorious grin on the intruder's face as he slowly raised the weapon, its muzzle pointed at his victim's heart. Suddenly a shot rang out, and every muscle in Nicholas's body tightened, expecting to feel the pain of the wound as the lead ball tore through him. But in that same instant he saw the cloaked figure jerk sideways, hit the banister, and topple over it, a loud crash filling the air when his body fell to the floor below.

It took Nicholas a moment to comprehend the fate of the dead man, but once he had he quickly came to his feet, his gaze locked on the slim figure dressed in white and standing twenty feet down the hall. She hadn't moved, and Nicholas wondered if the act of killing a human being had been too much for her.

"Amber?" he called out softly, moving toward her.

Her blue eyes moved from the spot where the man had fallen to look upon her husband. "I . . . I had to," she whispered, her words choked with tears. "He . . . he was going to shoot you."

Enveloping her in his arms, he hugged her to him. "Yes, my love." He kissed her brow, her cheek, then held her close again.

"I didn't want . . . I would have done . . ."

"Hush," Nicholas soothed. "It's over now."

"Is . . . is he . . . dead?"

Nicholas glanced down at the still body. "I would guess so. But I better make sure." He gently set her from him. "Stay here while I get a candle." He waited for her nod, then went into their bedchambers and returned a moment later, a long white taper held in his hand. But when he started down the stairs past her, she reached out to grab his arm.

"I'm coming with you."

"Are you sure?"

She nodded, clutching his arm more fiercely, and he understood her need to stay at his side. Smiling compassionately, he draped an arm around her shoulders, and together they descended the staircase. When they reached the intruder's unmoving shape, Nicholas stooped and touched a hand to his shoulder, pulling the man onto his back. His glassy stare looked upward.

"Oh, my God," Amber gasped. "It's Pierre Duehr."

"You know him?"

"Yes. He was one of the men Von Buren sent to kidnap me."

"Von Buren? But he's dead. Why would this man try to kill us now?"

"I—I don't know. Surely he felt no loyalty to the baron. Not enough to seek revenge."

Nicholas came to his feet. "Well, maybe the constable will have an idea. Let's get dressed and go find him."

He slipped an arm around her waist and guided them back up the stairs. When they reached the top, he chuckled softly.

"Whatever made you leave our room probably saved both

our lives. At the time I couldn't see its importance, but now I'm glad I didn't argue. What did you go after, anyway?"

"That," she said, nodding toward the hall table.

Nicholas's chin sagged. "My mother's vase! But Edgar said he had broken it."

Amber grinned, the terror of the moment forgotten. "Edgar stole it. He planned to sell it until you told him it wasn't truly worth a tuppence. Then he couldn't very well just hand it back to you."

Nicholas threw back his head and roared with laughter. "Poor Edgar. He never could seem to do anything right."

Amber shrugged. "Well, he did this time."

"He sure did," Nicholas agreed, hugging her. "And where did you find a gun?"

Realizing she still held the weapon in her hand, she lifted it for him to see. "I discovered it when I rummaged the closets for another of Kate's gowns to wear." She chuckled, lifting her eyes to look at him, and paused when she saw the shocked expression on his face. "What's wrong?"

"That's my father's pistol. It was supposed to have been destroyed in the fire. Where did you get it?"

The blood drained from her face. "Oh, Nicholas, I'm sorry. I would . . ."

"It's all right. You couldn't have known. Just show me where you found it."

Breaking free of him, she hurriedly entered the spare bed-chambers Dru Chandler had used as his own and rushed to the armoire and the hidden compartment. "I found it in here along with a diary of some kind. I didn't have time to read any of it then." She pulled it from its resting place and handed it to her husband, taking the candle he held out for her in turn. "Did it belong to your father, too?"

Tilting the book toward the flame's light, he opened the cover, a twinge of sorrow touching his heart when he recognized his father's handwriting. "Yes," he answered quietly and began to read.

The first entry was dated a year before Dru's death and outlined the success of Chandler Shipping Lines plus making a reference to his son's absence. Nicholas's throat tightened, the

578

old guilt surfacing again, and he forced himself to flip further ahead. Praying there was some clue to his father's questionable demise, he stiffened when he saw the date on the last page. April 10, 1804, the night of the warehouse fire.

"What is it, Nicholas?"

Her soft voice penetrated his private agony, and he swallowed the knot in his throat. "The last time he wrote in this was the night he died."

"What does it say?"

Nicholas drew in a deep breath, wondering if he had the strength to find out. But the years of uncertainty and suspicion about the way his father had died refused to let him close the book. He cleared his throat and began to read out loud.

"I've invited him here to have this out. Since there is a chance he bought the guns for other reasons, I must be sure before I inform the authorities. But somehow, I don't think I'm wrong. I think he is a gunrunner. And if it's true, I must be careful. Von Buren is an evil man."

"Von Buren!" Amber gasped. "My God, Nicholas, he killed your father."

"Yes, it seems so, doesn't it?" he growled, his eyes flashing fire. He paused a moment, then looked at the book again. "There's more," he said quietly, and continued to read. "I don't think he's in this alone and feel safe in assuming he won't come by himself. I'm not sure if his partner is who I suspect, but I did some checking on a man who came to my docks to pick up one of Von Buren's shipments whom I had not seen before, and, by the way, have not seen since. That particular load was marked 'tea,' but one of my men discovered guns in it when the crate was accidentally dropped. I knew who had ordered the shipment but wanted to see for myself who came for it. Through rumors, I learned he was possibly the illegitimate son of Nathaniel Cromwell and went by the name of . . ." Nicholas paused and looked up at Amber, surprise mirrored in his eyes.

"Who, Nicholas? Who was it?"

"Seth Tyler," he finished quietly.

Amber's breath seemed to leave her and she shook her head, refusing to believe. "It couldn't have been. He must have been wrong."

Numbly, Nicholas closed the diary and went to the window of the room to stare outside, a thousand possibilities whirling in his head.

"Nicholas, it couldn't have been Seth. I've known him—"

"How long, Amber? How long have you known him?" he asked, without turning to look at her.

Suddenly, Amber realized that neither she nor her sister knew anything about Seth's past, only that he'd appeared one day working in the general store at Jamestown three years ago. She bit her lip to stop its quivering.

"If he is indeed Nathaniel Cromwell's son and you and Andrea are his granddaughters, that makes you kin. And if he married one of you, he would inherit his father's estate, even though Cromwell left it to someone else."

"But . . . but maybe he didn't know," she argued, not wanting to accept the truth.

"Von Buren knew about the will before you. How do you suppose he found out, unless a member of the family told him?"

"But Von Buren wanted to marry Andrea. If Seth was the one after the estate, why would he allow the baron to marry her?"

Nicholas turned slowly to look at her. "I don't know, Amber. And there's only one way we'll ever find out for sure. We'll have to ask him. But I think what happened here tonight is enough proof to tie the two together."

"How?"

"Duehr worked for Von Buren. He tried to kill us both, and I think Tyler sent him. As long as you and I are alive, we have the right to half of everything in Cromwell's estate."

A deathly chill raced through her. "What about Andrea? Do you suppose he intends to . . . to kill her, too?"

"I don't know, Amber. It depends on whether or not he truly loves her. But I suggest we not take the chance. I had better change and pay Tyler a visit tonight." He straightened and started across the room.

"I'm going with you," Amber insisted.

"No. It won't be safe."

She grabbed his arm as he passed. "She's my sister, damn

you!" she shouted, and tears suddenly filled her eyes. "And you're my husband, Nicholas." Her words came softer. "I will be with those I love."

He stared at her a moment, then smiled, tucking her slender form within the circle of his arm as they walked from the room.

White satin robe tied tightly around her waist, Andrea stepped into the hallway outside the bedchambers she shared with her husband and started down the stairs, the candle she held lighting the way. The hall clock struck half past midnight, bringing a deeper frown to her troubled face. She had gone to bed alone some time ago when Seth told her he had work to do in the study and would retire later. Had the dying fire in the room not chilled the air and awakened her, Andrea would have slept until morning, never aware of when he had shed his clothes and slipped beneath the covers next to her. Since inheriting the estate, Seth had worked long hours both in the fields and behind his desk, and Andrea worried he did too much.

"Seth?" she called out when she reached the front hall at the end of the long staircase. She moved toward the study. "Are you still working, Seth? It's late."

The door to the room was open and she stepped inside, surprised to find it empty and no papers or books strewn about the desktop. The candle had burned low, and Andrea realized it had been a long while, if at all, since her husband had been in the study. Turning slowly, she decided to look in the parlor. He had many times chosen to read there, and possibly he had fallen asleep while doing so. Her frown disappeared. Yes, that had to be it. Her step quickening, she moved across the hall, intent on scolding her husband playfully for leaving her alone in bed to get cold without his companionship. She had just passed by the front entrance of the manor when the distant rattling of a carriage drew her attention, and she paused to listen. Who would possibly be out at such an hour? Surely they didn't come to pay a visit. Slowly she moved toward the window adjacent to the double front doors and pulled aside the curtain to peer outside. In the steady streams of moonlight she could see the buggy at the end of the lane, its lamps bouncing with the sway of the vehicle as it traveled closer. She stood transfixed and curious as she watched the coach pull up near the cobblestone walk leading to the house, an unexplainable apprehension tickling the hairs on the back of her neck. Had something happened to Seth, and they had come to tell her? The curtain fell back into place.

"Seth?" she called. "Seth, are you in the—"

A trio of raps against the door echoed in the hallway. Andrea froze. *Go away*, her mind demanded. *Go away!*

The knocking came again.

She spun around, tears welling in her eyes as she stared at the sealed portals. *Seth is in the parlor. He's all right. He's just sleeping.* She trembled and forced her feet to move. A shaky hand reached for the latch, and, from sheer determination to prove the bearer of bad tidings wrong, Andrea swung the door open.

"Oh, Amber," she half laughed, half cried when her gaze fell upon her sister standing there. "I thought—" The smoothness of her brow wrinkled when she saw Nicholas coming up the walk behind her. "What are you doing here?"

"We must talk," Amber said, stepping into the hallway. "Is Seth here?"

Andrea's worried gaze looked from her sister to Nicholas and back. "He's . . . he's in the parlor. What's wrong? Is someone ill?"

Nicholas followed Amber inside and closed the door behind them. "No one's ill, Andrea, but something is terribly wrong," he said quietly. "May we join your husband?"

She nodded nervously, then turned to lead the way, pulling up short when the light of her candle revealed an empty room. "I . . . I thought he was here." She glanced over at her sister. "He hadn't come to bed and I was looking for him when you came." She paused, then said, "Tell me what's wrong."

Nicholas moved to take the taper from her hand and light those in the candelabrum, flooding the room with a warm radiance before he went to the fireplace and began to stake several logs in the hearth. Within minutes the blaze chased away the chill in the air, and he stood, removing his cape as he watched Amber guide her sister to a chair and pull up another to sit next to her. Taking the bonnet from her head and untying the strings of her cloak, Amber tossed the garments on the nearby sofa. She turned back to look at Andrea, reaching for one of her hands.

"Someone broke into our house tonight and tried to kill us," she said as gently as she could.

"Oh, my God, who?" Andrea cried out, her thin frame shaking.

"His name was Pierre Duehr. He was one of the men Von Buren sent to kidnap me."

"Von . . . but he's dead!" Her troubled blue eyes glanced up at Nicholas. "You killed him, didn't you?" she asked, and he bowed his head a degree. She looked back at her sister. "Then what did he have to gain?"

"We had hoped you could help us decide," Amber continued.

"Me?" Andrea exploded. "How would I know anything?"

Not wanting to go on, for she knew how devastating the news would be, Amber looked up at her husband beseechingly. Understanding her need, he went to the small table near the sofa and poured a glass of wine from the decanter sitting there, handing it to Andrea.

"Drink this while I explain," he instructed, and waited until she had taken a sip. "We found a diary that belonged to my father. In it, he told of his discovery of gunrunners for the Indians, and he had proof Von Buren was one of them."

"But what has this to do with me? Or Seth?"

Nicholas glanced down at the black toes of his shoes. "Has Seth told you anything about his past, where he comes from, who his father was?"

"There was never any need," the deep voice from the doorway admitted, and all eyes turned to find Seth casually leaning a shoulder against its frame, a pistol held in one hand and aimed at Nicholas.

"Seth?" Andrea sobbed, starting to rise, but he waved her back. "What . . . what are you doing with that gun?"

"I plan to finish what Duehr couldn't."

"So you did send him," Nicholas observed.

Seth smiled with a nod. "And since you've come here and made my job easier, I feel I at least owe you an explanation. But I warn you, if anyone moves, I will see Mr. Chandler is the first recipient of my gift here." He waved the muzzle of the gun. "And from this distance, I assure you, I won't miss."

Terror filled Amber's heart at his announcement, and she mustered all the courage she could find not to look at her husband. If Seth Tyler had gone to so much trouble over a period of years, he would not hesitate to kill Nicholas if she even blinked an eye. She steeled herself to watch the man and not reveal her loathing of him by the expression on her face.

"When I was twelve years old, my mother fell ill. We had no money and could not afford a doctor to tend her. We had always lived that way, too poor sometimes to even have a decent meal. I watched her grow weaker, until one night I knew she would never see the sun rise again. I loved her more than anyone else in my life." He grinned hatefully at Andrea. "Even you, my dear wife," he said acidly, and laughed at the pain in her eyes. "Before she died, she told me why my father never lived with us or even came to visit. You see, he already had a wife and children. His name was Nathaniel Cromwell. You've heard of him, haven't you, Andrea?" His gaze swept the room briefly. "Your grandfather and the former owner of this plantation."

"Seth," she wept, "I don't understand."

"Of course, you don't. You're too stupid. That's why it made my plan so easy. When I learned the old man had died and left his estate to the twin daughters of *his* illegitimate daughter, I decided on a way to get what should have been mine. I would marry one of you and kill the other."

"Oh, my God," Andrea wailed in a rush of tears. "How could you?"

Seth grinned evilly.

"If that's all you had to do, why did you involve Von Buren?" Nicholas asked curiously.

"Because there was a catch. If the twins weren't found, the estate went to his true granddaughter, Heather Branford."

"Heather?" Amber exclaimed, looking at Nicholas.

"Yes. Heather wasn't aware of her grandfather's death, because Cromwell had disowned her mother years ago and never kept in contact. At the time I wasn't sure the Courtney twins were who he had named, either, and thus it left me in a bit of a bind. I couldn't very well marry two women, so I decided to find someone to help. I needed a man with money. One who could buy up all of Heather's debts and force marriage."

"The baron," Nicholas finished, waiting for Seth to nod.

"Once he forced Heather to marry him, we had planned to kill her. But she took care of that for us. Tsk, tsk," he mocked. "Dreadful accident." He shifted the pistol to his other hand. "Then all that was left were the twins. Von Buren was to marry Andrea and kill her sister." He laughed. "But by then I didn't need him. I knew Andrea was the heir and she had fallen in love with me. It was all so simple." He sighed. "It was, until you returned with your wife, alive and well."

Reminded of the circumstances of her kidnapping, Amber thought back to the time she had been held prisoner in the root cellar and had heard the voice of a man she could not see but thought she recognized. It had been Seth Tyler issuing commands the whole time. How could she have been so blind?

"May I ask how you got Von Buren to agree? He could have kept it all," Nicholas asked.

"Blackmail."

Amber and Nicholas exchanged puzzled glances.

"You see, Von Buren murdered his first wife in a fit of rage. I told him I found her diary, which implicated such a possibility, and that I would give it to the authorities if he didn't do exactly as I said. Of course, there wasn't such a thing, but the fool believed me anyway. Then I learned he was a gunrunner and discovered a better hold to have on the baron. I confiscated one of his shipments of guns, marked 'tea.'"

"We already knew that part of it."

Seth raised questioning brows.

"There was another diary, a real one. My father kept it. I wish I had found it sooner, because you wouldn't be standing

585

here now if I had."

"Ah, yes, Dru Chandler," he smiled. "If he had just kept his nose out of it, I wouldn't have had to kill him."

The cold admission of murder tore through Nicholas like a bolt of lightning, sparking each nerve ending and setting his wrath afire. Blinded by rage and the guilt he'd carried for over two years, Nicholas's entire body turned to granite, his nostrils flared, his blazing eyes locked on the man who had heartlessly killed his father. "You son of a whore." The words came low and filled with hatred, and he slowly reached around in back of him for the pistol he had hidden beneath his coat.

Amber knew his intent, for she had watched him load the gun and stuff it in the waistband of his breeches before they left the house. And she also realized there would not be enough time for him to draw it before Seth cut him down. In a desperate attempt to save her husband, she sprang from the chair and threw herself at him.

"No, Nicholas! Don't!" she screamed.

Knocking her aside with one arm, he reached for the gun as Seth quickly came to attention, his eyes wide, his hand trembling slightly. "Go ahead," he challenged loudly. "Nothing would give me more pleasure than to shoot you in the belly and watch you bleed like your father!" Pulling back the hammer, he sneered venomously when Nicholas held steady. "Yes, just like your father."

He raised the pistol high, his concentration so great that he failed to see the trim figure of a woman vault from her chair a split second before he squeezed the trigger. The powder exploded, hurling the lead ball through the air and catching Andrea in the chest as she shielded Nicholas with her body. The power behind it threw her backward into his arms, but her pain-filled eyes never broke their hold on Seth, the man she had loved, and the man with whom she had chosen to live out her life. How ironic that he would be the one to end it.

A second shot rang out almost immediately as Nicholas clutched the dying woman in one arm and fired upon the man with the pistol he had drawn too late. Seth Tyler crumpled to the floor, a victim of his own greed.

"Andrea!" Amber screamed, scrambling to her feet to aid her husband in lowering the delicate form to the sofa. "Oh, Andrea." Her throat tight, tears streamed down her face as she studied the gaping wound that quickly stained the satin whiteness of her sister's robe, and she wept uncontrollably, barely feeling the cool hand touching hers.

"Don't . . . cry," the weak voice begged, and Amber looked up to find her sister smiling. "All our . . . lives . . . you were the one . . . who was strong. Be so . . . now."

Amber angrily brushed at the tears on her cheeks.

"I . . . I loved him. . . ."

"I know," Amber sobbed.

"And . . . I couldn't . . . let him . . ."

"Don't talk," Amber begged, raising the hand to her lips.

"No . . . I must . . . Nicholas?"

Quickly kneeling down next to his wife, he smiled tenderly, his own suffering mirrored in his eyes. "Yes, Andrea. I'm here."

"I . . . can't ask you . . . to forgive him . . . just understand. Say you do . . . and I will rest . . . in peace."

Nicholas's heart had run the gauntlet of emotions in only a few short minutes, each more powerful than the one before. But as he stared down at the pale beauty of the face so much like his wife's, he discovered he no longer felt anything at all. His father's death had been avenged, his guilt removed, and life held the promise of happiness with the woman he called his wife. Now a dying woman asked only that he understand what drove her husband to do what he had, and Nicholas did, and he pitied him.

"I do, Andrea," he whispered, bringing a faint smile to her lips.

"Thank you."

"Andrea, please don't talk anymore. Save your strength. We'll send someone for the doctor," Amber begged.

Andrea closed her eyes. "No. Too late . . ."

"Don't say that!" Amber screamed. "You're not going to die! I won't let you!"

"For once . . . Amber . . . you'll not get . . . what you want."

Her dark blue eyes glanced up lovingly. "You . . . already have all you need. Love him . . . Amber. Love him for both of us." Her face twisted in pain, then relaxed. "Tell him your secret." Suddenly, Andrea's body stiffened. She sucked in a deep breath and closed her eyes, still for a moment before she relaxed again, her body quivering as her last breath of life escaped her.

Epilogue

July 9, 1807

"Nicholas, you had better hurry or we'll be late. Kate's wedding is in one hour, and you don't want to spoil it," Amber called up from the bottom of the staircase. "She's expecting you to give her away."

A moment passed before his tall figure filled the doorway to their bedchambers, a scowl on his handsome face as he fumbled uselessly with the black ascot around his neck. "Then I must plead surrender and beg your help." His arms fell resignedly to his sides, the satiny tie twisted in a lopsided knot. "I never could fix these things the way they're supposed to be."

Shaking her head, she lifted the heavy skirts of her bright yellow gown and started up the stairs. "What did you do before you married me?" she chuckled.

"Well, most of the time I simply didn't wear one. I guess that's why I decided to get married," he teased.

Amber came to an abrupt halt on the last step. "Just so you'd have someone to fix your tie?"

He shrugged. "Well, it sounds better than saying I simply wanted you in my bed."

"To others, maybe, but not me," she rebuffed.

"Ah, but we know the truth, don't we?" he grinned suggestively. "How long did you say we had before we had to be at the church?"

"Not *that* long," she laughed. "You and your lusty thoughts will have to wait."

Nicholas opened his arms to welcome her when she came within reach, but Amber firmly took his hand instead and led him back into the bedchambers where the light was better and she could adjust the ascot properly.

"You know," he said dreamily as he played with a tendril of yellow hair dangling over her ear. "I got to thinking about Andrea the other day."

"Oh?" Amber asked, concentrating on her task. "What about?"

"I was wondering how she knew you had a secret, or for that matter what it was."

She finished the perfect knot, fluffed up the fullness of the cloth, and stepped back to appraise her work. "It's quite simple. Andrea and I were twins. When one hurt, the other felt the pain. We could never hide anything from each other."

"I don't believe that," he disagreed, with a shake of his dark head.

"Oh, don't you? Then come with me." Without giving him a chance to answer, she took his elbow and guided him through the doorway leading to an adjacent room. They paused in the center of it and smiled lovingly over at the cribs near the window. "I never had a chance to tell her I was with child, yet she already knew."

"Ah-ha. See there. She was wrong. You weren't with child. You were with children," he proclaimed stubbornly.

Amber burst into laughter, remembered the sleeping twins, and quickly covered her mouth with her hand. "Go find your coat, you silly oaf, so we may be gone," she whispered, turning him around and giving him a gentle shove. She lingered a moment until he had disappeared from view and slowly looked back at the sleeping faces of her children. Coming to stand between their beds, she smiled down at the baby dressed in blue with dark tufts of hair on his head.

"Andrew Chandler," she whispered, "may you grow to be as bright and strong and handsome as your father." She turned to the other infant, a pretty pink bow tied in the single curl of its yellow hair. "Make your aunt proud of you, Andrea, my daughter, as I always was of her."

She bent, kissed each cherubic face, then stood and went to the window of the room, her eyes looking toward heaven.

"You were right, my sister. I do have all I need."